George E. Matthews

**The Men of New York**

Vol. I

George E. Matthews

**The Men of New York**
*Vol. I*

ISBN/EAN: 9783337169794

Printed in Europe, USA, Canada, Australia, Japan

Cover: Foto ©Raphael Reischuk / pixelio.de

More available books at **www.hansebooks.com**

# THE MEN OF NEW YORK:

A COLLECTION OF BIOGRAPHIES
AND PORTRAITS OF CITIZENS OF
THE EMPIRE STATE PROMINENT IN
BUSINESS, PROFESSIONAL, SOCIAL,
AND POLITICAL LIFE DURING THE
LAST DECADE OF THE NINETEENTH
CENTURY.

## VOL. I

BUFFALO, N. Y.
GEO. E. MATTHEWS & CO.
1898.

# PREFACE

TO KNOW the men of a time is the first requisite to an understanding of the time itself. Words alone can tell but half the story. No man is more than half comprehended by those who have never seen him. History becomes comprehensible to even a sluggish imagination when a visit is paid to a great portrait collection like that at Hampton Court or The Hague. Then the name that has been a mere abstraction on the printed page, takes a new life as the student gazes into the very features of the statesman or the warrior; and feels that in his time there was a living man, with blood as warm and mind as keen as has the friend by his side to-day. One portrait by itself cannot bring out this feeling of the integrity and continuity of humanity; but a collection of the contemporaries of any character makes his environment realizable, and therefore his personality more comprehensible.

The compilers of this collection of portraits and biographies have not deluded themselves into the belief that they were making history. They know that much of biography is but the raw material upon which history is founded, and that photographic portraiture is but one of the humbler branches of art; but they have felt that there was room and need for the preservation of some record of the men who were a great part of the life of a great state in these last years of a great century.

The labor has been longer and more engrossing than anyone anticipated when it began, but the result will, they trust, meet the approval of even the highest expectations. No effort has been spared to obtain the most complete and accurate information concerning each subject of a biography; and the portraits have been made with the greatest care from photographs in the majority of cases taken especially for the work.

The conditions inseparable from printing in parts have made it impossible to preserve the alphabetical arrangement throughout the two volumes; but each volume will be found to have a separate index, and in the second volume will be found a synoptical index of the entire work. In this index is given an outline of the biography of each subject, and also the occurrences since the original publication of the biography. As these biographies were written and published continuously during the years 1896 and 1897, this outline has been found needful in bringing the information up to the beginning of 1898.

In the first volume are included the biographies of citizens living in 1896 and 1897 in the western section of this state. The second volume is divided into several sections covering the rest of the state, and also contains the biographies of prominent citizens who died shortly before the work was undertaken. The synoptical index, also, will be found in this volume.

The compilers and publishers submit the work to the consideration of their friends and the public with the sincere belief that, though far from perfect, it will be found to be of permanent value, and by far the most monumental work of the kind ever undertaken. Certainly no expense has been spared to make it worthy of preservation.

# INDEX OF SUBJECTS IN Vol. I

# WESTERN SECTION

In the Western Section are published the biographies of subjects from the counties of Allegany. Cattaraugus. Chautauqua. Erie. and Niagara.

**Frank B. Goodyear** has achieved an unusual degree of success in the business world of Buffalo and northwestern Pennsylvania, where he has been an active figure for the past twenty-five years. He is of English and Scotch descent, and possesses the sturdy determination and shrewd common sense of both races. He is a son of Dr. Bradley Goodyear, formerly of Buffalo, and was born in Groton, N. Y., less than fifty years ago. His early education was obtained in the public schools, the academy at East Aurora, N. Y., and from private tutors.

On completing his education Mr. Goodyear taught a district school a few months, and later became a bookkeeper for Robert Looney, who operated extensive sawmills at Looneyville, N. Y. He was anxious, however, for a busy commercial career; and in 1872 he went to Buffalo, where his brother Charles had recently established himself as a lawyer, and embarked in the coal and lumber trade. Beginning at first on a small scale, he was soon able to enlarge his operations; and before many years became a prominent factor in these industries throughout the section tributary to Buffalo. Becoming convinced of the desirability of manufacturing his own lumber, he built, in connection with his father, two sawmills in northwestern Pennsylvania; and as this venture proved successful, he established others in different parts of the state, until he has built not less than fifteen sawmills and more than four hundred miles of railroad, which have been constantly employed in supplying the demands of his extensive trade.

In 1887 Charles W. Goodyear, who had been for many years a prominent attorney of Buffalo, gave up his law business; and the two brothers established the firm of F. H. & C. W. Goodyear, which for the past ten years has conducted a vast amount of business. In order to open up the regions of north western Pennsylvania, and to initiate the shipment of lumber therefrom, F. H. Goodyear in 1885 built at his own expense a little railroad known as the Sinnemahoning Valley, from Keating Summit, Penn., on the line of the Western New York & Pennsylvania railroad, into that part of the lumber regions where he was then operating. The Goodyear brothers owned thousands of acres of the finest hemlock forest in Potter county; and as their busy mills gradually devoured the timber and the hills grew bare, it became necessary to go farther for the supply of raw material, and more railroads had to be built in order to get the logs to the mills. For this purpose "the Goodyears," as the two brothers are familiarly called throughout that region, incorporated the Buffalo & Susquehanna Railroad Co., of which the earlier lines became a part; and extended the road as far east as Galeton and Ansonia. On New-Year's Day, 1896, another branch was opened from Galeton to Wellsville, Allegany county, N. Y. Mr. Goodyear is now the chief owner of the Buffalo & Susquehanna road, and has an important share in its management.

Mr. Goodyear's success in the conduct of his own commercial undertakings is evidence of his keen business foresight and marked executive ability. He has also had a part in the management of other important enterprises, notably the United States Leather Co., of which he is a director. Though so fully occupied with the demands of business, Mr. Goodyear is a progressive and public-spirited citizen, who may be counted on to help in any good cause. He has never interested himself actively in politics, and has never been a candidate for an elective office. In 1886 President Cleveland appointed him a commissioner to examine government lands on the line of the Northern Pacific railroad, and he discharged the duties of the position with his customary energy and ability.

Mr. Goodyear is well known in social circles in Buffalo; and is a member of several prominent clubs, including the Buffalo, Liberal, Ellicott,

*FRANK H. GOODYEAR*

Country, and Falconwood. He belongs, also, to the Manhattan and Lawyers' clubs of New York city.

*PERSONAL CHRONOLOGY—Frank Henry Goodyear was born at Groton, N. Y., March 17, 1849; was educated at East Aurora Academy; was bookkeeper and teacher in a district school in 1871; married Josephine Looney of Looneyville, N. Y., September 14, 1872; has engaged in the coal and lumber trade in Buffalo since 1872.*

* * *

**William H. Love** will be called a young man for some time yet; but he has already attained distinction, not only in the profession of law, but also in that of teaching and school administration. Born in Buffalo while the Civil War was raging,

he was educated in the public schools of the city, graduating from the high school with the class of '81. District Attorney Kenefick, Congressman Mahany, and Frederick A. Vogt, now principal of the high school, were members of the same class.

For the next ten years Mr. Love engaged in school teaching. Soon after his graduation from the high school he was appointed by Christopher G. Fox principal of school No. 29 at South Buffalo, and continued to teach there for four years. Appointed in 1885 to the principalship of school No. 33, he remained in charge of that institution for the next five years, developing all the while decided talent as a teacher and organizer of school work. When he went to school No. 33 it was comparatively small; but when he left it, in 1890, it was the largest school in South Buffalo, and one of the largest in the city. His next school was No. 13, in the central district of Buffalo, to which he was transferred in the fall of 1890. He remained there until February, 1892, when he succeeded James F. Crooker as superintendent of schools. Mr. Love was appointed to this important position by a commission consisting of Mayor Bishop, Comptroller Gavin, and Councilman Hanrahan. He was only thirty years old at the time, and the appointment was a striking tribute to his character as a man and capacity as an educator. He held the position until January 1, 1893. In the fall of 1892 he was unanimously nominated by the Democratic party to succeed himself as superintendent, but lost the election by a narrow margin after a hotly contested campaign.

While Mr. Love was in charge of the Buffalo schools the municipal ordinances relating thereto were revised under his advice and supervision. He also assisted materially in organizing the board of school examiners. Largely through his efforts a part of the public funds was set aside for the purpose of establishing kindergartens in Buffalo; and in recognition of his work in this regard he was elected the first honorary member of the Buffalo Free Kindergarten Association.

During the latter part of his teaching Mr. Love had been preparing himself to practice law. He filed his certificate as a student in the office of Cuddeback & Kenefick, and devoted his afternoons and

Saturdays to the study of law in their office. By the time he left the position of superintendent of schools his studies were far advanced, and he was able to pass the bar examination at Rochester in March, 1893. He was elected president of the class of lawyers admitted at that time. In April, 1893, he formed a partnership for the general practice of law with Daniel J. Kenefick, under the firm name of Kenefick & Love. This association has continued to the present time, and has prospered markedly as regards volume of business, success in litigation, and solidity of clientage. The firm has a diversified practice consisting of contested work in the courts, the settlement of estates, and general office business. Without having made special efforts to obtain that kind of work, they have come to enjoy a considerable clientage among fraternal and benevolent societies. They are the attorneys, for example, of the Knights of the Maccabees and the Buffalo Fire Department Beneficiary Association.

Mr. Love belongs to various social organizations, including the Knights of Columbus, Royal Arcanum, Buffalo Orpheus, and Knights of the Maccabees. He has been prominent in the counsels of the Democratic party for several years, and has taken an active part in campaigns as a platform speaker.

*PERSONAL CHRONOLOGY —* *William Henry Love was born at Buffalo November 18, 1862; was educated in the Buffalo public schools, graduating from the high school in 1881; was principal of various public schools in Buffalo, 1881-92, and superintendent of schools of that city in 1892; was admitted to the bar in 1893; married Helen A. Niendorf of Buffalo June 18, 1896; has practiced law in Buffalo since 1893.*

\*\*\*

**Morris Morey,** who has practiced law in Buffalo for upwards of thirty years, and has long been recognized as one of the leaders of his profession in that city, is a son of Joseph Morey, an Erie-county farmer. He received a common-school education, followed by a broken course of study at Oberlin College, from which he graduated in 1863. The next few years were divided between military service and study at the Albany Law School, and in 1865 he took up his residence in Buffalo, and began the practice of his profession.

In the early part of his professional career Mr. Morey devoted considerable time to public affairs. He served for a year as assistant city attorney, and for two years as assistant district attorney of Erie county, and in 1874 he was the Republican candidate for district attorney. Since that time he has held no public office, but has continued to practice his profession in Buffalo. In 1882 the Republican city convention nominated him for the office of mayor, but he declined for professional reasons to accept the nomination.

In 1885-86 Mr. Morey was chairman of a committee of nine who framed new rules for the government of Republican caucuses and conventions in Erie county. These rules aimed, by a registry of all Republican voters and other safeguards, to [...] all such voters full opportunity to vote at [...]

WILLIAM H. LOVE

caucuses, and to be represented in the conventions of the party. They were adopted by the county convention of 1886, and were quite successful for a time in securing these objects.

In the winter of 1892-93 Mr. Morey made an address, on behalf of various committees of citizens of Buffalo, before the assembly and senate committees on cities at Albany, in favor of the repeal of what were popularly known as the "sneak bills." These bills had been rushed hastily through the

NORRIS MOREY

legislature, they changed in an unusual and extraordinary manner the political control of the police board of Buffalo; and their passage produced a notable and wholesome uprising of public sentiment, which resulted in a political revolution at the city elections which followed.

*PERSONAL CHRONOLOGY— Norris Morey was born at Brant, Erie county, N. Y., July 20, 1848; completed his education at Oberlin (O.) College; served in the Union army, 1861-62 and 1864-65; studied law, and was admitted to the bar in 1866; was assistant city attorney of Buffalo, 1870-71, and assistant district attorney of Erie county, 1872-74; has practiced law in Buffalo since 1866.*

**George B. Stowits,** Buffalo's veteran school teacher, began his career in the public schools of that city in 1861, and is still actively engaged there at the age of seventy-five. In all these years his enthusiasm has never failed; and his most earnest efforts are still directed to the task of training the boys and girls in his charge to be true and loyal American citizens, as well as intelligent, well educated men and women.

Major Stowits was born in the village of Fort Plain, in the beautiful Mohawk valley. He was left an orphan in childhood, and was thrown upon his own resources; but he succeeded in securing a good fundamental education, and during a career of more than fifty years as a teacher he has constantly broadened and extended his mental equipment. After attending academies at Clinton and Whitestown, Oneida county, he studied law for a time in an office at Little Falls, N. Y.; but when he was twenty-one years old he began his long career as a teacher. His first field of labor was Starkville, Herkimer county; and he subsequently taught at Fort Plain, Waterford, Little Falls, Ilion, and Batavia. In the summer of 1856 he went abroad, and made a study of the educational institutions of England, Ireland, and Scotland.

January 1, 1861, Major Stowits went to Buffalo as principal of Public School No. 10. The troublous war times were already close at hand, and in the summer of 1862 he gave up his position as a teacher, and went to the front. Enlisting August 29 as a private in company H, 100th New York volunteers, he joined his regiment a few weeks later at Gloucester Point, Va. In December the command was ordered to the department of the South, and took part in the siege of Charleston and the bombardment of Fort Sumter. After serving in many of the most hard-fought engagements of the war, the 100th regiment was ordered back to Gloucester in the spring of 1864, and thence to Bermuda Hundreds. In the advance upon Richmond Major Stowits served as acting assistant adjutant general on the staff of the commanding officer; and in attempting to push forward his skirmish line closer to the enemy's works, he was shot through the right arm. Before the wound was well healed he returned to his regiment, and served on the brigade staff during the rest of the

G. Frederick Zeller

part of the time traveled considerably, buying and selling goods, and acting as Mr. Schoellkopf's confidential representative.

At the end of this time Mr. Zeller determined to go into business for himself. He was almost thirty years old; and had gained an excellent training in

G. FREDERICK ZELLER

sound business principles, as well as a thorough familiarity with the tanner's trade, from his long service with Mr. Schoellkopf, a business man of unusual ability. Accordingly he formed a partnership with George Laub, under the style of Laub & Zeller, and began the manufacture of leather on his own account. This association lasted for almost a quarter of a century, and was entirely successful. By the year 1889 Mr. Zeller became desirous of admitting to a share in the business his three sons, Henry C., J. Fred, and Edward G. Zeller. He therefore severed his connection with Mr. Laub, built a new tannery on Howard and Smith streets, Buffalo, and established the present firm of G. F. Zeller & Sons. Mr. Zeller maintains an active supervision of the entire

establishment, and devotes the same prudent and careful attention to every detail that has characterized the conduct of the concern from the beginning. Under the new management the business has prospered markedly, and the product of the Zeller tannery is known throughout the United States, and finds a wide and ready market.

Mr. Zeller's success in carrying on his own business has naturally brought him into prominence in the commercial life of Buffalo, and he has been called upon to take part in the management of various financial institutions. He has been vice president of the Citizens' Bank ever since its organization in 1890, and has contributed much to its high standing. He has been for many years a trustee of the Buffalo Savings Bank, one of the most solid institutions in the city; and he is actively interested in other business enterprises.

Though far from being a politician in any sense of the word, Mr. Zeller is a public-spirited citizen, and has taken part more or less in public affairs. In the fall of 1873 he was elected an alderman from the old 4th ward, Buffalo, and served for the ensuing two years, and until he moved out of the ward. He is best known in public life, however, as a fire commissioner, having been one of the most efficient members of that board for more than a dozen years. He was first appointed in 1884 by Mayor Scoville, and the appointment was particularly gratifying from the fact that it was received without any solicitation on Mr. Zeller's part. At the end of his term of six years he was reappointed by Mayor Bishop. In 1896 Mayor Jewett appointed him for a third term; but Mr. Zeller resigned six months later, feeling that he had served the city well and long in that capacity, and was entitled to be released from further duty.

Mr. Zeller is a life member of the German Young Men's Association of Buffalo and the Buffalo Orpheus, and belongs to various other societies.

*PERSONAL CHRONOLOGY — G. Frederick Zeller was born in Württemberg, Germany, February 8, 1836; was educated in German and American schools; married Barbara Mochel of Buffalo May 17, 1859; was in the employ of J. F. Schoellkopf, 1855-65; was an alderman of Buffalo, 1874-75, and a member of the board of fire commissioners, 1884-96; has conducted a tannery in Buffalo since 1865.*

**De Alva Stanwood Alexander** was born in Maine, but in early boyhood he went to Ohio with his mother, where, at the age of fifteen, he enlisted in the 128th Ohio volunteer infantry, serving three years, and until the close of the war, as a private soldier. Most young men would feel that such an experience was education enough, but Mr. Alexander deliberately returned to his native state, and prepared for college at Edward Little Institute in Auburn. He took his bachelor's degree from Bowdoin College in 1870, having as classmates James A. Roberts, comptroller of New York state, Dr. Lucien Howe, and Willis H. Meads, all of Buffalo.

After graduation Mr. Alexander went to Fort Wayne, Ind., where he taught in the public schools until he became one of the editors and proprietors of the Fort Wayne *Gazette*, a leading Republican paper of northern Indiana. Later, having disposed of his interest in this publication, he accepted a position on the Cincinnati *Gazette* as staff correspondent, with residence at Indianapolis. While so engaged he was elected secretary of the Republican state committee, holding the position for six years. It was also his good fortune at this time to be appointed clerk of the United States senate committee on privileges and elections by its chairman, Senator Morton, and to accompany the latter to Oregon during the investigation of the senatorial election in that state in the winter of 1876.

Mr. Alexander's connection with the newspaper was merely a stepping stone to the ranks of the legal profession. For his preceptor in the study of the law he had no less a master than Senator McDonald, under whose tuition he studied until admitted to the bar in January, 1877. He then formed a partnership with Stanton J. Peelle of Indianapolis, now judge of the Court of Claims in Washington. In 1881 Mr. Alexander, upon the recommendation of Senator Harrison, was appointed by President Garfield fifth auditor of the treasury department, and left Indiana for Washington. Here among other things he was required to pass upon and settle the accounts of United States ministers and consuls, of the internal revenue, of the Smithsonian Institute, of the census and patent offices, and the department of state — accounts amounting in all to upwards of $100,000,000 annually. A reform feature of his work was the

application of a system of checks upon consular fees, making it impossible for any consul, without discovery, to collect a fee and retain it. Mr. Alexander served under secretaries Windom, Folger, McCulloch and Manning. While residing in the national capital, he was elected and served as commander of the

*DE ALVA STANWOOD ALEXANDER*

Department of the Potomac, Grand Army of the Republic.

Mr. Alexander, attracted by the manifest advantages of Buffalo and by a law partnership with his college classmate, Mr. Roberts, moved thither in 1885. Three years afterward, when General Harrison had become a candidate for President, Mr. Alexander was invited to assist him, and for that purpose spent the entire campaign of 1888 at Indianapolis as his private secretary. In June, 1889, Mr. Alexander was appointed United States district attorney for the northern district of New York, and held the office until December, 1893, discharging successfully its responsible duties. The failure of two national banks and a large defalcation in the

Albany City National Bank, both of which occurred during Mr. Alexander's term, gave the district attorney ample opportunity for good work; and the fact that, of eight men indicted for these failures and this defalcation, seven were convicted and sent

*TRACY C. BECKER*

to the penitentiary, shows that the work of the office was well cared for.

Mr. Alexander has shown marked ability and capacity for affairs in whatever he has undertaken. Political life in its higher form has seemed to him a worthy ambition, and his time and thought, outside the business of his profession, have ever been subject to the demand of his party on the stump and in the work of organization. But while a strong partisan, he is no believer in party success at any cost, and he has identified himself with clean politics at all times. He is a member of the Buffalo and University clubs, and is well known and esteemed in social circles, at the bar, and in the plainer walks of life.

*PERSONAL CHRONOLOGY — De Alva Stanwood Alexander was born at Richmond, Me., July*

*17, 1846; served three years during the Civil War; was educated at Edward Little Institute, Auburn, Me., and at Bowdoin College, Brunswick, Me.; edited the Fort Wayne "Gazette," 1871–74; was admitted to the bar at Indianapolis in January, 1877; was fifth auditor of the treasury, 1881–85; was United States district attorney, 1889–93; married Alice Colby of Defiance, O., September 14, 1871, and Anne Lucille Bliss of Buffalo December 30, 1893.*

<br>

### Tracy C. Becker

**Tracy C. Becker** has attained a prominent position at the bar and in the public service at a comparatively early age. He was well prepared for the profession he adopted, and thus had to overcome none of those obstacles that retard, when they do not prevent, the success of ambitious men of limited education who undertake the practice of law. Mr. Becker has confined himself closely to his profession; and whenever he has accepted public office it has been because the position involved legal work, and was in line with his vocation.

Mr. Becker's studies preparatory for college were pursued at a private school in Albany, where he was fitted for Union College, graduating therefrom in the classical course at the unusual age of nineteen. He then entered the famous Albany Law School, studying office practice meanwhile with G. B. and J. Kellogg of Troy and S. W. Rosendale of Albany, and took his LL. B. degree in 1876. He was admitted to the bar the same year, and thus began practice when only twenty-one years old. The next year he came to Buffalo, where he has practiced ever since.

For four years Mr. Becker was one of the assistant district attorneys of Erie county, under District Attorney E. W. Hatch, now a justice of the Supreme Court. Mr. Becker was nominated for the office of city attorney in 1882, and came within two hundred votes of an election. In 1894 he was elected a member of the state constitutional convention, and served on several of the most important committees. As chairman of the committee on legislative organization, which apportioned the state senate and assembly districts, he took a leading part in embodying in the constitution provisions to prevent political gerrymandering. He was also a member of the judiciary committee and of the committee on cities, and rendered efficient aid both in committee and on the

floor of the convention in securing the adoption and
passage of the important amendments that were
ratified by the people.

In the field of municipal reform Mr. Becker has
been foremost among the citizens of Buffalo. He
served with Messrs. Milburn, Wilcox, Clinton,
Graves, and others as a member of the Buffalo Citizens' Association, which succeeded in obtaining from
the legislature in 1892, after several years of earnest
effort, a new charter for the city. Largely through
the efforts of the same gentlemen there followed,
three years later, the passage of the jury-reform bill
for Erie county — a measure which daily proves the
wisdom of its promoters, and which is of vast benefit
to the cause of justice. Mr. Becker was one of the
organizers of the Buffalo Law School, in which he
has lectured since 1886 on criminal law
and medical jurisprudence.

The esteem in which Mr. Becker is
held by his professional brethren is evidenced in their selection of him, for four
years as chairman of the executive committee, and for one year as president, of
the State Bar Association of New York.
Not only as a practitioner, however, is he
regarded highly ; for he has also gained
a reputation in the ranks of law writers.
In collaboration with Professor R. A.
Witthaus, and other medico-legal special-
ists, Mr. Becker has written a valuable
work, in four volumes, on " Medical Jurisprudence, Forensic Medicine, and Toxicology." His law practice is large and
growing, and he has appeared before all
the courts of this state during the last
decade in many important civil and criminal cases. He is a member of one of
the leading law firms in Buffalo, of which
Comptroller James A. Roberts is the
senior partner.

Mr. Becker is prominent in social life,
and is a member of various fraternal societies, Masonic lodges, and of the Buffalo
Club. He is a Presbyterian in religion
and a Republican in politics.

*PERSONAL CHRONOLOGY —
Tracy Chatfield Becker was born at
Cohoes, N. Y., February 14, 1855 ; graduated from Union College, Schenectady,
N. Y., in 1874, and from Albany Law
School in 1876 ; was admitted to the bar at Binghamton, N. Y., in May, 1876 ; married Minnie A. Le Roy
of Cohoes December 27, 1876 ; was 2d assistant district attorney of Erie county, 1884-85 ; was president*

of the New York State Bar Association in 1894 ;
practiced law in Buffalo since 1877.

## Charles F. Bishop

**Charles F. Bishop** owes his success in life
close attention to business, zeal and activity in
ing for all matters entrusted to him, and an hone
and a singleness of purpose from which nothi
could entice him. Firmness, shrewdness, boldne
and the strictest integrity are parts of his charact
He has never been known to fail in the discharge
the manifold duties that have devolved upon him
a business man, as mayor of the city of Buffalo
five years, or as a representative Mason, to whom
fraternity often looks for assistance and guidance.

When only thirteen years old, young Bish
sought and obtained employment in a retail groce

CHARLES F. BISHOP

This was the humble beginning of a business
that has continued to the present time with an ev
increasing and broadening success. For many ye
Mr. Bishop has been a leading wholesale dealer

tea, coffee, and spices, having established himself in
that business in 1869. He is interested in various
other business enterprises, is a director of the People's
Bank, and a trustee of the Western Savings Bank.

Mr. Bishop pursued the quiet tenor of his way
as a business man, making friends steadily and holding them firmly, with no thought or ambition for
public life, until 1887, when the Democratic party
insisted on making him its candidate for county
treasurer. The contest was unusually close, and
when the official count was made Mr. Bishop was
declared defeated by forty-one votes. Some of his
friends strongly urged him to contest the election;
but he declined to do this, having no desire for an
office so obtained. This forbearance increased his
popularity greatly, and, together with the strength
he had shown in the contest, made him his party's
candidate for mayor of Buffalo in 1889. He was
elected by a very large majority, and two years later
was re-elected, serving altogether five years as the
chief magistrate of Buffalo. To the discharge of the
many vexatious duties of that trying position he
applied plain, business methods, and gave the city
one of the most efficient administrations it had ever
known. His conscientious devotion to duty was
modest withal, and he brought about many reforms
and prevented many abuses of which the public
learned only incidentally. His idea of what a mayor
ought to be was aptly shown in an after-dinner address made at a banquet given to Grover Cleveland at
the Iroquois hotel on May 11, 1891, when he said
that the mayor should be a "handy man." That
was exactly what Mayor Bishop proved himself to
be for the taxpayers. Never for a moment did he
swerve from what seemed to him the right course;
and to his credit it may be added that what seemed
right to him seemed right to the majority of his
fellow-citizens as well.

Mr. Bishop is a Mason of high standing and great
popularity. He is a Knight Templar, and holds the
32d degree in the Ancient Accepted Scottish Rite.
He has been Master of Concordia Lodge and Eminent Commander of Lake Erie Commandery, No. 20,
Knights Templars. He was president of the board
of trustees of the Masonic Hall Association for five
years, and in that capacity won the highest praise,
formally expressed, of his associates. For four years
he was District Deputy Grand Master for the 25th
Masonic district, and as such had the honor of laying
the corner stone of the magnificent temple that is
owned by the fraternity in Buffalo. He is first vice
president of the Masonic Life Association of Western
New York, and has been treasurer of Ismailia Temple,
Nobles of the Mystic Shrine, ever since its institution.

*PERSONAL CHRONOLOGY— Charles Fred-
erick Bishop was born at Williamsville, N. Y., October 14, 1844; moved to Buffalo in his boyhood; attended the public schools until he was thirteen years
old; married Kate Moran of Buffalo August 6,
1865; was elected mayor of Buffalo in 1889, and
re-elected in 1891, serving five years altogether; has
conducted a wholesale business in tea, coffee, and
spices since 1869.*

- - - ***

## Wilson S. Bissell

is one of the group of
public men who have made Buffalo famous in the
political annals of the country. Four of the number, Presidents Fillmore and Cleveland and Messrs.
Hall and Bissell, have been lawyers, and by a unique
coincidence have occupied the same law office. Few
cities have sent so many men to fill the highest positions in state and nation as the city of Buffalo.
That the history of the country has been profoundly
influenced by these men is not an unwarranted statement growing out of local pride.

Mr. Bissell is a native New Yorker, and his home
has been in Buffalo since he was five years old, when
his parents removed thither from New London,
Oneida county. He had, therefore, the advantages
of an education in the public schools of the city;
and in his sixteenth year he was sent to New Haven,
Conn., to prepare for college in the famous Hopkins
Grammar School. He entered Yale College in
1865, and graduated with the class of 1869. Returning to Buffalo, he began the study of law in the
office of Laning, Cleveland & Folsom, and was
admitted to practice two years later.

As a lawyer his career has been marked by close
attention to work, faithfulness to clients, increasing
practice, and steady advancement in the respect and
esteem of his brethren at the bar. The office of the
counselor has been to him far more congenial than
the contentious life of the advocate; and as an office
lawyer he holds a high rank both because of his wide
knowledge of his profession, and especially because
of excellent business judgment, which has drawn to
him a large corporation practice. The law is, after
all, like any branch of science—a few broad principles and a great deal of common sense.

Mr. Bissell has been associated in partnership with
a number of distinguished men and strong lawyers.
His first partner was Lyman K. Bass. Later, Mr.
Cleveland joined the firm, which was known as
Bass, Cleveland & Bissell. After Mr. Bass retired
and Mr. Cleveland was elected mayor of Buffalo, the
firm became Cleveland, Bissell & Sicard. On his
election to the governorship Mr. Cleveland withdrew, and since then Mr. Bissell has been the senior

member of one of Buffalo's great law firms, the style to-day being Bissell, Sicard, Bissell & Carey.

Although so much and so intimately associated with a man now occupying the highest position in the gift of the American people, Mr. Bissell resolutely abjured politics beyond what strong party fealty required of him. An earnest Democrat, always ready with time and services to aid in the success of his party, he preferred the practice of his profession to the allurements of political life. In Mr. Cleveland's first term Mr. Bissell had the refusal of several honorable offices, but could not be tempted from his purpose to remain simply a lawyer. However, when his old partner was elected for a second term in 1892, and invited him into his cabinet, Mr. Bissell felt that an honor so high and unsought by him should not be put aside. Therefore he accepted the position of postmaster-general in Mr. Cleveland's cabinet, and made the most of the large opportunities for usefulness that a cabinet portfolio presents. When, after two years of service, he resigned for purely personal reasons, he left behind him in the post-office department a record for thoroughness, unfailing courtesy, executive ability, and practical reform unsurpassed by any of his predecessors. The good will of men of both parties followed him to his home.

Mr. Bissell is prominent in the social life of Buffalo. He is a member of the Buffalo Club, of which he was president in 1888. In all public movements his counsel and his influence are sought, and every worthy cause finds in him a supporter and a friend.

*PERSONAL CHRONOLOGY—Wilson Shannon Bissell was born at New London, N. Y., December 31, 1847; graduated from Yale College in 1869; married Louise Sturges of Geneva, N. Y., February 6, 1880; was admitted to the bar at Buffalo in 1871; was presidential elector-at-large on the Democratic ticket in 1888; was postmaster-general, 1893-95.*

⁂

**George Bleistein** is a remarkable example of the rapidity with which a young American can rise to positions of high responsibility when ability and favoring fortune go together. His school days were brief, ending when, at the age of fourteen, he left one of the Buffalo public schools, and entered the service of the Courier Company as office boy. That

was the beginning of his career, and the indication or promise up to that time future was to be. Success came marvel for in five years the office boy had be tendent, and in three years more, on Chas. W. McCune — or less than a dec

time when the lad of fourteen entered t ment — he was elected president of th From the foot of the ladder he had ga most round.

Rapidly won success imposes upon hi it a greater task than that which rests u whose rise is slower. In sustaining the sibilities that he assumed as president o Company, Mr. Bleistein has made evid session of qualities that explain and just ori' advancement. As a business man fested enterprise and wisdom in the im extensive affairs; while in public rela made his position and abilities a post for the welfare of the community in whi

While he has not been active in politics in the lower sense in which that term is often understood, he has taken a decided stand in political matters, and one which, from his position at the head of the company that publishes the leading Democratic newspaper of Buffalo, has contributed much to the

*GEORGE BLEISTEIN*

well-being of his fellow-citizens. That stand is for pure government and home rule in home affairs. When the Home Rule Democracy of Erie County sprang into existence in 1893, to battle with the influences that were committing the municipality and county to the power of a corrupt political machine, Mr. Bleistein was elected president of the organization. The effect of the movement was felt in state as well as in local politics, and to it belongs much of the credit for the victory won for good government at the polls in that year. Mr. Bleistein has never sought public office, and the only office which he has held is that of trustee of the City and County Hall in Buffalo — a position that he occupied for seven years, four of which were spent as chairman of the board.

Mr. Bleistein has furnished many proofs that he is a good citizen of Buffalo. Projects for advancing the interests of the city have always met with warm sympathy from him. He has given generously of both his means and his time and influence to such enterprises. Any movement with a benevolent object is sure to find in him an ardent supporter.

Mr. Bleistein is by nature one of the most social and companionable of men. Thus it happens that he has many friends, and is a member of many clubs. Among the social organizations to which he belongs are the Buffalo Club, the Saturn Club, and the Country Club (of which he is president), all of Buffalo; the Manhattan Club of New York city; and the Jekyl Island Club. He is a 32d degree Mason.

Mr. Bleistein is president of the Associated Press of the State of New York, and a director of the United Press of the United States.

*PERSONAL CHRONOLOGY* — *George Bleistein was born at Buffalo December 6, 1861; graduated from the public schools, after spending two years at a German school; entered the service of the Courier Company, in Buffalo, in 1876, becoming superintendent of the company in 1881 and president in 1884; married Mrs. Elizabeth Wells McCune of Buffalo April 28, 1886; was chosen president of Home-Rule Democracy of Erie County, N. Y., in 1893.*

\*\*\*

**Henry W. Brendel** is one of the younger lawyers and politicians of Buffalo who have taken an active and intelligent interest in the affairs of the city. Although of German descent, he was born in Buffalo, and was educated in the public schools of that city. His course of study was completed in 1873, and he was then called upon to choose his calling in life. To the young man just entering the arena of action in this way, the future presents many and varied possibilities. The world of business, with its intense activity, wide opportunities, and splendid rewards, calls loudly to him to cast in his lot with its followers, while the various professions offer their counter attractions with compelling force. Mr. Brendel, notwithstanding the obstacle of insufficient scholastic preparation, chose the study of law, and resolved to make actual work and training in a practitioner's office take the place of a law school. This plan he successfully pursued, acquiring a knowledge of the law under these adverse conditions in about the same time that some law schools require. He remained one year in the office of Hawkins & Fischer, and completed his studies in the office of Delavan F. Clark. Realizing the fact that in the case of young men a successful practice of the law is most easily obtained through a connection with some attorney already prominent, Mr. Brendel formed a copartnership with General James C. Strong in the fall of 1879. The firm was most successful, and conducted much important litigation. In the year 1891 this partnership was dissolved by mutual consent, and Mr. Brendel has since carried on his extensive practice alone.

Mr. Brendel has always been actively interested in Republican politics, and has served his party for a number of years as member of its executive committee, where his counsel and advice are much sought and are always valuable. While serving on this committee, he was chosen treasurer for three years, on account of his strict integrity and business and financial acumen; and he handled the funds of the organization in a manner highly satisfactory to the party managers. He has three times been nominated for the state assembly, but, living in a district strongly Democratic, he has been as many times defeated. These defeats he takes cheerfully and philosophically, realizing that the man who can say, " I have never held a political office," has escaped many of the discomforts of life.

Mr. Brendel is a member of St. Stephen's Evangelical Church, and takes great interest in its work. Inheriting from his German ancestors that love of music for which the race is so famous, he belongs to the Harugari, the Teutonia Maennerchor, and other singing societies. He can claim much credit for the magnificent results accomplished by the German-American musical societies — one of the noteworthy and creditable features wherein Buffalo is pre-eminent among the cities of the Empire State — where the divine art is rationally mingled with domestic and social enjoyments, and with that genial Teutonic *gemuthlichkeit* that seems at present impossible to the less gregarious and more egoistic, nervous Yankee. To the Teutonia Maen-

nerchor, the chief among these societies, Mr. Brendel has devoted his time and energy without stint; and in other ways as well he has contributed liberally of both his means and influence to the advancement of the musical art and the cultivation of a sound musical taste in the city of Buffalo. Thus, with greater effectiveness than by more pretentious agencies, has he helped forward and developed that true urban civilization which has made the Queen of the Lower Lakes a city of cosmopolitan culture.

*PERSONAL CHRONOLOGY* — *Henry H. Brendel was born at Buffalo December 10, 1853; was educated in the Buffalo public schools, began the study of law in 1875, and was admitted to the bar in January, 1879; was nominated for the state assembly in 1886, 1887, and 1889.*

HENRY H. BRENDEL

**John C. Bryant,** while earning a handsome competence for himself, has devoted his life to the welfare of others. As president of the Bryant & Stratton Buffalo Business College he has contributed no small share to the growth and prosperity of Buffalo, by the business training given at his institution to a host of young men, many of whom have become leaders in the business world. He can, therefore, look back upon his life with a degree of satisfaction that falls to the lot of comparatively few. Of good

JOHN C. BRYANT

old English stock, Mr. Bryant was brought to this country early in life. His education was begun in the common schools, and after a two years' course in the academy at Norwalk, Ohio, he determined to study medicine. For three years he devoted his entire time and all his energies to the study of that noble profession, and graduated from the Cleveland Medical College in 1846.

For the next ten years he was known as Dr. Bryant. His field of labor was in Amherst, Ohio, and here he was widely known and honored, both as a man and as a physician. Many a professional man has found, after a few years devoted to what he had expected would be his life-work, that there were

opportunities for remunerative usefulness in directions altogether unthought of. Such was the case with Dr. Bryant. It was in the fall of 1856 that he came to Buffalo and entered into partnership with his brother, H. B. Bryant, and his brother-in-law, H. D. Stratton, who had established business colleges in Cleveland in 1853 and in Buffalo in 1854, which were to become links of a chain of similar institutions afterward located in forty-four cities of this country and Canada. These places of business training became famous as the Bryant & Stratton business colleges. To the projectors of these schools it was evident that here was an unoccupied field. Young men had no opportunity to acquire a knowledge of business methods except by a slow course of training in some office or store; and even then they were not likely to gain an insight into the theory and practice of business so comprehensive and accurate as modern conditions demand. From the first it was the intention of Messrs. Bryant and Stratton to make their course of study cover not only the theory but also the practice of mercantile methods. How successful these business colleges have been, thousands of young men, who have gone forth from them equipped with a practical knowledge of business methods, can testify.

Since 1860 Mr. Bryant has been president of the Buffalo college, and under his watchful care the original system has grown and expanded until it has apparently reached the stage of perfection. Yet it has never been Mr. Bryant's habit to be satisfied with what was already accomplished. His motto might well have been "Progress," so closely has he lived up to that principle.

No author of practical text-books on bookkeeping and commercial law ranks higher than Mr. Bryant. He has given a great deal of time and intelligent thought to the preparation of his books; and the fact that they have a large circulation all through the United States and Canada, and are favorably known even in foreign countries, is an evidence of their great value.

*PERSONAL CHRONOLOGY*— *John Collins Bryant was born at Ebley, Gloucestershire, England, December 21, 1821; attended the Norwalk (O.) Academy two years, and studied medicine three years, graduating from the Cleveland Medical College in 1846; married Hannah M. Clark of Wakeman, O., May 21, 1851; practiced his profession at Amherst, O., 1847-56; came to Buffalo in 1856, and formed a partnership with H. B. Bryant and H. D. Stratton for the conduct of business colleges; has been president of the Bryant & Stratton Buffalo Business College since 1866.*

---

**S. Douglas Cornell** is the head of one of the best known and oldest families in Buffalo. He is a familiar figure on the streets of the city, and is one of the most popular men in its society. He is a gentleman in the best sense of the word, always courteous and affable, ever kind and considerate in his bearing toward others. Mr. Cornell was born in Fairfield county, Conn., but early in life came to Buffalo, where he, and his father before him, were identified for many years with the progressive business interests of the city. Mr. Cornell had the good fortune to be equipped for his life-work with an excellent education, begun at home, continued under the care of able and watchful tutors, and finished (scholastically speaking) at Hobart College, Geneva, N. Y., whence he graduated in 1860. Supplementary study brought him the degree of A. M. from the same institution in 1863.

Immediately after his graduation he began an active business career with his father, S. G. Cornell, who was a leading manufacturer of white lead — a business with which the name of Cornell was associated for a long period. His connection with the manufacture of this important product was interrupted for some time that he spent in Colorado as an agent for the examination of gold mines. In this specialty he was eminently successful, and in 1863 he published, as a result of his observations, a valuable pamphlet entitled "Prospects of Gold Mining in Colorado."

As Mr. Cornell's father desired the aid of his son in his rapidly expanding business, hitherto conducted under his own name, the young man returned from Colorado and devoted himself to the interests of the firm, which thus acquired the style of S. G. Cornell & Son. The firm was so known until 1867, when it was reorganized as the Cornell Lead Company. Under this style the business was successfully carried on until 1888, when Mr. Cornell retired from active pursuits.

Mr. Cornell early interested himself in the National Guard of the State of New York, and long and faithful service therein must be placed to his credit. In this connection he may be referred to as colonel, since that was his rank for a long time. He enlisted as a private in the 74th regiment, in which he soon became a non-commissioned officer. The attention of Brigadier General William F. Rogers was called to the faithful young officer, who was thereupon given a staff appointment as junior aide de camp. Mr. Cornell remained on the staff of General Rogers for fifteen years, while that officer was a brigadier general and afterwards a major general in command of the 8th division. After serving through various subordinate ranks, Mr. Cornell won the position of assistant adjutant-general and chief of staff with the rank of colonel. This position he retained until the

S. DOUGLAS CORNELL

reorganization of the National Guard and the abolishment of divisions.

Mr. Cornell is possessed of much histrionic talent and would undoubtedly have made a brilliant success had he adopted the stage as a profession. Buffalonians have had the pleasure on numerous occasions of seeing him in the entertainments of the Buffalo Amateurs — an organization that has acquired no little fame by reason of the finish of its performances and the high social standing of its members. For the former of these distinctions great credit is due Mr. Cornell, for he has been the stage manager of the organization from 1872 to the present time.

*PERSONAL CHRONOLOGY— Samuel Douglas Cornell was born at Glenville, Conn., December 2, 1839: graduated from Hobart College in 1860: married Lydia Hadfield of Buffalo January 29, 1862: spent about three years in Colorado, 1862-64, as agent for the examination of gold mines: took part in his father's lead business for two years after graduation, returned thereto in 1864, and remained in the business until 1888: served on the staff of brigadier general, afterwards major general, William F. Rogers, in command of 4th division, N. G., S. N. Y., for fifteen years, becoming assistant adjutant general and chief of staff, with rank of colonel.*

* * *

**William Caryl Cornwell** has done much to spread abroad the fame of Buffalo, for press dispatches often quote "W. C. Cornwell of Buffalo" as making a speech or reading a paper on some live topic before a gathering of bankers of state or national importance. Mr. Cornwell is known as one of the leading bankers of the country. Indeed, David A. Wells includes him among the six best conservative authorities on financial subjects, the other five so distinguished being David W. Stone, William B. Dana, William Dodsworth, Edward Atkinson, and Charles B. Fairchild. The fact is that Mr. Cornwell is a thorough master of the theory as well as the practice of banking, and when he speaks or writes on these subjects he is sure to have an attentive and appreciative audience.

Mr. Cornwell is thoroughly modern in his methods and ideas, and at the same time thoroughly sound. The best illustration of the truth of this is found in the great growth of the Bank of Buffalo, of which he was for fifteen years the cashier, and in that of the City Bank of Buffalo, which he organized in 1892, and of which he is president.

When Mr. Cornwell became cashier of the first-named bank it employed a few clerks, and used one room for the transaction of its business. When he left the bank it had a staff of thirty-five clerks, and was so cramped for room that it had been trying for some time to obtain a site for a building of its own. During his administration the business of the bank increased over 600 per cent, and its surplus earnings became greater than its capital, while its deposits

amounted to more than $4,000,000. In 1892, Mr. Cornwell withdrew from active connection with this bank, and organized the "City Bank, Buffalo, N. Y." This bank began operations in the spring of 1893 in the face of universal business depression: but the fall of the same year found the City Bank with deposits of $1,000,000, all accumulated within six months and during a panicky season. These facts certainly speak volumes for the skill of Mr. Cornwell as a banker, and for the confidence that the business men of Buffalo have in him. He was one of the organizers of the Buffalo Bankers' Association in 1881, and has been its secretary from the start. It was largely through him that the clearing house was formed in 1889, and made a part of the Association. He was the first chairman of the clearing-house committee, and held the position for three years. During that time he perfected two most important undertakings. One was the making of clearings on a cash basis instead of by draft: the other was the banding of the banks together for the issuance of clearing house certificates. This was effected in 1890 upon Mr. Cornwell's forecast of coming danger. The banks at that time passed a resolution for joint action, and all machinery was arranged for clearing-house certificates. The possibility of using these promptly saved the city from impending disaster on the fatal 26th of June, 1893. The resolution of 1890 ran as follows:

"In view of a possible money crisis at any future time, the Banks, members of this Association, for the purpose of sustaining each other and the business community, do hereby resolve. That A committee of five be elected, as hereinafter provided, to receive from Banks, members of the Association, bills receivable and other securities to be approved of by said Committee, who shall be and are hereby authorized to issue therefor to such depositing Banks loan certificates not in excess of seventy-five per cent of the securities or bills receivable so deposited (except in case of United States Bonds), and such certificates shall be received and paid in settlement of balance at the Clearing House; the obligations given for such certificates to bear interest at the rate of six per cent per annum."

In the larger field of state, national, and international banking, Mr. Cornwell has won a renown that might well be the envy of an older man. He took a very active part in bringing pressure to bear upon congress to secure the repeal of the purchase clause of the Sherman act. It was he who prepared forms of petitions, and sent them all over the country to banks, which in turn obtained the signatures of their customers, and forwarded the petitions to Washington. These collectively became known as the "Buffalo Petition." Mr. Cornwell's addresses and writings on financial subjects evince clearness of comprehension, soundness of view, and strength of logic. Among his writings are a pamphlet on "Free

Coinage"; an address before the American Bankers' Association in 1891, on "Canadian Bank Currency," in which he pointed out the errors in our own system, and predicted the disasters of two years later; papers on "Currency Reform and Bank Circulation" and "The Gold Standard," both ranking high among American economic writings; and "The Currency and Banking Law of Canada," a digest of the laws of Canada, recently published by G. P. Putnam's Sons.

Mr. Cornwell was one of the founders of the New York State Bankers' Association, and was its first president. So highly were his efforts in behalf of the institution and of sound money appreciated by his associates, that he was elected an honorary member of the council of administration. He has also been vice president for New York state of the American Bankers' Association; and in 1894 he was elected a member of the executive committee for three years.

Banking, however, does not occupy all of Mr. Cornwell's time. He is an artist of much ability, and a pleasant and discriminating writer on art topics. He studied art at the Julien school in Paris, and was a pupil of Lefebvre and Boulanger. He has produced many charming sketches and some work of a more ambitious character that has been highly praised. Mr. Cornwell has a summer home at East Aurora, seventeen miles from Buffalo, where he and his wife have surrounded themselves with everything that artistic natures can desire.

### PERSONAL CHRONOLOGY

*William Caryl Cornwell was born at Lyons, N. Y., August 19, 1851; attended the public schools of Buffalo; married Marian W. Loomis of Buffalo October 9, 1874; was cashier of the Bank of Buffalo, 1877–92; organized the City Bank of Buffalo in 1892, and has been president thereof since; was made the first president of the New York State Bankers' Association in 1894; was president of the Buffalo Society of Artists, 1894-96; was a member of the executive committee of the American Bankers' Association, 1894-96; has been Fund Commissioner of the Buffalo Fine Arts Academy since 1889.*

* * *

**Charles W. Cushman** is an example of a class of men fortunately by no means rare in our country — men whose activity and usefulness begin

early in life, and continue unceasingly to develop. Like many another high minded youth, Mr. Cushman left school to enter the army at the time of the Civil War. The fact that as a boy he was willing to forsake the easy and pleasant avenues of civil and business life for the far rougher paths of military

WILLIAM CARYL CORNWELL

activity, promised well for his character and for his chances of success in any business to which he might devote himself. He served as drummer boy in the Army of the Cumberland, and marched with Sherman to the sea. Service and sacrifice of this kind are never without their reward. The self-reliance, energy, and fortitude developed in camp life cannot fail to be valuable acquisitions to the character of any man; and these qualities, when developed early in life, as they were in Mr. Cushman's case, are likely to be permanent and most valuable characteristics of the man.

Soon after the close of the war, Mr. Cushman found an opportunity to put his ability to the test in the service of the Lake Shore & Michigan Southern railway. He must have stood the test excellently, for three years after entering the service of this corporation he was appointed to the office of general agent at Cleveland. This position he held for eight years — from 1872 to 1880. While so engaged, Mr. Cushman came to see the manifold advantages that

CHARLES W. CUSHMAN

might result from an association of railway-car interests. The project appeared both desirable and practicable, and in 1880 Mr. Cushman organized the Railway Car Association. At this time the prominence that Buffalo was destined to attain as a great railroad center was already foreseen by the more observant railroad men, and by Mr. Cushman among others ; and Buffalo was made the headquarters of the association. There are branches in the principal cities of the United States. Of this association Mr. Cushman has been president and general manager since 1880.

Some active business men seem to find no field too large for their capacities, no work too burdensome for their energies. In business, as in scholarship,

most men must specialize in these days of ever widening knowledge. But the vigor of the capable business manager overflows in numerous channels, and many kinds of business cognate to his special pursuit benefit by the diversity of his talents. Mr. Cushman's career admirably illustrates this statement.

He is president of the Columbian Equipment Company and president of the Standard Iron Works, both of Chicago, and stockholder and director in several other companies. He served on the staff of the commander of the Grand Army when General Fairchild was commander in chief.

Mr. Cushman has found continual relaxation in a great and constantly increasing devotion to Masonry. Rarely does an active man lack an avocation, and often the success and distinction that he wins in his chosen means of relaxation are parallel to his business attainments. That such has been the case with Mr. Cushman, and that he has found both pleasure and honor in his avocation, we may infer from the fact that in September, 1894, he was crowned a Sovereign Grand Inspector General of the 33d and last degree of Masonry.

*PERSONAL CHRONOLOGY—Charles Weeks Cushman was born at Cleveland, O., August 31, 1848 ; attended the Cleveland public schools and the Rockford (Ill.) High School ; spent two years in the army, 1864–65 ; married Georgie L. Doran of Chicago March 18, 1873 ; entered the service of the Lake Shore & Michigan Southern railway in 1869, and was general agent of the company, 1872–80 ; organized the Railway Car Association in 1880, and has been president thereof since.*

* * *

**Joseph P. Dudley** comes from good old New Hampshire stock. In every quarter of the globe and in every country the New Englander is found. As merchant and banker, as inventor and discoverer, as navigator and explorer, the Yankee is to the front. A man is what his ancestors have made him, in quality, but the particular form of development is determined by circumstances. This fact explains the inborn integrity and conscientious course pursued in the affairs of life by Joseph P. Dudley.

After a youth among the hills of the old Granite State, with only such educational advantages as the country schools and Pembroke Academy could give him, he began a business career that has culminated in a success so marked that he is recognized as an ideal type of business man. Mr. Dudley came to Buffalo in 1858, and embarked in the foundry business, continuing the same for three years. He then formed a partnership with J. D. Dudley and M. L. Dudley, the firm being Dudley & Co. and the business that of oil refining. The entire management was under the direction of Joseph P. Dudley, and the firm was very successful. In 1882 the oil business of Dudley & Co. was merged with that of the great Standard Oil Company of New York, the Buffalo business being known as the Star Oil Branch ; and since that time Mr. Dudley has been the general manager of the Standard Oil Company's vast interests in Buffalo and western New York. Probably no man among the many able managers who direct the affairs of the greatest corporation in this county, stands higher than Joseph P. Dudley.

It is but natural that a successful man like Mr. Dudley should be engaged in many enterprises, for profit, for pleasure, and for religious, educational, and philanthropic purposes. He is identified with many of the important institutions of Buffalo. He is a trustee of the Erie County Savings Bank with assets amounting to $20,000,000 ; director in the American Exchange and Hydraulic banks ; and director of the Ellicott Square Company, now erecting the greatest office building in the world.

Mr. Dudley loves his church. He is vice president and treasurer of the Lafayette Street Presbyterian Church Society, and has done as much for that church as any man ever identified with it. He has had charge of its music for a great number of years, and has an abiding interest and faith in the musical as well as the theological end of the church. He has always shown great interest in musical matters, having been identified with the Buffalo Musical Association since its organization, as director or as president. Mr. Dudley has been connected with most of the leading institutions of Buffalo, and in 1895 was president of the Buffalo Library. He is actively interested in the Historical Society, and is president of the board of managers of the State Hospital for Insane.

He is pre-eminently a society man ; that is to say, he is an intelligent man, who is fond of his fellow creatures, and loves to be with them. He is a member of the leading clubs of the city. He has been president of the Buffalo Club, and is now a director is vice president of the Ellicott Club ; he is a director of the Falconwood Club, and member of the Country Club, Liberal Club, Otowega Club, and several others. He is a generous giver to the poor, and the benevolent institutions of the city. Few are more popular, and no man has a keener sense of humor, a greater fund of anecdote and experience, and a livelier appreciation of the good things of than Joseph P. Dudley.

PERSONAL CHRONOLOGY — Joseph Plumbury Dudley was born at Candia, N. H., November 21, 1832 ; attended country schools, and graduated from Pembroke (N. H.) Academy in 1852 ; married Mary E. Underhill of Concord, Mass., in 18—

moved to Buffalo in 1858 ; engaged in the oil-refining business from 1861 until 1882 in the firm of Dudley & Co. ; has been manager of the Star Oil Branch of the Standard Oil Company since 1882.

**Henry P. Emerson** was born in the old Bay State town of Lynnfield, of the good New England stock that makes leaders everywhere. He prepared for college at the famous Phillips Academy, Andover, Mass., and distinguished himself at Rochester University by taking the senior essay prize.

*HENRY P. EMERSON*

He began his pedagogic career in 1871 as teacher of Greek and Latin in the State Normal School at Potsdam, N. Y. In 1874 he came to Buffalo as principal of the classical department of the Buffalo High School; and in 1883, upon the resignation of Professor Spencer, who had held the principalship of the school for twenty years, Mr. Emerson was appointed to that very responsible position. His work there quickly gave promise of striking success. Aroused by his efforts, the school alumni became enthusiastic over the project for the enlargement of the school, petitions were circulated among the citizens, and the city was induced to build an addition, costing nearly $60,000, to the old school building. The growth of the school during his administration was remarkable, for during the ten years that he occupied the principal's chair the number of pupils increased from three hundred to a thousand. But his greatest successes were not of this material sort. He exerted himself to create among the students a sentiment in favor of order, and they were thus led to respect the rights of others in the school; and oppressive and repressive measures were seldom necessary. In opposition to mechanical and bookish methods, he sought to arouse an enthusiasm for investigation and original work, and the scholarship of the school was materially improved. His morning talks were a feature to which many of his pupils look back as one of the happiest and most profitable experiences of their school life. It was his custom to give an informal talk, at least once a week, to the assembled school on some historical subject (suggested, perhaps, by an anniversary), or on current matters of interest in the outside world. In this way the boys and girls obtained definite and available information that they found most useful.

Appreciating his devotion to the cause of education and his entire fitness for the office, the Republican party in 1892 nominated him for superintendent of schools of the city of Buffalo. He was elected, and began his new duties January 1, 1893. One of his first reforms was the introduction of more modern text-books in English and in other subjects. He also turned his attention to that important branch of public instruction, the primary schools, and appointed a capable woman to oversee this whole work of primary teaching. The evening schools of the city had fallen sadly into disrepute, owing to their general inefficiency. Superintendent Emerson took these in hand with eminent success. He reduced their number from twenty-two to twelve, and placed them in charge of thoroughly qualified teachers; and as a result these schools have become most popular, and valuable opportunities for self-improvement have been given to all who choose to embrace them, while the cost of maintaining the schools has been materially reduced. Superintendent Emerson is an indefatigable worker, and labors incessantly in his office, in teachers' meetings, and elsewhere. He is a Napoleon of organization, and the wonderful system inaugurated by him in the Buffalo public schools is worthy the study of the educator.

In the meantime the scant leisure of so busy a professional life has been fruitful of supplementary achievements. A paper on "Latin in High Schools," read at the 1881 session of the State Teachers' Association, published by Bardeen of Syracuse, is a master piece among educational monographs; as is also his "Education of the Child," an address delivered before the public-school teachers of Buffalo. "A Summer in Europe," a collection of letters, written originally for the Buffalo *Courier*, is his breezy contribution to travel literature.

Professor Emerson is a member of the Baptist church; of the Alpha Delta Phi, Phi Beta Kappa, and Masonic fraternities; of the Buffalo Historical Society and the Society of Natural Sciences; and of the Liberal Club, the University Club, and the Saturn Club (all of Buffalo).

*PERSONAL CHRONOLOGY — Henry P. Emerson was born at Lynnfield, Mass., January 14, 1847; graduated from Phillips Academy, Andover, Mass., in 1867, and from Rochester University in 1871 with the degree of A. B., receiving the degree of A. M. from the latter institution in 1874; married Mary A. Estes of Middleton, Mass., August 4, 1874; came to Buffalo in the same year as teacher of Greek and Latin in the Central High School, of which he was appointed principal in 1884; was elected superintendent of education of the city of Buffalo in 1892, taking office January 1, 1893, for a term of three years; was re-elected to the same position in November, 1895.*

***

**Edwin Fleming** has devoted his life to newspaper work. He has not held office, political or other, nor has he sought it. He is a type of the journalist who respects his profession; who finds in it the opportunity for high usefulness to his fellow-men; who brings to it his best, allowing no distraction to come between; and who does it, and himself, honor.

In newspaper work, in a degree greater than that of most professions, the usefulness of the worker depends upon the breadth of his training. Mr. Fleming laid the foundation of his professional career in a university education, and supplemented this with systematic study after graduation. Leaving college with the degree of B. A., he afterward attended law lectures, and received from his *alma mater* in 1873 the degree of M. A. To his

college training he added later the education that comes of travel, devoting eighteen months to European sight-seeing. Since then the education received from books and from travel has been finely rounded out by the education in practical affairs that journalism so effectively provides.

Mr. Fleming's newspaper life began in the University of Michigan, where, in his junior and senior years, he was one of the editors of a college paper. To this experience he added, while still in college, the more practical training involved in correspondence for the Detroit *Post*. Immediately upon graduation he found a berth upon the *Post* as a reporter; in the winter of 1870-71 he had charge of the telegraph desk of the Detroit *Tribune*; later in 1871 he did special reporting for the latter paper

EDWIN FLEMING

in various parts of Michigan, afterward doing general newspaper work for the Kalamazoo *Telegraph* and the Jackson *Citizen* as well as for the *Tribune*. Thus he had a thorough training in different branches of

his profession before he went to Europe. On returning from abroad, he went to Washington, D. C.,
and became the Washington representative successively of the New York *Journal of Commerce*, of the
New York *Commercial Bulletin*, of the Detroit *Free
Press* (from 1875 to 1885), of the St. Louis *Republic*

*JAMES GILBERT FORSYTH*

(from 1881 to 1885), and of the Buffalo *Courier*
(from January 1, 1877, to 1885). Thus by easy
stages his way led to the editorship of the Buffalo
*Courier*.

The traits of this extensive training are apparent
in Mr. Fleming's work as a newspaper man. On
the one hand, he looks upon affairs with the breadth
of view of the scholar. On the other, he possesses the practical advantage given by a remarkably
wide acquaintance with public men — an acquaintance gained during a ten years' residence at the
national capital. The combination of these two
elements explains, in large measure, Mr. Fleming's
success in the editorial chair.

While his temper might be described as that of the
scholar, it must not be supposed that Mr. Fleming
takes no interest in politics. On the contrary, he
seems to find, and rightly, in politics the field of the
highest usefulness of a journalist. In his editorial
work he exhibits a judicial nature. He considers
coolly and deliberately, and when his
resolution is made carries it out fearlessly
to the end. He treats political matters
with a view, not to their temporary and
superficial aspect, but to their deeper
relations and significance. As might be
supposed, his work has been on the side
of good government, of honest elections,
and of political independence. He has
believed, and preached, that the right
thing is the best thing in the long run.

*PERSONAL CHRONOLOGY —
Edwin Fleming was born at West Lebanon,
Ind., December 11, 1847 ; graduated from
the University of Michigan in 1870 ; engaged in newspaper work of various kinds
for several Michigan papers until 1873 ;
after spending eighteen months abroad, went
to Washington as correspondent of New
York, Detroit, and St. Louis newspapers,
and of the Buffalo " Courier" ; married
Harriet L. Stone of Kalamazoo, Mich.,
April 29, 1884 ; has been editor of the
Buffalo " Courier" since June 1, 1885.*

**James Gilbert Forsyth** exhibits
the type of man in which singleness of
purpose and tenacity of determination are
exemplified in a marked degree. Half-
way measures are unknown to him. His
methods are direct and thorough, and he
devotes to every task such time as may be
needed for its proper and final execution.

Born in Buffalo April 17, 1832, he
went West at an early age, his boyhood being
spent in Kenosha, Wis. Here he received the
usual common-school education, but restlessness to
begin the more definite work of life caused him to
apprentice himself at the age of fourteen to the hardware firm of Marshall & Phelps, where he learned
the trade of tinman. After serving out the most
of his apprenticeship in the true old-fashioned style,
he was released by the dissolution of the firm and
went to Geneva, Wis., where he worked for a few
months at his trade before coming to Buffalo in
1852. After determined effort he secured a position
with Pratt & Co., then the leading hardware firm of
this section, with whom he remained until January

1, 1856, when he accepted a position with Sidney Shepard & Co., and was admitted to partnership in December, 1860. He has since devoted himself with unfaltering energy to the ever increasing interests of this well known house, whose business operations now extend over the entire country.

He was married on the 10th of March, 1857, to Miss Jane Elizabeth Dodge of Buffalo. He was one of the founders of Christ Church, later incorporated with Trinity.

*PERSONAL CHRONOLOGY James Gilbert Forsyth was born at Buffalo April 12, 1842; was educated in the public schools of Kenosha, Wis.; married Jane Elizabeth Dodge of Buffalo March 10, 1857; entered the service of Sidney Shepard & Co. of Buffalo in 1856; and has been a partner in the firm since 1860.*

...

## George S. Gatchell

George S. Gatchell has never seen an idle day since he became old enough to know what real work is. He belongs to the class of men who are happiest when they have most to do, and who justify the paradoxical saying, "If you want a thing done quickly, take it to a busy man." Mr. Gatchell is best known as a railroad man of wide experience and of great capacity; but his earlier military career is worth recalling. He went to the front with the 3d Pennsylvania cavalry, was present at the taking of Petersburg and at the surrender of Lee, and was mustered out of service August 7, 1865, as sergeant major of the 5th Pennsylvania cavalry. This army career was his first serious venture in life, and may safely be regarded as his first success.

Soon after the war, he accepted an opportunity to go out on the preliminary line of the Buffalo & Washington railroad as a rodman. This was the beginning of his connection with railroads. The Buffalo & Washington railroad, which afterward became the Buffalo, New York & Pennsylvania, and which is now the Western New York & Pennsylvania, was designed to open up a new territory for Buffalo, and its construction was watched with much interest. After taking charge of the construction of four miles of this road in 1866-67, Mr. Gatchell went to Michigan, where he ran the lines and had charge of part of the construction of forty miles of a road that ran from Grand Rapids to Muskegon. He then returned to this state, and ran the lines of the Rochester & State Line railroad in 1870 and 1871.

When work was resumed on the Buffalo & Washington railroad he was made assistant engineer, and in 1872 was made chief engineer. From this time Mr. Gatchell was identified exclusively with the development of the railroad system of western New York and northwestern Pennsylvania. Among the lines with the construction of which he was intimately connected were the Olean, Bradford & Warren narrow gauge, from Olean to State Line, and the Kendall & Eldred, from Eldred, N. Y., to Bradford, Penn. These roads tapped the oil regions, the rich, of southwestern New York and northwestern Pennsylvania, and ultimately became feeders for the

George S. Gatchell

Buffalo, New York & Pennsylvania railroad. The markedly excellent work that he had done in connection with these lines and the undoubted talent he had shown in the management of large interests, led to his appointment in 1879 as general superintendent of the Buffalo, New York & Pennsylvania railroad. For ten years, through several changes of management, he held this responsible position, discharging its trying duties with rare sagacity and executive ability. Mr. Gatchell left the railroad business in 1889 to become the general manager of the Buffalo Elevating Company.

When the charter of the city of Buffalo was revised with a view to correcting many existing evils, the department of public works was created under the control of three commissioners. This department has charge of all municipal construction, paving, street cleaning, water works, and public buildings, and is responsible for the proper expenditure of a large sum of money annually. When the first commission was created in 1892, Mayor Charles F. Bishop appointed Mr. Gatchell as the only Republican member of the board. Mr. Gatchell's long experience in dealing with important interests and with large bodies of men was of the utmost value to the commission, and it was not long before he became known as the " working member " of the board.

Socially Mr. Gatchell is a most companionable man. He is a leading member of the Buffalo Club.

*PERSONAL CHRONOLOGY— George Samuel Gatchell was born at Wheatfield, N. Y., January 16, 1847 ; attended the Lockport Union School until 1863, when he moved to Philadelphia ; enlisted in the 3d Pennsylvania cavalry in June, 1864, and served until the close of the war ; came to Buffalo in 1866, and engaged in railroad surveying ; was appointed chief engineer in 1872 of what is now the Western New York & Pennsylvania railroad, and was general superintendent of that company, 1879–89 ; married Sarah M. Ketcham of Buffalo October 15, 1874 ; was appointed a commissioner of public works of the city of Buffalo January 4, 1892, for a term of one year, and was reappointed January 4, 1893, for three years.*

•••

## James Fraser Gluck,

if the law were not his first thought, might be one of the foremost literary workers of the day. Indeed, as it is, his contributions to literature have been such as to give him high rank in that difficult sphere of attainment. He is a strong, vigorous writer, and the products of his pen are characterized by a literary finish that is rarely found outside the work of professional authors of repute. But the law has been his chosen profession ; and he has no reason to complain that his choice has not brought him substantial and deserved rewards.

Born at Niagara Falls in 1852, Mr. Gluck attended the common schools of that famous city, then a mere village. This was supplemented by courses of study at the grammar school of Drummondville, Canada, at Upper Canada College in Toronto, Ont., and at Cornell University, from which he was graduated in 1874, standing at the head of his class, and receiving the highest honor of the college — the Woodford prize. He was chosen president of his class, and has been re-elected to that office at every subsequent meeting of his class.

Mr. Gluck, after acting as editor of the first daily newspaper at Niagara Falls, the *Niagara Falls Register*, turned his attention to the law. He came to Buffalo, studied in the office of Laning & Willett, was admitted to the bar in 1876, and formed a partnership with A. P. Laning and Daniel H. McMillan in 1877. After the death of Mr. Laning the firm became successively Greene, McMillan & Gluck (1881–87), McMillan, Gluck & Pooley (1887–90), and McMillan, Gluck, Pooley & Depew (1890–18—). During all these changes the firm has been celebrated for its successful care of large corporate interests, which it has made its specialty. Railroads have sought its guidance, and among its chief clients have steadfastly been the great Vanderbilt interests represented in the New York Central, the Lake Shore, the West Shore, the Michigan Central, and other railroads entering Buffalo.

As a trial lawyer in railroad cases, Mr. Gluck stands pre-eminent in his profession. His ability was recognized by his selection some years since to fill the chair of the law of corporations in the Buffalo Law School, a branch of the University of Buffalo ; this position he still occupies.

Mr. Gluck has been active in numerous fields of labor. Like many lawyers, he has paid no little attention to politics, and during the exciting campaign of 1884 he organized the Central Republican Club of Buffalo, which attained a membership of over 2,500, and which was the largest campaign club ever formed in Buffalo. He is a favorite campaign speaker, and has made many addresses in Buffalo and throughout the state. Mr. Gluck is a brilliant and powerful orator, and has made on occasions of importance many addresses on literary and scientific topics that have won for him the highest praise, as regards both matter and manner. These addresses should receive permanent form in one or more volumes. Mr. Gluck is much sought, also, as an after dinner speaker.

Service of the highest importance in the cause of education has been rendered by Mr. Gluck during his long term as a trustee of Cornell University. Andrew D. White, formerly president of the university, has publicly given Mr. Gluck much of the credit for the establishment of the system of scholarships, whereby poor and meritorious students receive university aid for four years to the amount of $250 a year. The report on the condition of the university made by Mr. Gluck at the end of his first year as trustee seemed entirely to dissipate the dissatisfaction that had prevailed extensively theretofore among the alumni. Mr. Gluck had also much to do in stimulating the establishment of the school of philosophy at Cornell, which is now recognized as one of the most complete in the country. When President White retired, Mr. Gluck was prominently mentioned as his successor. This was justly regarded at the time as a striking tribute to the ability Mr. Gluck had displayed in all his relations with the institution. While curator of the Buffalo Library, Mr. Gluck made a collection of manuscripts, autograph letters of famous men, historical documents of value, and rare books ; and just before the close of his term of office he surprised and delighted the trustees of the library by presenting to them for the institution what many deem the most valuable collection of the kind in the country. As president of the Grosvenor Library, Mr. Gluck has pursued a liberal and progressive policy, and has done much to increase the public usefulness of that institution. The private library of Mr. Gluck is probably the largest private library in the city, and is distinctively rich in history, philosophy, science, and the classics of Greece and Rome.

*PERSONAL CHRONOLOGY.—James Fraser Gluck was born at Niagara Falls, N. Y., April 28, 1852 ; attended common schools, Upper Canada College, at Toronto, Ont., and Cornell University, graduating therefrom in 1874 ; studied law in Buffalo, and was admitted to the bar in 1876 ; married Effie D. Tyler, daughter of Professor Charles M. Tyler of Cornell University, June 15, 1877 ; was elected a trustee of Cornell in 1883 ; was curator of the Buffalo Library from 1885 to 1887 ; has been president of the Grosvenor Library, Buffalo, since 1885.*

- - -

**Charles W. Goodyear** is a shining example of the fact that a good lawyer makes a good business man, for he has attained marked success in both callings. The word failure has no place in any dictionary he ever conned. He has been successful in great undertakings because he is ready to take advantage of all opportunities that present themselves, and to make opportunities where they do not already exist. Shrewdness and courage go hand in hand with him ; and these, coupled with an industry that knows no rest, have won for him unusual success.

JAMES FRASER GLUCK

Buffalo first knew Mr. Goodyear as a resident in 1868. His education was obtained in the common schools of Erie county and at the Cortland (N. Y.) Academy. When he came to Buffalo he began the study of law in the office of Laning & Miller, continuing the study with John C. Strong. Admitted to the bar of Erie county in 1871, he immediately began the practice of law. For the first few years he was alone, but in 1875 he formed a partnership with Major John Tyler, which continued for two years. Until 1882 he was again without an associate, but in February of that year the firm of Goodyear & Allen (Henry F. Allen) was formed. Grover Cleveland, becoming governor of the state of New York January 1, 1883, retired from the law firm of

Cleveland, Bissell & Sicard, and Mr. Goodyear joined that firm. Thereafter, for four years, the firm of Bissell, Sicard & Goodyear was one of the most prominent in Buffalo.

For some years Mr. Goodyear was actively interested in politics, and the Democratic party in the

CHARLES W. GOODYEAR

city and the state was always glad of his services in whatever form they could be obtained. He served the people of Erie county as assistant district attorney from January 1, 1875, until October 1, 1877, having been appointed to that office by the district attorney, Daniel N. Lockwood. When Mr. Lockwood resigned to enter upon his term as representative in congress, Governor Robinson appointed Mr. Goodyear to serve out the balance of the year. These were the only political offices ever held by Mr. Goodyear. He was, however, actively interested in the movement that resulted in the nomination of Grover Cleveland for mayor of Buffalo and in his subsequent election to that office. Mr. Goodyear

had no small part in effecting the election of Mr. Cleveland to the office of governor of New York state; and he did yeoman's service in securing the nomination of Governor Cleveland for the Presidency in 1884. Since his retirement from the law Mr. Goodyear has not been actively engaged in politics.

In 1887, when he left the law, Mr. Goodyear associated himself with his brother, Frank H. Goodyear, in the lumber and railroad business. The firm of F. H. & C. W. Goodyear was organized May 1, 1887, and has been the foremost factor in the development of the lumber industries of northern Pennsylvania. The firm's interests in that section are vast. With the enormous output of 130,000,000 feet of hemlock lumber a year, the Goodyear brothers are the largest manufacturers of that commodity in the world. They have mills and works of various kinds throughout Potter county, Pennsylvania, and control many miles of railroads, which they have built to develop the territory. These roads are known as the Buffalo & Susquehanna, of which Mr. Goodyear is second vice president and general manager, and the Wellsville, Coudersport & Pine Creek, of which he is vice president.

With all his mammoth business interests, Mr. Goodyear finds time for other things. He is a Mason, a life member of the Buffalo Library, a trustee of the State Normal School in Buffalo, and a member of the Buffalo Club, the Falconwood Club, the Saturn Club, the Country Club, the Liberal Club, and the Acacia Club.

PERSONAL CHRONOLOGY— Charles Waterhouse Goodyear was born at Cortland, N. Y., October 15, 1846; completed his schooling at the Cortland Academy in 1865; came to Buffalo in 1868; was admitted to the bar in 1871; married Ella Portia Conger of Collins Center, N. Y., March 23, 1876; was appointed assistant district attorney of Erie county by Daniel N. Lockwood, taking office January 1, 1875; was appointed district attorney by Governor Robinson to fill an unexpired term October 1, 1877, holding office until January 1, 1878; retired from the practice of law in 1887 to enter the lumber and railroad business with his brother, Frank H. Goodyear.

***

**John C. Graves** has on more than one occasion shown the possession of those qualities that make the ideal citizen.    Fearless and resolute, actuated by no selfish motives, determined to do whatever is for the best welfare of the community, swerved from that purpose by no clamor of demagogues, — to him as much as to any one person Buffalo owes its present improved form of government. During all the years that this community struggled, through the Citizens' Association, of which General Graves is president, for a reformed charter, he stood in the forefront, receiving the brunt of the battle and successfully beating back the spoilsmen, who fought for a retention of antiquated methods of municipal government because in them were the greater opportunities for personal and political profit. For that labor General Graves finds recompense in the gratitude of those of his fellow-citizens who place business above politics, and in the consciousness of having performed an arduous task faithfully and well.

General Graves is a prominent figure in the commercial and social circles of Buffalo. He was educated to be a lawyer, but practiced his profession for only a few years, from 1862 to 1867, with his father, Ezra Graves, of Herkimer, N. Y. A year in Tufts College, near Boston, followed a preliminary training at Fairfield (N. Y.) Academy, and preceded a year at Union College, Schenectady, N. Y. His course was completed at Hamilton College, Clinton, N. Y., in 1862, when he received the degree of A. M. In December of the same year he was admitted to the bar. In 1867 General Graves took up his residence in Buffalo, engaging in business. He was active in commercial pursuits until 1874, when he was appointed clerk of the Superior Court — a position that he filled to the entire satisfaction of the judges of that important court and of the legal fraternity until 1886, when he resigned. General Graves then turned his attention to business, having large personal and trust interests confided to his care. He was one of the organizers of the Frontier Elevating Company, and was president of the company from 1886 to 1894. His greatest single interest is still in the grain-transfer and storage business; for he is president of the Eastern Elevator Company, which owns one of the largest and finest elevators in Buffalo harbor, renowned for the magnitude of its elevating capacity.

General Graves owes his title to twenty years' service in the National Guard of the State of New York. As colonel of the 65th regiment of Buffalo, he labored in season and out of season to bring that organization to a high state of efficiency. Great advances were made, not only in this direction, but also in the character of officers and men. He made popular a service that had been regarded by too many as detrimental to those engaged in it, surrounding himself with men of his own high ideals and thoroughness of execution. When a vacancy occurred in the position of commandant of the brigade, General Graves was, by reason of past achievements, the first choice for the position of general commanding the 8th brigade, including the 65th and 74th regiments in Buffalo and a number of separate companies in western

JOHN C. GRAVES

New York. He served in that capacity until the demands of business compelled his retirement.

The only municipal office that General Graves has held is that of member of the board of park commissioners, a body which controls the eight hundred acres of park lands in the city of Buffalo, and which, despite great pressure, rigorously excludes politics from its management. He has served on that board for twelve years.

*ALBERT HAIGHT.*

General Graves is actively interested in the Universalist church. He is a trustee of the Church of the Messiah, Buffalo, and of the general convention of Universalists of the United States. He is a Mason of high degree. He has been Master of Herkimer Lodge, and of Washington Lodge, No. 240, of Buffalo; High Priest of Keystone Chapter of Royal Arch Masons; is a member of Hugh de Payens Commandery, Knights Templars; and has been invested with all the degrees of Scottish Rite Masonry up to and including the 32d.

*PERSONAL CHRONOLOGY  John Card Graves was born at Herkimer, N. Y., November 18, 1839; attended various schools and colleges; was admitted to the bar in December, 1862; married Augusta C. Moore of Buffalo January 30, 1864; was clerk*

*of the Superior Court of Buffalo, 1874–86; was president of Frontier Elevating Company, 1886–94; has been a member of the board of park commissioners of Buffalo since 1884; has been president of the Citizens' Association since its organization in 1889.*

\*\*\*

**Albert Haight** enjoys a reputation second to that of no jurist in the state of New York. Practically his whole active life has been spent on the bench. Judicial honors came to him when he was only thirty years old. Promoted from the bench of the County Court of Erie county to the Supreme Court, he rose thence to the General Term, and thence to the Court of Appeals. If a high tribute were to be paid to Judge Haight, it would be necessary only to mention the facts already outlined : for no man unworthy of such honors could obtain them from the hands of his fellow-citizens. The record means that the laity as well as the legal profession were early impressed by the pre-eminent juristic ability of Judge Haight.

We hear much of the "judicial cast of mind." Sometimes the phrase means nothing. It ought to mean a great deal, and in Judge Haight's case it means all that the words imply. He has presided at an untold number of trials of causes at law, involving sums ranging from a trifling amount to millions of dollars ; and many principles of law have been adjudicated for the first time by him. Few judges can point to so satisfactory a record as can the subject of this sketch. His decisions have almost universally been looked upon as utterances from which it were useless to appeal. His statement of facts is clear and beyond dispute, his application of the law is direct and positive, and his deductions are characterized by the soundest logic.

Possessing these traits in so marked a degree, it is no wonder that Judge Haight made rapid progress on the bench. He was not even allowed to serve out his first term in the County Court, but was elected to fill the position of a justice of the Supreme Court for the 8th judicial district. Appreciating the legal knowledge and the judicial capacity and learning of Mr. Haight, Governor Grover Cleveland, himself a lawyer and a personal acquaintance of Judge Haight, though of opposite political faith, made him an associate justice of the General Term of the Supreme

Court for the fifth department. Mr. Haight has always been a man of intense activity, having that valuable faculty of doing a great deal without apparent effort, though never without careful study and consideration. During his entire term of service on the General Term he found time to hold occasional Circuit and Special Term courts. It is a significant fact that every appointment that has come to him has been from Democratic governors of the state, though Judge Haight himself is a staunch Republican. When the second division of the Court of Appeals was formed in order to clear up the work of the highest appellate court of the state, Governor Hill named him as one of the associate judges of that court. He remained in this position until the dissolution of the court, when he was reappointed to the General Term by Governor Flower. There he remained until he was elected to the Court of Appeals on the Republican state ticket in 1894. The Democratic party of the 8th judicial district paid him the high honor in 1880, on the expiration of his first term of office in the Supreme Court, of a joint renomination with the Republicans.

For the past twelve years Judge Haight has taken part in the decision of from four hundred to five hundred cases each year, and has written probably seventy-five opinions every year. These have been published in court reports and legal publications of all sorts, and are frequently cited as authorities.

The law is a hard mistress, and those who win her smiles must hesitate not in her service. Judge Haight is a firm believer in this truth, and his measure of success on the bench has been won through close application. The law is at once his work and his recreation: in it he finds his profit and his pleasure; to it he gives the best there is in him; from it he has received honors fairly won.

Judge Haight is a member of the Buffalo Club and of the Fort Orange Club of Albany, where he is always a welcome visitor.

*PERSONAL CHRONOLOGY — Albert Haight was born at Ellicottville, N. Y., February 20, 1842; attended district schools and Springville ( N. Y. ) Academy; married Angeline Waters of West Falls, N. Y. November 20, 1864; was elected successively supervisor from the second ward of Buffalo in 1869, 1870,*

and 1871, county judge of Erie county in 1872, and justice of the Supreme Court for the 8th judicial district in 1876; was re-elected Supreme Court justice in 1890; was appointed successively associate justice of the General Term of the Supreme Court for the fifth department by Governor Cleveland in 1884, associate judge of the second division of the Court of Appeals by Governor Hill in 1889, and associate justice of the General Term ( again ) by Governor Flower in 1892; was elected associate judge of the Court of Appeals in 1894.

•••

**William W. Hammond** has often been called to serve the people of his county in an official capacity, because he has always been faithful to their interests.

He was born upon a farm, and passed his early years there. He did the usual work of a farmer's

*WILLIAM W. HAMMOND*

boy, went to the common schools, such as a new country affords, and after reaching a suitable age walked six miles a day to get the better advantages offered by a "select" school. He closed his school career by a short attendance at Fredonia Academy. Before 1850 he taught school in Pennsylvania and Kentucky, and soon afterward went to Mississippi, where he turned his attention to the manufacture of lumber. Returning to his native county, he taught school again for a few years. Afterwards he conducted a country store, studying law at the same time. He came to Buffalo to finish his legal studies with the law firm of Sawin & Lockwood, and was admitted to the bar in 1861 in that city. After practicing law for two years at Angola, N. Y., he returned to mercantile pursuits for several years at Brant, N. Y. He was elected to the office of magistrate there; and for twelve years, from 1865 on, he was a member of the board of supervisors from that town, serving with the late Judge Sheldon and with Judge Haight, at present of the Court of Appeals.

In military affairs Mr. Hammond's interest is best shown by his fourteen years' connection with the National Guard of the State of New York. He enlisted in 1852. He went with the 67th regiment of the National Guard to Harrisburg, Penn., in 1863, when Lee's army was invading the state, and was on duty at Harrisburg when the battle of Gettysburg was fought. Mr. Hammond held a 1st lieutenant's commission while he was in the United States service, and was honorably discharged after about three months' duty. After his return he was elected captain of company C, 67th regiment, and held that rank when he left the militia service in 1866.

Mr. Hammond's popularity in Erie county was first shown in 1877, when he was elected county judge to succeed Albert Haight. He was twice reelected, serving twelve years in that important office. From 1890 until 1892 Mr. Hammond was a member of the law firm of Peck, Hammond, Peck & Hatch; for the next three years the style was Hammond & Hatch; and in 1895 the firm became Hammond & Werick.

He has spent much time in travel, and has supplemented the scant school advantages of his youth by wide reading and observation. He is interested in all church matters, and was a charter member, and for many years a trustee, of the Angola Congregational Church. He has been a member of the First Congregational Church of Buffalo since its organization. In all movements for higher citizenship and improved public service his voice and influence have always been on the right side. He has long been a member of the Buffalo Civil Service Reform Association, and he is a member of the Good Government Club of the ward in which he lives. In politics Mr. Hammond has been steadfastly Republican.

Mr. Hammond's eminence in his profession and his social position were not attained at a single bound, but rather came as a fitting reward to patient endeavor and continued achievements. He has seen Erie county change from a forest into a garden, and Buffalo has expanded under his eyes from a small city to a metropolis. Throughout these years, in all his dealings with his fellow-men, he has been painstakingly honest and conscientious. This fact, more clearly than any other perhaps, gives the keynote to Judge Hammond's long and successful career.

*PERSONAL CHRONOLOGY—William W. Hammond was born at Hamburg, N. Y., November 4, 1831, attended common schools and Fredonia (N. Y.) Academy; married Amy A. Hurd of Evans, N. Y., in 1854, and Louisa A. Hurd of the same place in 1861; was admitted to the bar in Buffalo in 1861; was a member of the National Guard from 1852 to 1866; was elected county judge of Erie county in 1877, and was re-elected in 1878 and in 1884; has practiced law in Buffalo since 1890.*

***

**William Hengerer** is a self-made man, having successfully applied his natal talents to the opportunities of his circumstances. Though born in Wurtemburg, Germany, he is essentially an American. His school education, obtained partly in Germany and partly in this country, ended with his fourteenth year. His father, however, was a Lutheran minister, poor in this world's goods, but possessing the character and qualifications of his calling; so that while Mr. Hengerer's school days were few in number, he had the great advantage of a sound home training, which is often more than equivalent to scholastic opportunities.

His family came to America while he was still a boy, and for twelve years he lived in Pittsburg, Penn. At the age of twenty-two he came to Buffalo, and entered the dry-goods house of Sherman, Barnes & Co., as a clerk, at six dollars a week. From this humble beginning, by force of industry, perseverance, and integrity, Mr. Hengerer has achieved his present position in the business, social, and political life of Buffalo. To call his success luck, would be to disparage hard work, pluck, and honesty. In 1874 his worth and ability were recognized, and he was admitted to the firm, which was then known as Barnes, Bancroft & Co. This was the style of the firm for eleven years, when a new organization took place, and the name of the firm was changed to Barnes, Hengerer & Co. The death of the senior partner, and the expansion of business consequent upon the evolution of dry-goods houses into the modern department stores, in time required a different organization ; and in 1895 a joint-stock company was formed, known as The William Hengerer Company, taking its name from the clerk who thirty-odd years before began on a salary of six dollars a week.

Only once has Mr. Hengerer's business career been interrupted, and then there was a break of two years, when he was engaged in the more serious business of helping to put down the Rebellion. He had been in Buffalo scarcely a month when the Civil War broke out, and President Lincoln called for troops. He did what thousands of men to-day earnestly wish they had done — he enlisted as a volunteer soldier. Mr. Hengerer was an alien born, but he showed the true spirit of an American patriot. He enlisted for two years as a member of the 21st regiment, N. Y. volunteers — the first regiment to go to the front from Buffalo. During its service it was part of the Army of the Potomac, and shared in its battles and its triumphs.

Returning home in 1863, Mr. Hengerer resumed his connection with Sherman, Barnes & Co., and steadily devoted himself to their interests. His life, however, has not been confined to the accumulation of wealth, to the neglect of his duties as a citizen and a member of society. His time, influence, and money have been freely given to every commendable object. In politics he is a "war Democrat," and his counsel and assistance are invariably sought by his party associates. While he has uniformly declined, owing to the cares of business, to consider nominations for elective offices, he has served the public for many years as park commissioner, and as trustee of the State Normal School.

Mr. Hengerer is a member of the English Lutheran church, and in all the philanthropic movements connected with church work in these days his name is among those relied upon for financial assistance. He is a Mason in high standing, having served as Master, High Priest, Commander, and District Deputy Grand Master. He has a life membership in both the Buffalo Library Association and the Buffalo Historical Society. He is a member, also, of the Liedertafel and Orpheus societies, and of the Buffalo Club.

Mr. Hengerer finds diversion from business in travel, and has visited Europe several times for rest and recreation. Unostentatious in his style of living,

cordial in his friendship, prompt and progressive in business, he has won his place in Buffalo by the same qualities he displayed when, at a critical time in the country's history, he donned the uniform of a volunteer soldier of the United States, and sacrificed everything to the call of duty.

*WILLIAM HENGERER*

*PERSONAL CHRONOLOGY*—*William Hengerer was born at Wurtemburg, Germany, March 2, 1849; attended common schools; came to the United States in 1849; served in the Union Army, 1861-63; married Louisa Duerr of Buffalo September 24, 1864; has been park commissioner of Buffalo since 1884, and trustee of State Normal School since 1885.*

***

**Nelson K. Hopkins** is a son of the Empire State. His father, General Timothy S. Hopkins, lived for many years at Great Barrington, Mass., but moved to Erie county in 1800, and purchased a farm near Williamsville, where the subject of this sketch was born March 2, 1816.

General Hopkins was appointed captain by Governor George Clinton in 1803, major by Governor Lewis in 1806, and lieutenant colonel by Governor Tomkins in 1811; and he served as brigadier general under Major General Hall during the war of 1812, but resigned his commission when peace was declared.

*NELSON K. HOPKINS*

The boyhood of Nelson K. Hopkins was spent upon his father's farm, where practical experience of many kinds supplemented the scant educational opportunities offered by the district school. When only seventeen, he secured the position of clerk and manager to the contractors then building the Macadam road between Williamsville and Buffalo. In this position he had entire charge of the accounts with over 400 men. After the completion of this work, Mr. Hopkins again turned his attention to his education, and in 1834 entered the academy at Fredonia, N. Y., where he remained two terms. He then spent two years at the Genesee Wesleyan Seminary at Lima, N. Y. Before entering this school young Hopkins had been elected captain of a company of militia at Williamsville, and while he was at the seminary his company was called out. Mr. Hopkins immediately started for the front, where he enlisted in the United States service with sixty of his men, and served in what was called the "Patriot War." He was stationed on the Niagara frontier, near the foot of Ferry street in Buffalo.

He next entered Union College at Schenectady, N. Y., where his brilliant work and the high honors with which he graduated in 1842 gave promise of those qualities that were to be developed when he was to battle with the actual realities of life. Upon his graduation Mr. Hopkins was elected to membership in the Phi Beta Kappa society — an honor conferred only upon students of the highest standing.

The legal profession has always attracted men of ambition and of keen and brilliant mind, and Mr. Hopkins made choice of it as his life-work. He entered the office of Potter & Spaulding, in Buffalo, as a clerk, and in 1846 was duly admitted to the bar in the city of New York. Thus began the career that has made him one of Buffalo's most honored sons. Mr. Hopkins has devoted himself to the practice of law continuously since then, with the single exception of four years spent at the state capitol, as comptroller. Mr. Hopkins has ever been a counselor rather than an advocate. Much of his practice has concerned the settlement of estates, the examination of titles, and the placing of investments — duties that fitted him well for the responsible position he filled so brilliantly in the service of the state.

Mr. Hopkins has always been a staunch Republican. After several years of service in Buffalo, as ward supervisor and as alderman, he was appointed collector of internal revenue of the Buffalo district by President Johnson in 1866. In 1871, without his knowledge or consent, he was nominated for state comptroller, and was elected by a handsome majority. He was called to the administration of the financial department of the state at a very critical period. Tweed and his accomplices were then in power, and they had sadly disorganized the finances of the commonwealth. The sinking funds had been despoiled to make good other appropriations, and in various ways the comptroller's department was greatly in need of reform. Mr. Hopkins addressed himself to the task with the painstaking care and unbending integrity that have characterized his public and private career; and, happily for the good of the state, he was well qualified for the work, both by natural ability and by legal training. His first annual report was greeted with applause, both for its clear elucidation of the financial condition, and for the evidence it bore that a *régime* of retrenchment had replaced that of extravagance. That men of all parties appreciated his services, was shown in 1873, when he was re-elected to the office he had filled so well, notwithstanding the defeat of every other candidate on the Republican ticket. During his four years of office, $6,500,000 that had been abstracted from the treasury in direct violation of the constitution was restored, and nearly $20,000,000 of the state debt was paid.

At the expiration of his second term of office, Mr. Hopkins returned to Buffalo and resumed his legal practice, which he has continued ever since. It is scarcely necessary to say that he is a prominent citizen there, and actively interested in the welfare of the city. He was one of the organizers of the present paid Fire Department, and for ten years occupied the honorable position of fire commissioner, where his services were of a careful and conservative nature that guarded the best public interests. For many years he was the attorney and a director of White's Bank, now the American Exchange Bank, of Buffalo; and he has always been identified with the prominent local clubs, organizations, and societies.

*PERSONAL CHRONOLOGY —
Nelson K. Hopkins was born at Williamsville, N. Y., March 2, 1816; attended
Fredonia (N. Y.) Academy and Wesleyan
Seminary at Lima, N. Y., and graduated
from Union College, Schenectady, N. Y.,
in 1842; was admitted to the bar at New
York city in 1846; married Lucy Ann
Allen of Buffalo in 1848, and Louise
Ann Pratt of Buffalo in 1855; was alderman in Buffalo, 1862-64; was appointed
collector of internal revenue by President
Johnson in 1866; was elected comptroller
of the state of New York in 1871, and was
re-elected in 1873; has practiced law in
Buffalo since 1846.*

···

**William T. Hornaday** has made a success of life in more directions than are open to most men. He is a naturalist of distinction, a taxidermist of the

first rank, and a traveler and hunter of renown. He stands high as an author, and as a business man he has won an enviable position.

Born with a love of nature, which his early life did much to foster, he sought employment when a young man in the famous natural history establishment of Professor Ward in Rochester, and there prepared himself for the work as a field naturalist in which he gained such distinction. His first venture in this line was in Cuba and Florida, where he won his spurs as a naturalist by discovering and describing the Florida crocodile, a genus quite distinct from the alligator. His success gave impetus to the desire to enter richer, if wilder and more dangerous, lands; and in 1876 he undertook an expedition to the West Indies and South America, where he made a large

*WILLIAM T. HORNADAY*

collection of strange fishes, beautiful birds, and horrible reptiles. On his return he went to Europe, and spent some time in study in various museums of science and art. His next trip was to the East

Indies. This was the most extensive expedition Mr. Hornaday ever made, and lasted nearly three years, during which he sent home the largest collection of specimens ever made in the Far East. His adventures in India, Ceylon, the Malay Peninsula, and Borneo, have been given to the public in a book entitled "Two Years in the Jungle," which was published in 1885, and ran through four editions.

Mr. Hornaday returned to Rochester in 1879, and three years later was appointed chief taxidermist of the United States National Museum at Washington. During the eight years in which he held that important position, it is not too much to say that he stood at the head of the profession. Many of the recent advances in the taxidermic art are due to him. He introduced the present very popular method of mounting large quadrupeds in groups and placing them amidst their natural surroundings. Some of his work — notably the group of buffalo which is such an ornament to the National Museum — has received the highest praise from the best authorities, and is a monument to his skill as an artist and his knowledge as a naturalist.

In 1889 Mr. Hornaday proposed the establishment by congress, on a grand scale, of a national zoölogical park at Washington, to be under the control of the Smithsonian Institution. He was forthwith detailed by the secretary to formulate plans and present them to congress. He did this with so much success that in the next two years congress appropriated $292,000 to carry out the scheme. Mr. Hornaday was appointed superintendent, and served the commissioners for one year in that capacity. When the park was finally placed under the control of the Smithsonian Institution, Professor Langley insisted on changes in its plans so sweeping that Mr. Hornaday resigned his position, severed his connection with the government, and came to Buffalo. Here he became interested in real estate, and with four other operators formed a close corporation called the Union Land Exchange, which has been the direct means of bringing a large amount of capital to Buffalo.

As a writer, Mr. Hornaday has interested the public in many subjects. His story of life in the East Indies has already been referred to. He has written a work on "Taxidermy and Zoölogical Collecting" that is a standard authority. His memoir on the "Extermination of the American Bison" (a government publication) attracted much attention. His contributions to various papers and magazines are well known and popular. His recent novel, entitled "The Man Who Became a Savage," which made its first appearance in the *Illustrated Buffalo Express*, possesses great merit and originality.

The æsthetic side of Mr. Hornaday's nature finds expression in an intense love for art. He is an excellent judge of paintings, and has begun to form a collection of works by American artists only.

*PERSONAL CHRONOLOGY — William Temple Hornaday was born near Plainfield, Ind., December 1, 1854; attended the public schools of Knoxville, Iowa, Oskaloosa (Iowa) College, and the Iowa Agricultural College; studied zoölogy, taxidermy, and museology in Rochester and in various European museums; traveled extensively from 1875 to 1879, visiting the West Indies, South America, and the Far East, making zoölogical collections; married Josephine Chamberlain of Battle Creek, Mich., September 11, 1879; was made chief taxidermist of the United States National Museum in 1882; proposed the establishment and prepared the plans of the National Zoölogical Park at Washington in 1888; has been engaged in the real-estate business in Buffalo since 1890.*

\* \* \*

**Harvey J. Hurd** is a striking example of the men whose capacity for work is such that they can be at once successful in business and actively interested in public affairs. He has been a thoroughly practical citizen, attending strictly to his private enterprises on the one side, and on the other assuming his full share of the duties that we all owe to the community in which we live. One of the encouraging signs of the times in our country to-day is the steady increase in the number of business men who are recognizing the fact that the state has a just claim to their services in some official capacity. It is in this way only that our politics can be made clean and respectable.

Mr. Hurd's father, Clark W. Hurd, was of Vermont stock, coming to Erie county in the '30's. He was one of the first settlers on the Buffalo Creek Indian reservation at Elma, where Harvey Hurd was born. The latter's early life was passed upon the farm, and his early education was obtained in the district school. To this was added an excellent training at the old Buffalo Academy and at Cornell University, from which he graduated in 1872. His commercial life has been confined to the lumber business chiefly, in which he is at present engaged in Buffalo, in company with his brother, James T. Hurd, under the firm name of Hurd Bros.

In 1890 and 1891 Mr. Hurd was president of the Buffalo Lumber Exchange. He is a member of the Buffalo Merchants' Exchange, and served for several years on the board of trustees of that institution. He is also a member of the Buffalo Builders' Exchange. He is part owner of the Buffalo Planing Mill Company, which operates one of the largest and best equipped plants in the United States, and is vice president of the company. Mr. Hurd is also a director of the Buffalo Loan, Trust, and Safe Deposit Company, and of the Lancaster Brick Yard Company. He is a life member of the Buffalo Library Association.

In public life Mr. Hurd has made a good record. Few men are able to manage many things well at the same time, but Mr. Hurd has shown ability as a legislator as well as in the walks of mercantile life. He was first elected to the legislature in 1877, and served altogether four years. His principal work in the assembly was in connection with the Erie canal. For three years he was chairman of the canal committee, and directed his efforts towards securing the adoption of a constitutional amendment making the canals free from tolls. His services in this matter have not been forgotten in western New York.

Mr. Hurd was a member of the legislature in 1881, when the memorable resignation of Mr. Conkling from the United States senate, together with that of Mr. Platt, unexpectedly rendered the election of two senators necessary. The Republican party, with which Mr. Hurd has been identified, was divided into two factions — one favoring the return of Mr. Conkling to the senate and the other opposing such return. A long and bitter fight followed in the legislature. Mr. Hurd was a strong admirer of the New York senator, and supported him to the end. This trait of adhering to a friend or to a cause is a marked one in his character.

Mr. Hurd is an ardent Republican, and has taken an active interest as one of the managers of the party in Erie county. For several years he was chairman of the Republican general committee. He is at present a member of the Republican state committee, representing the 33d senatorial district, and is a member of the executive committee of the state committee.

In social life Mr. Hurd is eminently companionable. He is a member of the Buffalo Club and of the University Club, and is a 32d degree Mason. While the cares of business leave little time for diversions, his life is not in any sense one-sided.

*PERSONAL CHRONOLOGY— Harvey Jetson Hurd was born at Elma, N. Y., February 28, 1849; was educated at Buffalo Academy and at Cornell University, from which he graduated in 1872; was a member of the New York legislature, 1878–81; has been engaged in the lumber business in Buffalo since 1880.*

**E. H. Hutchinson** is one of the men who make themselves valuable in the community in which they live. Thoroughly imbued with the progressive spirit of the age, he is to be found in the front rank of those who are working for the material and moral welfare of the world. Endowed with large re-

*HARVEY J HURD*

sources, he has numerous and varied business interests. Unlike many people blessed with means, Mr. Hutchinson is liberal with both his energy and his money. No worthy charity appeals to him in vain ; no public movement that has for its object the eradication of some political or moral evil need lack his influence. He is a public-spirited citizen in the fullest meaning of the term, and he has made many personal sacrifices to serve his fellow citizens. Sturdy in mind and purpose, no unworthy motive ever turned him from the path of duty. When his way is seen clearly, it is pursued to the end, no matter what obstacles are to be overcome.

Mr. Hutchinson's business life began when he was eighteen years old, ill health having forced him to abandon a course of study preparatory for college. His first venture was as a partner in the firm of L. W. Drake & Co., provision dealers and pork packers. In the summer of 1875 their slaughterhouse at East Buffalo was burned, and the fire was followed by a dissolution of partnership. But so energetic and re-

F. H. HUTCHINSON

sourceful a man as Mr. Hutchinson had already shown himself to be could not long remain idle, and in a few months he had established an advertising agency. To this he soon added the job-printing business. Under his fostering care and wise management this business grew steadily and prospered exceedingly. Mr. Hutchinson continued it alone until 1890, when Harry C. Spendelow became his partner. This association was unbroken until January 1, 1895, when Mr. Hutchinson retired, the Spendelow Printing Company succeeding F. H. Hutchinson & Co.

Mr. Hutchinson is interested in many business enterprises in Buffalo. He is a director of the Marine Bank, and a stockholder of the Bank of Buffalo; and serves as a trustee of the Buffalo City Cemetery. A number of fine business blocks, flats, and apartment houses have been erected by him. In many directions his influence is felt, and every where his counsel and his energy of execution are desired and sought. He is a manager of the Church Charity Foundation of the Protestant Episcopal Church in Buffalo, and is a life member of the Buffalo Historical Society, the Buffalo Orphan Asylum, and the Buffalo Library. No more cheerful giver is known to many charitable and benevolent institutions of the city, and he is always one of the first to respond to any special call for aid. As a loving memorial to his father, John Martin Hutchinson, and to his mother, Eunice Alzina Howard Hutchinson, he has recently built the Hutchinson Memorial Chapel of the Holy Innocents, which has been presented to the Church Charity Foundation.

Men of Mr. Hutchinson's stamp make ideal public servants, and it is certainly to be regretted that he has found it impossible to give the city as much of his time as his fellow-citizens would like. A Democrat in politics, he was yet elected, because of his personal popularity, to a seat in the board of aldermen for the old 10th ward, the strongest Republican ward in the city. He served one term of two years.

When John M. Hutchinson died August 17, 1886, there was a popular demand for the appointment of his son to succeed him as member of the board of fire commissioners. No convenient opportunity to effect this came until February 24, 1891, when Mayor Charles F. Bishop was pleased to make the appointment. The father had served the city for years with a singleness of purpose and an unexcelled faithfulness, and it was felt that the son would do the same. The other members of the board at once paid a tribute to the father by choosing the capable son as their chairman. Unfortunately the younger Hutchinson's connection with the Fire Department ceased in two years, because he was compelled by ill health in his family to absent himself from Buffalo for a considerable period of time, and he felt it unjust to the city to hold the position under such circumstances. He has still a keen interest in everything pertaining to the Fire Department, and the members of the force in all grades of service have a warm regard for their former commissioner.

Mr. Hutchinson delights in travel, and has visited all parts of the United States and the greater part of Europe.

Several fraternal organizations know E. H. Hutchinson as a brother. He is a member of Ancient Landmark Lodge, No. 441, F. & A. M.; Adytum Chapter, No. 235, R. A. M.; Keystone Council, No. 20, R. & S. M.; Hugh de Payens Commandery, No. 30, K. T.; Ismailia Temple, Nobles of the Mystic Shrine; and Orient Lodge, A. O. U. W.

*PERSONAL CHRONOLOGY—Edward Howard Hutchinson was born at Buffalo March 7, 1852; attended various public and private schools; married Jeanie Blanche Ganson of Buffalo September 25, 1872; was alderman from the old 10th ward, 1888–89; was appointed a Fire Commissioner February 24, 1891, resigning October 3, 1893.*

***

**Christian Klinck** is one of Buffalo's most enterprising citizens, and stands among the foremost on the list of men of Teutonic descent who have made for themselves fame and fortune in their adopted country. Mr. Klinck is a native of Germany, where he received a good common-school education, and learned his trade as a butcher. The narrow world of German provincialism, with its hopelessness of any great success, proved too small for the ambitious lad, and at the age of seventeen he determined to seek his fortunes in the new world. Accordingly he set sail for America, intending to settle in Cincinnati, Ohio; but when he reached Buffalo he was unable to pay his railroad fare further, and, making a virtue of necessity, he sought work there, which he obtained at the munificent rate of six dollars a month. Notwithstanding this small beginning, his German thrift and industry enabled him, in six years, to amass sufficient capital to go into business for himself; and from that time forth his path was always forward and upward. At first he conducted the business of a general butcher, but in 1868 he took up a specialty, opening a pork-packing business that was destined to become one of the greatest establishments of its kind in the United States. From the start he had to contend with competition of the keenest kind. There were wealthier and stronger firms which, had they been able, would have crushed the life out of the new concern; but it was

based upon the principles of business integrity, and an iron will was behind it. Few men could have been successful in this enterprise, but Mr. Klinck was one of the few. He was honest, industrious, prudent, far-seeing, and resolute; and because he possessed these characteristics, because he rejected all offers to compromise or combine, because he refused to be swayed from his original purpose, he won the battle, and is to-day one of the kings of pork packing in the country. His establishment is situated on Depot street, near William, in East Buffalo. The yards cover over eighteen acres, and the mammoth buildings are equipped with the most complete machinery and the most improved appliances. Some idea of the magnitude of the business may be gained from the fact that between two and three hundred

CHRISTIAN KLINCK

men are there employed, turning out a product that annually amounts to over $3,000,000.

Mr. Klinck has not only flourished financially, but he has prospered politically as well, so far as he has found time for such pursuits. In 1864, yielding to the solicitations of his friends and neighbors, he entered the political arena as candidate for alderman of the old 13th ward in Buffalo, and served his constituents faithfully for two years, when he retired. For nearly thirty years he remained out of politics,

*ERASTUS C. KNIGHT*

but at the expiration of that time representative citizens waited upon him, and induced him to become a candidate for councilman; and he was elected by a most flattering majority. In this capacity Mr. Klinck has brought to the service of the public those rugged qualities of sterling integrity, steadfastness of purpose, and keen discrimination that have brought him success in private life. To be fair and just is the self-evident purpose of his action in all matters of legislation. Though at times others have differed from him and taken opposite grounds, none have ever impugned his motives or suggested for a moment that his intentions were other than the purest.

Mr. Klinck is interested in many financial and business enterprises aside from those immediately under his personal control. He is a director of the Citizens' Bank and of St. John's German Orphan Asylum, and is a stockholder in the Live Stock Exchange and in the Crocker Fertilizer Company.

*PERSONAL CHRONOLOGY.— Christian Klinck was born in the Bavarian village of Schonenburg, Germany, February 6, 1844; moved to the city of Zweibrucken ( also in Rhenish Bavaria) in 1849, where he learned his trade as a butcher; came to America and settled in Buffalo in 1850; established a pork-packing business in 1868; was alderman from the 13th ward, Buffalo, 1864-65; was elected a member of the Buffalo board of councilmen in 1893, and was made president of the board January 6, 1896.*

...

**Erastus C. Knight** attained his present high position in finance and politics by reason of undoubted merit and ability. His ancestors were New Englanders, of the revolutionary type, his great grandfather, Seth Cole, having moved from Chesterfield, Mass., to the shores of Lake Erie near Dunkirk in 1805. Mr. Knight's grandfather, Erastus Cole, was a volunteer in the war of 1812, and was present at the burning of the city of Buffalo in 1813. Mr. Knight's own father was a substantial business man of Buffalo, and very likely the son inherited some of his father's business capacity. At all events, Mr. Knight's career shows an unbroken chain of advancement such as unmistakably indicates some powerful and adequate cause in antecedent conditions.

A thorough education was one of the factors of Mr. Knight's success. Having taken a course in a commercial college, he had a theoretical and practical knowledge of business methods before he entered active business. On the completion of his studies, he accepted a position in the wholesale house of Bell Brothers, produce commission merchants, of Buffalo. Later he broadened his experience with men and places by going on the road as a traveling salesman for the same firm — one of the finest schools of practical business knowledge. In 1880 he started in business for himself, and became senior member of the firm of Knight, Lennox & Co., produce commission merchants, with whom he was successfully engaged for seven years.

Usually a man is loath to change when once he has established himself in a profession or branch of

mercantile industry. But Mr. Knight concluded
that the opportunities were greater in a field different
from that first chosen by him, and in 1887 he withdrew from the foregoing firm, and embarked in the
real-estate business. To this he added the occupation of a builder in 1892, when he formed a partnership with Oliver A. Jenkins, under the firm name of
Jenkins & Knight. Mr. Knight is also a partner in
the firm of Sloan, Cowles & Co., proprietors of excursion steamers and summer resorts.

In politics Mr. Knight has been prominently identified with the Republican party. Before the city of
Buffalo was redistricted he was nominated for supervisor in the old 11th ward, and was elected ; and two
years later he was renominated from the new 24th
ward, and was elected. He was chosen for a third
time in 1893, serving as chairman of the board during the session of 1894. In the fall of
that year he received the nomination for
comptroller of the city of Buffalo, and
was elected by a round majority, assuming
the duties of the office January 1, 1895.
The country is learning that the successful business man is most likely to manage
wisely the affairs of a municipality. Experience in commercial life is what we
need in the administration of nearly all
public offices, and it marks an advance in
practical wisdom when a community
selects a business man for what is essentially a business office. The city of Buffalo, therefore, may well congratulate itself
on Mr. Knight's accession to the office of
comptroller. His administration has been
marked by sound business judgment, faithfulness to the interests of the public, and
uniform courtesy to the patrons of the
office. In public and in private capacity
alike, Mr. Knight has in large measure the
respect and good will of his fellow-citizens.

*PERSONAL CHRONOLOGY—
Erastus Cole Knight was born at Buffalo
March 1, 1857 ; attended the public schools
and Bryant & Stratton's Business College ;
engaged in the produce commission business
with William C. Lennox, 1880-84 ; married Mary Elizabeth Cowles of Buffalo May
14, 1884 ; established a real-estate business
in 1887, and formed a partnership with
Oliver A. Jenkins in 1892 ; was elected
supervisor of the old 11th ward of Buffalo in 1889, and
was re-elected in the new 24th ward in 1891 and 1893,
serving as chairman of the board in 1894 ; was elected
comptroller of the city of Buffalo in November, 1894.*

**John H. Lascelles,** though a newcomer to
Buffalo, is already thoroughly identified with the
business interests of the city. He is a banker of
long experience and of great ability, and is so regarded by his fellow-financiers. His career in the
field in which he has won so marked a success began
when he was eighteen years old. At that time he
entered the service of the Lake Shore Bank of Dunkirk, N. Y., his native town. Beginning in the lowly
capacity of "trotter," where the power of literally
"getting there" right on time is the one thing
needful, he rose by degrees to more important positions, serving in the various grades of clerkships,
absorbing speedily a thorough knowledge of banking methods, and acquiring a mastery of the science
of finance. For eight years his connection with the
Lake Shore Bank was unbroken, and he severed it

JOHN H. LASCELLES

only to accept a flattering offer from a rival institution, the Merchants' National Bank of Dunkirk,
which wished to make him its cashier. This was in
1882. Ten years of his active business life were

spent with this bank — years fraught with success for both the bank and its cashier. During this period Mr. Lascelles became known in circles beyond Dunkirk as a careful and conservative but shrewd bank manager. He had proved himself fully equal to every emergency and to all demands, and it was plain that the limit of his capacity was far from reached. Accordingly, when that old, solid institution, the Marine Bank of Buffalo, stood in need of an assistant cashier, Mr. Lascelles was chosen for the place. He accepted the position, and moved to Buffalo October 15, 1892. His election to the position of cashier soon followed, and this place he now fills to the eminent satisfaction of the officers and directors of the bank and of its many customers. A bank cashier must be affable, yet firm; must know when to acquiesce and when to refuse; must at no time offend those with whom his bank has dealings; must be alert to protect the bank, and ready to listen to all propositions from its customers; must know the financial standing of those who come to him; and must see that the machinery of the institution runs without jar. Mr. Lascelles has all the necessary qualities highly developed, and they make him an ideal man for the place he fills. He still retains a connection with the Merchants' National Bank of Dunkirk, of which he is vice president.

Banking has not absorbed all of Mr. Lascelles' time and attention. Having a broad outlook and a wide interest in men and all their affairs, he has to meet demands for his services in many directions. During his long residence in Dunkirk he devoted himself somewhat to politics. This was largely a labor of love, as he is a Democrat, and as Chautauqua county is a hotbed of Republicanism. It is said, by the way, that there is more politics to the square inch in that county than in any other in the state of New York, and it is only natural that Mr. Lascelles became infected with the prevailing disease. Still, he is not a violent partisan, and does not place party above good government. His personal popularity in Dunkirk was evidenced by his triumphant election as city treasurer, an office that he held for several consecutive years. For six years he served as a member of the board of education, of which he was also treasurer at different times. When he ran for county treasurer on the Democratic ticket, he was, of course, defeated; but he received the largest vote of any of his party's candidates.

One who is willing to give of his time and energy for the benefit of others always has plenty of such opportunities for self-sacrifice thrust upon him; and so it has been with Mr. Lascelles. He has performed many duties cheerfully with no thought of recompense. One

of the organizers of the Dunkirk Savings & Loan Association, he served it as treasurer from the date of its organization until he moved to Buffalo. He is now serving his third year as treasurer of the Buffalo Board of Trade and of the Merchants' Exchange.

Mr. Lascelles is a member of various social organizations, including St. Mary's Lyceum of Dunkirk, the Buffalo Orpheus Singing Society, and the Buffalo Catholic Young Men's Club.

*PERSONAL CHRONOLOGY— John Henry Lascelles was born at Dunkirk, N. Y., March 4, 1856; attended the public schools of Dunkirk; was elected cashier of the Merchants' National Bank of Dunkirk in 1884; married Annie Moran of Buffalo on Thanksgiving Day, 1885; was elected assistant cashier of the Marine Bank of Buffalo in 1892; has been cashier of the same bank since 1893.*

***

**John Laughlin** is a native of Erie county, N. Y., and a man to whom that county and the state as well is much indebted for public service. After taking a four years' course in the Lockport Union School (an institution that has played a prominent part in the intellectual development of western New York), Mr. Laughlin read law in the office of Richard Crowley of Lockport. In the spring of 1881 Mr. Crowley moved to Buffalo, and Mr. Laughlin, who had just completed his legal studies, accompanied him and was admitted to the bar in Buffalo. He at once became managing clerk in the office of Crowley, Movius & Wilcox, and two years later became Mr. Crowley's partner in the firm of Crowley & Laughlin. Soon after, Mr. Crowley went to New York city, and Mr. Laughlin formed a copartnership with Joseph E. Ewell. Wilbur E. Houpt was taken into the firm a little later, and the style became Laughlin, Ewell & Houpt.

In 1887 Mr. Laughlin was nominated for state senator to fill a vacancy on the Republican ticket, and was elected. He was re-elected in 1889, but was defeated in 1891, though he ran ahead of his ticket. He was a delegate to the Republican national convention in 1888, where he warmly advocated Depew's candidacy, and was the last man in the New York delegation to give up "our Chauncey." Mr. Laughlin's service in the legislature was marked by earnest efforts to effect needed and practical reforms in different departments of the government. Like all men of advanced views, he not infrequently found himself in a minority; but on many points he has had the satisfaction of seeing his ideas prevail in the end.

Throughout his two terms in the senate, Mr. Laughlin was a member of the judiciary committee,

He was also chairman of the canal committee, and advocated liberal appropriations for the improvement of the state canals, believing that they are an important factor in the prosperity of the commonwealth. He prepared and introduced a revision of the police-excise laws of Buffalo, and of the Buffalo public school act; and these measures, though defeated when originally presented, were subsequently embodied in the revised charter of the city of Buffalo, which passed the senate in 1891 chiefly through Mr. Laughlin's efforts.

Another of Mr. Laughlin's practical reforms has been more widely operative by reason of its embodiment in the new constitution of the state of New York. We refer to the change in the method of conducting elections whereby municipal offices, concerning which the "personal equation" counts for so much, are filled in odd years, while state and national offices, in which great public questions play so important a part, are filled in even years. Such an arrangement obviously simplifies issues, promotes political purity, and generally serves the cause of good government.

While in the senate, Mr. Laughlin devoted much time and thought to the subject of text-books in the public schools. His own experience suggested to him the need of reform in this particular, and his later observation only strengthened the earlier conviction. He saw the lack of uniformity in the books used in different schools, and the frequent changes involved in the attempt of each school board to improve on the choice of its predecessor. All this he regarded not only as a serious hardship in a pecuniary way to people of moderate means, but also as a positive obstacle to the pupil's progress. His plan was thoroughly comprehensive in its scope, and provided for the creation of a commission to select books, purchase copyrights, and prepare originals when necessary. The books could thus be obtained by the state at the lowest possible rates, and were to be furnished to the pupils without charge; and the books were not to be changed except at stated periods and for adequate cause. This measure was defeated in the senate; but one consequence of the movement was the adoption of free text-books by Buffalo and by some other places in the state.

Since his retirement from the senate Mr. Laughlin has devoted himself assiduously to the law, and has built up a large general practice in both the state and the United States courts. He has been especially successful as a trial lawyer, where his talent as a public speaker has come into effective play. Though out

*JOHN LAUGHLIN*

of active politics, Mr. Laughlin maintains his interest in public affairs. He is called upon in every campaign to deliver addresses, and usually does so.

*PERSONAL CHRONOLOGY— John Laughlin was born at Newstead, Erie county, N. Y., March 14, 1856; was educated in the district schools of Erie and Niagara counties, and in Lockport Union School; was admitted to the bar in 1881; was elected state senator in 1887, and re-elected in 1889; has practiced law in Buffalo since 1881.*

● ● ●

**Loran L. Lewis** has been prominent at the bar and on the bench of western New York for nearly forty years. During all that time his record has been one of which any man might well be proud, and which few men may hope to equal. Coming to Buffalo when it was little more than a large village, he has seen it grow and prosper, and has been a part of its growth and prosperity. While the law has claimed his first attention, he has been an active

LORAN L. LEWIS

figure in various enterprises that have done much to build up and make great the Queen City of the Lakes.

Born in Cayuga county, N. Y., in the quarter-century year, Mr. Lewis spent his early life in the central part of the state, and his education was begun in the city of Auburn. He was quite a young man when he determined to study law, and was only twenty-three years old when admitted to the bar. Then, as now, the question of location was an important one for the young lawyer to decide. Loran L. Lewis, after looking carefully over the field, determined to come to Buffalo. He arrived in that city in 1848, and it has been his home ever since. He did not have to wait long for clients, and his

progress when once begun was continuous. He formed a partnership with C. O. Pool in 1854, and with several others afterward — with George Wadsworth, Wm. H. Gurney, A. G. Rice, Adelbert Moot, and with his own son, George L. Lewis. The firm name of Lewis, Moot & Lewis is best known to the younger generation of Buffalonians.

Politics at one time demanded much of Mr. Lewis's attention, and his services to the Republican party were rewarded in the fall of 1869 with a nomination to the state senate. The voters of Erie county endorsed the nomination, and Mr. Lewis had a seat in the highest legislative body of the state of New York for four years, having been returned for a second term in 1871. From the end of that period of service Senator Lewis, as everyone then called him, remained a private citizen until January 1, 1883, when he took his seat on the Supreme Court bench, to which he was elected from the 8th judicial district. For thirteen years he presided with dignity, fearlessness, impartiality, and unusual ability over many trials, some of grave importance, and others of slight interest to any but the parties at suit. For the last four years of his service on the bench Judge Lewis was honored with the appointment as a member of the General Term, and distinguished himself there by many valuable decisions. During the period of his life passed at the bar, Mr. Lewis was known as a trial lawyer of the highest rank. His examinations were marked by a searching directness that permitted nothing to be left hidden; his opponent always dreaded his shafts of sarcasm; and his appeals to the jury were eloquent, logical, and eminently successful. It is still said among the lawyers of Buffalo that there has never been, in the history of the Erie county bar, any other advocate who won so large a proportion of his cases before the jury as Mr. Lewis, and that when he went upon the bench he was regarded as an advocate unequaled in persuasiveness.

Judge Lewis is interested in several of the banking institutions of Buffalo, being a director and vice president of the Third National Bank, and a director of the German-American Bank. He has found recreation in farming, and is the owner of a handsomely equipped farm at Lewiston, where he spends much of his leisure time.

*PERSONAL CHRONOLOGY— Lucan Lude-
wick Lewis was born at Mentz, Cayuga county, N. Y.,
May 9, 1825; came to Buffalo in the fall of 1848;
was admitted to the bar in 1848; married Charlotte
E. Pierson of East Aurora, N. Y., June 1, 1852;
was elected state senator from the Erie county district
in 1869, and was re-elected in 1871; was elected
judge of the Supreme Court in the 8th judicial district
in 1882, and served as such until 1895, when he retired by limitation of age.*

●●●

**Hardin Heth Littell** is a splendid type of a
most important class of men — the class which has
had the largest part in the material development of
our country, and which constitutes, together with
nature and with inventive genius, the real cause of
that development. These are the men who possess
in a conspicuous degree what is known
as executive ability—that rare and choice
quality of brain matter which enables the
owner to organize men and things into a
perfectly-oiled, swift-running, and fric-
tionless machine, performing immense
amounts of work almost automatically.

Such a man in a marked degree is
Hardin H. Littell. Educated very in-
adequately—"none at all," as he says
himself jocosely—Mr. Littell was obliged
to begin work when most boys are beginning their Caesar and their algebra. He
essayed first the dry-goods business, and
later, after the family had moved to Louisville, Ky., assumed a more ambitious
place in a jewelry store. Few men are
fortunate enough to find at once the
special kind of work for which they are
best adapted, and our present subject
offers no exception to this general rule.

At nineteen Mr. Littell really began his
career, for it was at that age that he entered
the service of the Louisville City Railway
Co., as a clerk in the treasurer's office.
In the following year he was promoted to
the position of assistant superintendent,
and at the age of twenty-two he became
superintendent. He remained in charge
of the Louisville city railways for nearly
a quarter of a century, in which time the
system was very much extended and improved. The change from horse to electricity as the motive power was made in part in the
later years of his work in Louisville.

In the decade 1880-90 the city of Buffalo grew
beyond all precedent in many ways, and especially in

the matter of population. Such a period is particularly trying for a street railway system, and the
owners of the Buffalo street railways deemed it of
the first importance to find somewhere a thoroughly
capable man to cope with this state of affairs in the
management of their property. Such a man they
found in Mr. Littell. He was elected in May, 1891,
president of the Cross-town Railway Co., vice president of the Buffalo Railway Co., and general manager of both companies. He assumed the duties of
these positions in the following month. Under his
administration the prosperity of the companies has
been marked, while the operation of the system from
the standpoint of the public has been greatly improved and brought to a high degree of excellence.
The service was doubled in mileage in three years,
and all parts of the city and suburbs were brought

*HARDIN HETH LITTELL*

into close touch with each other through a network
of electric lines.

Mr. Littell's time and energy have been given
chiefly to the companies directly under his care; but

numerous other enterprises have received the benefit of his wide experience. For a number of years he has been president of the Cincinnati Inclined Plane Railway of Cincinnati. He is director and vice president of the Buffalo, Bellevue & Lancaster railroad. He is a director in the Bellevue Land Co., also. Notwithstanding his departure from Louisville, Mr. Littell has retained his position as director in the Louisville Railway Co., as well as a directorate in that highly successful institution, the German Bank of Louisville. He is also a director still in the Columbia Finance and Trust Co. of Louisville.

*PERSONAL CHRONOLOGY.— Hardin Heth Littell was born at Corydon, Harrison county, Ind., August 5, 1845 ; attended country schools until the age of twelve : married Nellie Burton Green of Logansport, Ind., April 26, 1876 ; entered the service of the Louisville City Railway Co. in 1864, and became superintendent of the company in 1867 ; has been general manager of the Buffalo street-railway system since June, 1891.*

***

**Daniel H. Lockwood** is a Buffalonian whose fame and reputation are national. He is known as a politician of great ability, as a legislator of keen intelligence, as a lawyer of deep learning, and as a shrewd man of affairs. He has long held a conspicuous and honorable position at the bar of Buffalo and among the public men of the Empire State.

Born in a small country town, with none of the advantages of wealth, and bereft of his father at an early age, he found the usual difficulty which young men of limited means and high ambition experience in obtaining a college education. But he possessed such tenacity, determination, and persistency that he swept all obstacles from his pathway, and finally graduated from Union College in 1865.

Mr. Lockwood had early been attracted to the law, and shortly after graduation he entered the office of Judge Humphrey in Buffalo, and was admitted to practice before the Supreme Court of New York in 1866. The wisdom of his choice of a profession soon became evident ; for to strong reasoning powers, forcible expression of ideas, and unfailing tact, he added capacity for work and untiring zeal in the preparation and presentation of cases. During the thirty years in which he has followed his profession many important causes have been entrusted to his care, and many notable victories have been won by him in the courts. That he is a careful, sound, and conscientious counselor, and an able, eloquent, and convincing advocate, is amply evidenced in the gratifying measure of professional success attained by him.

As a business man Mr. Lockwood stands high, and his shrewdness and good judgment, conservative yet fearless, are acknowledged by all. He has an active interest in a number of commercial enterprises. He is president and manager of the Akron Cement Works, one of the leading industries in this line ; vice president and manager of the Buffalo Sewer Pipe Company ; president of the Buffalo, New York & Erie railroad ; and a director of the Merchants' Bank, and of the Third National Bank, both of Buffalo.

To the people at large, however, Mr. Lockwood is best known through his long connection with public affairs. He has always been a Democrat and an ardent supporter of Democratic principles. He has a wide reputation as a campaign speaker of unusual force and eloquence. During his early days in party service, it was not unusual for him to make half a dozen campaign speeches to as many different audiences in a single evening. He is said to have a wider personal acquaintance with the people of western New York than any other man in the country.

Soon after coming to Buffalo Mr. Lockwood took an active part in political affairs. In 1871 he was nominated for district attorney of Erie county ; and though he was defeated, his great popularity carried him 1,500 votes ahead of his ticket. Three years later he was again nominated, and this time was elected. Before his term of three years expired he was called upon to accept a higher honor — membership in the 45th congress. This body assembled in October, 1877, and was destined to figure largely in one of the most serious and momentous political contests in the history of the country. The Tilden-Hayes election controversy is still fresh in the public mind, and is even yet hardly ripe for the pen of the historian ; but the part played by the great actors in that scene stands out in higher relief with the passage of time, and to have been intimately connected with that event is an experience a man might properly covet. It was Mr. Lockwood's fortune to serve in that memorable congress. Though one of the youngest representatives, his speech on the Democratic side of the question attracted the attention of his fellow-members, and is one of the really valuable contributions to the literature of the great controversy.

On the expiration of his congressional term Mr. Lockwood resumed the practice of his profession, associated in partnership with Judge Humphrey, but did not cease his active participation in what has always seemed an allied branch of the law — civic affairs. He was too good a manager, too wise a counselor, too willing a worker, to be relieved from public service. In 1880 he was a delegate to the Democratic national convention at Cincinnati, which nominated General Hancock for President. In the same year Grover Cleveland was elected mayor of Buffalo, and Mr. Lockwood made the nominating speech. Two years later, as a delegate to the Democratic state convention, Mr. Lockwood placed Grover Cleveland in nomination for the office of governor. In 1884, at the Democratic national convention in Chicago, Mr. Lockwood presented the name of the same man for the Presidency of the United States.

Having been appointed by President Cleveland United States district attorney for northern New York, Mr. Lockwood brought to the office the same legal acumen that characterized his private practice. After holding the position for three years, he resigned in 1889. In the following year he was elected to congress again, and in 1892 he was re-elected. In both congresses Mr. Lockwood served on important committees, and repeated his earlier success in that body. He cared for the interests of his constituents with fidelity and unflagging zeal. He drafted an immigration bill that was regarded by many authorities as affording the best protection to American labor ever devised.

*PERSONAL CHRONOLOGY —*
*Daniel Newton Lockwood was born at Hamburg, N. Y., June 1, 1844 ; graduated at Union College, Schenectady, N. Y., in 1865 ; was admitted to the bar in May, 1866 ; married Sarah B. Breton of Buffalo October 18, 1870 ; was district attorney for Erie county, 1875–77 ; was a delegate to Democratic national conventions in 1880 and 1884 ; was United States district attorney for the northern district of New York, 1886–89 ; was a member of the 45th, 52d, and 53d congresses (1877–79 and 1891–95) ; was nominated for lieutenant governor of New York state in September, 1894.*

•••

**Willard Francis Mallalieu** has carried the gospel over a larger part of the world than most living clergymen. He has journeyed from north to south, zigzagged from Norway to Mexico, and belted the globe, tending the scattered flocks of the Methodist fold. He is the embodiment of physical and mental vigor consecrated to religious work. These qualities he comes by honestly, inheriting on

his father's side the blood of the Huguenots exiled from France, and on his mother's side that of a Puritan family who helped to found Salem. Bishop Mallalieu's youth was favored with the superior educational opportunities of the oldest section of the country, and he was thus enabled to enter the minis-

DANIEL N. LOCKWOOD

try the same year in which he graduated from college, excellently equipped for the grave responsibility of that profession. He quickly rose to influential prominence in the important Massachusetts stations to which he was assigned. In 1867 he proved his devotion to pastoral work by declining the presidency of Central Tennessee College, to which he had been elected. In 1875 he visited Europe for the purpose of studying certain phases of social, religious, and educational life. In 1876 he was elected assistant secretary of the Freedman's Aid Society, but declined the position. He was repeatedly sent by the New England Conference as delegate to the General Conference of the Methodist Episcopal church, and to the Conference of 1884 he was elected by the largest vote ever given to a delegate. This Conference proved memorable in Mr. Mallalieu's career, as it placed him on the exalted roll of Methodist bishops. He was thus removed from the presiding eldership that he had filled during the two preceding years; but he added a solid pillar to the Methodist episcopate.

*WILLARD FRANCIS MALLALIEU*

From this time Bishop Mallalieu's work took on a quickly expanding character. His episcopal residence was in the South, where he chose New Orleans for his home. It is not farfetched in this connection to point to the wonderful growth in recent years of the Methodist Episcopal church in the South. Because of its abolitionism, this church was not tolerated in that part of the country a quarter of a century ago; but there are now over a half million members of the Methodist church south of the old line. During his eight years' residence in New Orleans, Bishop Mallalieu held Conferences from Delaware to Texas, and spared no effort to further the conversion and education of the freedmen.

In pursuance of the duties of his office Bishop Mallalieu went to Europe in 1888, and presided over Conferences from Naples to Throndheim in Norway, and from Switzerland to the Black Sea. In the following year he went to Mexico, to inspect missions and hold Conferences. In 1892 he undertook a world-encircling episcopal itinerary in behalf of the foreign missions of his church. Sailing from San Francisco by way of Honolulu, he traveled in Japan, Korea, and China, visiting Peking and adjacent cities. He went to Shanghai next, and up the Yangtse-Kiang river to Kew Kiang and the heart of the empire. Returning, he visited the city of Foochow and many other localities in the Fuhkien province. Singapore, Ceylon, Madras, and Calcutta were then visited in turn. He next went up the Ganges fifteen hundred miles, inspecting mission work in many of the great cities, and crossed the country via Delhi to Bombay. He returned by way of the Red Sea and Egypt, with occasional stops at points in southern Europe.

Action has been the keynote of Bishop Mallalieu's successful ministry. Ever alert, quick in thought and sympathy, and remarkably affable in manner, his work both as pastor and bishop has endeared him to all. While in the pulpit, Bishop Mallalieu was in constant demand in the lecture field; and he has been a frequent contributor to both the religious and the secular press. In 1874 he received the degree of D. D. from East Tennessee Wesleyan University, and in 1892 the degree of LL. D. from New Orleans University.

*PERSONAL CHRONOLOGY—Willard Francis Mallalieu was born at Sutton, Mass., December 11, 1828; was educated at various preparatory schools and at Wesleyan University, Middletown, Conn., whence he graduated in August, 1855; married Eliza F. Atkins of Sandwich, Mass., October 14, 1858; had pastorates of the Methodist Episcopal church successively at Grafton, Chelsea, Lynn, Charlestown, Boston, and Worcester (all in Massachusetts); was appointed presiding elder of the Boston district of the New England Conference in April, 1882; was elected bishop of the Methodist Episcopal church in 1884; lived in New Orleans from 1884 until 1892, when he moved to Buffalo.*

**Edwin G. S. Miller** represents a class of men that are called in the West by the name, meaningful to Americans at least, of "hustlers." Some men seem born with activity and enterprise sufficient for two, and cover as much in a brief span of life as others in twice the number of years. Modern life accomplishes more in a day than was even possible before the age of stenographers, typewriters, and improved facilities of communication and transportation. This undoubtedly accounts in part for the vast volume of business that certain men perform to-day; but nevertheless the personal element is still a large factor as regards both the quantity and the quality of the work done.

Mr. Miller's forty-odd years have been spent entirely in Buffalo, where he was born and educated, in which his business training was begun, and in which his commercial successes have been achieved. After a common-school education (the equipment of most American boys) Mr. Miller took up the occupation of bookkeeper — one of the best forms of discipline for anyone entering upon a mercantile career — and became an employee in the office of George Urban & Son, proprietors of the Roller Flour Mills. His capacity for business and his demonstrated worth to the firm were soon recognized, and in 1874 he was admitted into the partnership. He then extended his business relations, and in the year 1884 became manager of the Gerhard Lang Brewery. His conduct of this establishment has been highly successful, and the output from the malt house has steadily increased. In December, 1895, Mr. Miller added yet another enterprise to his various projects by purchasing an important interest in the Buffalo *Enquirer*. Most men would be taxed to the utmost with the cares of so much business, but Mr. Miller is blessed with a splendid physique, executive ability, and untiring industry. He is at one or the other of his offices early and late, keeping longer hours than most men in positions like his.

In financial circles Mr. Miller is an active and yet conservative force, seeking lines of investment and development that have a permanent future. He is a director in the People's Bank, the German-American Bank, the Buffalo Loan, Trust & Safe Deposit Co., and the Buffalo Savings Bank. When a movement for increased street-car facilities was set on foot, and capital began seriously to examine the field, Mr. Miller was among the foremost in giving his influence and support to the scheme; and when finally a company was organized to build a new railway line, he became the first president.

Despite this busy career, Mr. Miller has found time for those political duties too often neglected by men of affairs. While never a candidate for office — for he would have no time to perform its functions — his counsel and spare hours have always been at the service of his party. He is a Democrat in political belief, and was chosen by the Democratic state convention of 1892 to be one of the presidential electors; and he helped cast the vote of the state for Mr. Cleveland.

*EDWIN G. S. MILLER*

In social life Mr. Miller is essentially a home man, though a member of the Buffalo Club and of the Ellicott Club. He is a member of St. Louis Church, and is identified with its philanthropic work.

Courteous in his demeanor, reliable in business, and cordial in his hospitality, he stands among the foremost of Buffalo's active and progressive men of to-day.

*PERSONAL CHRONOLOGY— Edwin G. S. Miller was born at Buffalo March 9, 1854; was educated in common schools; married Annie E. Lang*

*EDWARD H. MOVIUS*

*of Buffalo in June, 1884; was a Democratic presidential elector in 1892; has been a partner in the firm of Urban & Co. roller flour mills since 1874; manager of the Gerhard Lang Brewery since 1884; and part owner of the Buffalo "Enquirer" since December, 1895.*

•••

**Edward H. Movius** is a student, a lawyer, and a man of affairs. He is known as one of the foremost professional men of Buffalo, and as a thorough, painstaking, and capable worker in whatever he undertakes. To these traits of character he owes his great success. Though born in Michigan, Mr. Movius has practically been a Buffalonian all his life. His early scholastic training was obtained in various private schools in Buffalo, at Russell's Military Academy, New Haven, Conn., and at Phillips Academy, Exeter, N. H. Shortly after finishing his studies at Exeter in 1867, he went to Europe and took a course at the famous University of Heidelberg, Germany, from which he graduated in 1869, with the degrees of Doctor of Philosophy and Master of Arts. Afterward he determined to adopt the law as his profession, and took a course in the law school connected with Hamilton College at Clinton, N. Y., receiving there the degree of LL. B.

He began at once the active practice of his profession, and has continued the same with unbroken success up to the present time. He read law in the offices of those masters, E. Carleton Sprague and Delavan F. Clark, both now dead, and brought to his life-work a mind well grounded in the principles of the law and thoroughly trained in the application of those principles to intricate problems. The firm names of Crowley & Movius, of Allen, Movius & Wilcox, and of Movius & Wilcox have been prominent in many matters of much legal importance. Since the dissolution of the last-named firm in 1892, Mr. Movius has practiced alone.

When the West Shore railway was projected from New York to Buffalo, paralleling the lines of the New York Central, Mr. Movius was appointed one of the attorneys of the company, and as such rendered service of the utmost value. This company bought millions of dollars' worth of property, and Mr. Movius passed on the greater part of the titles of land purchased in Erie and Genesee counties. He continued as the attorney of the West Shore road until about the time of its reorganization and lease to the Central. He was also one of the attorneys for the commissioners of the state reservation at Niagara in their condemnation of valuable lands taken by the state "for the purpose of restoring the scenery of the great Falls to its natural condition," and of establishing there a park that should be free to all mankind for all time. In that capacity Mr. Movius passed on the titles of all land taken by the state.

From 1887 to 1889 Mr. Movius served in the very trying position of receiver of the First National Bank of Buffalo, which had been wrecked by its president. Here he displayed in a marked degree unusual ability as a lawyer and as a man of business. To his efforts was largely due the satisfactory closing of the affairs of that unfortunate institution.

When President Cleveland was looking about for the right kind of material to compose the board of United States mineral-land commissioners he picked out Mr. Movius as one of the three members for the Helena (Mont.) land district. Theirs was a most difficult and delicate task. How well they are discharging their duties is evidenced in the Montana papers, one of which, the Helena *Independent*, said on August 23, 1895: "Starting out inexperienced and unfamiliar with their duties, with natural prejudice against them because they were strangers in a strange land, the mineral-land commissioners, one and all, have discharged their duties with fidelity, earnestness, and impartiality. They have done a great work, and have won deserving and lasting gratitude from all parties interested."

The social side of Mr. Movius's nature is highly developed, and he is a welcome visitor at the many clubs and societies of which he is a member. Among these are the University Club of New York, the University Club of Buffalo, the Buffalo Club, of which he has been vice president, and the Montana Club of Helena, Mont.

*PERSONAL CHRONOLOGY* — *Edward Hallam Movius was born at Ypsilanti, Mich., October 19, 1848; was educated in various preparatory schools in this country, and graduated from the University of Heidelberg, Germany, in 1869 with the degrees of Ph. D. and M. A.; graduated from Hamilton College law school, Clinton, N. Y., in 1878; married Mary Lovering Rumsey of Buffalo September 26, 1877; was appointed receiver of the First National Bank of Buffalo in 1887; was appointed by President Cleveland one of the board of three United States mineral-land commissioners in the Helena (Mont.) land district in April, 1895.*

**Nathaniel Willis Norton** is one of the best known of the younger members of the bar of Erie county. Coming to Buffalo fresh from his law studies, a comparative stranger in the city, he nevertheless, by reason of natural ability and untiring diligence, soon attained a practice that was the envy of many new disciples of Kent and Blackstone.

The excellent common-school system of Maine afforded young Norton his first knowledge of books. When nineteen years old he entered Nichols Latin School at Lewiston in his native state, and there devoted himself industriously to a course of study that would adequately fit him for college. Mr. Norton spent his freshman year at Bates College; but Dartmouth was more to his liking, and he entered the sophomore class of that institution in 1875. Three years of hard study at Hanover brought him to that epochal time in the lives of all college men — graduation day. His duties at Dartmouth had been discharged with fidelity, and the bachelor's degree was conferred upon him in due course.

Immediately after leaving college Mr. Norton was elected principal of the high school at Ware, Mass. This appointment was very creditable to the young

NATHANIEL WILLIS NORTON

graduate, and might easily have encouraged him to adopt teaching as his profession. But it was no part of Mr. Norton's scheme of life to remain a schoolteacher; he had other aims, and the law was his ambition. He taught school for one year only, therefore, and devoted all his spare time to the study of the fundamental principles of law. At the end of that period he entered the Albany Law School, from which he graduated with the degree of LL. B. in May, 1880. His admission to the bar, at Albany, followed at once.

Mr. Norton came to Buffalo the same year, believing that the place was a thriving, growing, bustling city, where the legal profession was not overcrowded at the top — and the top was the place that Mr. Norton determined to reach, if intelligence, industry, and a mastery of his profession could put him there. How well he has succeeded the record of the past fifteen years amply demonstrates. For the first five years Mr. Norton practiced law alone, but in April, 1885, his brother, Roswell M., joined him; and in January, 1895, a second brother, Herbert F. J., was admitted to the firm.

While thoroughly devoted to his profession, Mr. Norton has identified himself with the general concerns of the community, and many enterprises and organizations of a public and semi-public nature have received the benefit of his support, his counsel, and his example. He is a member of the Buffalo Historical Society, the Buffalo Library, the German Young Men's Association, and the Merchants' Exchange. He is a trustee of the Buffalo Orphan Asylum. He is also a prominent member of the Buffalo, Saturn, and University clubs. He has long been an ardent believer in the principles of the Republican party, and is a leading member of the Buffalo Republican League. At the same time he does not believe that party advantage should be placed before public good; and honest politics, as the phrase is, finds in him a hearty advocate. His party services were rewarded by an appointment as assistant United States district attorney under Colonel D. S. Alexander, who was appointed by President Harrison. Mr. Norton ably filled this position for a year and a half during 1889 and 1890, when the demands of his private practice compelled his resignation. This is the only public office he has held.

*PERSONAL CHRONOLOGY — Nathaniel Willis Norton was born at Porter, Me., March 3, 1854; spent one year at Bates College, but graduated from Dartmouth College, in 1878; was principal of Ware (Mass.) High School, 1878-79; married Mary Estella Miner of Buffalo June 30, 1880; was assistant United States district attorney, 1889-90-; has practiced law in Buffalo since 1880.*

* * *

**Daniel O'Day** is an example of what pluck, energy, and perseverance, coupled with ability, all properly directed, will do for a man. Starting with no advantages, without influential friends to back him, with nothing in fact but native talent, a determination to succeed, and a willingness to work hard at whatever he could find to do, this man early in life reached a position of affluence and influence. Some people might say that Mr. O'Day had opportunities that come to but few men. This may be so, but he worked for those openings for advancement, seized them when they came within his reach, and had previously qualified himself, by untiring energy, to make the most of them. No obstacle ever came in Daniel O'Day's pathway that he was not ready and willing to overcome by hard work and persistent effort. This is the secret of his business success. He is, furthermore, a public-spirited citizen, engaged in many enterprises of a public or a private nature. His friends are numbered by the thousand, for he is a popular man, personally, socially, and politically. He is a member of various social organizations in both Buffalo and New York. Though an ardent Democrat and a liberal contributor to his party's funds, he has never held political office, except as a presidential elector.

Born in Ireland, Mr. O'Day was brought to this country when a small child. His early life was passed on a farm in Cattaraugus county, New York. Here he spent his days as do most boys brought up in like conditions. His education, acquired in the broad field of the world, had its foundation in the public schools. Farming was not at all to his liking, and when he was eighteen years old he moved to Buffalo to begin his struggle with the world. His first employment was found with the New York Central railroad as a messenger. In this humble position his faithful application and his natural capacity and intelligence were displayed so far as opportunity offered. They were rewarded, too, by successive promotions, until, after a lapse of three years, young O'Day attained the position of shipping clerk.

Though the main business of his life was to concern transportation interests, Mr. O'Day did not find railroading so congenial that he was satisfied to continue in that line. In 1865 the oil excitement in the rapidly developing fields of Pennsylvania permeated every part of the East, and in Buffalo, so near the scene of operations, the excitement was naturally intense. The shipping clerk became infected, resigned his position, packed his few belongings, and soon was in the thick of the fight. Perhaps because of his railroad training, perhaps by chance, his attention was early directed to the transportation of oil. It was a great problem in those days. Railroads were few and hard to reach, and teaming was expensive and a vexation to the soul. Pipe-lines had been projected, some of which had proved failures, while others had shown that the method could be economically and successfully applied. Mr. O'Day early became connected with one of the pioneer lines, the Empire Transportation Company. So active was he in furthering its interests, so shrewd was his counsel, that he soon held an important position in the company.

Mr. O'Day's connection with the Standard Oil Company dates from 1870. It is largely to him that this great company owes its wonderful system of pipe-lines, which have their beginning at thousands of wells scattered over thousands of acres of land, and which end at the seaboard. It was some years after pipe-lines were successfully used to convey oil from the wells to refineries located in the oil country, that it was deemed possible to transport this product over long distances by the same method. Daniel O'Day was one of the first to suggest that this might be done. He saw no reason why the company should not send its petroleum from the fields to the seaboard through pipes, using pumps of great force as the motive power. This idea eventually resulted in the construction of the line that now extends from Olean, N. Y., to Bayonne, N. J. Mr. O'Day is the virtual head of the mammoth pipe-line interests of the Standard Oil Company. He is vice president of the United Pipe-Lines Company, and of the National Transit Company.

Though Mr. O'Day, long a Buffalonian, has moved to New York since the death of his first wife in 1890, he has still large interests in the Queen City, and may be seen there frequently. He is president of the People's Bank, of the General Electric Company, and of the Buffalo Natural Gas Fuel Company. He is also interested in other concerns, and is a large owner of Buffalo real estate.

*PERSONAL CHRONOLOGY— Daniel O'Day was born at Kildysart, Ireland, February 6, 1844; was brought to this country early in life, and lived at Ellicottville, N. Y., until 1862; was with the New York Central railroad, 1862-65; went to Pennsylvania oil fields in 1865, and ultimately became manager of the Standard Oil Company's pipe-lines; married Louise Newell of Boston in 1870 and Mary Page of Nova Scotia in 1892.*

**Roswell Park**, though only forty-three years old, is one of the most distinguished of the men whose names appear upon the annals of medicine in western New York; and this is no slight distinction, when the statement concerns a locality that has been the home of such teachers and practitioners of

*DANIEL O'DAY*

national reputation as Austin Flint, Frank Hastings Hamilton, James P. White, and Julius F. Miner.

Dr. Park might be taken as an illustration of what Dr. Holmes says of the influence of a fine ancestry. His father, the Rev. Roswell Park, D. D., graduated at the head of his class at West Point in 1836, and did important work in the corps of engineers of the United States army for some years; then became professor of chemistry and physics in the University of Pennsylvania; and finally entered the church and became, in 1852, founder and first president of Racine College. On the other side, Dr. Park is descended from a race with a bent, like that of R. L. Stevenson, for engineering. His mother, Mary B. Baldwin of Woburn, Mass., was a descendant of the Baldwin family, so many representatives of which became famous engineers in the eastern part of the country, and left monuments of their skill all along the Atlantic coast. Dr. Park's ancestors on both sides were prominent in the War of Independence, and several of them were officers.

*ROSWELL PARK*

With such a family history, it would not have been surprising if Dr. Park had become an engineer. Instead, he decided to follow the study of medicine. After a general education at Racine College, he graduated from the Chicago Medical College (Northwestern University), adding to his preparation for his profession the valuable experience of two and a half years' service as *interne* in the two largest hospitals in Chicago. At twenty-five Dr. Park began his work as a teacher, having received an appointment, in 1877, as demonstrator of anatomy in the Woman's Medical College of Chicago. The next year he was appointed to the same position, and later to that of assistant professor of anatomy, in the Chicago

Medical College. In 1882 he was made lecturer on surgery in the Rush Medical College. In 1883 he was called to the chair of surgery in the Buffalo Medical College; this position, with that of surgeon to the Buffalo General Hospital, he still holds. His ability as a teacher has been widely recognized.

Dr. Park's reputation, however, is not confined to his work in the class-room and as a practitioner. If the record stopped here, it would leave out a very important part of his career. He is a deep student, and has won fame as a writer upon medical topics. The list of the papers that he has published in the last twelve years fills fourteen pages of manuscript. Among the chief items is a volume of "Lectures on Surgical Pathology," which appeared in 1892. He has in preparation, and will soon publish, a volume of lectures on the history of medicine; and a treatise on surgery, in two volumes, of which he is editor, and to which he has been a large contributor. He has written many encyclopedia articles and popular lectures. His signature appears at the foot of many of the medical articles in Johnson's "Universal Cyclopedia." He is a member of the New York Academy of Medicine, the American Medical Association, the American Surgical Association, the American Orthopedic Association, the American Association of Genito-Urinary Surgeons, the German Congress of Surgeons (*Deutsche Gesellschaft für Chirurgie*), and various other professional societies. He was made an honorary member of the American Academy of Medicine in 1895, and is now president of the Medical Society of the State of New York. He is a member of all the local scientific societies. Among the degrees that he has received are A. M., Racine College, 1875; honorary M. D., Rush Medical College (Lake Forest University), 1892; and honorary A. M., Harvard, 1895.

At the age of forty Dr. Park had attained a national reputation. He is not only a good student and a voluminous writer in his profession, but is also a man of the world, actively concerned in everything that makes life interesting. He is a man of the widest sympathy. His social nature, and the extent and diversity of his interests, appear in the fact that he has been an officer of the Buffalo, Saturn, and University clubs of Buffalo; that he has been president of the Buffalo Musical Association; that he is a member of the University and Reform clubs of New York city; that he has been president of the 21st Ward Good Government Club, and vice president of the Council of Confederated Good Government Clubs of Buffalo. In years past Dr. Park was for some time president of the Chicago Electrical Society, and later of the Buffalo Microscopical Society. In 1895 Governor Morton made him one of the managers of the Buffalo State Hospital. Dr. Park has also held many other positions of honor and responsibility.

*PERSONAL CHRONOLOGY — Roswell Park was born at Pomfret, Conn., May 4, 1852; graduated from Racine (Wis.) College in 1872, and from the Chicago Medical College with the degree of M. D. in 1876; married Martha P. Durkee of Chicago June 1, 1882; served upon the faculty of the Woman's Medical College of Chicago, the Chicago Medical College, and Rush Medical College, successively, 1877–84; was called to be professor of surgery in the medical department, University of Buffalo, and surgeon to the Buffalo General Hospital, in 1884; was elected president of the Medical Society of the State of New York for 1895–96.*

•••

**William H. Pitt** has an important place in the history of the petroleum industry, and is an excellent illustration of the truth that one of the chief factors in the material development of our country to-day is the man of science. He was born and brought up on a farm — a circumstance that he has looked back upon not with regret, but with pleasure. The oldest boy in a farmer's family of ten children — more than half of them girls — is generally not overburdened with opportunities for advancement. So it was with young Pitt. His education had to be for the most part what he made it himself, and he early determined that it should be the best possible under the circumstances. He worked and taught and studied, in accordance with shifting conditions, for twelve years, finally graduating from Union College in 1860. He was then twenty-eight years of age — somewhat older than the average collegiate at graduation; but he had been forced to interrupt his studies continually for the purpose of meeting his current expenses by means of teaching; and he had

the solid and enduring satisfaction of knowing that all the expenses of his education had been paid by himself.

Once through college, Professor Pitt returned to teaching, all the while continuing the study of various branches of science. He was principal of the high school at Spencer, N. Y., for two years; then held a similar position at Angelica (N. Y.) Academy; next served as superintendent of education at Warren, Ohio, for two years; and then returned, as principal, to Friendship (N. Y.) Academy, where he had once taught. From there he came to Buffalo in September, 1872, to take the professorship of physics and chemistry in the high school. He built up both departments, added largely to their apparatus, and finally resigned his position in 1890, after eighteen years of useful work, on account of the

*WILLIAM H. PITT*

growing demands of other interests. He still retained, and yet occupies, the chair of general physics and chemistry in the medical department of Niagara University, to which he was called in 1884.

Professor Pitt, during all these years of teaching, was still a student, devoting his leisure moments to scientific research. In 1863 Union College gave him the degree of A. M.; in 1879 the medical department, University of Buffalo, that of M. D.; and in 1886 Alfred University that of Ph. D. His scientific knowledge furnished at last the basis of important developments in the petroleum fields. He became interested in the subject of oil at the time of the early excitement in Pennsylvania, and studied carefully the geological and chemical problems relating to the production and the manufacture of oil. His suggestion that oil would be found further north and east of the Oil Creek district was followed by the opening of the Bradford field in 1876. In 1880 he declared that petroleum existed along the line dividing the head waters of the Allegheny and Genesee rivers. His theory led O. P. Taylor, the pioneer of the Allegany county field, to "wild-cat" in the locality pointed out by Professor Pitt. An immensely rich territory was discovered, Richburg and Bolivar sprang into fame as oil towns, and millions of dollars' worth of oil was produced; all of which redounded to Professor Pitt's reputation for excellent judgment, but was otherwise of no advantage to him.

But he was more fortunate later in profiting from the fruits of his knowledge. For a long time the oil produced in the Ohio and Canadian fields was of little use, except for fuel, on account of the large proportion of sulphur that it contained. Professor Pitt applied himself to the problem of utilizing this nearly valueless product. After many fruitless experiments, he at last hit on a practical method of refining the oil; and the result has been a revolution in the petroleum industry in Ohio. Formerly the Lima oil was sold at fifteen cents a barrel. To-day certificates for the same oil are sold at the exchanges for about ninety cents. If the man who makes two blades of grass grow where only one grew before is a public benefactor, the man who invents a process by which any of the earth's products are made doubly useful should be placed in the same category. Professor Pitt's process is in use, with entire success, at the Paragon Oil Refinery at Toledo, Ohio, of which he is the consulting chemist. This position and his duties as lecturer at Niagara University have occupied all his attention in recent years.

Professor Pitt has written mostly on scientific questions. Papers from his pen have appeared in the Buffalo Medical Journal and other periodicals, and in the proceedings of the American Association for the Advancement of Science. He has described and illustrated several new fossils from the water-lime formation in the neighborhood of Buffalo—among them the first pterogotus, it is believed, found in this country. He has belonged to the Buffalo Society of Natural Sciences for many years, doing original work on the Journal and adding specimens of his own discovery to the society's collections.

PERSONAL CHRONOLOGY—William Hudson Pitt was born at Short Tract, N. Y., September 8, 1841; prepared for college at Alfred (N. Y.) Academy, and graduated from Union College, Schenectady, N. Y., in 1860; married Mary Elizabeth Church of Friendship, N. Y., May 18, 1861; was superintendent of education at Warren, Ohio, 1867-68; was professor of physics and chemistry in the Buffalo High School, 1872-90; was State Analyst of Foods and Drugs, 1881-82; has been professor of general chemistry and physics in the medical department of Niagara University since May 26, 1884.

***

**Charles A. Pooley** is known as one of the soundest lawyers in the city of Buffalo. It is no small praise to say this, for it is an undisputed fact that the bar of Buffalo contains among its members some of the best lawyers in the state of New York. To win a recognized place among these legal lights one must be well-read in the law, and must be able to apply legal principles correctly and promptly to all questions arising. The fact that the firm of which Mr. Pooley has long been an active and distinguished member cares for large corporate interests is itself a guarantee that he is an able and astute lawyer.

Mr. Pooley has always lived in Buffalo. He attended Public School No. 4, and graduated from the Central High School in the class of 1873. This was the end of his scholastic training. Upon his graduation he entered the lumber business, in which he continued for three years. Not finding this employment strictly congenial and having an ambition to adopt a profession for which he felt a special aptitude, Mr. Pooley began the study of law on January 1, 1876. Devoting himself diligently to Blackstone and Kent, he was admitted to the full privileges of the bar in April, 1879. He began at once the active practice of law in connection with the firm of Laning, McMillan & Gluck, having completed his studies in the office of the late Senator A. P. Laning. He has continued with that firm through its various changes—Greene, McMillan & Gluck, McMillan, Gluck & Pooley, and McMillan, Gluck, Pooley & Depew—to the present time.

As an evidence of the high esteem in which Mr. Pooley is held by his fellow members of the bar, the fact may be cited that when a vacancy occurred on the bench of the Supreme Court for the 8th judicial district, caused by the elevation of Judge Albert Haight to the Court of Appeals on January 1, 1895, Mr. Pooley was strongly endorsed for the appointment. The petition to Governor Morton in his favor was signed by lawyers of all shades of political opinion; and the mere fact that he was endorsed in this manner to succeed a jurist of the recognized standing of Judge Haight is as great a compliment as could well be paid to a man of his profession. That he was not appointed was undoubtedly due largely to political exigencies, Governor Morton deeming it best to select for the place a man from another part of the judicial district. In the summer of 1895 Mr. Pooley was prominently mentioned as a candidate for the Republican nomination to a place on the bench of the Supreme Court.

Mr. Pooley is a trustee of the law library of the 8th judicial district, having been appointed to that honorable position by the Supreme Court. He has likewise been a director of the Buffalo Library, serving for three years.

Always a faithful worker in the interest of any cause with which he has connected himself, Mr. Pooley has been highly honored by the Free Masons. He is a Past Master of DeMolay Lodge, No. 498, and served a term as District Deputy Grand Master of the Masons of the state of New York for the 25th Masonic district.

*PERSONAL CHRONOLOGY—Charles A. Pooley was born at Buffalo November 17, 1854; was educated in the public schools of Buffalo; engaged in the lumber business, 1873–75; was admitted to the bar in April, 1879; married Carrie Adams, daughter of S. Cary Adams of Buffalo, June 4, 1884; has practiced law since 1879 with the firm of McMillan, Gluck, Pooley & Depew and their predecessors.*

— •••

**Cyrus K. Porter** has made an honorable reputation in two distinct lines of activity. He has been a successful architect and builder, and he is the founder of the order of Royal Templars of Temperance. His life has been twofold, having been devoted both to his vocation and to movements for the uplifting of his fellow-men. Practical work and judicious philanthropy have occupied his time and thought; and self-seeking has had no place in his plans for the betterment of society. Recognizing

the great evil that lies at the root of so much human misery and crime, he has combated this evil in public and private with every rational weapon at his command. He has not allowed himself to be carried away by the cause he advocates, but has avoided fanaticism, and appealed to the reason of men.

CHARLES A. POOLEY

Though a native of New York state, Mr. Porter is of an old New England family that has contributed generation after generation to the ranks of the country's scholars and public men. His education was obtained in common schools, and, as he characteristically says, "in the workshop." He began his apprenticeship as a builder on the day General Taylor was elected President — November 7, 1848. Having mastered the mechanical part of building, he next undertook the theoretical study of the subject, and in due time he became an architect. For two years he was employed in the office of the resident engineer of the Chicago waterworks. Business then took him to the province of Ontario, and ten years elapsed before he returned to western New York.

It was in 1865 that Mr. Porter came to Buffalo to live. The American block, which had just been destroyed in a memorable fire, was then rebuilding, and he was made superintendent of construction in connection with that work. In the following year he formed a partnership with H. M. Wilcox under

*CYRUS K. PORTER*

the firm name of Wilcox & Porter; but he soon bought out his partner's interest, and has since carried on his profession alone or in company with his son. He has paid particular attention to designing schoolhouses, churches, and public buildings, such as permit the exercise of bold ideas and original conceptions. He has frequently competed for public buildings, and has won several important premiums — notably the second premium for the War, State, and Navy Department Building at Washington and a like premium for the City Hall, Quebec, Canada. Among the prominent buildings of Buffalo planned and constructed by him are Trinity Church, St. Patrick's Church, the new municipal buildings, and the Builders' Exchange.

Mr. Porter has been no less active in the cause of temperance than in the practice of his profession. He is among the foremost reformers in devising methods of promoting sobriety in all classes of the people. His work in this direction has attracted the attention of the Prohibition party, which has placed him in nomination several times upon its ticket. He has always been a Republican, having cast his first ballot for John P. Hale, in 1852. He is not, however, a hidebound member of that party, but has exercised the high prerogative and duty of "scratching" the names of objectionable candidates.

The fraternal side of Mr. Porter's character is evidenced in the number of societies to which he belongs. He is an Odd Fellow, a Free Mason, a Good Templar, a Son of Temperance, a United Workman, and a Royal Templar of Temperance. All his leisure has been spent in temperance work, the one interest he has had at heart outside the practice of his profession.

*PERSONAL CHRONOLOGY—Cyrus Kinne Porter was born at Cicero, N. Y., August 27, 1828; was educated in common schools; learned the builders' trade, and became an architect in 1855; founded the order of Royal Templars of Temperance in 1870; went to Buffalo in 1865, and has practiced his profession there since.*

* * *

**Pascal P. Pratt** has added lustre and prestige to a family name already so distinguished that the mere maintenance of the patronymic unimpaired would have been a noteworthy achievement. When the century now closing had barely begun to run its course Captain Samuel Pratt, grandfather of Pascal P. Pratt, brought his family from Vermont to Buffalo in an old-fashioned coach, said to be the first carriage ever seen in Erie county. Captain Pratt had an important part in shaping the frontier history of Buffalo, and his sons, one of whom was twice mayor of Buffalo, contributed their share in making the family name a part of the best history of western New York.

Pascal P. Pratt, so descended, really deserves three biographies — one as a business man, another as a banker, and a third, perhaps most important of all, as a public-spirited citizen. Regarding him first from a business standpoint, we may note the fact that he began his commercial life, in the hardware business, at the age of sixteen, after having made the most of educational opportunities that would now be deemed scanty. In this business he remained as clerk and partner for half a century, finally retiring from the famous firm of Pratt & Co. in 1885, in order to devote more time to banking duties that were becoming increasingly burdensome. Side by side with the hardware business there grew up under Mr. Pratt's masterful hands other industrial concerns hardly less important. The house of Pratt & Letchworth, founded in 1845, and the Buffalo Iron & Nail Company, organized in 1857, are cases in point. Without resort to details, Mr. Pratt's business life may be characterized as having been ideally successful: he has furnished lucrative and pleasant employment to thousands of contented workmen, and he has at the same time secured a fair return for invested capital.

As a banker Mr. Pratt's career has been equally distinguished. With the Manufacturers' and Traders' Bank of Buffalo he has been identified from the very beginning, over forty years ago, when he was made director and vice president. The latter office he held until 1885, when he was elected to his present office, that of president. He has also been a director of the Bank of Buffalo, of the Third National Bank of Buffalo, and of the Bank of Attica.

Most interesting to the general reader, and perhaps most pleasing to himself, is Mr. Pratt's life on the side of public services and civic honor. A list of the offices of trust and responsibility held by him would quite exhaust the space at our disposal. Educational and religious institutions, political and charitable organizations, as well as the city and the state, have asked him freely for the benefit of his business sagacity, mature judgment, and ripe experience. The Buffalo Female Academy, the Young Men's Christian Association, the North Presbyterian Church, the Buffalo Orphan Asylum, and numerous other institutions of his native city have been greatly aided in their work by his head and heart. Well might a careful biographer, in summing up the character of Mr. Pratt, write the following: "A just and devoted husband and father, a true friend, and active in all the years of a pure and useful life in whatever would inure to the benefit of humanity, no

man better represents the character of the good citizen. And thus it is that the city of Buffalo, gratefully appreciating his devotion to its best interests, and the example of a stainless life, honors him, in the dignity of his manhood, with its confidence and respect."

*PERSONAL CHRONOLOGY— Pascal Paoli Pratt was born at Buffalo September 15, 1819; was educated at Hamilton (N. Y.) Academy and at Amherst (Mass.) Academy; married Phoebe Lorenz of Pittsburg September 1, 1845; was a Republican presidential elector in 1874, chairman of the Buffalo Park Commission from 1869 to 1879, and one of the three commissioners appointed by the Supreme Court in 1883 to appraise the value of the property taken by the state for the Reservation at Niagara Falls; has been president of the Manufacturers' and Traders' Bank of Buffalo since 1885.*

PASCAL P. PRATT

**T. T. Ramsdell** is one of the most widely known men in Buffalo to-day. Unlike many of the prominent citizens of this changing and rapidly growing city, Mr. Ramsdell was born and educated

here, and has spent his whole life here ; and he gives
to the many enterprises for the advancement of his
native city that hearty co-operation and interest
which might be expected from one of her loyal sons.
As a boy he attended the public schools of the
city, and later spent three years in Professor Briggs's

*THOMAS T. RAMSDELL.*

classical school, from which he graduated in 1871.
In 1873 he began his business life as a clerk in the
wholesale boot and shoe house established by his
father in 1857, and he has ever since been connected
with this firm. At that time the business was conducted by his father, Orrin P. Ramsdell, and by
W. H. Walker. In 1877 Mr. Walker retired from
the firm, and T. T. Ramsdell and his brother, Albert
N., were taken into partnership. Albert N. Ramsdell died in the following year, and in 1879 W. C.,
G. W., and S. M. Sweet were admitted to the firm, and
the business took the present style of O. P. Ramsdell,
Sweet & Co. O. P. Ramsdell and G. W. Sweet
have since died, and T. T. Ramsdell is now the

senior member of the firm. To the maintenance and
development of this already extensive and prosperous
business, Mr. Ramsdell has devoted himself with persistent energy ; and as a result the firm to-day is one of
the most solid and highly respected in Buffalo, and
one of the largest of western New York in its line.

Mr. Ramsdell has never sought nor
held political office, but his interest in
political affairs is keen, and his influence
is always exerted on the side of good
government and needed reform. He is
an active member of the Republican
League, which he served as president in
1894, and to which he devotes much time
and energy.

He is also prominent in all the movements for enhancing the prosperity of his
native city. The great scheme for bringing Niagara Falls water power to Buffalo
is a notable case in point. When this
was only an idea, Mr. Ramsdell foresaw
the immense industrial, domestic, and
municipal benefits inherent in the scheme,
and he identified himself actively with the
promotion of the project — with the prac-
ticalization of the idea. He was appointed a member of Mayor Jewett's
advisory committee to consider the practical business use of the great power within
the limits of Buffalo. Mr. Ramsdell is
a director of the Ellicott Square Company, the corporation that erected the
Ellicott Square Building, which is one of
the finest architectural features of the
city of Buffalo. He is also a director of
the Merchants' Exchange, of the Board
of Trade, and of the Bell Telephone
Company of Buffalo.

Mr. Ramsdell has not confined his
attention to projects for the material
prosperity of the city. He is a member of the
Westminster Church, the Buffalo Library, the Buffalo
Historical Society, the Buffalo Fine Arts Academy,
and the Buffalo Society of Natural Sciences. He is
a director of the Buffalo General Hospital. Membership in the Buffalo Press Club, the Country Club,
and the Buffalo Club, evidences his interest in social
matters, and rounds out on an important side his
character as a successful business man and public-
spirited citizen.

*PERSONAL CHRONOLOGY— Thomas T.
Ramsdell was born at Buffalo March 15, 1854 ;
graduated from the Buffalo Classical School in 1871 ;
began business in 1873 as a clerk for O. P. Ramsdell*

*& Co., wholesale dealers in boots, shoes, and rubbers;
became partner in this firm in 1877; organized the
present firm of O. P. Ramsdell, Sweet & Co. in
1879; married Louise Miller of Sterling, Ill., November 10, 1881.*

...

**James A. Roberts** began life in the back-
woods of Maine. He was "raised on a farm," as
the saying is — a statement that conveys to all Americans a mental image perfectly intelligible and meaningful. He resolved to obtain a college education,
and to effect this he underwent the most rigorous
self-denial. He taught school in winter, worked in
the fields in summer, and practiced the strictest
economy at all times. At one particularly trying
stage of his college finances he contracted to haul a
large number of logs to market, and fulfilled the contract on time by arising at
four o'clock every morning and starting
into the woods with two yoke of oxen.

If it be true, as some competent judges
assert, that a young man who enters college with plenty of money to spend is
really handicapped thereby in the race
for college honors, we may understand
why our teacher-farmer-contractor student was able to graduate from Bowdoin
at the head of his class.

One reason for this success, in the face
of obstacles that would have disheartened
most men, may be found in the fact that
young Roberts brought to his college
duties a matured mind and a character
that had been strengthened by experiences quite unusual in the case of so
young a man. When he would naturally
have entered college the Civil War was
raging fiercely, and he determined to exchange his books for the soldier's knap-
sack. He enlisted in 1864, when only
seventeen, in the 7th Maine battery, and
served with the Army of the Potomac
until the surrender at Appomattox.

After leaving college Mr. Roberts
taught school in Portland for one year
and in Buffalo for three years, studying
law at the same time. He abandoned
teaching on his admission to the bar,
and devoted all his energy to the practice
of law and the promotion of various business enterprises. At that time Buffalo was about to
enter upon a period of extraordinary growth in population and of wide expansion in industrial affairs, and
she needed professional men of the highest class to
complement her material prosperity. Mr. Roberts
was quick to realize the significance of these conditions and to take advantage of them, and he soon
became prominently identified with the city of his
adoption. Coincidentally with wide learning, literary culture, and intellectual attributes of a high
order, Mr. Roberts possesses an intensely practical
turn of mind, which has been of the utmost value in
his professional work and in his highly successful
business operations. In the organization and the
conduct of banking, street-railroad, electric-lighting,
and real-estate enterprises, Mr. Roberts has shown
a marked genius for business.

In political life Mr. Roberts has attained decided
success without the sacrifice of self-respect or of any
quality that should be dearer than the highest measure

*JAMES A. ROBERTS*

of success as sometimes estimated. He has not
always been prominently before the public in political matters, but he has always been allied with the
best element of his party, and has always given that

element the wisest and most patriotic counsel. He has been an ardent civil-service reformer, and has done yeoman's service in the advance of that cause. As comptroller of the state of New York, Mr. Roberts has splendidly improved the opportunity to show how important that office may be made in the hands

*SHERMAN S. ROGERS*

of a capable and a thoroughly upright public official. Without attempting the difficult feat of forecasting the political future, the statement may safely be made that Mr. Roberts' career in the world of politics has not yet reached its zenith, if honesty of purpose, independence of character, fearlessness of judgment, and broad-minded statesmanship of the highest type count for anything with the people of the Empire State.

*PERSONAL CHRONOLOGY—James A. Roberts was born at Waterboro, Me., March 8, 1847; fitted for college at Auburn, Me., and graduated from Bowdoin in 1870; was admitted to the bar at Buffalo in 1875; married Minnie Pinco of Calais, Me., in 1871, and Martha Dresser of Auburn, Me., in*

*1884; was representative in the state assembly, 1879-80; was elected comptroller of the state of New York in 1893, and was re-elected in 1895.*

***

**Sberman S. Rogers** has served the law and his fellow-men all his days. He began the endless study of legal science at an early age, and enjoyed an important practice before young men nowadays have received their diplomas. After practicing three years in his native town of Bath, N. Y., Mr. Rogers sought the wider opportunities promised in the city of Buffalo. This was in 1854 when Buffalo contained fewer than 50,000 people, but when evidences of its later greatness were clearly apparent. There Mr. Rogers has lived for more than forty years — a shining light in his profession, an ornament to his city, and a distinguished honor to his state and country.

Of Mr. Rogers as a practitioner hardly any words of praise could be deemed extravagant. The Buffalo bar has a very splendid history, and includes among its illustrious members two presidents and many famous jurists; but it may be said without fear of contradiction that Mr. Rogers' success as a lawyer in western New York has rarely or never been surpassed. Rogers, Bowen & Rogers, Bowen, Rogers & Locke, and Rogers, Locke & Milburn have been names to conjure with in the annals of the Buffalo bar; and the subject of this sketch has been a tower of strength to these firms as regards weight of legal counsel, brilliancy of pleading, and solidity of clientage.

The lawyer's calling, more than any other, paves the way for political preferment, and abundant evidence of this may be found in the career before us. Early in life Mr. Rogers was a Democrat in political belief, but at the outbreak of the Civil War he became a Republican, and has so remained. At various times Mr. Rogers has been strongly supported for high political offices, such as the governorship and the United States senatorship, and these might easily have come to him under conditions slightly different. Political and personal independence, however, and absolute integrity, such as characterize Mr. Rogers, are not the best motive power in the operation of office-actuated "machines." Whenever the popular voice has been heard, the tone has been loud and unmistakable. In 1875, for example, Mr. Rogers consented to run as state senator in a district that had gone heavily Democratic two years before, and in which Republican defeat seemed inevitable ; but he was elected by the largest majority ever given to a senatorial candidate in the district. In the same way, when he ran for lieutenant governor, he received more votes than any other candidate on the ticket.

Mr. Rogers' influence in national politics has been felt through his active and consistent advocacy of reform in the civil service. For many years he has been a member of the executive committee of the National Civil Service Reform League, rendering great service under the captaincy of his intimate personal friend, the late George William Curtis. Mr. Rogers has in fact for years been deemed in Buffalo the typical anti-spoilsman, having been president of the local reform organization, as well as an officer in the National League. To no other citizen does Buffalo owe so much for its place in the front rank of civilized communities as regards the distribution of municipal patronage.

Mr. Rogers has been a director of the Bell Telephone Company of Buffalo, director and vice-president of the Bank of Buffalo, president of the Fine Arts Academy, and president of the board of trustees of Calvary Presbyterian Church. He has been prominently identified with almost every literary and benevolent society in Buffalo, and with the intelligent and cultured side of the city in general.

Mr. Rogers has found time in the intervals of his busy life as a lawyer and a statesman to cultivate the arts. He is a connoisseur in painting and music, and his literary style is most charming. Unfortunately for his admirers, it is only in occasional addresses and now and then in a magazine article that he has displayed his gifts in pure literature.

*PERSONAL CHRONOLOGY—Sherman S. Rogers was born at Bath, N. Y., April 16, 1830; prepared for college, but entered a law office at the age of sixteen without further scholastic training; married Christina Cameron Davenport of Bath January 6, 1858; was appointed a member of the commission to revise the constitution of the state of New York in 1872; was elected state senator in 1875; was nominated for lieutenant governor in 1876, on the ticket headed by E. D. Morgan; has practiced law in Buffalo since 1854.*

**Charles A. Rupp** was thrown on his own resources early in life, and began his business career when he was fifteen years old. How well he has succeeded in his efforts to build up a business every resident of Buffalo knows. For many years he has been closely identified with the best interests of the city, and many flourishing enterprises are due to his sagacity, energy, and faith. As a young man he was not averse to turning his hand to any honorable occupation however lowly. During the war and while attending the public schools he sold papers on the streets, and worked at various small jobs. His first permanent employment, however, was as a "trotter" for the old Buffalo City Bank, which was located in the Ætna building on Commercial street. This section of the city was then the business center.

*CHARLES A. RUPP*

for the chief material interests of the town were in its lake and canal trade. It was only natural for Mr. Rupp to drift into employment connected with this trade, and he was soon hard at work as a tallyman and clerk for forwarding firms. It is seldom that a young man at the outset of life finds the business to which he is best suited, and Mr. Rupp was not so favored. He soon abandoned the forwarding business, and worked as a clerk in a dry-goods store and later in a variety store; and it was not until 1868 that he found the vocation in which he was to make his mark.

In the year mentioned he was employed by Henry Rumrill, a leading contractor and builder, to keep his books and to act as confidential clerk. He liked the business, and soon evinced an ambition to acquaint himself with its practical details. To accomplish this he attended night schools of architecture and mechanical drawing, and even worked for a time at brick laying. His enthusiasm, ambition, and determination to master the practical knowledge necessary to become a contractor found encouragement from his employer, and in 1874 he was admitted to a partnership. This lasted for fifteen years, or until Mr. Rumrill sold his interest to his son, Henry Rumrill, Jr. The firm name of Rumrill & Rupp remained unchanged until 1893, when the partnership was dissolved. Since then Mr. Rupp has conducted his business alone as a mason, builder, and contractor. Many extensive contracts have been successfully carried out by Mr. Rupp and his partners, and their work has found a place in a large number of the best buildings that adorn the city of Buffalo.

Mr. Rupp has been active in politics, and his advice and support have been eagerly sought by his party. His entrance into public life was made in 1884, when he was elected an alderman from the 11th ward. He served two years. For the next seven years he held no public office, but in 1890 he was appointed a civil-service commissioner. This position carries with it a great deal of hard work and no corresponding recompense beyond the gratitude of all believers in honest, efficient government, and the satisfaction involved in the faithful discharge of duty. When the citizens of Buffalo rose in their might, in 1891, and vindicated the principle of home rule, Mr. Rupp was appointed one of the police and excise commissioners. Their first duty was to cleanse the police force of the city of partisan politics, and Mr. Rupp had an important part in this work. In the fall of 1894 he ran for the office of commissioner of public works, but shared in the general defeat of his party at that time.

Mr. Rupp has been active in various other directions. He is a Mason and a Knight Templar, and is active in a number of business associations. He is president of the Builders' Exchange Association,

a stock company that owns the fine building occupied by the Builders' Exchange. That project was carried to a successful completion largely through the efforts of Mr. Rupp. He has been vice president of the National Association of Builders of the United States, and was elected president thereof at the convention held in Baltimore in October, 1895.

Some years of Mr. Rupp's life were devoted in part to the State Guard. He enlisted as a private before the war closed, and held various positions, finally becoming lieutenant colonel of the 65th regiment in 1873. He resigned after a service of thirteen years.

*PERSONAL CHRONOLOGY*—*Charles Albert Rupp was born at Buffalo April 1, 1850; attended the district schools; married Nellie Pilot of Buffalo September 11, 1872, and Anna T. Henafelt of Buffalo October 2, 1889; was elected alderman on the Democratic ticket in 1881; was appointed a civil-service commissioner in June, 1890, and a police and excise commissioner March 1, 1891; entered the service of Henry Rumrill, builder and contractor, in 1868, and formed a partnership with him in 1874; has been in business alone, as builder and contractor, since 1893.*

●●●

**Stephen Vincent Ryan,** bishop of the Catholic diocese of Buffalo, is revered by the priests under his authority, beloved by all his people, and honored by all classes in the city of which he has for nearly thirty years been a resident. Strict in his exaction of church authority, firm in his control of the great interests in his charge, he has yet no harshness in his character, and benevolence and kindness are the foundation stones of his rule. His influence is naturally most weighty; and his voice is always heard in behalf of whatever makes for the highest moral welfare of the community.

A little Canadian town, Almonte, Ontario, was the birthplace of Stephen Vincent Ryan, and January 1, 1825, was his natal day. When he was yet a child his parents removed to Pottsville, Penn., and there young Ryan spent his youth. He was early attracted to the priesthood, and when his parents consented to fall in with his bent, he was sent to St. Charles's Seminary at Philadelphia for a classical course. This was in 1840. While there he made the acquaintance of the fathers of the Mission of St. Vincent de Paul, and expressed a desire to enter their community. In 1844 he was sent to their college at Cape Girardeau, Mo., and afterward to St. Mary's of the Barrens, Perry county, Mo., when that institution became the mother house of the Vincentians. While at Philadelphia he served as one of the acolytes in the cathedral at that place, and thus had the honor of participating in the consecration of Bishop Kenrick. When Mr. Ryan was ordained to the priesthood in St. Vincent's Church, St. Louis, Archbishop Kenrick conducted the august ceremony. Father Ryan at once entered upon the discharge of the duties pertaining to his holy order, and brought to them rare intelligence and unflagging industry. He was untiring in his devotion to the interests of the order of the Mission, and it was not long before he took a leading part in the grand work carried on by the Lazarist fathers. In 1857 he was appointed Visitor, or head, of the order in the United States. To him was due the successful establishment at Germantown, Penn., of the Vincentian Seminary, which is now the headquarters of the Vincentian army of devoted missionaries, the mother house of the Eastern Province, and the residence of the Visitor of the order in America. On several occasions Father Ryan crossed the ocean to consult with the Superior General of the order in Paris concerning the welfare of the Vincentian congregation in America.

Father Ryan's eminent success in all matters placed in his care had attracted so much attention that when Bishop Timon of the Buffalo diocese died in 1867 it was freely prophesied that Father Ryan would be his successor. His appointment came from the Holy See a little later, and he was duly consecrated November 8, 1868. His administration of the constantly growing diocese of Buffalo has met with the entire approval of his superiors, and, as has been said, he has endeared himself to priests and people alike. His wonderful popularity was shown a few years since, on his return from a journey to Rome, when he received a welcome home such as is extended to but few men. The churches in this great diocese number more than one hundred and sixty and the priests more than two hundred. Under his zealous care there have grown up three seminaries, five colleges, twenty academies, over seventy parochial schools, and seventeen charitable institutions.

*PERSONAL CHRONOLOGY — Stephen Vincent Ryan was born January 1, 1825, at Almonte, Ont.; was taken by his parents when a child to Pottsville, Penn., where he grew up; was sent to St. Charles's Seminary, Philadelphia, in 1839, to begin a course of study to fit him for the priesthood; was*
*ordained at St. Louis in 1849; was consecrated bishop of the Catholic diocese of Buffalo November 8, 1868, and has lived there since.*

•••

**Henry H. Seymour** illustrates vividly, on his intellectual side, what is known as the "legal mind."

STEPHEN VINCENT RYAN

A disposition to get to the root of the matter, to push aside nonessentials and get down to fundamental causes, is a marked characteristic of his mental processes. This legal cast of mind, joined to a strong, wholesome faith in his fellow-men, is perhaps the distinguishing trait of his character. While yet a student in Cornell University, he was attracted to the philosophic study of history; and his interest in the subject has continued ever since, and has been stimulated by extensive foreign travel.

Mr. Seymour's college career was a brilliant one, and on his graduation from Cornell University he received one of the Goldwin Smith prizes, then deemed the highest rewards in the gift of the university. After a season of study and travel abroad, he returned to Mount Morris and began the reading of law. He studied law in the offices of his uncles, McNeil Seymour and George Hastings — two of the most widely known lawyers in the Genesee valley — and was admitted to practice in 1874. He then went abroad again, and spent over a year in further

*HENRY H. SEYMOUR*

study and sight-seeing. In 1876 he returned to this country, and opened a law office in Buffalo, where he has since practiced.

It has ever been Mr. Seymour's desire to elevate the standard of legal education. He has filled the position of lecturer on the law of agency and partnership in the Buffalo Law School ever since the formation of that institution, and in that capacity has sought to impress upon the students the importance of the fundamental principles of the law. Statutes may change with every session of the legislature, but the great legal principles do not vary, and every statute must ultimately rest upon them. He urges his students to think for themselves, and to attach

more importance to independent and well-considered reasoning than to mere text-book knowledge.

Mr. Seymour has never held, and has not cared to hold, any public elective office. He has been a consistent independent Democrat in political opinion, and has filled numerous public trusts in a creditable manner. He has been for many years one of the bar examiners for the judicial department in which he lives, and since 1889 he has been commissioner of jurors for the northern district of New York in the United States District Court. For the latter office he was selected by Judge Coxe, who made the appointment in recognition of Mr. Seymour's strong faith in the jury system and strong desire to see it maintained and strengthened rather than abolished. In 1895 Mr. Seymour was appointed deputy commissioner of jurors for Erie county, under a reform-jury act passed in that year. He has been a bulwark of strength to the jury system against the attacks that have lately been made upon it in various quarters. Admitting that the system has faults, he contends that these may be remedied by wise legislation, and that the institution as a whole has rightly been regarded as one of the pillars of constitutional liberty.

Mr. Seymour's extensive travels in the old world have given him ample opportunity to broaden his general culture, and to round out his legal knowledge by a study of comparative constitutions. On one of his visits to England he enjoyed, through the courtesy of Lord Chief Justice Coleridge, the somewhat unique privilege of sitting beside that official all one day while he held his court in the Law Courts in the Strand. Such an honor, and many other opportunities to note the workings of the law in the mother country, were naturally highly prized by the young American lawyer.

Mr. Seymour is a prominent member of Buffalo clubs. He is chairman of the house committee of the University Club and of the library committee of the Buffalo Club.

*PERSONAL CHRONOLOGY— Henry Hale Seymour was born at Mount Morris, N. Y., October 27, 1849; prepared for college at Mount Morris Academy; after one year in Dartmouth College entered Cornell University, from which he graduated in 1871 with the degree of Bachelor of Science; studied law at Mount Morris, and was admitted to the bar in 1874;*

*served as judge advocate of the 4th division N. G. S. N. Y., 1880–85; was appointed commissioner of jurors for the northern district of New York state in the United States District Court in 1889, and deputy commissioner of jurors for Erie county in 1895; has practiced law in Buffalo since 1874.*

\*\*\*

**T. Guilford Smith** finely typifies, in his career and in his character, the material prosperity of our country and the conquest of man over nature by which that prosperity has been attained and promoted. The intelligent and persistent development of our natural resources by men especially adapted for the work by reason of native ability and technical training, has characterized our industrial history as a whole, and especially the chapters relating to coal, iron, and steel. Few men have had a larger and more important part in this work than T. Guilford Smith.

A thorough scholastic training, both general and technical, paved the way for Mr. Smith's life-work. His father took great pains with his education, obtaining special instruction for him in French, German, and the sciences, in addition to the regular courses in the public and private schools of Philadelphia. When he graduated from the Central High School there in 1858, he was the salutatorian of his class, and five years later the same institution gave him the degree of Master of Arts. To the general education obtained in Philadelphia, he added the special training of a civil engineer, which he obtained at the Rensselaer Polytechnic Institute at Troy, N. Y.

Mr. Smith began his business life in the engineering department of the Philadelphia & Reading railroad, and finally became resident engineer of the company in the Mahanoy district of the anthracite coal fields. He resigned from the road in 1865, and spent the next four years as general manager of the Philadelphia Sugar Refinery. He was then connected, as consulting engineer, with railroad and mineral projects in various parts of the country; and in 1872 he visited Europe in connection with railroad enterprises. His appointment as secretary of the Union Iron Company of Buffalo brought him to that city in 1873. He has lived there since.

After five years in the service of the Union Iron Company, Mr. Smith became western sales-agent of the Philadelphia & Reading Coal & Iron Company, and afterward organized the firm of Albright & Smith, sales-agents for New York and Canada for the same company. This arrangement with the Reading Company continued until 1892, when the company bought out Albright & Smith, and Mr. Smith's long connection with the anthracite coal trade ceased. For more than thirty years he had been more or less intimately connected with the mining, transportation, and sale of anthracite coal in the interest of the Reading Company. In 1889 Mr. Smith became sales-agent for Carnegie, Phipps & Co., since merged into the Carnegie Steel Company, Limited; and he is still connected with that company. He is also vice president of the New York Car Wheel Works, of the St. Thomas (Ont.) Car Wheel Works, of the Canada Iron Furnace

*T GUILFORD SMITH*

Company (Radnor, Que.), and of other industrial enterprises.

Mr. Smith's life-work has thus been identified with iron, steel, and coal; and his experience of the needs of these great industrial factors has led him to devote much of his energy to the cause of protection to American industry. He has never lost faith in this cause, and deems the necessity for a protective policy as strong to-day as it was years ago.

Most men of force and character have an avocation which affords an outlet for their overflowing energy; and Mr. Smith is a case in point. While these important extractive industries have been the chief concern of his business life, the cause of education has received his best attention, and may fairly be regarded as his avocation. He has found no incongruity, as engineer and man of affairs, in cultivating the love of letters that began in his early life. His interest in educational matters culminated in his election by the state legislature in 1890 as a regent of the University of the State of New York. This is a life position, and he will thus have the opportunity, as long as he lives, of assisting in the development of education in this state. In 1891 Mr. Smith was made chairman of the Museum committee, which has charge of the geological and other surveys of the state and of the state Museum. This position brings him into close touch with all matters affecting the mineral resources of the state and the exhibition and study of those resources at the Museum.

Ever since his graduation from the Rensselaer Polytechnic Institute Mr. Smith has had membership in various engineering societies, and has always taken a lively and an intelligent interest in them. In 1894 he traveled extensively in Europe and the Orient, and acted as a delegate from the American Society of Civil Engineers to the International Congress of Medicine and Surgery in Rome. Mr. Smith belongs to many literary and scientific societies, including the Academy of Natural Sciences of Philadelphia, the Union League of Philadelphia, the Franklin Institute, the American Institute of Mining Engineers, and the Historical Society of Pennsylvania. He is president of the Charity Organization Society of Buffalo, vice president of the Buffalo Fine Arts Academy, and president of the Buffalo Library. In 1894 he was made an honorary member of the Phi Beta Kappa, by Hobart Chapter.

*PERSONAL CHRONOLOGY — Thomas Guilford Smith was born at Philadelphia August 27, 1840; graduated from the Central High School of Philadelphia with the degree of B. A. in 1858, and from Rensselaer Polytechnic Institute in 1861; married Mary Stewart Ives of Lansingburgh, N. Y., July 14, 1864; was with the Philadelphia & Reading railroad as civil engineer, 1861–65; was general manager of the Philadelphia Sugar Refinery, 1866–69;*

*was secretary of the Union Iron Co. of Buffalo, 1873–78; was sales-agent of the Philadelphia & Reading Coal and Iron Co., 1878–92; has been sales-agent of the Carnegie Steel Co., L't'd, since 1889; has been regent of the University of the State of New York since 1890.*

## E. G. Spaulding

**E. G. Spaulding** — lawyer, financier, statesman — is Buffalo's "Grand Old Man." Born in the same year with Gladstone, he bears the burden of fourscore and seven with faculties unimpaired. What a long, eventful, and useful career has been his, honorable alike to himself, to his state, and to the nation! Jefferson was President, the second war with England was still to be fought, Napoleon's sun was at its zenith, seventeen states, with less than seven millions of people, comprised the American Union, Buffalo was a mere village — when Mr. Spaulding first saw the light.

Apart from a common-school education, Mr. Spaulding may justly be called a self-made man. His early days were spent on his father's farm in central New York; but he was ambitious to become a lawyer, and on attaining his majority he began the study of law in Batavia, N. Y. Admission to the bar was not so easy and direct in those days as now. First the applicant was admitted to the Court of Common Pleas; later he was eligible to the office of attorney of the Supreme Court; and finally he might become counselor of the Supreme Court and of the Court of Chancery. After being admitted to practice before the Court of Common Pleas, Mr. Spaulding came to Buffalo, in 1834, an entire stranger and without so much as a letter of introduction. Such a beginning, however, befits a man who relies on his own talents and industry. He soon obtained a position as law clerk in the office of a leading firm, and in due time became an attorney and counselor of the Supreme Court, and opened an office for himself. His success was rapid and on a large scale. After fourteen years at the bar he retired from the legal profession to begin a business career. Mr. Spaulding was instrumental in securing the removal from Attica to Buffalo of two banks that have become widely known as reliable money institutions — the Commercial Bank and the Farmers' and Mechanics' Bank. Of the latter institution he was made president. This banking experience was destined to prove invaluable in another field of usefulness, to which he was called in the same decade by the suffrage of his fellow-citizens at a time of national peril.

Along with his private cares and manifold labors, Mr. Spaulding has frequently accepted the duties and responsibilities of public office. He has been city clerk, alderman, and mayor of Buffalo, member of the legislature, state treasurer, and representative in congress. As mayor, nearly half a century ago, he adopted a system of sewerage for the first time in the history of the city; in the legislature, and as treasurer, he was a potent factor in the development of the Erie canal; in the 31st congress of the United States he stood among the stoutest opponents of slavery, and favored the admission of California as a free state; in the 36th and 37th congresses, extending from 1859 to 1863, he was again a member of the house of representatives, and served on the most important committee of that body — the committee on ways and means. The nation was in the midst of the great Civil War; its resources were taxed to the utmost; there seemed no way for the government to maintain its credit and meet its obligations. The wisest statesmen pondered the perplexing problem in vain till Mr. Spaulding conceived of the "greenback" as the nation's salvation, made necessary and constitutional by stress of war. Mr. Spaulding introduced the bill for the adoption of the greenback as legal tender, and the national currency banking bill, both of which became laws; and their author has since been known as the "Father of the Greenback." In later years, Mr. Spaulding gave to the world a full account of this important legislation in a "History of the Legal Tender Paper Money issued during the Great Rebellion." In so high estimation was he held as a financier, that upon the resignation of Mr. Chase President Lincoln, it is said, would have appointed Mr. Spaulding secretary of the treasury, if New York had not been already represented in the cabinet by Mr. Seward.

Since his retirement from public life, Mr. Spaulding has devoted his business time to a bank presidency, the presidency of the Buffalo Gas Company, and to various enterprises of a financial character. He has sought at the same time to vary the routine of business by filling in his leisure with diversions suited to his age, chief among which have been the building and improvement of his beautiful summer home at River Lawn on Grand Island. At the Centennial Celebration in Philadelphia, he delivered the address to the bankers' association on "One Hundred Years of Progress in the Business of Banking." In

social life he has long been a conspicuous figure. He is a member of the Buffalo Club, and though less active before the public than in years gone by, he retains an adequate interest in the current of passing events.

*PERSONAL CHRONOLOGY* — *Elbridge Gerry Spaulding was born at Summer Hill, N. Y.,*

E. G. SPAULDING

*February 24, 1809; received a common-school education; was admitted to the bar at Batavia, N. Y., in 1834; was city clerk of Buffalo in 1836, alderman in 1841, and mayor in 1847; married Antoinette Rich of Attica, N. Y., in 1837; was member of the state legislature in 1848; was representative in the 31st, 36th, and 37th congresses (1849–51 and 1855–63); was treasurer of New York state, 1854–55; has been president of the Farmers' and Mechanics' Bank since 1850.*

***

**Seth S. Spencer** may be said to resemble one of those wheels in a great, complicated machine, which, though inconspicuous to the beholder, are none the less essential to the smooth and perfect working of the mechanism. As a rule, in every large city, the men who are the real factors in many mercantile and commercial establishments, banks, and factories are not the men best known in the community, popularly speaking. Mr. Spencer belongs to this class of quiet, unassuming men, whose ability

*SETH S. SPENCER*

and character are fully realized and appreciated only by those who have social or business relations with them. For many years he has successfully managed one of the largest manufacturing bakeries in the United States, so that to-day the name of the founder of the business has become a household word in western New York. Since Mr. Spencer has been at the head of this business the output from the factory has more than doubled in volume — a most creditable showing in these days of keen and active competition.

Mr. Spencer is a native of New York state, having been born in Genesee county less than sixty years ago. His educational opportunities were such as a country school afforded, supplemented by a course in

the Rural Seminary, at East Pembroke, N. Y. Although ambitious to do so, he was without the means to enter college and prepare himself by advanced instruction for the legal profession, which he hoped to make his vocation. Taking advantage of spare hours in his regular occupation, he read law in the offices of F. J. Fithian and William Dorsheimer, both noted lawyers in their day, and was admitted to the bar in 1865.

Stress of circumstances, however, prevented him from practicing law. As early as 1857 he had turned his attention to telegraphy, and on mastering this craft he secured a position as local agent and telegraph operator at the railroad station in Lancaster, N. Y. His duties in this connection brought him into contact with the railway mail service, then in its infancy, but destined to be rapidly developed and widely extended in the course of the following decade. In 1861 Mr. Spencer obtained an appointment as a railway mail clerk, and for two years he "ran" between Elmira and Buffalo. Promotion then brought him the route from Buffalo to New York city, one of the most important in the service, which he retained for ten years, or until his resignation in 1873. Whatever may be said of some positions under the government, that of the railway mail clerk is by no means a sinecure. The work is exhausting in an extreme degree, and is often rendered more difficult by the poor facilities provided by railroads. Only a man of vigorous constitution, quick eye, and alert mind is fitted for the position; and the fact that Mr. Spencer endured the labor and strain for twelve years is proof of his sound constitution and capacity for hard work. After retiring from the railway mail service, he became associated in business with Robert Ovens, manufacturing baker, to whose daughter he had been married in 1870, and who was at that time engaged in building up in Buffalo the industry that now bears his name. In 1883 Mr. Spencer assumed the entire management of the business, which he has since conducted on an increasingly large scale and with corresponding success, displaying an energy and method that have marked him as one of Buffalo's most enterprising and farsighted men of affairs. Free from ostentation, and devoted to the responsibilities he undertakes, Mr. Spencer enjoys the respect and confidence of the business world, and is held in high esteem by his neighbors and fellow-citizens. In politics he is a Republican, but he has generally exercised his prerogative to vote for the best man irrespective of party lines, when no great principles were at stake. Mr. Spencer attends the Lafayette Street Presbyterian Church, and is one of the trustees thereof; he is also a member of the Merchants' Exchange and of the Buffalo Club.

*PERSONAL CHRONOLOGY — Seth S. Spencer was born in the town of Batavia, N. Y., August 25, 1838; was educated in country schools and at Rural Seminary, East Pembroke, N. Y.; was a railway mail clerk, 1861–73; was admitted to the bar in 1865, but never practiced law; married Mrs. Agnes J. Derrick of Buffalo December 22, 1870; has been manager of the R. Ovens Branch U. S. Baking Co., Buffalo, since 1883.*

* * *

**Mathias Strauss** shows by his career what a man starting without means or influence can achieve through hard work, brains, and honest dealing. Born nearly sixty years ago in Remich, grand duchy of Luxemburg, Germany, he secured a limited education; and at the age of fourteen, allured by glowing reports from America, persuaded his parents to leave their fatherland and seek a new home and fortune across the sea. No writer can adequately describe the pathos, the hope and fear, the complete change that accompanies the sundering of old friendships, the parting with familiar places and objects, and the launching out into an untried world of a family from one of the old countries. It is an experience never to be forgotten. Mr. Strauss recalls it the more vividly because the " promised land " so eagerly sought proved a keen disappointment in many respects. Wages were low and work was scarce; and the prospect of a strange land, a stranger tongue, no friends, and no business was exceedingly disheartening to the newcomers.

Young Strauss realized that his parents, with a large family, had come to this country chiefly on his account, and he resolved to take upon his shoulders all the burden they could bear. For over a hundred years in the old country, his father and grandfather had carried on in their native town the business of wool and sheep-leather manufacturing. So naturally he applied for work with his father in the

same business here, and both obtained employment in the sheepskin tannery of Breithaupt & Schoellkopf of Buffalo — the father at 75 cents, and Mathias at 37½ cents a day. Bitterly regretting that he had left his native country, the young man determined nevertheless to make the most of his opportunities and to do his full duty to his parents, whom his youthful enthusiasm had brought to the United States. He was glad of the chance to work and to learn a trade; and so diligently and intelligently did he apply himself to his duties that in five years he was promoted to be foreman of the department for dyeing and finishing fancy-colored sheep leather, and was regarded as the best man in that line in Buffalo.

To every industrious and faithful young man an opportunity such as he wishes finally comes. When Mr.

*MATHIAS STRAUSS*

Strauss was twenty-four years old, the firm for which he worked was dissolved, and the tannery became vacant. On a capital of two hundred dollars, which he had slowly accumulated, he rented the old establishment, and started in business for himself. He there laid the foundation for the immense business which came to him with the passing years, and which to-day requires a large force of men and huge buildings for its adequate operation. Mr. Strauss attributes much of his success, especially at the beginning of his career, to the influence of his wife, who was Miss Elizabeth Brosart, daughter of Charles Brosart. As an illustration of Mr. Strauss's continued activity, pluck, and energy, the fact may be cited that when his establishment was burned to the ground in the spring of 1895, he set to work at once to rebuild, kept all his workmen employed at full wages, and in six months had the great plant again under roof and in complete operation. Two of Mr. Strauss's sons are employed in the business : John A. is head bookkeeper, and Charles is foreman and buyer.

Not only has Mr. Strauss impressed himself upon the community as a manufacturer and employer, but he has also served the people of Buffalo in a political capacity, as an active, progressive citizen. He has twice been elected a councilman, and in performing the duties of that office he has been faithful to his own ideals, and has done at all times what he believed would meet the approval of the people and the taxpayers of the city, in common with whom he has large and varied property interests affected by public action. In politics he is an ardent Democrat.

Mr. Strauss has been active in church, social, and philanthropic work for many years. A member of St. Mary's Roman Catholic Church, one of the founders of a church, an orphan asylum, and a working boys' home, he has shown his devotion to religious and charitable institutions and their wants. He is a member of the Old German Society of Buffalo, and an honorary member of the Knights of St. John, thus maintaining in addition to business relations a broad participation in the moral and social life of the community, and proving himself in every way a worthy citizen of the country of his adoption.

*PERSONAL CHRONOLOGY—Mathias Strauss was born at Remich, Germany, April 15, 1836; married Elizabeth Brosart of Buffalo November 15, 1859; was elected councilman of the city of Buffalo for the year 1892, and again for the years 1894-95; went to Buffalo in 1856, and has been engaged there since in the manufacture of leather and wool.*

* * *

**Charles R. Sweet** has long been one of the recognized, quiet-working forces in the commercial, social, and political life of Buffalo. A man may be no less a factor in a community because he is naturally

unobtrusive, devoted to business affairs, and opposed to notoriety of every sort. Mr. Sweet is a type of a class of men happily to be found in all our large cities, who constitute the strong, conservative element, whose influence and support are always sought whenever any great enterprise or important measure is under consideration or is being projected.

Among the things that determine success in life are parentage, place of birth, education, and opportunity, for none of which are we primarily responsible. What we make of the " raw material " of life, as it may be called, is really the sum total that the individual can claim as his own. Applying this standard impartially, it is possible to estimate the credit due to any given person. Mr. Sweet was fortunate in being born of old New England stock, amid the picturesque scenery of Berkshire county, Mass. What education he was able to secure was limited to the three " R's," and had to be obtained in the winter months when there was no work on the farm. But the training of the home supplied a discipline and a standard of living that schools, and colleges even, do not undertake to furnish. His life was that of the farmer's son — an apprenticeship that has proved of invaluable benefit in fitting young men for the practical work of the world.

In 1862, when twenty-six years of age, Mr. Sweet made Buffalo his home, and engaged in the transportation business on Central wharf. Here, undoubtedly, he gained many of those traits of accurate dealing, and that sound business judgment, which have characterized his career in the more difficult and responsible field upon which he entered in 1884, when he became president of the Third National Bank of Buffalo — a position he continues to occupy.

A busy life has left him little leisure for many diversions so agreeable to those who have time for them. Mr. Sweet has, however, realized that he had duties as a citizen as well as a business man, and every public movement commending itself to his judgment has received his active support. A Democrat in politics, he has influenced his party in the right direction on all occasions : and his personal interest in local affairs, together with his readiness to contribute of his time and means to his party's success, has given him a power in the community that he has always employed for its good. Though frequently urged by his friends to be a candidate for various offices, he has uniformly declined, and has never accepted a distinctly political office.

One public office, however, he did consent to fill in 1892, when he was appointed by the governor of New York one of the nonpartisan board of General

Managers having charge of the manifold representation of the Empire State at the World's Fair in Chicago in 1893. The complete and successful exhibit of New York at that superb exposition is a matter of history, and the volume and variety of the work performed by the General Managers is best illustrated by their comprehensive report to the state legislature, comprising a detailed account of the labors of the board.

Mr. Sweet was president of the Buffalo Board of Trade when that institution was still on Central wharf. He was president of the Young Men's Association before it was changed to the "Buffalo Library." He served many years as one of the trustees of the City and County Hall, having been appointed to that position by the Superior Court. He served many years, also, as trustee of the State Normal School at Buffalo. He was one of the organizers of the Citizens' Gas Company, and is now vice president of the same. He was one of the organizers of the Delaware Avenue Methodist Church, and is president of the board of trustees of that institution. He has been connected with many associations of a religious and philanthropic character.

*PERSONAL CHRONOLOGY—Charles Augustine Sweet was born at Hancock, Mass., February 16, 1836; was educated in country schools; went to Buffalo and engaged in the transportation business in 1862; was a member of the board of General Managers for New York state at the World's Fair, 1894; has been president of the Third National Bank of Buffalo since 1881.*

***

**James Tillinghast** may be justly regarded as a typical American railroader, though his diversified experience in connection with the transportation industry has rarely been paralleled in this or any other country. He began at the bottom of the ladder, and ended at the top; and the story of his life is at once interesting, instructive, and inspiring.

Mr. Tillinghast inherited his mechanical ability from his father, and as a schoolboy spent much of his leisure time in his father's machine shop, where he became practically conversant with the use of tools and the methods and processes of mechanical work. At the age of fifteen he entered a country store in Brownsville, N. Y., as a clerk. A year later he accepted a similar position at Dexter, N. Y.,

where his duties included, besides clerical work, making fires, sweeping the store, waiting on customers, and keeping track of a miscellaneous stock of drugs, hardware, dry goods, groceries, and notions. For all this he received the princely sum of eight dollars a month.

CHARLES L. SWEET

In 1843 Mr. Tillinghast embarked in the lake trade, making his first venture as supercargo of a sailing vessel that carried passengers and freight from Sackett's Harbor to Chicago. The passengers supplied their own provisions, and slept in the hold. On the return trip he brought a cargo of wheat, which was the second that had ever been shipped from Chicago to Buffalo. Mr. Tillinghast soon abandoned this lake traffic, and engaged in business with his father for several years; but in 1851 he began the railroad career in which he was to attain such success. Beginning as extra fireman on a gravel train, he became assistant superintendent of the Rome & Watertown railroad the following year; and since that time he has held high official positions on almost every important railroad in this part of the country. Few men have had a more varied experience. His energy and good judgment won for him positions of trust, and these he always filled with faithfulness and zeal. He entered the service of the New York Central road in 1865, at the request of its presi-

*JAMES TILLINGHAST*

dent, Dean Richmond, and was appointed superintendent of the western division. He soon made the acquaintance of Commodore Vanderbilt, who had recently acquired a large interest in the road, and was making his first trip of inspection over it. The great railway king at once recognized Mr. Tillinghast's unusual ability, and the friendship that then began grew with advancing years, and ended only with the death of Mr. Vanderbilt. When Commodore Vanderbilt acquired a controlling interest in the "Central," he made Mr. Tillinghast general superintendent, with headquarters at Albany; and this position he held until 1881, when he was appointed by William H. Vanderbilt assistant to the president. By

that time the tonnage of the road had increased tenfold from the figures of 1865, when Mr. Tillinghast first became connected with the road.

In 1878 and 1879, in addition to his other duties, Mr. Tillinghast filled the double position of president and general manager of the Canada Southern railway; and it was owing chiefly to his exertions that the Dominion parliament passed laws that saved the road from bankruptcy, and enabled it to be reorganized without loss to the stockholders. In 1883 Mr. Tillinghast was vice president of the Niagara River Bridge Company, and superintended the erection of the cantilever bridge built by that company and opened for traffic during that year.

All the important offices held by Mr. Tillinghast have come to him unsolicited. It is worthy of notice, moreover, that he has never demanded a fixed sum for any services rendered, but has relied upon the zeal with which he served his employers to secure for him adequate compensation. His good judgment and reliability, in all emergencies and under all circumstances, have earned for him the respect and esteem of railroad officials far and near, and of the general public as well. He is a man of few words, exceedingly quiet and undemonstrative in manner; but a deep thinker, and a man of action and determination. He is affable and kindly in his intercourse with all, and is noted for his generous hospitality and other social virtues.

*PERSONAL CHRONOLOGY— James Tillinghast was born at Cooperstown, N. Y., May 8, 1822; was educated in the public schools; engaged in business, 1841–42, and in lake traffic, 1843–46 and 1862–64; was assistant superintendent of the Rome & Watertown railroad, 1852–56, superintendent of motive power of the Northern Railway of Canada, 1856–62, division and general superintendent of the Central-Hudson railroad, 1865–81, and assistant to the president of that road in 1881; was president of the Wagner Sleeping Car Co., 1884–87; married Mary Williams of Limerick, N. Y., October 4, 1843, and Mrs. Susan Williams of Buffalo July 25, 1882.*

***

**Robert C. Titus** has for many years of his life served his fellow-men. For nearly twenty years he has held various important positions of trust, and in each one he has discharged the duties imposed upon him so faithfully that his record is without a blemish,

Born in a little Erie-county village, Judge Titus passed the early years of his life amid surroundings that called for great sacrifices and much labor. He worked on a farm and attended district schools by turn. At last the opportunity came for a course in Oberlin College at Oberlin, Ohio, and this chance to broaden out and to satisfy some of the ambitions that had long possessed the young man, was eagerly seized. He did not, however, graduate from this institution, but returned to Buffalo, and began the study of law. Thus was gratified an earnest desire. The young man applied himself to the study of the principles of law with so much zeal and persistence that in 1865 he was admitted to the bar with high honors.

The next thirteen years of his life were spent in the practice of his profession, either alone or with others. During this time Judge Titus had drifted into politics, and soon became one of the favorite campaign orators of the Democratic party, whose platforms and principles he warmly endorsed. His personal popularity and his eminent party services appropriately led to a nomination for district attorney of Erie county, and he was triumphantly elected to that office in the fall of 1877. The duties of this office were filled during the next three years with honor to himself, and to the entire satisfaction of the people. When his term expired he resumed private practice. His party, however, soon called upon him to stand as the leader of its county ticket, and in the fall of 1881 he was elected state senator from the 31st district, which then included the whole of Erie county. He served with so much distinction that he was re-elected in the fall of 1883, thus representing Erie county in the highest legislative body of the state for four years. During that time he was a member of the judiciary and other important committees, on which he rendered valuable service. He was a faithful friend of the canals during his career in the legislature, and stood by the Erie canal, which has done so much in the development of the state, against all the attacks made by its enemies.

A vacancy about to occur on the bench of the Superior Court of Buffalo gave Mr. Titus's party friends another opportunity to show their regard for him, and he was nominated in the fall of 1885 for the honorable position thus available. His election

followed, and since that time Judge Titus has presided with impartiality and dignity at many important trials in Buffalo. In the course of time he became chief judge of the court, and held that position when the Superior Court was abolished, and its judges took seats on the bench of the Supreme Court January 1, 1896.

Judge Titus has for many years been a prominent and honored member of the Masonic fraternity, and has been a leader in its many beneficent works. At the meeting of the Supreme Council of Sovereign Grand Inspectors General, 33d and last degree, Ancient Accepted Scottish Rite, held in Buffalo in September, 1895, he was made an honorary member of that body. He is a director of the Masonic Life Association of Western New York, and is treasurer of the Acacia Club, the largest purely social club of

*ROBERT C. TITUS*

Masons in this country. This club has beautiful rooms in the Masonic Temple at Buffalo.

*PERSONAL CHRONOLOGY— Robert Cyrus Titus was born at Eden, N. Y., October 24, 1839;*

*attended Oberlin College ; married Arvilla R. Clark of Gowanda, N. Y., August 22, 1867 ; was admitted to the bar at Buffalo in 1865 ; was district attorney of Erie county, 1878–80 ; was state senator for Erie county, 1882–85 ; was elected judge of the Superior Court of Buffalo in the fall of 1885 ; was chief judge*

*AUGUSTUS FRANKLIN TRIPP*

*of that court at the time of its absorption into the Supreme Court January 1, 1896, when he became a member of the bench of the Supreme Court.*

•••

**Augustus Franklin Tripp** is the head of one of the most important industrial establishments of Buffalo. In business circles he is known as a man of great worth of character, and of a wonderful grasp of details that makes him a perfect master of anything to which he gives his attention. The firm of Sidney Shepard & Co., of which he is the senior member, is known far and wide as a large producer of tinware and house-furnishings, and to Mr. Tripp is due in no small measure the success that the firm has made in the business world. This concern has a mammoth factory in Buffalo, to which Mr. Tripp has devoted himself for nearly forty years ; and he has reduced its methods to a system that is almost perfection. The firm has also a large warehouse and distributing center in Buffalo ; and a subsidiary firm, styled C. Sidney Shepard & Co., has headquarters in Chicago. Mr. Tripp is one of the men who do things without making any noise about it. Careful, prudent, and sagacious in a marked degree, he has succeeded where others might have failed.

Born the son of a farmer, in a little Vermont town, young Tripp spent his early years helping his people wring the necessities of life from the stony and ungenerous soil of the Green Mountain State. His ambition to attain something better than appeared in the East led him to leave home for what was then the Far West, and in 1844 he bade good-by to the friends of his boyhood, and started out to make his fortune. He went to Buffalo by the canal-packet line, and after a hasty look over the new city, which was in later years to be the scene of his business triumphs, he boarded a lake steamer for Fairport, Ohio. Thence he went to Painesville, in the same state, and there obtained a job cleaning up the machinery of an old oil mill. This job completed, he went to Cleveland, where he secured employment in the office of the Cuyahoga Steam Furnace Co. He remained here until 1847, when he returned to Buffalo to take a position with the firm of John D. Shepard & Co., owners of steam-engine works and a large foundry. Two years later, when this firm passed out of existence, Mr. Tripp returned to Ohio, and established himself in business at Painesville under the firm name of Steele Bros. & Tripp, and at the same time in Buffalo with his brothers-in-law under the firm name of A. F. Tripp & Co. This partnership was dissolved in 1852, and Mr. Tripp then entered the service of Sidney Shepard & Co. as clerk and bookkeeper. Here he displayed so much energy and intelligence in the discharge of his duties, and was so quick to grasp the details of the business and so efficient generally, that after five years he became a partner in the concern, and has been actively interested ever since.

Outside of his business, Mr. Tripp is preëminently a home man. This does not mean that he is not interested in all that pertains to the welfare of his city and of his fellow-men. His sympathy for the unfortunate has often found expression in his support of many Buffalo charities that have learned to look upon him as a friend in need. But Mr. Tripp never lets the right hand know what the left is doing. Unostentatiously he pursues his way through the world, leaving on all sides evidences of the sterling worth of his character.

*PERSONAL CHRONOLOGY— Augustus Franklin Tripp was born at New Haven, Vt., September 30, 1822; went West in 1840 — first to Painesville, O., and thence to Cleveland; went to Buffalo in 1847, and entered the employ of John D. Shepard & Co.; engaged in business with his brothers-in-law in Ohio, 1850-52; married Mary M. Steele of Painesville, O., August 17, 1847, and Caroline M. Brown of Chelsea, Mass., January 22, 1868; entered the service of Sidney Shepard & Co. of Buffalo in 1852, and has been a member of the firm since 1857.*

***

### George Urban, Jr.,

is recognized as one of the potent factors in the commercial and political life of Buffalo. He is a splendid example of the modern business man. Enterprise, industry, sound judgment, and integrity have been the foundation stones of his success. He has not confined himself to one thing, but has shown his ability and capacity in several fields. Happily, the rise and development of corporations have enabled a vigorous and resourceful man to engage in many enterprises at the same time. A large part of every business and profession is made up of routine and relatively unimportant details, which require neither skill nor foresight, and which can safely be left to subordinates; while the talents of the manager or owner, thus relieved from petty annoyances and cares, may be employed far more effectively with weightier matters. The man who knows how to make this division of work economizes his time, and is enabled to take part in the conduct of banks and other organizations in addition to his particular business.

Mr. Urban is the son of a Buffalo pioneer in the flour and milling business, and was born in 1850 in a house just opposite the Urban mill. He was educated in the public schools of Buffalo, and at the age of eighteen entered his father's establishment. Two years later he was made a partner in the firm. His father retired from business in 1885, and the firm of Urban & Co. now consists of George Urban, Jr., E. G. S. Miller, and W. C. Urban, a brother of the senior partner. For fifty years the Urban family have been in the flour business, and have made their excellent brands of flour household names.

In financial circles and among the promoters of enterprises on a large scale, Mr. Urban is well known from his connection with banking institutions and electrical companies. He is president of the Buffalo Loan, Trust & Safe Deposit Co., and a director in the Merchants' Bank and the Bank of Buffalo. He has devoted much attention to electric lighting and to electricity as a power in manufacturing and transportation, and he is connected with several companies concerned in electrical development. He is

*GEORGE URBAN, JR.*

vice president of the Buffalo General Electric Co. and a director of the Buffalo Railway Co., of the Depew Improvement Co., and of the Buffalo, Bellevue & Lancaster Railway Co.

Mr. Urban's business occupations have not made him neglectful of his political obligations, and in taking an active part in local politics he has rendered his native city an important service. While he never would accept public office, Mr. Urban was chairman of the Erie county Republican general

*GEORGE WADSWORTH*

committee during the eventful years 1892-95; and to his skillful organization, his executive ability, and courageous demand for high standards of fitness in public officials is due in large measure the triumph of the people at the polls, and the complete rout of the spoilsmen and demagogues who had so long ruled the Queen City. Increasing business cares have since caused Mr. Urban to retire from active politics, but he can always be counted on by the friends of honest municipal government, and his influence for good on Republican politics is felt throughout the state.

*PERSONAL CHRONOLOGY — George Urban, Jr., was born at Buffalo July 12, 1850; was educated in the public schools; entered the firm of Urban*

*& Co., millers, in 1870; married Ada E. Winspear of Buffalo in October, 1875; was chairman of the Republican county committee, 1892-95.*

* * *

**George Wadsworth** enjoys an enviable genealogical distinction. He is a descendant of William Wadsworth, who came from England in the ship "Lion," and landed in Boston September 18, 1632. William Wadsworth was one of Parson Hooker's company that traveled through the wilderness and settled Hartford, Conn., in 1636. Joseph Wadsworth, of "Charter-Oak" fame, was a son of William Wadsworth, though not in direct line with the subject of our sketch. Everyone remembers from his school days the striking incident of the imperiled charter in the dark days of the Connecticut colony—how Sir Edmund Andros, acting under orders of the King, attempted to take away the liberal charter of the colony, and how a Wadsworth extinguished the lights, seized the precious document, and hid it in the hollow of an oak. One of Mr. Wadsworth's great-grandfathers was a colonel of the Connecticut troops during the Revolution, and an intimate friend of Washington and of Lafayette. To such early champions of freedom, and to others like them, Mr. Wadsworth may trace his lineage.

Born in the delightful old town of Litchfield, Conn., he received his early education in one of the "little red schoolhouses" so famous in their day. After pursuing more advanced studies in neighboring academies, he took up the occupation of teaching, which has so often been used by ambitious young men as a stepping-stone to one of the professions. At the same time he began to study law, and when his means at length permitted, he undertook a course of study in a law office in Litchfield. In the earlier part of the century Litchfield had a wide reputation as a legal center, and attracted to its famous law school students from every state. It was here that John C. Calhoun, John M. Clayton, and many other eminent men studied law, and that Judge Reeve and Judge Gould, the author of the noted work on Pleading, delivered their celebrated lectures for years.

On the completion of his law studies Mr. Wadsworth was admitted to the bar of Connecticut; and in the same year, having removed to New York city, he was admitted to the bar of the Empire State. The following year, 1852, he went to Buffalo, and after a preparatory experience as a law clerk, opened an office for himself. There for more than forty years he has been engaged in the active practice of an arduous profession.

Mr. Wadsworth has acted upon the belief that he who would be a thorough all-round lawyer can find little time for diversions or pursuits not connected with the main object of his vocation; and that, while one's life may be thereby confined, one is nevertheless a real factor in the development of the community. Consequently he has avoided extensive participation in public affairs; but at times he has contributed services of permanent value to the public, when the office concerned was in the line of his profession. He was at one time city attorney, was twice nominated judge of the Superior Court of Buffalo, and was a member of the commission consisting otherwise of John G. Milburn, Joseph Churchyard, and Spencer Clinton, to revise the charter of the city of Buffalo — a work that reflected credit upon both the revisers and the city.

A great part of Mr. Wadsworth's legal practice has concerned the intricate domain of real property and the settlement of estates — departments of the law in which he stands high as a man of sound business judgment. During his long career at the bar he has been professionally associated in partnership relations with some of the best known members of the local bar — with such men as Benjamin H. Williams, Loran L. Lewis, Truman C. White, and Nelson K. Hopkins.

Mr. Wadsworth is thoroughly American in his habits and tastes, and preserves the characteristics of his New England training. He is a lover of old books, fond of gaining instruction by travel, solid and resolute in his political convictions. He is a member of the First Presbyterian Church, the Republican League, and the Sons of the American Revolution, and a Past Master of the Ancient Landmark Masonic Lodge, besides holding membership in several social clubs, such as the Buffalo and the Ellicott. His life has been well-rounded, honorable to himself, and useful to the city in which he lives.

*PERSONAL CHRONOLOGY—George Wadsworth was born at Litchfield, Conn., March 10, 1830; attended common schools and academies at Litchfield and Danbury (Conn.); was admitted to the bar of Connecticut and of New York in 1851; married Emily O. Marshall of Utica, N. Y., in June, 1858; was city attorney of Buffalo, 1860–61; has practiced law in Buffalo since 1852.*

...

**Richard A. Waite** is a distinguished member of a profession that unites, in a greater degree than any other perhaps, the graces of art and the demands of utility. Architecture is among the very oldest, if it be not indeed the most ancient, of the professions, since the first builders, in a rude way to be sure, practiced a kind of architecture. As for historic times, it is known that the earliest remains of any people evidence a more developed state in architecture than in any other department of human knowledge. Temples and tombs proclaim the fact that man in

RICHARD A. WAITE

remote ages devoted his time and thought to material creations evolved from the workings of imagination and from the longing to embody in physical forms the ideas of the mind.

Mr. Waite's special strength lies in the fact that he combines a theoretic with a practical knowledge of building. Previously to entering upon his chosen career he devoted considerable time to mechanical engineering, thus laying a broad foundation for the more artistic work he was to take up. He had such masters as Ericsson, of "Monitor" fame, and John Kellum, New York's most prominent architect in the sixties.

Mr. Waite is an Englishman by birth, having been born in what is now a part of London; but he came to the United States when a lad, and was educated in the public schools here. He has pursued his profession in Buffalo since 1871, and has established a wide reputation among his professional brethren, who are best qualified to appreciate the value and merit of his work. His first building of any magnitude was the German Insurance Co. edifice, at the corner of Main and Lafayette streets, Buffalo. Other structures of importance in the same city designed by him are the Women's Union, Music Hall, the Grosvenor Library, Pierce's Palace Hotel (since destroyed by fire), and the General Myers mausoleum at Forest Lawn.

To get an adequate idea of the scope and extent of Mr. Waite's achievements as an architect, one must study the work that he has done away from his home and even from his adopted country, Canada, and especially the city of Toronto, has his master pieces, which rank among the most important and successful examples of the highest class of modern architecture. For six years, commencing in 1886, Mr. Waite was engaged in the planning and the construction of the Ontario Parliament buildings at Toronto. This was a stupendous undertaking, and the brilliantly successful execution of the work quickly and justly gave Mr. Waite a high position in the ranks of his profession. This magnificent structure, known in its entirety as the Parliament and Departmental Buildings, includes within its walls over 76,000 square feet, and shows in all its architectural details vigorous, masterful, and highly artistic treatment. Not the least noteworthy feature of the work is the fact that the undertaking was entirely completed promptly, and within the original estimates. The Toronto *Globe* truly remarks that "the completion of such a building without extras or disputes is probably a unique and unprecedented occurrence; and no other instance is known of a public edifice of such magnitude erected at so small a cost."

While the Parliament building must be regarded as Mr. Waite's *chef-d'œuvre*, for the present at least, the account of his professional achievements would

be quite incomplete, if the record were to stop here. He is said to be the first American architect employed by Her Majesty's government, and probably no other American architect has received so many important commissions from Her Majesty's subjects. In the construction of buildings for banks and insurance companies Mr. Waite has especially distinguished himself. He designed buildings for the Western Assurance Co. at Toronto, the Canada Life Assurance Co. at Hamilton, Toronto, and Montreal, the Standard Life Assurance Co. at Montreal, and the head offices of the same company at Glasgow, Scotland. The Bank of Hamilton at Hamilton, Ont., and the Canadian Bank of Commerce at Toronto, together with the *Mail and Empire* building at Toronto, are notable additions to Mr. Waite's list of architectural triumphs. Among his works in western cities may be mentioned the Oliver Opera House (and office building) at South Bend, Ind.

*PERSONAL CHRONOLOGY— Richard Alfred Waite was born at Camberwell, county of Surrey, England, May 14, 1848; came to the United States and settled in Buffalo in 1856; married Sarah E. Holloway of Buffalo September 22, 1869; has pursued the profession of architecture in Buffalo since 1871.*

***

**William D. Walker** belongs to the class of business men that give stability and character to the community in which they live. Not widely known beyond a circle of friends and business associates, and not seekers for fame or official honors, these men yet influence and shape the public sentiment that determines the social, commercial, and political standards of the people. The talkers of the world have not often been its workers, and as the tendency of the age asserts itself, the practical man of affairs is becoming more and more the typical American citizen.

Mr. Walker is the son of Stephen Walker of Utica, N. Y., a prominent mechanic and builder of his day, who moved to Buffalo in 1832, when William was six years of age. Buffalo had then a population of a few thousand only, and was regarded as decidedly "out West." The stagecoach or the Erie canal, recently completed, afforded the only means of travel to the East. The public school system was not then developed in Buffalo, and Mr. Walker's education was obtained in private schools and in the Buffalo Academy. At the age of eighteen, having decided to follow a business career, he entered the employment of Orrin P. Ramsdell, who was one of the pioneers in the wholesale shoe business in western New York. After serving several years as a clerk,

Mr. Walker found that his worth to the house was recognized ; and in 1856 he was admitted to a part nership in the concern. This connection continued until 1876, when the copartnership was dissolved, and Mr. Walker engaged in business for himself.

The wholesale boot, shoe, and rubber house then established has become one of the largest and most reliable firms in this section of the state. Its trade extends not only over New York, Pennsylvania, and Ohio, but also into the far western states. In 1887 Mr. Walker, finding his business growing to large proportions, admitted to partnership Edward C. Walker and William A. Joyce ; and Stephen Walker was added to the firm in 1893. All these men were experienced in the business, and their accession to the firm gave ad ditional strength to a house already noted for its resources.

Success in one commercial field in variably leads to enlarged opportunities in the business world, since men who have conducted their own affairs safely will naturally be sought to care for the inter ests of others. Mr. Walker as a financier has duplicated his success as a business man. In 1884 he was elected to the position of president of the Merchants' Bank of Buffalo ; and so faithfully and sagaciously has he discharged the duties of this responsible office that the bank has been enabled to pay regularly an annual dividend of six per cent, and has accumulated in addition a surplus of two hundred thousand dollars.

In politics Mr. Walker is an ardent Republican, and while never an office-holder or office-seeker, he has always responded to the calls of his party. In 1888 he was nominated for presidential elector on the Repub lican ticket.

Mr. Walker maintains an active connection with educational, philanthropic, and religious institutions. He is a trustee of Hobart College, vice president of the Buffalo General Hospital, and warden of St. Paul's Church. He is also vice president of the Fidelity Trust & Guaranty Company, and of the Merchants' Exchange. In all these positions of trust and responsibility he is noted for disinterested action, fidelity, and unimpeachable integrity.

*PERSONAL CHRONOLOGY— William Henry Walker was born at Utica, N. Y., August 20, 1836 ; was educated at the Buffalo Academy ; entered the wholesale shoe house of O. P. Ramsdell in 1854, and was associated in partnership with him, 1856-76 ; married Edith Kimberly of Buffalo October 21, 1869 ; was nominated for presidential elector in 1888 ; has conducted the wholesale boot and shoe business of Wm. H. Walker & Co. since 1876.*

WILLIAM H. WALKER

**John B. Weber** has lived much in few years. He has been equally successful in different lines of activity —in business, in public office, and in financial affairs. He is a native of Buffalo, and was born in a favorable time to test his mettle and capacity ; for he was in his nineteenth year when President Lincoln called for troops.

Among the many grand regiments sent into the field by the Empire State, none was more famous than the Ellsworth regiment, popularly known as "The Avengers," composed of men representing every ward and town in the state. The members were selected by boards of examiners, and Mr. Weber was chosen from the seventh ward of Buffalo. One of the examiners expressed the fear that Mr. Weber could not stand the hardships of camp and battle. How little this examiner appreciated the staying powers of the young soldier is realized when the fact is stated that Mr. Weber was never sick a day during the war, nor obliged to fall out of line on a march. He was made a corporal, and being the smallest man

*JOHN B. WEBER*

physically in the company, received the sobriquet of the "Little Corporal."

Mr. Weber saw active service in the field. He was present at the siege of Yorktown, and was made 2d lieutenant soon after that event. He took part in the "Seven Days' Fight" before Richmond, and at Gaines's Mill he received special mention for meritorious combat. Later in the war, when the 116th New York regiment took the field, Mr. Weber joined it as adjutant. He was subsequently made acting assistant adjutant general of Chapin's brigade, and was with his command in the memorable fight at Port Hudson. About this time he was offered the colonelcy of a Massachusetts regiment or, in case he preferred to do so, was authorized to organize a colored regiment. He chose the latter course, and in 1863, when less than twenty-one years old, he was made colonel of the 89th United States colored infantry; and as Colonel Weber he fought to the end of the war.

On the restoration of peace he returned to Buffalo, and engaged in business as a grain commission merchant. Later in life (1880-81) he was a member of the firm of Smith & Weber, wholesale grocers. His public career, however, must have our chief attention. He was first nominated for sheriff of Erie county in 1870, but was defeated by Grover Cleveland by fewer than three hundred votes, Mr. Weber running nearly twelve hundred votes ahead of his own ticket. He ran again in 1873, and was elected by two thousand plurality. Meantime he had been appointed deputy postmaster, and had filled that office for three years. In both these positions he displayed excellent judgment, and faithfully discharged the duties devolving upon him.

But higher honors were in store, and in the same year when his old antagonist for sheriff was elected President, Mr. Weber took his seat as a representative in congress from the 33d New York district. He was re-elected in 1889, and during both terms proved himself a capable representative and a public-spirited legislator. He interested himself especially in the improvement of our canals by federal aid on condition that they should be free. He was a member of the subcommittee charged with the drafting of a bill to settle the Pacific railroad indebtedness, his colleagues on the committee being ex-Speaker Crisp, and Mr. Outhwaite of Ohio. In the year following his retirement from congress Mr. Weber was appointed by President Harrison to the responsible office of commissioner of immigration at the port of New York. While in this position he was sent to Europe at the head of a commission to make an investigation into the sources and causes of immigration. His special field was Russia, and the part of the report dealing with that country was widely discussed, and was translated into French. The work is prohibited in Russia, though it understates rather than exaggerates the evils considered.

Mr. Weber is a vigorous, clear, and dispassionate writer, and he is the author of numerous articles and reports, chiefly on canals and the immigration problem. He is a member of the G. A. R., the Union League Club of Brooklyn, the Buffalo and Ellicott clubs, and is a Free Mason. Since his withdrawal from official life he has been cashier of the American Exchange Bank, and has repeated in this new field the success that has attended all the undertakings of his active career.

*PERSONAL CHRONOLOGY — John B. Weber was born at Buffalo September 21, 1842; was educated in the public schools and the Central High School of Buffalo; enlisted as a volunteer soldier in the Union army in August, 1861, and served three years; married Elizabeth J. Farthing of Buffalo January 7, 1864; was assistant postmaster at Buffalo, 1871-74, sheriff of Erie county, 1874-76, representative in congress, 1885-89, and commissioner of immigration at the port of New York, 1890-93; has been cashier of American Exchange Bank of Buffalo since 1894.*

\*\*\*

## Charles Barker Wheeler has

for years been a deep and earnest student of civil-service reform. As a member of the civil-service commission of Buffalo and as chairman of that board, he has done work of incalculable value to the cause of pure politics. The time has long since gone by when the reform movement can be successfully and openly attacked by petty politicians; yet those who stand for a better civil service, who represent the principle that municipal government is not spoils politics, know full well that eternal vigilance is the only safeguard. How true Mr. Wheeler has been to the trust given to his care, how many annoyances he has been subjected to because of his faithfulness, how many covert attacks he has warded off with the aid of his associates — only those know who come into an intimate contact with the civil-service commission. He has labored at all times for an extension of the governing principle of merit, until he has the satisfaction of seeing nearly all departments of the city government under the operation of civil-service rules and regulations. Silas W. Burt of the state civil-service commission said lately that in the application of the reform to the city service, Buffalo was a model for all other cities in the state.

Mr. Wheeler is a lawyer by profession and an active practitioner. He has been such since 1876,

when he was admitted to the bar. Going to Buffalo three years prior to his admission, after graduating from Williams College, Mr. Wheeler entered the office of Sprague & Gorham, where he assiduously studied the mysteries of the law. On his admission to the bar he at once began the practice of his profession. His thoroughness in all things, his accurate knowledge of law, his care in preparing cases, his logical presentation of the same, and his clearness before judge or jury early attracted the attention of older lawyers. Because of these marked characteristics as a legal practitioner Mr. Wheeler was admitted to partnership in 1882 by Sherman S. Rogers and Franklin D. Locke, retaining his connection with this firm for three years. During this time many important cases were handled by him; and it need hardly be added that he won his full share of victories.

*CHARLES BARKER WHEELER*

With broadened experience and ripened judgment Mr. Wheeler in 1885 began to practice alone, and has remained without a partner since. He is regularly retained by a number of business men of extensive

interests, some of whom came to know him and to
appreciate his worth while he was a partner with
Messrs. Rogers and Locke. He is a faithful student
of the law, and thinks the time not wasted that is
devoted to a patient acquirement of all the details of
legal learning. In this particular he is an example

matter, and bears down upon the judgment of the
"twelve good men and true" in an irresistible
manner. In a legal argument before a court his
facts are again presented fairly and forcibly, and his
contentions supported by citations always relevant to
the matter under consideration.

If one were asked to give in a word
the secret of Charles Barker Wheeler's
success in life, that word would be " thoroughness."

*PERSONAL CHRONOLOGY —
Charles Barker Wheeler was born at
Poplar Ridge, Cayuga county, N. Y.,
December 27, 1851; graduated from
Williams College with the class of 1874;
was admitted to the bar in 1876; married
Frances Munro Rochester of Buffalo June
28, 1884; was appointed member of the
Buffalo civil-service commission March 11,
1889, and was elected chairman of the
board February 3, 1892.*

•••

**Truman C. White**, a justice of
the Supreme Court, is a son of the late
Daniel Delevan White and Alma Wilber,
and comes from good New England
stock. Elder John White, who settled in
Cambridge, Mass., in 1632, and who was
a member of the famous Thomas Hooker's
congregation, was Mr. White's paternal
American ancestor. His American ancestor on the other side was George
Wilber, who lived near Danby, Vt., early
in the 18th century. Truman White
and Stephen Wilber, the grandparents of
Justice White, were pioneers in Erie
county, having settled there in 1810.

Mr. White attended the public and
"select" schools of his neighborhood,
and taught two winter terms in the village

*TRUMAN C. WHITE*

for many other lawyers who fail to appreciate the
fact that only constant and intelligent application
will fit them for a successful battle in court. Mr.
Wheeler is an excellent trial lawyer as well as a sound
counselor. He never finds it necessary to bully and
hector witnesses in his endeavor to bring out all that
will be of advantage to his side of a case. His examination is marked by an admirable clearness; he
knows exactly the object to be attained and the most
direct and positive way of reaching it. In cross-
examination he is equally expert, and shrewdly fights
his way to the desired end. When presenting a case to
a jury he indulges in no mere oratory, but marshals
his facts in strong array, sweeps away all extraneous

school of Langford, Erie county. He also spent
a part of the years 1859-60 at the Springville
Academy, intending to complete a course of study
there; but the breaking out of the Civil War
caused a change in his plans. In September, 1861,
he enlisted as a private in the 10th regiment New
York volunteer cavalry for three years or during
the war. He held the noncommissioned office of
quartermaster sergeant in his company from August
5, 1862, to March 4, 1863, and that of orderly or
1st sergeant from March 4, 1863, to February 9,
1864, when he was promoted to the rank of 1st
lieutenant. In January, 1864, he re-enlisted in the
field for the remainder of the war, served with his

regiment until the war ended, and was mustered out of service at Syracuse in July, 1865.

Justice White's name has long suggested legal rather than military associations, and his heart was set upon the law from an early day. While in the army he read Blackstone and Kent, but of course could not pursue his legal studies effectively under such conditions. On his return to civil life he spent some months in the oil regions of Pennsylvania, and in January, 1866, entered the law office of Judge Stephen Lockwood in Buffalo as a student, and soon afterward became a student and managing clerk in the office of Edward Stevens, then one of the most brilliant and successful lawyers in western New York. In November, 1867, Mr. White was admitted to the bar, and immediately opened an office on his own account. He had scarcely become settled in his new quarters, however, when his former preceptor tendered him a partnership on very liberal terms. The offer was accepted, and the firm was known as Stevens & White. Mr. Stevens having died in August, 1868, Mr. White from that time until he was elected a judge of the Superior Court of Buffalo in 1891, was associated successively with George Wadsworth, Nelson K. Hopkins, and Seward A. Simons in the practice of the law. Mr. White attained high rank as an active practitioner at the bar. He enjoyed the confidence and regard of all who knew him; and his practice was extensive, varied, and successful in a marked degree.

Though a strong Republican in politics, Mr. White is not a partisan, and when he was first nominated for a place on the bench of the Superior Court of Buffalo in 1885, he received the support of men of both parties, and failed of election by a minority of only fifty-seven votes in a total of thirty-three thousand. When placed in nomination for the same office in 1891, he received a majority of over four hundred votes in a year when nearly all the city and county Democratic tickets were elected by large majorities, the mayor, or head of the Democratic city ticket, being elected by a majority of 4,587. This was remarkably strong evidence of the esteem in which his fellow-citizens held him at that time, and his career on the bench has been such as to increase that esteem. Apt learning, legal ability, unquestioned integrity of purpose,

and a well balanced temperament have characterized and distinguished Mr. White's judicial career.

*PERSONAL CHRONOLOGY—Truman Clark White was born at Perrysburg, N. Y., April 30, 1840; attended country schools and Springville (N. Y.) Academy; enlisted in the 10th New York cavalry in 1861, and served throughout the war, being discharged in July, 1865, as 1st lieutenant; was admitted to the bar in Buffalo in November, 1867; married Emma Kate Haskins of Buffalo February 10, 1869; was elected judge of the Superior Court of Buffalo in the fall of 1891, serving until January 1, 1896, when, on the abolishment of the Superior Court, he took his seat on the bench of the Supreme Court.*

...

**Thomas L. Bunting** is a living proof that the boy who has it in him can win success in the

*THOMAS L. BUNTING*

country as well as in the city. His own life has shown that it is not necessary to leave the village for the larger field of the city, if one desires to build up a profitable business. Of course the chances are

fewer in the country, but that fact contributes so
much more to the credit of the man who takes advantage of them. Like so many other country boys,
Mr. Bunting taught school while he was finishing his
education. After leaving the Springville Academy
in 1863 he moved to Hamburg, in Erie county, and
has lived there ever since, having closely identified
himself with the material welfare of that thriving
town. He embarked early in mercantile business,
and in 1868 established a general store. Close and
intelligent application won him success, and he is
now the owner of the largest store of its kind in
western New York. His establishment is popularly
known as " Six Stores in One."

Always on the lookout for opportunities to widen
his field, Mr. Bunting became identified with the
canning business in 1881, and to his business insight
is largely due the great measure of prosperity that
has come to the Hamburg Canning Co. This concern has mammoth plants both at Hamburg and at
Eden, in Erie county. Its capital stock is $100,000,
and its yearly output is three and one-half million
cans of fruits and vegetables, equivalent to five hundred car-loads. It finds markets in all states of this
country and in many foreign cities. Mr. Bunting is
interested in various other companies. He is vice
president of the Bank of Hamburg, a stockholder in
the Hamburg Planing Mill Co., president of the local
water and electric light company, and president of the
Hamburg Investment & Improvement Co., which has
done much for the development and improvement
of the town. All of these enterprises have the benefit
of Mr. Bunting's sagacity and business judgment.

Mr. Bunting is a Democrat in political faith, and
has manifested a deep interest in honest politics. He
was elected to the 52d congress from the 33d New
York district in 1890, and served his term with
much distinction. It was during this time that the
discussion over the proposed changes in the tariff
laws was at its highest point. The McKinley law
had been passed in 1890, and the 52d congress,
which assembled in 1891, and which was Democratic, made a great effort to overthrow the principle
of protection. Mr. Bunting arrayed himself with
the tariff reform forces, took a leading part in the
debates, and became recognized as one of the best
authorities on that side concerning tin plate. His
connection with the canning business, in which he
was a large consumer of tin cans, gave him a practical knowledge of the subject, and he wrote many
articles for the press and for the Tariff Reform Club.
When his term expired his party endeavored to give
him a renomination, but he positively refused to
return to Washington.

Mr. Bunting is a member of the Presbyterian
church, of the Free and Accepted Masons, of the
Royal Arcanum, and of the Ancient Order of United
Workmen.

*PERSONAL CHRONOLOGY—Thomas Lathrop Bunting was born in the town of Eden, N. Y.,
April 24, 1844; received his education at a district
school and the Springville Academy; taught school in
1861-63; married Bettie Maria Newton of East
Hamburg, N. Y., September 8, 1869; established a
general mercantile business in Hamburg, N. Y., in
1868; became manager of the Hamburg Canning Co.
in 1881; was a member of the 52d congress (1891-
93); has lived in Hamburg since 1863.*

---

**Charles S. Cary** is a prominent character in
the political, social, and business circles of western
New York. An academic education, together with
a close study of law, science, literature, and mankind, has given Mr. Cary that tact and farsightedness needed by the successful politician, business
man, and lawyer. Of commanding presence and
great mastery of language, he not only impresses one
by his physical perfection, but also wins one's confidence at once by his quaint, bluff, and yet adroit
manner of speech. Thoroughly schooled in all the
practice of the law, he has gained a clientage in
Olean and the oil country second to none; and Cary
& White, Cary & Bolles, and Cary, Rumsey &
Hastings, have always appeared as counsel in important cases on the court calendars of the 8th
judicial district. During the forty-five years of his
practice he has attended every term of the Supreme
Court held in his county.

In political life Mr. Cary has been a Democrat.
President Lincoln, however, recognizing his ability,
appointed him commissioner of enrollment for the
32d district in 1863; and during the years 1865-66
he was collector of internal revenue for the same district. In 1872 he was nominated by the Democrats
for representative in congress, and received a majority of the legal votes in the district comprising Chautauqua and Cattaraugus counties. The Republican
ballots in Chautauqua county, having been printed
" For Member of Congress " instead of " For Representative in Congress," as required by law, were
invalid, and Mr. Cary might have had the whole
vote thrown out, and might thus have been seated by
congress. He was strongly urged to do so, and it
would have been an easy matter to give Mr. Cary
his seat, the Democratic party having a large majority in the house of representatives at that time. But
he would not permit this, and refused to take advantage of the technicality. This act alone brought him

many friends in the Republican party, and he was able in 1883, when he received the nomination for member of assembly at the hands of the Democrats, to overcome a large Republican majority and to win the election. In the same year he was nominated by the Democratic judicial convention for the 8th judicial district for justice of the Supreme Court, and ran eleven thousand ahead of the party ticket. In 1886 President Cleveland, seeking to inaugurate reforms in the governmental supervision of the Pacific railroads, appointed Mr. Cary one of the national commissioners. In this capacity he served one year, when the President made him solicitor of the United States treasury. Mr. Cary held this office until the close of President Cleveland's first term. At the Democratic state convention at Syracuse in 1895 he was strongly urged to accept the nomination for secretary of state, but refused to allow the use of his name.

In railroad circles of western New York and Pennsylvania Mr. Cary has long been prominent, having been president of the Olean, Bradford & Warren, the Kendall & Eldred, and the Olean & Bolivar railroads. He is now vice president of the Coudersport & Port Allegheny railroad. He is favorably known in banking circles, having been an incorporator of the Exchange National Bank of Olean and a director in that institution from the time of its foundation. He has retained in abundant measure the confidence and esteem of the community of which he has so long been an active member.

*PERSONAL CHRONOLOGY—*
*Charles S. Cary was born at Hornellsville, N. Y., November 25, 1823; graduated from Alfred (N. Y.) Academy in 1843, and from the National Law School, Ballston Spa, N. Y., in 1850; married Sarah A. Mitchell in 1850; was appointed commissioner of the board of enrollment by President Lincoln in 1864; was collector of internal revenue, 1865-69; was a member of the state assembly in 1884; was appointed commissioner of Pacific railroads in 1886, and solicitor of the United States treasury in 1887; has practiced law in Olean since 1850.*

• • •

**Willard A. Cobb** has been a lifelong student of men and affairs. He is especially noted as a journalist who has faithfully served the state in official positions. He has been an active force in the formation of a sound and healthy public opinion in western New York on every prominent question that has arisen during the last twenty-five years. He has labored with pen and voice for the success of principles constituting the basis of all good government.

*CHARLES S. CARY*

As a preparation for his career he had the advantage of an excellent education. He was fitted for college at Rome (N. Y.) Academy and at Dwight's Rural High School, Clinton, N. Y., and pursued a four years' course at Hamilton College, having among his classmates Elihu Root, Franklin D. Locke, and other men who have since achieved distinction. Having chosen journalism as his profession, Mr. Cobb at once began his apprenticeship in the practical school of the reporter. He accepted a position on the Chicago *Post*, and was then successively assistant editor of the Racine *Advocate*, city editor of the Utica *Morning Herald*, editor of the Dunkirk *Journal*, and finally editor in chief of the Lockport *Daily Journal*.

Were it not for the absorbing work connected with a modern newspaper, Mr. Cobb might have made his mark in pure literature. His letters from Europe during a year's travel abroad exhibited such powers of description and faculty of imparting information in an interesting way as have made the

*WILLARD A. COBB*

reputation of many writers. His letters from Italy upon the economic, political, and religious conditions of that country, and especially his account of an interview with Leo XIII., recently elected Pope, were in great demand by the press.

His experience abroad, coupled with his wide knowledge of practical problems in education, equipped him in a marked degree for the high office conferred upon him by the legislature in 1886, when he was elected a regent of the University of the State of New York. The duties of this position were fully appreciated and faithfully discharged until 1895. He was appointed by Governor Morton in that year one of the three civil-service commissioners of the state, and thereupon resigned from the board

of regents, the law forbidding him as commissioner to hold any other official position.

Though always a strong Republican, an active party worker, and a member of the state committee and of numerous state and local conventions, Mr. Cobb has proved himself an impartial, efficient, and progressive member of the board. At the first meeting of the new commission he was elected president. It has been said by a high authority — one of the United States civil-service commissioners, in fact — that under Mr. Cobb's administration more has been accomplished than by any former state civil-service commission.

Mr. Cobb has been called upon frequently to speak before teachers' associations and editorial conventions, and has always delivered addresses worthy of the occasion. He has been at all times a hard and energetic worker, and has impressed himself upon his day and generation. Few men are more widely or more favorably known throughout the state.

Mr. Cobb is a bachelor, and lives in an apartment flat in Lockport.

*PERSONAL CHRONOLOGY—Willard Adams Cobb was born at Rome, N. Y., July 20, 1842; graduated from Hamilton College in 1864; was a regent of the University of the State of New York, 1886–95; has been president of the State Civil Service Commission since 1895; has edited the Lockport "Daily Journal" since 1871.*

...

**John T. Darrison** is one of the most popular citizens of Lockport. Although still a young man, he long since made his mark in the community in which he has lived all his life. He is identified with its interests in many ways, and has done his full share in promoting its welfare. His fellow-citizens delight to do him honor, for he has shown himself faithful in small things as well as in great. No interest committed to his care is allowed to suffer from want of attention and of wise counsel. This is true of him, not only as concerns things that have to do with the material and municipal welfare of the city, but also as regards its charities. Mr. Darrison is a man of the people, true to himself and true to others.

It is because of these qualities that he has so often been called upon to occupy positions of great trust and responsibility. He has been prominent in the municipal affairs of the city for some years.

His first public office was that of alderman, in which he rendered services of so valuable a character that he was next chosen to be a member of the board of supervisors. Here, again, his plain common sense and strict business methods were so marked that in 1892 he was elected mayor of the city, holding that office for two years. His administration was eminently satisfactory to the people of Lockport. At present he is one of the railroad commissioners of the city; a member of the board of education; treasurer of the Lockport & Buffalo Railway Co.; and active in an official capacity in various local institutions.

All that John T. Darrison is he owes to his own efforts. He was born in Lockport, and obtained his education in the public schools of that city. When sixteen years old he started out for himself by becoming an apprentice in the composing department of the Lockport *Journal*. But the opportunities there seemed limited, and when, two years later, a chance came to engage in the flour and feed business, young Darrison was glad to make a change. Unremitting and careful attention to the business in all its details has been followed by a success that could have been only dreamed of in the beginning. The business has grown steadily and surely, until now Mr. Darrison is at the head of an establishment that occupies three commodious stores equipped with the best appliances for handling, in the most approved manner and with the utmost dispatch, the special kind of merchandise concerned. These stores are the center of distribution for a very large trade in western New York. The seed department is particularly well organized, and has business in all parts of the country.

While developing his private business, Mr. Darrison has been fully alive to the opportunities in other directions. He has done his part in local enterprises of a public nature, the successful operation of which has resulted in benefit to the city of Lockport. He is a stockholder in the Lockport & Buffalo Railway Co., the Thompson Milling Co., and the United Indurated Fibre Co.

*PERSONAL CHRONOLOGY—John Thomas Darrison was born at Lockport, N. Y., October 29, 1855; was educated in the public schools; married Laura A. Lambert of Lockport September 29, 1880; was elected alderman of Lockport in 1885, mayor* in 1892, and school trustee in 1895; was appointed supervisor in 1886, member of the board of health in 1889, civil-service commissioner in 1890, railroad commissioner in 1894, and a member of the board of education in 1895; has conducted a flour, feed, and grain business in Lockport since January, 1874.

*JOHN T. DARRISON*

**Ben. S. Dean** is as well known throughout a large part of western New York as any newspaper editor in that section. This fame is not due to his newspaper work alone, but in great part to his activity in politics. He is a man of positive ideas, who always has the courage of his convictions, and never hesitates to make them known. Such a man cannot fail to impress himself upon any community in which he lives. He may make foes — a positive man always does that — but he is never without friends. In fact, he derives more philosophic satisfaction from the opposition of enemies than pleasure from the support of friends. In politics it is often a compliment to a man that Mr. So-and-So opposes him.

We think of Mr. Dean nowadays as an old Chautauquan, since he has long been a resident of Jamestown; but he was born in Randolph, Cattaraugus county. His early education was obtained in the common schools. When someone asked him where his education was completed, the answer was thor-

*BEN S. DEAN*

oughly characteristic — "It has never been completed; I am still a student." Being still a student, Mr. Dean is a growing man; it is only the man that knows it all who ceases to develop.

In 1878, when only eighteen years old, Mr. Dean became a member of the firm of Sampson, Kittell & Dean, who published a paper called the *Register* at Emlenton, Penn. He next associated himself with the Rev. J. J. Keyes in the publication of the Sunday *Mirror* at Olean, N. Y. This partnership continued through 1881 and 1882. From Olean Mr. Dean went to his native town of Randolph in the year last named, and there, in partnership with G. W. Roberts, published the Randolph *Register*. Here he remained until May, 1885. Jamestown was then, as

it is now, a bustling, growing city, the metropolis of Chautauqua county, and the seat of many prosperous manufactories. The place seemed to offer a fine field for another live newspaper, and in November, 1885, Mr. Dean formed the News Publishing Company, and established the Jamestown *News*. Of this paper he has been editor ever since, with the exception of five months in 1894, when he served as a member from Chautauqua county of the state constitutional convention. This is the only office to which Mr. Dean has ever been elected, and the only one for which he was ever a candidate.

Mr. Dean is an ardent Republican in political belief, and his journalistic work is largely in the line of political writings. He handles all subjects of that nature with a directness of purpose that can never be mistaken. A spade is a spade to him, and he never hesitates to call things by what he conceives to be their proper names. He has a large fund of information on many subjects, and his editorials command wide attention. Though often attacked, he is ever ready with reply, and a controversy is very much to his liking. Besides his journalistic writings he has contributed politico-economic articles to various publications.

Outside of his newspaper work Mr. Dean's activities have been mostly devoted to politics. He has been an earnest worker both with the leaders and in the ranks. Sometimes he has been with the controlling interests of his party and sometimes against them, but with one exception he has acquiesced in the decrees of the party conventions in nominations. The fight he led in this exception resulted in the defeat at the polls of the candidate opposed by him.

Mr. Dean is a firm believer in the free coinage of silver on a basis of sixteen to one, and in governmental ownership of essential monopolies. He is opposed to ballot reform, high license, and civil-service reform, all of which he terms "fads." However much others may differ from him on these subjects, it must be conceded that he is honest and fearless in his opposition.

*PERSONAL CHRONOLOGY— Benjamin S. Dean was born at Randolph, N. Y., May 10, 1860; began work as a newspaper writer in 1878; married Emile C. Blasdell of Attica, N. Y., June 23, 1884; was elected a member of the state constitutional* convention in 1883; organized the News Publishing Company in 1885, and has edited the Jamestown "News" since.

\*\*\*

**William Caryl Ely** owes his success as a lawyer and man of affairs to an indomitable will controlled by sound judgment, wide knowledge, and practical experience. When once he has grappled with a problem, he holds on till a solution is obtained. He has been the projector, organizer, and promoter of a number of important undertakings in the electrical field, and has succeeded in the face of great discouragements. He has had the faith and the energy that, united, overcome all obstacles. The law, it has been truly remarked, has to-day become a business. The old-time, slow going, pedantic man of books would be out of place in a modern law office or court room. In his stead has come the quiet, accurate thinker, well grounded in the principles and practice of the law, but possessing in addition a mind adapted to the complicated forms and involved methods of the commercial world as it exists to-day.

To speak of Mr. Ely as a business lawyer seems natural. Yet he is something more than that, for he is a successful advocate, and has the valuable gift known in the profession as a judicial mind. But his work in connection with such corporations as the Niagara Falls Power Co. and the Buffalo & Niagara Falls Electric railway exemplifies and emphasizes the practical side of Mr. Ely's character. He was one of the five original promoters and incorporators of the power company. He prepared and had charge of the legislation pertaining to its original charter, and assisted in preparing and had charge of all subsequent legislation; and he has been a trustee and local counsel of the company from its organization. He was the principal promoter of the railway company, and carried the enterprise to a successful end despite the panic of 1893–95, which threatened at one time to block the project. He is president of the company.

Mr. Ely is a native of the Empire State, and received the greater part of his elementary and college training within its borders. After a sound preliminary education he took up the study of law, and was admitted to the bar at East Worcester, N. Y., where he practiced for three years

before settling in Niagara Falls. His career as a lawyer has been unusually successful and brilliant, and the firm of Ely, Dudley & Cohn, numbering among its clients many important corporations and manufacturing companies, has to-day the most extensive legal business in Niagara county.

Legislation and law are so intimately connected that lawyers naturally constitute the most numerous class in all legislative bodies. The law, more frequently than any other profession, leads to politics, and Mr. Ely has been an active and prominent member of his party for many years. He has served as supervisor and as assemblyman, and in 1891 he received the Democratic nomination for justice of the Supreme Court. While in the legislature he was nominated by his party for speaker, and was the leader of the minority on the floor. He is treasurer of the Demo-

WILLIAM CARYL ELY

cratic state central committee, and is also one of the executive committee of that organization. Although thus closely interested in politics, Mr. Ely has declined nominations for offices that would be likely to interfere with his paramount duties as an attorney and counselor at law. His profession has been first with him, as it must be with every lawyer who is determined to win the respect and confidence of his clients and his brethren at the bar.

In social life Mr. Ely holds a high position, and has hosts of friends. He is a member of the Masonic order, and has been a vestryman of St. Peter's Episcopal Church since 1886. In college he was a member of the Chi Phi fraternity.

*PERSONAL CHRONOLOGY—William Caryl Ely was born at Middlefield, N. Y., February 25, 1856; was educated at Cooperstown (N. Y.) Union School, Girard (Pa.) Academy, Delaware Literary Institute (Franklin, N. Y.), and Cornell University; was admitted to the bar in 1884; married Grace Kehler of Cobleskill, N. Y., February 14, 1884; was a member of the state assembly, 1883-85; has practiced law at Niagara Falls, N. Y., since 1885.*

* * *

**Thomas T. Flagler** has had a thoroughly American career — American both in breadth and variety of experience, and in the rewards that have followed upon energy, intelligence, and thrift. His educational advantages were limited to what the common schools afforded nearly three-quarters of a century ago. His first paid employment began when he was eleven years old, and was in a bark mill connected with a tannery. The compensation was board and one shilling a day. From six months' labor he saved ten dollars, which he deposited in a New York savings bank. When he withdrew the deposit, after attaining manhood, the original sum had been fully doubled by interest. At sixteen Mr. Flagler was apprenticed to the printing trade in the office of the Chenango *Republican*, Oxford, N. Y., at a compensation of board, washing, mending, and forty dollars a year. When his employer died two years afterward, Mr. Flagler formed a partnership and bought the paper. His cash capital was seventeen dollars. For two years he rode one day each week over the Chenango hills and valleys distributing the paper to the subscribers. After five years' experience in the newspaper business, he sold his interest in March, 1836, and went westward to Lockport with $1,200, the profits of his labor, securely belted about his body.

Lockport was thenceforward Mr. Flagler's home. For about two years he worked as a journeyman printer, earning the current wages of eight dollars a week. In September, 1838, he bought the Niagara *Courier*, again embarking in the newspaper business on his own account. The *Courier* was a Whig paper, and brought him into active participation in politics. Seward and Marcy were opposing candidates for governor, and Mr. Flagler took an active part in the canvass, not only in his paper, but also by accompanying the Whig candidate for congress about the county and speaking with him at public meetings. This speaking tour doubled the subscription list of the *Courier*. Mr. Flagler also took a prominent part in the presidential campaign of 1840. He made the dedicatory address at the completion of the log cabin at the junction of old and new Main streets in Lockport, before an immense throng of people. Millard Fillmore, elected vice president four years later, delivered an address on the same occasion.

In 1842 and again in 1843 Mr. Flagler was elected to the state legislature. The first year he was chairman of the committee on grievances, and the second year he was a member of the committee on canals. Only two men are now living who antedate Mr. Flagler in assembly membership.

In 1842 Mr. Flagler sold his newspaper, and engaged in the hardware business, retaining an interest therein for twenty-seven years. In 1849 he was elected treasurer of Niagara county, and held the office for three years. In 1852 he was chosen representative in congress for the district embracing Niagara and Orleans counties. He took part in the struggle over the Kansas-Nebraska bill, and was one of the hundred who voted against it because it repealed the prohibition of slavery in those territories. He was almost unanimously re-elected to the next congress, the 34th (1855-57), and took part in the memorable ten weeks' contest over the speakership that ended in the election of Nathaniel P. Banks. Out of the disorganization of parties typified in this contest sprang the Republican party. In 1860 Mr. Flagler was returned to the legislature, and became chairman of the committee on ways and means, and of a special committee which unavailingly proposed legislation preventing railroad discrimination. In this term of the legislature Mr. Flagler took a stand in advance of his time by returning, unused, railroad passes presented to him. He was the only member who did this. The list of Mr. Flagler's public offices closes with his service as a member of the constitutional convention of 1867-68.

In his own community Mr. Flagler has held many positions of trust and honor. He has been, from the beginning, a director of the Lockport Hydraulic Co., which has expended large sums of money in making the surplus canal water, taken from the head of the locks, available for water power. He has thus been instrumental in building up Lockport and making it a manufacturing town. Among the industries so created by this company is the Holly

Manufacturing Co., organized by Mr. Flagler in 1859 with a capital of $20,000, of which he furnished half. He was made president at the beginning, and has held the office ever since, building the concern into an institution of national reputation. Other enterprises with the organization of which he was connected are the Lockport Gaslight Co., established in 1854; the Niagara County Bank, organized in 1856; and the Lockport & Buffalo railroad, now leased by the Erie. Without seeking the position, Mr. Flagler has been called almost invariably to the presidency of the business organizations with which he has been connected. For many years he has stood at the head of eight such organizations. He has shown in many ways his interest in the well-being of Lockport, and lately gave the city a dwelling house for use as a hospital. The city has named the institution the Flagler Hospital.

Mr. Flagler has been active in religious matters since his early manhood, having united with the Congregational church in Oxford in 1831. He was elected a ruling elder of the Presbyterian church in Lockport in 1840, and still holds the office after fifty-five years' service. From 1853 to 1876 he served as Sunday-school superintendent, being finally released at his own request and made honorary superintendent for life. When the presbytery of Niagara was incorporated in 1875, Mr. Flagler was elected to the board of trustees, and has been president of the board since.

*PERSONAL CHRONOLOGY —*
*Thomas Thorn Flagler was born at Pleasant Valley, N. Y., October 12, 1811; after attending country schools, was apprenticed to the printing trade at Oxford, N. Y., in 1827; became publisher of the Chenango " Republican " in 1829, and of the Niagara " Courier " in 1838; was elected to the New York legislature in 1842, 1843, and 1860; was treasurer of Niagara county, 1849; was representative in congress, 1853-54; was a member of the constitutional convention of 1867-68; has lived in Lockport, N. Y., since 1836.*

<hr />

**R. U. U. Franchot** has the honor of being the first man elected to hold the office of mayor of the city of Olean. A study of the census report of 1890 reveals the interesting fact that of the increase of five thousand in the population of Cattaraugus

county in the previous ten years, almost the entire number may be credited to Olean, the slight losses and gains in the other portions of the county about offsetting each other. As a result of this increase of population, Olean applied for and obtained a city charter, and the first election of officers for the new

*THOMAS T. FLAGLER*

city was held in February, 1894. When a community first takes its place among the cities of a great state it is of the utmost importance that it choose for its chief magistrate a man who will administer the municipal affairs with due dignity and with sound business judgment. The voters of the city of Olean chose Mr. Franchot, who had been for nearly twenty years one of its well known and highly respected citizens, prominently identified with its business, political, social, and religious interests.

Mr. Franchot is not a native of western New York, but was born in Otsego county, and was educated in Schenectady. He prepared for college there, at Union School, and graduated from Union College in the class of 1875 with the degree of B. A. At that time the oil fields of Pennsylvania offered a tempting opening for ambitious young men, and Mr. Franchot, like many others, turned aside from the professional paths to which his college training invited him, and embraced a commercial career, trusting to industry and natural ability to win suc-

N. V. V. FRANCHOT

ress. Immediately after his graduation he went to Millerstown, Penn., where he was employed by a pipe-line company as gauger, and afterwards as division superintendent. After spending two years in Millerstown he was able to begin business for himself as an oil producer. He went to Olean, and formed a partnership with his brother and with A. N. Perrin, under the firm name of Franchot Bros. & Co. In 1888 Mr. Perrin sold out his interest in the business, and the firm has since been known as Franchot Bros.

Mr. Franchot has always been a staunch Republican, and he served his party well, as chairman of the county committee for three successive years, and as delegate to the national convention at Minneapolis

in 1892. He was honored by the nomination for mayor in 1894, in recognition of his executive ability and of his consistent devotion to the principles of the Republican party.

Mr. Franchot is a prominent figure in the business life of Olean, and is in the forefront of all the schemes for advancing the prosperity of the city. While still maintaining his interest in the firm that bears his name, he is at the same time president of the Olean Improvement Co., and a director of the Olean Electric Light & Power Co., and of the Exchange National Bank of Olean.

Mr. Franchot has not allowed himself to become so occupied with his numerous business cares as to neglect the other aspects of our complex nineteenth-century life. He has been active in the work of St. Stephen's Episcopal Church ever since he first came to Olean, and for many years has been a member of its vestry. He is president of the City Club of Olean, and a member of the Sigma Phi fraternity of Union College. He was elected a life trustee of Union College in June, 1895. He is a nonresident member of the Genesee Valley Club of Rochester, and of the University Club and the Sigma Phi Club of New York city.

*PERSONAL CHRONOLOGY—Nicholas Van Vranken Franchot was born at Morris, Otsego county, N. Y., August 21, 1855; was educated at Union School and at Union College, Schenectady, graduating from the latter institution in 1875; married Annie Coyne Wood of Warren, Penn., November 5, 1879; was elected mayor of Olean, N. Y., in February, 1894; has been in business in Olean, as an oil producer, since 1878.*

* * *

**Joshua Gaskill** has been prominently connected with the growth of Lockport for over thirty years, and has done much to enhance its material development and prosperity. Born in the town of Royalton, Niagara county, N. Y., his education was begun in the district schools, and continued in Lockport Union School, Wilson Collegiate Institute, and Gasport Academy. For three years he taught a district school in the winter, and worked on his father's farm in summer, accumulating sufficient funds in this way to enable him to enter the University of Rochester in the spring of 1856. We prize most what costs us the most effort, and Judge Gaskill, having worked hard to obtain a college education, naturally made good use of the opportunities that it offered: and when he was graduated in 1859 he received the highest honors of his class. The same year he began the study of law in the office of George D. Lamont of Lockport, and after completing the required course of reading, was admitted to practice in the courts of Niagara county at the December term of 1860. In 1862 he opened an office in Lockport, where he has lived and practiced ever since, with the exception of six months, in 1862–63, when he practiced law in Saginaw, Mich., with William H. Sweet. In the spring of 1863 he returned to Lockport, and formed a partnership with Andrew J. Ensign, which lasted until 1868. Since then Judge Gaskill has practiced alone. Notwithstanding the infirmity of deafness, which has for many years prevented him from trying cases in court, and has excluded him from several of the most lucrative sources of professional income, he has built up and maintained a large and varied practice, of which important litigations form no inconsiderable part. He has also devoted much time, since his retirement from active political life in 1878, to the training of students for the profession to which he is such an honor. In this he has been most successful. Thirteen young men who gained their knowledge of law in his office are now in active practice, and without exception they have been successful in their profession: while one has attained great eminence.

Judge Gaskill retired from political life when still a young man, but between the years 1865 and 1878 he held many important offices in the city and county. In the former year he was appointed first city clerk of the newly made city of Lockport, and held the office for two years. In the same year he was made clerk of the board of supervisors of Niagara county for one year. In the spring of 1870 he was elected treasurer and tax collector of the city of Lockport, and in the following year was nominated for the office of surrogate of Niagara county, to which he was elected, and in which he served the full term of six years.

Judge Gaskill's study of the law has been constant and diligent, and in addition he has devoted much

time to literary, scientific, and philosophical subjects. He has written and published numerous poems, lectures, and addresses. He was the poet at the annual meeting of alumni of the University of Rochester in 1865, and one of the essayists of the New York State Bar Association in 1880. He was one of the founders of the Upsilon chapter of the Psi Upsilon fraternity at the University of Rochester. He is a member of the New York State Bar Association, and was one of the earliest members of the American Association for the Advancement of Science.

*PERSONAL CHRONOLOGY—Joshua Gaskill was born at Royalton, N. Y., November 4, 1835; was educated at the Lockport Union School, Wilson Collegiate Institute, Gasport Academy, and the University of Rochester, from which he graduated in 1859;*

*JOSHUA GASKILL*

*was admitted to the bar in 1860; married Salome Cox of Lockport, N. Y., May 25, 1863; was appointed city clerk of Lockport in 1865, and clerk of the board of supervisors of Niagara county the same year; was elected treasurer of Lockport in 1850, and surrogate of Niagara county in 1851; has practiced law in Lock port since 1853.*

\*\*\*

**Eleazer Green,** a shrewd lawyer and an honest and successful business man, has long been one of

*ELEAZER GREEN*

the central figures of Chautauqua county life, and one of the leading men of the city of Jamestown.

Educated in the common schools of Busti and Harmony, both country towns of Chautauqua county, and afterward at the old academy at Westfield and the Albany Law School, this "Harmony boy" (as he is called by his admirers from that town) has won an enviable position in professional, business, and political circles. In May, 1868, Mr. Green was admitted to the bar, and came to Jamestown, where he acted as clerk in the law office of Cook & Lockwood for two years. At the end of that interval he opened an office for himself in the same town, where he has ever since resided, and where he has built up a large and successful practice. The following

well known law firms have had the benefit of Mr. Green's ability and experience: Barlow & Green (Byron A. Barlow); Green and Prendergast (the late James Prendergast); Green, Prendergast & Benedict (James Prendergast and Willis O. Benedict); Sheldon, Green, Stevens & Benedict (Porter Sheldon, Frank W. Stevens, and Willis O. Benedict); Green & Woodward (John Woodward); and the present firm of Green & Woodbury, Mr. Green being associated with Egbert E. Woodbury, surrogate of Chautauqua county.

The legal profession readily lends itself to business pursuits, and Mr. Green's career amply exemplifies the fact. His real-estate operations have been on an extensive scale, and his numerous successful ventures in this direction have marked him as a farsighted investor. One of his most successful efforts was the reclaiming of swamp lands on the northern shore of Lake Chautauqua, and the creation of "Greenhurst on Chautauqua," a picturesque and popular resort, named in his honor. In keeping with his interest in lake-shore property have been his public-spirited efforts in establishing the artificial propagation of muskellunge (a kind of pike) at Chautauqua Lake. To this end Mr. Green has devoted time, money, and energy, and the successful establishment of the industry is the result.

In politics Mr. Green is a Republican, and while he has been a prominent and influential member of his party, he has also won the esteem and confidence of all political parties. When, therefore, in 1894, he consented to become a candidate for mayor of Jamestown, he received 2,979 votes out of a total of 3,325, although there were two other candidates in the field. In 1895 Mr. Green was a candidate for district attorney of Chautauqua county, and although there were two other candidates before the Republican county convention, he was nominated on the first ballot by a large majority, and was elected in the following November.

Mr. Green holds many offices of trust. He attends the Congregational church, and is one of its active supporters.

*PERSONAL CHRONOLOGY—Eleazer Green was born at Remsen, N. Y., March 16, 1846; was educated at Westfield (N. Y.) Academy and at the Albany Law School, from which he received the degree of Bachelor of Laws in 1868; married Mary E. Brown of Jamestown, N. Y., November 5, 1873; was elected clerk of the village of Jamestown in 1875, and mayor of the city of Jamestown in 1894; was elected district attorney of Chautauqua county in 1895; has practiced law in Jamestown since 1870.*

• • •

**Robert J. Gross** was thrown early in life upon his own resources, and has achieved success by his own energy. He was born in a village of Ontario, Canada, and his schooling was limited to about five years in the common schools of his native place. Before he entered his teens he had taken up the study of telegraphy, and while a mere boy he began to support himself. He served as telegraph operator for the Montreal Telegraph Co. and the Dominion Telegraph Co. at Brighton, Ont., and later engaged in the railway service in a similar capacity. The hours were long and the work was hard; but it is precisely such conditions that prove and develop character. Mr. Gross's abilities and perseverance were equal to the test, and his progress was steady.

He continued in railway employment until 1882. The service called him to various places, and March, 1873, found him at Dunkirk, N. Y., as train dispatcher for the Erie railroad. While there he came under the observation of Horatio G. Brooks, founder of the Brooks Locomotive Works of Dunkirk. Widening opportunities, due to the recognition of his abilities, called Mr. Gross to more important positions in the railway service in the West. Thence he returned in March, 1882, to form a partnership with Mr. Brooks, M. L. Hinman, and others connected with the Brooks Locomotive Works. His rise there, like that of his earlier career, has been continuous and rapid; and he is now the vice president of the company. His business has made him an extensive traveler, as well in foreign lands as in this country; and he has been instrumental in the introduction of the American locomotive into Cuba and Brazil.

Mr. Gross's business ability and energy have been called into use by other institutions than the Brooks Locomotive Works. Since May, 1890, he has been president of the United States Radiator Co. of Dunkirk; and upon the organization of the Hartford Axle Co. of Dunkirk in January, 1895, he was chosen a director. Since

January, 1893, he has been president of the Young Men's Building Association, Limited, of Dunkirk. This association, with a view to the improvement of the city, built and has conducted the fine Hotel Gratiot in Dunkirk.

Though he has not sought office, Mr. Gross has been an active and public-spirited citizen, and has taken a citizen's proper interest in political duties. He is an earnest Republican, and in 1883 served as chairman of the Republican committee of Chautauqua county — one of the strongest Republican counties in the Empire State. Since June, 1893, he has been a member of the board of water commissioners of Dunkirk — a life position that is considered one of the most honorable distinctions within the power of the municipality to bestow. In all matters concerning the prosperity of the city Mr. Gross takes an

*ROBERT J. GROSS*

active interest. Since January, 1895, he has been vice president of the Dunkirk Board of Trade, a body devoted to the advancement of the city in its manufacturing and commercial relations.

Mr. Gross has a wide circle of friends. He is a member of the Union League Club of Chicago, the Old Time Telegraphers' Association, the American Railway Master Mechanics' Association, and the Engineers' Club of New York city. He is a Mason of the 32d degree, and belongs to the order of the

CHARLES E. HEQUEMBOURG

Mystic Shrine. He has been a trustee of the First Presbyterian Church of Dunkirk since 1883.

*PERSONAL CHRONOLOGY— Robert J. Gross was born at Brighton, Canada West, November 21, 1850; received a common-school education; was in the telegraphic and railway service, 1864-82; married Helen E. Wheeler of Milwaukee, Wis., June 24, 1887; has been a partner in the Brooks Locomotive Works, Dunkirk, N. Y., since 1882.*

***

**Charles E. Dequembourg** possesses in a marked degree the qualities of self-reliance, courage, and inflexibility of purpose. Apply these characteristics mentally to the branches of activity wherein his energy has found an outlet, and it is easy to understand why he has been a successful contractor upon a large scale, and an instrument in the development of important material interests.

Mr. Hequembourg began life in the village of Dunkirk, N. Y., and received a common-school education there, in Dansville, N. Y., and in Warren, Penn. To this education he added an experience gained in the war, having been mustered, as a boy of eighteen, into the 68th regiment, company D, N. Y. N. G. After receiving an honorable discharge at the expiration of his term of enlistment, he entered the quartermaster's department of the Army of the Cumberland, where he was employed until after the close of the war. Since then he has been engaged in business in various capacities as mechanic, clerk, contractor, and civil engineer.

His first large contract was the erection, for the board of education, of the second-ward schoolhouse in the village of Dunkirk. The next year he put up the first brick schoolhouse built in the city of Titusville, Penn. In 1871 he constructed the Dunkirk waterworks. In 1873-74 he built the Hyde Park waterworks, near Chicago. In 1879 he erected, with associates, the St. James hotel at Bradford, Penn., which was the second brick building in the place, but which was so well constructed that it holds its own among the later buildings of the city.

As a natural result of his location, Mr. Hequembourg became interested in oil development. He was one of the early operators in the Bradford oil fields, and has since been concerned in oil and gas production in many other parts of the country. In 1878 he built, with others, the plant of the Bradford Gaslight & Heating Co.— the first corporation in this country to supply natural gas to a municipality for both illumination and heat. In 1880 this company, of which he was president and engineer, installed a gas pumping station of 6,000,000 cubic feet daily capacity at Rixford, Penn., to pump gas to the city of Bradford. This was at that time the only plant in the world pumping gas through a pipe-line. Later he was instrumental in carrying out the same idea upon a much larger scale. As president and engineer of the Columbus Construction Co., he undertook in 1888 the building of a natural-gas pipe-line connecting the gas fields of Indiana with the city of Chicago. In 1892 the corporation completed and turned over to the owners — the Indiana Natural-gas & Oil Co. and the Chicago Economic Fuel Gas Co. — the largest and longest natural-gas pipe-line system in the world, fully equipped with modern pumping stations and appliances ; and the plant is now in successful and profitable operation.

Mr. Hequembourg has exhibited, as a citizen and in official life, the same qualities of progressiveness and firmness of purpose that have characterized his business career. Though his political affiliations have always been Republican, he was chosen mayor of Dunkirk, a Democratic city, by a large majority over the Democratic candidate. His election was due in great part to a movement, outside of party lines, to make fitness and not politics the controlling element in municipal affairs. The application of business methods to municipal politics proved here, as elsewhere, eminently satisfactory. His administration was marked by a large increase in local patriotism, and exercised much influence upon the prosperity of the community. At the election in March, 1895, Mr. Hequembourg was re-elected mayor without opposition. The only other public office he has held is that of civil engineer of Dunkirk. He has also rendered public service to that city as president of the Commercial Association.

Mr. Hequembourg has been a member of the Masonic fraternity for many years. He is a Knight Templar and a 33d degree Mason, belonging to the body known as the Ancient Accepted Scottish Rite Masons as organized by Ill. Joseph Cerneau in 1807. Mr. Hequembourg is Commander in Chief of Dunkirk Consistory, No. 34.

*PERSONAL CHRONOLOGY — Charles Ezra Hequembourg was born at Dunkirk, N. Y., July 9, 1845 ; was educated in the common schools ; served in the United States army from 1863 to the close of the war ; married Harriet E. Thurber of St. Louis, Mo., July 31, 1872 ; was an early operator in the Pennsylvania oil fields, and a pioneer in the development of natural-gas transportation ; was elected mayor of Dunkirk in March, 1894, and again in March, 1895 ; has been engaged in business, chiefly as civil engineer and contractor, in Dunkirk since 1875.*

\* \* \*

**William M. Irish** has earned no less than three reputations, each of them enviable. The first is that of one of the most actively useful citizens of

Olean, N. Y. ; the second is that of an able manager of public institutions ; the third and most distinctive is that of a high authority in the complicated business of oil refining. To this business Mr. Irish has devoted over half of his sixty-odd years ; and both his experience and knowledge, which is as scientific as it is practical, place him among the experts whose opinions are frequently called for in the various departments of oil refining.

Mr. Irish was a Yankee boy, who began earning bread and butter at thirteen years of age. For eleven years thereafter he worked in a grocery, finally leaving that business to accept a clerkship in the New Bedford (Mass.) custom house. He retained this position through the Pierce and Buchanan administrations — 1853-61. He began his connection with the oil industry, first with the Fairhaven

*WILLIAM M. IRISH*

Oil Co., and then with the New Bedford Oil Co., holding the office of superintendent for two years in each concern. In 1865, with more experience and skill than were generally possessed by those who flocked to the oil country, Mr. Irish decided to invest his talents where the promise of return was greatest. Arriving at the oil district, he immediately became treasurer and superintendent of the Wamsutta Oil Co. in Venango county, Penn. Since that time he has occupied similar positions in several other companies, including the Octave Oil Co. at Titusville, Penn., and the Acme Oil Co., to which the former company sold out. He is now general manager of the Acme Works, which are owned by the Standard Oil Co.

Wherever he has lived Mr. Irish has been prominently identified with the best interests of the community. In his native town, in Titusville, and in Olean, he has served long and with distinction as a member or as president of school boards. In connection with the requirements of this office, as he regards the matter, he has carried on courses of study resulting in a broad culture that has been at once a satisfaction in itself and a source of power. Mr. Irish was the president of the first board of water commissioners in Olean during the construction of the city waterworks. That his acquaintance with the scientific side of municipal management is by no means narrow is proved by the fact that he has for several years been a member of the local board of health, and is now its president. Other conspicuous positions, such as that of vice president of the Olean Electric Light & Power Co. and of the Board of Trade, indicate the commercial talents possessed by Mr. Irish. Altogether it may be said that Olean is healthier, better taught, better lighted, and better watered, because of Mr. Irish's residence within its borders.

Executive ability such as that of Mr. Irish has not been allowed by state officials to go to waste. Governor Cleveland appointed him to a directorate on the board of the State Hospital for the Insane, located at Buffalo, and Governor Hill reappointed him. Mr. Irish is an attendant of the Presbyterian church. His spare time is devoted to efforts to promote the social and educational interests with which he is identified, or to study connected with these interests.

*PERSONAL CHRONOLOGY — William Mitchell Irish was born at Fairhaven, Mass., July 3, 1829; attended district schools in early youth; was clerk in a grocery, 1842–54; married Sarah Jane Dunham of Fairhaven December 11, 1851; was a custom-house clerk, 1853–61; was superintendent of oil concerns, 1861–65; was treasurer and superintendent of Wamsutta Oil Co., McClintockville, Penn., 1865–72, and of Octave Oil Co., 1872–76; has lived at Olean, N. Y., since 1880 as manager of the Acme Oil Works.*

**Charles Z. Lincoln** has done his part in making the fame of the Cattaraugus-county bar. On many occasions he has shown his fellow-lawyers the value of fundamental training in the principles of the law and of persistent research into legal history. Mr. Lincoln at present holds the important position of chairman of the New York commission of statutory revision, to which he was appointed by Governor Levi P. Morton in January, 1895. In virtue of this office he is also the confidential legal adviser of the governor. How important this position is may be seen from the fact that every bill passed by the legislature is referred to Mr. Lincoln for his opinion as to its constitutionality and its other legal aspects, and many bills have been amended, at the governor's suggestion, to meet the objections raised by Mr. Lincoln to the form or phraseology or requirements of the bill. Mr. Lincoln is also chairman of the commission to revise the code of civil procedure. As may be inferred from the facts already cited, his legal attainments are of a high order.

He is a son of Vermont, though he has lived in Cattaraugus county since his early childhood. His mother died when he was four years old, and his father when he was eight, and he was left to fight his way in the world as best he could. The story of his life resembles that of so many successful men, in recounting efforts to obtain an education under the most adverse conditions. He ultimately succeeded in taking an incomplete course at the Chamberlain Institute at Randolph, N. Y.; but his school attendance stopped at this point.

Determining to study law, Mr. Lincoln entered the office of Cary & Jewell, of Olean and Little Valley, in 1871, and three years later was admitted to the bar. In August, 1874, he opened an office in Little Valley, where he has practiced ever since. His time and advice have been freely given to the community in which he has lived, and in which he is honored. For four years he represented the town of Little Valley on the board of supervisors; twice he has been president of the village of Little Valley, and once trustee of the same; and for seven years he served as a member of the village board of education.

When the 32d senatorial district needed a sound man, an able thinker, and a hard worker to represent it in the constitutional convention that sat in this state in 1894, Mr. Lincoln was chosen. It is not too much to say that he was a force in that body of able men, and was early recognized as one of the best of the constitutional lawyers who joined in guiding the action of the body. He served on a number of very important committees, including those on apportionment, privileges and elections, and civil service.

Mr. Lincoln has a ready pen. A series of articles on "Young Men in Politics" which he wrote in 1884 proved very popular, and attracted considerable attention throughout his section of the state. He has also written much on legal and historical topics for newspapers and legal journals during the last twenty years; and in 1893 he wrote a history of the bench and bar of Cattaraugus county. At his home in Little Valley he has a fine library, particularly rich in subjects of history and law. Outside the practice of his profession he has found his chief recreation in the study of history, especially the branches that have a leaning toward the law. He is likewise a master of the philosophy of law. The education that was denied him in his youth has been won as he went along. He is a thorough student, and is remarkably well grounded in the law of the ancient Romans. His lectures and addresses on law and history involve immense research, and are in great demand.

Though so thoroughly devoted to the law, Mr. Lincoln has never neglected his social duties. He is a member of the Ancient Order of United Workmen, and of the Methodist Episcopal church.

*PERSONAL CHRONOLOGY— Charles Z. Lincoln was born at Grafton, Vt., August 5, 1848; was educated in the common schools and at Chamberlain Institute, Randolph, N. Y.; married Lusette Rumsteel of East Otto, N. Y., November 12, 1874; was a member from the 32d senatorial district of the state constitutional convention in 1894; was appointed chairman of the commission of statutory revision and governor's confidential legal adviser, by Governor Morton, January 2, 1895; was appointed chairman of the commission to revise the New York code of civil procedure June 15, 1895; has practiced law at Little Valley, N. Y., since 1874.*

* * *

**Robert H. Marvin** is a business man, a progressive citizen, a man whose name stands among the first in good causes — in short, one of the men who help generously to make the wheels go round in whatever community they live. As he has spent his whole life in Jamestown, he has the unusual good fortune of seeing about him the fruition of the efforts he has put forth during a remarkably active career.

With such preparation as could be obtained from public and private schools, a course at Hartwick

CHARLES Z. LINCOLN

Seminary, Otsego county, N. Y., and the training of a business college, Mr. Marvin began his career. He started in business life as a bookkeeper, and soon after became manager of the business of his father, the late Judge Richard P. Marvin. This position he held for nearly twenty-five years. He also became connected with the lumber business, and organized the firm of Marvin, Rulofson & Co., which still continues under his management. To give a detailed account of the business interests with which Mr. Marvin has been identified, and to recount the labors prompted by the philanthropic, patriotic, and fraternal instincts of his character, would require more space than our present limits allow. Merely brief mention can be made of the efforts that have rendered him a potent and valuable factor in the community.

The city of Jamestown has to thank Mr. Marvin's active public spirit for a number of the civic advantages that it enjoys. He was chairman of the committee that formed the charter under which the city was organized; he first set on foot the movement that resulted in free mail delivery there; he was largely instrumental in supplying the city with good water; he organized the local telephone company, and was for years its president; he has been a volunteer fireman in the Jamestown fire department, and

ROBERT N. MARVIN

chairman, vice president, and president of the State Firemen's Association. In addition to local services rendered to the Republican party as supervisor, delegate to conventions, and nominee for state senator, he served as elector on the Republican ticket in 1884

Mr. Marvin's brain has been prolific in conceiving and carrying out commercial ventures that have contributed to the prosperity of the community. The Jamestown street railway, the Chautauqua Lake railway, and other enterprises are indebted to him as promoter, incorporator, or president. He was an incorporator of the Lakewood Land & Improvement Co., whose holdings border beautiful Lake Chautauqua, and is a director of the company. He holds a

similar position in the Wyckoff Harvester, Mower & Reaper Co., in the Preston Farming Co., and in the Chautauqua County National Bank.

In the midst of these manifold business interests Mr. Marvin has found opportunity to serve his fellows in other ways as well. As chairman of the committee to raise funds for the Gustavus Adolphus Orphanage, as a member of the advisory board of the Women's Christian Association, and as advisory member of the State Charities Aid Association, he has proved himself the friend of the unfortunate. He is a trustee of the James Prendergast Library Association of Jamestown, and is a lover of books and works of art. He is one of the charter members of the Jamestown Club, and was for eighteen years its president. He is a member of Mt. Moriah lodge, F. & A. M., and of the A. O. U. W.; an honorary member of the 13th Separate Company, N. G., S. N. Y.; a member of the Chautauqua County Historical Society, and of the Sons of the Revolution. With the death of Mary A. Prendergast ended the historic family of the founder of Jamestown — James Prendergast, from whom the town was named. The property accumulated by him and his descendants has gone into permanent monuments, such as the Prendergast Library, and the beautiful stone church that adorns the city of Jamestown. Mr. Marvin was one of two executors of the Prendergast estate.

*PERSONAL CHRONOLOGY—Robert Newland Marvin was born at Jamestown, N. Y., October 14, 1845; attended public and private schools, Hartwick Seminary, and Bryant & Stratton's Business College, Buffalo; began business as bookkeeper, and later became manager of his father's business; organized the lumber business of Marvin, Rulofson & Co. in 1870, and has been manager of the same ever since; was Republican candidate for state senator in 1881, and presidential elector in 1884; married Mary Elizabeth Warner of Jamestown February 6, 1890.*

**C. D. Murray** has an interesting and significant lineage. His father, Dauphin Murray, was sheriff of Steuben county, New York, and participated in the war of 1812; while his grandfather fought at Bunker Hill and in other revolutionary battles. On the maternal side the line is equally distinguished, including General Sedgwick, governor of Jamaica, and other notable men. Mr. Murray himself has had an interesting and varied career. When he was only nineteen years old the California gold fever broke out, and the subject of our sketch joined the westward tide of emigration, and in due season reached San Francisco. It is hard at the present time to picture the scenes of those days. Men flocked to the Pacific coast from all over the country — some overland by wagon and others around the Horn — and all acquired, if not tangible riches, at least a wealth of experience. Young Murray, however, did not become a miner, but confined his attention to business pursuits. Finding no other opening, he obtained employment as a drayman, and as soon as he had saved a little money bought a dray for himself. A year later he engaged in the produce commission trade as a member of the firm of Murray & Foster. The firm carried on an extensive business, and Mr. Murray made two voyages to Australia with cargoes of lumber. Such an experience was full of interest in those early days, before the steam vessel and the cable had dispelled the romance connected with that distant land.

Mr. Murray was called East in 1855 by the death of his father, and engaged in the lumber business at Hinsdale, Cattaraugus county, for several years. The commercial depression following the panic of 1857 and especially a strike on the Erie railroad preventing the shipment of lumber, brought business reverses to Mr. Murray, and he was forced to abandon the lumber business and begin over again. He obtained a position as railway mail clerk on the Erie road, traveling between Hornellsville and Dunkirk, and employed all his spare time in the study of the law.

In 1860 he was admitted to the bar, and at once opened a law office in the town of Hinsdale, where he practiced for four years. At the end of that time he removed to Dunkirk, where he has won for himself a position at the bar and in public life that has made him a conspicuous figure in western New York.

Municipal affairs have occupied a large share of Mr. Murray's time and thought. He has served one term as mayor of Dunkirk, and has been repeatedly nominated for high offices by the Democratic party, of which he is an ardent supporter. He has been a delegate to several state conventions,

and to the national convention of 1884 that nominated Grover Cleveland for president. The district in which he lives is strongly Republican in politics, and Democratic success there is of the nature of a forlorn hope. Mr. Murray has nevertheless accepted the nomination of his party for the state assembly, and twice for representative in congress, and has greatly reduced the majority of his opponents whenever he has run. In 1870, for example, he came within three hundred votes of election from the 33d congressional district, which usually gives a Republican majority of six thousand. This fact attests Mr. Murray's popularity at home, and shows the estimate placed upon him by those who know him best.

In educational matters Mr. Murray has been an important factor in Dunkirk. As president of the board of education for seven years, he has contributed

C. D. MURRAY

more than his fair share of work and care to a task that often proves thankless. The internal improvements of the city have also received his attention; and he demonstrated his value to the city not only

as mayor but as president of the board of water
commissioners. He is president of the Merchants'
National Bank and of the Hartford Axle Co., and
vice president of the United States Radiator Co.
He is a communicant and senior warden of St. John's
Episcopal Church. A conservative business man, an

*S. FREDERICK NIXON*

earnest and upright citizen, he enjoys the esteem of
a large circle of friends, and the confidence of his
fellow-citizens.

*PERSONAL CHRONOLOGY — Charles De
Kalb Murray was born at Guilford, N. Y., May 4,
1841 ; received a common-school education ; engaged in
commerce in San Francisco, 1850–55 ; married Orpha
A. Bandfield of Hinsdale, N. Y., May 29, 1860 ;
was admitted to the bar at Buffalo in 1860 ; was
president of the board of education of Dunkirk, N. Y.,
1875–79 and 1884–86 ; was first president of the
board of water commissioners, in 1871, and mayor of
the city in 1889 ; was nominated for congress in 1870
and 1872, and for the assembly in 1884 ; has practiced law in Dunkirk since 1864.*

**S. Frederick Nixon** affords a good example
of what a young man can accomplish in politics, if
he have suitable talents, energy, and ambition. Before
Mr. Nixon was thirty years old he had made a name
in the state legislature as a political leader. He did
not owe his eminence to subserviency, moreover ;
for he stands among the most prominent
of those who insist upon uncontrolled and
independent action on the part of political
leaders.

The main facts in his career outside of
politics can be quickly narrated. He was
born in the village of Westfield, and graduated from the village academy in 1877.
Then he spent four years at Hamilton
College, Clinton, N. Y., graduating in
1881 with the degree of B. A. The next
year he passed with the Vermont Marble
Co., at Sutherland Falls, Vt. Then he
returned to his native place, and has been
engaged in business there ever since as a
member of the firm of Nixon Brothers,
manufacturers of monumental work and
building stone. In connection with his
brother he has also extensive farming and
vineyard interests in the Chautauqua grape
belt.

Like most men who have won distinction in public life, Mr. Nixon very early
showed a taste for political affairs. He
also displayed an unusual talent for leadership. Thus it happened that, when little
past his majority, he had already become
a prominent figure in local politics. Before he was twenty-four years old he was
elected trustee of the village of Westfield
— a surprising mark of confidence in the
case of one so young. Two years later, in
1886, he was elected supervisor, and has
since continued to represent the town of Westfield,
one of the richest in Chautauqua county, upon the
county board. During four terms, 1892–95, he was
chairman of the board of supervisors.

Mr. Nixon was introduced to the field of state
politics when, in 1887, he was chosen to represent
the 1st district of Chautauqua county in the state assembly. He has served altogether in six legislatures.
After his first term in 1888, his district sent him back
to Albany for the terms of 1889 and 1890. He was
elected to the legislature of 1894 to represent the
whole of Chautauqua county, the two earlier districts
having been consolidated under the apportionment
act of 1892. He was re-elected to the following legislature, and when the county was once more subdivided

under the new constitution, he was chosen as the first representative of the new 2d district. Mr. Nixon has been, from the beginning, a conspicuous figure on the Republican side of the assembly. He has served on many important committees, including those on ways and means, railroads, insurance, and general laws. In the legislature of 1896 he was chairman of the railroad committee, held the second place on the committee on ways and means, and had membership in minor committees. He was chairman of the Republican caucus committee at the organization of the assembly, and his name has been proposed more than once for the speakership. Upon the floor he is one of the ablest of the Republican leaders. Among the constructive measures for which he is responsible is the legislation under which a system of horticultural schools has been established in the state. Mr. Nixon is best known, however, for his independence. He is a leading representative of the spirit of opposition to one-man domination within his party, and as such is one of the most prominent figures in the politics of western New York.

Mr. Nixon was a member of the Chautauqua-county Republican committee for five years, and served as chairman during the presidential campaigns of 1888 and 1892.

*PERSONAL CHRONOLOGY— Samuel Frederick Nixon was born at Westfield, N. Y., December 5, 1860; received his early education at the Westfield Academy, and graduated from Hamilton College in 1881; married Myrtle Hunting Redfield of Westfield May 21, 1885; was member of the state assembly, 1888–90 and 1894–96; has been supervisor of the town of Westfield since 1886, and was chairman of the Chautauqua-county board of supervisors, 1892–94.*

**Jerome Babcock,** member of assembly from the 1st Chautauqua district, has taken a prominent part in the politics of his county for more than twenty years. He represented the town of Busti in the board of supervisors back in the '70's and again in the later '80's. He is now serving his second term in the assembly, having served ten years ago for the first time. Probably no other act of his official life has attracted so wide attention as his introduction, at the beginning of the 1896 session of the legislature, of a

resolution calling on the state comptroller for an explanation of his action in issuing bonds for the canal loan with the stipulation that both principal and interest should be paid in gold. Unlike most eastern politicians, Mr. Babcock is a firm believer in silver, and he was determined to show the courage of his convictions even though he stood alone. As the event proved, he did stand alone. He made an elaborate speech in support of his resolution, holding the attention of his colleagues and even eliciting considerable applause. No speech during the session received more notice from the press of the state. But when the vote came, Mr. Babcock was the only member recorded in the affirmative. His character is well shown by this incident. He knew that he had the unpopular side, and that he could expect no support; but he was determined to record his views,

*JEROME BABCOCK*

Mr. Babcock has known what it is to work with his hands as well as with his head. He was born in Chautauqua county somewhat more than sixty years ago, and country boys of that day were put to work about as soon as they got out of the cradle. He attended the common schools in his neighborhood, and went to work for himself as soon as he was old enough, as a farm hand. But his ambition demanded a more profitable return for his labor, and he soon betook himself to Pennsylvania, and engaged in the

CHARLES A. BALL

lumber and oil business on the Allegheny river. This was his occupation for ten years. Having become a man of family, he felt the need of a business that would be more settled, and would take him away from home less, and he accordingly bought a farm in Sugar Grove, Warren county, Penn. This was his home, and a farmer's life his calling, for the next eight years. While at Sugar Grove he was president of the school board for four years, and also served for two years as president of the Union Agricultural Society. He was at heart a New Yorker all this time, notwithstanding his absence from the state of almost a quarter century, and he availed himself of a good opportunity to sell his farm and return to his native town of Busti. Here he devoted himself

successively to the hotel business, to mercantile affairs, and to farming; and here his political career really began. As his acquaintanceship in Chautauqua county extended, he naturally became more and more interested in Jamestown and its people; and he finally established himself there in 1889. He is now recognized as one of the most prominent citizens of the place, as is shown by the fact that he was elected an alderman of Jamestown in the spring of 1895.

*PERSONAL CHRONOLOGY— Jerome Babcock was born at Busti, N. Y., July 21, 1843; spent his early manhood in Pennsylvania, in the lumber and oil business and in farming; married Celia O. Smith of Sugar Grove, Penn., January 1, 1864; was supervisor from Busti, 1874-75 and 1887-88; was elected a member of the assembly in 1885 and in 1895; was elected alderman of Jamestown, N. Y., in March, 1895; has been in business in Jamestown since 1889.*

\* \* \*

**Charles A. Ball** has been a very influential man in state politics for a number of years. Those who have an intimate knowledge of the inside workings of political affairs well appreciate this, though Mr. Ball is not among the men whose names are most frequently heard in connection with such matters. This is partly because he is a modest man, preferring to keep his personality in the background and let only his work show. He has a wide acquaintance with men and an accurate knowledge of affairs in both the state and the nation, and he has come to be regarded as an indispensable assistant about headquarters in both state and presidential campaigns.

It was Senator Fassett who discovered the abilities of Mr. Ball, and made him known to the political managers of the state. When Mr. Fassett first went to the senate, Mr. Ball held a committee clerkship in the legislature. Mr. Fassett made him his private secretary. As the party leader in the senate, Mr. Fassett naturally had close relations with politicians in all parts of the state. He found in Mr. Ball not merely a competent clerical employee, but a trustworthy and reliable friend as well. His services were so valuable that when Mr. Fassett became secretary of the Republican national committee, in 1888, he chose Mr. Ball as his assistant. Thus the latter obtained opportunities for extending his acquaintance and his sphere of usefulness, which he improved so well that in the next national campaign he was again called upon to serve as assistant secretary, though the secretary this time was not his friend Mr. Fassett, but Louis E. McComas of Maryland. Mr. Ball has retained, meanwhile, his connection with the state senate. He was index clerk for two years, and during the greater part of the last six years he has been assistant clerk under John S. Kenyon. He has never accepted a nomination for an elective office, though he has twice been the unanimous choice of the Allegany-county delegates for state senator.

Mr. Ball was born on a farm in Allegany county about forty-six years ago. He attended the country and village schools, the Almond Academy, and the Dickinson Seminary at Williamsport, Penn. He is a self-made man, having educated himself and supported himself since his thirteenth year. He intended to go to Heidelberg, Germany, to complete his education ; but his father's death, which occurred when Mr. Ball was within six weeks of graduation at Dickinson Seminary with the degree of A. B., caused a change in this arrangement. Mr. Ball abandoned his plans for completing his education, and took charge of his father's business, which was that of a carriage manufacturer at Wellsville, N. Y. After some years he gave up this occupation, and became interested in oil production. He now has important holdings in the Allegany field.

Mr. Ball is a broad-minded, public-spirited citizen. He has interested himself especially in the matter of preserving the fish, game, and forests of the state, and has rendered important service in this work.

*PERSONAL   CHRONOLOGY—*
*Charles Alley Ball was born at Almond, Allegany county, N. Y., December 19, 1850; was educated in Almond Academy and in Dickinson Seminary, Williamsport, Penn.; married Clara M. Pooler of Wellsville, N. Y., October 1, 1873; was index clerk of the senate, 1888–89, and assistant clerk, 1890–91 and 1894–97; was assistant secretary of the Republican national committee in 1888 and 1892; has lived at Wellsville, N. Y., since 1874.*

•••

**Frank L. Bartlett,** president of the Exchange National Bank of Olean, comes of sturdy English stock, his grandfather having removed to this country and settled at Belfast, Allegany county, when the locality was almost an unbroken wilderness.

Mr. Bartlett's early education was limited to the public schools of his native village, supplemented by a course at Friendship Academy. His business career began at the age of twenty-one, when he became a clerk in the First National Bank of Cuba, N. Y. Here his efficiency early won the confidence and esteem of his employers, and soon opened to him a broader business field. Within a year he entered the Exchange National Bank of Olean, where his ability and untiring energy have gained him rapid promotion. Attaining successively the positions of bookkeeper, teller, cashier, and president, he thoroughly mastered the duties and details of each in turn. Mr. Bartlett possesses a combination of

FRANK L. BARTLETT

qualities which would insure success in any business calling he might seek, but which seem peculiarly fitted for the profession of his choice. To his good business judgment, his keen perception of men and events, his untiring industry and devotion to the interests in his charge, is due, more than to anything else, the uninterrupted success and increasing prosperity of the Exchange National Bank of Olean. Mr. Bartlett is the largest stockholder in the institution.

WILLIAM BROADHEAD

These qualities have also brought their due reward in other enterprises in which he has become interested. Among these may be mentioned the Eastern Oil Co. of Buffalo, of which he is a director and the treasurer.

Mr. Bartlett has always been interested in public affairs and especially such projects and enterprises as tended to enhance the prosperity and well-being of his locality. He was largely instrumental in the organization of the local Board of Trade, whose efforts have secured the location in Olean of many important manufacturing industries. He has ever been zealous in the support of every project for the improvement of his city in a material, moral, or aesthetic way.

Socially Mr. Bartlett is noted for his good-fellowship and uniform courtesy ; and he and his charming wife dispense hospitality and charity with a generous hand.

Mr. Bartlett is affiliated with the Odd Fellows and the Masons, being a member of St. John's Commandery, K. T., of Olean, and Ismailia Temple of Buffalo. He attends the Presbyterian church.

*PERSONAL CHRONOLOGY — Frank Le Verne Bartlett was born at Belfast, Allegany county, N. Y., December 25, 1858 ; entered the banking business in 1879 ; moved to Olean, N. Y., in 1880 ; became cashier of the Exchange National Bank, Olean, in 1885 ; married Fannie E. England of Tidioute, Penn., July 15, 1886 ; has been president of the Exchange National Bank, Olean, since January 1, 1895.*

* * *

**William Broadhead,** the founder of the worsted manufacturing industry in Jamestown, N. Y., is a Yorkshireman by birth. At the age of ten he was apprenticed to learn the weaver's trade in his native town of Thornton. Before and during his apprenticeship he attended the common and evening schools at Thornton, but his education has been mainly that of the factory and of practical business life. On completing his apprenticeship at the loom he went to work in his father's blacksmith shop, where he remained until he became of age.

He was twenty-four years old when he emigrated to the United States, going to Busti, Chautauqua county, N. Y., where his uncle, the Rev. John Broadhead, was then living. He secured work in the shop of Safford Eddy at Jamestown, and within two years had married. About two years after his marriage he formed a partnership with his father-in-law, Adam B. Cobb, for the manufacture of scythe snaths and grain cradles. The business gradually extended to include other farm implements, and when it was divided, after ten years, Mr. Broadhead continued alone the manufacture of axes, pitchforks, and edge tools.

As his capital accumulated, and the need of providing business for his sons developed, Mr. Broadhead opened a merchant-tailoring establishment, taking his eldest son, and later a younger son, into partnership. This business was continued for fourteen years.

Mr. Broadhead had reached his fifty-third year before he revisited his old home in England. The trip marked an epoch, not only in his own business career, but also in the development of Jamestown. The dimensions to which worsted manufacturing in Yorkshire had grown since he learned the weaver's trade on a hand loom, impressed him with the idea that the business might profitably be undertaken in Jamestown. For the purpose of carrying out this idea he formed a partnership with Joseph Turner of England and William Hall of Jamestown. The necessary machinery was imported, a factory was built, and by January 1, 1874, the firm was making worsted dress goods. The enterprise was successful from the start, but owing to some disagreements Mr. Broadhead and Mr. Hall were compelled to dissolve partnership. Mr. Broadhead withdrew, and in 1875 began the erection of a new mill, in which his sons became partners. Three years after it was finished, the merchant-tailoring business was sold, and the firm gave its whole attention to worsted manufacture. A second mill, and afterward a third and fourth, became necessary to accommodate the growing business. The present large factory at Jamestown employs some seven hundred hands. Though he has passed his seventy-seventh year, Mr. Broadhead continues the active superintendence of his property.

Mr. Broadhead has many investments besides his manufacturing plant. He has built and now owns no fewer than twenty-five business places on Main street in Jamestown. His firm built, and are now operating, the Jamestown electric street railroad. He has been a director of the First National Bank of Jamestown for eighteen years, and vice president for ten years.

His extensive manufacturing interests have naturally made him an ardent protectionist and a Republican, but he has never held public office. In his native town he belonged to the Wesleyan Methodist church, and on his removal to Jamestown he joined the Methodist Episcopal church, as most like the Wesleyan. He was a strong abolitionist, however, and when his church endorsed slavery, before the war, he left it and formed a Wesleyan society. This organization was given up some years later, and Mr. Broadhead then became a member of the First Congregational Church. He is a man of

exemplary habits, and is especially proud of the fact that never in his life has he used tobacco or liquor.

*PERSONAL CHRONOLOGY—* William Broadhead *was born at Thornton, Yorkshire, England, February 17, 1819; emigrated to the United States in January, 1843; married Lucy Cobb of Jamestown, N. Y., October 29, 1845; was a manufacturer of edge tools in Jamestown, 1847–61; conducted a merchant-tailoring establishment in Jamestown, 1864–78; built, with others, the Jamestown Worsted Mills in 1874; built worsted mills himself in Jamestown in 1876, and has conducted the same since.*

\*\*\*

**Jason D. Case,** one of Franklinville's most prominent and public spirited citizens, has been all

*JASON D. CASE*

his life a resident of Cattaraugus county. Born in the town of Lyndon, and educated in the district schools of that town and in Rushford Academy, he settled in Franklinville at the age of twenty-six, immediately after his marriage, and has made that town his home ever since.

His first knowledge of business was gained in aiding his father, an extensive dealer in farm produce, when but sixteen years of age. For two years he traveled about the country, buying butter, cheese, eggs, wool, etc., and at eighteen assumed charge of his father's large dairy farm. Four years later he was engaged as superintendent of an oil company near Pleasantville, Penn., which he managed for three years to the entire satisfaction of the company; and at the expiration of that time he succeeded in disposing of the property most advantageously.

In December, 1872, Mr. Case was asked to take the management of a private bank then organizing in Franklinville. He undertook the work, and soon made it evident that he had found his true vocation. When, in 1877, this private enterprise was succeeded by the First National Bank of Franklinville, the second institution of its kind in Cattaraugus county, Mr. Case became its cashier and active manager; and he has held that responsible position until the present time. He has devoted to the work keen business foresight and a special aptitude for financial affairs; and the remarkable success of the institution ever since its organization is due to his indefatigable efforts more than to any other one cause. This bank easily holds the first place among similar institutions in its vicinity, and is to-day one of the solid financial establishments of western New York. When the Bank of Ellicottville was started, a year after the First National Bank of Franklinville, Mr. Case became one of its directors, and he has held the position ever since. In addition to this, he has been president of the Citizens' Bank of Arcade from its organization in 1883; and he makes frequent visits there, in order to maintain an active supervision of all the details of its management. It will thus be seen that Mr. Case is a prominent figure in banking circles in the neighborhood in which he resides, and it is not surprising to learn that he is a large owner of bank stock in that vicinity. He is also a director of the People's State Bank of Mazo Manie, Wis.

Although Mr. Case has devoted his best energies to banking, he has been interested in the production of oil ever since his early experience as superintendent of the company in Pennsylvania; and more recently he has been instrumental in forming the Manufacturers' Gas Co. of Bradford, Penn., of which he is a director. In connection with W. H. Odell and A. K. Barrow he has operated some Pennsylvania oil property very successfully. He was influential in forming the canning company of Franklinville, and is a director of the new Conklin Wagon Co. at Olean.

Franklinville possesses one of the most beautiful cemeteries in western New York, and this is due largely to Mr. Case's efforts — first, in promoting the organization of the Cemetery Association in 1878, and ever since in the active interest he has taken in its management, as trustee and treasurer.

Mr. Case has been for many years a prominent member of the Free and Accepted Masons.

*PERSONAL CHRONOLOGY—Jason D. Case was born at Lyndon, N. Y., October 5, 1847; was educated in the district schools and in Rushford (N. Y.) Academy; began business in 1863 as assistant to his father, an extensive produce dealer; accepted a position as superintendent of an oil company in Pennsylvania, in 1869; became manager of a private bank in Franklinville, N. Y., in 1874; married Helen C. Morgan of Cuba, N. Y., January 27, 1874; has been cashier and manager of the First National Bank of Franklinville since 1877, and president of the Citizens' Bank of Arcade, N. Y., since 1884.*

•••

**Josephus B. Clark** presents a career interesting in various ways. An active business man in Jamestown, N. Y., for fifty-five years, the war-time president of the board of trustees of the village, a member of the board of education for twenty-one consecutive years, and a trustee of the First Baptist Church for forty-four years — such a man must have led a life of great usefulness, and must have commanded the respect and confidence of his townspeople in an unusual degree.

Mr. Clark is a representative of that sturdy New England stock from which so much of the best blood of western New York has come. He was born in Worcester county, Mass., in President Monroe's first term. He attended the public schools of his native village, and was afterwards sent to school at Salem, Mass., and at Winchester, N. H., thus obtaining a good education in the common branches of learning. His studies were interrupted, however, at an early age, when he went West, as New Englanders of that time regarded western New York. He arrived in Chautauqua county in 1830, and obtained a little more schooling before taking up the serious business of life.

Mr. Clark settled in Jamestown in 1835, and has lived there since with the exception of about two years in his early manhood, which were spent in New Orleans, Cincinnati, and Pittsburg. When only twenty-two years old, he engaged in the foundry and machine-shop business in Jamestown. He had two partners at first, and there were frequent changes in the firm during its early years; but he retained his interest throughout, and since 1857 he has conducted the business alone.

Mr. Clark was early recognized as a public-spirited citizen who had the interests of his town at heart. Two years before the war his townspeople elected him a member of the board of trustees — Jamestown was a village then — and he held this office continuously for ten years. Throughout the war he served as president of the board. The duties of the position at such a crisis were far more important than in the ordinary times of peace. Jamestown, as one of the principal places in Chautauqua county, was naturally a center for enlistment and for the collection of the heavy taxes made necessary by the war. Moreover, when the nation was calling for so great sacrifices, unusual prudence and conservatism were necessary in the management of local affairs. Jamestown justly looks upon Mr. Clark as one of the men who laid the foundations for the present prosperity of the city.

Mr. Clark takes a characteristic New England interest in the welfare of the public schools. In 1870 he was elected a member of the board of education, and served in this office for twenty-one consecutive years: for fifteen years he was president of the board.

From early life he has been an attendant of the Baptist church. He was chosen a trustee of the First Baptist Church of Jamestown in 1852, and still holds that position. He is also a member of the Chautauqua County Historical Society, and is one of its executive committee.

*PERSONAL CHRONOLOGY—Josephus H. Clark was born at Petersham, Mass., December 1, 1819; was educated in the public schools; moved to western New York in 1839; married Jane E. Marsh of Panama, N. Y., July 14, 1851; was trustee of Jamestown, N. Y., 1859–69, and member of the board of education, 1870–91; has conducted a foundry in Jamestown since 1841.*

* * *

**Asa Stone Couch** has devoted his life to the study, teaching, and practice of medicine. He ranks among the foremost expounders and defenders of homeopathy in the United States. In medical conventions, in the press, and before legislative committees, he has vigorously upheld the tenets of the "new school," and has demanded for its practitioners, against fierce opposition, the public rights

and opportunities accorded to the "old school." The warfare between allopathy and homeopathy has lost much of the intensity that characterized it when the renowned Hahnemann first enunciated his famous principles of medicine. The new school has demonstrated its right and its power to exist, and has

*JOSEPHUS H. CLARK*

obtained a recognized standing before the law. It may be said without exaggeration that this condition of things has been brought about by Dr. Couch as much as by any one man. His voluminous writings on this burning question in medical science have given him fame and reputation wherever the controversy between the old school and the new has been carried on. In addition to his controversial works he has written numerous books and pamphlets on the doctrines and methods of homeopathy, besides occasional papers and articles on subjects connected with the education and qualifications of physicians.

Dr. Couch has an ancestry noted in the fields of medicine and education, and he inherited in an unusual degree those qualities of mind that mark the patient investigator and man of science. After an academic and a classical training in the Westfield Academy and the Chamberlain Institute, he took up the study of medicine under the supervision of two eminent physicians of Vermont. He attended

ASA STONE COUCH

courses of study at both allopathic and homeopathic institutions, and graduated from the Homeopathic Medical College of Pennsylvania in 1855. He immediately entered upon the practice of his profession in association with Professor Gardner of Philadelphia. In the same year his *alma mater* appointed him demonstrator of anatomy and assistant surgeon.

With this rich experience added to his theoretical studies, the young doctor concluded to devote his entire time to practice. He returned to his native county in New York, and opened an office in Fredonia, where he has practiced for forty years. The esteem in which he is held in his profession and in the community in which he lives, is best attested by

the positions of trust and honor to which he has frequently been summoned. He was for several years vice president of the Homeopathic Medical Society of the State of New York, and for one year its president. He was one of the founders of the Chautauqua County Homeopathic Medical Society and of the Homeopathic Society of Western New York.

In 1877 he was appointed professor of special pathology and diagnosis in the Hahnemann College and Hospital in Chicago, where his lectures were noted for depth of thought, broad knowledge, and painstaking research. His professional brethren showed their estimation of his ability by recommending him to the regents of the University of the State of New York for the honorary degree of Doctor of Medicine, which was promptly conferred upon him, in 1879; and in 1891 the Homeopathic Society of the state nominated him for the state board of homeopathic medical examiners, to which he was duly elected by the state regents. Dr. Couch was chosen president at the first meeting of the board, and was appointed examiner in pathology and diagnosis.

In 1894 by Governor Flower, and again in 1895 by Governor Morton, Dr. Couch was commissioned one of the managers of the Collins Farm Homeopathic Hospital for the Insane. He is very much interested in the work of this institution, and means to make it, so far as he can, second to no similar establishment in the world in perfection of detail for hospital purposes.

As a popular lecturer Dr. Couch enjoys a wide reputation, presenting complicated subjects in a simple, intelligible way. He has lectured before the Buffalo Society of Natural Sciences, and he delivered the opening address before the World's International Homeopathic Congress held at Atlantic City in 1891. Dr. Couch's whole life has been one of unceasing activity in the practical and theoretical branches of his profession; and he is to-day, in consequence, justly regarded as a complete, all round physician and scientific man.

*PERSONAL CHRONOLOGY — Asa Stone Couch was born at Westfield, N. Y., October 22, 1833; was educated t Westfield Academy and Chamberlain Institute; graduated in medicine from the Homeopathic Medical College, Philadelphia, in*

1855; married Martha L. Sherman of Westfield April 2, 1857, and Mrs. Ellen S. Barrett of Dunkirk, N. Y., February 6, 1878; was appointed a member of the state board of homeopathic medical examiners in 1891; has practiced medicine in Fredonia, N. Y., since 1856.

...

**Albert G. Dow** of Randolph, N. Y., was born of Puritan parents at Plainfield, Cheshire county, N. H., August 16, 1808. He was the eighth of the ten children of Captain Solomon and Phoebe Dow, who removed from Hartland, Vermont, to Genesee county in 1816.

Albert Dow's father died in Pembroke, N. Y., in 1822, and soon after Mr. Dow, in his fifteenth year, began the battle of life on his own account, and commenced a business career that has continued uninterruptedly for over seventy years. He lived a year in Batavia, where he learned the shoemaker's trade; next went to Panama for a short time; and then settled in Silver Creek, Chautauqua county, in 1827, which continued to be his home for nearly twenty years. Here he conducted a shoe business until January, 1840, when he entered the hardware business, having George D. Farnham for a copartner. This partnership continued about a year, and on its dissolution Mr. Dow opened a hardware store at Sinclairville. In the fall of 1842 he resumed the business at Silver Creek in partnership with Horatio N. Farnham, and this continued until his removal to Randolph in 1845. In 1843 he had opened a dry-goods store at Randolph, his nephew, James Nutting, being associated with him. This store they conducted as copartners until 1851. Upon his removal to Randolph he opened there a hardware store that he continued until 1863; his son Warren was his partner during the last three years.

In 1860 he established a private bank in Randolph, which was the first institution of the kind in that section; and from that time he has been prominently identified with the banking interests of Cattaraugus county. From 1875 to 1880, the last five years of Mr. Dow's banking in Randolph, his son, Charles M. Dow, now of Jamestown, N. Y., was an active partner. In 1881 Mr. Dow organized the Salamanca National Bank at Salamanca. He was the principal stockholder and president of the institution until 1890, when he resigned the presidency, but continued to be a director.

Since then he has not been actively engaged in business, but has devoted himself to the care of his investments and the enjoyment of a well-earned rest.

All through his extended business career he has found it a pleasure and deemed it a duty to interest himself in public affairs, and he has discharged faithfully and well the duties of various public offices. He was a Democrat up to the time of the Civil War. Like so many others he changed his party affiliations at the outbreak of the war, and since 1861 he has been a Republican and an active and unswerving member of that party. He was early elected to local offices in Silver Creek, and acted as justice of the peace for eight years in Randolph. He served as supervisor of that town for ten years. In 1863 and

*ALBERT G. DOW*

1864 he served as a member of the legislature from the 2d district of Cattaraugus county, and in 1872 he was elected state senator, representing what was then the 32d senatorial district. In all these positions he displayed the good sense and faithful devotion to duty that characterized him in private affairs.

Mr. Dow has always been actively interested in religious work and in educational movements. When a young man he united with the Presbyterian church in Silver Creek, and upon his removal to Randolph

GRANT DUKE

he joined the Congregational church of that village, of which he has ever since been a member, and in which he has often served in official capacities.

In 1850 he was active in the organization of the Randolph Academy (now Chamberlain Institute), which has been a power in the intellectual and moral development of western New York ever since its foundation. He was one of the original trustees of this school, and has held that office uninterruptedly up to the present time.

Mr. Dow's strong personality, sound judgment, purity of character, honesty of purpose, and conscientiousness in the discharge of duty, has won the respect and admiration of a large circle of

acquaintances and the friendship of all classes in the community in which he lives.

*PERSONAL CHRONOLOGY— Albert Gallatin Dow was born at Plainfield, N. H., August 10, 1808; carried on a shoe business in Silver Creek, N. Y., 1827–40, and a hardware business, 1840–45; married Freelove Mason of Batavia, N. Y., October 4, 1829, and Lydia A. Mason April 24, 1850; engaged in the hardware business in Randolph, N. Y., 1845–53; established a private bank in Randolph in 1860; was member of assembly, 1863–64, and state senator in 1873; was president of the Salamanca (N. Y.) National Bank, 1881–90.*

★★★

**Grant Duke** is one of the most prominent figures among the younger generation in his native town of Wellsville, N. Y. So large a majority of our promising young men follow Horace Greeley's advice and "go West," or turn their backs on the country to seek the more extended field of activity offered by some large city, that it is a pleasure to read the story of a life like Mr. Duke's. It is a fortunate thing for the prosperity of the nation that there are cases, like this one, where young men of ability and enterprise are content to devote their talents to the development of the smaller towns.

After attending the common schools of Wellsville, Mr. Duke spent two years at the Pennsylvania Military Academy at Chester, Penn., and one year at Alfred University, and finally took a course at a business college in Rochester. He was thus well equipped as regards both general culture and practical commercial training when he began the business of lumbering and oil producing with his father. The name of Duke is well known in southwestern New York and northwestern Pennsylvania, for in that region William Duke, the father of our subject, and four of his brothers, had been engaged all their lives in these industries. The town of Duke Center, Penn., was named for them, and practically owned and controlled by them for many years. At present Mr. Duke and his two brothers are associated with their father, and their interests throughout Allegany county are varied and extensive.

Mr. Duke is an ardent Republican, and is devoted heart and soul to the interests of his party. He is full of enthusiasm for all plans looking toward the improvement of the village of Wellsville and the county of Allegany. When the Allegany County Firemen's Association was organized he was made the first president : and he is president of the Wellsville hose company, which is named in his honor. His popularity in his native place was abundantly proved by his election, in 1894, as president of the village, although his opponent was deemed one of the strongest men in the town. He was re-elected in 1895, and his fellow-townsmen have every reason to be satisfied with his successful administration of the affairs of the village ; for he has displayed great executive ability, and has made one of the best presidents the village ever had.

Mr. Duke has traveled extensively in the United States, and has thus expanded his sympathies and interests, and gained that knowledge of men and affairs which is so desirable, and which the man who has lived all his days in a small community sometimes fails to acquire. His genial good-fellowship is amply evidenced by the number of clubs and fraternal organizations to which he belongs. He is a member of the Hornellsville Club, the Acacia Club of Buffalo, the Genesee Club of Wellsville, DeMolay Commandery, No. 22, of Hornellsville, the Damascus Temple of Rochester, the Knights of St. John and Malta, and other organizations. He is an Episcopalian.

*PERSONAL CHRONOLOGY—Grant Duke was born at Wellsville, N. Y., June 1, 1864 ; was educated at the Pennsylvania Military Academy and at Alfred University ; married Anna B. Taylor of Wellsville March 24, 1884 ; was president of the village of Wellsville, 1894–95 ; has been engaged in business in Wellsville and Allegany county, as lumber merchant and oil producer, since 1884.*

* * *

**John E. Dusenbury** has expended the efforts of a vigorous and varied business life upon interests centered in Portville, N. Y., where he was born and has always resided. He had only the education afforded by district schools and a course at Binghamton Academy, but he was endowed with a generous equipment of common sense and sagacity. He has recognized each opportunity that came to him, and has made the most of it, until he now controls extensive and varied concerns.

Mr. Dusenbury's father, in partnership with William F. Wheeler, carried on for many years a country store in connection with a large lumber business, and young Dusenbury, on attaining his majority, became proprietor of this store. Two years later, on the death of his father, Mr. Dusenbury, together with his brothers, succeeded to a partnership in the firm, which then became known as Wm. F. Wheeler & Co. Later on, the firm added the manufacture of leather to its previous undertakings, and finally the production of oil. In these successive developments Mr. Dusenbury has contributed a large share of enterprise and executive ability.

The qualities that make a man successful in manufacturing pursuits or in general business are likewise of great value to a bank official, and it is not strange that Mr. Dusenbury was a prime mover in the estab-

*JOHN E. DUSENBURY*

lishment of the First National Bank of Olean, twenty odd years ago, and that he has been actively connected with the institution ever since. Upon the death of his father's old partner, William F. Wheeler, in

1893, Mr. Dusenbury succeeded him as president of the institution.

Mr. Dusenbury has no liking for the scramble in which those desirous of the emoluments of office too often engage ; but he has been willing to serve the public when called upon, as is proved by his ten

*MILTON M. FENNER*

years' incumbency of the office of town supervisor. He has also remained aloof, as a rule, from all societies or fellowships, which many men find necessary to satisfy the social instincts of their nature. He is, however, an attendant of the Presbyterian church.

One diversion in which Mr. Dusenbury finds relaxation from the perplexities of a complicated business is that of horse raising and training. With a particular liking for the fine points of well-bred horse flesh, he has given some attention to horse breeding as an avocation, and now owns an establishment of this kind.

PERSONAL CHRONOLOGY— *John E. Dusenbury was born at Portville, N. Y., June 10, 1836 ; was educated in common schools and at*

*Binghamton (N. Y.) Academy ; commenced business as a country merchant in Portville in 1858 ; engaged in lumbering in the same place in 1860, and later in the manufacture of leather and in the oil business ; married Hattie A. Foster of Chili, N. Y., in February, 1861, and Delle V. Mather of Southwick, Mass., in July, 1869 ; established, with others, the First National Bank of Olean, N. Y., in 1874, and has been president of the same since 1893.*

Milton M. Fenner is a farmer's boy who has risen to success in medicine, business, and politics. He was born at South Stockton, Chautauqua county, and until he was eighteen years old divided his time between farming and such schooling as he could get in the district schools. Then he set himself in earnest to obtain an education. He went to Ellington Academy at Ellington, N. Y., and then to Allegheny College at Meadville, Penn. Finally he entered the Eclectic Medical Institute at Cincinnati, and graduated therefrom in 1860, at the age of twenty-three, with the degree of M. D. Throughout his school career he paid his way by teaching.

For about a year after graduation Dr. Fenner practiced medicine in Michigan, first in Goodrich and then in Flint. Then he decided to enter the army. He enlisted, in 1861, in the 8th Michigan volunteer infantry, served as hospital steward, and was afterward promoted successively to the rank of 2d and 1st lieutenant. In 1863 he was appointed assistant surgeon in the United States navy. Finally he retired from the service, in 1864, to devote himself to private practice, and returned for this purpose to his native county, settling at Jamestown. There he remained until 1869, when he moved to Fredonia, N. Y., which has since been his home. He conducted a general practice until 1872, and still carries on an office practice. In 1872 he began the manufacture of proprietary medicines, in which he has met with great success.

Dr. Fenner has held various official positions in the line of his profession. He was consulting surgeon to the Chautauqua County Insane Asylum from 1866 to 1869. During the same years he was physician to the poor for Jamestown, and from 1869 to 1872 he held a similar office in Fredonia. He was United States examining surgeon from 1870 to

1872, and in 1871 and 1872 was president of the Eclectic Medical Society of the State of New York.

This summary of Dr. Fenner's professional career would alone show him to be a busy man; but he has found time to do many other things. He is secretary and treasurer of the Dunkirk & Fredonia Railroad Co., and has been its manager since 1880. The company maintains an electric street-railroad between Fredonia and the neighboring city of Dunkirk, and carries on incidentally the business of commercial electric lighting and steam heating. Dr. Fenner is also engaged in grape and miscellaneous farming. Each branch of his business — manufacturing, street-car management with its accessories, printing (the Globe Printing House), and farming — is organized by itself; but the general supervision of the whole falls upon him. He is a director of the Hubbard Company, the Fredonia National Bank, and the Merchants' National Bank of Dunkirk; is a member of the local board of the State Normal School at Fredonia; and was formerly the president of the Life and Reserve Association of Buffalo.

Dr. Fenner is most widely known through his political connections. He is an earnest Republican, has been prominent as a leader in local politics, and has held various offices. He served his town as supervisor — its highest office — two terms, in 1878 and 1879. In 1880 his district sent him to the legislature as its assemblyman, and the following year he was re-elected. In 1890 and 1891 he was deputy collector of customs of the port of New York.

*PERSONAL CHRONOLOGY—Milton Marion Fenner was born at South Stockton, N. Y., July 28, 1847; was educated in the public schools, Ellington (N. Y.) Academy, and Allegheny College, Meadville, Penn.; graduated from the Eclectic Medical Institute at Cincinnati in 1869; married Georgianna L. Grandin of Jamestown, N. Y., June 5, 1866, and Florence E. Boudeson of Jamestown March 28, 1883; served in the Union army and navy, 1861-64; practiced medicine in Michigan, 1859-61, and in Jamestown, 1864-69; was member of assembly, 1881-82, and deputy collector of customs at the port of New York, 1890-91; has practiced medicine in Fredonia, N. Y., since 1869, and carried on the manufacture of proprietary medicines there since 1872.*

**Benjamin Flagler** is an excellent type of the class of citizens to whose progressive spirit and untiring energy is due in large measure the material development of the Empire State. This is the class that possesses the ability to organize, and the skill and means to carry out successfully, large operations in the commercial and mechanical fields of industry. In this day of gigantic undertakings, requiring for their execution large numbers of men and vast expenditures of money, there is in every community an urgent demand for men of executive ability and high integrity.

Such a man is Mr. Flagler in the community in which he lives. He was educated in the district school and in the Lockport Union School. With this training added to his natural mental endowments, he began his business career. This, however, was

*BENJAMIN FLAGLER*

destined to be arrested soon by a call to higher duty. The great Civil War interposed between him and his personal interests and commercial prospects. It found him a young man in prosperous condition, married, settled in business, looking forward to the steady-going course of commercial and domestic life. The war found many other young men similarly circumstanced. Some heeded the call of their country, and quickly volunteered their services; others turned a deaf ear to the summons of the nation. Mr. Flagler proved himself a true patriot. He enlisted in the first regiment raised in Niagara county, and served in the model Army of the Potomac until honorably discharged for disability.

Mr. Flagler was for many years connected with the customs service, holding the offices of inspector, deputy collector, and collector at Suspension Bridge, N. Y., during a period of twenty-three years. While in these positions he established a reputation for courtesy, accuracy, and fidelity that commended him to all classes having business at the custom-house.

Upon his retirement from public service Mr. Flagler directed his efforts to financial enterprises. He became president of the Suspension Bridge Bank on its organization in 1886, and has continued at the head of that institution since then. Another field of activity which he entered about the same time was that of street railways; and he was elected president of the first surface road operated in Suspension Bridge. The development of electric power from Niagara Falls, so long a matter of speculation, has now become a demonstrated fact. Among the men deserving of credit and gratitude for this grand illustration of man's dominion over nature, is Mr. Flagler, who was one of the incorporators of the Niagara Falls Power Co., and who has been its vice president since 1891.

Outside business relations Mr. Flagler maintains a worthy and useful connection with various organizations of a social, religious, and philanthropic character. He is a Mason of the highest rank, and Past Grand Master of the order in New York state. For many years he was a trustee and the treasurer of De Veaux College. His political affiliations are with the Republicans, and he has been honored by his party through Governor Morton, of whose staff he is a member, being chief of ordnance with the rank of brigadier general. In politics as in business, Mr. Flagler carries into practice the sound principles of individual opinion and strict integrity.

*PERSONAL CHRONOLOGY— Benjamin Flagler was born at Lockport, N. Y., December 10, 1844; was educated in public schools; married Martha J. McKnight of Newlane, N. Y., November 9, 1859; served in the Union army, 1861-64; settled in Niagara Falls, N. Y., in 1864; was in the customs service at Suspension Bridge, N. Y., as inspector,* deputy collector, and collector, 1864-86; has been president of Suspension Bridge Bank since 1886, and vice president of Niagara Falls Power Co. since 1891.

***

**William B. Henderson** of Randolph, N. Y., has won advancement and honor by holding fast to one good profession for a lifetime. At sixteen years of age he entered Fredonia Academy, then the leading institution of its kind in western New York. At eighteen he was teaching. By dint of attending schools when he had the opportunity and teaching between times to earn the means therefor, he was able, at the age of twenty, to graduate from the State Normal College at Albany.

After receiving his diploma Mr. Henderson went to Randolph, N. Y., where for two years more he taught school to defray expenses while studying law. This preparation resulted in his admission to the bar at Buffalo in 1852. Since then Mr. Henderson has practiced his profession continuously at Randolph with but one change in the name of his firm. His first partnership was with J. E. Weeden, upon whose retirement in 1859 Mr. Henderson associated himself with Alexander Wentworth; and to the present day the firm name is Henderson & Wentworth. As he says himself, "Neither politics nor pleasure nor other business has ever interfered with the practice of my profession."

Professional devotion, however, has not absorbed the whole individuality of Mr. Henderson. He has been ready to contribute his talents to public service, if the office came without any seeking on his part. That he has not been more in public life is due to the fact that he has always belonged to the Democratic party, which has not been uppermost in western New York. When only twenty-three years of age Mr. Henderson was nominated for the office of treasurer of Cattaraugus county. He was appointed county judge by Governor Tilden to fill a vacancy, in 1875. At the next election he was his party's choice for the same office, and succeeded in reducing the Republican majority in the county from three thousand to about three hundred. Shortly afterward Governor Tilden again placed him in office, this time as justice of the Supreme Court for the 8th judicial district. That he was popular in his own community was shown by his selection as president of the centennial celebration of his county, which occurred at Olean July 4, 1876. Three years later he was nominated as state senator; and close upon this honor came that of representing his state as alternate delegate at large in the Democratic national convention that nominated Hancock and English at Cincinnati in 1880. Governor Robinson had been elected delegate at large, and Mr. Henderson was elected his alternate, and at the governor's request Mr. Henderson attended in his stead.

Mr. Henderson holds a directorate in the First National Bank of Salamanca, in the People's Bank of East Randolph, and in the State Bank of Randolph, of which he was for ten years president of the board of directors. Successive preferments, political or professional, have attested the high esteem in which both his ability and his integrity are regarded at home and in official circles.

Two very important trusts have been assigned to Mr. Henderson and faithfully discharged by him. For many years he was the legal adviser of Benjamin Chamberlain, the founder of Chamberlain Institute, and was thus intimately acquainted with that gentleman's philanthropic and educational ideas. Since 1876 Mr. Henderson has been president of the board of trustees of Chamberlain Institute, and has carried out the beneficent projects of the founder with distinguished success. For a period almost equally long he has been president of the board of trustees of the Western New York Society for the Protection of Homeless and Dependent Children. To this worthy charity he has given his most earnest thought and labors. Under his guidance a "Home" has been built which now cares for about one hundred and forty children, and in which they are educated and trained until homes are found for them.

*PERSONAL CHRONOLOGY—*
*William H. Henderson was born at Tully, N. Y., December 4, 1828; was educated at Fredonia Academy and at the State Normal College at Albany, N. Y.; was nominated for treasurer of Cattaraugus county in 1851; was appointed county judge of Cattaraugus county in 1875, and justice of the Supreme Court for the 8th judicial district in 1876; was delegate to the Democratic national convention in 1880; married Anna M. Morris of Ellicottville, N. Y., June 3, 1858, and Emily A. Thompson of Randolph, N. Y., July 9, 1885; has practiced law in Randolph since 1852.*

**Frank W. Higgins** has a large part in the business and political life of southwestern New York, as his father had before him. As the owner of three stores in Olean, in addition to various mining and

lumber interests in the West, and as representative of the 50th senate district in the legislature, Mr. Higgins gives in his daily life evidence of great energy and unusual power of concentration and organization.

His education began in the district school of his native town, and was continued in the seminary at

*WILLIAM H. HENDERSON*

Pike, Wyoming county, and in the Riverview Military Academy at Poughkeepsie. At the age of eighteen he began business life in Chicago as the western sales-agent of an eastern refinery of lubricating oils. He continued this business for only a short time, going from Chicago to Denver, Col., where he spent parts of the years 1875 and 1876. Returning again to the middle west, in November, 1876, he bought an interest in the mercantile firm of Wood, Thayer & Co. at Stanton, Mich. The following year he purchased the interests of his partners, and continued the business in his own name.

Mr. Higgins's father, O. T. Higgins, was at this time extensively engaged in mercantile business in Olean and other towns of western New York and northern Pennsylvania. The firm of Higgins, Blodgett & Co., in which the elder Higgins was senior partner, had nine stores scattered through this territory, chiefly at Olean. In February, 1879, Mr. Higgins sold his interests in Michigan, and bought a partnership in this firm; and after five years he

*FRANK H. HIGGINS*

bought the Olean stores from his partners, and he now owns three stores in Olean. His talent for organization is such that he has been able for the last eight years to devote most of his time to pine and iron lands in Michigan, Wisconsin, and Minnesota, where he has large holdings.

Mr. Higgins took an early interest in politics. He was elected a delegate to the Republican national convention at Chicago in 1888. In 1893 he was nominated and elected state senator from what was then the 32d district, consisting of Allegany, Cattaraugus, and Chautauqua counties. His service was distinguished by strict integrity, close attention to legislative business, and honest independence. Thus he early acquired strong influence, and before the close of his term was recognized as among the leaders in the upper house at Albany. His constituents showed their appreciation of his services by giving him a renomination without opposition, his district, the 50th, consisting under the new constitution of Cattaraugus and Chautauqua counties. The Democrats, Prohibitionists, and Populists of his district made no nominations against him, and his re-election lacked little of being unanimous. He is chairman of the important committee on taxation and retrenchment, to which the famous Raines excise bill was referred in February, 1896.

Mr. Higgins attends the Episcopal church. He has been Eminent Commander of St. John's Commandery, No. 24, of Olean, and is trustee of the Randolph Home for Friendless Children and of the Chautauqua Assembly. He has always taken deep interest in the growth and improvement of the city where he has his home, and of the surrounding locality.

*PERSONAL CHRONOLOGY— Frank Wayland Higgins was born at Rushford, N. Y., August 18, 1856; was educated in the public schools and at Riverview Military Academy, Poughkeepsie, N. Y.; was in business in Chicago and in Denver, 1874–76; was in business at Stanton, Mich., 1876–79; married Kate C. Noble of Sparta, Wis., June 5, 1878; was a delegate to the Republican national convention in 1888; was elected state senator in 1894 and re-elected in 1895; has conducted a general mercantile business in Olean since 1879.*

\*\*\*

**John William Humphrey, Jr.,** has led an active, energetic life, full of enterprise and usefulness. He was born in New England, in the thriving town of New Britain, Conn., less than half a century ago. At an early age he was sent to boarding school at Saybrook, Conn., a delightful old village situated on Long Island sound at the mouth of the Connecticut river. His parents having moved to Chicago, his elementary education was completed in the public schools of the western metropolis. Then he entered the Northwestern Seminary at Evanston, Ill., to prepare for Beloit College, where he finished his scholastic studies.

At the age of twenty-one Mr. Humphrey launched out into business, acquiring a half interest in an oil well at Pithole, Penn. He soon extended his operations in the oil district, and became interested in valuable properties near Titusville. The allied business of coal mining also engaged his attention, and this he carried on with a partner under the firm name of Humphrey & Co. He next devoted a period of two years to manufacturing at Erie, Penn., and retired from the coal and oil business. About this time railroading became attractive to him, and for some months he was in the service of the New York, Pennsylvania & Ohio railroad at Meadville, Penn.

In 1877 Mr. Humphrey chose a new and entirely different field for his activities and talents, becoming the proprietor of the Tuna Valley House at Bradford, Penn. This was the beginning of his career as an owner and a manager of hotels. He soon purchased the St. James hotel, which he carried on successfully for several years, when he disposed of it, removed to Jamestown, N. Y., and acquired possession of the hotel that now bears his name — the Humphrey House. The success of this hotel is proof of Mr. Humphrey's ability. Few kinds of business require so many and varied talents as hotel-keeping. It demands brains, executive ability, and velvety tact. The hotel has assumed in modern life an importance undreamed of in the days when travel was limited to short distances. Hotels are the homes of a large class of people. To meet the wishes of the traveling public and to provide for their wants, is a task that taxes a man's resources at all points. Mr. Humphrey has set a high standard for the conduct of his hotel, and has maintained that standard under all circumstances, however trying.

In addition to his hotel business Mr. Humphrey, since his father's death in October, 1893, has carried on the manufacture of carriages and implements, a business that his father had built up to large proportions.

Political affairs have always interested Mr. Humphrey, and while he has not sought office, he has been an active Republican in both state and national politics. He is a Mason of the 32d degree and a Knight Templar.

*PERSONAL CHRONOLOGY— John William Humphrey, Jr., was born at New Britain, Conn., December 5, 1846; was educated in various preparatory schools and at Beloit College, Beloit, Wis.;* *was an operator in oil and coal in Pennsylvania, 1868–72; married Mary E. Irwin of Erie, Penn., October 41, 1872; was engaged in the hotel business at Bradford, Penn., 1877–82; purchased the Humphrey House at Jamestown, N. Y., March 1, 1883, and has conducted the same since.*

* * *

**J. R. Jewell** is prominent in legal circles in Cattaraugus county, where he has practiced his profession with distinguished success for nearly thirty years.

After an education received at Rushford and Arcade academies, both well-known institutions of southwestern New York, in 1865 he entered the law office of Cary & Bolles in Olean as a student. Two years later he was admitted to the bar. The firm with which he had studied was one of the most

*JOHN WILLIAM HUMPHREY, JR.*

successful in the county, and the fact that Mr. Jewell was immediately admitted to partnership shows that he had already displayed marked ability. The new firm of Cary, Bolles & Jewell established itself in

Little Valley, which had just been made the county seat, and remained there for the next six years.

It was during his first year in Little Valley, and when he was little more than twenty-five years old, that Mr. Jewell achieved his first brilliant success, and established his reputation as a lawyer of splendid

*J. R. JEWELL*

promise. Throughout Cattaraugus county men of middle age and over still remember the "celebrated Burdick case," as it was called. The man was indicted for the murder of a negro, and was convicted. The public sentiment against him was so strong that the judge before whom the case was tried committed an error in his charge to the jury, and on this ground Mr. Jewell obtained for his client a second trial. Here, too, the prisoner was convicted, but his indefatigable young lawyer succeeded in having the sentence commuted by Governor Hoffman to imprisonment. Mr. Jewell conducted the entire case without the aid of other counsel; and the legal learning, tact, and untiring perseverance that he displayed at once

brought him into prominence, and secured for him the beginnings of the lucrative practice that he has since enjoyed. Although he has not confined himself to criminal cases, it is worthy of note that during his professional life he has defended twelve men who were on trial for their lives, and not one of them has been executed.

In 1883, when Judge Bolles retired from the firm, Mr. Jewell returned to Olean, and was associated with Mr. Cary, and later with his brother, M. B. Jewell. Since 1893 he has practiced alone.

Mr. Jewell is a stanch adherent of the Democratic party, and received a nomination for district attorney in 1873. His county was strongly Republican, and he was of course defeated; but he ran about four hundred votes ahead of the party ticket. This is the only political office for which he has ever been a candidate; but in August, 1894, he was appointed by President Cleveland United States agent for the Indians of New York state, and this position he still fills.

A very notable achievement in the practical application of the law of real property has recently been accomplished by Mr. Jewell. Congress having authorized the secretary of the interior to negotiate with a land company for the purchase of whatever title, if any, the company had in the lands of the Seneca nation of Indians in New York state, Mr. Jewell was called upon to investigate the title of the lands in question. The merits of the case were exceedingly difficult to ascertain, as the controversy went back to the year 1624, when the state of Massachusetts claimed the territory. Grants were made of certain rights by Massachusetts and by New York before the constitution of the United States was adopted, and after that conveyances were made under the grants from the two states. The determination of the title at this time, therefore, was a most difficult legal problem; and the proper solution of the problem by Mr. Jewell, to the satisfaction of the United States government and of eminent lawyers interested in the case, must be regarded as striking evidence of his legal ability. He presented an exhaustive report on the subject, which was approved by the United States department of justice and adopted by it; and this report will be a permanent record in the archives of the government, and will doubtless have a most important influence, in case the question shall ever arise again.

Outside of his profession Mr. Jewell finds interest and recreation in farming. He owns a small farm not far from Olean, to the management of which he devotes considerable attention, and from which he derives much pleasure. Mr. Jewell is not a member of any church, but his sympathies are with the Methodists.

*PERSONAL CHRONOLOGY — Joseph R. Jewell was born at Machias, N. Y., April 15, 1842; was educated in the district schools and in Rushford and Arcade academies; was admitted to the bar at Buffalo in 1867; married Julia E. Lamper of Conewango, N. Y., September 5, 1870; practiced law in Little Valley, N. Y., 1867-74; was nominated for district attorney of Cattaraugus county in 1874; was appointed United States agent for the New York Indians August 20, 1894; has practiced law in Olean since 1874.*

...

**W. H. Mandeville**, the son of John Drake Mandeville and Susan Mandeville, is an excellent type of the men who have made our country what it is to-day — one of the world's greatest nations; for, as is well known, it is not the few phenomenal geniuses who raise a people to the foremost rank among the families of the earth, but the solid rank and file of intelligent, educated, energetic, and public-spirited citizens, who are always ready to help forward any project for good in the community in which they live.

Mr. Mandeville has been all his life most prominently connected with the insurance business, that great feature of our modern life which, as has been well said, is more than almost any other typical of our American civilization. Engaging first in this business when a young man, with his father, in Belmont, N. Y., he moved soon afterward to Olean, which has ever since been his home. In a few years he became prominent in insurance circles, and was elected president of the Cattaraugus-county board of underwriters; this position he has held for the past thirty years.

Mr. Mandeville has not confined himself, however, to insurance interests. His active spirit has caused him to identify himself with the business of the country in those special enterprises that characterize

our age. He was one of the incorporators of the Lima Natural Gas Co. of Lima, O., and of the Ohio Oil Co.; and for twenty years he has been actively engaged in the production of petroleum.

We are sometimes tempted to think that one of the faults of our bustling, go-ahead, nineteenth-century life is that each man thinks only of himself, and not always even of what is best for himself in the broadest and truest sense. In this respect Mr. Mandeville certainly has not failed, for his interest in all public enterprises for the good of the community is well known. Everyone nowadays realizes the importance of education and the general diffusion of knowledge, and the two most potent factors to this end are the public school and the public library. The man who helps forward either of these two institutions is doing

W. H. MANDEVILLE

a great work for posterity, and Mr. Mandeville, in his connection with the library at Olean, has shown a most intelligent appreciation of this fact. He was one of the original members of the Olean Library, and for many years its president. Since its reorganization as the Forman Library he has been one of its managers, and his well-directed efforts have had much to do with the success of the institution.

*PERSONAL CHRONOLOGY— William Howard Mandeville was born at Millport, Chemung*

GEORGE W. PATTERSON

*county, N. Y., August 15, 1841; was educated in the public schools of New York city and of Belmont, N. Y., and at Rushford Academy; entered the insurance business in 1865, in partnership with his father, at Belmont, N. Y.; married Helen L. Eastman of Nashua, N. H., August 22, 1872; has been engaged in the insurance business in Olean, N. Y., since 1865.*

* * *

**George W. Patterson** will be held in honorable remembrance by the people of Westfield long after he has passed away. His greatest service to the village is the founding of the Patterson Library, a work in which he is still engaged. His sister, Hannah W. Patterson, left for this purpose a legacy of $100,000, the application of which was entrusted

to his care. Had the library never been undertaken, however, Mr. Patterson would still be long remembered for his services in the perfecting of land titles. The Chautauqua land office of the Holland Land Company was located at Westfield, and Mr. Patterson's father was its agent. Since 1879 Mr. Patterson has himself been the owner, legatee, and grantee of the remaining property of the Holland and Chautauqua land companies for Chautauqua county. The books, records, maps, and papers of the office have been in his possession, and have been kept with scrupulous care. In consequence, he has often been called on for evidence of the discharge of mortgages, and for quitclaim deeds to perfect titles, when land-office deeds have not been recorded in the county clerks' offices. Many Chautauqua-county land owners have been saved great trouble and expense by the care and system with which Mr. Patterson has preserved the important papers that have come under his charge.

Mr. Patterson was born on a farm in Livingston county, N. Y. His father determined to give him a liberal education, and he was fitted for college at the Temple Hill Academy, Geneseo, the Westfield Academy, and the Genesee Wesleyan Seminary at Lima. At the age of eighteen he entered Dartmouth College, where he graduated in 1848 with the degree of A. B., and from which he received his A. M. three years later. For the purpose of completing his education, and not with any view to practicing, he entered a law office in Buffalo, and studied about two years. His father had moved to Westfield with his family in 1841, and here, ten years later, our subject entered business life by becoming a member of the firm of Waters & Patterson, manufacturers of edge tools, shovels, forks, and hoes. He retired from this business in 1854, and moved to Corning, where he became cashier of the Geo. Washington Bank. After four years he became president of this institution. The bank failed in the great financial panic of 1873–74; but Mr. Patterson was fully discharged of all claims by creditors of the bank. He then, in 1876, returned to Westfield, where his later years have been devoted to the benevolent works described above, to his personal interests, and to the executorship of four estates averaging over $300,000 each.

Mr. Patterson's connection with public affairs has been limited to the towns in which he has lived. He was a member and president of the board of education of Corning from 1867 to 1876, and a village trustee one term. His election to the latter office was significant of the respect in which he was held. Though a Republican, he received a large Democratic vote, and was chosen acting president of the village by his colleagues, all of whom were Democrats. He was also treasurer of the Hope Cemetery Association of Corning from 1859 to 1876. He drew the preliminary plans for the first waterworks of Corning and for the building of the Corning Free Academy. He also made the plans for the Westfield waterworks, and is a member of the board of water commissioners, having served as president thereof since 1888.

Mr. Patterson was a member of the Amphictyon Association of the Genesee Wesleyan Seminary, and of the Zeta chapter of the Psi Upsilon and the Phi Chi Delta fraternities of Dartmouth College. He was a vestryman in the Episcopal church at Corning, and fills the same office at Westfield. He has frequently contributed articles to newspapers on topics of interest, and has collected with a view to publication genealogical *data* of more than fifteen thousand persons, descendants of his own and his wife's ancestors. Mr. Patterson's father was lieutenant governor of the state in 1848–50, and his son is a professor in the University of Michigan at Ann Arbor. Four generations have borne the name George Washington Patterson.

*PERSONAL CHRONOLOGY—George Washington Patterson was born at Leicester, N. Y., February 25, 1826; was educated at various preparatory schools (Temple Hill Academy, Westfield Academy, and Genesee Wesleyan Seminary) and at Dartmouth College, graduating therefrom in 1848; studied law in Buffalo, 1849–50; engaged in the manufacture of edge tools at Westfield, N. Y., 1851–54; was cashier of the Geo. Washington Bank at Corning, N. Y., 1854–58, and president, 1858–75; married Frances De Etta Todd of Toddville, N. Y., September 17, 1861; has lived in Westfield since 1876; has been owner, legatee, and grantee of the Holland and Chautauqua land companies since 1859.*

**Jesse Peterson** has long been a conspicuous figure in the business and political life of western New York. He removed from his native town of Belfast, N. Y., to Lockport in 1858, and that city has ever since been his home and the scene of his business enterprises. After a somewhat limited early education, which extensive travel in his own country and in Europe and Africa has amply supplemented, Mr. Peterson at the age of eighteen embarked upon the sterner activities of life. He engaged first in the business of a contractor, and for five years devoted himself to this work. During this time, notwithstanding his youth, he carried out several important works, such as the tunnel for the Hydraulic Company of Lockport, and the main portion of the waterworks of the city of Toledo, Ohio.

*JESSE PETERSON*

Mr. Peterson next turned his attention to manufacturing, and in this field, which has ever since claimed his attention, his greatest success has been attained. His first venture in this new sphere of activity was made as half owner of the Penfield Block Co. of Lockport, N. Y. While connected with this concern he built up and extended the business until it became the largest of its kind in the world. This early achievement is characteristic of Mr. Peterson's whole career, since he has always been able to outstrip competitors in any industry to which he has turned his attention.

While occupied with the affairs of the Penfield Block Co., Mr. Peterson's attention was drawn to a field just beginning to attract the notice of capitalists — the manufacture of wood pulp. In this he perceived a fine opening for his business enterprise, and he established a plant accordingly in Lockport. Since 1883 he has been proprietor of the Cascade Wood Pulp Mills. A further development of this industry is found in the manufacture of wares from the hardened, or indurated fiber of the wool. In 1885 Mr. Peterson became president of the Lockport Indurated Fiber Co., which has since been consolidated into the Indurated Fiber Co. of New Jersey, with a capital stock of $750,000. It is the largest establishment of its kind in the world.

Mr. Peterson has never been ambitious for public office, but he stands high in the esteem of his party, and was honored by a place on the Democratic electoral ticket in 1888, when President Cleveland was a candidate for re-election.

Mr. Peterson has not failed, in the midst of a busy career, to broaden his knowledge and liberalize his mind by extensive travel in many parts of the world; indeed, this has been his chief recreation and one great interest outside of business. He has visited nearly every city of any importance in Europe, and has extended his travels into the less frequented regions of northern Africa, exploring the coast as far east as Tunis and spending considerable time in the Great Desert. But he has not committed the fault of which many an American is guilty — that of neglecting the places of interest in his own land and devoting his attention solely to exploring the old world. His extensive travels in the United States have familiarized him with the wonderful natural beauties of the country, as well as with the great cities, whose phenomenal growth and enterprising spirit are full of interest to a man of Mr. Peterson's progressive character. Gifted by nature with a fine voice and a love of music, Mr. Peterson has given considerable recreative attention to musical societies.

Mr. Peterson is a fine specimen of physical manhood, being six feet and two inches tall and of proportionate build and weight. He has reached his present position of prosperity and influence through a happy combination of sound judgment and sagacity with that venturesome spirit which, in this age of sharp competition, has become essential to great success.

*PERSONAL CHRONOLOGY — Jesse Peterson was born at Belfast, Allegany county, N. Y., October 1, 1850; was educated in Lockport (N. Y.) Union School; married Arabella A. Brown of Lockport January 29, 1874; was half owner of the Penfield Block Co. of Lockport, 1875–85; has been engaged in the manufacture of wood pulp and indurated fiber in Lockport since 1884.*

\*\*\*

**Jerome Preston** is one of the men to whose energy, determination, and business acumen Jamestown, N. Y., owes its growth and prosperity. He is the kind of man that is of great value to any community, alive to all its interests, and prepared at all times to shoulder his full responsibility as a citizen. The moral welfare of the city as well as its material advancement has found an ever energetic supporter in Mr. Preston. In whatever direction his duties lay, he brought the full force of his strong nature to bear in their discharge. Conscious of his own rectitude, he has proceeded on a straight line, turning neither to the right nor to the left, intent only on fulfilling his obligations as a man and a citizen.

Mr. Preston is a Pennsylvanian by birth, but moved to Chautauqua county, New York, early in life. When twenty years old he formed a partnership with V. C. Clark under the firm name of Clark & Preston, and opened a general country store in the Chautauqua-county village of Busti. This connection continued for four years, until 1859, when, desiring a larger field for his operations, he moved to Jamestown. There he has since resided, an active force in the business, political, social, and religious circles of that city. His first venture there was of a rather ambitious nature, for, with DeForest Weld as a partner, he opened one of the largest dry-goods stores in the town. Constantly alive to all opportunities for widening his sphere of activity, and having unlimited faith in the future of the village, Mr. Preston was soon engaged in various branches of trade. Among his copartnerships were those of Preston, Harrington & Co and Kent, Preston & Co., firms that will readily be recalled by all the older residents of Chautauqua county.

Jamestown was near enough to the oil fields to feel the influence of the early excitement there, and in 1862 Mr. Preston, in connection with Lewis Andrews, built the first oil refinery of which the city boasted. For several years thereafter this firm continued to refine oil, Mr. Preston at the same time retaining a large interest in the dry-goods and clothing business. For many years Jamestown has been noted for its woolen mills, and for the past twenty-eight years Mr. Preston has been identified with that important industry. Throughout this long period he has been one of the managers of the Jamestown Woolen Mills, which have been conducted during most of this time under the firm name of Allen, Preston & Co.

Mr. Preston early began to take a lively interest in things political, and when only twenty-one years old he was elected town clerk of the town of Busti. Later he served as a trustee of the village of Jamestown, and was also a member of the board of education. For two years he represented the town of Ellicott, in which Jamestown is located, on the board of supervisors of Chautauqua county. In all these positions he was faithful to the trust reposed in him, and guarded carefully the affairs of the people he represented. In 1871 he was called to higher honors and responsibilities, being elected a member of the assembly from the 2d Chautauqua district. This was a reform legislature, and among its members who afterward became famous the country over were Samuel J. Tilden and David B. Hill. In many respects this legislature failed to command the respect of the people, but Mr. Preston's course was such as to win the praise of his constituents. One of the local papers said of him after the legislature adjourned:

"Mr. Preston has taken a straightforward, conscientious course at Albany, honorable both to himself and to the district. He has gained the respect of his fellow members, and accomplished much to retrieve the dilapidated reputation of the district and county on account of former venality and corruption. Mr. Preston would go to Albany again with a wide acquaintance and with something of a state reputation, not only for honesty but for ability and strict attention to his legislative duties."

A tribute equally warm and deserved appeared in the New York *Times*, contributed by a Queens-county member of the same assembly. Mr. Preston thus retired from office with a record that has often been held up since as an example for other ambitious men.

For almost the whole period of his active life Mr. Preston has been a communicant of the First Baptist Church of Jamestown. In behalf of this society

in particular and the cause of Christianity in general, he has been an active worker. He believes that church membership means something more than church attendance and a yearly contribution, and he has always acted up to that belief. For over thirty years he was clerk and treasurer of the society men-

*JEROME PRESTON*

tioned, retiring from those offices in December, 1895. As a mark of appreciation, he was unanimously re-elected to the offices from which he resigned, pending the election of his successor. He has also been a force in Sunday-school work, and for a third of a century has been superintendent of the school connected with the First Baptist Church. He was the first president of the first Young Men's Christian Association formed in Jamestown, and has been a director of the present association since its organization.

*PERSONAL CHRONOLOGY—Jerome Preston was born at Farmington, Penn., January 28, 1834; attended common and select schools and the Jamestown (N. Y.) Academy; married Hannah Broadhead of*

*Busti, N. Y., June 4, 1856; conducted a general store in Busti, 1854–59; was elected member of assembly from the 2d Chautauqua district in 1871; has been engaged in mercantile and manufacturing pursuits (dry goods, oil refining, Jamestown Woolen Mills, etc.) in Jamestown, N. Y., since 1859.*

*EDGAR PIERPONT PUTNAM*

**Edgar Pierpont Putnam** is one of the men to whom the nation owes a lasting debt of gratitude. With a patriot's impulse he sprang to his country's defense in the hour of its peril, and followed the flag from the outbreak of rebellion until the last gun of the enemy was spiked; he faced rebel bullets in repeated battles, and was twice wounded; and when armed resistance was quelled, he returned to peaceful industry as unpretentiously as many another unsung hero of the Civil War.

Though only seventeen years old, young Putnam was among the foremost to respond to Lincoln's first call for troops, enlisting as a private in the 9th New York cavalry. While other boys of his age were at school or taking their first lessons in business, he was in the army in Sheridan's cavalry, learning the hard lessons of war, in camp, on the march, and in the field. For four long years he served his country under the stern discipline of arms, mustered out among the last, as he had enlisted among the first. Mr. Putnam's career as a soldier was distinguished and meritorious. Enrolled as a private, he won, by his excellent bearing and services, successive promotions to the rank of corporal, sergeant, 1st lieutenant, captain, and brevet major; and all this before he was twenty-one years of age. He was noticed by federal authorities for his gallantry, and congress voted him a medal of honor for " distinguished conduct in action." This flattering mark of approval was bestowed upon comparatively few, and only in recognition of exceptional merit. Major Putnam saw hard fighting, and carries the scars of two wounds received upon the battlefield.

In the year following the close of the war Major Putnam was appointed United States deputy surveyor, and went to Minnesota, where he remained in this branch of federal service nine years. He then returned to his native county to enter private business as a book and drug dealer. He soon received the appointment of postmaster of Jamestown, N. Y.

In 1888 he was elected clerk of Chautauqua county, and served in that capacity three years. Major Putnam has not sought the preferment which a grateful government has been glad to bestow upon those who made heroic sacrifices to save it, and which would have been his for the asking. He has been content to accept offices that came to him as a free tender on the part of his fellow-citizens. He has been active in promoting the interests of the party under whose leadership the principles for which he fought were established. He has been repeatedly, and is now, chairman of the Republican committee of his county, and is valued as a wise and patriotic counselor.

For the past few years Major Putnam has given his attention to private enterprises, such as a directorate in the Chautauqua County National Bank. He is an esteemed member of various military organizations, from the most general to those numbering only the pick and flower of brave veterans, including the Grand Army of the Republic, the Union Veteran

Legion, the Loyal Legion, and the Medal of Honor Legion. He is also a Mason and a Knight Templar.

*PERSONAL CHRONOLOGY— Edgar Pierpont Putnam was born at Stockton, Chautauqua county, N. Y., May 4, 1844; was educated in common schools; enlisted as a private in the 9th New York cavalry in September, 1861, and served until the close of the war; was United States deputy surveyor in Minnesota, 1866-75; married Eppie Mace of Jamestown, N. Y., February 2, 1878; was clerk of Chautauqua county, 1889-91; has lived in Jamestown since 1875.*

...

**William Richmond** has made a record as a successful business man and trustworthy public official. A great part of his best thought and effort has been expended in the performance of duties of a municipal character. The city of Lockport, where he resided for over twenty years, repeatedly honored him with executive and administrative offices. He served that community as alderman four years, water commissioner three years, trustee of the board of education six years, and mayor of the city one year. In all these positions of trust and responsibility Mr. Richmond displayed thorough knowledge, business methods, and fidelity — attributes much too rare in the annals of city government. A sound practical judgment has guided him through difficulties that would have proved a stumbling-block to most men, while his tried integrity has stamped him as a man upon whom the people can rely in all emergencies.

Though possessing the true traits of an American citizen, Mr. Richmond is not a native of the United States, having been born in England, where his childhood was passed, and where all his schooling was obtained. He attended a private school in Worcestershire till he was fifteen years of age, when he was brought to this country by his father. His uncle was already established in business in Lockport, N. Y., and at his request Mr. Richmond took up his residence with him in 1867. Mr. Richmond soon displayed business capacity of a high order, together with an affable disposition, both combining to gain for him warm friends and numerous admirers. Such a man finds it hard to keep out of politics for any length of time. Popularity eventually brings to its possessor nominations for political office. Mr. Richmond proved no

exception, and for fourteen years he served the city in the different offices mentioned.

Having filled so acceptably many local trusts, he soon became one of the party leaders in western New York, and his time and counsel have been freely bestowed in every important campaign of recent years. In recognition of his prominent standing as a business man, a public official, and a Democrat, he was appointed by President Cleveland collector of customs for the district of Niagara, and assumed the duties of his first federal office March 4, 1893. In this position he has given the same care and thought to the public business that characterized the performance of his duties in local offices.

Meantime Mr. Richmond has been engaged in the business to which he succeeded on the death of his uncle in 1873. As a business man he has

WILLIAM RICHMOND

shown himself prudent and conservative, and by wise management has earned for himself distinct financial success and an excellent reputation in commercial circles.

In social and fraternal walks of life Mr. Richmond is likewise prominent. He is a member of Niagara Lodge, No. 375, F. & A. M., Lockport, and of Lockport Council, Royal Arcanum. He is a communicant of the Protestant Episcopal church. In all his relations to society, to the state, and to

*WALTER L. SESSIONS*

the church, he has proved himself a man of genial nature, public spirit, and philanthropic impulses.

*PERSONAL CHRONOLOGY— William Richmond was born at Milton, Worcestershire, England, October 6, 1837; was educated at a private school in England; came to the United States in 1864; married Mary McGill of Lockport, N. Y., October 12, 1870; was alderman in Lockport, 1881-83 and 1889-91, mayor of Lockport, 1883-84, water commissioner, 1884-87, and trustee of the board of education, 1888-89 and 1891-95; has been collector of customs at Niagara Falls since March 4, 1895.*

•••

**Walter L. Sessions** is a leading representative of one of the most famous families in southwestern New York. For more than forty years he has been among the foremost in the politics of Chautauqua county. Always a strong Republican, he has served his party, his state, and his country repeatedly, holding positions which are a guarantee of his great force of character and of the high esteem in which he is held by his fellow-men. Away back in the '50's he was elected a member of the assembly, and held the office for two years. During his second year he was chairman of the committee on ways and means, which is the most important committee of the house. This position made him the leader of the majority, and put him in direct line for the speakership, had he gone back for another term.

Just at the close of the decade, the year Lincoln was elected President, the name of Mr. Sessions is found in the list of members of the state senate. Another gap of five years, and he is again found in the senate and again leader of the majority as chairman of the finance committee, the most important in the upper house, as the committee on ways and means is of the lower house. Most men are content to obtain this leadership in the legislature after many years of unbroken service, and such experience is usually deemed necessary to familiarize a man with the fine points of parliamentary practice requisite to successful guidance of the controlling party. Mr. Sessions, it will be observed, obtained leadership in both the assembly and the senate after having served in each only one term. Moreover, his two terms in the senate were not consecutive.

Reference to the *Congressional Directory* will show the name of Walter L. Sessions among the members of the 42d congress, which met in the third year of Grant's first administration. Again his name appears as a member of the 43d congress, elected in the exciting Grant-Greeley campaign — the most interesting, perhaps, in the history of the Republican party. There were famous men in those two congresses. James G. Blaine was speaker of both, and James A. Garfield was a leader on the floor. The New York delegation included such men as Henry W. Slocum, Samuel S. Cox, Fernando Wood, Clarkson N. Potter, John H. Ketcham, William A. Wheeler, Ellis H. Roberts, and Thomas C. Platt. Important measures were before congress, and the sessions were often exciting. The "salary grab" bill, raising the compensation of members of congress fifty per cent and giving them $5,000 for back pay, is a case in point. Mr. Sessions voted against this measure, and returned the money to the treasury. Another noteworthy bill was that abolishing mileage for members of congress, which the house passed and the senate allowed to drop. Mr. Sessions voted for this bill. Reconstruction questions had not yet passed out of congressional notice; and the greenback question, which has been handed down to present times, was just beginning to demand attention. It is interesting to note that a bill providing for the cancellation of greenbacks and substitution therefor of notes payable in gold two years after issue, was lost in the house of the 43d congress by a vote of 79 to 160, with Mr. Sessions recorded in the negative. The most far-reaching legislation of this period, however, was the famous currency law of 1873, containing the clause that is regarded in some quarters as having surreptitiously demonetized silver.

Ten years after his retirement from the 43d congress, Mr. Sessions took his seat in the 49th congress. This was the year in which Grover Cleveland first became President.

Mr. Sessions is a New Englander by birth, his father having moved from Brandon, Vt., to an unimproved farm in Clymer, Chautauqua county, in 1835. Mr. Sessions went to the common schools and to the Westfield Academy. He took up his present residence in Panama in 1846, so that his entire manhood has been spent there. He was admitted to the bar in 1849, and began practice in Panama immediately. His only partnership, which was formed in 1886 and continued six years, was with John Woodward, now justice of the Supreme Court. Mr. Sessions has served his county as school commissioner and supervisor. He was a member of the board of General Managers of the New York state exhibit at the World's Columbian Exposition at Chicago. Aside from his law practice, Mr. Sessions has been extensively engaged in the tanning and currier business and in lumbering.

*PERSONAL  CHRONOLOGY—*
*Walter Loomis Sessions was born at Brandon, Rutland county, Vt., was educated in the common schools and in Westfield (N. Y.) Academy; married Mary R. Terry of Clymer, N. Y., in 1848; was admitted to*

*the bar in 1849; was member of assembly, 1853–54, state senator, 1860–61 and 1866–67; member of congress, 1871–75 and 1885–87; has lived in Panama, Chautauqua county, since 1846.*

***

**Hiram Smith** is a splendid type of the American citizen. His grandfather was one of the pioneers of western New York, having settled in Chautauqua county in 1810. His father helped clear the forests and break land for farms where now are populous communities. Hiram was the eldest of fourteen children, seven boys and seven girls. He received his education in the district school and Fredonia Academy. His first business experience was obtained as clerk in his father's establishment at Smith's Mills. In 1839 his father started a branch store at Great Valley, in Cattaraugus county, and sent Hiram there

*HIRAM SMITH*

to take charge of it. The country had not then fully emerged from the great panic of 1837, and it was very difficult to realize money from produce, business having sunk in a great degree to its primitive basis

of exchange of commodities. Hiram soon had a
large amount of timber to the credit of the house,
and in 1840 these logs were run to the mills and
rafted to Cincinnati. In all these transactions the
young man displayed so much business ability that
in 1843 his father made him his partner, under the
firm name of Rodney B. Smith & Co. For eighteen
years they conducted an extensive and a successful
general merchandise business.

The outbreak of the Civil War found Mr. Smith
in the prime of his vigorous manhood. The nation's
call met a patriotic response on his part. He enlisted
in 1861, and served till the close of the war, retiring
with the rank of major. Mr. Smith was connected
with the quartermaster general's department, and
had the responsibility of accounts aggregating many
millions of dollars; but so accurate and honest
was his dealing with the government that he was one
of the comparatively few officers who were able,
when mustered out of service, to accept the generous
offer of the government of three months' extra pay
on presentation of certificates of nonindebtedness.

After the close of the war Mr. Smith moved to St.
Louis, where he engaged in mercantile business.
The climate there proved detrimental to the health
of his family, and he returned to New York state in
1867, settling in Jamestown, where he has since
resided. For the past quarter of a century he has
been engaged there in the insurance business, and
though now well advanced in years, he is as active
and energetic as many men in middle life.

Mr. Smith has taken an active interest in politics,
and served two terms in the New York legislature
before the war. He was for several years town clerk
of Hanover, N. Y., and filled one term of six years
as supervisor of the same place. In 1884 and again
in 1890 he was the Democratic nominee for congress
from the 34th district, and received the united support of his party. As a citizen and neighbor Mr.
Smith is regarded with high honor in Jamestown,
for his upright life, strict attention to business, and
just dealings with all men.

PERSONAL CHRONOLOGY—Hiram Smith
was born at Hanover, N. Y., October 25, 1819; was
educated in the district school and Fredonia Academy;
engaged in general mercantile business, 1836–61; was
elected to the state legislature in 1859, and re-elected in
1860; served in the Union army, 1861–65; was
nominated for member of congress from the 34th district
in 1884 and 1890; married Melissa P. Love of Forestville, N. Y., September 10, 1844, and Anna L. Gray
of Jamestown, N. Y., September 10, 1894; has lived
in Jamestown since 1867, and has been engaged in the
insurance business there since 1879.

**Almon A. Van Dusen** inherited an honorable name, which he has borne without blemish as a
lawyer and citizen. Our best critics are those who
have the fullest opportunity to study us in all our
relations to society; and if the good opinion of
one's neighbors is a source of happiness in life, Mr.
Van Dusen must derive great satisfaction from the
high esteem in which he is held in his community.

Mr. Van Dusen made no mistake when he chose
the law for his profession, and it would be hard
to picture him in any other calling. His success
has been all the more praiseworthy because he has
overcome no small obstacle in the lack of a collegiate
training. His elementary education was obtained in
the public schools of Jamestown, N. Y., and was
followed by a course in the Randolph Academy,
which enjoyed a favorable reputation as a preparatory
school. Having decided to become a lawyer, he
entered the office of Alexander and Porter Sheldon,
at Jamestown. After mastering Blackstone and Kent
and the dull routine of the law clerk, he was admitted to the bar in November, 1866, and three
years later was admitted to practice in the United
States District Court. He then formed a partnership in Sherman, N. Y., and as junior partner of the
firm of Benson & Van Dusen began the slow and
arduous work of building up a clientage and winning
a name in his profession. He moved to Mayville,
N. Y., in 1871, and has since practiced his profession
there. He has been senior partner in the firm of
Van Dusen & Martin since 1886.

Wherever he has resided, Mr. Van Dusen has
shown special interest in the cause of education, and
has done much to promote the welfare of the community. During the four years that he lived in
Sherman he held the position of president of the
board of education, and devoted much time and labor
to the task of elevating and improving the condition
of the public schools of the village. It was largely
through his instrumentality that a new schoolhouse
was built, in spite of much opposition. After his
removal to Mayville Mr. Van Dusen continued his
public-spirited efforts, and the handsome school
building of that village, as well as the system of waterworks, affords ample evidence of his devotion to
the public good.

In 1890 Mr. Van Dusen was elected to the bench
as judge of the County Court, and his record in
connection with this election is one of which he
may well be proud. He declined to resort to the
use of money or any other unworthy means of securing votes, preferring to rely entirely upon his personal
popularity and fitness for the office. He gave to the
county one of the most dignified and respectable

canvasses it had known for years. The result proved the truth of the old saying that "Honesty is the best policy," for he was elected on the Democratic ticket by a majority of 889 in a county where the normal Republican majority is 5,000. Mr. Van Dusen as a judge may be praised in unstinted measure. When he was promoted to the bench he took with him the ripened experience of a large and varied practice, an innate judicial balance, and the confidence of lawyer and layman alike. His record as county judge very properly commended him to his political associates, and in 1895 he was nominated by the Democratic party for judge of the Supreme Court.

Mr. Van Dusen is a vestryman of St. Paul's Episcopal Church of Mayville, and a member of the Holland Society of New York.

*PERSONAL CHRONOLOGY—Almon Augustus Van Dusen was born at Jamestown, N. Y., January 4, 1843; was educated in public schools and in Randolph Academy; was admitted to the bar in 1866; married Jettie E. Merchant of Brocton, N. Y., January 30, 1871; was appointed judge of the County Court of Chautauqua county January 2, 1890, and was subsequently elected to succeed himself; was nominated for judge of the Supreme Court in 1895; has practiced law in Mayville since 1871.*

•••

**C. P. Vedder** has had an enviable career. Every man, it is said, has at least one opportunity in life to demonstrate just what he really is. His use of that opportunity becomes the test by which he is ever after judged. The Civil War was such an opportunity to men now in middle life or beyond. To go to the front, leaving family, friends, and fortune behind, to suffer, and perchance to perish — this was the test that confronted the generation born before the war. In their number was Mr. Vedder. He had spent his boyhood on a farm at Ellicottville, N. Y. In early manhood he worked on the Erie canal, was a raftsman on the Allegheny river, finally shipped as a sailor before the mast, and rose to the position of captain at the early age of nineteen. All this time he was saving money to pay for an education, and the outbreak of the war found him a student in Springville Academy. But his ambition for a college course was not to be gratified. He decided that his duty lay in responding to the call

of his country. He closed his books, and left the academy to enter the practical school of war, enlisting as a private soldier in the 154th regiment, New York volunteers.

Mr. Vedder's service in the field was long and meritorious. He served from 1862 to the close of

*ALMON A. VAN DUSEN*

the war, and fought at Chancellorsville, Wauhatchie, Lookout Mountain, Missionary Ridge, siege of Savannah, and Bentonville. He was wounded at the battle of Rocky-Faced Ridge, was confined in Libby prison, and participated in Sherman's immortal march to the sea and through the Carolinas. He was promoted to be 1st lieutenant and captain, and for "gallant and meritorious conduct at the battle of Lookout Mountain" he was brevetted major in the regular army; and "for bravery in the campaign to Atlanta" he was promoted to be lieutenant colonel of volunteers.

Returning to his native state, Colonel Vedder studied law and was admitted to the bar. His success in civil life as a lawyer, a business man, and a legislator has been as complete and conspicuous as his record in the army was honorable and brilliant. He occupied the responsible position of register in bankruptcy for eight years. He filled the office of United States assessor of internal revenue for two years, and was state assessor for three years. How

*C. P. VEDDER*

faithfully he performed the duties of these various offices is best proved by repeated elections to the assembly and senate at Albany.

In the legislature Mr. Vedder made a splendid record. He was first chosen to the lower house in 1872, and took a leading part in the debates and deliberations of that body. He was chairman of the committee to draft articles of impeachment against Judge Barnard, of Tweed-Ring notoriety, and was one of the managers at the trial of that official, evincing in both capacities legal ability of a high order and wide knowledge of parliamentary procedure. In 1875 he was elected to the senate ; and it is no exaggeration to assert that no man there did more than he to lighten the burdens of taxation upon

those least able to bear them. He was the author of the laws taxing gifts, legacies, and collateral and direct inheritances, and requiring corporations to pay for the privilege of organization in the Empire State. As a result of these measures millions of dollars have been paid into the treasury, and a permanent source of revenue has been provided for the state.

Mr. Vedder was chosen a delegate at large to the constitutional convention of 1894, and served on several important committees. Of the thirty-three amendments proposed by the convention and adopted by the people, he drafted and introduced four. Too much cannot be said of the sagacity, zeal, and untiring devotion to the public interests displayed by Mr. Vedder in every position of trust and responsibility to which the people have called him. The constitution and the laws of the state alike attest his wisdom and his worth.

In the business world Mr. Vedder has also been a conspicuous factor. He is president of many corporations, including the State Bank of Norwood, the New York & New Jersey Ice Lines, the Elko Mining, Milling & Manufacturing Co., and the Falls Electric Power & Land Co. In politics he is a Republican. He is a member of the Presbyterian church, of the G. A. R., and of the Masonic order. His social clubs are the Holland Society, the Republican Club, and the Lawyers' Club, all of New York city.

*PERSONAL CHRONOLOGY— Commodore Perry Vedder was born at Ellicottville, N. Y., February 24, 1838 ; was educated at Springville (N. Y.) Academy ; served in the Union army, 1861-65, rising to the rank of lieutenant colonel ; was admitted to the bar in 1866 ; was register in bankruptcy, 1867-75 ; was United States assessor of internal revenue, 1869-71 ; was member of the assembly, 1872-75, and state senator, 1876-77 and 1884-91 ; was state assessor, 1880-83 ; married Bettie E. Squires of Springville, N. Y., September 2, 1862, and Mrs. Genevieve A. Wheeler of Chicago July 12, 1892.*

**Alexander Wentworth** received the hardy training of a farm boy, for his parents moved from Aurora, Erie county, when he was only four years old, to Ellicottville, N. Y., and soon after to a farm in the town of Randolph, N. Y. Practically his whole life has been spent in Randolph, and he is a representative of the class of men who are content to cast in their lot in places that offer but modest attractions, and who, by force of ability and persistent effort, at length achieve a substantial competence and high standing in the community.

Mr. Wentworth's educational opportunities were of the limited kind usually available for the country boy of half a century ago; but he used them to the very best advantage, and it is doubtful if the young man of to-day who goes through a preparatory school and a college without special effort on his own part, derives as much benefit from the experience as did young Wentworth from his hardly won privileges. For a time Mr. Wentworth paved the way to each winter's study by a summer of hard but healthful work on the farm. At seventeen he substituted teaching for the farm work, but continued his study during spring terms at the Randolph Academy. At nineteen he began reading law, and carried on all three occupations as best he could for the next three years. It speaks well for his natural ability and for the excellent use he made of his opportunities, that he was able to complete his legal studies at the age of twenty-two. He was admitted as an attorney and counselor at law at the General Term held in Buffalo in May, 1859. An interesting fact which Mr. Wentworth recalls in this connection is that President Cleveland was one of the class admitted to the bar at this term.

Mr. Wentworth had pursued his legal studies in the office of Weeden & Henderson of Randolph, and on admission to the bar he at once formed a partnership with William H. Henderson, under the name of Henderson & Wentworth, Mr. Weeden retiring from the firm. This connection has lasted ever since. The firm, consisting of two men so able and so public-spirited as Mr. Wentworth and Mr. Henderson, has naturally become a power in Cattaraugus county, and has had a wide influence upon public affairs. Their business is largely what is termed in the profession "litigation," and is varied and extensive, and they give to it their undivided attention. Mr. Wentworth's son, Crowley, a graduate of Princeton, was admitted to the firm January 1, 1896. Mr. Wentworth has no taste for politics, and has never sought nor accepted a political nomination. But he is not unmindful of his duties as a citizen, and

when important interests are involved and there is "no politics in it," he is at times active and aggressive. He has been willing to serve the community as president of his village and in similar positions.

Mr. Wentworth is a prominent member of the Masonic fraternity. He has been Master of Randolph Lodge, No. 359, F. & A. M., most of the time for the past twenty years; and he was District Deputy Grand Master of the 26th Masonic district from 1874 to 1880. At the latter date professional engagements compelled him to decline the reappointment that was tendered to him. These offices came to him without effort on his part, and as a spontaneous testimonial of the esteem in which he is held by his brother Masons.

*PERSONAL CHRONOLOGY— Alexander Wentworth was born at Aurora, Erie county, N. Y., July 26, 1837; was educated in common schools and*

*ALEXANDER WENTWORTH*

*at Randolph Academy; was admitted to the bar at Buffalo in 1859; married Ellen C. Crowley of Randolph, N. Y., October 10, 1859; has practiced law in Randolph since 1859.*

**Alfred J. Barnes** is one of Buffalo's energetic bankers and agreeable men of business. He has had a thorough training in financial matters, and is a conservative, industrious, and courteous official. Commercial life often seems uneventful and made up entirely of routine; but closer observation shows

ALFRED J. BARNES

that a successful mercantile career demands the same qualities requisite in more stirring pursuits. Good judgment, courage, and a high sense of honor are as essential in the sphere of finance as in any other field of human activity.

Mr. Barnes is a native of Troy, N. Y., and was educated in the public schools of that city. His earliest business experience was in association with his father, who conducted a large steam-fitting and plumbing business in the city of Troy. He desired a different occupation, however, and when a position was offered him in the Manufacturers' National Bank of his native city, he eagerly accepted it. He entered the service of that institution at the foot of the ladder, and by faithful attention to his duties worked

his way up through the different clerical grades until he became general bookkeeper. He continued in this position for nine years.

Early in the '80's Mr. Barnes retired from the bank, and engaged with a local business concern. But his training and predilection was for finance, and in 1883 he went to Chicago, and accepted a place in the Continental National Bank of that city. With this institution he remained ten years, attaining the responsible position of chief clerk. His success in Chicago won him a valuable reputation, and led to his engagement in Buffalo in 1893 as cashier of the City Bank.

While Mr. Barnes's residence in Buffalo has been comparatively brief, he has nevertheless taken rank already as a shrewd and active financier, a capable official, and affable gentleman in all the relations of life. He is a member of the Ellicott and Independent clubs, and a Republican in his party affiliations. His circle of acquaintance in business and social life is rapidly extending, and he has the satisfaction of knowing that no community is more open to receive a man of his character than the Queen City.

*PERSONAL CHRONOLOGY—Alfred Joseph Barnes was born at Troy, N. Y., July 12, 1856; was educated in the public schools of that city, and received a technical training in the Gurley Mathematical Instrument Works of Troy; was employed in the Manufacturers' National Bank, Troy, 1874-82, and in the Continental National Bank, Chicago, 1884-93; married Margaret L. B. Bowles of Riverside, Cook county, Ill., October 21, 1893; has been cashier of the City Bank, Buffalo, since 1893.*

\* \* \*

**Stephen O. Barnum** has been a factor in the mercantile life of Buffalo for fifty years. He went there in 1845, when the main avenue of travel was by canal, and established himself in a business that has been known for half a century all through his section of the state as "Barnum's." That all-embracing, *sui-generis* term, "Yankee notions," best describes the mammoth stock of merchandise that Mr. Barnum's establishment provides. He has catered to the rich and the poor, to the large and the small, to men, women, and children. At all seasons of the year Barnum's has been a center of trade.

Especially dear to the children has been the place, for Santa Claus has made his headquarters there ever since Stephen O. Barnum arrived in Buffalo. In this half-century of business activity Mr. Barnum has ever been in the forefront of the battle, alive to the interests of his customers, careful to ask only for his due, honorable in his dealings with all men.

When Mr. Barnum's school days were ended at the academy in his native city of Utica, he became a clerk in the Utica post office. There he remained for two years, when he entered the Oneida Bank of Utica as discount clerk. Here his business training was continued until his father made him a partner in what was known as "Barnum's Bazaar," where he obtained an insight into a business that he has successfully followed all his life. He remained with his father for several years, until, thinking it time to start out for himself, he made way for his younger brothers. Buffalo was then coming into notice as a growing commercial city, and the opportunities that it afforded seemed to the young man just what he needed. Thither he went, therefore, with a stout heart, determined to succeed if untiring effort and steadfastness of purpose would avail.

When he had been in business a short time a brother, Richard Smith Barnum, joined him in partnership; but after a few years Richard went to Chicago, and there entered into business with another brother, Ezra S. Their business was of the same general nature as that in which Stephen was engaged in Buffalo, and which the father conducted in Utica. The great Chicago fire brought heavy loss to Stephen, who had become largely interested in the Chicago venture by the death of his brothers. Since then Mr. Barnum has given his main attention to his Buffalo business, but he has found opportunity to serve other interests, having been at different times a director of the Western Transportation Co., the American Exchange Bank, and the Empire Salt Works of Warsaw, N. Y.

While taking such interest in public matters as is the duty of all good citizens, Mr. Barnum has never sought nor held political office. In his younger days, however, he took a more active part in affairs than he has taken of late. At one time in the early history of the city the rivalry between the different fire companies became so great that more attention

was given by their members to fighting each other than to fighting fires. The situation became so scandalous at last that the city council was obliged to disband the companies and to call for volunteers to fill their places. Mr. Barnum was one of the volunteers, and ran to more than one fire. Before his removal to Buffalo he was a member of the Utica fire department. He was also a lieutenant in the Utica Citizens' Corps, and is now an honorary member of that organization.

*PERSONAL CHRONOLOGY—Stephen Osborne Barnum was born at Utica, N. Y., January 13, 1816; was educated in the public schools; began business in Utica in partnership with his father in 1838; married Elizabeth Chatfield of Utica May 18, 1841; has carried on a general notion business in Buffalo since 1845.*

STEPHEN O. BARNUM

**Lewis J. Bennett** has built for himself an enduring monument in Buffalo in the beautiful residence district known as Central Park, of which he is the founder. This is a part of the city that has not been left to grow up at haphazard.  It was conceived and laid out on a broad plan, with an eye mainly to the future.  Instead of waiting, as has usually been the case elsewhere, for the houses to be built and the residents to come and determine the character of the section, Mr. Bennett planned Central Park from the

The laying out of the park took four years, and required for improvements alone an expenditure of nearly $300,000.

Like many other prominent citizens of Buffalo, Mr. Bennett is not a native of the city.  He was a country boy, having been born in Schenectady county, New York.  His education was limited to attendance at the district school, and when its meager facilities had been outgrown, at the larger village school of Fort Plain, N. Y.  At the age of eighteen Mr. Bennett entered business, buying a partnership in the grocery firm of Chapman, Peek & Co., at Fultonville, N. Y.  At first he was only the "Co."; but three years later Mr. Peek withdrew, and the firm name became Chapman & Bennett.  In two years more Mr. Bennett had become the senior partner, the firm embracing Wm. R. Chapman, Wm. W. Kline, and Lewis J. Bennett ; and the style was changed to L. J. Bennett & Co.  So it remained until 1866, when Mr. Bennett moved to Buffalo.  While a resident of Fultonville, in 1861, Mr. Bennett was appointed collector of canal tolls, and held the position for two years.  In 1865 he was elected supervisor for the town of Glen, in which the village of Fultonville is located.  His good standing with his townspeople is evidenced by the fact that, though he was a Republican, he received a majority of 184 votes in a town in which the ordinary Democratic majority was 60.

Soon after moving to Buffalo Mr. Bennett established a general contracting business, in partnership with Andrew Spalding and John Hand.  This was continued for five years.  In 1877 he organized the Buffalo Cement Co., Limited.  He was elected the first president of the company, and still holds the position.

Mr. Bennett is a Universalist in religion and a prominent Mason.  He holds membership in the following orders:  Fultonville Lodge, No. 531, F. & A. M.; Johnstown Chapter, No. 71, R. A. M.; and Apollo Commandery, No. 15, K. T., at Troy He was a charter member of the Fultonville Lodge, and was its first treasurer.  Mr. Bennett's long and active business career has been varied by only one notable vacation, which was taken in 1894-95, when he made a tour of the world.  While on this trip he

*LEWIS J. BENNETT*

first as a high class residence district.  Broad macadam streets were laid out, sewer, water, and gas mains constructed, and wide, deep lots platted, before any building was permitted.  Then, whenever a lot was sold, a minimum cost was fixed of the house to be placed on it.  As a consequence, Central Park contains some of the finest, most modern houses in Buffalo, and its general topographical features make it one of the acknowledged beauty spots of the city.  Only a man with strong faith in the future of Buffalo, sound business judgment, and a public spirit that refused to yield one iota of a general plan for the sake of temporary advantage, could have carried to a successful completion such an enterprise.

sent home frequent letters, which were published for the benefit of his friends.

*PERSONAL CHRONOLOGY— Lewis Jackson Bennett was born at Duanesburg, N. Y., July 7, 1833; was educated in the public schools; conducted a general store in Fultonville, N. Y., 1854–56; married Mary Francelia Spalding of Johnstown, N. Y., October 6, 1857; moved to Buffalo in 1866, and engaged in the business of a contractor; organized the Buffalo Cement Co. in 1877, and has been president thereof ever since.*

...

**John Blocher** is a worthy representative of the men, more numerous in this country than elsewhere, who are the architects of their own fortunes; who rise by their own exertions from obscurity to distinction, and attain success in spite of adverse circumstances.

Mr. Blocher's ancestors belong to the class known as the "Pennsylvania Dutch," who were accustomed to the toil of the fields, and disciplined in the school of economy and frugality. Mr. Blocher's father settled on a farm in Cayuga county, New York, in 1823. In addition to farming he furnished supplies to the contractors engaged in building the Erie canal. This business brought him into western New York; and he was so favorably impressed with the country that he bought a farm at Clarence in Erie county. This was the year after John Blocher's birth. As most of the farm was heavily timbered, young Blocher was early enlisted in the work of clearing the forest. His life was like that of the average farmer's boy, consisting of incessant labor in summer followed by three months' schooling in winter. The school was a log house with a big open fireplace at one end, in which huge logs from the surrounding forest were burned. Mr. Blocher was but ten years old when his father died, leaving him the youngest of a family of three children. Life now became more difficult for the afflicted family, but continual toil and a spirit of self-reliance carried them through. When there was no work at home John was hired out to neighboring farmers, and the scanty wages were carefully saved and laid by as a nest egg for the future.

At twelve years of age John's school education ended, and he was apprenticed to the tailoring trade.

In six years he had a shop of his own. This he ultimately turned into a ready-made clothing house, to which in time he added a stock of dry goods, groceries, and the other accessories of a country store. Mr. Blocher had thus established himself as a prosperous merchant when the war broke out. It was hard to leave his business, but his patriotism demanded the sacrifice, and he enlisted as a volunteer soldier in the 74th New York regiment. After a year's active service in the field he was honorably discharged, and sent home on account of impaired health. He was now obliged to pursue an outdoor occupation, and for a year he engaged in farming and the lumber business. In this way he regained sufficient health to warrant his resuming a sedentary occupation. He accordingly moved to Buffalo, and

*JOHN BLOCHER*

began in a small way the manufacture of boots and shoes, in partnership with his brother-in-law, Mr. Neff. Their capital was small, and patrons were yet to be found; but untiring industry, dauntless pluck, and strict integrity soon brought the firm a fair measure of prosperity. Two years later Mr. Blocher opened a factory of his own in the Rumsey block on Exchange street. Here his business steadily grew, until it required several large shops and two hundred operatives. A noteworthy fact in Mr. Blocher's career as an employer, creditable alike to head and heart, is that he has never had a serious disagreement with his employees. For many years he had for a partner his only son, whose early death was a terrible blow to his parents. Together they had worked harmoniously to build up an extensive business, and had accumulated a comfortable fortune.

Since his son's death Mr. Blocher has retired from active business, and now occupies himself chiefly with his property at Williamsville, where he has a country home, and has laid out pleasure grounds for the public. He is president of the Buffalo & Williamsville electric railroad, and deals to some extent in real estate and loans. His leisure is spent at his country home and among his books. Mr. Blocher is a well-informed and widely read man, history being his favorite study. Those who know him intimately are aware that he possesses talents which, if cultivated at the proper time, would have distinguished him. He has the inventive faculty, and has taken out many patents. He is a man of original ideas. The mausoleum that he erected in Forest Lawn cemetery in memory of his son embodies his own idea. Nay, he fashioned the models with his own hands. He had tried many artists, but all failed either to grasp his idea or to carry it out successfully. But Mr. Blocher knew what he wanted, and was determined to have it. Rejecting the ideal creations of the artists, one of which represented Mr. Blocher as a togaed Roman, he sought to sculpture the real man. Without previous training in art, he worked for months over his models, and at last produced clay figures so perfect in design that the marble workers of Italy were astonished by the skill displayed. Out of purest Carrara marble, famed from classical ages, the forms of Mr. Blocher, his wife, and son were hewn just as they existed in life, and exactly as Mr. Blocher desired. He wished to construct a memorial unique in conception, permanent in its quality, and calculated to convey to remote ages a true representation of men and women as they appear to day, in their proper stature, dress, and lineaments. In this design he has admirably succeeded.

Mr. Blocher is a Republican in politics, but always votes for the best man. In 1896 he celebrated the fiftieth year of his long and happy wedded life. He

is a member of the Delaware Avenue Methodist Episcopal church, and in philanthropic work is a generous and cheerful giver.

*PERSONAL CHRONOLOGY—John Blocher was born at Scipio, N. Y., July 22, 1825; was educated in district schools; conducted a general store at Williamsville, N. Y., 1851–61; married Elizabeth Neff of Williamsville April 20, 1846; enlisted in the Union army in 1864, and served one year; established a boot and shoe factory in Buffalo in 1865, and has been connected with that industry since.*

\*\*\*

**Patrick Cronin** has achieved distinction, not only as a preacher and a theologian, but also as an orator, an essayist, a professor, and an editor. Few men in Buffalo are better known or more popular, at home and abroad.

Father Cronin is a native of Ireland, and possesses in large measure the warm-hearted generosity and readiness to help those in need which are characteristic of his countrymen. He was born in Limerick county, near the banks of the Shannon, Ireland's most famous river; and his early education was received in the schools of Adare, in his native county. When he was fourteen years old, he came to the United States with his father, his mother having died years before. His college training was received at St. Louis University, and from there he went to St. Vincent's College, at Cape Girardeau, Mo., to prepare for the ministry. He was ordained to the priesthood in December, 1862, by Archbishop Kenrick, in the cathedral at St. Louis, and served for the next eight years under his episcopal jurisdiction, first as assistant in the Church of the Annunciation, St. Louis, then as pastor of a church in Hannibal, Mo., and finally as pastor of the Church of the Immaculate Conception, St. Louis.

In 1870 Father Cronin was called to occupy the chair of Latin and *belles-lettres* in the Seminary of Our Lady of Angels, now Niagara University, at Suspension Bridge, N. Y. His marked literary ability and general culture rendered him well fitted for this position. While there he made his first venture in journalism, a field in which he was to distinguish himself later. He became editor of the college paper, which was printed in the institution, and known as the *Niagara Index*.

In October, 1873, Father Cronin went to Buffalo. Bishop Ryan had begun work there five years before as head of the diocese, and Father Cronin became one of his most valued and trusted priests. For nearly a quarter of a century they lived under the same roof, where under the guidance of his bishop Father Cronin found inspiration for his work.

During all that time Father Cronin has been editor of the *Catholic Union and Times*, the official organ of the diocese of Buffalo, and in that capacity his literary talents have had full scope. He has also made good use of the opportunities thus afforded to advance the cause of Home Rule for Ireland, so dear to the hearts of patriotic Irishmen the world over. He has taken an active part in this agitation, and was the first vice president of the Land League in the United States. His services in this connection have won for him the enthusiastic friendship and admiration of his fellow-countrymen abroad.

An account of Father Cronin's life would be incomplete that made no mention of his work as a poet. Though he has never collected his productions in a volume, he has written and printed many poems that give evidence of decided talent. There is little doubt that, had he been free to devote his time to this pursuit, he would have won lasting fame as a poet. He has also delivered lectures and addresses on many subjects in many places. Perhaps the most famous are the oration at the O'Connell centenary at Detroit, a speech at the Columbian World's Fair, and an address before the New York State Bar Association at Albany. In June, 1891, Father Cronin received the degree of LL. D. from the University of Notre Dame, South Bend, Ind.

*PERSONAL CHRONOLOGY —  Patrick Cronin was born at Pallaskenry, Limerick county, Ireland, March 1, 1835; came to the United States in 1849; was educated at the St. Louis University and at St. Vincent's College, Cape Girardeau, Mo.; was ordained to the priesthood at St. Louis, Mo., in 1864, and was connected with various parishes in that state until 1870; was professor in the Seminary of Our Lady of Angels, Suspension Bridge, N. Y., 1870–72; has been editor of the "Catholic Union and Times," Buffalo, since 1874.*

* * *

**John Cunneen** has demonstrated what perseverance in study and an honorable ambition can accomplish in this country, where a fair field is given to their possessor. Born in Ireland, he came to America when a boy, and, like many others of his nationality, embraced the rich opportunity here afforded to rise in the world by dint of industry and talent. He obtained his elementary education in

private schools in Ireland, and after coming to the United States attended for a time the Albion (N. Y.) Academy. Having secured all the preliminary training his limited means could afford, he settled down to the study of law, was duly admitted to practice, and at once, in January, 1874, opened an office at

PATRICK CRONIN

Albion. During his term of legal clerkship, and for several years after his admission to the bar, Mr. Cunneen was clerk of the board of supervisors for Orleans county. He also served one term as collector of taxes of Albion. Aside from these positions he has never held any political office, though he was twice nominated by the Democratic party for district attorney. As an evidence of his popularity, it may be remarked that on the second occasion he came within twenty-six votes of an election in a county where the usual Republican majority was over one thousand.

For sixteen years Mr. Cunneen practiced his profession at Albion. His learning, industry, and integrity drew to him a numerous and important clientage. He recovered the largest verdict ever won by a lawyer in that county, amounting to nearly $500,000, in a case tried in the United States Circuit Court for the northern district of New York. His success in jury trials has been exceptional in the record of cases won

*JOHN CUNNEEN*

In 1890 Mr. Cunneen sought a wider field for the exercise of his legal talents, and settled in Buffalo. In company with Charles F. Tabor, William F. Sheehan, and Edward E. Coatsworth, he formed a law partnership under the firm name of Tabor, Sheehan, Cunneen & Coatsworth. Two of his partners were more or less absorbed in public affairs, and a great share of the work devolved upon Mr. Cunneen. In 1894 the firm was dissolved, and Mr. Cunneen became the senior member of the firm of Cunneen & Coatsworth. His well-merited success gained at Albion has followed him to Buffalo, and he has appeared in many of the most important causes in Erie county during the past five years, and is recognized as a lawyer of marked ability.

Apart from his chosen profession Mr. Cunneen has displayed a taste and bent for journalism. While at Albion he conducted successfully a weekly paper, and he has on many occasions been a contributor to the press. He has thus been an active factor in two professions, and both have naturally led him into the field of politics. Law and journalism are the most frequented roads to public position and political prominence. Mr. Cunneen has displayed an interest in politics in the best sense of the word. A strong adherent of the Democratic party, he has been active among its leaders on the stump, in his paper, and in conventions, and he is recognized as an honest, astute, and indefatigable worker, seeking not his own preferment but the success of his cause. He is a member of the Democratic state committee, and one of the chief men of his party in Buffalo. In social life he is held in high esteem, and is a member of the Buffalo and Ellicott clubs. The duties of an exacting profession, however, have left him little time for pursuits and pastimes not connected in some degree with his life-work — the study and practice of law.

*PERSONAL CHRONOLOGY— John Cunneen was born at Enis, Ireland, May 18, 1848; came to the United States in 1861, and settled in Albion, N. Y.; was admitted to the bar at Rochester in 1874; married Elizabeth E. Bass of Albion January 26, 1876; practiced law in Albion, 1874–90, and has practiced in Buffalo since 1890.*

•••

**Ganson Depew** is a genuine Buffalonian, having been born and educated in the Queen City, and having lived there always. He attended the public schools of Buffalo, and graduated from the high school in 1884. He was president of his class, and was also class orator. Additional evidence of Mr. Depew's popularity is afforded by his election, in the year of his graduation, to the office of vice president of the High School Association, which numbers over two thousand members.

Without resort to either college or law school, Mr. Depew soon after his graduation from the high school entered the law office of Greene, McMillan & Gluck as a student. This firm was one of the foremost at the Erie-county bar, and hardly any office could have been found that was better fitted to train and instruct

a student in general and corporation law. Mr.
Greene, one member of the firm, afterward became
leading counsel of the Lake Shore & Michigan
Southern railway; Mr. Gluck has long lectured on
the law of corporations in the Buffalo Law School;
and the firm as a whole is known far and wide for
its vigilant and able guardianship of large corporation interests. Thus Mr. Depew had an unusually
fine opportunity to become minutely and thoroughly
acquainted with railroad and general corporation
law. This department of legal science he had
determined to make his specialty, and the connection
with Greene, McMillan & Gluck was correspondingly
valuable to him. He made rapid progress in his
legal studies under the favorable conditions noted,
and in 1887 he was admitted to the bar at Buffalo.
He continued in the office that had served
his student purposes so well, and in 1890
his fidelity and ability were rewarded by
admission into the firm with which he
had so long been associated. The style
then became McMillan, Gluck, Pooley &
Depew, and the firm continues to-day as
it was then organized. The legal interests of some of the largest corporations
in the country are committed to this
firm — such corporations as the New York
Central & Hudson River railroad, the
West Shore railway, the Lake Shore &
Michigan Southern railway, the Michigan
Central railway, the Rome, Watertown &
Ogdensburg railway, the Western Union
Telegraph Co., and the Equitable Life
Assurance Co. of New York city.

The same earnestness, perseverance,
and faithfulness that marked Mr. Depew's
early career at school have been characteristic of the man, and have been
embodied in his professional work. Although still a young man and only
recently started on his career, he may
confidently be regarded as one of the
coming legal lights of western New York.
Two relatives, whose names he bears,
were long leaders of the bar in New
York state, and in the careers of his
cousin, John Ganson, and of his uncle,
Chauncey M. Depew, there is much to
encourage and spur him onward in his
profession.

Mr. Depew is a member of St. Paul's Episcopal
Church; of Ancient Landmark Lodge, No. 441,
F. & A. M.; of Adytum Chapter, Royal Arch
Masons; of the Sons of the American Revolution;

and of the Buffalo, Saturn, Liberal, and Ellicott
clubs. He was elected a director of the Buffalo
Library in 1892 and again in 1895, receiving on each
occasion the highest vote of any of the candidates.

*PERSONAL CHRONOLOGY* — *Ganson
Depew was born at Buffalo March 6, 1866; was
educated in the public schools, and graduated from the
high school in 1884; studied law in the office of
Greene, McMillan & Gluck in Buffalo, and was admitted to the bar in 1887; became a member of the
firm of McMillan, Gluck, Pooley & Depew in 1890;
married Grace E. Goodyear of Buffalo November 15,
1894.*

* * *

**Samuel G. Dorr** comes of a lineage that insures to him public spirit and devotion to civic duty.

*GANSON DEPEW*

The name Dorr is doubtless of German origin, but
in the seventeenth century a representative of the
family lived in the western part of England, whence
Edward Dorr came to Boston somewhere about 1670.

Dr. Dorr's middle name is that of one of Connecticut's oldest families, several members of which held the office of governor. Edmund Dorr, one of Dr. Dorr's ancestors, moved to Connecticut in the early part of the eighteenth century, and there married into the Griswold family. Another of his ancestors

SAMUEL G. DORR

was Captain Matthew Dorr of revolutionary fame, who did heroic service at the battle of Saratoga, and whose regiment was officially praised by General Gates. A son of Captain Matthew Dorr, named Samuel Griswold, was the American inventor who patented a wheel of knives, which, in connection with the spinning jenny, was destined to revolutionize the business of cloth manufacture. This son, while introducing his machinery in England, died of poison presumably administered by persons bent on frustrating any improvement that would decrease the number of people employed in cloth manufacturing.

Dr. Dorr, like his father, has been a business man and a physician. He was born at Dansville, N. Y., and received a liberal education at Nunda (N. Y.)

Academy and at the Albion State Academy in Wisconsin. Upon his graduation from the latter institution he returned to New York state, and ran a flour mill at South Dansville, which he had bought of his father. Not being of age, Mr. Dorr was unable to execute legal papers, and such complications arose that he wound up the business, after having assumed obligations amounting to over $10,000, every penny of which he ultimately paid to his creditors. When the Civil War broke out, and President Lincoln called for 75,000 troops, Mr. Dorr enlisted within forty hours thereafter. Unfortunately he was prevented from going to the front by an attack of diphtheria, which left him an invalid for a year. In 1863 he was appointed by Governor Seymour recruiting agent for half of Livingston county, a position in which he rendered valuable service during the rest of the war.

After the war Mr. Dorr went to the oil regions in Pennsylvania, and engaged in the business of refining oil, in partnership with Charles Twining, at Oil Creek. The cooperage business soon proving more attractive, they established works for the manufacture of barrels at Waterford, Penn. Mercantile life, however, was not to Mr. Dorr's taste, and the force of heredity asserted itself. He went to Buffalo, and matriculated in the medical department of the University of Buffalo in 1873, receiving his doctor's degree two years later. Once established in the practice of his profession, Dr. Dorr won quick success, for he possesses in addition to medical knowledge a kindly disposition that is in itself a tonic to the afflicted. During the administrations of mayors Brush and Cleveland he held the position of police surgeon. No physician is better known or more highly esteemed in the neighborhood in which he lives than Dr. Dorr. He is a member of all the leading medical societies in the state, and for years has been a consulting physician at one of Buffalo's largest hospitals.

As a political factor Dr. Dorr is a power in his community, and is invariably found with the active forces of good government. Two things have constituted his political creed — the abolition of slavery and the purification of politics. The former he has lived to see accomplished; the latter is being wrought out at the present time, slowly it is true, but no less certainly. He abhorred slavery as a man ; as an American he abhors political dishonesty. He has been an active Republican from the days of Fremont. Lincoln was the idol of his life, and the picture of the martyred President graces the most conspicuous wall of his living room. While a resident of Waterford, Penn., he was burgess of the town, and organized its first fire department. In Buffalo he has been elected supervisor, and was once nominated for councilman. In 1888 he was chosen an alternate delegate to the Republican national convention at Chicago. He is a stanch protectionist. In fact, adherence to that doctrine may be called a family trait, resulting perhaps from the destruction of his grandfather's cloth factory by the repeal of a tariff law soon after the war of 1812.

Dr. Dorr is a trustee of the Sentinel Methodist Church, a member of the Masonic fraternity, and of many benevolent and literary societies.

*PERSONAL CHRONOLOGY —*
*Samuel Griswold Dorr was born at Dansville, N. Y., May 30, 1840 ; was educated at Nunda (N. Y.) Academy and Albion State Academy in Wisconsin : conducted a flour-milling business at South Dansville, N. Y., 1859–64 ; married Rebecca Bradley of Dansville July 7, 1864 ; engaged in oil refining and in cooperage in Pennsylvania, 1865–72 ; graduated from the medical department of the University of Buffalo in 1875, and has practiced medicine in Buffalo since.*

---

**Charles French Dunbar** deserves the title of "Pathfinder" in recognition of his great services to commerce and navigation. He exemplifies the truth and power of hereditary influence. It is no mere coincidence that men of his blood invented and operated the first steam dredging apparatus with a revolving crane, and that he gave to the world the first successful submarine drilling machine. Deep harbors and channels are to water traffic what massive iron bridges are to railway transportation. If there were no way to deepen shallow places, modern vessels could no more enter some of our chief ports than could a mogul engine cross an old-fashioned wooden bridge ; and since large vessels and heavy engines are now a necessity of commerce, the man who facilitates their use does a notable service.

Mr. Dunbar received a common-school education, supplemented by a high-school course of a year or more ; and his whole life has been devoted to study and learning in the practical school of affairs. His knowledge of the dredging business began early, for he was only fourteen years old when he was fireman on a dredge engaged in digging the Des Jardins canal in Ontario, where his father was foreman. His father having turned his attention to railroad construction, young Dunbar worked for him for several years on the Utica & Watertown, the Hamilton & Toronto, and the Grand Trunk roads. He then went to Missouri, and helped build the first railroad west of the Mississippi river — the Hannibal & St. Joseph. He was subsequently employed in running the preliminary line of the St. Joseph & Council Bluffs railroad. With this rich experience he went

*CHARLES FRENCH DUNBAR*

to Buffalo in 1860, where his father was clearing out the entrance to Buffalo creek. Since that time his career has been substantially the history of deep water navigation.

In 1863 Mr. Dunbar formed a partnership in the dredging business with Franklin Lee, under the firm name of Lee & Dunbar, by the terms of which Mr. Dunbar was to have charge of the mechanical part of the work. This firm was instrumental in deepening the channels and harbors at Buffalo, Dunkirk, Erie,

*GUSTAV FLEISCHMANN*

Conneaut, Ashtabula, Sandusky, Toledo, and Port Colborne on Lake Erie; St. Clair Flats, Port Huron, Bay City, and Au Sable on Lake Huron; Wilson, Big Sodus, Little Sodus, Pultneyville, Oswego, and Toronto on Lake Ontario; and Ogdensburg on the St. Lawrence. The firm had, in addition, important contracts on the Welland and Murray canals.

It was at Port Colborne that Mr. Dunbar perfected his drilling machine. He had taken the contract to deepen the mouth of the Welland canal. The undertaking was regarded as so hazardous that many of his friends predicted ruin for him; and the Canadian government, doubting his ability to fulfill the contract, demanded a penalty bond of $25,000.

With the aid of the new invention, however, the contract was satisfactorily performed. Then Mr. Dunbar contracted with the United States government to excavate the Lime Kiln Crossing at Detroit. This undertaking was likewise most formidable, and a bond of $200,000 was required from the contractor.

The work was much retarded and endangered by navigation, and required twelve years for its completion. Mr. Dunbar next excavated and deepened the Haylake Channel for a distance of over two miles, securing a depth of twenty-one feet instead of nine as before. In short, it may be said that Mr. Dunbar has left his mark on the principal ports of the Great Lakes, and has profoundly influenced the commercial welfare of many cities.

The success and usefulness of Mr. Dunbar's invention have been acknowledged by engineers of the highest character. General O. M. Poe made the invention the subject of a paper read before the American Society of Engineers, and in a letter to Mr. Dunbar's son said, "I regard his [Mr. Dunbar's] adaptation of the method of drilling and blasting rock under water as one of the great feats of modern engineering."

Mr. Dunbar retired from the dredging business in 1895, and now enjoys a well-earned leisure. He finds much pleasure in literature, and is the author of a drama that was brought out in Buffalo in 1884, and was favorably received by the public. While not active in politics, he is a firm Republican, having cast his first vote for Abraham Lincoln. During his residence at Erie, Penn., he served one term of two years in the common council. He has devoted much time and attention to trotting horses, and is well known on the circuit. He has a large circle of friends, to whom he is endeared by his worth, and freedom from ostentation.

*PERSONAL CHRONOLOGY— Charles French Dunbar was born at Boston, Mass., January 6, 1829; was educated in public schools; married Mrs. Lucille DeWolf Berston of Pelham, Ont., October 28, 1864; carried on a dredging business in Buffalo, 1860-95; invented a submarine drilling machine in 1873.*

\*\*\*

**Gustav Fleischmann** is one of the many sons of the old world who have attained prosperity in this new land, and have contributed their full share to the growth and development of their adopted country.

Mr. Fleischmann was born less than fifty years ago in Vienna, Austria. He came to the United States at the age of sixteen, and obtained employment with the firm of Casoni & Isola in New York city as a marble cutter and designer, at the same time attending night schools and Cooper Institute, and pursuing his studies in mathematics and drawing to fit him for the profession he had adopted. He was obliged to abandon this vocation, however, on account of ill health; and in 1869 he went to Cincinnati, and entered the firm of Goff, Fleischmann & Co., of which his brothers, Maximilian and Charles, were members. There he thoroughly learned the business of a distiller and yeast manufacturer. When he had perfected his knowledge of this industry, and was ready to establish himself in business, Mr. Fleischmann began to consider the question of location. The Buffalo of twenty years ago was a different place from the city of to-day, as regards both population and commercial prosperity; but the elements of her future greatness were there, and it was not difficult for a farsighted and sagacious man to appreciate her superior advantages. Mr. Fleischmann accordingly went to Buffalo, and engaged in the distilling business under the firm name of Frost & Co. A year later Mr. Frost retired, and Mr. Fleischmann formed a partnership with E. N. Cook, under the style of E. N. Cook & Co. This connection lasted until 1893, when Mr. Fleischmann bought out Mr. Cook's interest in the business, and organized the Buffalo Distilling Co., of which he has since been the proprietor.

The successful business man of the present day is able to carry on an amount of business that would have been deemed entirely impossible by even the most active man of half a century ago. It is not surprising, therefore, that Mr. Fleischmann is president of the Meadville (Penn.) Distilling Co., and of the Frontier Elevating Co. of Buffalo, in addition to his ownership of the Buffalo Distilling Co. He also held, for some years, the presidency of the Merz Universal Extractor and Construction Co.; but this position he resigned in favor of his brother, when the main office of the company was moved from Buffalo to New York city.

Mr. Fleischmann is a member of Meadville Lodge, B. P. O. E. His chief interests are now in Buffalo, and he is the owner of some fine residence property in that city. His greatest recreation from the engrossing cares of business is in hunting, to which he is passionately devoted. He is a member of the Adirondack League Club, and brings home several fine deer each fall as trophies of his marksmanship.

*PERSONAL CHRONOLOGY—Gustav Fleischmann was born at Vienna, Austria, March 22, 1850; came to the United States in 1866; married Emily Robertson of New York city August 24, 1880; has been engaged in the distilling business in Buffalo since 1877.*

\*\*\*

**Edward C. Hawks,** the son of Thomas S. Hawks, is a lawyer of standing and a man of business

*EDWARD C. HAWKS*

affairs. In the branch of the law covering real estate he is an especially well-qualified counselor. He has confined himself almost exclusively to office practice in recent years, and to the care of his personal interests, and is rarely seen in court. He has, how ever, figured in important litigation, and as city attorney of Buffalo was engaged in several exciting and momentous contests. As a trial lawyer he was an adversary at once full-armed and unfaltering, and when convinced that he was in the right nothing could move him from the position he had taken. But the continual struggle of the court room, the delays in bringing causes to trial, and the disproportion of the issue to the time and labor involved, have made the office of counselor more attractive to most lawyers in these busy days than the pleading of cases at the bar.

A Buffalonian by birth and education, Mr. Hawks has taken more than ordinary interest and pride in the growth and development of the city. He graduated from the Central High School, and studied law in the office of Sprague & Fillmore, then one of the leading law firms of western New York. For seven years he was managing clerk of their large legal business, and had entire charge of the real-estate transactions of the Erie County Savings Bank, a client of the firm. After this thorough and extensive experience, Mr. Hawks opened an office of his own.

While never a seeker for political office as a means of livelihood, Mr. Hawks in the early part of his legal career had, as nearly every energetic lawyer at some time has, an ambition for public life. Usually a short experience in that direction cures the aspirant, and sends him back to his profession a wiser if not a sadder man. Mr. Hawks held the office of city attorney two years, and frankly admits that that sufficed him so far as public office was concerned. Yet it is just such men who ought to be in office, for they have the welfare of the community at heart, and discharge their duties conscientiously. Mr. Hawks's term as city attorney was marked by a distinguished service to Buffalo. A generous council had voted to sell a railroad corporation the South Channel land for $12,000, and directed the city attorney to facilitate the transfer. Mr. Hawks, who knew the property to be worth far more than the price named, demurred to the authority of the council over him, regarding himself as the attorney of the city, and not of one of its departments. Consequently he refused to effect the transfer. Thereupon the common council attempted to oust him from office on written charges, and he was formally tried before Mayor Brush. The mayor dismissed the charges as entirely unfounded. It may be added that the railroad company did not get the property for $12,000, but paid the city, for less than half of it, $150,000.

Private affairs have engrossed Mr. Hawks's attention in recent years, and he has become largely interested in land improvement and grain elevators. Richmond avenue may almost be said to have been laid out and improved by him. He was one of the builders of the International elevator at Black Rock, and is interested in grain elevators elsewhere. In business he has the same courage and backbone that he displayed as a city official. When the forgeries and rascalities of the Sherman brothers threatened to ruin several Buffalo banks and permanently injure the city's grain commerce, Mr. Hawks with two associates assumed a liability amounting to more than half a million dollars, and thus re-established the confidence of shippers and financial houses in the integrity and soundness of the local elevators. Mr. Hawks has immense land holdings in Massachusetts, owning five miles of sea beach at West Gloucester. In connection with his property there, he has given much thought to road building, and published a series of articles on "Good Roads and How to Build Them."

Mr. Hawks is prominent in many of Buffalo's literary and art societies, and is an honorary member of the Art Students' League — an unusual distinction. He is a Fellow of the Buffalo Society of Artists, and a member of the Merchants' Exchange.

*PERSONAL CHRONOLOGY — Edward Clinton Hawks was born at Buffalo July 26, 1846; graduated from the Central High School in 1865; was admitted to the bar in 1869; was city attorney, 1880-81; married, on June 5, 1879, Amanda Smith of Buffalo, a lineal descendant of Richard Smith, Jr., the crown patentee of Narragansett, Rhode Island, 1641; has practiced law in Buffalo since 1874.*

\*\*\*

**Henry Wayland Hill,** the son of Martha P. Hall, Hill and of Dyer Hill, a member of the Vermont state legislature in 1849-50, is a country boy who has risen to prominence as a lawyer and legislator. He was born in the Green Mountain State, where he passed his youth on his father's farm. He took a four years' classical course at the University of Vermont, graduating therefrom with honors in 1876. He received the degree of A. B. at this time, and was admitted to membership in the Phi Beta Kappa society. Four years later his *alma mater* conferred upon him the degree of A. M.

After his graduation Mr. Hill was principal of the academy at Swanton, Vt., for two years, and then accepted a similar position at Chateaugay, N. Y. During his career as a teacher he organized a college preparatory course in the academies at Swanton and Chateaugay, and fitted several classes for college. His standing among educators was recognized by his election to a term as president of the Franklin County N. Y. Teachers' Association.

While he was occupied in teaching, Mr. Hill devoted his leisure hours to the study of law, and successfully passed the New York state bar examination in 1884. In that year he moved to Buffalo, and became a member of the law firm of Andrews & Hill. As a lawyer his career has been marked by unusual skill in the conduct of legal business. He has also taken an active interest in civic affairs, and is among the best known of Buffalo's younger generation of public men. He has the qualities that bring success in the arena of political activity.

In the fall of 1893 Mr. Hill was elected a delegate to the New York constitutional convention, and served in that body on the suffrage, education, and civil-service committees. He was an able and a useful member of the convention, and was selected as one of the committee of five to determine the order of business, and arrange the calendar of the convention. He formulated several of the amendments that are now a part of the fundamental law of the state. To Mr. Hill is due in large part the amendment for improving canals. He organized sentiment in its favor, made one of the principal speeches on the subject, and after the convention had taken adverse action on the proposition, he secured a reconsideration of the matter and the passage of the amendment.

One of Mr. Hill's most eloquent and scholarly speeches in the convention defended the use of the Niagara river for power purposes. Among other things, he said :

"The diapason of Niagara is being translated into the hum of industry. The music of nature will continue, while the factories of Buffalo, Rochester, and the smaller cities of western New York pulsate in unison with the waters of the great cataract. Shall Niagara remain but the rendezvous of poets and wedding tourists, and its waters be permitted 'to flow on unvexed to the sea,' or shall they be utilized for the good of man? The beauties of Niagara will remain, the charm of the thousands who visit it, although its potent energies be conserved to contribute to the welfare of humanity. Hitherto, Niagara has spent its great energies in vain, and now that the time has come when they may be made to propel the wheels of industry, it is proposed to prohibit the latter by constitutional inhibition. Why not prohibit the use of the waters of the Hudson, the Mohawk, the Susquehanna, or the St. Lawrence? Why not erect a barrier to the use of all the waters of the state? Why not deny to commerce access to Lake Champlain, Lake Erie, or the inland lakes of the state? Natural streams of water, ever since the morning of time, have been made to serve the purposes of man.......... The legislature

may be entrusted to grant only such franchises for the use of the waters of Niagara river as will be for the interest of the people of the whole state."

Mr. Hill's services in the convention and on the stump were noteworthy and duly appreciated, for they led to his nomination and election to the legis-

*HENRY WAYLAND HILL*

lature of 1896 by a plurality of 4,860, the largest Republican plurality received by any member of the New York assembly in that year. The press of Buffalo strongly supported his candidacy, declaring him to be "the peer of any man that ever went to the assembly from Erie county." Mr. Hill was assigned to the committee on affairs of cities and the committee on canals. The latter assignment was particularly appropriate, because Mr. Hill had strongly advocated, in 1895, the measure whereby the state appropriated $9,000,000 for canal improvement. He has shown himself to be an earnest legislator, seeking at all times courageously to represent the interests and to record the wishes of his constituents, and strenuous in the advocacy of measures favoring Buffalo and its expanding commerce. Mr. Hill is an active Republican, and for several years has been a member of the Erie-county Republican committee, and of the Buffalo Republican League. He is a believer in home rule for cities, and spoke ably on that subject in

*EDWARD J. HINGSTON*

the constitutional convention. He is also an earnest promoter of the commercial interests of the state.

Mr. Hill has done much work of a literary character, and has delivered many addresses of an educational or historical nature. Especially noteworthy is his address, delivered before the Buffalo Historical Society, on the " Development of Constitutional Law in New York." Mr. Hill is much given to the philosophic study of the development of civil institutions, and this address, covering the subject from the ancient Roman codification in the Twelve Tables to the latest aspects of organic law in the Empire State, shows deep research and wide learning. Mr. Hill is recording secretary of the Buffalo Historical

Society, and a member of the State Bar Association and of the University Club of Buffalo.

*PERSONAL CHRONOLOGY — Henry Wayland Hill was born at Isle La Motte, Vt., November 14, 1853; prepared for college in the public schools, and graduated from the University of Vermont in 1876; was principal of Sosanton (Vt.) Academy, 1877-79, and of Chateaugay (N. Y.) Academy, 1879-84; married Miss Harriet Augusta Smith of Sosanton August 14, 1880; was admitted to the bar at Albany in 1884; was elected member of the New York constitutional convention in 1894, and of the New York assembly in 1895; has practiced law in Buffalo since 1884.*

**Edward J. Hingston** has had a unique experience. He was born in the United States, and educated in England, where his mother's family resided. His original intention was to pursue a literary occupation, and he was ambitious to win distinction in the field of journalism. In early years he showed a predilection for books and study, and for several years taught school in Liverpool. But fate had in store for him a decidedly practical career, and to-day he is a member of the firm of Hingston & Woods, celebrated in Buffalo and all lake ports as skillful dredgers and contractors for foundation and sewer work.

Thomaston, Maine, was Mr. Hingston's birthplace, but his childhood and youth were spent in England, where he attended the National School at Liverpool. Having returned to America at eighteen years of age, and settled in Buffalo, he concluded to follow the advice of his ship-building uncle, and learn the latter's trade. In this occupation he spent five years, and the experience thus acquired has proved of distinct service in his present line of business. Additional valuable training followed this, as he became bookkeeper for a leading firm of Buffalo dredgers, holding the position for ten years. He then embarked in the business for himself, in partnership with Arthur Woods, under the firm name of Hingston & Woods.

The specialties to which Mr. Hingston has devoted his energies are dredging, excavating, and laying water mains and submarine structures. An enumeration of the important contracts undertaken and successfully carried out by him and his partner would fill a page. Among the more noteworthy achievements of the firm may be mentioned the Lehigh Valley slips at Buffalo, the inlet pier of the Buffalo waterworks, water mains at Rochester and Erie ; and similar mains for Syracuse at Skaneateles lake. Extensive rock-removal contracts at Oswego, Buffalo, Erie, Sault Sainte Marie, and New Brunswick, N. J., have been successfully fulfilled. In this business are employed a large force of men, with twelve dredges, tugs, mud scows, pumping barges, etc.

Mr. Hingston is also interested in other enterprises. He is a member of the firm of Leh & Co., dock builders, and for several years has been senior member of the firm of Hingston, Rogers & O'Brien, known as the International Dredging Co. Mr. Hingston is an active, forceful man, with executive ability and strict methods of business. His success has been well earned, and his ability has been demonstrated by the diverse and difficult pursuits he has followed, in all of which he has proved himself capable and competent. His leisure hours are devoted to literary studies, and were it not for the exactions of business, some form of literary activity would be most congenial to him as a life occupation. Mr. Hingston is a Free Mason, and a member of the Lafayette Street Presbyterian Church and of the Buffalo and Oakfield clubs.

*PERSONAL CHRONOLOGY—*
*Edward J. Hingston was born at Thomaston, Me., January 22, 1844 ; was educated in the National Schools, England ; taught school at Liverpool, 1858-62 ; returned to the United States, and settled in Buffalo in 1862 ; learned the shipbuilder's trade, 1862-67 ; married Mary E. Rees of Buffalo July 22, 1872 ; has been engaged in the dredging business in Buffalo since January 1, 1878.*

...

**William H. Hotchkiss,** though still a young man, even if the term be narrowly interpreted, has already made a name for himself, and accomplished much good in a field of usefulness cultivated too little by men of his standing and capacity. He is a type of the young professional men, of liberal education and well-developed talent, who interest themselves in public affairs for the public good. He was prepared for college at Glidden's Classical School in Jamestown, N. Y., going from there to Hamilton

College, where he graduated at the age of twenty-two with the degree of A. B. He secured the much coveted Phi Beta Kappa key, besides honors in literature, oratory, debating, Greek, Latin, and mathematics, and delivered the Head prize oration and Latin salutatory. Three years after his graduation, his college conferred on him the degree of A. M.

Law was the profession that Mr. Hotchkiss had chosen for himself, and with a view to obtaining a practical knowledge of legal procedure as early as possible, he accepted, after completing his college course, the appointment of clerk of the Surrogate's Court of Cayuga county, at Auburn, N. Y. The surrogate at that time was John D. Teller, whose name became familiar throughout the state by his candidacy for judge of the Court of Appeals on the

*WILLIAM H. HOTCHKISS*

Democratic ticket in 1895. Mr. Hotchkiss served as clerk two years, 1887–89. Meantime, in 1888, he was admitted to the bar. Judge Teller took him into partnership, and he practiced at Auburn, in the firm of Teller & Hotchkiss, till 1891. He then moved to the larger field of Buffalo, where he entered into partnership with E. L. Parker, and where he has since pursued his profession. The firm of Parker & Hotchkiss has risen rapidly in both influence and volume of business, and now ranks among the leading

CHARLES R. HUNTLEY

commercial and banking law firms of Buffalo. Mr. Hotchkiss is a lecturer on the law of personal property in the Buffalo Law School.

The great problems of municipal government, so long neglected in American cities, were just beginning to receive serious public attention when Mr. Hotchkiss began the real work of his manhood. To the study of these problems he addressed himself with the energy of youth, the earnestness of strong convictions, and an honest desire to serve right purposes. He has contributed articles frequently to the *Review of Reviews*, *Munsey's*, *Outing*, and the Buffalo *Illustrated Express*, his range of subject including travels as well as municipal problems. In the latter field, however, he has become recognized

as an authority. He wrote a pamphlet monograph on "Urban Self Government" in 1892, and has since delivered numerous lectures on that and kindred subjects. His interest in politics has been in the line of promoting ideas, rather than in the actual work of machines. He took an active part in exposing the ballot frauds in Buffalo in 1892, and has served as secretary of the committee on law and legislation of the Buffalo Citizens' Association for three years. He is also an active member of the Buffalo Republican League, having served two years on the executive committee, and one year as editor of its organ, *The Opinion*. He is a member of Chi Psi college fraternity, and served as editor in chief of its magazine, *Purple and Gold*, from 1886 to 1890. He belongs, also, to the Sons of the American Revolution, the Buffalo Club, the Liberal Club, the Independent Club, and the New York State Bar Association. Especially worthy of mention is his work in connection with the drafting of the reform charter of Buffalo.

*PERSONAL CHRONOLOGY— William Horace Hotchkiss was born at Whitehall, Washington county, N. Y., September 7, 1864; was educated at Glidden's Classical School, Jamestown, N. Y., and Hamilton College, Clinton, N. Y. from which he graduated in 1886; was clerk of the Surrogate's Court of Cayuga county, 1887–89; was admitted to the bar in 1888; has practiced law in Buffalo since 1891; married Katherine Tremaine Rush of Buffalo April 25, 1895.*

...

**Charles R. Huntley** belongs to the electric age. Within the memory of young men a new science, and a new profession and industry, have sprung into existence, revolutionizing the world in many of its features, destined evidently to transform the mechanics of life. The magician's wand has been outstripped in this epoch of practical wonders. We live in an age of pioneers into the most extensive and promising realms that have ever invited the genius of man. Electricity has attracted to its service a class of men marked by keen activity and American optimism. The science seems to have no place for old-fashioned people. Those who serve it must be like it—quick and full of force. Such a man is Charles R. Huntley.

Mr. Huntley went to Buffalo a few years ago to accept the position of secretary of what was then the

Brush Electric Light Co. This company was subsequently changed to the Buffalo General Electric Co., of which Mr. Huntley is now general manager. Into his position he has thrown all the energy and enthusiasm of a vigorous mind and body. While making no pretense to inventive power, he has successfully striven to master the commercial side of electricity, and to understand it thoroughly as a commodity. It sounds strange to talk of the summer cloud's flash as a commodity, but to Mr. Huntley it is merely that and nothing more. His business is to sell electricity at so much a horse power. This requires careful computation of the cost of every kilo of electricity, for in no industry is competition keener, or figured down to a closer basis, than in this of furnishing electric power.

Few men are better known in the electrical world than Mr. Huntley, and his standing among his associates is attested by his election to the office of president of the National Electric Light Association, composed of eight hundred members. He was chiefly instrumental in bringing the yearly convention of that body to Buffalo in 1892. He is a frequent contributor to electrical journals, and is a member of the American Institute of Electrical Engineers.

Previously to connecting himself with his present business, Mr. Huntley had experience in the oil fields of Pennsylvania, where he was the agent of the Standard Oil Co. At one time he was in the brokerage business at Bradford, Penn., and while a resident of that city became prominent in its local affairs. He was elected school comptroller for four years. He served a term also as select councilman. These positions he filled from a sense of civic duty. He is a supporter of the Democratic party, but he has not sought nominations, nor interested himself in politics beyond what the duty of every voter requires.

Mr. Huntley is a native of the Empire State, and was born at Winfield, Herkimer county, where his father was a merchant. He was educated in the district school, and graduated from the Free Academy at Utica, his parents having moved to that city. His first business training was obtained as a clerk in a hardware store. Next he entered the service of Remington & Sons, the famous gun and typewriting-machine makers. He continued here for several years, until the oil excitement

in Pennsylvania attracted him to the Keystone State. Wherever Mr. Huntley has lived he has won hosts of friends, and he is a member of the principal social clubs of Buffalo. He is a Mason in high standing, and is a member of the Episcopal church.

*PERSONAL CHRONOLOGY—Charles Russell Huntley was born at Winfield, N. Y., October 14, 1854; graduated from Utica Academy in 1870; was engaged in the hardware business and with Remington & Sons, Ilion, N. Y., 1870–77; married Ida L. Richardson of Buffalo June 12, 1878; was agent of the Standard Oil Co. in Pennsylvania, 1877–84; conducted a brokerage business at Bradford, Penn., 1884–88; has been connected with the Buffalo General Electric Co. and its predecessors since 1888.*

*WILLIS K. JACKSON*

**Willis K. Jackson** is a type of the younger class of Buffalo business men whose energy and foresight have had much to do with the remarkable growth of the city in the last twenty years. Entering business there just at the time when the "Buffalo boom" was setting in, his rapid advance may almost be deemed representative of that of the town. And yet nothing has been further from Mr. Jackson's line of work than mere booming or speculating. His has been rather the substantial work of the manufacturer and trader, whose enterprising spirit, reaching out constantly after new business, and making the city the center of operations that cover a considerable part of the country, has given to the growth of Buffalo the substantial and permanent character that is its chief distinguishing feature.

Mr. Jackson is only about thirty-five years old. Born in the West, he reversed the advice of Horace Greeley and went East, though he can hardly be held responsible for that, since he was but six years old at the time. His education was obtained in the Buffalo public schools, from which he graduated at the age of sixteen. With the energy of a youth who finds himself freed at last from school fetters, young Jackson sought and found employment with the Tug Association on Central wharf. This, however, occupied him only during the summer. The months at his disposal during the season when navigation on the lakes was closed, he determined to use to improve his education, and he accordingly entered Professor Herman Poole's Practical School, where he took a full commercial course, besides a special course in higher mathematics. This occupied two winters, his summers, meantime, being employed on Central wharf, first with the Tug Association, and then with forwarding and commission houses. After this Mr. Jackson worked for five years in a mercantile office.

When he was twenty-five years old he became connected with the cooperage business of his father-in-law, Thomas Tindle, who gladly availed himself of Mr. Jackson's business training and talents, taking the young man into his business at first on a salary and within a short time as a partner. The branching out of the firm into manufacturing dates from 1892. The first mill was built at Saginaw, Mich. The experiment of making their own stock in the very region where the material grew turned out so well that the Saginaw mill was soon duplicated by one at St. Charles. Then another was built at Bellaire, another at Gaylord, and finally a fifth at Alba. Thus the products of five large cooperage factories in the Michigan forests are brought to Buffalo for distribution by this single firm.

Mr. Jackson early became interested in military matters, enlisting as a private in Company D, 65th regiment. He was afterward transferred to Company F, and won rapid promotion. In the six years of his service he passed through the grades of corporal, 2d sergeant, 1st sergeant, 2d lieutenant, and 1st lieutenant. Though he has never been ambitious for political honors, he is an earnest Republican, and a member of the Buffalo Republican League. He belongs to the Asbury Methodist Church, and is esteemed and respected by a large circle of social and business acquaintances.

*PERSONAL CHRONOLOGY* — *Willis K. Jackson was born at Edgerton, Wis., September 22, 1861; moved to Buffalo in 1867, and was educated in the public schools there; was employed in forwarding and commission houses and in a mercantile office, 1877–86; married Annette Tindle of Buffalo September 22, 1880; has been a member of the firm of Tindle & Co., cooperage manufacturers, since 1888.*

***

**William Pryor Letchworth** has devoted his life, for more than a quarter of a century, to philanthropic public service. His parents were members of the Society of Friends, whose lives were those of quiet usefulness; and the boy, looking out upon the larger world before him, early determined that if in God's providence the way should open, his own efforts and means should be devoted to the betterment of his fellow-men.

Going to Buffalo from New York in 1848, Mr. Letchworth established with Samuel F. and Pascal P. Pratt the firm of Pratt & Letchworth, manufacturers of saddlery hardware and malleable iron. He was managing partner of that prosperous and constantly enlarging business until 1869, when he felt that he might retire from its engrossing cares, and devote his time to those works of usefulness that were the polar star of his life's endeavor. In intervals of rest he had profited by foreign travel, for which his literary tastes, and his cultivated habits of close and constant observation, had well prepared him. His interest in Buffalo affairs had always been most active. For three years he was the president of the Buffalo Fine Arts Academy, and contributed much to its success. He served also as president of the Buffalo Historical Society, and was active upon many local boards.

In 1873 the board of state commissioners of public charities, organized under the laws of 1867, was changed by statute, and became the state board of charities; and in April of that year Mr. Letchworth was appointed by Governor Dix commissioner of the 8th judicial district, to fill the vacancy caused by the death of Dr. Samuel Eastman. In these new and unexpected duties his sympathies were at once aroused by the pitiable condition of homeless and destitute children, of whom a considerable percentage were at that time in the county and city almshouses throughout the state, exposed to the most degrading associations; and he resolved that he would not rest until those unfortunates were removed from the vicious influences of that poisoned moral atmosphere. During 1873 he effected much in reforming this abuse, and in the annual report of the board to the legislature in March, 1874, he prepared that suggestive portion relating to child-saving work in which he directed attention to the great abuse of rearing children in poorhouses. In January, 1875, he made an important report on the subject, the details of which covered every poorhouse and almshouse in the state except the immense establishment in New York county containing about 800 children, which was reserved for further examination. In his report Mr. Letchworth recommended that all children between the ages of two and sixteen years be removed from these institutions, and placed in families or asylums suited to their care and education, and that their admission to pauper establishments be forbidden in the future. The recommendation was adopted, and an important act was passed during the session, which has come to be known as the "Children's Law." The county of New York subsequently appealed to the legislature for exemption from the law; but when Mr. Letchworth's report on the county institutions was made in January, 1876, which completed his report of the whole state, the appeal was denied, and this long standing abuse in the New York state system was completely abolished.

In 1876 Mr. Letchworth submitted an exhaustive report on the condition of homeless children in the various reformatory institutions of the state. These were 136 in number and provided for about 18,000 children, and with only two exceptions Mr. Letchworth had personally visited every institution. He presented authoritative information regarding each that proved of the highest value in forming and instructing public opinion as to the best methods of conducting this important branch of charitable work. From year to year his labors were continued, and his painstaking investigations and matured opinions proved of such worth that his published reports and addresses have become acknowledged authorities in the wide domain covering the relations of the state to the dependent classes.

In 1874 he had been elected vice president of the state board of charities, and upon the death of J. V. L. Pruyn, in 1878, he was unanimously elected president. From the beginning of his public service he has devoted his entire time to the work without compensation.

*WILLIAM PRYOR LETCHWORTH*

His attention was turned at this time to the care of the insane, and he deemed it of importance to learn from personal observation the methods adopted elsewhere. In 1881, accordingly, he spent several months in Great Britain and on the continent, giving his entire time to the inspection of European institutions, and seeking information that might aid him in his duties. Upon his return, his work upon "The Care of The Insane in Foreign Countries" was published, and found immediate recognition by alienists throughout the United States as a valuable treatise for their information and guidance. Its clear judgments and practical suggestions accomplished much good in our state hospitals and private asylums.

After holding the position for a decade, Mr. Letchworth voluntarily retired from the presidency of the board of charities, feeling entitled to a release from responsibilities so long sustained. He continued, however, to be a member of the board, as commissioner for the 8th judicial district. He has

*THOMAS LOTHROP*

devoted his time in recent years to official duties, to the exacting requirements of an extensive correspondence, and to the preparation of many valuable publications relating to public charities. Largely through his efforts the state has established at Sonyea, near Mount Morris, the Craig Colony for the care and treatment of epileptics. His country home at Glen Iris, at the Falls of the Genesee, has been a busy center for charitable work, extending far beyond the borders of his own state, wherever the needs of his fellow-men have sought recognition and help.

*PERSONAL CHRONOLOGY—William Pryor Letchworth was born at Brownville, Jefferson county, N. Y., May 26, 1823; engaged in manufacturing in Buffalo, 1848-69; was appointed a member of the state board of charities in April, 1873, vice president in June, 1874, and president in March, 1878; was president of the National Conference of Charities, September, 1884; received the degree of Doctor of Laws from the University of New York "for distinguished service to the state" February 9, 1894.*

***

**Thomas Lothrop** is one of the most distinguished practitioners of medicine in Buffalo, a city that supports several medical colleges, and is noted for its skilled physicians and surgeons. Dr. Lothrop's ancestors were among the earliest settlers of New England, and he is a lineal descendant of the Rev. John Lothrop, who came from England and settled in Scituate, Mass., in 1634. Dr. Lothrop prepared for college under private tutors, graduated from the Liberal Institute at Clinton, N. Y., in 1855, and entered the same year upon a three years' course of medical study at the University of Michigan. From the medical department of that institution he received the degree of M. D. in 1858. The next year he went to Buffalo to practice his profession.

His life in Buffalo began under favorable auspices, for he was invited to take charge of the professional work of Dr. John D. Hill, an eminent physician in his day, who desired a European vacation from his labors. On Dr. Hill's return Dr. Lothrop opened an office at Black Rock, where he practiced for eleven years, and established his reputation. Moving back to the center of the city in 1871, he has since been actively engaged in practice, and in the performance of his professorial duties at Niagara University. His has been a busy life. In addition to practicing and teaching medicine, he has been, since 1879, senior editor of the Buffalo *Medical and Surgical Journal*. He is physician in chief of St. Francis Hospital and the Women's Hospital; consulting physician of the Hospital of the Sisters of Charity, the Providence Retreat, and the Erie County Hospital; Fellow of the American Association of Obstetricians and Gynecologists; and he was appointed by Governor Flower in 1892 a manager of the Buffalo State Hospital.

Dr. Lothrop has been deeply interested in the eleemosynary institutions of Buffalo, especially as regards the medical aspect of such establishments. Outside the immediate practice of his profession, he has devoted time and study to the beneficent work of the Church Charity Foundation of Buffalo, of which he is president, and to the cause of education in general and of medical training in particular. His long connection with the medical department of Niagara University, dating from its establishment, has made him an earnest advocate of higher standards of study and teaching for those who are to become physicians and surgeons. The esteem in which he is held by the members of his profession was evidenced by his election in 1893 as president of the Buffalo Academy of Medicine.

Dr. Lothrop served one term as superintendent of education of Buffalo, in 1870-72, and has never lost his interest in the city schools. In 1890 he was appointed a trustee of the State Normal School at Buffalo. In all the many offices and positions of responsibility held by him, Dr. Lothrop has shown rare faithfulness, capacity for work, and executive ability. He is one of the strong men of his profession and of the city of Buffalo. Niagara University has conferred upon him doctorates of medicine and of philosophy. In politics Dr. Lothrop is a Democrat, but he has never taken an active part in political affairs except when nominated and elected superintendent of education.

*PERSONAL CHRONOLOGY—Thomas Lothrop was born at Provincetown, Mass., April 16, 1836; graduated from the Liberal Institute, Clinton, N. Y., in 1855, and from the medical department of the University of Michigan in 1858; was superintendent of education, Buffalo, 1870–72; has practiced medicine in Buffalo since 1858; has been professor of obstetrics in the medical department of Niagara University since 1883.*

•••

## Louis William Marcus

was elected surrogate of Erie county when only thirty-two years old, and he is probably the youngest man that ever held the office. When one remembers that this is the third county in the state as regards size and population, and that the work of the surrogate is correspondingly important, one can appreciate the confidence that the voters have placed in this young man. Mr. Marcus has not been long in office, but he has already shown such grasp of details, talent for concentration, and equipoise of judgment, as give assurance of a successful and highly creditable term of service.

Louis W. Marcus is a thorough Buffalonian. He was born in the Queen City, and there he has always lived. This fact explains why he has become so fully imbued with the spirit of the place. He loves Buffalo, and his enthusiasm for his native city has won friends for Buffalo and for himself. His early education was obtained in the Buffalo schools and in Williams Academy. After graduating from the high school he entered Cornell University, where he obtained the degree of LL. B.

He naturally turned his mind toward the law; ambitious youth commonly find this the most attractive of the professions. After exhaustive study, he was admitted to the bar when twenty-five years old. His first partnership was formed in 1890, when he made one of the firm of Swift, Weaver & Marcus. Two years later Mr. Swift withdrew, and

*LOUIS WILLIAM MARCUS*

the firm continued as Weaver & Marcus until the death of Mr. Weaver in February, 1894.

Mr. Marcus has taken a strong interest in politics ever since his majority, though his part until recently

has been that of the citizen rather than of the politician. When the time came for the election of a
new surrogate of Erie county, in the fall of 1895,
there was a general feeling of revolt from machine
politics, which had once wrecked the Republican
party in the county, afterward the Democratic, and

*JOSEPH B. MAYER*

which was then beginning to reappear in the Republican party. The feeling expressed itself in a desire
to choose Republican candidates from outside the
ranks of the older and more familiar politicians.
For the office of surrogate, as for other offices, the
people demanded an infusion of new blood, a candidate of independent character, who should feel
that his sole obligations were to the people who
had elected him. It was in response to this demand
that the county convention placed in nomination
Louis W. Marcus. It was not done without a sharp
struggle, but the triumph was all the more notable
for the opposition that had preceded it. The same
faith in Mr. Marcus's ability and honesty that had

led to his nomination secured his election by a large
majority.

Judge Marcus stands high as a Mason, holding
membership in Ancient Landmark Lodge, No. 441,
F. & A. M., and Adytum Chapter, Buffalo Consistory, 32d degree. He is also a member of the Independent Order of Red Men. While in
college he joined the Delta Kappa Epsilon
fraternity, and has since become a member of the D. K. E. Club of New York.
In the social life of Buffalo he figures as
a prominent member of the new and
growing Phoenix Club, of which he is
president.

*PERSONAL CHRONOLOGY—
Louis William Marcus was born at Buffalo
May 18, 1864; was educated in the Buffalo schools and Cornell University; was
admitted to the bar in 1888; married Ray
R. Dahlman of Buffalo November 19,
1889; was elected surrogate of Erie county
in November, 1895.*

\*\*\*

**Joseph B. Mayer** is a promoter
of new enterprises. He is a representative of a class of men in the modern world
who find unplowed fields for capital to
develop. Invention and enterprise have
gone hand in hand under the guidance of
such men as Mr. Mayer, who blaze the
way for industry and progress. The past
decade has witnessed a marvelous expansion of American cities. The trend of
humanity has set in that direction, and
there has been an ever increasing demand
for more room in urban communities. To
supply this demand, vast tracts of waste
or farm land must be reclaimed from
nature and transformed into city lots.
Along this line of commercial activity
Mr. Mayer has expended effort and capital in recent
years. He has organized and successfully managed
syndicates, which have purchased large sections of
land around Buffalo, improved it, and put it upon the
market. The transportation problem has also received
attention from him, for nothing is more essential to
the development of suburban property than easy and
cheap means of access. Therefore Mr. Mayer is
interested in street railroads, and was a promoter
of the Buffalo Traction Company, whose vigorous
fight, in 1895-96, to secure a franchise in Buffalo,
is a matter of local history.

Mr. Mayer was born in Baden, Germany, but
came to the United States before he had attained

his majority. He received a thorough elementary education, and graduated in 1866 from the Freiburg gymnasium, an institution of the same relative rank as the American high school or academy.

Mr. Mayer settled in Buffalo in 1868, and for many years was engaged there in the business of importing diamonds. He was associated with Louis Weill from 1872 until 1876, when the partnership was dissolved. Mr. Mayer continued in the business until 1891, and built up one of the largest and most important establishments of the kind in the country outside of New York city. He made trips to Holland twice each year, purchasing there unset stones in large quantities. The manifest destiny, however, of the Queen City impressed itself upon Mr. Mayer, and his attention was gradually turned in the direction of real estate. In this field of enterprise his operations have been on a large scale, and his sagacity, perseverance, and tact have enabled him to conduct to favorable results the many important projects in which he has figured.

In politics Mr. Mayer is a Democrat, and is always ardent in the support of his party; but he has uniformly declined to accept nominations for elective offices. He accepted, however, in 1895, an appointment from the mayor of Buffalo as a civil-service commissioner. He is president of the Temple Beth Zion, the leading Jewish congregation in Buffalo; and is a member of the Masonic fraternity, and of the Ellicott and Liberal clubs. He is a life member of the German Young Men's Association, a member of the council of the Charity Organization Society, and actively interested in the free kindergartens and many kindred organizations. He has been an extensive traveler, having been all over the United States, and visited many European countries.

*PERSONAL CHRONOLOGY—Joseph B. Mayer was born at Baden, Germany, January 4, 1849; graduated from the high school of Freiburg, Germany, in 1866; came to the United States in 1868, and began business as a diamond importer in Buffalo; married Belle Falck of Buffalo July 15, 1874; has been engaged in the real-estate business in Buffalo since 1891.*

●●●

**Willis H. Meads** is a prominent member of the Erie-county bar; but he is equally well known for his interest in all matters pertaining to the public

good. He is a "down-Easter" by birth, and his early education was acquired in the schools of his native town. He prepared for college at Limerick Academy and Nichols Latin School, entered Bowdoin College at Brunswick, Me., in 1866, and graduated therefrom in 1870 with the Bachelor of Arts degree. Three years later he was honored with the Master of Arts degree by his *alma mater*. While in college he was a member of the Psi Upsilon fraternity, and upon graduation was elected a member of the Phi Beta Kappa fraternity. Mr. Meads has a studious nature, and he naturally turned his talents to teaching. He went to Buffalo soon after he left college, and for a period of ten years was principal of one of the public schools there. Mr. Meads studied law while teaching, and in 1880 he was admitted to the bar, and resigned his position in the

*WILLIS H. MEADS*

public schools. Soon afterward he became the junior member of the law firm of Kennedy, Roberts & Meads, which was dissolved in 1881. For about four years after this he practiced law alone, and then associated himself with George T. Quinby under the firm name of Quinby & Meads. Later the firm was changed to Quinby, Meads & Rebadow, and so continued until its dissolution in 1893.

Aside from his connection with the legal profession, Mr. Meads has associated himself with many of

*HERBERT MICKLE*

the well known institutions of Buffalo, and is prominent in fraternal and club circles. He is a member of the Queen City Lodge, F. & A. M., and of the Adytum Chapter, R. A. M. He is a prominent member of the University, Buffalo, and Acacia clubs, and is actively interested in the Buffalo Historical Society and the Society for the Prevention of Cruelty to Animals.

Mr. Meads has only once been a candidate for political honors. He had always been interested in the cause of education, and especially in the advancement of the public schools, and in 1881 he received the Republican nomination for superintendent of education for the city of Buffalo. How well he ran may be seen in the fact that while Grover Cleveland

was elected mayor of the city at this time by a Democratic majority of 3,700, Mr. Meads was defeated by fewer than 150 votes.

The reputation for honesty and ability that Mr. Meads had gained during his long and successful career in the practice of law in Buffalo brought him, in 1895, an important appointment. The jury system of Erie county was then in a very unsatisfactory condition, and a law had been passed to correct the evil. This law vested the appointing power in the justices of the Supreme Court residing in the county, and in the county judge; and by them Mr. Meads was appointed commissioner of jurors. The office is a very important one, and Mr. Meads was selected from a large number of candidates to fill the position. Since his appointment he has given his whole energy and ability to the task before him, and has brought the once-distrusted jury system of Erie county to a high standard.

*PERSONAL CHRONOLOGY— Willis Howard Meads was born at South Limington, Me., February 22, 1846; attended Limerick (Me.) Academy and Nichols Latin School, Lewiston, Me., and graduated from Bowdoin College in 1870; was principal of Public School No. 18, Buffalo, 1870–80; married Martha Rose of Buffalo December 24, 1872, and Louise Collingnon of Buffalo January 6, 1880; was admitted to the bar at Buffalo in 1880; was Republican candidate for superintendent of education of Buffalo, 1881; was appointed commissioner of jurors for Erie county in 1895.*

...

**Herbert Mickle,** though still a young man, has attained an enviable position among the medical fraternity of Buffalo, and has established a reputation for learning and skill that insures to him a distinguished career in the years to come. He is a member of a family well known in literary and scientific circles in Canada, and inherits a taste for poetry from his ancestor, William Julius Mickle, who flourished as a Scottish poet, 1735–88, and who is best known by his translation of Camoens's *Lusiad.*

Born at Guelph, in the province of Ontario, Dr. Mickle received a thorough collegiate and medical education to fit him for his chosen profession. He graduated from Upper Canada College, Toronto, at the unusually early age of sixteen, and at once entered Trinity Medical School in the same city. In 1881 he received the degree of Bachelor of Medicine from Trinity College, Toronto; and the same year went to England, and entered St. Bartholomew's Hospital Medical School, in London, where he pursued additional studies for two years. At the end of that time he was made a member of the Royal College of Surgeons and Physicians of London, and received the degree of Doctor of Medicine from Trinity College, Toronto.

After this long and thorough course of preparation, combining the advantages of the old world and the new, Dr. Mickle returned to America, in 1883, and established himself in Buffalo. Although he had devoted so much time to his medical studies, he had scarcely passed his majority when he began his professional career in Buffalo. He was at once appointed house surgeon to the Emergency Hospital, and demonstrator of anatomy in the medical department of Niagara University. Two years later he was made lecturer on pathology in the same institution, then professor of anatomy, and finally professor of surgery; and this position he still fills. Of hospital practice, so valuable to a physician, Dr. Mickle has always had a large share. He is at present attending surgeon to the Hospital of the Sisters of Charity, St. Francis Hospital, the Emergency Hospital, and the Church Home, and consulting surgeon to the Buffalo Women's Hospital.

His duties in connection with these various institutions, together with his private practice and his lectures at the university, would seem more than enough to occupy the time of one man; but Dr. Mickle has also given some attention to literature in connection with his profession, and he was at one time assistant editor of the Buffalo *Medical and Surgical Journal*.

Dr. Mickle finds healthful relaxation from the wear and tear of professional life in his interest in athletic sports of different kinds. He has been an active member of the Buffalo Yacht Club, the Buffalo Cricket Club, and the Buffalo Athletic Club. He is also a member of Hiram Lodge, No. 105, Free and Accepted Masons, and attends the First Presbyterian Church.

*PERSONAL CHRONOLOGY—Herbert Mickle was born at Guelph, Ontario, April 30, 1861;* graduated from Upper Canada College, Toronto, in 1877, and from Trinity Medical School, Toronto, in 1881; married Susette L. Ross of Brooklyn July 27, 1892; has practiced medicine in Buffalo since 1883; has been professor of surgery in the medical department of Niagara University since 1891.

***

**Adelbert Moot** ranks with the foremost of Buffalo lawyers. A studious, painstaking, conscientious man, he has won his way by his own efforts, based upon untiring energy and a strong moral purpose. He is a man whom his fellows respect, because they believe that he strives to be right and to do right. Though he has never sought public office, he has been prominent in politics, and has been a lifelong Republican. He loves his country first, however, and his party afterward. He deems

*ADELBERT MOOT*

it the citizen's duty to keep his party clean if he can, and if he cannot, to punish it for its sins, rather than have his fellow-citizens suffer by its mistakes or its crimes. Acting on these high principles, he is naturally a reformer. The Civil Service Reform Association holds him among its most active and earnest members. When the Good Government Club movement in this state began, he was among the first to identify himself with it. The agitation for sound money found in him a ready and an eager advocate. When the election frauds of 1892 were brought home to the people, and a citizens' association was formed to prosecute the malefactors, Mr. Moot was retained at once as one of the principal lawyers for the association. He was thus actively engaged at that time in the work of purification of the city.

Mr. Moot was a country boy, born among the hills of famous Allegany county. When he had exhausted the resources of the schools in his neighborhood, he followed the usual course of country boys by going to the nearest village school, which in this case was at Belmont. Afterward he attended the academy at Nunda, and then the State Normal School at Geneseo. Thence he went to the Albany Law School, where he took his degree. He was admitted to the bar on his twenty-second birthday.

He began practice a few months later in partnership with George M. Osgoodby at Nunda. Two years thereafter the firm moved to Buffalo, and Mr. Moot thus plunged into the struggle of city practice much earlier than do most country-bred lawyers. Lacking the advantage of an extensive acquaintance, he made up for this drawback by exceptional ability and a disposition to work hard. The Nunda firm of Osgoodby & Moot became, in Buffalo, Osgoodby, Titus & Moot, by the accession of Judge Titus. Three years later Mr. Moot withdrew to enter the firm of Lewis, Moot & Lewis, with which he remained twelve years. During this period was achieved the substantial success that won for him his high place at the Buffalo bar. In 1893 he entered his present firm, known as Sprague, Moot, Sprague & Brownell. He has had charge of many important cases in the courts of Erie county, and his practice, it need hardly be added, has assumed large proportions. He is a member of the American Bar Association and of the New York State Bar Association, and is also connected with the law department of the University of Buffalo.

Mr. Moot has found time for extensive reading and study, outside his profession, in the general field of literature, science, and history. As an aid to these pursuits, he has joined the Thursday Club, the Liberal Club, the Buffalo Historical Society, and the Society of Natural Sciences. His only social club is the Saturn. He belongs to the Church of Our Father (Unitarian).

*PERSONAL CHRONOLOGY—Adelbert Moot was born at Allen, Allegany county, N. Y., November 22, 1854; was educated in public schools and the Albany Law School; was admitted to the bar at Albany in 1876; practiced law at Nunda, N. Y., 1877-79; married Carrie A. Van Ness of Cuba, N. Y., July 22, 1882; has practiced law in Buffalo since 1879.*

\*\*\*

**William H. Orcutt** was a distinguished member of the Middlesex-county bar in Massachusetts before he moved to Buffalo, and became a citizen of the Empire State. In his new home Mr. Orcutt has already won a high place in the ranks of his profession, and among the influential factors of the city's intellectual and social life. Mr. Orcutt is a Bostonian by birth, and had the benefit of a thorough training in the public schools of his native city, and of the neighboring city of Cambridge. Educated under the very eaves of America's greatest university, it was quite natural that he should enter Harvard College. His course there was most creditable, and he took rank with the best scholars in his class, graduating eighth in a class of 108. This high stand made him eligible for membership in the Phi Beta Kappa society, composed of the brainiest men of all the leading colleges of the country. Mr. Orcutt was prominent also in athletics, and is a fine illustration of the fact that a man can attain to high scholarship, and yet participate in the athletic sports of his college.

After completing his classical course, Mr. Orcutt entered the law school of the university, and at the end of two years received the degree of LL. B. He entered at once upon a twenty months' clerkship in the office of Brooks & Ball of Boston. In 1875 he was admitted to the Massachusetts bar, and in that year began to practice for himself in Boston. He was there engaged in the duties of his profession continuously until 1882, when he was appointed by Governor Long judge of the District Court in the county of Middlesex. This was a life position, and as the court was located in Cambridge, the shire city of that county, Mr. Orcutt's duties were performed there, until he resigned his office and moved to Buffalo.

Mr. Orcutt took up his residence in the Queen City under most favorable auspices. He became a member of the law firm of Roberts, Alexander, Messer & Orcutt, now changed to Roberts, Becker, Ashley, Messer & Orcutt, one of the largest legal firms in western New York. In the comparatively short time that he has lived in Buffalo, Mr. Orcutt has impressed the bar and the community as a man of wide intelligence, a clear and deep thinker, endowed in an exceptional degree with hard sense, deliberate judgment, and absolute integrity. To these sterling qualities he adds a dignified presence and courtly manners. In public affairs Mr. Orcutt has been less conspicuous in Buffalo than he was in Massachusetts, and has confined himself closely to his law practice, doubtless from an inherent modesty and dislike to obtrude himself in the affairs of a somewhat strange city; but Buffalo has need for the very services which he is most competent to render, and which in Cambridge he did render.

While a resident of Cambridge, Mr. Orcutt gave twelve years of efficient and unrewarded service to the public schools of that city. The cause of education has been his special study outside the law, and he has devoted time, in a manner worthy of the highest praise, to the betterment of the system. It is such service that really tests a man's loyalty to American institutions. His practical sense has been displayed in providing manual training schools, and in shortening the time and simplifying the courses of study in preparatory schools so as to give to pupils who can spend but a few years in school the greatest variety of training compatible with sound principles of instruction. Mr. Orcutt has written frequently on educational topics, and is master of a logical, forceful style. He is a member of the Buffalo and Ellicott clubs, and is an attendant at the Delaware Avenue Baptist Church.

*PERSONAL CHRONOLOGY—William Hunter Orcutt was born at Boston, Mass., November 15, 1847; was educated in the public schools of Boston and Cambridge, and graduated from Harvard College in 1869; studied law at Harvard Law School, and was admitted to the bar of Massachusetts in 1875; practiced law in Boston, 1875-82; was appointed judge of the District Court in Middlesex county in 1882; married Leafie Sloan of Buffalo June 4, 1889; has practiced law in Buffalo since 1889.*

---

**Maurice B. Patch** has made applied science the study of a lifetime, and has become a recognized authority on the subject of metallurgy. He is a son of the Pine Tree State, and has enjoyed the double advantage of a broad education in the East and a large practical experience in the West. After completing a public-school training at Lowell, in a state famous for its educational system, he pursued a course in mining and engineering at the Massachusetts Institute of Technology, which has sent out many of the scientific leaders of the day. He graduated thence in 1872 with the degree of Bachelor of Sciences.

*WILLIAM H. ORCUTT*

Mr. Patch chose as a field for his talents and attainments the remote western regions containing the mines for whose exploitation he had equipped himself. Accordingly, the very year of his graduation found him settled at Georgetown, Col., carrying on his profession as a mining engineer. For two years he remained there, surveying mining properties and working in the various departments of his calling. He then accepted an offer from the Detroit & Lake Superior Copper Smelting Co., and became the chemist of the company at Houghton, Mich. While in this position Mr. Patch was able to follow a line of original research which had always been attractive to him, and which he has pursued untiringly, until he is now among the foremost copper metallurgists in the country. During these same years he was also establishing a wide reputation as a mine surveyor, chemist, and practical operator in mining and smelting, and in all the branches of his profession. Consequently, when the well-known Calumet &

but his work has been solely in the interest of the corporations by which he has been employed, and which naturally desire to keep secret the processes that they have perfected. For this reason Mr. Patch has never been able to write anything for publication, and the general public has not profited, except indirectly, by his research.

Mr. Patch has been a prime mover in several successful financial undertakings. While residing in Michigan he helped to organize two banks, the First National at Lake Linden and the Superior Savings Bank at Hancock, and was a director in both until he left the state. He is now a director of the Niagara Bank of Buffalo, and is interested in several mining companies. He is a member of the American Institute of Mining Engineers, and of the Engineers' Society of Western New York. He is a member and vestryman of St. John's Episcopal Church, Buffalo.

*PERSONAL CHRONOLOGY—Maurice Byron Patch was born at Otisfield, Me., June 8, 1852; was educated in the public schools of Lowell, Mass., and graduated from the Massachusetts Institute of Technology in 1872; was employed as a mining engineer in Colorado, 1872–74; married Emily Isabella White of Lowell July 6, 1875; was chemist of the Detroit & Lake Superior Copper Smelting Co., 1874–86, and superintendent of the Calumet & Hecla Mining Co.'s works at Lake Linden, Mich., 1886–90; has been superintendent of the Buffalo Smelting Works of the same company since 1891.*

MAURICE B. PATCH

Hecla Mining Co. was preparing to install a smelting plant at Lake Linden, Mich., they sought Mr. Patch as designer and superintendent of the work. He accepted the position, moved to Lake Linden, and remained there for five years, completing this contract and carrying on work in his special line. At the end of this time he received a flattering offer from the same company to undertake similar work for them at Buffalo. He went to that city in January, 1891, and became superintendent of the company's works there; and he still holds this position.

In connection with his special branch of science, Mr. Patch has done much original work, and has made many discoveries of great practical utility;

**John W. Robinson,** president of the Robinson Bros. Lumber Co. of North Tonawanda, N. Y., is one of the solid, conservative business men whose life shows the rewards that may be obtained from prudence, close attention to business, and strict integrity. The Tonawandas constitute one of the chief centers of the lumber trade in the United States. The fact is due to the efforts of such men as Mr. Robinson, who have had the foresight and courage to invest their capital in the development of this important business at the foot of the lakes.

Mr. Robinson has been the architect of his own fortunes. At the age of fourteen he was left to care for himself. His education was therefore necessarily limited to such as could be obtained at the common schools, supplemented by attendance at night schools and by careful reading. He first went to Buffalo when about seventeen years old, remaining there and thereabouts for a few years. His father had been engaged in the lumber business, and it was natural for the son to concern himself with the same industry. Then he went to Detroit, and obtained employment with one of the large lumber manufacturers there. By his fidelity, intelligence, and determination to master the business, he soon obtained the best position at the disposal of his employers.

But he was not satisfied to remain working for others. Having acquired a thorough knowledge of the calling and a moderate capital, he became interested with his brothers in the wholesale lumber business in Detroit. The concern began operations in a small way, but was at once successful and grew steadily. Having concluded that their business could be carried on more advantageously at North Tonawanda, the company moved thither in the latter part of 1888. One of Mr. Robinson's brothers retired from the firm before the removal of the business from Detroit. The other died June 30, 1889. Mr. Robinson soon afterward purchased the interest held by his brother, and for the last few years has been practically the sole owner of the business. In 1891 he brought his family to Buffalo, and has maintained his residence there since. He is now known as an upright citizen, and a firm and enthusiastic believer in a greater Buffalo.

As soon as he went to Tonawanda Mr. Robinson began to take a prominent part in promoting the welfare of the place, and especially of the trade in which he was engaged. He has frequently been called upon to visit both the national and state capitals in the interest of the Twin Cities. He has been twice elected president of the Tonawanda Lumberman's Association, serving in that capacity during the great strikes of 1892 and 1893, and conducting the affairs of the association with the sagacity and firmness which finally resulted in an amicable adjustment of all disputed matters. He has served as vice president of the Lumber Exchange Bank, North Tonawanda, for several years, and has also been twice elected president of the National Association of Wholesale Lumber Dealers.

In private life Mr. Robinson is of quiet, unassuming manners, and is approachable by both old and young. He is fond of outdoor sports, and is an expert angler. He is an official member of the Delaware Avenue Methodist Church, and takes great interest in charitable and religious work. He was one of the founders and supporters of the Buffalo Ophthalmic Hospital. He is a member of the Buffalo, Acacia, and Liberal clubs, and the Buffalo Historical Society. He is also a Knight Templar, a 32d degree Mason, and a Noble of the Mystic Shrine. In politics he is a Republican, and takes pride in attending the primaries, believing that this duty is as important as voting, and should be discharged by every good citizen. He has never aspired to political office.

*PERSONAL CHRONOLOGY—John Willoughby Robinson was born in Simcoe county, Ontario, October 14, 1848; married Matilda Oxenham*

JOHN W. ROBINSON

*May 22, 1874; was connected with the lumber business in Detroit, 1873-88; established a lumber business at North Tonawanda, N. Y., in 1888, and has lived in Buffalo since.*

**Charles F. Tabor** is a Buffalonian whose reputation is at least state-wide. That he is thus generally and favorably known is due to the fact that he was the head of the state legal department for four years, and as attorney general had the disposal of a large number of complicated questions,

*CHARLES F. TABOR*

and the preparation and presentation in court of several cases of the greatest importance.

Mr. Tabor is a native of the Wolverene State, but he was brought to Erie county, New York, when about two years of age. He received what was then deemed a good education, attending various academies in western New York that had more than a local reputation. Finishing his school course in 1860, he began at once the study of law; and in November, 1863, he was admitted to the bar. While studying law Mr. Tabor also taught school for three winters. In 1868 he formed a copartnership with Thomas Corlett, afterward a justice of the Supreme Court. This connection continued for six years. Then Mr. Tabor practiced alone until 1883, when

he formed a partnership with William F. Sheehan. The firm was afterward enlarged by the admission of E. E. Coatsworth and John Cunneen, and became one of the best-known firms in western New York. Since Mr. Sheehan moved to New York, in the fall of 1894, Mr. Tabor has been associated with L. C. Wilkie.

Like so many lawyers, Mr. Tabor has been for many years intimately connected with politics. He is a Democrat and a strong party man. He has held many public offices, the first of which was that of commissioner of excise for Erie county. He was also a member of the board of supervisors of Erie county, representing the town of Lancaster. He spent two years in the legislature, sent thither by a majority of the voters of the 4th district of Erie county. This was in 1876 and 1877. In 1885 he was appointed deputy attorney general of the state of New York, and served as such for two years. His work here brought him prominently into view, and gave him the Democratic nomination for the position of attorney general. He was triumphantly elected in 1887 and re-elected in 1889. After the expiration of his four years of service at the head of this important department, he returned to Buffalo and resumed his large private practice.

While acting as attorney general Mr. Tabor was called upon to handle a number of notable cases. One of these involved the constitutionality of the so-called electrocution law, which substituted death by electricity for hanging as the capital punishment of the state. This law was fought with great vigor. The large electrical companies united in opposing it, and it was charged that, impelled by commercial reasons, they supplied the means for fighting the law. They were lacked, moreover, by a strong public sentiment, many people believing that electricity was not sufficiently well understood to be used in taking human life. The case was not settled until the Supreme Court of the United States passed upon it. Mr. Tabor came off triumphant. Another important victory was won by Mr. Tabor in the case that established the state's right to tax corporations for doing business in this state, although their capital might be invested in government bonds.

Mr. Tabor also succeeded, while attorney general, in obtaining the decision of the Court of Appeals of this state, that the great sugar trust, formed by the union of different corporations for the purpose of controlling the product and price of refined sugar, was in violation of corporate law, and in securing judgments vacating the charters of the different corporations that had entered the syndicate.

*PERSONAL CHRONOLOGY — Charles F. Tabor was born at White Pigeon, St. Joseph county, Mich., June 28, 1841; was admitted to the bar in 1863; married Phebe S. Andrews of Pembroke, N. Y., December 24, 1864; was member of assembly, 1876–77, deputy attorney general, 1880–81, and attorney general, 1888–91; has practiced law in Buffalo since 1865.*

* * *

**Thomas Tindle** was a Yorkshire lad who came to America to seek his fortune, and who, for the past thirty years, has made his home in Buffalo.

His education was obtained in the common schools of his native place, and ended with his fourteenth year. He possessed an energetic, ambitious spirit, and after a few years' work in England he determined to seek the wider opportunities that a newer country afforded. Accordingly, at the age of nineteen, he came to the United States. He settled in St. Lawrence county, New York, and followed the occupation of a farmer there for the next ten years. But his instincts were those of the trader and manufacturer, and in the spring of 1865 he disposed of his farm, and became foreman for J. H. Crawford & Co., a firm of canal forwarders at Oswego, N. Y.

This proved to be the turning point in his career — the first step which led him ultimately to Buffalo, and to the extensive and prosperous business that he now carries on. He had been with Crawford & Co. only a year when they moved their headquarters to Buffalo, taking him with them. Two years later the firm discontinued business, and Mr. Tindle obtained employment with Toles & Sweet, canal forwarders and dealers in cooperage stock. There he remained for the next twelve years, becoming purchasing agent and salesman, and learning many details of the cooperage business.

In this industry Mr. Tindle discerned a favorable opening, and in January, 1880, he began business for himself as a jobber. A few months later he

extended his operations, and began the manufacture of cooperage stock at mills in Canada. After five years he sold his interest in these mills, and for the next few years devoted his entire attention to his jobbing business. In 1888 his son-in-law, Willis K. Jackson, was taken into partnership, under the firm name of Thomas Tindle & Co. Under Mr. Tindle's shrewd and careful management the business grew rapidly, and it soon became necessary to undertake once more the manufacture of the stock in which the firm dealt. Five mills, therefore, all located within easy reach of the Michigan forests, were successively built or otherwise acquired. They turn out a vast amount of cooperage stock, all of which is handled by the firm at its Buffalo headquarters. In addition, a large amount of stock is bought from

*THOMAS TINDLE*

other manufacturers, including the entire output of several stave mills in Canada. The firm of Tindle & Co. sells its products all over the country, from Maine to California, though New York,

Pennsylvania, Wisconsin, and Minnesota constitute its principal markets.

Such a business affords ample scope for the talents and energies of any man, and Mr. Tindle has wisely confined his attention to it for the most part. He is, however, a director of the Niagara Bank, a member

ANSLEY WILCOX

and trustee of Asbury Methodist Episcopal Church, and a member of the Ancient Order of United Workmen.

*PERSONAL CHRONOLOGY — Thomas Tindle was born at Broomfleet, Yorkshire, England, April 3, 1856; was educated in common schools in England; came to the United States in 1855, and engaged in farming in St. Lawrence county, N. Y.; was agent for canal forwarders in Buffalo, 1855-80; married Harriet Braithwaite of Ogdensburg, N. Y., April 5, 1856; has carried on a jobbing and manufacturing business in cooperage stock at Buffalo since 1880.*

* * *

**Ansley Wilcox** is still a young man, having barely passed two score years; but a strong personal force, displayed in all his dealings with his fellow-men, has given him a place in the esteem of the community that few men attain at his age. Endowed with an acute sense of right and wrong in public affairs, and with a sturdy determination to do a lion's share toward the correction of the political and social abuses of the times, Mr. Wilcox has closely identified himself with all the reform movements of recent years, and has been a tower of strength to the cause of good government. He is a type of the best citizenship to be found in American life.

Born near Augusta, Ga., just before the breaking out of the Civil War, young Wilcox spent his boyhood amid some of the most stirring scenes of that great and fierce struggle. In the last year of the war his family left the South, and finally settled in Connecticut, which was his father's native state. The second ten years of his life were passed at New Haven, first in attending a preparatory school, and afterward as a student at Yale College. Then came a year of rest and travel, succeeded by a year of post-graduate study at University College, Oxford, England.

Having moved to Buffalo in 1876, and been admitted to the bar two years later, Mr. Wilcox began a brilliant career, and soon attained a foremost rank among the lawyers of western New York. For ten years the firm of Allen, Movius & Wilcox was one of the strongest at the Buffalo bar. Mr. Wilcox, while a forcible and brilliant speaker, has devoted most of his time and attention professionally to office rather than to the trial of cases in the courts. He enjoys a large and lucrative practice.

Mr. Wilcox has never had any aspirations in the direction of office holding, and many phases of political life are particularly distasteful to him. Independence has been his watchword from the start, and the independent movement in national politics beginning in 1884, appealed most strongly to him, and had his heartiest sympathy and support. He was a leader of the movement in his part of the state.

Outside of politics, also, Mr. Wilcox has labored energetically for the cause of reform. The Buffalo Charity Organization Society — an association which has been the forerunner of many similar societies in the country, and which is founded on the principle that the best way to aid the poor is to help them to help themselves — counted him among its first and most active members. The unqualified success of this practical charity owes not a little to his energy and devotion to its interests.

In the social life of Buffalo Mr. Wilcox has been conspicuous. He is a prominent member of the Buffalo Club, and was its president in 1893; and has taken a more or less active part in many societies, both social and charitable, of his city. For ten years he has regularly delivered a course of lectures at the University of Buffalo, where he has the professorship of medical jurisprudence. While in college and in the early years after graduation, Mr. Wilcox wrote several magazine articles; but in recent times he has found little leisure for purely literary work.

*PERSONAL CHRONOLOGY — Ansley Wilcox was born at Summerville, Ga., January 27, 1856; prepared for college at Hopkins Grammar School, New Haven, Conn., and graduated from Yale College in 1874; studied at University College, Oxford, England, 1875-76; was admitted to the bar in 1878; married Cornelia C. Rumsey of Buffalo January 17, 1878, and her sister, Mary Grace Rumsey, November 20, 1883; was in the firm of Crowley, Movius & Wilcox, 1882-84, in that of Allen, Movius & Wilcox, 1884-92, and in that of Movius & Wilcox, 1892-94; has been associated with Worthington C. Miner since early in 1894.*

**Edward Appleyard** is a self-made man, whose life illustrates the power of will and honest effort to cope successfully with adverse circumstances. In speaking of him it is difficult to state the facts of his life without seeming to intrude upon his privacy, for he belongs to the class of men who prefer that their work shall be the criterion of their worth. Mr. Appleyard was born in Yorkshire, England, within sight of the home of the famous Brontë family of novelists. He attended the parish school a short time; but at the early age of eight years was put to work in a factory for half a day, and at thirteen was taken from school altogether and employed in a mill. The boy had, however, learned enough at school to want to know more, and with the aid of night schools and by home study he filled out a given course, took a government examination, and received a certificate.

About this time he was apprenticed to Messrs. Butterfield Brothers of Bradford, England, to learn the business of a worsted spinner. When twenty-five years old he embarked in business for himself, associating his brother with him a few years later. In the fall of 1872 arrangements were made with William Broadhead for the manufacture of alpaca goods in the United States. The next year, from plans drawn by Mr. Appleyard, the great plant of the Jamestown Worsted Mills was established, and put in operation under his management. In 1876, having severed his relations with this company, he returned to England, and procured for William Broadhead & Sons an equipment for alpaca manufacture. The plant thus established has grown to mammoth proportions, and to-day constitutes one

*EDWARD APPLEYARD*

of the most valued and important industries of Jamestown. Mr. Appleyard is superintendent of the works.

Not only in mercantile life, but also in social, literary, and religious circles, has Mr. Appleyard been active. He was the first president of the Sons of

St. George, and is a contributor to the journal of that body. He is the author of the "History of the Methodist Church in Jamestown," and of numerous poems, among which "An Ode to Sympathy" is highly regarded by critics. He is a member of the Methodist Episcopal church, a local preacher,

*CHARLES H. CORBETT*

and a Sunday-school superintendent. He was elected a delegate to the General Conference held in New York in 1888. His continued interest in education is evidenced by his position as trustee of Allegheny College.

In politics Mr. Appleyard is an ardent Republican. While never a seeker for office, he has served for three years as president of the board of health of Jamestown, regarding his incumbency of that position as a duty to the public. In all the varied relations of his full and active life he has the confidence and respect of business men and neighbors, and can be truly classed among the strong, conservative forces of American citizenship.

*PERSONAL CHRONOLOGY— Edward Appleyard was born in the parish of Keighley, Yorkshire,* *England, April 15, 1840; was educated in the parish school and by private study; was apprenticed to a firm of worsted spinners in 1855, and began business for himself in 1865; married Isabella Stott of Halifax, England, July 15, 1868; has been engaged in worsted and alpaca manufacture at Jamestown, N. Y., since 1874.*

***

**Charles H. Corbett** has had an unusually successful business career, and is deservedly popular in the political and social life of the town of Sherman, where he has lived for the past thirty years. For a quarter of a century the firm of Hart & Corbett, of which he is a member, has carried on a dry-goods and general-merchandise business in Sherman. The concern has steadily grown and prospered, and this is due in large measure to Mr. Corbett's energy and ability. He has known how to provide for the wants of the public, and has spared no effort to that end; and thus his business success may be regarded as fairly earned.

Political honors are not easily obtainable by a Democrat in Chautauqua county, but Mr. Corbett has shown that personal popularity and special fitness for public life can overcome even so great odds as confront Democrats in that stronghold of Republicanism. Three years after his removal to Sherman he was elected town clerk, and served for three years, 1874–76. In 1882 and 1883 he acted as supervisor for the town of Sherman, and in the fall of 1882 he was elected to the legislature from the 1st assembly district of Chautauqua county by a majority of 986 votes. In the legislature he was made chairman of the committee on charitable and religious institutions. His advice and assistance are highly valued by his fellow-Democrats, and he has been for four years chairman of the Democratic county committee, and is at present its treasurer. He is also a member of the Democratic state committee.

Mr. Corbett was a country boy, born in Chautauqua county and brought up on a farm. He attended the district schools and Westfield Academy, and then took a full commercial course at the Eastman Business College, Poughkeepsie, N. Y. He thus acquired an excellent theoretical business training, which he at once proceeded to put to practical use. He entered the dry-goods house of J. T. Green of Sherman as a clerk, and remained there five years.

At the end of this time he determined to launch out for himself. He accordingly bought the interest of J. M. Coveney in the well-established firm of Coveney & Hart, and began the successful business career outlined above.

Mr. Corbett has taken an active part in all public affairs in Sherman. He was one of the organizers of the State Bank there, and is its vice president. He is also treasurer of the school board of the town, and chief of the fire department. In the Masonic and other fraternities he is a prominent member. In 1891 he was Grand Master of the Ancient Order of United Workmen of the State of New York, and he has been for five years a member of the Grand Lodge finance committee, of which he is at present chairman. He is a Mason of the 32d degree, and a member of the following organizations: Olive Lodge, No. 575, F. & A. M.; Westfield Chapter, No. 230, R. A. M.; Dunkirk Council, No. 25, R. & S. M.; Dunkirk Commandery, No. 40, K. T.; Ismailia Temple, O. N. M. S.; and others.

*PERSONAL CHRONOLOGY—*
*Charles H. Corbett was born at Mina, N. Y., October 5, 1845; was educated in district schools and Eastman Business College, Poughkeepsie, N. Y.; was clerk in a dry-goods store at Sherman, N. Y., 1866-71; married Narcissa Dutton of Sherman May 14, 1869; was elected member of assembly in 1882; has conducted a dry-goods and general-merchandise business at Sherman since 1871.*

**William J. Glenn** has achieved prominence in life at an unusually early age. The Empire State has produced few sons who have displayed more activity, energy, and ambition. In his brief career he has occupied himself in various pursuits, and has succeeded in so marked a degree that each occupation has become the stepping-stone to a higher one. He has been both printer and editor, and is an all-round newspaper man. His education was not so thorough as he desired, but he made the most of his opportunities in the village school at Dansville, and later at Wellsville Academy, from which he graduated at the age of seventeen years.

After finishing his school life he went to work as a printer in the office of the Wellsville *Reporter,* which was then edited by the late Enos W. Barnes.

Having learned the printer's trade, and acquired experience in the management of a newspaper, Mr. Glenn purchased the well-known Cuba *Patriot,* in company with Walter J. Beecher. In this work he soon made himself a factor in the public affairs of western New York, and though he had just reached his majority, older men admired his ability, diligence, and zeal.

Newspaper men and lawyers are naturally attracted to participation in political affairs. Mr. Glenn has always been a devoted follower of the Republican party. When only twenty-one years of age he was elected secretary and treasurer of the Allegany-county Republican committee, and held the position four years. Subsequently he was elected chairman of the same committee, and served in this capacity two years. After the inauguration of President

*WILLIAM J. GLENN*

Harrison Mr. Glenn became a candidate for the office of postmaster at Cuba. He was appointed, and duly confirmed by the senate, in the spring of 1889, and held the position for nearly five years

He was called to party service in 1890 as a member of the Republican state committee for the 34th congressional district, to which he was re-elected five times. The election of a Republican house of representatives in 1894 was followed by the re-organization of the executive offices of the body

CHARLES HICKEY

at the opening of the 54th congress in December, 1895. The members of the New York delegation in the house selected as their candidate for the position of doorkeeper William J. Glenn of Cuba, and after a spirited contest Mr. Glenn was nominated in caucus for the office, and was duly elected. The position is one of great responsibility, and involves the care of much government property, and the supervision of a large force of employees. Mr. Glenn is probably the youngest man ever chosen to the office — a fact that attests the esteem and respect of his friends and supporters. His success in securing this responsible post has done much to increase his prominence in the ranks of Republican party leaders in western New York.

Mr. Glenn believes in fraternal societies, and is a member of several such organizations, including Cuba Lodge, No. 306, F. & A. M.; Valley Point Chapter, R. A. M., Cuba; St. John's Commandery, K. T., Olean; Star Tent, No. 12, K. O. T. M., Cuba. He attends the Episcopal church.

PERSONAL CHRONOLOGY—
*William Johnson Glenn was born at Dansville, N. Y., July 4, 1862; was educated in common schools and at Wellsville (N. Y.) Academy; learned the printer's trade, and worked on newspapers, 1879–83; married Jessie A. Goodrich of Wellsville December 31, 1882; became one of the proprietors and editors of the Cuba "Patriot" January 1, 1883; was postmaster of Cuba, N. Y., 1889–94; was elected doorkeeper of the house of representatives of the 54th congress in December, 1895.*

———   •••   ———

**Charles Hickey**, county judge and surrogate of Niagara county, has risen by his own unaided efforts, and in the face of many obstacles, to a high place in the regard of the community. This becomes the more noteworthy when it is remembered that Judge Hickey is not yet forty years old, and that, owing to lack of scholastic opportunities in early life, he was in his twenty-eighth year when admitted to the bar.

Judge Hickey is a native of Niagara county, and his early education was received in the district schools of the town of Somerset. His father died when Charles was a young lad, and his mother was left with no means and with a large family on her hands. Under such circumstances each one must do his part, and from the time he was ten years old Charles worked for the neighboring farmers whenever there was work to be done. He had, however, a great desire to obtain an education; and in the winter months, when farm work was not pressing, he made good use of such opportunities as the country schools afforded. When he was seventeen years old he decided to try his fortunes in the West, and betook himself to the lumber regions of Michigan, where for two years he was engaged in rafting logs on the rivers, and in general work in the mills and pine woods of that state. He then returned to his native county, and spent two years in the service of the Rome, Watertown & Ogdensburg railroad, where he was employed in construction work and on gravel trains.

He was now a young man of twenty-one, with considerable experience in different kinds of work; but his earnings up to this time had been freely given to his widowed mother, and the fulfillment of his desires for a better education and a more important place in the world seemed still far off. Feeling that the time had come when, if ever, he should devote himself to these ends, he entered Lockport Union School. He was obliged to interrupt his course of study from time to time to earn money by teaching, and in this calling he met with such success that in a short time he was chosen president of the Niagara County Teachers' Association. But he had determined to become a lawyer, and while still in school he began reading law in the office of John E. Pound. Finally, in 1884, he was admitted to the bar. The following year he commenced practice in Lockport as a member of the firm of Hickey & Hopkins; and for the past ten years his practice has grown steadily, and he has established an enviable reputation for ability, fairness, and integrity. He practiced alone from 1891 till 1894, when he formed a partnership with Augustus Morris, under the firm name of Hickey & Morris, that lasted until Judge Hickey's elevation to the bench January 1, 1896.

Like many able lawyers, Judge Hickey has given considerable attention to politics. Soon after his admission to the bar he was elected justice of the peace for the city of Lockport, but resigned after one year's service. Later, in 1892, he was appointed city attorney of Lockport, and held the position until he became county judge. The people of Lockport have cause to be grateful to him for his skillful care of their interests during these four years, for in all that time not a single judgment was rendered against the city. Judge Hickey was elected to his present office by a majority of 2700, probably the largest ever received by a candidate in Niagara county. He is the first person to hold the combined offices of county judge and surrogate in his county; and the prediction may safely be made that he will fill the responsible position with credit and distinction.

Judge Hickey is a Mason and an Odd Fellow, and is president of the Odd Fellows' Home Association

of New York state, which maintains an institution at Lockport.

*PERSONAL CHRONOLOGY—Charles Hickey was born at Somerset, Niagara county, N. Y., April 18, 1857; was educated in district schools and at Lockport Union School; was admitted to the bar in October, 1884; married Frances C. Lambert of Lockport November 25, 1886; was city attorney of Lockport, 1892-95; practiced law in Lockport, 1885-95; has been county judge and surrogate of Niagara county since January 1, 1896.*

---

**Edward Daniel Loveridge** of Cuba, N. Y., has already passed the "three score years and ten" allotted as an ordinary lifetime; but as a practicing lawyer and president of a bank, he gives ample evidence that his days of usefulness are not yet over

*EDWARD DANIEL LOVERIDGE*

Mr. Loveridge was born before the close of the first quarter of the century, among the Litchfield hills of Connecticut, and there he passed his youth. Having completed his preparatory studies, he entered

Trinity College, Hartford, and studied there for two years. He then left college, having determined to become a lawyer, and began his legal studies at Lexington, Va. He had thus the benefit of a more varied experience of men and places than usually falls to the lot of the young law student. He was admitted to the bar in March, 1853, at Rochester, and from that time his life has been passed in western New York.

At first he opened an office alone at Castile, Wyoming county, and there obtained his first practical knowledge of the life of a lawyer. About three years later, in May, 1856, he moved to Cuba, and entered into partnership with his brother, Noah P. Loveridge. For ten years the brothers worked together to build up a practice, but at the end of that time Noah moved to Michigan, and for a little more than a year Edward practiced alone. He then associated with him in his practice Harlan J. Swift, now of Buffalo, and this connection lasted fifteen years. For the past ten years he has practiced in partnership with John C. Leggett. Mr. Loveridge has thus been actively engaged in the practice of his profession for more than forty years, and has conducted a vast amount of legal business.

Aside from the law, Mr. Loveridge's greatest interest has been banking. He has been president of the Cuba National Bank for twenty-eight years, and his successful management of the affairs of that institution reflects great credit upon his business ability. Other similar institutions have been glad to avail themselves of his counsel, and he has been for many years a director of the Citizens' National Bank of Friendship, N. Y.

Mr. Loveridge has always taken great interest in public affairs, and in his younger days he played a prominent part in the political life of his neighborhood. He served as member of assembly in the legislatures of 1862 and 1863, and was a delegate to the Republican national convention of 1864. He was supervisor of the town of Cuba for two years. In 1876 he was nominated for representative in congress.

Mr. Loveridge has been for years a member of the Masonic fraternity, and has taken an active part in its affairs. He is a Knight Templar, and for three years (1874–76) was Commander of St. John's Commandery, No. 24, Olean; and for fourteen years he was High Priest of Valley Point Chapter, Cuba. He is a member of the Episcopal church.

*PERSONAL CHRONOLOGY— Edward Daniel Loveridge was born at New Milford, Conn., December 11, 1824; completed his education at Trinity College, Hartford, Conn.; studied law, and was* admitted to the bar in 1853; married Frances Emily Bartlett of Granby, Mass., October 19, 1854; practiced law at Castile, N. Y., 1854–56; was member of assembly, 1862–64; has practiced law at Cuba, N. Y., since 1856; has been president of the Cuba National Bank since 1868.

...

**James Low** has served his country in military and in civil stations. To an intensely practical life he has added a deep interest in public affairs, and has long been a prominent factor in his community. Though not American-born, he has made a record of which any American might justly be proud. His parents, originally from Scotland, went to Niagara county from Toronto, Canada, when he was only two years old, so that all his early educational training was obtained in the United States. He attended the common schools of Lockport and Lewiston, and was for three years a pupil in the Collegiate Institute at Wilson, N. Y. This excellent education he turned to account in the very matter-of-fact business of farming, as well as in teaching district schools in the winter for seven years. He continued in these occupations until appointed deputy collector and inspector of customs for the district of Niagara in 1861, an office he resigned a year later to enter the military service of the United States.

Mr. Low had been foremost in recruiting company B of the 129th New York volunteers, and when it was organized he was commissioned 1st lieutenant, and mustered into the service August 22, 1862. He went at once to the front, and took part in the defense of Baltimore and in the West Virginia campaign. Two years later he joined the Army of the Potomac, and was present at the memorable battles of Spottsylvania, Tolopotomy, North Anna, Cold Harbor (where he was wounded), and Hatcher's Run. He was also present at the siege of Petersburg, and at the surrender of Lee at Appomattox. During his service he was twice promoted, first to the rank of captain and afterward to that of major, retiring with the latter rank at the close of the war.

When peace was restored, Major Low returned to New York state, and was soon appointed by President Johnson postmaster at Suspension Bridge. In this position he gave such satisfaction that he was reappointed by President Grant in 1870.

In state affairs Major Low has taken an active interest, and has three times represented the 2d district of Niagara county in the assembly, serving the people intelligently and faithfully. He is an ardent and vigorous Republican, and has been repeatedly honored when his party has been in power in the nation, by appointments to federal offices. President Arthur made him United States consul at Clifton, Ontario, and President Harrison appointed him collector of customs for the district of Niagara. He held the latter office for five years. Since the expiration of his term he has conducted the business of a coal merchant, and has carried on a farm.

At home Major Low has served for six years as president of the board of education of Suspension Bridge, and has devoted time and attention to securing a high standard in the schools under the care of the board. He attends the Congregational Church, and has been for many years president of its board of trustees. He is a member of the A.O.U.W., the Knights of Honor, the G. A. R., and the Loyal Legion. His neighbors and townsmen look to him for leadership in every movement having a worthy object in view. Conservative in his ideas, he is nevertheless open to conviction on every question arising in the course of public and political events ; and he has thus won and retained the confidence of all who know him.

*PERSONAL CHRONOLOGY—
James Low was born at Toronto, Canada,
January 24, 1846 ; was educated in the
public schools of Niagara county, N. Y.,
and Wilson (N. Y.) Collegiate Institute ;
married Amanda Barnes of Cambria,
N. Y., March 25, 1858 ; served in the
Union army, 1862–65 ; was appointed
postmaster at Suspension Bridge, N. Y.,
in 1865, and was reappointed in 1870 ;
was member of assembly, 1879–81, United
States consul at Clifton, Canada, 1882–
87, and collector of customs for the district of Niagara,
1890–95 ; has carried on the business of a coal merchant at Niagara Falls since 1875.*

*JAMES LOW*

**Charles Henry Miller,** member of assembly in 1896 from the 1st district of Cattaraugus county, is a native of that county, and has spent his whole life there.

Mr. Miller was born in the town of Machias, near the close of the first half of the century. Like all country boys of that day, he received his early educational training in the district school, which he began to attend at the age of four years. At the outbreak of the Civil War Mr. Miller was a youth of seventeen, attending school, and looking forward to

a useful commercial career. He gave up all his personal plans, however, and enlisted in the 105th regiment New York volunteers. In the campaign of 1862 he participated with his regiment in all the battles from Cedar Mountain to Antietam. His regiment suffered so much in these engagements that it was consolidated, in March, 1863, with the 94th New York volunteers, then commanded by General Adrian R. Root of Buffalo. In this regiment Mr. Miller served at the battle of Gettysburg, and in Grant's campaign before Petersburg and Richmond.

Having been honorably discharged from the army, Mr. Miller resumed his education, spending several years in the academy at Arcade, N. Y., and at Griffith Institute, Springville, N. Y. He then took up the occupation of teaching, and devoted himself to this profession during the winter seasons for twelve years. At the end of that time he moved to Delevan, N. Y., and engaged in the business of a furniture dealer and an undertaker, in partnership with George H. Whiting, under the firm name of

Miller & Whiting. This connection lasted for twelve years. During this time Mr. Miller was appointed to the railway postal service. The position of mail clerk on a railroad is one that requires close application, and great accuracy and quickness. Mr. Miller was connected with the service for four years,

CHARLES HENRY MILLER

traveling on various roads, including the Western New York & Pennsylvania, the New York Central, and the Erie; and during his term of service was promoted, upon his record in competitive examinations, through all the several grades from mail-route messenger to head clerk.

In 1882 Mr. Miller associated himself with D. D. Smith in the drug and grocery business, at Yorkshire, N. Y. The interests centering in a country store are many and varied, and no branch of knowledge comes amiss there. Mr. Miller's training as a mail clerk was useful to him, for he was made deputy postmaster, and had charge of the Yorkshire post office.

Always a strong Republican, Mr. Miller had long been prominent in county affairs before he was called to represent the people in the legislature of the state. He was first elected a member of the board of supervisors of Cattaraugus county in 1877, and since that time he has served on the board thirteen years. In 1894 he filled the responsible position of chairman of the board. His well-known devotion to the best interests of the county received a fitting recognition when, in 1895, he was unanimously chosen the Republican candidate for member of assembly from the 1st Cattaraugus district, and was duly elected. In the session of the legislature that followed he was a member of the important committee on taxation and retrenchment, and of the committees on banks and excise.

Mr. Miller is a trustee of the Methodist Episcopal Church of Yorkshire, and a member of Arcade Lodge, No. 419, F & A. M., and of Delevan Lodge, No. 616, I. O. O. F.

*PERSONAL CHRONOLOGY— Charles Henry Miller was born at Machias, N. Y., June 2, 1844; served in the Union army, 1863–65; was educated at Arcade (N. Y.) Academy and Griffith Institute, Springville, N. Y.; engaged in business in Delevan, N. Y., 1872–84, and in the railway mail service, 1872–76; established a drug and grocery business at Yorkshire, N. Y., in 1882, and has carried on the same since; married Emma L. Williams of Arcade, N. Y., December 19, 1877; was chairman of the board of supervisors of Cattaraugus county in 1894, and member of assembly from the 1st Cattaraugus-county district in 1896.*

**Arthur B. Ottaway** proves by his career that a young man can win success at home. The essential conditions of success are character, energy, and ability; and these factors will be decisive anywhere.

Mr. Ottaway has spent his whole life in Chautauqua county. He was born in Mina, among the Chautauqua hills not far from the Pennsylvania line, and was brought up on a farm. His early education was acquired in the district school and at Sherman Academy. In 1873 he moved to the village of Westfield, and attended the academy there, graduating at the age of twenty one. His training had included preparation for a college course; but this was abandoned, and his subsequent education was such as one gets in the practical school of life, while earning one's own living.

Like many country boys who purpose entering the professions, Mr. Ottaway's first resource on graduation was teaching school. He followed this occupation for some time, meanwhile preparing for the law. Later he prosecuted his studies in the office of William Russell at Westfield, and finally, in 1879, was admitted to the bar. Mr. Ottaway's career since then has been that of a successful lawyer. At first he was a member of the firm of Russell, Dickerman & Ottaway, as junior partner. Subsequently this firm dissolved, and Mr. Ottaway for a time practiced alone. He is now the senior partner in the firm of Ottaway & Munson of Westfield.

The law often proves a stepping-stone to politics, and so it was in Mr. Ottaway's case. He was always an active Republican, quick at making friends, energetic ; and by a natural course of events he was nominated, in 1883, for district attorney of Chautauqua county. He was elected, and served from 1884 to 1887 with credit to himself and the county. After his administration of this office he retired to the care of his large and growing general practice. Mr. Ottaway has been engaged in many important trials, and is one of the best-known members of the bar in Chautauqua county. He has served for several years as attorney for the board of supervisors of the county.

One of the leading characteristics of Mr. Ottaway's career is the interest he has taken in matters pertaining to the welfare of Westfield and its institutions. He has always been active in village affairs. He served for many years as one of the vestrymen of St. Peter's Episcopal Church of Westfield. He is a Mason.

*PERSONAL CHRONOLOGY—
Arthur B. Ottaway was born at Mina, Chautauqua county, N. Y., May 8, 1854 ; was educated in the district schools, and at Sherman and Westfield academies, graduating from the latter institution in 1873 ; taught school, studied law, and was admitted to the bar in 1879 ; was district attorney of Chautauqua county, 1884–87 ; has practiced law in Westfield, N. Y., since 1879.*

\*\*\*

force of industry, perseverance, and character. There is something in the practical training and in the surroundings of farm life that inculcates a sturdy self-reliance and stimulates ambition ; and the fact is aptly illustrated in the career of Mr. Stearns.

He received his elementary education in the district school of his native Chautauqua-county town, and completed his studies in the Forestville Free Academy. For the two years following his graduation he taught school, thus acquiring the discipline in method and accuracy so essential in the profession of law, which he soon decided to make his vocation. Before he began his legal studies, however, he spent a year in the Bradford oil region in Pennsylvania, where he had the supervision of a large strip of oil territory. This work failed to prove congenial, and he returned to Chautauqua county, to enter upon a

*ARTHUR B. OTTAWAY*

## Lester Forrest Stearns grew

to manhood on his father's farm. His early life was similar to that of many boys, who, born and bred in the country, fit themselves for a profession, and win fame and reputation in large fields of usefulness by

course of legal study at Forestville. Later he moved to Dunkirk, where he finished his studies in the office of C. B. Bradley, then district attorney. Admitted to the bar in 1882, Mr. Stearns at once opened an office for himself. In 1884 he formed a partnership with Walter L. Kinsley that lasted until 1889. Since then he has been the senior partner in the legal firm of Stearns & Warner. Mr. Stearns has taken pains from the beginning to acquire the best books bearing upon his profession, and he now has a

LESTER FORREST STEARNS

large and valuable law library. Here he has ready at hand a vast amount of information otherwise attainable only at the cost of much time and effort.

Although Mr. Stearns has not yet passed the meridian of life, he has built up a very large and important practice in the northern part of Chautauqua county, numbering among his clients about all the leading concerns of Dunkirk. Men do not entrust weighty interests to lawyers as a matter of friendship, but seek the best talent anywhere obtainable ; and the large number of important clients who look to Mr. Stearns for legal advice demonstrates the wisdom of his choice of profession. His success, however, while rapid, has not come without corresponding effort and faithfulness on his part.

The judicial cast of Mr. Stearns's mind has been recognized in his nomination for the office of special judge of the County Court — a nomination he felt constrained to decline. Subsequently he was nominated and elected to the office of special surrogate, and served for three years in that responsible position.

His popularity has been likewise attested by two elections to the office of district attorney, which he has held six years in all. He has been prominently mentioned for judicial honors, and his friends are desirous of seeing him on the bench. In politics he is a Republican, but he has never been guilty of carrying partisanship into the duties of any public position that he has been called upon to fill.

To his active professional duties Mr. Stearns has added those of a progressive citizen. He has taken a keen interest in municipal affairs, and to his enterprising efforts in large part the city of Dunkirk is to-day indebted for its municipal system of electric lighting. He has also interested himself in the improvement of the streets and harbor of Dunkirk, and every movement for the public good finds in him a warm supporter and a zealous champion.

PERSONAL CHRONOLOGY— Lester Forrest Stearns was born at Villanova, Chautauqua county, N. Y., July 25, 1856 ; graduated from Forestville Free Academy in 1878 ; was admitted to the bar at Dunkirk, N. Y., in 1882 ; was elected special surrogate in 1884 ; was elected district attorney in 1886, and re-elected in 1889 ; married Mary M. Hiller of Dunkirk July 16, 1889 ; has practiced law in Dunkirk since 1882.

***

H. Miner Wellman has had a remarkably successful career thus far ; and as he is not yet thirty years old, it may safely be assumed that the future has a much greater measure of prosperity in store for him.

Mr. Wellman was born in the town of Friendship, Allegany county, where he still lives. His early education was received in a private school, but he soon entered Friendship Academy, and took a five years' course there. Having exhausted the educational resources of his native town, at the age of sixteen he entered Hopkins Grammar School at New Haven, Conn., to prepare for college. Two years later he entered Yale University, and graduated in the class of 1888 with the degree of A. B.

After this absence from home of six years, Mr. Wellman returned to Friendship, a young man of twenty-two, well prepared, by means of the excellent education he had received, to begin the actual work of life. In the fall succeeding his graduation he entered, as a clerk, the First National Bank of Friendship, of which his father was cashier. He was soon chosen a director of the bank; and after an experience of little more than a year, on the death of his father, he succeeded him as cashier. This office involved a heavy responsibility for so young a man; but Mr. Wellman has proved himself an able financier, and during the six years of his management the bank has prospered in a most satisfactory manner. His excellent qualifications for the position of a bank official have led to his selection as vice president of the First National Bank of Cuba, N. Y., and as a director of the First National Bank of Salamanca.

Like so many other enterprising men in Allegany county, Mr. Wellman is interested in the production of oil, and his operations in the town of Wirt have been highly successful. He has also become interested in mining in Colorado, and is treasurer of the Columbia-Menona Mining Co. of Telluride, Col. He is secretary and treasurer of the Ontario Improvement & Gas Co., Limited, of Honeoye Falls, N. Y.; president of the Friendship Water Co., and of the Phoenix Gas Co. of Seneca Falls, N. Y.; and a director in the Williams & Werner Co. of Rochester. Thus it will be seen that Mr. Wellman, though he has spent his life in a country town, is as far as possible from the traditional type of villager; and is, in fact, an active, enterprising business man with extensive and varied interests.

In politics Mr. Wellman is a thorough Republican. Though he has never been a candidate for a political office, he has served his party in many ways. He acted as secretary and treasurer of the Allegany county Republican committee during the presidential campaign of 1892, and has been a delegate to county, senatorial, and state conventions. In 1895 he was chairman of the Allegany-county delegation to the national convention of the Republican League at Cleveland.

In social, fraternal, and religious circles alike, Mr. Wellman is active and popular, thus rounding out and completing his character as a business man and a public-spirited citizen. He is a member of Psi Upsilon college fraternity; Master of Allegany Lodge, No. 225, F. & A. M., of Friendship; and a member of Valley Point Chapter, R. A. M., of Cuba, N. Y.; of St. John's Commandery, No. 24, K. T., Olean, and of Ismailia Temple, Nobles of the Mystic Shrine, Buffalo. He is a member of the First Baptist Church of Friendship. As a trustee of Cook Academy, Havana, N. Y., he demonstrates in a practical way his interest in the cause of education.

*PERSONAL CHRONOLOGY* — *Asher Miner Wellman was born at Friendship, N. Y., November 14, 1866; prepared for college at Hopkins Grammar School, New Haven, Conn., and graduated from Yale in 1888; became a clerk in the First National Bank*

*A. MINER WELLMAN*

*of Friendship in 1888, a director in 1889, and has been cashier of the same bank since 1890; married Hattie Prior Baldwin of Saxtons River, Vt., June 28, 1893.*

**John Woodward**, who finds himself, at the age of thirty-six, a member of the Supreme Court of the state of New York, was born at Charlotte, Chautauqua county. He is a son of Daniel S. and Cornelia Lake Woodward; a grandson of John Woodward, who served in the assembly from Chautauqua

*JOHN WOODWARD*

county in 1835; and a great-grandson of John Woodward, who fought before the Heights of Abraham in the French-Canadian war, and who served in one of the Massachusetts regiments during the revolutionary war. Early in the century this latter John Woodward moved to Genesee county, New York, afterward taking up his residence in Chautauqua county, where his descendants have carved out for themselves careers worthy of his name. Mr. Woodward's grandmother on his mother's side was Sarah Mather, a lineal descendant of Cotton Mather.

In his infancy Mr. Woodward's parents left Chautauqua county, taking up a residence in Michigan, whence they moved to Kansas in 1870, where his father died. The family returned to Chautauqua county in

1871, the mother yielding up her life at Fredonia in the same year. From that time Mr. Woodward made his home with Henry C. Lake, his mother's brother, who has long been a conspicuous figure in the politics of Chautauqua county. Working his way along, taking employment in the village stores and on the neighboring farms, Mr. Woodward graduated from the Fredonia Normal School in 1878, and began reading law in the office of Morris & Lambert in that village in the same year, afterwards attending the law school of the University of the City of New York, and graduating therefrom in 1881. He was admitted to the bar at Poughkeepsie in the same year, and began the practice of his profession in Fredonia. In August, 1883, he moved to Jamestown to practice law there; and in 1886, on the incorporation of the city of Jamestown, he became its first city attorney, filling the position for two years. He was appointed to a vacancy on the board of supervisors in 1887, holding the place by successive elections until 1892, when he was elected district attorney of Chautauqua county. He held this position during the term, and in January, 1896, was appointed a justice of the Supreme Court by Governor Morton.

Judge Woodward is a member of the Jamestown Club, the Knights of the Maccabees, the Elks, the Citizens' Club of Fredonia, the Ellicott Club of Buffalo, the Orpheus Singing Society of the same city, and the Camp Dent Fishing Club of Allegany county. He takes an active interest in all matters of a public or quasi-public character.

John Woodward is not a plodding student of the law in the abstract; not a cowardly searcher after precedents, in an effort to make new conditions conform to old measurements. He seeks rather to energize modern jurisprudence by compelling it to meet a broadening conception of justice and equity. To him the law is the servant of society, to be administered impartially as between its members, in the interests of equal justice; and he has the courage to assert so much of a new doctrine as may be necessary in his judgment to this end, thus aiding in that evolution of the law which is essential to its highest development.

Personally Judge Woodward is genial and thoroughly likable, so that it is easy to understand his widespread popularity.

*PERSONAL CHRONOLOGY — John Woodward was born at Charlotte, Chautauqua county, N. Y., August 19, 1859; received a common-school education, and graduated from the Fredonia Normal School in 1878; graduated from the law school of the University of the City of New York in 1881, and was admitted to the bar the same year; practiced law in Fredonia, N. Y., 1881-84; married Mary E. Barker of Fredonia May 26, 1886; was city attorney of Jamestown, N. Y., 1886-88, member of the board of supervisors of Chautauqua county, 1887-92, and district attorney of Chautauqua county, 1892-95; was appointed a justice of the Supreme Court of the state of New York in January, 1896.*

\*\*\*

**S. Cary Adams** illustrates in his life the potency of character and lofty ambition. Under circumstances that would have daunted most young men, and with few opportunities, he laid the foundation for success in a profession where continual study and expanding knowledge are essential. His education in schools was meager, and confined to elementary grades. He never had the benefit of collegiate training. In its place he substituted a course of private study, and thus gained a knowledge and mental discipline that fitted him ultimately for the practice of law. Though he was not admitted to the bar until middle life, the preceding years were so employed as to prove valuable to him in his professional career. He was brought into contact with the practical affairs of life, and acquired a wide business experience. At the age of sixteen he learned the carpenter's trade, and for several years followed this calling during the summer months. In the winter he taught in district schools, and devoted himself to study. His interest in education extended beyond teaching, and for six years he filled the position of superintendent of schools for the town of Collins, N. Y., having under his charge over twenty schools.

Mr. Adams has had a long and varied experience in municipal and county affairs, and is an authority on questions relating thereto. He was supervisor of the town of Collins two terms, and was subsequently elected clerk of the board of supervisors of Erie county for two years. During the year 1857 he was a member of the state assembly from the 4th Erie county district.

In 1859 Mr. Adams was appointed deputy county clerk of Erie county, and moved to Buffalo. In the same year he began a course of legal study, reading his Blackstone and Kent whenever he could find a spare hour. In this way he acquired the legal knowledge necessary to pass the bar examination, and he was admitted to practice in 1863. His efficiency and popularity as deputy county clerk led to his nomination for county clerk in 1864; but he was defeated by fewer than 100 plurality, though he polled the largest vote on his ticket. As a lawyer Mr. Adams has made a specialty of commercial law. He was led into this branch of the profession by his relations with the well-known houses of Pratt & Co. and Pratt & Letchworth, whose confidential agent and legal adviser he was for nearly a score of years. He was also a trustee and secretary of the Buffalo

S. CARY ADAMS

Iron & Nail Co., which was part of Pratt & Co.'s establishment. His charge of the legal affairs of these houses sent Mr. Adams into most of the northern states east of the Missouri, and familiarized him

with the legal procedure of many states. Since the
dissolution of the firm of Pratt & Co. in 1886, Mr.
Adams has devoted himself to general law practice.

In his political affiliations Mr. Adams has been an
ardent Republican since the formation of that party.
For several years he was a member of the Republican

*JAMES A. ALLEN*

county committee, and served one year as its chairman. He has, however, never sought office, and
has frequently declined nominations when urged
by his friends to accept them. Mr. Adams is
prominently identified with philanthropic work in
Buffalo. He served as a trustee of the Children's
Aid Society for a number of years, and has been a
managing director of the Queen City Society for
the Prevention of Cruelty to Children since its
organization in 1879. He has been connected with
the Wyoming Benevolent Institute as trustee and
secretary since 1883.

*PERSONAL CHRONOLOGY— Samuel Cary
Adams was born at Federal Stores, town of Chatham,
N. Y., December 22, 1819; was educated in common*

*schools; taught school winters and worked as a car-
penter summers, 1841–50; married Harriet White
of Collins, N. Y., October 20, 1842; was superintendent of schools of Collins, 1846–52, supervisor
1852–54, and clerk of the board, 1854–55; was member
of assembly in 1857, deputy county clerk of Erie county,
1859–64, and deputy collector of customs,
1865–67; moved to Buffalo in 1859, and
was admitted to the bar in 1864; was
employed as confidential agent and legal
adviser for the firm of Pratt & Co.,
1867–86, and has conducted a general law
practice in Buffalo since 1886.*

**James A. Allen** was a Connecticut
boy, born in the delightful town of New
London, famous for its magnificent harbor
and historic associations. In his tenth
year he left his native New England,
and moved with his parents to New York
state. His studies, begun under a
Yankee schoolmaster, were continued at
Sinclairville, Chautauqua county, in the
select school of E. H. Sears, who subsequently practiced law and became a
judge. From this school Mr. Allen
entered Fredonia Academy, and completed his education. In the meantime
he had taken up the study of law in the
office of Judge E. F. Warren. Like
many ambitious young men, he was
obliged to work his way in the world.
He taught school in the winter, and in
the summer assisted his father at home
while continuing his studies. He learned
thus to economize his time, and employ
profitably every hour of the day. His
career is an illustration of the fact that
any youth with an earnest ambition can
find opportunities to make himself the kind of man
he wishes to be.

In the fall of 1852 Mr. Allen entered the law
office of Welch & Hibbard of Buffalo as a student,
and when twenty-two years of age was admitted to
the bar, thus placing his foot on the first round
of the ladder that was to lead him to success and
prominence. He opened an office in Sinclairville,
and was so fortunate as to succeed to the law practice of Albert Richmond, newly elected surrogate
of Chautauqua county. The professional field, however, was limited, and Mr. Allen decided that a
city offered greater attractions in the way of legal
business. Accordingly, he settled in Buffalo in 1861,
where his practice has grown both in the number

of his clients and in the importance of his causes. He has appeared before the highest courts of the country, including the United States Supreme Court at Washington. For three years of his professional life Mr. Allen was associated in partnership with Asher P. Nichols, once state comptroller.

Mr. Allen has so earnestly confined himself to his office and his profession that he has never figured in public life as either an office holder or a candidate for office. His leisure outside his legal studies has been devoted to literature. He is fond of the Latin classics, has studied French, and is conversant with its literature. He has also devoted some time to the study of German literature, through the translations of such masters as Carlyle. Though not an author of books, Mr. Allen has written many articles for the press, which have appeared on the editorial pages of leading papers.

Above all things, however, Mr. Allen is a student of the law, and is deeply versed in its history and literature. Of recent years his chief work has been in connection with that intricate branch of the profession relating to patents and copyrights. Numerous cases of this class have taken him far and wide over the United States. He has appeared before United States courts at Portland, Boston, New York, Albany, Utica, Detroit, Grand Rapids, and Chicago. He argued the first patent cause heard before Judge Wallace after the latter's appointment as a judge of the United States Court, and the last patent case ever decided by Judge Blatchford of the United States Supreme Court. Mr. Allen has been connected with some of the most notable patent cases tried in New York state. The calendars of the circuit courts attest his prominence in the field of federal practice. He is domestic in his tastes, delighting in his family and in a choice circle of friends and acquaintances.

*PERSONAL CHRONOLOGY—James Albert Allen was born at New London, Conn., January 19, 1844; was educated in the common schools of New London, a select school at Sinclairville, N. Y., and at Fredonia (N. Y.) Academy; was admitted to the bar in 1856; practiced law in Sinclairville, 1856-64; married Jeanie Pauline Mack of Buffalo November 5, 1862; has practiced law in Buffalo since 1864.*

**Philip Becker** was not born in Buffalo, but his long residence therein, his prominent part in the business of the city, and his civic honors, have made him one of the most prominent citizens of the place.

He was born at Oberotterbach, a town in Bavaria on the river Rhine, in 1830. His early education was obtained in local schools, in the classical school of his native province, and in two years' study in France. He came to the United States in 1847, going directly to Buffalo from New York, via Albany and the Erie canal. He first found employment in Buffalo as a clerk in a grocery, at the very modest salary of four dollars a month and board. He brought to his employment the same energy and determination to succeed that have characterized all his business life. Soon after reaching manhood he opened a store of his own, only a few doors from his

*PHILIP BECKER*

present establishment, and founded the great business that has been so long and favorably known to the people of Buffalo under the name of Philip Becker & Co.

The remarkable success that has attended Mr. Becker's business career has not come by chance, but has been the result of hard and intelligent work, right living, and honest frugality. Mr. Becker's acquaintance in Buffalo is probably as large as any man's. While building up his own business he has had many opportunities to lend a helping hand to others, and the kindly way in which he has rendered such aid has won for him a host of friends.

Mr. Becker's energy, uprightness of character, kindliness, and success attracted the attention of the citizens of Buffalo, and they have frequently honored him with public office. In 1876 and 1877 he was mayor, and gave the city a thoroughly satisfactory and businesslike administration. In 1886 he was again mayor, and served four years. During this period he continued the business methods that he had introduced in his previous term. His record as mayor is a creditable one, and his administration was of great value to the city. No mayor has ever been more faithful to the people's interests than he.

Mr. Becker was a presidential elector in 1888. In 1891 his name was strongly presented to the Republican state convention for the nomination as governor. He was a delegate to the Republican national convention in 1876, and again in 1892. He was one of the commissioners in charge of the erection of the City and County Hall, a building of which Buffalonians are proud, not only for its beauty, but also for the fact that it is one of the few great public buildings that have been honestly constructed. Since Mr. Becker's retirement from the mayor's office December 31, 1889, he has declined to accept any political position.

Mr. Becker has been connected with many of the public institutions of Buffalo, notably with the Music Hall enterprise. The erection of this building, in fact, was due largely to his generosity, wide acquaintance, untiring energy, and personal influence. He was president of the great Saengerfest which was held in Buffalo in 1883, and caused the building of the first Music Hall.

Mr. Becker was one of the original members of the Buffalo German Insurance Co., and since February, 1869, he has been its president. The great success that attended this enterprise, and the growing demand for more good insurance companies, led Mr. Becker, in 1896, to organize a new institution in Buffalo, known as the Buffalo Commercial Insurance Co. The lines on which he has organized this association, together with the persons whom he has interested therein, insure the success of the enterprise. The stockholders have unanimously elected Mr. Becker the first president of the new company.

In 1852 Mr. Becker was married to Miss Sarah Goetz, and their beautiful home on Delaware avenue is the gathering place of numerous friends. Mr. Becker is a member of many of the charitable and scientific societies of Buffalo, and he is always a contributor to any enterprise requiring public benevolence.

*PERSONAL CHRONOLOGY—Philip Becker was born at Oberotterbach, Bavaria, in April, 1830; was educated in German and French schools; came to the United States and settled in Buffalo in 1847; married Sarah Goetz of Buffalo in 1852; was mayor of Buffalo, 1876–77, and 1886–89; was presidential elector in 1888; has been president of the Buffalo German Insurance Co. since 1869; has conducted a wholesale grocery business in Buffalo since 1854.*

\*\*\*

**Albert D. Briggs** has spent his entire professional life, covering a period of twenty five years, in Buffalo, and has achieved no small measure of success as a general practitioner; although, as he expresses it, he has "never had time to get rich." Realizing the value of concentration of effort, Dr. Briggs has never been interested, either directly or indirectly, in any business or occupation outside his profession; but has devoted all his energies to his private practice, and to the duties of the various public offices that he has been called upon to fill.

Dr. Briggs was born in what is now Town Line, Erie county, and began his education at the district school. Later he attended the Batavia Union School, and the academy at East Aurora, and finally the Genesee Wesleyan Seminary at Lima, N. Y. His medical studies were pursued at the University of Buffalo, from which he received the degree of M. D. in 1871.

During his student days in Buffalo Dr. Briggs had come to appreciate the advantages of the city as a place of residence and a field for the exercise of his medical skill, and he decided to cast in his lot there permanently. Accordingly he opened an office in Buffalo immediately after his graduation. Within a few months he received an appointment to the newly established office of *post-mortem* examiner for Erie county, and held the position for more than three years. Meanwhile he was appointed city physician for the second district. In 1880 and 1881 he was health physician for the city, and discharged the duties of the office so well that he was reappointed in 1881, and served for four years. During this second term the office of registrar of vital statistics was created at the suggestion of Dr. Briggs. He was appointed registrar, and as such organized that useful department of the city government.

Dr. Briggs has been a member of the National Guard for many years. In October, 1879, he was appointed assistant surgeon of the 65th regiment, with the rank of 1st lieutenant, and in less than two years he was promoted to be surgeon of the regiment, with the rank of captain. In April, 1883, he received the rank of major, and this he still retains. In all these years of his connection with the regiment his interest therein has never failed, and he may be regarded as one of the men who have helped to raise the tone of the National Guard, and to win for it the high place in the esteem of the community that it now occupies.

For sixteen years Dr. Briggs has filled the office of state medical examiner for the Ancient Order of United Workmen, and in that time he has examined nearly fifty thousand applications for life insurance, or an average of about ten a day. This duty, in addition to his private practice and his service to the city and to the National Guard, has made Dr. Briggs a notably busy man even in this busy age. He holds membership in a great number of the societies that are so helpful in keeping a physician abreast of the times, and bringing him into contact with other bright men in his profession. Among such societies may be mentioned the American Medical Association, the American Public Health Association, and the Association of Military Surgeons of the United States, as well as the New York State Medical Association, the Buffalo Academy of Medicine, and the Erie County Medical Society. He is also a Mason, belonging to Washington Lodge, No. 240.

*PERSONAL CHRONOLOGY— Albert Henry Briggs was born in the town of Lancaster, N. Y., September 9, 1842; was educated in various schools and academies, and graduated from the medical department of the University of Buffalo in 1871; married Sarah America Baker of Andover, N. Y., June 7, 1864; was health physician of the city of Buffalo, 1880–81 and 1884–87; has practiced medicine in Buffalo since 1871.*

∴

**Edward Clark** is a typical American citizen, in the broadest and best sense of the term. Without the initial advantage of wealth or position, and with only the education of the public schools, he has achieved an honorable name in his profession, and

has earned the gratitude of his fellow-citizens by his active interest in many problems relating to public health and public welfare. Such men as he illustrate and justify the phrase, "a self-made man," and confer upon it the honorable meaning that it has acquired in popular speech.

*ALBERT H. BRIGGS*

Dr. Clark was born in Buffalo forty-odd years ago, and has spent practically his whole life there. His education was begun in the district schools of West Seneca; but he afterwards graduated from Public School No. 27 in Buffalo, and attended the high school for two years. As he was ambitious to become a physician, and had not the means to obtain a medical education, he taught school for several years, and thus obtained sufficient money to enable him to attend medical lectures at Cincinnati in 1875 and 1876. He then returned to Buffalo, and after several years more of combined teaching and study, received his degree from the medical department of the University of Buffalo with honors. This happened on February 25, 1880.

Since then Dr. Clark has followed his profession in Buffalo, and has built up an extensive practice. He has been attending surgeon at the Erie County Hospital ever since its organization, and was for two years a member of the executive committee of the staff of that institution.  He served for five years as

EDWARD CLARK

lecturer and demonstrator of anatomy in Niagara University, and at the end of that time was offered the professorship of anatomy, but declined the honor. Dr. Clark has written many articles and pamphlets for publication, not only on purely professional subjects, but on sanitary questions as well.

After serving as physician at the county jail, as *post-mortem* examiner, and as sanitary inspector for the health department of Buffalo, Dr. Clark was appointed health physician of the city in 1888, and filled the office for two years.  In the discharge of the duties of this responsible position he was vigilant, prompt, and efficient, and won the esteem and confidence of his fellow citizens irrespective of party.  One of his first official moves was to make a strenuous effort to

secure better school accommodations on the east side of the city ; and it was largely owing to him that several new buildings, with improved methods of ventilation and general sanitation, were erected.  He also deserves the gratitude of the people for his successful handling of the smallpox that broke out in Buffalo during the first year of his office. Such emergencies test severely a man's strength, and the fact that Dr. Clark was able to cope with this dread disease and avert an epidemic speaks well for his skill and executive ability.

In 1890 Dr. Clark was nominated for member of the board of councilmen, but was defeated, though he received over 4000 more votes than the Republican candidate for mayor.  In the spring of 1894 he was appointed by Mayor Bishop a member of the advisory committee on street cleaning and the disposal of garbage, and in this position he displayed the same devotion to the best interests of the community that has characterized his entire public service.

Dr. Clark is fond of music and art, as well as of outdoor sports and amusements.  He is a Mason, and Past Master of Erie Lodge, No. 161, F. & A. M., and a member of the Acacia Club.  He attends the Delaware Avenue Methodist Church.

*PERSONAL  CHRONOLOGY—Edward Clark was born at Buffalo October 28, 1852; was educated in the public schools; graduated from the medical department of the University of Buffalo in 1880; married Nellie M. Daniels of Buffalo May 1, 1884; was health physician of the city of Buffalo, 1888-90; has practiced medicine there since 1880.*

✻✻✻

**Myron D. Clark** was born in Erie county, New York, in what is now the town of Elma, though it was at the time of his birth a part of Lancaster.  Not many years before, the first house and a sawmill had been built, and the dozen Indian families who occupied the clearings in the vicinity were the only neighbors of the owners of the mill. When the boy reached school age, the prosperity of the town was assured, and the place was taking on an important air, as befitted a community soon to boast of a railway in its immediate vicinity — the Buffalo & Washington, now the Western New York & Pennsylvania.  The present town of Elma was organized in

1857 from territory taken from the towns of Lancaster and Aurora.

The district school at Elma was unusually well taught, and prepared its pupils to enter the Genesee Wesleyan Seminary at Lima, N. Y., on whose roll Mr. Clark was registered from 1868 to 1870. Preferring then to pursue a practical business course, he went to Buffalo, and took up the curriculum of Bryant & Stratton's Business College. Here he received his diploma, when he was eighteen years old. He put his training into immediate use by engaging in the lumber business. This occupation, together with farming, brought him substantial returns, but he had other aims in view for his life-work. Entering the law office of M. A. Whitney of Buffalo, he studied with characteristic persistency until prepared for admission to the bar. After five years' practice alone he formed a partnership with Frederick Howard, and the firm has since been known as Howard & Clark.

Mr. Clark has been clerk of the board of supervisors of Erie county, twice supervisor from the town of Elma, chairman of the Erie-county board of supervisors, and a member of the state assembly. While in the assembly he was a member of two important committees—those on judiciary and excise. He was defeated by a close vote for re-election to the assembly, by reason of the Democratic apportionment of 1892, when the district that he then represented was changed by the addition of two large wards of the city of Buffalo, and was thus made largely Democratic. The welfare of the Republican party has always been a matter of great interest to Mr. Clark, and he has represented the town of Elma on political committees ever since his majority. He is, and has been for several years, a member of the Republican general committee of Erie county.

From the coming of the early settlers dates the beginning of Free Masonry in Erie county. In 1807 there were a sufficient number of Masons in Buffalo, then called New Amsterdam, to warrant the establishment of a Masonic lodge, although the first lodge was not founded until 1812. Blazing Star Lodge, No. 694, of which Mr. Clark is a member, is located at East Aurora. He is also an Odd Fellow, belonging to Aurora Borealis Lodge; a member of the Ellicott Club, Buffalo, a new business men's dining and social club in Ellicott Square; and a frequent attendant at the Acacia Club. This organization is an important Masonic club, occupying the entire third floor of the Masonic Temple, Buffalo. The club derives its membership, which is limited to six hundred, from the Masonic fraternity of Buffalo and vicinity. To be eligible one must be a Master Mason in good standing. Mr. Clark is an earnest member of the order, belonging to a chapter of Royal Arch Masons in addition to Blazing Star Lodge.

*PERSONAL CHRONOLOGY—Myron Henry Clark was born at what is now Elma, N. Y., June 30, 1854; was educated at Genesee Wesleyan Seminary, Lima, N. Y., and Bryant & Stratton's Business College, Buffalo; married Mary Eliza Bancroft of Elma May 24, 1876; was admitted to the bar in 1884; was clerk of the board of supervisors of Erie*

*county in 1881, supervisor of the town of Elma, 1886–87, chairman of the Erie-county board of supervisors in 1887, and member of assembly in 1892; has practiced law in Buffalo since 1884.*

**Emory P. Close,** though his success is due primarily to his own efforts, owes not a little to his environment. His training in the public schools of Buffalo was cut short by his acceptance of a position as assistant in the Buffalo Young Men's Association Library, where he made good use of the

EMORY P. CLOSE

advantages afforded. Always fond of reading, he had here rare opportunity to indulge his taste for good books, and the influence was both helpful and stimulating. History, biography, mental philosophy, and English literature, he enjoyed and studied ; and his acquaintance with books and authors enabled him to select the best works in the different fields. Many moments of leisure came during the long hours in which the library was open, and they were all improved. Among other books he read "David Copperfield," and a passage therein greatly influenced his subsequent career. This was the account of David's arduous struggle with shorthand and final mastery of the art—a feat that Dickens deems equal to acquiring six foreign languages. Mr. Close

determined to learn stenography, and finding in the library a copy of Graham's *Handbook*, he applied himself to the study. At that time, in 1875, there were not more than five or six stenographers in Buffalo, and these were engaged principally in the courts. Mr. Close sought no instruction, but applied himself diligently to his text-book, and in a year he had mastered the science, and was ready for the more difficult task of acquiring a high rate of speed. His ambition was to fit himself for the highest grade of professional work. This demanded at least a superficial knowledge of the many subjects that are frequently involved in legal controversy.

At the age of seventeen Mr. Close resigned his position at the library, and entered the office of Slocum & Thornton, official stenographers for the Supreme Court of the 8th judicial district. Before he was twenty-one he established an office of his own, and soon after formed a partnership with one of his former employers, organizing the well-known firm of Thornton, Briggs & Close. In 1884 Mr. Close was elected official stenographer of the state assembly by the Republican caucus of that year, and reported all the debates in that body. He was re-elected without opposition by the assemblies of 1885, 1886, and 1887.

His official life at Albany brought Mr. Close into contact and acquaintance with senators and assemblymen, state officers, and leading politicians, and familiarized him with legislative methods and procedure. Having reached the topmost round in the stenographic ladder, and established a reputation as one of the most rapid and correct reporters in the United States, he turned his thoughts to a wider field. His relations with the courts and legislature led him naturally to the legal profession, and he determined to study law. During the last three years of his stenographic work he utilized his spare moments, generally at night, in legal study, until his admission to the bar in 1886.

Not until 1888 did Mr. Close enter upon the practice of the profession that was to be his life-work. He found the law a jealous mistress, demanding devotion of head and heart. He has given his entire thought and effort to his profession, and in the eight years of his practice has already earned for himself a reputation for tireless energy and legal ability. In jury cases especially he must be regarded as one of the most successful lawyers at the Erie-county bar. His regular practice began in the firm of Close & Fleischmann; and upon the election of Manly C. Green as justice of the Supreme Court, Mr. Close formed a partnership with Judge Green's former partner, William L. Marcy, under the style of Marcy & Close. This association still continues.

Mr. Close has always been deeply interested in the success of the Republican party, and has been a favorite campaign speaker throughout Erie county. For political office, however, he has no ambition, preferring the laurels won in his profession. He is a member of the Masonic order, affiliated with Ancient Landmark Lodge. He belongs to the Buffalo Club and the Acacia Club, and is president of the Republican League, one of the leading party organizations of the state.

*PERSONAL CHRONOLOGY—*
*Emory P. Close was born at Buffalo December 14, 1859; was educated in the public schools; was assistant librarian of the Young Men's Association Library of Buffalo, 1874-77; was Supreme Court stenographer for the 8th judicial district, 1880-88, and official stenographer of the New York state assembly, 1884-87; married Etta S. Cobb of Buffalo January 7, 1885; was admitted to the bar in 1886, and has practiced law in Buffalo since 1888.*

***

# Edward E. Coatsworth

is prominent among the rising young lawyers and well-known men of Buffalo. He was born there less than thirty years ago, and was educated in the common schools, attending Public School No. 4, and graduating from the high school. Having decided upon the law as his profession, he immediately entered upon a course of legal study, and was admitted to practice by the General Term of the Supreme Court soon after completing his twenty-first year. This is an unusually early age at which to gain admission to the bar, and is a striking proof of the maturity of his mind.

Mr. Coatsworth next added to his theoretical knowledge of the law a thorough familiarity with court rules and procedure by a period of service as managing clerk in the office of Tabor & Sheehan. With such ability and success did he conduct the clerical affairs of the office, that he was admitted to a partnership in the firm May 1, 1888. Two years later the firm was enlarged by the admission of John Cunneen. The two senior partners were much engaged in public affairs, and the volume of the work of the firm fell upon Messrs. Coatsworth and Cunneen. On the removal of Mr. Sheehan to New York the partnership was dissolved, and Mr. Coatsworth united with Mr. Cunneen in forming a new partnership under the name of Cunneen & Coatsworth. This firm has been deservedly successful, and has built up a substantial and reputable clientage comprising many important business concerns and private corporations.

Mr. Coatsworth has wisely held aloof from active participation in politics, thus economizing his time and energy for the zealous pursuit of his profession. He has avoided the mistake of so many bright young

*EDWARD E. COATSWORTH*

men, who seek office and busy themselves with party politics, to the neglect of their life occupation. But Mr. Coatsworth is far from being a bookworm. No man takes more interest in healthy recreation than

he ; and his connection with numerous societies and
clubs attests the fact that he does not neglect the
social side of life.  He is particularly fond of aquatic
sports, and is a member of the Buffalo Yacht Club
and the Buffalo Canoe Club, seeking in this way to
take the exercise so essential to every man pursuing a

EDWARD L. COOK

sedentary vocation and engaged in head work largely.

In the Masonic fraternity Mr. Coatsworth stands
high, and is a devoted member of the brotherhood.
He belongs to all the Masonic bodies of Buffalo,
both York and Scottish rites, and has taken all the
degrees from the first to the thirty-second inclusive.
He is also a Knight Templar and a Noble of the
Mystic Shrine, and holds membership in the Royal
Arcanum and the Acacia Club.

*PERSONAL CHRONOLOGY— Edward
Emerson Coatsworth was born at Buffalo November 5,
1866; was educated in the public schools, graduating
from the high school; was admitted to the bar January 6,
1888; married Emma Marion Blocking of Buffalo June
25, 1891; has practiced law in Buffalo since 1888.*

**Edward L. Cook** deserves honorable mention
in the list of Buffalonians who have been instrumental in building up the Queen City, and making
it the healthful and beautiful place of residence that
it is to-day.  He was born in Buffalo and has lived
there all his life, barring an absence of three years
as a volunteer soldier in the Union army.
His early life was that of the city boy.
He attended the grammar school, and
later the Central High School.  To this
instruction he added a winter's training
as a teacher, thus solidifying the knowledge previously acquired.

Abandoning teaching for business, Mr.
Cook became connected as bookkeeper
with the firm of Hardiker & Toye, who
then carried on a large plumbing business
in Buffalo.  He remained with them till
the summer of 1862, when he enlisted in
the 100th New York regiment, donned
the blue uniform, and marched to the
front in defense of the Union.  He served
to the end of the war, and rose from the
ranks to the grade of captain, receiving a
commission as major by brevet after he
was mustered out.  At one time he was
detailed to duty on the staff of General
Dandy, the brigade commander.  He was
still a young man when the war closed,
but the three years spent in the army are
numbered among the most valuable of his
whole life.  In this respect Mr. Cook
is like most soldiers, who would not
exchange their war experience for any
other.

On returning from the field Mr. Cook
entered the service of the New York Central & Hudson River railroad, and filled
a clerkship with that company.  His old
business training, however, asserted itself, and after
a while he became bookkeeper for a plumbing house
conducted by T. W. Toye, one of his first employers.  His faithfulness and ability brought in the
course of years their proper reward, and he was made
a partner by Mr. Toye under the firm name of
T. W. Toye & Co.  Finally Mr. Cook branched
out in business in his own name, and for the past
eighteen years he has been at the head of one of
the largest and most complete plumbing, heating,
ventilating, and lighting establishments in Buffalo.

Mr. Cook is connected with numerous social and
benevolent organizations, and is an active member
of each.  He has long been prominent in the Grand
Army of the Republic, the Union Veteran Legion,

and the Military Order of the Loyal Legion. He is a member of DeMolay Lodge, F. & A. M., and of the Acacia Club. All societies and clubs having a patriotic or philanthropic object find in him a warm supporter and friend. His name is identified with the Good Government Club, the Society for the Prevention of Cruelty to Animals, the Liberal Club, and the Charity Organization Society. In short, Mr. Cook is not only a man of business, but a man of affairs generally, recognizing his obligations to society, and meeting them by hearty co-operation to the full extent of his time and power.

*PERSONAL CHRONOLOGY— Edward L. Cook was born at Buffalo March 29, 1849; was educated in the public schools; was bookkeeper for a firm of plumbers, 1859-62; served in the Union army, 1862-65; married Mary E. Moffett of Portageville, N. Y., June 16, 1869; became a member of the firm of T. W. Toye & Co., plumbers, in 1870, and has conducted a similar business under his own name since 1878.*

**George W. Cothran** has risen to his present eminence through indomitable energy and inborn ability. When he was four years of age his father died, leaving his mother with a small and heavily encumbered farm and a family of thirteen children, of whom George was the youngest. Until he was sixteen years old the routine of farm work, study at the neighboring school, and lessons with an elder brother, filled his time. Removing to Lockport, he devoted the succeeding four years to acquiring a practical knowledge of several branches of the mechanical arts. In these he evinced decided skill, and his ability to draw plans of wooden, iron, and stone structures has often been of service in his law practice in causes involving such questions.

The young man's ambition to study law saw promise of fulfillment when Phineas L. Ely of Lockport took him into his office. After three years' faithful application Mr. Cothran was admitted to practice in all the courts of New York state. His examination was unusual: it was conducted by three judges in open court, and he answered correctly all the questions with a single exception. After a year spent with his preceptor, Mr. Cothran opened a law office in

Lockport in 1858, and met with most gratifying success until he was interrupted by the call to arms in 1861.

Organizing battery M, 1st New York volunteer light artillery, he was commissioned its captain, and went at once to the front. The record of this battery is that it never lost a gun in all the great battles or lesser engagements in which it took part. An eight hours' fire at Antietam was one of Captain Cothran's memorable experiences. Another was the exposure to a twenty-four hours' rain, which brought on sciatica, and obliged him to resign his commission and return home. From the effects of this he has never fully recovered. After the battle of Antietam Captain Cothran was recommended to President Lincoln, by every commissioned officer in the 11th army corps, for promotion for meritorious service in

*GEORGE W. COTHRAN*

the field; but political considerations prevented him from receiving this richly deserved honor.

On leaving the army in 1863, Mr. Cothran took up the practice of his profession in Buffalo, and soon achieved an honored place in the bar of western New York. He has been connected with many important litigations. In 1869-72 he conducted what was known as the "penalty litigation" against the New York Central & Hudson River Railroad Co. for exacting excess of fare; and the result com-

WILLIAM H. CUDDEBACK

pelled a reorganization of the passenger tariffs of nearly all the railroads in the country, and prevented their demanding more than legal rates. In 1879 Mr. Cothran went to Chicago, to help unravel a railroad complication, and made that city his home until 1885, when he returned to Buffalo. He has practiced there ever since.

In 1877 Baker University of Kansas conferred on Mr. Cothran the degree of LL. D. because of his scholarly work in editing and annotating the sixth edition of the revised statutes of the state of New York, in three volumes containing nearly 4000 pages. In 1879 he did a similar piece of work for the revised statutes of Illinois, and this has been edited biennially since, and is a standard authority.

Mr. Cothran is the author of two practical and helpful books entitled "Law of Supervisors" and "Law of Assessors and Collectors." He has frequently contributed in lighter vein to the pages of popular periodicals.

Among the educational institutions that have benefited from Mr. Cothran's liberality is the Buffalo College of Physicians and Surgeons. He was its first president, and for a considerable period occupied the chair of medical jurisprudence.

Mr. Cothran's beautiful home in Buffalo is a veritable picture gallery and art emporium. There is probably no larger collection of music and musical literature to be found in America than his. His private library covers the whole range of literature, a unique feature being a collection of rare books on the origin, formation, and progress of religious ideas. His law library is said to be the most thoroughly annotated of any in Buffalo.

*PERSONAL CHRONOLOGY—George W. Cothran was born at Royalton, Niagara county, N. Y., February 25, 1844; was admitted to the bar in 1857; served in the Union army, 1861-64; married Jennie W. Mann of Buffalo May 26, 1864; was county judge of Erie county in 1877; edited, annotated, and wrote several valuable books, 1875-89; has practiced law in Buffalo since 1864, with the exception of several years' practice in Chicago, 1879-85.*

***

**William H. Cuddeback** comes of old Dutch stock, and his ancestors settled in the Empire State soon after it passed under the control of the English. Many of his lineage have figured in the local annals of the state; several served in the revolutionary war, and took part in the fighting that occurred in the Minisink territory, when the settlers were attacked by the famous Indian chieftain, Joseph Brant. Mr. Cuddeback's father was a delegate to the constitutional convention of 1846, a member of the state assembly, and county clerk of Orange county. Public affairs have proved attractive to his family, and naturally enough Mr. Cuddeback has devoted the time not required in his profession to active participation in the management of his political party in Buffalo. He is prominently identified with the "regular" Democracy; and for two years was chairman of the Democratic general committee, and gave freely of his time and effort to promote the success of his party. The divisions and dissensions in the Democracy in the Queen City are matter of history, but Mr. Cuddeback has the respect of all factions.

Mr. Cuddeback was born in the delightful county of Orange, in New York state, and received an academic education in the town of Goshen, to which his parents had moved. He entered Cornell University at the early age of sixteen, and spent four years there. He chose the law as his profession, and was admitted to practice at Poughkeepsie, N. Y., in May, 1877. At first he practiced alone for a short time at Goshen, where he became a justice of the peace. Then for seven years he was associated with Henry A. Wadsworth of Orange county. But like all ambitious young men, Mr. Cuddeback longed for the marts of trade and commerce. He realized the fact that to obtain business one must go where business is. Accordingly he cast around for a new location, and, drawn by the obvious advantages of Buffalo, moved thither in 1885. In 1889 he formed a partnership with Daniel J. Kenefick, at present district attorney of Erie county, that lasted four years. In 1895 Mr. Cuddeback associated himself with Joseph V. Seaver, county judge, and is at present connected with Eugene P. Ouchie. Since establishing himself in Buffalo Mr. Cuddeback's law practice has grown steadily, and he has to-day a recognized position at the bar of Erie county.

Meanwhile he has become one of the leaders of the Democratic party in the western part of the state. His only public office has been that of manager of the Craig Colony for epileptics at Sonyea. He was first appointed to this office by Governor Flower, and, though a strong Democrat, he has been twice reappointed by Governor Morton—a striking proof of his efficient administration of the office.

Mr. Cuddeback is a Mason, and holds membership in Ancient Landmark Lodge, No. 441, Free and Accepted Masons. He is well known in club circles, belonging to the Saturn Club, the Ellicott Club, and the Acacia Club.

*PERSONAL CHRONOLOGY—William Herman Cuddeback was born in the town of Deer Park, N. Y., March 25, 1854; was educated at* Goshen Academy and Cornell University; was admitted to the bar in 1877; practiced law at Goshen, N. Y., 1877–85; was chairman of the Democratic general committee, Buffalo, 1895–96; has practiced law in Buffalo since 1885.

**Thomas Dark** has led a laborious, useful, and honorable life. Born in the parish of Bitton, county of Gloucester, near Bristol, England, about the time printing machines were invented, and a year before the battle of Waterloo was fought, Mr. Dark's career has extended over the most remarkable period in the world's history. His place has been among the toilers. From his early days he was accustomed to heavy labor, since he went to work for his father, a contractor and builder, at the age of ten, thus learning the mason's trade. Too young to carry on the

*THOMAS DARK*

business of his father on the latter's death, Mr. Dark left his home and went to Bristol, where he worked at his trade under master builders. While there some of his father's old patrons sent for him to do a job of masonry, and from this beginning Mr. Dark developed into a building contractor. At first he put up dwelling houses, for the most part, but afterward his specialty became municipal work — the construction of bridges, culverts, waterworks, gas tanks, sewers, and the like.

After a score of years spent at his trade in England, Mr. Dark made up his mind to seek the richer opportunities of a new country by going to America. He arrived in Buffalo with two of his sons April 1, 1857, in the midst of universal business depression. At first the outlook was discouraging, and Mr. Dark sought employment in Canada. He soon returned to Buffalo, and, in order to become acquainted with the customs of the place and people, secured work on the new post office then building at the corner of Washington and Seneca streets. Mr. Dark's readiness to accept work under a " boss " when he had long been an employer himself, is characteristic of the man. Idleness he has always abhorred.

About this time, seeing an advertisement inviting proposals for building a stone culvert across Louisiana street, Mr. Dark put in a bid, and secured the work. From that day he has been prominent among the contractors of Buffalo, where he has performed many large contracts for corporations and individuals. The foundations of numerous public and private structures are the work of his brains and hands. In all his undertakings he has applied the same principles of dealing in the case of the public as in that of a private citizen, and has never been classed among contractors who grow rich on public jobs.

In 1873 Mr. Dark planned and constructed the Titusville, Penn., waterworks. For nearly thirty years he has taken a deep interest in the water supply of Buffalo. He received the first premium, $2000, offered by the city of Buffalo in 1869 for the best plans and specifications for the improvement of the waterworks. Mr. Dark's ideas, however, were not carried out by the city and contractors, and he has always insisted that the work was very badly done. He contends that the Buffalo water supply is entirely inadequate to the needs of a growing community, and constitutes in some respects a distinct menace to the prosperity of the city. He compiled and published, in 1895, a fifty-page pamphlet on the Buffalo waterworks, entitled " History of a Great Failure." His contention in brief is that the existing system and plant are radically defective ; that the practice of supplying water in its crude state to consumers, by direct pumping service from the river, is a ridiculous and dangerous novelty in hydraulic engineering ; that the mains which deliver water for domestic use should be filled from reservoirs

supplied by filter beds, the latter receiving the water in its crude state from a separate pumping main ; that the present inlet pier, receiving well therein, and tunnel thence to the pumping station, were badly constructed, at a cost monstrously in excess of the proper cost of good construction ; that the water supply is now, under certain conditions easily fulfilled, polluted by sewage and street washings ; that the water supply at certain seasons may be cut off, to the great danger of the city, by slush ice — partly cut off, as it is every year, wholly cut off, as it may be under conditions foreseeable and not unprecedented ; that the inlet is located in the wrong place, and should have been built far out in the lake, where pure water can be obtained at all seasons without danger of a water famine from the clogging of the inlets by slush ice. Without particularizing further Mr. Dark's plans, it may be said that his pamphlet on the subject, his original estimates, diagrams, and specifications — all of which will be deposited in the archives of the Buffalo Historical Society — will be exceedingly useful to future students of the Buffalo water supply, and will constitute an interesting chapter in the history of municipal government.

Mr. Dark embodies the best traits of the English character — industry, independence, and devotion to the acquisition of knowledge. He is a fine type of the self-made and self-educated man. His school days were few ; but he has succeeded by perseverance and economy of time in enlarging his mental horizon until he has become an intelligently informed man in a variety of lines. Close observation and sound judgment have been his guides. He is fond of reading and travel. He wrote, in the form of a diary, an account of a European trip made with several members of his family in 1893. This narrative was published at the request of friends, and the book is thoroughly enjoyable, affording a delightful picture of English home life.

*PERSONAL CHRONOLOGY — Thomas Dark was born at Kingswood, near Bristol, England, December 21, 1814 ; received an elementary education, and learned the mason's trade ; married Eliza Willis of Kingswood in 1844 ; came to the United States, and settled in Buffalo in 1857 ; has been a mason and building contractor in England and the United States since 1844.*

•••

**Oliver J. Eggert** has led a markedly useful and successful life along important and difficult lines of commercial activity. He was born in the Keystone State, but was taken during his infancy to Erie county, New York, and has lived ever since in or near Buffalo. He was unable to carry his education beyond the common schools, and even that advantage was cut off at the age of sixteen, when he began business life as a clerk in a Buffalo grocery. Three years of this service gave him considerable insight into the elements and principles of business, and thus paved the way for the partnership formed in 1847 with his father, Christian Eggert. They established a general store in the Erie-county village named from their family Eggertsville, and built up there a flourishing trade. Mr. Eggert remained in the business until 1862, when he sold his interest and retired.

In the same year the sheriff of Erie county, Robert H. Best, offered the position of under sheriff to Mr. Eggert. The latter had been so much absorbed in business before this that he had found little time for public office; though he had been elected, in 1858, clerk of the Erie-county board of supervisors. He accepted the position of under sheriff, and fulfilled its duties so effectively that he was himself elected sheriff two years later on the Democratic ticket for the term 1865-67. The responsibilities of this higher office were unflinchingly met and adequately discharged, and Mr. Eggert attained a reputation for integrity and business ability that materially promoted his subsequent success. Since his retirement from the sheriff's office he has not been in public life, except that in 1871 he was appointed police justice to fill a vacancy.

Mr. Eggert's earlier career thus related has been almost forgotten, and people nowadays think of him as a financier, and more particularly as a man widely informed in the great business of insurance. In 1867 a corporation was organized in Buffalo entitled the Buffalo German Insurance Co., to carry on the business of fire underwriting. Mr. Eggert has been identified with this enterprise from the very beginning, having been one of the incorporators and one of the first directors of the company. He held no active executive position, however, until 1874, when Alexander Martin resigned the position of secretary, and Mr. Eggert assumed the duties of the office. In the twenty and more years during which he has continued to hold this position, the affairs of the Buffalo German Insurance Co. have prospered exceedingly. The reason for this cannot be found exclusively in the secretary of the company, because the other

offices and the general management of the institution have been vested in able hands. There is no doubt, however, that the important duties assigned to Mr. Eggert have been most faithfully and efficiently performed, and the success of the business must be ascribed in large measure to him. When he became

*OLIVER J. EGGERT*

secretary the assets of the company were about $447,000 and the net surplus $141,000. By July 1, 1896, the assets had risen to $1,850,000 and the surplus to $1,250,000. These comparative figures demonstrate clearly the success of the company since Mr. Eggert became its secretary. The insurance business necessarily occupies the chief share of Mr. Eggert's time and thought, but he is also a trustee and second vice president of the Erie County Savings Bank. Mr. Eggert's thorough knowledge of financial subjects and sound judgment in matters connected therewith are of great value in the conduct of banking affairs.

*PERSONAL CHRONOLOGY — Oliver Jefferson Eggert was born at Petersburg, Penn., October 31, 1828; received a common-school education;*

conducted a general store at Eggertsville, Erie county,
N. Y., 1837-42; married Susan Frick of Eggertsville November 15, 1849; was appointed under sheriff
of Erie county in 1862, and was elected sheriff for the
years 1865-67; has been secretary of the Buffalo German Insurance Co. since 1874.

*JOSEPH FOWLER*

**Joseph Fowler** has practiced medicine in
Buffalo nearly a quarter of a century, and has thus
built up an enviable reputation, both professionally
as a general practitioner and socially as a cultured
gentleman and thoroughly likable associate. He has
served the public efficiently in positions of much
importance, and is widely known, outside the circle
of his immediate practice, as a man of character and
responsibility.

Dr. Fowler was born in Saratoga county, New
York, shortly before the middle of the century, in
the township of Clifton Park. His ancestors were
among the early settlers of that part of the state,
and both his parents and grandparents were likewise born in the same community. His preparatory

education was obtained at Half Moon Academy in
his native town. He was unable to enter upon professional studies at the usual and most convenient
stage of life, and followed the example of so many
eminent men by basing his higher education on the
foundation of preliminary teaching. He undertook
this work at the age of eighteen, and
continued to teach for four or five years.
At the end of that time his resources
were such that he was able to carry out
his plans to fit himself for the medical
profession; and in 1869 he left Saratoga
county for the other end of the state,
matriculating in the medical department
of the University of Buffalo. Taking his
degree in 1873, he began practice in
Buffalo at once, with the happy results
stated in our opening paragraph.

The early career of a young physician
in a large city, without special prestige,
family connections of value, or other
favoring circumstance, is likely to be
somewhat thorny; and Dr. Fowler had
no magician's wand with which to dissi-
pate the natural and inevitable drawbacks
of his early professional environment.
His progress, however, was rapid, and
the conditions quickly changed for the
better. The "personal equation" counts
for much in the physician's calling,
and Dr. Fowler's engaging manners and
genial disposition doubtless helped him
onward in the struggle for success. As
early as 1881 he was elected one of the
coroners for Erie county, and served a
term of three years. He has always
been a consistent Republican in political
affiliations, and has been prominently
mentioned at various times in connec-
tion with important offices at the certain or possible
disposal of his party. His name was before the
convention on more than one occasion as that of
a suitable candidate for the office of superintendent
of education for the city of Buffalo, and in 1889 he
received the Republican nomination for the office.
He was appointed by Mayor Becker, in 1886, surgeon
to the department of police, and has since discharged
the duties of that office with ability and zeal.

Dr. Fowler believes in supporting professional
societies, and belongs to several, including the New
York State Medical Association and the Erie County
Medical Society. For ten years he was on the
medical staff of the Sisters of Charity Hospital.
He believes thoroughly, too, in fraternal associations

unprofessional in scope, and has taken advanced standing in the ranks of Masons, Odd Fellows, and similar societies.

*PERSONAL CHRONOLOGY—Joseph Fowler was born in Clifton Park township, Saratoga county, N. Y., May 4, 1847; was educated in the schools of his native town; taught school, 1864-69; married Cornelia F. Cowles of Buffalo in 1861; graduated from the medical department of the University of Buffalo in 1874; was elected a coroner of Erie county in 1881; was Republican candidate for superintendent of education of Buffalo in 1889; was appointed surgeon of the department of police in 1886, and has held the position since; has practiced medicine in Buffalo since 1874.*

***

**Joseph E. Gavin** has displayed in the management of private business and public affairs the characteristics and qualities of a successful financier. Born in Buffalo, he is thoroughly familiar with the history and development of the city, in which indeed he has been no insignificant factor. A genial disposition, intelligent comprehension of business details, executive ability, and fidelity to duty, have commended Mr. Gavin to the attention and confidence of the commercial classes of the city and its people generally. He is in the very prime of a vigorous manhood, progressive, popular, and self-reliant. What he has already accomplished augurs a successful and an honorable future.

Mr. Gavin was educated in the public schools of Buffalo, and pursued his collegiate studies at St. Joseph's College in that city and at St. Michael's College, Toronto, from which he graduated shortly after attaining his majority. After completing his studies he entered the coal and wood business with his father, on whose death he succeeded to the entire business. In the course of several years Mr. Gavin had the satisfaction of seeing this enterprise grow to large proportions under careful and judicious management.

It is, however, in the field of politics and public affairs that Mr. Gavin is best known, and has won the greatest distinction. His temperament is such that he rejoices in the ups and downs of political contests, and is never discouraged by defeat nor unduly elated by victory. In Mr. Cleveland's first administration Mr. Gavin was a customs inspector at Buffalo, and served the public faithfully and well in

that capacity. Meanwhile he was making himself felt as a power in local affairs, and in recognition of his strength and ability the Democratic party in 1891 nominated him for comptroller of the city of Buffalo. His election followed by an overwhelming majority, attesting the popularity of the candidate.

Mr. Gavin's record in the office of comptroller is one to which he can always look back with justifiable pride. In this position he established a permanent reputation as a thorough executive officer and an astute financier. Men of both parties applauded his administration of the city's fiscal affairs. He negotiated several municipal loans to the great advantage of the city. His skill in this direction elicited the praise of financial journals of repute throughout the United States. He placed one loan in New York city at the remarkably low rate of two and one half

*JOSEPH E. GAVIN*

per cent. It was Mr. Gavin who, as comptroller, saved the city over $100,000 by his discovery that the fines collected from criminals had been paid into the county treasury, instead of to the city. Mr.

Gavin's career in the office of comptroller was so successful that upon the expiration of his term the council, pursuing an unusual course, adopted a resolution of public approval ; and the press, irrespective of party, complimented him on the good service he had rendered to the city and the people of Buffalo.

FRANK T GILBERT

Mr. Gavin was again the candidate of his party in 1894, this time for congress. It was the Republican tidal wave year, and the Republican candidate won, though by a margin so narrow as to justify the claim of Mr. Gavin's friends that a different result would have been reached, but for the mistake of many voters who cast the state ballot containing only the names of state candidates.

Since retiring from the comptroller's office Mr. Gavin has been engaged in the bond business, and has handled successfully over ten million dollars' worth of bonds, including several issues of the city of Buffalo and other municipalities, part of the $9,000,000 state canal bonds, and over $1,000,000 of the last issue of Government 4's.

Mr. Gavin is a member of numerous societies of a social and benevolent character, and is one of the men who can be counted on in behalf of every patriotic and worthy movement.

PERSONAL CHRONOLOGY—*Joseph Edward Gavin was born at Buffalo November 14, 1855 ; was educated in public schools, St. Joseph's College, Buffalo, and St. Michael's College, Toronto ; married Sarah E. Cando of Buffalo October 31, 1881 ; was customs inspector at Buffalo, 1885-89, and comptroller of the city, 1892-94 ; has been engaged in the coal and wood business in Buffalo since 1884.*

***

**Frank T. Gilbert** was born in Brooklyn, and began his education in the public schools of that city. Later he attended the public schools of Phoenix, N. Y., whither his parents had moved, as well as Falley Seminary, at Fulton, N. Y.; and at the age of eighteen he received his diploma from Ames's Commercial College in Syracuse.

When about twenty years of age Mr. Gilbert commenced his business career in a country store in Phoenix, in partnership with his father. After a short but successful business experience, he entered the law office of C. W. Avery of Phoenix, as a student, and remained with him about two years, when he abandoned the study of the law and returned to commercial pursuits. He accepted a position as bookkeeper with one of the large shipping houses of Buffalo, having moved to that city in 1871. From then until 1880 he was in the employ of William Avery & Co., L. P. Smith & Co., and Lothridge, Gallagher & Co.—firms that were doing a large shipping business at that time on the Buffalo docks.

When William W. Lawson became sheriff of Erie county in 1880, Mr. Gilbert was appointed one of his deputies, and served in that capacity for one year. At that time John B. Weber resigned his position as under sheriff, and Mr. Gilbert succeeded him, holding the position during the remainder of Sheriff Lawson's administration, as well as during that of Sheriff Koch, who succeeded Mr. Lawson. Mr. Gilbert has only once been a candidate for public office. In 1885 he was nominated on the Republican ticket for sheriff of Erie county, and at the November election he was chosen by a plurality of nearly

3000 votes. His long experience as deputy sheriff and under sheriff had fitted him well for this responsible position, and he displayed in the higher office the same ability that had characterized his conduct in the subordinate positions.

At the expiration of his term of office Mr. Gilbert again gave his attention to business matters. He became interested in various commercial and manufacturing enterprises, and spent much of his time, especially during the winter, in Florida, where he acquired a large quantity of valuable real estate, and where he now has profitable orange groves. When George H. Lamy became sheriff of Erie county in 1895, he urged Mr. Gilbert to become under sheriff. Mr. Gilbert accepted the appointment, and still holds the position.

Aside from his business and official connections, Mr. Gilbert is one of the best-known members of the Masonic fraternity in western New York. He is Past Master of Washington Lodge, No. 240, Free and Accepted Masons. He is a member of Keystone Chapter, No. 163, Royal Arch Masons, of which he is also Past High Priest. He is Eminent Commander of Hugh de Payens Commandery, No. 30, Knights Templars. He is Illustrious Potentate of Ismailia Temple, ancient Arabic Order Nobles of the Mystic Shrine. He is a member of Keystone Council, No. 20, Royal and Select Masters, and a 32d degree Mason, belonging to the Buffalo Consistory. Mr. Gilbert is especially proficient in all the beautiful ceremonial work of these Masonic lodges.

Mr. Gilbert has always been a Republican, and has taken an active interest in politics and in all public matters, and he has occasionally written for the press upon public questions of the day. He is not a member of any religious denomination, but is a regular attendant at the Unitarian Church, and is in hearty sympathy with its principle — the Fatherhood of God and the brotherhood of man.

PERSONAL CHRONOLOGY — *Frank T. Gilbert was born at Brooklyn October 1, 1846; was educated in the public schools, at Falley Seminary, and at Ames's Commercial College, Syracuse; married Helen A. Briggs of Phoenix, N. Y., October 10, 1866; engaged in business in Phoenix, 1868-69; studied law, 1869-71; went to Buffalo in 1871, and engaged in mercantile pursuits until 1880; was appointed*

deputy sheriff of Erie county in 1880 and under sheriff in 1881, and was elected sheriff in 1885; has been under sheriff of Erie county since January 1, 1895.

***

**Charles A. Gould** is one of the young men who by their own unaided energy and perseverance have worked their way to wealth, social position, and prominence. He was born in Batavia, N. Y., where he passed his boyhood. He was educated in the public schools of his native town, and prepared himself for college. He was unable, however, to carry out his plans in this regard, as his father met with business reverses. Thrown thus upon his own resources, Mr. Gould naturally turned his thoughts toward Buffalo, the largest city in his vicinity; and thither he went in 1869, a young man of twenty, to earn his own livelihood.

CHARLES A. GOULD

He was first engaged with a large mercantile firm, and there gained the business experience that was to be so beneficial to him in after years. Gradually he began to take an active part in politics. There was a stirring local campaign in Buffalo in 1870, and Mr. Gould's interest in political matters dates from that time. He showed taste and decided ability for public affairs, and it was not long before he had become prominent in local Republican councils. In 1878 he was appointed deputy postmaster of Buffalo, and served in that position for two years. Then he was appointed collector of customs for the district of Buffalo Creek, by President Garfield, and served from 1880 to 1884, when the Democrats came into power with the first election of President Cleveland. During all these years Mr. Gould was one of the leaders of his party in Erie county, taking a prominent part in many Republican campaign organizations, and acting for many years as a member of the Republican county committee.

With Mr. Gould's retirement from office there began a third period in his life. He had been an accountant and a public official. He now became a manufacturer, and in this field he has since continued with steadily growing success and prosperity. He bought an interest in the Henry Childs Steam Forge in South Buffalo, which he ran for a number of years with marked success. In 1887 he purchased ground at Black Rock, and built a large steam forge of his own, which he equipped with the very best modern appliances for the manufacture of shafting, locomotive driving axles, car axles, links and pins, and other railway appliances. Success attended the new undertaking.

Soon after the erection of this new plant he took up the manufacture of what is now known as the Gould automatic coupler. He was not satisfied with placing the Gould equipment on American railways, but in 1895 succeeded in introducing it abroad, and it is now in use on several of the largest railways of England. In fact, the Gould system seems likely to become the standard for English railways, and to change entirely their old method of vestibuling cars. The Gould Coupler Co. was organized with Mr. Gould as its president. Later the Gould Steel Co. of Anderson, Ind., was formed, with Mr. Gould as president of this latter concern, also. Since 1889 Mr. Gould's home has been in New York city, where the main offices of these companies are situated.

A picturesque episode of Mr. Gould's life is the establishment of the town of Depew. Need of better railroad facilities led him to look about for a new site, which he found near the village of Lancaster, N. Y. Within three years a tract of farming land ten miles from Buffalo was transformed into a thriving industrial community of several thousand people. In this transformation Mr. Gould has been one of the chief factors; and he was the originator of the

general plan. The Buffalo Investment Co. was formed with Mr. Gould as president, and about 1300 acres of land were bought. The New York Central road took 100 acres for new shops; and the Gould Coupler Co. took 50 acres, on which they erected one of the largest malleable iron works in the country. The forge at Black Rock was destroyed by fire in the summer of 1895. It was a disheartening loss, but Mr. Gould with indomitable push immediately decided to rebuild at Depew with increased facilities and modern appliances.

Personally Mr. Gould is of a very social nature. He is a lover of yachting, and is commodore of the Douglaston Yacht Club, as well as a member of the New York, American, and Larchmont yacht clubs. Other organizations of a social nature with which he is connected are the New York Athletic, Republican, and Engineers' clubs of New York city; the Buffalo and Ellicott clubs of Buffalo; the Chicago Club; the Manufacturers' Club of Philadelphia; and the Flushing Club of Flushing. He is a generous giver to church and benevolent objects. He is senior warden of the Episcopal Church of the Holy Nativity in New York city, and is president of St. Andrew's Free Hospital for women at Harlem.

*PERSONAL CHRONOLOGY* — *Charles Albert Gould was born at Batavia, N. Y., January 13, 1849; was educated in public schools; went to Buffalo in 1869, and began work as an accountant; married Adelaide Stocking of Batavia September 1, 1869; was deputy postmaster of Buffalo, 1878-79, and collector of customs there, 1880-84; went into business for himself as a partner in a steam-forge company in 1884, and later established a forge of his own; is president of the Gould Coupler Co. of Depew, N. Y., and the Gould Steel Co. of Anderson, Ind.*

\* \* \*

**S. S. Green** is an eminent physician of Buffalo, whose life has been somewhat more varied and active than that of most professional men. He is a lineal descendant of Samuel Green, who came to this country from England in 1630, and settled in Boston. Dr. Green is a native of Vermont, and is one of a family of fourteen children. He received his primary education in the common schools and in local academies, and then attended Nine Partners' Friends' College at Washington, N. Y. He had determined to become a physician, but as he was without means to carry on his medical studies he now taught school for two years to obtain the necessary funds. He then entered the medical department of the University of Michigan, and after a year there became a medical student in the University of the City of New York, from which he graduated in 1861 with honors.

The Civil War was at its height when Dr. Green took his degree, and his first step after graduation was to offer his services to the government as assistant surgeon in the navy. Perhaps he inherited a patriotic nature from his ancestors, one of whom was General Nathanael Greene, one of the most distinguished officers of the Revolution, who received from congress a gold medal and a vote of thanks for his brilliant military achievements. Dr. Green was appointed acting assistant surgeon in the United States navy, and after a few weeks at the Brooklyn Navy Yard he was ordered to New Orleans, where he reported to Admiral Farragut for duty. He was assigned by him to the United States steamer "Arizona," afterwards Admiral Thatcher's flagship. Dr. Green served on board the "Arizona" for one year, and was then promoted to the post of examining surgeon, and charged with the examination of men who were transferred from the army to the navy. While performing the duties of this position he was stricken with yellow fever, and for over three weeks was confined in the naval hospital at New Orleans. Seven men died around him, but his excellent constitution rescued him from the terrible grasp of the disease. He resumed his post of duty, and served in the navy until he was honorably discharged at the close of the war.

Dr. Green then turned his attention to general practice, and settled in Lagrangeville, N. Y., where he devoted himself for several years to the arduous duties of a country physician. In 1873 he was appointed surgeon on the vessel "Charles H. Marshall," sailing between New York and Liverpool; and he subsequently filled a similar post on the "Alaska," running between Panama and San Francisco. Finally, in 1875, he moved to Buffalo, and has ever since practiced there with gratifying success. For six years he was one of the district physicians of the city, and proved himself an able and energetic public servant. He is a member of the Erie County Medical Society, the New York State Medical Association, the American Medical Association, and the International Medical Congress. It need hardly be added that Dr. Green holds a prominent place in his profession.

In 1888 Dr. Green gratified his fondness for travel by making a trip around the world. He crossed the country via the Canadian Pacific railway to Vancouver, B. C., and thence made his way south through the Puget-sound region and along the coast of Southern California and Mexico. Returning to San Francisco, he took steamer for Japan, and continued his course west through the Orient, traveling 3000 miles in India alone.

S. S. GREEN

Dr. Green has won considerable local fame as a sportsman, and has made many hunting trips to the Canadian forests. On such an excursion he shot one of the largest moose ever known. The head of this magnificent animal adorns the rooms of the Acacia Club, Buffalo, and is one of the finest specimens of its class anywhere on exhibition. Dr. Green is also a lover of good horses, and owns some of the best trotters in Buffalo.

Dr. Green is an active member of the G. A. R., and an officer of Bidwell-Wilkeson Post, No. 9, of Buffalo. He is a member of the A. O. U. W., the Red Men, the Royal Templars of Temperance, and the Acacia Club. He is prominent in Masonic circles, having received the 32d degree in the

Scottish Rite, and attained membership in the following Masonic bodies: Queen City Lodge, No. 358, F. & A. M.; Keystone Chapter, No. 162, R. A. M.; Keystone Council, No. 20; Hugh de Payens Commandery, No. 30, K. T.; and Ismailia Temple, Nobles of the Mystic Shrine. He is a member of

DEVILLO W. HARRINGTON

Calvary Presbyterian Church, and is closely identified with the social and philanthropic life of Buffalo.

*PERSONAL CHRONOLOGY—Stephen Squire Green was born at Starksboro, Vt., January 6, 1839; studied medicine at the University of Michigan, and received the degree of Doctor of Medicine from the University of the City of New York March 4, 1864; served as a surgeon in the United States navy, 1864-65; married Charlotte S. Cornell of Gaysville, Vt., January 6, 1869; has practiced medicine in Buffalo since 1875.*

•••

**Devillo W. Harrington** has devoted his life to the study and practice of medicine. He was born at Sherburne, N. Y., where his early education

was received. To obtain a higher education, and prepare himself for the profession of medicine, he taught school for several years, and at one time was principal of the Sherburne Academy. He was ready to enter college when the Civil War broke out, and was thus called upon to choose between private interests and public duty. The choice was not difficult for him, as he came of an American lineage noted for patriotism and civic spirit. Instead of entering college he enlisted in the Union army, and served for three years as a volunteer soldier. He was for one year in the 7th corps under General Dix, and two years in the 1st New York dragoons. He was twice wounded on the field of battle. When the war ended he was honorably discharged from service, and returned to his native town.

Having devoted to the cause of his country the years he had intended to pass in college, he now felt obliged to forego a classical training. Taking up, therefore, the study of medicine directly, he entered the medical department of the University of Buffalo, from which he received the degree of M. D. in 1871.

Dr. Harrington's career as a physician is part of the medical history of Buffalo for the past quarter of a century. By honorable and professional means he has acquired a large practice; and has been invited to act as physician at various institutions, and to assume the duties of a professorship in the medical department of his *alma mater*.

To a theoretic knowledge of medicine Dr. Harrington had the opportunity to add the most practical knowledge, by his appointment in the year of his graduation as resident physician of the Buffalo General Hospital. For nine years he was the attending surgeon of the Hospital of the Sisters of Charity, and for the past ten years he has been consulting surgeon of the Buffalo General Hospital. In 1886 he was elected a member of the medical faculty of the University of Buffalo, and a professor in the subject of genito-urinary and venereal diseases. He had previously held the position of lecturer on clinical surgery in the same institution, and his advancement attests the regard of his associates for him as a teacher and a man learned in his subject.

Dr. Harrington is a constant worker, of methodical habits, keenly appreciative of the value of time; and he finds no leisure for political or club life. He is a member, however, of all the leading medical associations.

*PERSONAL CHRONOLOGY — Deville White Harrington was born at Sherburne, N. Y., October 24, 1844; attended district schools, and taught for several years; served in the Union army, 1862-65; graduated from the medical department of the University of Buffalo in 1871; married Annie Scott of Buffalo October 10, 1875; has practiced medicine at Buffalo since 1871.*

•••

**Louis B. Hart** has won a prominent place in public notice, at an age when many young men are still casting about to decide what their life-work shall be; for he is now but twenty-seven years old. He has made every year tell, and has wasted no time on things that were not worth while.

At the age of fifteen he had completed the course of instruction offered by the public schools of Lockport, and had begun the study of stenography. Since the time when Tiro, the celebrated slave, acted in the capacity of secretary to the great orator Cicero, a century before Christ, inventing a set of characters for recording his patron's eloquence, the art of stenography has been made a stepping-stone to higher things by many an ambitious youth. Patience, a reliable memory, coolness of nerve, and power of physical endurance, are requisites for success in the hieroglyphic art; and these qualities Mr. Hart possesses in a marked degree. The speed and accuracy which he readily attained helped him at once to a position in the office of E. M. & F. M. Ashley, prominent lawyers of Lockport. In this legal atmosphere it was natural enough that his thoughts should turn towards the study of law, but he wisely decided to adhere to his task until the requisite funds should be laid by. A twelvemonth passed, and he was invited to become the private secretary of Senator McMillan at Albany. This opportunity to see the inside workings of the state legislature was not to be considered lightly, and he accepted. The year was full of interesting experiences, but Mr. Hart was not to be deterred from the study of law, which he had now fully decided to undertake. He therefore returned to Lockport to study in the office of Ellsworth & Potter, acting

at the same time as their stenographer. All through his studies he did double duty in this way.

Mr. Hart's appointment as stenographer to the grand jury of Erie county by District Attorney Quinby occurred in the month of his twenty-first birthday, and he held that position four years. He was then promoted to be managing clerk, and was reappointed to that office the following year by District Attorney Kenefick. In the meantime his devotion to his law studies remained unchanged. He became a special student at the Buffalo Law School, and was admitted to the bar in 1892. On January 1, 1896, he was appointed clerk of the Surrogate's Court by Louis W. Marcus.

*PERSONAL CHRONOLOGY — Louis Bret Hart was born at Medina, N. Y., March 30, 1869; was educated in the Lockport schools and the Buffalo*

*LOUIS B. HART*

*Law School; was admitted to the bar in 1892; was stenographer and afterward clerk to the grand jury of Erie county, 1890-95; has been clerk of the Surrogate's Court of Erie county since January 1, 1896.*

**John R. Hazel** secured a great advantage in this rushing age by gaining admittance to the bar at his majority; so that now, though only in his thirty-sixth year, he has spent nearly half his life in the pursuit of the law. Perseverance, industry, and pluck have been the characteristic qualities of his

JOHN R. HAZEL

career; and these always win in a land of opportunity, no matter what unfavorable circumstances may hinder their possessor.

Mr. Hazel is a Buffalonian by birth. He was obliged to leave school at the early age of twelve and begin work. He first obtained employment in White's Edge Tool Works, and remained there two years. His next position was in the law office of James C. Fullerton, then assistant city attorney. Here he found work that was not only congenial, but led to something higher. By attending night school, and using every opportunity to cultivate his mind, he fitted himself for the study of law; and in time was admitted to the bar, and became the partner of his former employer and preceptor. The law office

has been the training school and stepping-stone of some of the ablest lawyers America has produced — men who have made up for the lack of collegiate training by zealous home and office study.

The firm of Fullerton & Hazel was soon increased by the addition of Tracy C. Becker, and became Fullerton, Becker & Hazel. This professional partnership continued for eight years. Mr. Hazel then associated with himself Frank A. Abbott, and he is now the senior member of the firm of Hazel & Abbott. Mr. Hazel has been a busy lawyer, and has seen his practice grow steadily ever since his admission to the bar. He is a hard worker, and conscientiously serves the interests of his clients.

Mr. Hazel is an active Republican, and has been repeatedly honored by his party. In 1891 he was nominated for member of the state assembly, and though the normal Democratic majority in his district was 1500, he came within 150 votes of election. In 1894 he was appointed by Comptroller Roberts commissioner of corporation tax. Mr. Hazel has been a member of the Republican state committee since 1892, and is active in many local Republican clubs. He served as secretary of the Republican general committee of Buffalo for nearly ten years. This party service was fittingly rewarded by his election, in 1896, as a delegate to the Republican national convention at St. Louis.

Mr. Hazel is a member of St. Louis Church, Buffalo, is connected with many social and benevolent organizations, and has a wide circle of friends in both professional and social life.

*PERSONAL CHRONOLOGY—John Raymond Hazel was born at Buffalo December 18, 1860; received a common-school education; studied law, and was admitted to practice April 7, 1882; was appointed commissioner of corporation tax in 1894; was a delegate to the Republican national convention at St. Louis in 1896; has been a member of the Republican state committee since 1892; has practiced law in Buffalo since 1882.*

• • •

**Herbert M. Hill** is one of the best-known theoretical and practical chemists in the country. He fitted himself for his present work by a thorough course of preliminary education. After the training obtainable in the district schools of his native place, and in the grammar and high schools of Watertown, N. Y., Dr. Hill entered Hamilton College, whence he was graduated in June, 1879, with the degree of A. B. For the last two years of his college course he was assistant in charge of the chemical laboratory at the college, and in 1879–80 he took a postgraduate course at Hamilton in chemistry and mineralogy.

Dr. Hill's first engagement in teaching was a professorship of Greek and Latin in the Cortland (N. Y.) Normal School, to which he was appointed in 1880. He went to Minnesota the same year as second in charge of a party sent out by eastern capitalists to prospect for iron. This trip resulted in the establishment of mines at Tower on Vermilion lake in northern Minnesota. On his return Dr. Hill was appointed professor of natural sciences and mathematics in the high school at Watertown, N. Y.—a position that he filled acceptably for eight years. At the end of this period he was deservedly honored by an appointment as principal of the school.

But higher honors awaited him. The Buffalo Medical College stood in need of a thoroughly capable man to be its professor of chemistry and toxicology, and after carefully scanning the field the faculty offered the place to Dr. Hill. He accepted the offer, and since 1889 has been a resident of Buffalo, where his many estimable qualities and his intellectual attainments have made him an honored citizen. Besides the position already mentioned, Dr. Hill is professor of general and analytical chemistry in the Buffalo College of Pharmacy, and professor of general chemistry in the Buffalo Dental College. These three colleges are departments of the University of Buffalo.

From 1885 to 1889 Dr. Hill was chemist to the state dairy commission, and he now ably fills the position of city chemist of Buffalo. He has many commissions in the realm of applied chemistry as related to the industries. He is consulting chemist for the Iroquois Chemical Works, the Victor Mineral Spring Co., and the Milsom Rendering & Fertilizer Co. He has also figured as an expert in a number of criminal cases. Among his field experiences may be mentioned a trip to the Ontario gold fields that he made as an expert in 1895.

Since his graduation from Hamilton College Dr. Hill has been twice honored by his *alma mater*: in 1882 he received the degree of Master of Arts, and in 1890 that of Doctor of Philosophy.

Dr. Hill is a thorough student, and his connections outside the active practice of his profession are largely with organizations allied thereto. He is a member of the American Chemical Society, the American Microscopical Society, the Buffalo Society of Natural Sciences, the Buffalo Microscopical Club, and the Engineers' Society of Western New York.

*PERSONAL CHRONOLOGY—Herbert Malcolm Hill was born at Burrs Mills, Jefferson county, N. Y., May 19, 1856; graduated from Hamilton College in 1879; married Amanda Elizabeth Isdell of Watertown, N. Y., June 1, 1880; was a professor in the Watertown High School, 1881–85, and principal*

*HERBERT M. HILL*

*thereof, 1888–89; was chemist to the state dairy commission, 1885–89; has lived in Buffalo since 1889, holding professorships in different departments of the University of Buffalo.*

**Alvin A. Hubbell** has practiced medicine in
Buffalo for sixteen years, and for the last thirteen
years has devoted himself exclusively to diseases of
the eye and ear.    In this specialty he has attained
great distinction.    He has kept in touch with the
leading oculists, not only of this country but also of

ALVIN A. HUBBELL

Europe, and his studies have twice taken him
across the Atlantic, where he has visited the leading
ophthalmic hospitals of Birmingham, London, and
Paris.    He has had occasion to perform many difficult operations, the most notable of which, perhaps,
outside of his ophthalmic surgery, occurred only two
years after his graduation, when he performed
laparotomy for intussusception of the intestines —
the fourth operation for this disease in the United
States.    He has added materially to the appliances
for the practice of his specialty.    He devised an improved electro-magnet, in 1884, for extracting steel
from the interior of the eye.    Another invention is
a new form of car scissors, designed for him by
George Tilman & Co. of New York.    He has

received high honors from numerous medical societies, and from Niagara University, the medical department of which he was foremost in organizing.
This university conferred on him, in 1886, the *ad
eundem* degree of M. D., and in 1893 the higher
degree of Doctor of Philosophy.

Dr. Hubbell's grandparents were pioneer settlers of western New York, as
their ancestors were of the American continent.    He traces his descent to Richard
Hubbell, who emigrated from England
in 1645, and settled in Fairfield, Conn.
Dr. Hubbell was the eldest of four children.    His early education was obtained
in the common schools, and in Randolph
Academy (now Chamberlain Institute) at
Randolph, N. Y.    He also taught school
several years in the intervals of his own
tuition.    At the age of eighteen he began
reading medicine, continuing the study
under different physicians in Cattaraugus
county for three years.    Among his preceptors was Dr. Thomas J. Wheeler of
Rutledge (now Conewango), at that time
one of the most eminent practitioners in
western New York.    Dr. Hubbell then
attended medical lectures in Philadelphia
for two years, and at the age of twenty-
three began general medical practice in
Leon, Cattaraugus county.    Not satisfied
with the education already acquired, after
six years of practice he entered the medical department of the University of Buffalo, whence he graduated February 23,
1876, winning one of the Millard Fillmore cash prizes for the best thesis.    He
then returned to his general practice at
Leon ; but his interest in eye and ear
diseases soon induced him to move to
Buffalo, where he could specialize these subjects.
With what success he has done so has already been
shown.

Dr. Hubbell actively supports many professional
societies, including the Buffalo Medical Union, the
Buffalo Academy of Medicine, the Buffalo Ophthalmological Society, and the Erie County Medical
Association.    He belongs, also, to the New York
State Medical Association, and to the Medical Association of Central New York, of which he has been
president.    The American Medical Association likewise has his name on its membership roll, as well as
the American Ophthalmological Society, the highest
association of its kind in the country.    Dr. Hubbell
was a member of the Ninth International Medical

Congress held in Washington city in 1887, of the Pan American Medical Congress held in the same place in 1893, and of the International Ophthalmological Congress held in Edinburgh in 1894. He belongs to the Buffalo Society of Natural Sciences and to other scientific bodies. He is a member of the society of the Sons of the Revolution, his paternal great-grandfather, Ezbon Hubbell, and his maternal great-grandfather, William Farnsworth, having served in the revolutionary war.

After helping to organize the medical department of Niagara University, Dr. Hubbell was appointed professor of ophthalmology and otology therein, and was elected secretary of the faculty. He has since retained these positions, and is an earnest advocate of higher medical education. He is attending surgeon to the Charity Eye, Ear, and Throat Hospital of Erie county, and is eye and ear surgeon to the Hospital of the Sisters of Charity, and most of the other important hospitals in Buffalo.

Dr. Hubbell has been a frequent contributor to professional publications on subjects relating to his specialty. He is associate editor of the Buffalo *Medical Journal*, and has published in that periodical many articles of a technical nature. Several of his papers have appeared in the *Transactions* of the New York State Medical Association, the *Archives of Pediatrics*, the *New York Medical Journal*, the *Archives of Ophthalmology*, the *Ophthalmic Record*, and other professional publications. An address introductory to a course of medical lectures was published by Peter Paul & Bro. of Buffalo in 1888.

*PERSONAL CHRONOLOGY—Alvin Allace Hubbell was born at Conewango, N. Y., May 1, 1846; was educated in common schools and Randolph Academy; studied medicine at Philadelphia, 1867–69; began practice at Leon, Cattaraugus county, in 1869; married Evangeline Fancher of Leon June 5, 1872; graduated from the medical department of the University of Buffalo in 1876; practiced general medicine in Buffalo from 1880 to 1883, and has since confined his practice to diseases of the eye and ear; has been professor of diseases of the eye and ear in the medical department of Niagara University, and secretary of the faculty of that department, since its organization in 1883.*

**John Hughes** is a leading factor in what is peculiarly an American enterprise — the live-stock commission business. Success in this industry requires sound judgment, square dealing, and an accurate knowledge of the markets. Mr. Hughes came to the United States from Ireland when a child, so that his education and training were for the most part distinctly American. He made his home in Buffalo, where he attended the public schools, and subsequently pursued a course at Bryant & Stratton's Business College, to fit himself for mercantile life. His educational advantages were limited, for he was dependent on his own exertions; but he made good use of such opportunities as came within his reach.

The business career of Mr. Hughes has been confined almost entirely to the buying and selling of live stock, and in this he has met with deserved

*JOHN HUGHES*

success. He first entered the business in 1866, becoming associated with Edward Swope at East Buffalo. To-day Mr. Hughes is a partner in the firm of Swope, Hughes, Waltz & Benstead, one of the largest concerns in western New York operating in live stock. Buffalo stands next to Chicago in the extent and variety of its live-stock products, and is one of the greatest markets of the world. This fact is traceable, partly to the natural and geographical advantages of the city, but largely to the energy and business sagacity of such men as Mr. Hughes.

While steadily devoting himself to the demands of a growing business, Mr. Hughes has maintained a commendable interest in local affairs. In political convictions he is a zealous Democrat, but always tempers his politics with sterling sense and proper respect for the opinions of others. In short, he believes in using the same standard of honesty and courtesy in politics as in business. He has never sought for political office, having too many business cares to permit the discharge of exacting official duties. He has, however, served as a park commissioner of Buffalo, having been appointed by Mayor Bishop. In this position he has given the city the benefit of those qualities that have made him so uniformly successful in business affairs.

Mr. Hughes is connected with many of the moneyed institutions of Buffalo, and three corporations have called him to their boards of directors — the Milsom Rendering & Fertilizer Co., the Irish-American Savings and Loan Association, and the People's Bank. He has been a director of the latter institution ever since its organization. He is also a member of the Merchants' Exchange, and is president of the East Buffalo Live Stock Exchange Co. With the tireless energy of the true Irishman, Mr. Hughes renders efficient service in these varied positions, notwithstanding the engrossing cares of his private business. He is a Roman Catholic, and a member of the Catholic Mutual Benefit Association and of the Catholic Legion.

*PERSONAL CHRONOLOGY — John Hughes was born at Dunmore, Kilkenny county, Ireland, about 1842; came to the United States and settled in Buffalo in 1853; was educated in the public schools and Bryant & Stratton's Business College; married Mary Duffey of Buffalo July 10, 1864, and Elizabeth Lovett of Buffalo May 8, 1884; has been engaged in the live-stock commission business since 1866.*

•••

**Sherman S. Jewett** is a sterling type of American manhood. Of magnificent presence, fine mental endowment, and lofty character, he naturally stands among the foremost men of his community. The son of a farmer, he spent his earliest years amid the labors and pastimes of rural life. In the summer he worked in the fields, where doubtless

he laid the foundation of his robust constitution; in winter he attended the district school, and there acquired the essentials of a sound education, though the curriculum was limited. At the age of fifteen he acted as clerk for his half-brother, who owned a small country store in Moravia, N. Y. Realizing the lack of opportunity in a village, and encouraged by the suggestions of his relatives, he determined to go to Buffalo and seek work with his uncle, Isaac W. Skinner, who owned a foundry there and manufactured plows and mill machinery. In company with a neighbor who was taking a load of produce to market, Mr. Jewett walked to Jordan, where he took passage on a packet, and thus reached his destination via the Erie canal. This was in 1834, when Buffalo had only 12,000 inhabitants.

The young man, on presenting himself to his uncle, was set to work painting plows and cleaning castings. For one winter he attended Silas Kingsley's High School, still remembered by old inhabitants. Afterwards he learned the molder's trade, and then acted as a clerk in his uncle's warehouse until Mr. Skinner was burned out. Mr. Jewett was now in his nineteenth year, but he had so diligently improved his time that he was invited to form a copartnership with Franklin Day and Francis H. Root, under the firm name of Day, Root & Co. They erected a small foundry on Mississippi street, Buffalo, took off their coats, and went to work. In a few years, by withdrawals and reorganization, Mr. Jewett alone remained of the original partners. He continued the business by himself for several years, when Mr. Root again became a partner, the style of the new firm being Jewett & Root. This partnership continued for thirty-five years, and was altogether successful, requiring after a time a Chicago branch, and winning an enviable reputation in the mercantile world. Upon the dissolution of the firm of Jewett & Root in 1878, a new company was formed, which has since been known as Sherman S. Jewett & Co. Mr. Jewett has always been energetic in the personal management of his business, and his hand is still (July, 1896) at the helm. His name is a household word everywhere.

Mr. Jewett's success in his own line of business has naturally brought him into relations with the financial world. He has been one of the organizers of several of Buffalo's strongest banks. He was president of the Bank of Buffalo until 1892, and a director of the Manufacturers' and Traders' Bank for over thirty years, and of the Marine Bank for over twenty years. He has been a director of the Columbia National Bank since its organization in 1892. His reputation for financial ability and strict integrity received a notable recognition at the time of the great Chicago fire. That conflagration proved disastrous to insurance companies all over the United States. In Buffalo three companies — the Western, the Buffalo City, and the Buffalo Fire and Marine — were placed in bankruptcy, and by the action of the Chicago creditors Mr. Jewett was appointed assignee of all. He applied himself to his great task with such zeal that in three years he received his official discharge from the work, which he completed to the entire satisfaction of all parties concerned.

In railroad circles Mr. Jewett has been a quiet but influential factor. He was one of the earliest promoters of the Buffalo, New York & Philadelphia railway, a director for fourteen years, and president from 1876 to 1881. His management of this property was masterly in the highest degree, as he raised the road from practical bankruptcy to prosperity, returning to the city of Buffalo its entire investment in the road — $700,000. He has been a director of the New York Central railroad since 1884, and president of the Western Transit Co. since 1883.

By virtue of the services of Captain Joseph Jewett in the War for Independence, Mr. Jewett is a member of the society of the Sons of the American Revolution.

Religious and philanthropic institutions have ever found in Mr. Jewett a generous contributor and steadfast friend. His loyal and unselfish support of the Young Men's Association made it a success. Unostentatious in his giving, he is prudent in the bestowal of assistance, always requiring that the object be a worthy one, and that the means contributed to it be wisely expended. Mr. Jewett finds relaxation from business cares in the rod and line, and Izaak Walton never had a more devoted disciple.

In politics Mr. Jewett is an original Republican. He was thrice elected to the common council, and acted as mayor *pro tempore* on several occasions. His services to the city at that time were exceedingly valuable, and the council adopted his plan of creating both the Ohio and Erie basins, the advocates of each of which desired to destroy the other. In 1876 he was nominated for congress without his knowledge, but ill health compelled him

to decline. In 1880 he was a presidential elector, and helped cast the vote of New York for Garfield and Arthur. The organization of the Buffalo park system was planned at his house, and he has been a member of the board of park commissioners from the beginning.

*SHERMAN S. JEWETT*

*PERSONAL CHRONOLOGY* — *Sherman Skinner Jewett was born at Moravia, N. Y., January 17, 1818; was educated in district schools and at Kingsley's High School in Buffalo; went to Buffalo in 1834, and began work in a foundry; married Deborah Dusenberry of Buffalo August 14, 1849; was a member of the common council, 1845, 1846, and 1848; has been park commissioner since the organization of the board in 1871, and president of the board since 1879; has carried on the foundry business, alone or in partnership, since 1836.*

**Herman T. Koerner** developed early in life the artistic talent that has brought him success in his chosen calling of lithography. As a youth, in the public schools of Brooklyn, his native city, his aptitude for drawing and designing resulted in his capturing all the prizes for which he competed; and at the close of his school life, in 1870, he naturally became an apprentice to the lithographic business in New York city, where for several years he devoted

*HERMAN T. KOERNER*

himself to close study, and acquired considerable knowledge of the various branches of the art. The enormous development of the art of illustration, for both literary and commercial uses, gave ample scope to his talents, and he soon launched out for himself, establishing an office in New York city, and executing work for the lithographic trade. In 1876 he accepted a situation in Buffalo, and in 1878 assumed a position of importance in the establishment of which he is now the head, where his talent and industry rapidly pushed him to the front rank of practical lithographers. On the death of the junior member of the firm, Mr. Koerner was admitted to a share in the business, and on the death of the founder of the house, he became senior member of the firm of

Koerner & Hayes. Since that time this well known house has grown to large proportions, representing a capital of half a million dollars, and employing over five hundred operatives.

A number of important and valuable inventions, used chiefly in the various processes of lithography and printing, have been the fruit of Mr. Koerner's active and versatile mind; and his services in this direction have received substantial recognition in both trade and scientific circles.

While actively engaged in his engrossing duties as the chief artist of his own establishment, Mr. Koerner's artistic tastes have found other outlets in great variety. He had a thorough training in music in early life, and is a fine performer upon both the piano and violin, as well as a singer of taste. His genius in music is creative, also, and he has been a prolific composer of both vocal and instrumental music. He is well known in the musical circles of Buffalo as an enthusiastic amateur and musical director, and as the leader for seven years of the Mendelssohn Club.

Among his other occupations Mr. Koerner has frequently furnished to the illustrated press vivid and pungent cartoons upon local and general subjects. In this line of work he is peculiarly happy. He has strong opinions upon public affairs, and his pencil treatment of them is direct and striking. His manner of drawing shows decided individuality, and is instantly recognizable by those who have once seen it. His cartooning has been done *con amore*, but should he devote himself to it entirely, Mr. Koerner would easily attain high rank among satiric picture teachers of the day. Almost as clever with his pen as with his pencil, Mr. Koerner contributes to the press pointed articles upon current topics, which always show a grasp of the subject, and treat it in an original and entertaining manner. His numerous brochures and treatises on lithography, discussing the subject in both its practical and its abstract aspects, have been extensively copied, translated, and printed in this country and abroad.

As secretary and treasurer of the National Lithographers' Association for nearly a decade, he has rendered invaluable services in behalf of his profession.

*PERSONAL CHRONOLOGY — Herman Theodore Koerner was born at Brooklyn November*

*9, 1855; was educated in the public schools of that city; moved to Buffalo in May, 1876, to take a position as lithographer in the establishment of Cosack & Co.; married Georgia M. White of Buffalo May 41, 1877; has been a member of the firm now styled Koerner & Hayes since August, 1881.*

●●●

**George D. Lamy** is a true son of western New York, and though he has wandered at times, there he has found his greatest success in life. His quiet, unassuming manners conceal executive ability of a high order, and only to those who know him best is his full worth revealed. He was born in the old Lamy homestead at East Eden in Erie county, where his grandfather, George Lamy, settled in 1829, and where his father, Henry Lamy, died in 1895. Mr. Lamy acquired a good common-school education as a foundation for his battle with the world, and was for a time a student at the well-known Springville Academy. His first venture in business life was made in 1862, when he went to Buffalo and became a clerk in a grocery. After remaining in this position about a year, he saw greater opportunities for advancement in another direction, and turned his attention to the transportation industry on the Great Lakes. He remained in this business for eight years, becoming in that time the owner of one vessel and part owner of another.

His ambition still unslaked, Mr. Lamy resolved to go to that El Dorado, where, according to Horace Greeley, fortune awaited every man who would grow up with the country. Mr. Lamy spent nearly two years in the West, mostly on the plains, and had many experiences of an interesting character. He was present at the driving of the golden spike that marked the completion of the Union Pacific railroad. But the West did not have sufficient attractions to keep this eastern-bred young man, and soon his face was set in the direction of more advanced civilization.

After returning to Buffalo he received an appointment as a keeper in the Erie-county penitentiary, managed at that time by Charles E. Felton, who has since become known as an expert penologist. Mr. Lamy at once proved himself the possessor of those qualities that are so necessary in one who is responsible for the care and conduct of imprisoned men.

When Mr. Felton was called to a larger field, found in the superintendency of the House of Correction at Chicago, he induced his able assistant to accompany him. Mr. Lamy was made chief keeper of that important institution, and for eight years he filled with entire success this trying and responsible position.

A desire to return to Buffalo led Mr. Lamy to accept the appointment of office deputy under Sheriff W. W. Lawson after that official's election in 1880. When Mr. Lawson was succeeded by Harry H. Koch, at the end of three years, Mr. Lamy was retained in his position; and when Frank T. Gilbert was elected sheriff in 1886, he recognized Mr. Lamy's fitness and ability by promoting him to be under sheriff. This position he filled also during the term of Oliver A. Jenkins.

*GEORGE H. LAMY*

Mr. Lamy's long service in the sheriff's office had qualified him in a marked degree for the head position there, and in 1892 he received the Republican nomination. This was a bad year for that party, however, and he went down with the rest of the ticket. Two years later he was once more his party's candidate, and was elected by a solid majority of 13,299 votes in the county of Erie — a certain indication of his personal and political popularity.

WILLIAM F. MACKEY

PERSONAL CHRONOLOGY — George H. Lamy was born at East Eden, Erie county, N. Y., March 16, 1846; attended district schools and Springville Academy; went to Buffalo in 1862, and engaged in lake traffic, 1863–71; was chief keeper at the House of Correction, Chicago, 1871–76; married Lana C. Keller of North Boston, N. Y., April 16, 1874; was appointed office deputy by the sheriff of Erie county in 1880, and under sheriff in 1886; has been sheriff of Erie county since January 1, 1895.

* * *

William F. Mackey, like thousands of other bright young men brought up in the smaller towns, was attracted by the manifold advantages of a great city, and in early manhood settled in Buffalo. In the twelve years that he has spent there he has interested himself actively in public affairs, and has become well known both in his profession and beyond it.

Mr. Mackey is a native of western New York, and was born at Albion, Orleans county, late in the '50's. His early education was obtained in the private and public schools of his native village. In 1869 his parents moved to Middleport, Niagara county, and he attended the public schools there for three years. Then he took a four years' course at Lockport Union School, from which he graduated in 1876.

The legal profession possessed decided attractions for the young man, and he began at once to prepare himself for it, entering the office of the well-known firm of Ellsworth, Potter & Brundage in Lockport, as a student. When Judge Brundage withdrew from the firm Mr. Mackey continued his studies with him, and after admission to the bar, in 1879, he remained in the office as managing clerk. He continued to fill this responsible position until 1883, when Judge Brundage moved to Buffalo. For a short time Mr. Mackey practiced alone at Lockport; but in 1884 he, too, yielded to the magnet-like attraction of a large city, and moved to Buffalo.

It requires no small amount of courage and determination on the part of a young lawyer to make a place for himself in his profession without forming an alliance with some older man whose reputation is already established; and the difficulty is considerably increased if the young aspirant for fame and fortune be a stranger in the community. But Mr. Mackey was equal to the task before him, and for several years he worked alone, with ever increasing success. Finally, in 1890, he associated himself with John C. Draper, Jr., under the firm name of Mackey & Draper, and this partnership still continues.

Mr. Mackey's greatest interest outside his profession is in the domain of politics, so fascinating to many lawyers. He has taken an active interest in public affairs ever since he left school, and his party has gladly availed itself of his services. Before he left Lockport he was the Democratic candidate for district attorney of Niagara county, but was defeated with the rest of his ticket. Soon after his arrival in Buffalo he took an active part in the formation of the Cleveland Democracy. He was its president in 1887, 1888, and 1892, and has been especially interested in the organization ever since. In 1888 he was his party's candidate for the coveted position of representative in congress, but was defeated by John M. Farquhar by a majority of about 1600. In December, 1890, Mr. Mackey's devotion to the Democratic cause was rewarded by an appointment as assistant city attorney, and he held the position for three years, until his election as assistant United States attorney in 1893. This position he still holds.

Mr. Mackey is not actively connected with the many social and fraternal organizations of the day, but finds in politics all the relaxation he needs from the cares of his profession. He is a member of Buffalo Lodge, No. 21, B. P. O. E.

*PERSONAL CHRONOLOGY—William Fleming Mackey was born at Albion, N. Y., January 3, 1858; graduated from Lockport Union School in 1876; was admitted to the bar in 1879; married Ella L. Robinson of Cambria, N. Y., November 10, 1877; practiced law at Lockport, N. Y., 1879–84; was assistant city attorney of Buffalo, 1890–93; has been assistant United States attorney since 1893; has practiced law in Buffalo since 1884.*

\*\*\*

**Peter P. Miller** has long been active in the business life of Buffalo. His entire career has been devoted to practical objects, and he has done much to increase the material prosperity of his native city. With the exception of a few years' schooling, he is a self-educated man. He began early the task of making his own way in the world. Having learned the machinist's trade in the Buffalo Steam Engine Works, he graduated from the shop to the steamboat. He became connected with the Western Transportation Co., and for a time was assistant engineer on one of their screw propellers. Subsequently he was promoted and made chief engineer of the steamer "Free State." Finally the company made him chief engineer of its entire fleet. As a practical engineer Mr. Miller rendered most efficient service to the Transportation Co., and at the time of its dissolution in 1884 he was holding the responsible position of superintendent, and was also a director in the company.

In the following year Mr. Miller entered a new field, in which he was also destined to achieve

success. He became secretary and treasurer and managing director of the Citizens' Gas Co. of Buffalo. He had been connected with this company as a director ever since its organization in December, 1873. He has also extended his business relations in several quarters. He is a director in the American Exchange Bank and the Buffalo General Electric Co. His practical mind was early attracted to the electrical field, and in addition to the directorates mentioned he is president of the F. P. Little Electrical Construction & Supply Co. He also retains his interest in lake commerce, and is a member of the Lake Carriers' Association, as well as manager and part owner of the Red Star line of steamers of Buffalo. Mr. Miller was among the first engineers to recognize the value and feasibility of compound engines, and he introduced the first one of the kind on

*PETER P. MILLER*

the lakes in the case of the steamer "Susquehanna."

In politics Mr. Miller's affiliations are with the Republican party, and in 1869–70 he represented the 4th ward in the common council. In recent years increasing business cares have caused him to take a less active interest in public affairs so far as they relate to politics ; but his convictions on questions of the day are strong and well founded.    Mr. Miller is naturally of a retiring disposition, content with doing his duty as it appears to him from day to day.

*JAMES MOONEY*

He is a man of unflinching courage and of quick resolve, and displayed these qualities to great advantage at the memorable burning of the American block in January, 1865.   Three firemen had lost their lives, and the conflagration threatened to spread and become general    At this juncture Mr. Miller concluded that heroic measures were needed, and with a quantity of giant powder he entered and blew up the structure, thus preventing the fire from spreading. Mr. Miller is a prominent Free Mason, and is a member of a number of lodges in Buffalo.   He is also a member of the Buffalo Club and of the Merchants' Exchange.

*PERSONAL CHRONOLOGY— Peter Paul Miller was born at Buffalo November 20, 1837 ; was*

educated in the public schools of the city ; learned the machinist's trade, and became engineer on lake steamers ; was superintendent of the Western Transportation Co., and a director in the company, 1860–84 ; has been secretary, treasurer, and managing director of the Citizens' Gas Co. since 1885.

\*\*\*

**James Mooney** has made his name synonymous in Buffalo with enterprise, business energy, and public spirit. He possesses a rare combination of tact and push, and when once he has embarked on an undertaking knows no such word as fail.   He is of Celtic origin but of American training ; and unites in himself the suave but independent spirit of his race with the shrewd and progressive character of the native American. As a young man he was dependent largely on his own resources for success ; but he was ambitious, and laid a foundation of character and ability sufficiently broad and stable to support subsequent eminence and fortune.

Mr. Mooney took up his residence in Buffalo about forty-six years ago, and received his education in the public schools of that city.   His early ambition was to practice law, and he began a course of legal study in the office of the late Charles D. Norton.   But Mr. Mooney soon concluded that his talents lay in another field, and he put aside his law books to engage in the real-estate business.   Few men in Buffalo have been more fully identified with the development of the city than he.   At a time when land improvement was hardly conceived, he showed his faith in the destiny of his adopted city by expending time, money, and energy in reclaiming and laying out vast tracts of realty that are now within the limits of the city. Rare judgment and courage were required in such undertakings, but the reward has been commensurate with the outlay.

Mr. Mooney has long been an active factor in public affairs.   While not an office-seeker, he has been called upon frequently to fill public positions of trust and responsibility, and in every case he has fulfilled the duties imposed upon him in a business-like manner.   He was one of the original park commissioners of Buffalo, and served in that capacity for fifteen years.   For five years he was one of the commissioners of the State Reservation at Niagara

Falls, and proved himself watchful of the public interests, and conscientious in the discharge of his duties. In 1891 he was appointed by Mayor Bishop commissioner of public works, and this position he still holds.

In recent years Mr. Mooney has devoted considerable attention to building, and in the grand structure known as the Mooney-Brisbane building he has reared a lasting monument, creditable alike to himself and to the city of Buffalo. He has not confined his activities to mercantile lines. Causes appealing to his patriotism and his sense of justice have ever found in him an ardent supporter and a champion. He was one of the leading spirits in the Irish Land League of America, and was its president from 1881 to the time of its consolidation with the Irish National League. Loyalty to race and traditions has ever been a characteristic of men of Irish lineage, and this loyalty Mr. Mooney possesses in a high degree. For all that, his stanch Americanism is none the less marked and active, and he is a fine example of the true meaning of the appellation Irish-American — loyal to his native land, but true to the land of his adoption.

*PERSONAL CHRONOLOGY—James Mooney was born in Queen's County, Ireland, and came to Buffalo in 1850; was educated in the public schools; married Ellen L. McRoden of Rochester in 1874; has carried on a real-estate business at Buffalo since 1860; has been commissioner of public works of the city of Buffalo since 1891.*

\*\*\*

**Charles J. North** is a fit representative of the men who, from very humble beginnings and without help, work their way up to success and a place of honor in the community. His early years were passed in circumstances that gave little hint of what the future was to be. He was born on a farm far up in Clinton county, in which all of his great-grandparents had been pioneers. Perhaps the best part of his inheritance consisted of the qualities that he derived from a long line of Puritan and Quaker ancestors, one of whom, George Soule, was a signer of the "Compact" in the cabin of the "Mayflower."

In the panic of 1857 Mr. North's parents were reduced to distress; and insufficient food, fuel, and clothing made the winter one to be remembered. He was at that time thrown upon his own resources. His education was limited to what he had received in the district school, and to attendance for two or three winters at a private school, where he built the fires, shoveled the snow, and swept the schoolrooms, in payment for his tuition. However, he was an eager reader; and by sitting up nights after his day's work was done, and studying the few schoolbooks at his command, he made up in part for the limitations described.

Thus meagerly prepared, the boy set out with a stout heart to work his way upward. He earned his living by laboring as a farm hand until the spring of 1873, when he went to Buffalo, a total stranger, with a few hundred dollars, saved by the utmost denial, as his total capital. Having found employment in

*CHARLES J. NORTH*

an insurance office, he quickly mastered the details of the business, and secured the confidence of his employers to such an extent that within a short time he was promoted to the most responsible position in the office. After that advancement was easy. In 1879 he succeeded his former employer in the business, and two years later formed the insurance partnership of North & Vedder, which still continues. His history since then has been one of steadily increasing prosperity.

The guiding purpose of Mr. North's life has been, not to serve selfish ends, but to be of use to the world. He has never held nor sought office, but has always endeavored to do his duty in a quiet way as a citizen, in everything advancing the public good. He was an original member of the Buffalo Republican League, was one of six supporters to promise it the necessary financial backing when a permanent organization was planned, and served for two terms as vice president and chairman of the executive committee. He has been vice president of the Buffalo Association of Fire Underwriters, is a director of the Homestead Savings and Loan Association, and a director of the Exchange Elevator Co. He is treasurer of the First Presbyterian Church Society, a director of the Oakfield Club, a councilor of the Buffalo Historical Society, and a member of various other societies and institutions of a semi-public nature. He is especially interested in the study of colonial history and genealogy. He is a member of the Sons of the American Revolution, and of the New England Historical Genealogical Society.

*PERSONAL CHRONOLOGY—Charles Jackson North was born at Chazy, Clinton county, N. Y., May 14, 1845; was educated at the district school, with a few terms in a private school; worked as a farm hand, 1862–74; was a clerk in an insurance office in Buffalo, 1874–79; married Dora C. Briggs of Buffalo June 30, 1881; has carried on an insurance business since 1879, and since 1881 has been a member of the firm of North & Vedder.*

•••

**James Osborne Putnam** has a lineage consistent with and prophetic of his own splendid career. His earliest American ancestor was John Putnam, who came from England in 1634 and settled in Salem, Mass. The family prospered from the beginning, soon acquiring large landed property in Salem, and taking an important part in the affairs of Massachusetts Bay. The branch of the family with which we are immediately concerned moved to Vermont in colonial times, and Mr. Putnam's father was born in Brattleboro. He joined the westward procession, and settled in Attica, N. Y., in 1817. There James O. Putnam was born the next year, on Independence Day.

After studying at Hamilton College in 1834–35, Mr. Putnam entered, as a junior, the Yale class of 1839, first absenting himself a year from college on account of ill health. He then entered upon the study of law in his father's office. Harvey Putnam was himself a distinguished man, serving for many years in the state senate and the national house of representatives; and his son could hardly have found, especially in those days of inefficient law schools, a better guide along the difficult road to legal learning. With such advantages of tuition, Mr. Putnam easily obtained admission to the bar in 1842. He then moved to Buffalo and began practice at once. In the early years of his professional work he devoted a good deal of attention to railroad interests, which were already beginning to have an important place in the economic conditions of the country. In 1844 he became secretary and treasurer, and in 1846 attorney and counselor, of the Attica & Buffalo and Buffalo & Rochester railroad companies. These positions he retained until the consolidation of the companies with the New York Central railroad.

Comparatively early in life Mr. Putnam became prominent in public affairs, and he had not lived long in Buffalo before his pre-eminent fitness for positions of trust was recognized. In 1851 he was appointed postmaster of the city by President Fillmore, and held the office through the administration. In 1853 he was elected state senator, and attained national fame by his speeches in the legislature. His most notable work in that body was the authorship of a bill requiring the title of church real property to be vested in trustees. A serious controversy had arisen between the bishops of the Roman church, who contended that the title to every church estate should be vested in the bishop of the diocese, and certain congregations, particularly that of St. Louis of Buffalo, which insisted upon independence in their temporalities. The issue thus raised vitally affected the principles of religious freedom, and intense interest was taken throughout the country in the result of the controversy. It is not too much to say that Mr. Putnam's speech of January 30, 1855, in the New York state senate led to the almost unanimous passage of his bill by the legislature. The speech was a model of resistless logic, and was delivered with burning eloquence. It was read everywhere, and the orator acquired fame in a night from one end of the country to the other.

Mr. Putnam was in those days a conservative Whig. He went further, however, than that branch of his party in his opposition to slavery; and some of his most powerful speeches concerned the "irrepressible conflict." He was at one time identified with the American party, and he was its candidate for the office of secretary of state in 1857. In 1860 he was one of the two Lincoln presidential electors at large for New York state.

Throughout the war Mr. Putnam was consul at Havre, France, having been sent thither by President Lincoln in 1861. Paris was a rallying-point for loyal Americans on the continent, and Mr. Putnam was frequently called to the capital on national anniversaries and other patriotic occasions. He wrote the address of American citizens abroad to their government at the time of Lincoln's assassination. He delivered a notable oration in Paris on Washington's Birthday, 1866. Mr. Putnam was again sent abroad in the service of the government in 1880, receiving an appointment as minister to Belgium from President Hayes. While filling this mission he was appointed by the United States government its delegate to the International Industrial Property Congress held in Paris in 1881.

The foregoing sketch, of necessity largely statistical, etches lightly the outline of a career that deserves and needs for its proper portrayal a line engraving by a master hand. Beginning life when the century was young, Mr. Putnam has passed through a youth of ambition and preparation, a manhood of struggle and achievement, an age of dignity and honor. Throughout his long career he has been an intellectual and a moral force ever strongly exerted in behalf of right. Every good cause has received support from him, and has gathered added impetus from his contact with it. By pen and voice and personal effort, he has helped forward the good work of the world. The graces and charm of his oratory linger in the memory of thousands. For years no public occasion of importance in Buffalo was complete without his presence and his inspiring interpretation of the meaning of the day. A volume of "Orations, Speeches, and Miscellanies," published in Buffalo in 1880, shows the wide range of his sympathy, the soundness of his judgment, the nobility of his ideals.

*PERSONAL CHRONOLOGY—James Osborne Putnam was born at Attica, N. Y., July 4, 1818; studied at Hamilton and at Yale colleges; was admitted to the bar in 1842, and began the practice of law in Buffalo; married Harriet Palmer of Buffalo January 5, 1842, and Kate F. Wright of Woodstock, Vt., March 15, 1855; was postmaster of Buffalo,*
*1851–54, and state senator, 1854–55; was United States consul at Havre, France, 1861–66, and United States minister to Belgium, 1880–81; has been member of the council of the University of Buffalo since its organization in 1846, was for many years its vice chancellor, and is now its chancellor.*

*JAMES OSBORNE PUTNAM*

**Edward R. Rice** was born in Indiana, but he is of New England descent on both sides, his great-grandfather having fought for the colonial cause in the Revolution. Combining the tireless energy of the West and the business sagacity of the East, Mr. Rice has built up a commercial house with a wide and splendid reputation for enterprise, fair dealing, completeness, and general responsibility.

The son of a Methodist minister, Mr. Rice received an early home training that insured useful citizenship and an honorable business career. He attended the common schools of Warsaw, N. Y., and was graduated from the Batavia High School when only fifteen years of age. Having determined to pursue a mercantile career, he became a clerk in a retail boot and shoe store in Batavia, and a year later moved to Rochester, to accept a position in a wholesale boot and shoe house in that city. He has been identified with the rubber boot and shoe business ever since he first began to work. He has made a specialty of this business, and no man is more familiar

EDWARD R. RICE

thru he with every detail of the trade, and with the varying phases of the market.

After this experience in retail and wholesale houses, Mr. Rice felt sufficient confidence to embark in the business for himself, and he became the senior member of the firm of Rice & Abell, wholesale dealers in rubber boots and shoes at Dunkirk, N. Y. This firm conducted a satisfactory business for six years, when Mr. Rice made up his mind that Buffalo offered facilities for shipping and advantages for enlarging trade superior to any other city between New York and Chicago. Accordingly he moved to Buffalo in the spring of 1887, and established himself on Pearl street, until the requirements of an expanding business demanded larger quarters for the storage and display of goods. This increase in business can be safely attributed to Mr. Rice's energy, farsightedness, and organizing capacity. He possesses that quality, so valuable in a merchant, of impressing customers with his fairness and sincerity — an impression in this case that does not belie the reality.

Mr. Rice's present business establishment comprises a six-story warehouse and a block seven stories high, perfect in its arrangements and adapted for the convenient handling of rubber boots and shoes, to which he confines his business exclusively. He has a branch house at Detroit, and another at Duluth. This extensive business is carried on by Mr. Rice alone.

Though an exceedingly busy man, Mr. Rice is mindful of the fact that in a country like ours where political responsibility rests upon the people, every citizen should make public affairs part of his private concern. He is one of the men of independent action, who, in the last dozen years, rising above party considerations, have endeavored to rescue the politics of our municipalities from the control of the spoilsmen. A reform has undoubtedly been effected in American cities within the past decade, and this has been due to the activity of business men in local affairs. Mr. Rice has been prominent among this class in Buffalo. He was appointed civil-service commissioner by Mayor Bishop, and served for nearly four years, until pressure of business compelled him to resign. But he continues his interest in this reform as a member of the executive committee of the Civil Service Reform Association. To him also is due in large part the organization of the Good Government Club of Buffalo, which has done so much in securing needed reforms. At present he is a member of the central council of this club, representing the 24th ward of the city.

Mr. Rice devotes considerable attention to philanthropic movements and organizations that commend themselves to his judgment. He is a member of the council of the Charity Organization Society of Buffalo, a trustee of the Homeopathic Hospital in that city, and president of the Elmwood School, one of the best private institutions in the state. That his mental horizon is not narrow is shown by his membership in the Liberal, Thursday, Saturn, and Buffalo clubs, as well as in the Buffalo Society of Artists and the Buffalo Historical Society. In every relation of life, commercial, political, and social, Mr. Rice is noted for earnestness, thoroughness, and uprightness.

*PERSONAL CHRONOLOGY—Edward Russell Rice was born at Nashville, Ind., June 21, 1856; was educated in common schools, and graduated from the Batavia High School; was a clerk in boot and shoe houses in Batavia and Rochester, 1871–81; conducted a wholesale boot and shoe house in Dunkirk, N. Y., 1881–87; married Mary Langley Fullagar of Dunkirk October 18, 1884; has conducted a wholesale rubber boot and shoe house in Buffalo since 1887.*

...

**William Richardson** has lived a long and busy life, unsullied by a single questionable transaction. All through his career he has adhered steadfastly to the honest principle of avoiding debt, and never incurring obligations that he was not sure of being able to meet at maturity. Pessimists are fond of disparaging the practical utility of the Ten Commandments in commerce and in politics; but Mr. Richardson's life is a refutation of this demoralizing doctrine. He has engaged in business and in public affairs, and has never felt it necessary, in order to achieve success, to depart from the pathway of integrity and honor.

Mr. Richardson comes of New England stock. He was born in the old town of Attleboro, Mass., more than seventy-five years ago. Since the year of his birth the country has passed through nineteen presidential campaigns, and as many different Presidents have occupied the White House at Washington. During the period covered by his life the United States has witnessed its most marvelous growth in population, industry, and wealth. Mr. Richardson's parents moved from Massachusetts to Pennsylvania when he was an infant. There were no great railroads then, and the family traveled overland in a wagon. After a short residence in the Keystone State they moved to De Witt, N. Y., where Mr. Richardson's boyhood was passed on a farm. The Erie canal, a mighty enterprise of engineering skill for those days, was then in process of construction, and for several years Mr. Richardson was employed by one of the state

contractors charged with repairing the canal between Syracuse and Chittenango. Later he helped build the reservoir covering about 600 acres of land near Cazenovia, as a supply basin for the canal. This employment acquainted him with river and harbor work, and he next became engaged in dredging operations at Detroit.

Hitherto Mr. Richardson had been an employee. He now became a contractor, and had charge of the construction of a large piece of embankment for the Great Western railroad. He also entered the dredging business, and carried on the first work of this kind ever done on the St. Clair Flats in the Detroit river. He also dredged out the channel at Green Bay, Wis. The volume of business on the Erie canal had grown to such proportions by the year 1854 that an enlargement was rendered necessary between Tona-

*WILLIAM RICHARDSON*

wanda and Black Rock, and Mr. Richardson was employed by the state to do this work. He had now an established reputation as a skillful, conscientious contractor, and he secured many commissions from the United States government for the improvement of harbors on the Great Lakes. Steadfast application to his chosen pursuit brought him a competence, so that he was able to retire from active affairs in 1890.

Mr. Richardson has not only been an upright business man, but he has made a fine record for

*AUGUSTUS F. SCHEU*

devotion to civic duties. He has been an efficient member of the board of supervisors of Buffalo, and for three years he was a member of the common council. He is esteemed in financial circles for his sound judgment and conservative views, and holds directorates in the People's Bank and in the Niagara Bank.

*PERSONAL CHRONOLOGY— William Richardson was born at Attleboro, Mass., January 5, 1841; was educated in common schools at De Witt, N. Y.; married Ann O'Day of Buffalo in November, 1852; engaged in canal repairing and in dredging, 1850-90; was a member of the common council of Buffalo, 1884-87; has lived in Buffalo since 1850.*

**Augustus F. Scheu** comes of an old and respected Buffalo family, founded more than half a century ago by Solomon Scheu. The latter arrived in Buffalo in 1844, having come to this country from Germany five years earlier, and soon attained prominence in both business and political affairs. He was elected mayor, and held other offices of trust and importance, and made his name known not only in municipal but also in state politics. The traditions of broad mindedness and integrity left by Solomon Scheu have been maintained by his son, Augustus F. Scheu.

Born in Buffalo a little more than forty years ago, Mr. Scheu's whole life has been associated with the city. He is one of the young men who have made the "new Buffalo" what it is. The salient facts of his life can be quickly related. He was educated in the city schools and at the Buffalo Normal School. Upon his graduation he immediately entered the malting business established by his father in 1860. Since the death of the latter in 1888, Mr. Scheu has continued the management of the business for the benefit of the estate.

The name of Scheu has stood high in the annals of the Democratic party in Buffalo for many years. Mr. Scheu came naturally by his interest in politics, and he has been prominent in the councils of the local Democracy. He has been a counselor rather than a seeker for office. He received the Democratic nomination for sheriff of Erie county in 1885, but that is the only time he has appeared before the public as a candidate. He also served for a time as police commissioner. He has represented the 33d congressional district on the Democratic state committee for several years — a field in which he has shown excellent capacity for organization.

The most striking characteristics of Mr. Scheu as a man are his liberality of view, his integrity, and his disposition to believe in the good intentions and honesty of others. These are the qualities by which he is known among his fellow-citizens. He has given many proofs of disinterested devotion to public enterprises aimed at promoting the well-being and happiness of his native city. For several years he served as one of the park commissioners. He has also devoted much time and energy to the Buffalo grade crossing commission, of which he is now a member.

As might be supposed from this sketch of his personal characteristics, Mr. Scheu is a man of wide acquaintance and many friends. He is of a very social nature, and is affiliated with many societies. He is a trustee of the Charity Organization Society and of the Exempt Firemen's Association of Buffalo. He is an active member of the Buffalo Club, and belongs to the Orpheus and Liedertafel singing societies. He is also a member of Omega Lodge, No. 259, I. O. O. F. His religious affiliations are with the German United Evangelical St. Paul's Church of Buffalo.

*PERSONAL CHRONOLOGY— Augustus F. Scheu was born at Buffalo November 7, 1855; was educated in the public schools and at the Buffalo Normal School, from which he graduated in 1872; married Anna Frances Kraft of Buffalo January 8, 1879; was the Democratic candidate for sheriff of Erie county in 1885; entered the malting business with his father in 1874, and has managed the business since 1888.*

***

**A. P. Southwick** has never been satisfied with the present. Looking into the future, and seeing there something worth striving for, he has pushed forward, determined to attain his end. It is the dissatisfied men, as distinguished from the discontented, who make their mark in the world, and contribute something to its progress.

Dr. Southwick was born in Ashtabula, Ohio, and spent his youth there, acquiring a high-school education. Soon after attaining his majority, however, he left his native place for the greater advantages apparently offered by Buffalo. This was in 1849, in the early days of steamboating on the Great Lakes, when there were few railroads to compete for business to the West. Buffalo was then preëminently a commercial city, the terminus for all lake traffic, and naturally an attractive place for an ambitious and pushing young man who had already learned something of the duties and responsibilities of a steamboat engineer. For sixteen years Dr. Southwick devoted himself to the engineer's vocation, finally reaching the important position of chief engineer of the Western Transit Co.

Even then his ambition was not satisfied. He had reached the top of his calling, but he felt that there were better things in other directions. After some hesitation he took up the study of dentistry,

and in 1862 he decided that it was time for him to make a name for himself in his chosen profession. A successful record of over thirty years, broken only by the lapse of a twelvemonth, has made him one of the best-known members of the profession in the state. He was active in the organization of the State Dental Society in 1868, and was one of the first candidates for a diploma to appear before the society's board of censors. In 1877 Dr. Southwick was elected to that board, and became soon afterward its president. He retained the presidency until August 1, 1895, when the law was changed, creating a board of state commissioners, and Dr. Southwick was made president of this board. When the department of dentistry of the University of Buffalo was organized, Dr. Southwick, by reason of his long experience and undoubted ability, was chosen to the

*J. P. SOUTHWICK*

important position of clinical professor of operative technics. He has written frequent papers on professional subjects, and his views are always received with respect by his brethren.

Though dentistry has been Dr. Southwick's profession, it has by no means been his only occupation. He is actively interested in all that concerns his fellow-men. He is a deep thinker, and is positive in his opinions. To Dr. Southwick more than to any other man, probably, is due the law that

*JAMES B. STAFFORD*

substituted electricity for the rope in cases of capital punishment in the state of New York. Becoming convinced that hanging is brutal, he promulgated his views as widely as possible, and the agitation traceable directly to him resulted in the creation of a state commission "to investigate and report upon the most humane and practical method of carrying into effect the sentence of death in capital cases." The members of this commission were Elbridge T. Gerry, Alfred P. Southwick, and Matthew Hale. They reported in favor of killing by means of the electric current, and in the face of the greatest opposition their recommendations were adopted. Dr. Southwick in this way won the *sobriquet* of " Old Electricity."

Like all good citizens, Dr. Southwick takes a deep interest in public questions, but his active participation in politics has been confined to two occasions when his party forced nominations upon him, once for alderman and once for councilman. He is of a genial disposition, and is a member of the Buffalo Club and of other social organizations.

*PERSONAL CHRONOLOGY— Alfred Porter Southwick was born at Ashtabula, O., May 18, 1826; was educated in the public schools; engaged in the steamboat business, 1844-54, becoming chief engineer of the Western Transit Co. at Buffalo in 1855; married Mary M. Flinn of Buffalo May 26, 1874; has practiced dentistry in Buffalo since 1862.*

**James B. Stafford** has had a career that is full of inspiration to young men with a noble ambition to succeed. He was compelled to leave school when but eight years of age, began to earn his living a few years later as an errand boy, and advanced step by step until to-day he stands in the front rank of Buffalo's business men. Yet he is only about forty-three years of age.

Hard work, undaunted perseverance, studious habits, quick adaptability, and uncompromising integrity, may be set down as the mainsprings of Mr. Stafford's success. As a boy he won the confidence of substantial men with whom he came in contact; and as a man he made rapid headway when he started in business for himself. When other boys played after work he applied himself to books, and in time made up for the lack of early education. In maturer years he has been a voracious reader; and when he took the high place in the community that his industry and public spirit had earned, he was mentally fitted to adorn it. "Knowledge," he has been heard to say, " is easily carried, and it is a man's best possession."

Mr. Stafford was born of Scotch-Irish parentage, in Dublin, Ireland. On the death of his mother, when he was eight years of age, he was brought to the United States by his father, and soon afterward found employment in the store of S. N. Callender, a Buffalo grocer. The boy rapidly mastered business methods, and was well equipped at his majority for a business career. To John H. Jones, now president of the Buffalo Fish Co., Mr.

Stafford is indebted for encouragement and assistance in taking his first important step in commercial life. The firm of Jones, Stafford & Co. was formed, consisting of Messrs. Jones, Stafford, and C. A. Trevalee, and they originated the subsequently famous Fulton Market. Some years later Mr. Stafford became sole proprietor of this fine establishment. Afterwards his brother, Richard H. Stafford, was taken into the business, the firm becoming James B. Stafford & Bro. The brothers conducted the Fulton Market until 1892, when they sold out to Faxon, Williams & Faxon. In the meantime Mr. Stafford had erected a substantial four-story brick building at the corner of Pearl and Church streets, which was the home of the Fulton Market for many years.

Mr. Stafford retired from the grocery business to become president of the Security Investment Co. of Buffalo, which was formed by a number of leading citizens for the purpose of transacting real-estate business on a large scale. Mr. Stafford's entire time is devoted to the management of the company's extensive affairs.

There is another side to Mr. Stafford's life besides the one most open to public gaze. His private life is singularly happy. He is devoted to his wife and children, and spends almost all his leisure hours with them. He has never been induced to become a clubman. He is, however, a member of the Masonic fraternity. He and his family are deeply interested in church affairs, attending the Methodist church. The many charitable and religious movements of Buffalo have found in Mr. Stafford an ardent and a generous supporter. He has never aspired to political office, but takes an active interest in municipal affairs. He has had a leading part in public movements for the benefit of the community in which he lives, and well deserves his reputation as an ideal citizen.

*PERSONAL CHRONOLOGY—*
*James Bluett Stafford was born at Dublin, Ireland, September 23, 1854; came to the United States in childhood, and settled in Buffalo in 1864; married Henrietta Ella Holloway of Buffalo June 14, 1878; carried on a grocery business, with various partners, 1874-92; has been president of the Security Investment Co. of Buffalo since 1892.*

**Richard H. Stafford** has an established reputation in mercantile and financial circles in the city of Buffalo. His commercial training has been long and thorough, and he is familiar equally with the practical and the theoretical sides of business operations. Mr. Stafford was born and reared in Dublin, Ireland, a city famed for the high standing and ability of its mercantile class. After obtaining a sound elementary education in the schools of his native city, he came to the United States the year the Civil War broke out. He took up his residence in Buffalo the same year, and entered the employ of S. N. Callender, then the leading grocer of the city. He remained with Mr. Callender five years, when he secured a more attractive position with another house engaged in the same line of business. In this second position he also remained five years.

RICHARD H. STAFFORD

Mr. Stafford was now a young man of twenty-three, and had already won a reputation for capacity, integrity, and faithfulness under two successive employers. Meanwhile his brother, James B. Stafford, had met with such success that he decided to embark in business on his own account, and he invited his brother Richard to take charge of the financial part of Fulton Market. After working for his brother six years, Richard received, one Christmas morning, a substantial recognition of the value of his services

WILLIAM THURSTONE

in the form of a present of a third interest in his brother's business. Under the management of the Stafford brothers, Fulton Market throve, and its owners prospered. Mr. Stafford continued this business association with his brother till 1892, when they sold out to the house of Faxon, Williams & Faxon.

Mr. Stafford now directed his attention to a new field, in which success has crowned his efforts. In company with his brother, he helped to organize the Security Investment Co. of Buffalo, of which he has since been treasurer.

In his relations with business men, Mr. Stafford is noted for his frank dealing and obliging disposition. In church and Masonic work, he is unusually active

for a man so engrossed with business cares, and no good movement in Buffalo fails to receive his encouragement and support. In Masonic circles he has attained high honors, being a Knight Templar in Lake Erie Commandery, No. 20, a 32d degree member of the order of Ancient Accepted Scottish Rite Masons, and a Noble of the Mystic Shrine. Mr. Stafford is president of the board of trustees of the Richmond Avenue Methodist Episcopal Church, and in that position has done notable service in developing the association from a struggling mission to a prosperous and influential church.

PERSONAL CHRONOLOGY — Richard H. Stafford was born at Dublin, Ireland, August 10, 1848; was educated in the common schools of Dublin; came to the United States and settled in Buffalo in 1861; was a clerk in grocery houses, 1861–72; was associated with his brother in the management of Fulton Market, 1878–92; married Ella S. Gatchell of Medina, N. Y., October 29, 1877; has been treasurer of the Security Investment Co. of Buffalo since 1892.

•••

**William Thurstone** was twenty-eight years old when he came to this country, a sturdy, hearty Englishman, ready to grapple with whatever fate his adopted land might have in store for him. He was not the sort of immigrant for whom Uncle Sam has only a half-hearted welcome — immigrants who claim that the world owes them a living, but who do nothing toward collecting the debt. He had served a seven years' apprenticeship as printer to the Honorable Stationers' Company of London, had been a reporter for several London newspapers, and had become proprietor of the *Horticultural Journal*.

With such an equipment Mr. Thurstone did not need to wait long for employment. The first money he earned in Buffalo was by setting type on the city directory, and he was soon after engaged as compositor by the *Commercial Advertiser*, and later by the *Express*. Printers in those days were not paid for their intervals of waiting for "copy," and after setting the single column of local items there was often a long, profitless delay before work could begin on the telegraphic dispatches. The time from ten or eleven o'clock at night until two or three in the morning was frequently spent in watching for the possible arrival from New York of English news, which came by steamer, and was then transmitted by wire. When a notification was received that a steamer had been sighted, its arrival and the news it carried were waited for. Mr. Thurstone was too ambitious to yield passively to such enforced idleness, and he seized the opportunity to do the work of a reporter in these intervals. He was connected in this twofold way with the *Express*, the *Courier*, and the *Commercial Advertiser*; and finally became commercial editor of the *Courier*, retaining this position twenty-two years. His pluck and industry had now advanced him from a position where, according to the custom of those days, wages were paid two thirds in store produce and the rest in current and uncurrent money (the latter sometimes suffering two or three per cent discount) to one of independence.

When Mr. Thurstone was appointed secretary of the Board of Trade thirty-three years ago, the institution was too poor to pay more than a dollar a day for his services. His fidelity and devotion have done much to make that body the power it is to-day, and he is still its trusted secretary. He has also been secretary of the Merchants' Exchange for fourteen years.

The United States bureau of statistics is indebted to Mr. Thurstone for much thorough and painstaking work, including many reports on the commerce of the Great Lakes and western New York, and one on the railroad and canal systems of the state of New York and the Dominion of Canada, published in the United States public documents. For over thirty years he has furnished statistical matter for boards of trade, commercial conventions, newspapers, and pamphlets, and ranks as an expert in this line. He has also contributed extensively to the editorial columns of New York and Chicago magazines.

Politics has claimed a large share of his attention, as would be expected from so public-spirited a citizen. Twice nominated for alderman in the old 9th ward, he failed of election because the district was so strongly Republican; but it is noteworthy that his election as supervisor was the only Democratic victory ever achieved in that ward.

Loyal to the church of his native land, Mr. Thurstone has been identified in Buffalo with the Church of the Ascension and St. John's, serving in the former as vestryman and treasurer, and in the latter as vestryman and warden.

*PERSONAL CHRONOLOGY—William Thurstone was born at London, England, February 21, 1826; was educated in a private school; was apprenticed as printer, 1840–47; married Mary Anne Dillon of Hereford, England, June 1, 1848; came to the United States in 1854, and settled in Buffalo in 1855; occupied various positions there on the "Express," "Courier," and "Commercial Advertiser," 1855–85; has been secretary of the Board of Trade since 1864, and of the Merchants' Exchange since 1882.*

\*\*\*

**James W. Tillinghast** is widely known in the important sphere of commercial telegraphy, and

*JAMES W. TILLINGHAST*

he has rendered valuable service to the public by his efficient management of one of the largest telegraph offices in the country — that of the Western Union company at Buffalo.

Mr. Tillinghast is a native of the Empire State, and knows the lay of the land within all its borders as perfectly as others know their immediate locality. His business has made topography one of his strong points. Receiving his early education at private and public schools in Rome, N. Y., he completed his academic training at the Fort Edward Collegiate Institute. He began his commercial life at Toronto, a few years before the Civil War, as a clerk for his father in the office of the Northern Railway of Canada. With characteristic enterprise and industry he took up the study of telegraphy as an outside diversion, having no idea at the time that this pursuit would become the work of his life. In 1861, however, he went to Pittsburg, and entered the service of the Western Union Telegraph Co. as an operator. While engaged in that capacity his time was largely taken up with the handling of cipher dispatches passing between the western armies of the Union and the war department at Washington. His duties became so exacting and severe that his health failed, and by the advice of his physicians he abandoned active telegraphic work in 1863. The next year he moved to Madison, Ind., as manager of the telegraph office there. Less arduous duties in a quieter scene brought about a gradual restoration of health, and Mr. Tillinghast found himself strong enough in the spring of 1865 to become assistant manager of the Western Union office at Buffalo. During a part of that year he was located at Erie, Penn., as manager of the Western Union office there, but he returned to Buffalo in the fall. Five years later he was placed at the head of the office, and has occupied that position continuously since.

In 1868 the general agent of the New York Associated Press formed a rival organization, and with several agents of the old association left it without notice. Mr. Tillinghast was at once appointed agent of the Associated Press at Buffalo, invested with full charge of the service west and south of that point, and clothed with supreme authority. So complete was the rout of the new association that it quickly abandoned the field, and Mr. Tillinghast resumed his position with the Western Union. For the services then performed for the Associated Press he received a vote of thanks from the executive committee, and a personal letter from every member of the committee praising his work in the highest terms. This period is the only break in his long connection with the Western Union since he entered the service in Pittsburg in 1861.

Mr. Tillinghast is much attached to Buffalo, and has more than once declined offers of promotion involving residence elsewhere. He has the respect of his business associates and the confidence of the community, both in large measure. He is the only son of James Tillinghast, for many years a famous official of the Central-Hudson railroad.

*PERSONAL CHRONOLOGY — James W. Tillinghast was born at Brownville, N. Y., November 5, 1844; was educated at Rome Academy and Fort Edward Collegiate Institute; commenced business as clerk in the office of the Northern Railway of Canada at Toronto, in 1858; entered the service of the Western Union Telegraph Co. at Pittsburg, Penn., in 1861; married Sara A. Dannals of Pittsburg October 6, 1863, and Mrs. Anna Kelley of Lockport, N. Y., February 1, 1868; has been manager of the Western Union telegraph office at Buffalo since 1870.*

...

**Greenleaf S. Van Gorder,** though not yet beyond middle life, has made himself an important factor in public affairs. His career is an inspiring example to every American youth, and illustrates anew the truth of the time-worn proverb, " Where there's a will there's a way." He was thrown upon his own resources in early boyhood, and his surroundings were such as to develop the best qualities in an ambitious young man. To be born in an intelligent community, having intercourse through library, school, and press with the current events of the world, is no mean inheritance. The small town and the village rival the great cities in their contribution to the ranks of the professions, and of the leading business men of the country. The boy born in the city is surfeited with opportunities, and too often does not sufficiently appreciate them; but the country boy makes the best of the few at his command.

Mr. Van Gorder was educated in the common schools of Geneseo, and received further training in Angelica Academy and the academic department of Alfred University. He supported himself, meanwhile, by farm work, teaching, and any other resource that presented itself. He is not a graduate of any school except, as he himself puts it, the " school of experience." Having secured all the preliminary education within his means, Mr. Van Gorder began the study of law in the office of Sanford & Bowen of Angelica, one of the leading firms in Allegany county. He was admitted to the bar at a term of the Supreme Court held in Buffalo, and began the practice of his profession at Pike, Wyoming county. By industry, energy, and perseverance, he has attained high rank among the members of the bar in his part of the state.

Political advancement, as well as professional success, has marked Mr. Van Gorder's career. He is a

Republican in politics, and has been a delegate to many conventions of his party. He was elected town clerk of Pike, and held the position four years. This was his entrance into the arena of political activity, in which he was destined to become a prominent actor. After holding the office of supervisor of Pike for five years, he was elected a member of the state assembly from the county of Wyoming for 1888 and 1889. While in the assembly he served as a member of the important judiciary committee. Representing Wyoming county, the center of the western New York salt fields, he started a movement that resulted in the amendment of the constitution of the state, providing for the sale of the state " salt reservation " at Syracuse, and thus removing the state as a competitor against the private capital employed in the salt industry in western New York. The strong fight made by Mr. Van Gorder on this question made him a prominent figure in what was then the 30th senatorial district, composed of Livingston, Niagara, Genesee, and Wyoming counties. In the fall of 1889 he was elected state senator with but little opposition, and was re-elected two years later. In the senate, also, he was a member of the judiciary committee. In both houses Mr. Van Gorder proved himself a painstaking servant, and performed his duties with credit and distinction. He was identified with much important legislation. He was the author, for example, of one of the best and most far-reaching laws ever placed upon the statute books of the state — namely, the act to prevent any peace officer or police official from engaging in the manufacture or sale of intoxicating liquors. In the session of 1893 he was the author and introducer of the " Bi-partisan Election Inspectors " bill, which subsequently, in 1895, became a law of the state.

Mr. Van Gorder's activities have not been confined to politics or his profession. He has taken a deep interest in educational matters, and for many years has been one of the trustees of Pike Seminary. He is also director and president of the State Bank of Pike, and thus has come into contact with financiers in western New York. He is a member of several fraternal orders, and of the Holland Society of New York. June 1, 1896, Mr. Van Gorder entered into a copartnership for the practice of law at Buffalo,

and is now a member of the firm of Bartlett, Van Gorder, White & Holt. In all his relations as a lawyer, a banker, and a public man, he enjoys the esteem and confidence of those who know him.

*PERSONAL CHRONOLOGY—Greenleaf Scott Van Gorder was born at York, Livingston county,*

GREENLEAF S. VAN GORDER

*N. Y., June 2, 1855 ; received a common-school and an academic education ; studied law, and was admitted to the bar June 15, 1877 ; moved to Pike, N. Y., August 7, 1877 ; married Eva E. Lyon of Pike August 29, 1878 ; was supervisor of Pike, 1883-88, member of assembly, 1888-89, and state senator, 1890-93 ; practiced law at Pike, 1877-96 ; has been president of the State Bank of Pike since January, 1894 ; has practiced law at Buffalo since June 1, 1896.*

\*\*\*

**Harrison Needham Vedder** is less than forty years old, but he has already, by dint of energy and close application to business, won for himself a high place among the substantial business men of Buffalo. The insurance firm with which he is connected is regarded as one of the leaders in its line. But Mr. Vedder is not among those who selfishly confine their energies to their own personal interests. He is a man of public spirit, interested especially in promoting the business welfare of the city. He has long been one of the most active members of

HARRISON NEEDHAM VEDDER

the Merchants' Exchange; he was chairman of its postal committee in 1895, and is now serving his second term as trustee of the institution. On the social side he is greatly interested in yachting, and is perhaps as well known for his connection with this sport as for his business enterprises. He helped to organize the Buffalo Yacht Club, and was its commodore for three years, 1883–85.

Mr. Vedder is a genuine product of Buffalo. He was born and educated there, served his business apprenticeship there, married there, and has always lived there. He began attending school at the age of six, and was able to continue his education until he was fourteen years of age. Young as he was, he then began to earn his own living. He entered the

insurance office of Captain E. P. Dorr, where he remained three years. Thus early did he gain an experience in the business that has proved his highway to success.

After leaving Captain Dorr young Vedder went to work as a clerk for the insurance firm of Smith, Davis & Clark. Here he continued five years, thus devoting altogether eight years to the insurance business as an employee before branching out for himself. He was now a young man of twenty-two, and ambitious for more rapid progress than seemed possible in the position that he was then occupying. He had been prudent and economical, and had saved some money. He had, besides, formed an extensive acquaintance, which is of considerable value to a young man entering almost any calling, and of decided value to one embarking in the insurance business.

Mr. Vedder did not immediately, however, enter business for himself. For a brief time he abandoned insurance altogether, becoming chief clerk for the Western Elevating Co. But after about a year of this business he returned permanently to insurance, forming a partnership with Charles J. North that has since continued.

Mr. Vedder is active in the Masonic fraternity, and has attained distinction therein. He is at present Senior Warden of Ancient Landmark Lodge, No. 441, F. & A. M. He is also a member of Adytum Chapter, No. 235, R. A. M., and of Hugh de Payens Commandery, No. 30, K. T. He takes an interest in the study and preservation of local history, and is a life member of the Buffalo Historical Society.

*PERSONAL CHRONOLOGY— Harrison Needham Vedder was born at Buffalo September 11, 1858; was educated in the public schools; was clerk in an insurance office, 1872–80; married Ida Eliza beth Loveridge of Buffalo September 14, 1881; has been a member of the insurance firm of North & Vedder since 1881.*

***

**Francis G. Ward**, recently appointed superintendent of the water bureau of the city of Buffalo, is a man of thorough experience in the conduct of vast enterprises. He is a factor and product of this intensely practical age, which hesitates at nothing, from harnessing Niagara to divorcing continents.

Mr. Ward belongs to the generation reared since the close of the Civil War. He received his preliminary education at the Rectory School in Hamden, Conn., and when still a child was sent to France, and placed in the *Institution Cousin* and *Lycée Bonaparte*, Paris. There he remained four years, acquiring not only a careful scientific education, but as well a thorough knowledge of the French language. The rumblings of the coming struggle between France and Germany were already in the air, and Americans residing in Paris felt it wise to return home before the storm broke in all its fury. So young Ward came back to the United States, and prepared to enter the Annapolis Naval Academy, to which he was appointed a cadet in 1872. His stay in his native country, however, was not long, for he soon returned to Europe, declining the cadetship. After another year spent abroad in study Mr. Ward returned home, and entered the employ of the Laflin & Rand Powder Co., whose Buffalo representative he became in 1875. After two years in this business he resigned to accept a position with the New York Central & Hudson River railroad. He began his railroad apprenticeship in the arduous and responsible position of night yardmaster and train dispatcher at the Grand Central station in New York city. He was with the Central in various important capacities for seven years, when he became assistant manager of the Harlem line.

Mr. Ward's experience in railroading, and his skill in handling large bodies of employees, coupled with his scientific training and command of the French language, commended him to the favorable notice of the *Cie Universelle Canal Panama*, which was engaged in building the canal across the isthmus of Panama; and he was offered the superintendency of the Panama railroad, then owned by that company. He thereupon resigned from the Harlem line, and accepted the position under the French company. After spending two years at the isthmus, he was ordered to Paris and made manager of the railroad department of the canal company, and a member of the construction committee of the Turkish-Asiatic railroad. In connection with these interests he remained abroad until 1889, when he obtained leave of absence, and returned to Buffalo to look after personal matters. These he found so much disordered

as the result of his long absence, that he felt obliged to resign his position with the canal company, and to devote his whole attention to his affairs on this side of the water.

In military circles Mr. Ward is well known. For twelve years he was a member of the 7th New York regiment, and as a member of the 74th regiment, of Buffalo, he became captain, lieutenant colonel, and inspector of the 8th division. While at Panama he was for three years acting colonel of the battalion formed of employees of the Panama railroad located at Aspinwall. Among the many souvenirs of Mr. Ward's residence at Aspinwall, one he values very highly. After the destruction of that city by fire in 1885, Mr. Ward rebuilt the entire plant of the canal company, including wharves, railroad tracks, and the streets belonging to the French govern-

*FRANCIS G. WARD*

ment. In recognition of his distinguished service, and upon the recommendation of M. Rousseau, councilor of state, who inspected the work, Mr. Ward was made the recipient of a Sèvres vase, with a letter of thanks from the French government. In political and social life Mr. Ward is an active factor in Buffalo. He is closely identified with the Republican party, and has been one of its local managers in several campaigns. He is a member of the Sons of the American Revolution; and in

HENRY WEILL.

the Masonic order he has been Master of Ancient Landmark Lodge, Captain General of Hugh de Payens Commandery, and Lieutenant Commander of Buffalo Consistory.

PERSONAL CHRONOLOGY—*Francis Grant Ward was born at Jordan, N. Y., March 8, 1856; was educated in the United States and France; was in the employ of the Laflin & Rand Powder Co., at New York and Buffalo, 1875–76, and of the New York Central & Hudson River railroad, 1877–85; was employed by the " Cie Universelle Canal Panama," at Aspinwall and elsewhere, 1885–89; married Christine Meday at Rutherford, N. J., November 3, 1886; was appointed superintendent of the bureau of water of Buffalo in May, 1896.*

**Henry Weill** is an excellent representative of the class of citizens concerned in the oft-repeated compliment that the best blood of Europe has gone to make the present development of the United States. Born and educated in a foreign country, he brought to the land of his adoption an appreciation of the importance of industry such as can be felt only by those who have seen the greater poverty of the old world. To this, perhaps, more than to any other one thing, is due the business success he has achieved. He has been a tireless worker, shrewd, methodical, and with a ready talent for grasping opportunities. He has built up a large importing business, besides aiding materially in the development of Buffalo real estate.

Mr. Weill is about forty-nine years old. His father was a real-estate dealer in the little town of Mittersholtz, Alsace, and Henry was kept steadily at school until he was sixteen years of age. During this time he went through the public schools, and obtained the French degree at the college in Schlestadt. He looked forward to a mercantile pursuit, and after leaving college became a clerk in a wholesale dry-goods house in Mulhouse, Alsace. The experience here gained was valuable, especially as he was promoted rapidly, and was thus enabled to learn different branches of the business. When about twenty years old he determined to seek the broader opportunities and better rewards that could be found on this side of the Atlantic. He tried New York for a time, but finding no suitable opening went to Buffalo; and there his fortune has been made. He engaged first in selling cloth to country tailors, and was reasonably successful, but after a short time became attracted by the jewelry business. It was not the line in which he had experience, but his ready adaptability enabled him quickly to master its details, and by hard work and honest dealing he rapidly built up a prosperous trade. In 1881 he decided to try manufacturing, and went to Chicago for this purpose. He established there a jewelry factory, the principal product of which was gold rings. After about two years he returned to Buffalo, and established the business of a diamond importer, which he followed up to 1892.

Observing the rapid growth of Buffalo, Mr. Weill was one of the first to realize the possibilities that lay in real-estate operations. He bought a tract of land at North Buffalo, developed it, and made it one of the most desirable residence sections of the city. About five years ago he entered the banking business by helping to organize the Metropolitan Bank, of which he has been president since 1893.

Mr. Weill fills an important place socially, and has been of great help in building up several of the popular social organizations of the city. A notable case in point is the Orpheus Society, which he joined when it was founded, having previously been a member of the Liedertafel. He is also a charter member of the Phoenix Club, and is chairman of the building committee, which now has in hand the work of erecting a new clubhouse on Franklin street. He belongs to the Washington Lodge of Masons, and to several other social organizations. He has been a trustee of Temple Beth Zion for twenty two years, and its president for four years.

Mr. Weill has never held political office. He was elected a member of the executive board of the Orphan Asylum of Western New York at Rochester.

*PERSONAL CHRONOLOGY—*
*Henry Weill was born at Muttersholtz,*
*Alsace, France, December 17, 1847;*
*graduated from the college de Schlestadt,*
*Academie de Strasbourg, in 1863; emi-*
*grated to the United States in 1867; mar-*
*ried Fannie Shire of Buffalo October 16,*
*1870; carried on a wholesale jewelry*
*business in Buffalo, 1868–92; has been*
*president of the Metropolitan Bank of Buf-*
*falo since 1893.*

\*\*\*

**George W. Wheeler** exemplifies in his career the value of devotion to an idea : when a mere boy he decided to be a lawyer, and a successful one ; and his plan has become an achievement.

Mr. Wheeler's paternal grandfather was an Episcopal clergyman, for many years in charge of the famous parish of Shrewsbury, N. J., whose historic church has stood for two hundred years, and bears in its walls many bullet holes made at the time of the Revolution. The ancient communion service of the parish was the gift of Queen Anne. The name of Mr. Wheeler's maternal grandfather, Samuel Birdsall, is prominently connected with the progress of Seneca county, New York. He held various public offices, from supervisor to congressman, and during De Witt Clinton's administration was judge advocate on the governor's staff.

Mr. Wheeler's parents were people of culture, and his early years were spent in an atmosphere of refinement well calculated to foster his naturally studious habits. His father, a graduate of Hobart College, was for a time his tutor. The thorough course of instruction mapped out for the young pupil was ended by the father's untimely death. The mother was unable to provide the means for further education, and the boy's ambition for a professional life seemed in danger of being thwarted. Through the influence of friends, and because of his grandfather's service in the Episcopal church, he gained admission to De Veaux College, and received a four years' course there without expense to his widowed mother.

After his graduation the problem of self-support confronted Mr. Wheeler, and the legal profession still seemed far from his grasp. He secured a

*GEORGE W. WHEELER*

position with the well-known firm of Sidney Shepard & Co., and later with Pratt & Letchworth, carefully saving as much as possible, to hasten the time when he might begin his law studies. After four years he entered the office of Laning & Willett of Buffalo, and three years later, on October 10, 1879, was admitted to the bar at Rochester from the office of Barrows & Viele. On New Year's Day, 1880, he opened an office in Buffalo. Since then numerous important cases have been entrusted to him, and the successful

CHARLES E. WILLIAMS

manner in which he has conducted them has brought him deserved eminence in his profession. In the fall of 1895 he was a candidate for the nomination for county judge on the Republican ticket. His many friends felt that his elevation to the bench would be a fitting tribute to his worth and ability, but he failed to receive the nomination.

Mr. Wheeler is one of the founders of the Thursday Club, which is devoted to the study of men and things of a literary character. The club grew out of a reception and banquet given in 1883 to commemorate the one hundredth anniversary of the birth of Washington Irving. The success of the celebration called forth a general desire for the formation of a permanent organization, and the Thursday Club was

the result. In January, 1884, Matthew Arnold lectured under its auspices at Concert Hall, and the proceeds of the lecture were given to the building fund of the Buffalo Library.

Mr. Wheeler is a Past Master of DeMolay Lodge, No. 498, F. & A. M., and a Past Regent of Fillmore Council, No. 823, R. A. He is an Odd Fellow as well. He also holds the honored position of trustee of De Veaux College, in which he has taken an active interest ever since he was a student there.

*PERSONAL CHRONOLOGY* George Welles Wheeler was born at Niagara Falls, N. Y., September 1, 1856; was educated at De Veaux College; was admitted to the bar October 10, 1879; married Jennie F. Farrar of Buffalo October 17, 1882; has practiced law in Buffalo since 1880.

**Charles E. Williams** is a Buffalonian by birth, and has spent his whole business life in that city. He has been one of the fundamental, thorough-going workers who have done so much to make Buffalo a great modern city in all respects. His father was a prominent contractor, and the subject of this sketch was for many years engaged with him in the building business.

Mr. Williams was educated in the public schools of Buffalo, and at that well-known private institution, the Heathcote School. After completing his course at the high school, he entered his father's office as bookkeeper, retaining the position for three years.

Having resolved to obtain a technical education, he went to Germany, and pursued a two years' course of study at the celebrated Stuttgart Polytechnic Institute. His work there was devoted, for the most part, to engineering, architecture, and kindred subjects.

Upon his return to this country in 1876, he was taken into partnership by his father, under the firm name of Wm. I. Williams & Son, general contractors and builders. In 1882, after the dissolution of this firm, he entered into partnership with D. W. McConnell, under the style of Williams & McConnell. Among the big contracts undertaken and successfully carried out by this firm was the great reservoir at Charlottesville, Va.

Mr. Williams has paid much attention to the important problem of street paving, and he has extended his business interests in that direction. He is president of the German Rock Asphalt & Cement Co., Limited, which has laid many miles of smooth asphalt pavement on the streets of Buffalo. He laid the first Medina-blockstone pavement on a concrete base ever put down on a public thoroughfare. He was the contractor for the construction of the government-breakwater extension at the port of Buffalo in 1884.

On the death of his partner, Mr. McConnell, Mr. Williams organized a new firm, of which he is the senior member—Williams, McNaughton & Papst. This firm is largely engaged in the paving and general contracting business, and is interested in the grade-crossing changes now going on at what is known as "the Terrace" in the city of Buffalo. This work is extremely important, as it will permit the trains of the Central-Hudson, Lake Shore, Michigan Central, and other railroads to enter the Union Station at Buffalo without crossing at grade several streets whose congested traffic is now so endangered.

Mr. Williams is treasurer of the Buffalo Dredging Co., vice president of the Buffalo Floating Elevator Co., and president of the McConnell Catch Basin Co.

Not only in business circles is Mr. Williams active and prominent, but equally in social and military affairs is he a factor. For five years he was a member of old company D, Buffalo City Guards, and for an equal period was quartermaster of the 74th regiment, National Guard of the State of New York. He is a Scottish Rite Mason of the 32d degree, a life member of the Buffalo Press Club, and a member of the Buffalo Republican League.

*PERSONAL CHRONOLOGY—Charles Edwin Williams was born at Buffalo February 21, 1852; was educated in the public schools and the Heathcote School of Buffalo, and the Polytechnic Institute, Stuttgart, Germany; has carried on the business of a paving and general contractor at Buffalo since 1876.*

---

**James R. Austin** came to manhood in the midst of stirring times, and began early in life an active and a varied career. He has lived in the West, the South, and the East; has been a soldier, a manufacturer, and a business man in different lines; and the best part of it all

is that substantial success has attended him from first to last. He was born in Milwaukee shortly before the middle of the century. His parents were among the first settlers of that prosperous city, and they are both living there still, at ages very advanced.

Mr. Austin's education was good so far as it went, but it might have gone farther without violating the proprieties. After attending the public schools and the Milwaukee Military Academy, he made his choice between college and countingroom by accepting, at the age of sixteen, a clerkship in the wholesale dry-goods house of Bradford Bros. This was the second largest concern in the Northwest, and the salary was $800 a year. In normal times young Austin might have been content to plod along in the usual rut of an entry clerk; but the times were altogether abnormal, and the young man was impatient to have a

*JAMES R. AUSTIN*

more active part in the great drama of history then unfolding.

In February, 1864, therefore, he enlisted as a private in company A of the 39th Wisconsin volunteer infantry, and went to the front. He was captured in August, 1864, in the course of Forrest's raid on Memphis, Tenn. After hasty transfers from one prison pen to another, he was finally landed in a closely packed, open stockade, ridiculously styled "Castle Morgan," at Cahaba, Ala. Here he suffered all the miseries of exposure, starvation, nakedness, sickness, and needless cruelty implied in the more familiar name of Andersonville. His life was barely saved by a fortunate exchange in October of the same year, and in January, 1865, he was mustered out of service. He then returned to Milwaukee, and after regaining health resumed his position in the house of Bradford Bros. They had continued his salary during his army service, after the manner of a few other patriotic and generous concerns.

Reversing the usual procedure, Mr. Austin went due East in February, 1866, to take a position in the Boston agency of the New York Life Insurance Co. Subsequently succeeding to the management of this branch of the business, he conducted the agency for five years with conspicuous success. His office, indeed, is said to have received and remitted to the home office the largest amount of premium payments of any agency in the country.

After engaging for some time in mining and in the manufacture of agricultural implements, Mr. Austin decided to make Buffalo his home, and to embark in real-estate ventures in that promising city. He went thither, accordingly, in 1889, having previously made investments there, and having for a long time studied the situation, and noted the favorable aspects of the same. Associating himself with A. J. Riegel in the firm of Austin & Riegel, he built up a large business in a magically rapid way. In less than a year the firm sold over $3,000,000 worth of farm property. These operations led to the establishment, in 1892, of the Security Investment Co. of Buffalo, which includes among its directors and stockholders some of the most successful bankers and business men of the city. At the beginning James B. Stafford was elected president and James R. Austin vice president; and both these efficient officers have since been annually re-elected to their respective positions.

Mr. Austin is a Sir Knight of the Masonic order. He is also a member of Bidwell Wilkeson Post, No. 9, G. A. R.; of the Buffalo Merchants' Exchange; and of the Ellicott Club.

*PERSONAL CHRONOLOGY— James Russell Austin was born at Milwaukee, Wis., July 26, 1847; was educated in public schools and Milwaukee Military Academy; was clerk in a wholesale dry-goods house in Milwaukee, 1863-64, with the exception of a year*

*spent in the Union army; was agent and manager of a life-insurance agency at Boston, 1866-78; engaged in mining and in the manufacture of agricultural implements, 1879-89; moved to Buffalo in 1889 and began real-estate operations; has been vice president of the Security Investment Co. of Buffalo since its organization in 1892.*

•••

**August Becker** is young in years, though well matured in the practice of his profession. A man who secures an early start in the quickened and busy life of this nineteenth century has an incalculable advantage over those who enter the race even a few years later in life. Mr. Becker not only made an early start as a lawyer, but has forged ahead in his profession at an age when others are just beginning to acquire practice.

Mr. Becker is a native of Buffalo, where he was born two years after the great Civil War was brought to a close. He obtained his education in the public schools of the city, and after a thorough preparatory training in the elementary English branches he entered the office of Greene, McMillan & Gluck, one of the strongest legal firms of western New York. This firm was subsequently styled McMillan, Gluck & Pooley, and was noted throughout the state for its skill in that modern and intricate branch of the profession known as corporation law. No better training school for legal culture could be found, on account of the experience of the firm, its valuable library, and the prestige and traditions of the office. Mr. Becker served a busy and faithful apprenticeship with this firm, acquiring a sound practical knowledge, as well as a broad and comprehensive theory, of the law, particularly as related to corporations. He was admitted to the bar at Rochester, at a term of the Supreme Court held in that city in October, 1888, a few months after his majority.

After a further period spent in familiarizing himself with the routine of a law office, Mr. Becker began the practice of his profession in the city of his birth in July, 1891, and practiced alone for one year. A striking feature of the legal profession is the tendency of lawyers to associate themselves in legal firms, and specialize their work. In this way doubled experience, increased clientage, and greater prestige are obtained; for it is as true in law as in any other business that two heads are better than one. Mr. Becker was quick to recognize this advantage, and he formed a partnership with Charles C. Farnham of Buffalo, under the firm name of Becker & Farnham, that has continued until the present time.

Mr. Becker is distinctly a student of the law, and for a young man is deeply versed in legal literature. He has already figured as an author, having issued in conjunction with James Fraser Gluck a work known as "Gluck & Becker on Receivers of Corporations"; and the volume has been so well appreciated by the legal profession that a second edition of the work is now in press.

Mr. Becker has wisely chosen to hold himself aloof from the distractions of a political career, realizing the wisdom of the old adage against having too many irons in the fire. Nor has he sought through social affiliations to gain practice, having relied for success upon industry, and entire devotion to a noble profession.

*PERSONAL CHRONOLOGY— August Becker was born at Buffalo August 10, 1867; was educated in the public schools of that city; studied law in the office of Greene, McMillan & Gluck, and was admitted to the bar in 1888; has practiced law in Buffalo since 1891.*

***

**M. H. Birge** was born more than ninety years ago in Chittenden county, Vermont. His whole life, from his resourceful youth to his vigorous old age, illustrates the Puritan virtues in various ways, and it is not surprising to find that his ancestors were descended from one of the Plymouth Pilgrims. In the early years of the century educational opportunities were few, and Mr. Birge obtained rather more training than most young men in attending the district schools and the village academy. At the age of twenty he entered upon a business career that was destined to last sixty-six years. Obtaining a position as a clerk in a general store at Middlebury, Vt., in 1826, he learned the business rapidly, and at the end of three years felt able to start in on his own account. He did so, accordingly, April 1, 1829, carrying on a general store successfully for about five years.

Mr. Birge had too much Puritan blood in his veins, and was too good a Yankee, to remain satisfied with the slow-going life of a Vermont country town, and in 1834 he joined the endless procession of westward emigrants. His original purpose was to go to Chicago, but he was so much pleased with Buffalo that he decided to cast in his lot with the 15,000 people

then resident there. On October 15, 1834, he opened a store on Main street devoted to dry goods, paper hangings, and general merchandise.

Hardly had Mr. Birge become fairly established in his new venture when the financial crash of 1837, one of the most serious in the history of the country,

*AUGUST BECKER*

descended upon him. Failures abounded in every branch of trade, and many of his customers paid him little or nothing. He was unable, therefore, to meet his own obligations. He did not on that account take advantage of the bankruptcy law to force upon his creditors a fractional payment of their claims; but paid them what he could at once, promising to pay all in time. This promise he kept faithfully. By 1846 he had paid off the last obligation dollar for dollar, and was even with the world and at peace with his conscience. The struggle had been long and at times disheartening; but virtue is its own reward, and Mr. Birge must have been repaid many-fold for his self-sacrifice during the fifty years since elapsed.

Before the middle of the century Mr. Birge's business had resolved itself into the wall-paper trade exclusively, and for many years he carried on one of the largest stores in this line in western New York. Up to 1879 he handled stock manufactured by others; but in that year, in connection with his sons,

M. H. BIRGE

and under the firm name of M. H. Birge & Sons, he began the manufacture of paper hangings. His long experience in the business and minute acquaintance with wall-paper stock assured in advance the success of the new enterprise. On June 1, 1892, after having built up the business to large proportions, Mr. Birge disposed of his interest to his sons. He has since lived in retirement from active affairs, enjoying the leisure and rest to which he was years ago entitled.

*PERSONAL CHRONOLOGY— Martin Howland Birge was born at Underhill, Vt., July 30, 1806; was educated in district schools and the village academy; was clerk in a general store at Middlebury, Vt., 1826-29, and carried on a similar store on his own account, 1829-34; married Elizabeth Ann Kingsley*

*of Sheldon, Vt., October 21, 1830; opened a general store in Buffalo in 1834; established the manufacture of wall paper in 1879, and remained at the head of the firm until his retirement in 1892.*

<br>

**Spencer Clinton,** years ago a leader at the Erie-county bar, and now one of the most distinguished lawyers in the Empire State, belongs to an historic family. His grandfather on the maternal side was John C. Spencer, secretary of war under President Tyler and an eminent jurist. His grandfather on the other side, De Witt Clinton, was mayor of New York city, governor of New York state, and United States senator. But for him the Erie canal might never have been built, and certainly would not have been built until many years after its actual construction. Mr. Clinton's own father, George W. Clinton, was one of the ablest lawyers of his day.

Spencer Clinton was born in Buffalo, and has always lived there. His education was obtained in public and private schools in Buffalo, Brockport, and Albany. Colleges were not so numerous and accessible at the time of his youth as now, and Mr. Clinton did not have the benefit of a collegiate course. Having determined to study law, he entered the office of Solomon G. Haven for that purpose, and subsequently carried on his reading under William Dorsheimer. He made rapid progress in his studies, and was admitted to the bar in the October term of 1860, when twenty-one years of age.

Measured by the standards of to-day, when many men destined for the law are not even out of college at that age, Mr. Clinton made a prompt beginning on his life-work; and his progress was still further accelerated early in his professional career by an appointment as assistant United States district attorney under his former preceptor, William Dorsheimer. In this position Mr. Clinton had a chance to show his legal ability, and he discharged the duties of the office for several years with brilliant success. In 1868 he formed a partnership with Charles D. Marshall for the general practice of the law. This association has been maintained ever since, and has been altogether successful. Others have been admitted to the firm at various times, but the original partnership has not been severed. Since 1893 Adolph Rebadow, who studied as a young man in the office of Marshall & Clinton, has been a member of the firm, and the present style is Marshall, Clinton & Rebadow. The firm is one of the strongest in western New York, and transacts an immense amount of legal business. Mr. Clinton is everywhere regarded as a lawyer of great sagacity, wide learning in the law, and sound judgment.

Though deprived himself of systematic training in a law school, Mr. Clinton believes thoroughly in such institutions. He has taken an active interest in the Buffalo Law School, having been one of the organizers of the institution, and having lectured therein ever since its foundation. He has been attorney for the Buffalo grade-crossing commissioners since 1887, and has done all that he could, aside from his professional interest in the matter, to expedite and discharge in the best possible manner the important work of this commission. He is one of the trustees of the Buffalo Savings Bank and a director of the Third National Bank. As executor of two large estates, he represents the C. J. Wells elevator and the Bennett elevator in the Western Elevating Association.

Mr. Clinton has been absorbed in his professional work, and has studiously avoided public office. In 1887, however, he permitted himself to become the Democratic nominee for state senator ; and he was much relieved by the success of the opposing candidate. The episode is worth mentioning because readers will remember how freely and frankly the opposing press acknowledged Mr. Clinton's ability and high character. The National Democratic state convention, held at Brooklyn September 24, 1896, nominated him by acclamation for the position of associate judge of the Court of Appeals.

In social life Mr. Clinton has enjoyed the position to which his professional attainments and personal character would naturally entitle him. He is a prominent member of the Buffalo Club, and was its president in 1885. He is a member of St. Paul's Episcopal Church.

*PERSONAL CHRONOLOGY—*
*Spencer Clinton was born at Buffalo June 29, 1839 ; was educated in public and private schools ; studied law, and was admitted to the bar in 1869 ; was assistant United States district attorney, 1866–68 ; has practiced law in Buffalo since 1868.*

**George A. Davis** can enjoy in full measure the satisfaction that comes from the gratification of an honorable ambition. Nowhere but in America, perhaps, would a life like his be possible ; but even in this favored land it requires ability and determination for a young man entirely dependent on his own resources to become a successful lawyer and public man before he has reached his fortieth year.

Mr. Davis was born in Buffalo, and is a thorough Buffalonian, though of late years he has been actively identified with one of the suburban towns. His education was received in the Buffalo public schools ; and he doubtless used the opportunities there all the more faithfully because the lack of money made the acquisition of an education somewhat difficult. On the completion of his school course, he learned the trade of a picture-frame maker, and worked at that

*SPENCER CLINTON*

long enough to get a little money ahead. But he had determined to become a lawyer, and as soon as circumstances permitted he left the workman's bench for a law office. He became a student in the office of Day & Romer, Buffalo, and applied himself so diligently to the task of gaining the necessary knowledge of the law that in three years he was admitted to the bar.

Mr. Davis at once opened an office in Buffalo, and has practiced there continuously since. The same

GEORGE L. DAVIS

energy and ability that gained for him admission to his profession at the early age of twenty-two, in spite of obstacles that would have disheartened a less determined man, have brought him success in his chosen calling; and he has already established a reputation as an able attorney.

Public affairs have interested Mr. Davis greatly for many years. Before he was thirty he was a member of the Erie-county board of supervisors, representing the 9th ward of the city of Buffalo for two years. On his removal to Lancaster in 1887, he was elected supervisor of the town, and proved so able a guardian of the interests of the community that he has held the office ever since. In the years 1889, 1894, and 1895 he was chairman of the

board of supervisors, being the unanimous choice of his colleagues of both political parties; and he made an admirable presiding officer, and displayed unusual executive ability. In 1890 he was nominated for representative in congress from the 33d congressional district. This was a year of defeat for the Republican party, however, and Mr. Davis failed of election by a small majority. In 1894 he was a delegate to the state constitutional convention. There he was made a member of the committees on banking, insurance, and military, and did good work in each. In 1895 he was elected, by a majority of nearly 6000 votes, to represent his district, the 49th, in the upper house of the state legislature; and on the organization of that body he became a member of the committees on judiciary, commerce, navigation, penal institutions, and Indian affairs, acting as chairman of the latter.

Such a record for a comparatively young man indicates uncommon talent for public affairs, and this Mr. Davis undoubtedly possesses. It is safe to predict that further honors are in store for one who has already served his fellow-citizens so acceptably.

Mr. Davis is well known, also, from his long connection with the National Guard. Enlisting as a private in the 74th regiment in 1877, he rose through all the intermediate grades until he became commander of the regiment; and this position he retained for a number of years. He is a 32d degree Mason, belonging to the Buffalo Consistory, and a Knight Templar in Lake Erie Commandery. Since his removal to Lancaster he has taken an active interest in Trinity Episcopal Church there, and is at present one of its wardens.

*PERSONAL CHRONOLOGY — George Allen Davis was born at Buffalo August 5, 1858; was educated in the public schools; studied law, and was admitted to the bar in 1880; married Lillie N. Grimes of Lancaster, N. Y., June 4, 1885; was a member of the constitutional convention in 1894, and was elected state senator in 1895; has been a member of the Erie county board of supervisors since 1885; has practiced law in Buffalo since 1880.*

***

**Benjamin Folsom,** well known in western New York as a member of the bar, and throughout the country as the representative from the United

States in an important foreign station, was born in Wyoming county, New York, in 1847. The Folsom family has an interesting genealogy, beginning in this country with the landing of John Folsom in 1638 at Hingham, Mass., and directly traceable from him to the present generation. After receiving his preliminary training in the Attica Union School and Wyoming Academy, Mr. Folsom prepared for college at Genesee Wesleyan Seminary at Lima, N. Y., and entered the University of Rochester in the fall of 1867. He took the classical course there, and graduated in 1871 with honors, obtaining the degree of Bachelor of Arts, and afterward receiving from the same institution the degree of Master of Arts.

Mr. Folsom at first contemplated a journalistic career, and he went to Europe as a newspaper correspondent in the summer of his graduation. He seems, however, to have agreed with Thiers's doubtful praise of journalism as "a very good profession if you get out of it in time"; for he soon changed his plans, and after serving on the staff of the New York *World* until the fall of 1872, began the study of law in the office of Bass & Bissell, Buffalo. He made rapid progress in this work, and was regularly admitted to the bar in October, 1875. For the next two years he strengthened his grasp of legal principles, and obtained further insight into the actual conduct of litigation, by service in the city attorney's office as managing clerk. Opening an office in Buffalo on his own account in 1878, he began the active practice of the law, and continued the same with marked success until November, 1886.

An appointment as United States consul at Sheffield, England, received at that time, caused a long interruption in his law practice. He remained at Sheffield about seven years, resigning the consulate in 1893 for the purpose of returning to this country, and looking after his real-estate interests in California and in Omaha, Neb. The extraordinarily rapid growth of Omaha vastly increased the value of the estate of his father, the late Benj. R. Folsom, and the care and development of this property, together with its partition and division, required Mr. Folsom's personal attention. Having adjusted his affairs in the West, he returned to Buffalo and resumed the practice of law.

In political matters Mr. Folsom has allied himself with the Democratic party. He has served in the ranks, and has never sought a nomination for office. For many years before his residence in England he was secretary and treasurer of the board of trustees of the City and County Hall, Buffalo; and in that capacity he arranged and systematized the accounts of the institution in the way that they are now kept.

Mr. Folsom is a member of the Masonic order, belonging to Washington Lodge, No. 240, Buffalo, and to Talbot Chapter of Rose Croix, Scottish Rite, Sheffield, England. He is a member, also, of the University Club, Buffalo, St. George's Club, London, and the Sheffield Club, Sheffield. He is much interested in the history of his family, and is engaged in a study of the Folsom genealogy.

*BENJAMIN FOLSOM*

*PERSONAL CHRONOLOGY*—*Benjamin Folsom was born at Folsomdale, Wyoming county, N. Y., December 5, 1847; graduated from the University of Rochester in 1871; served as newspaper correspondent, 1871-72; studied law, and was ad-*

mitted to the bar in 1875; practiced law in Buffalo,
1878–86; was United States consul at Sheffield,
Eng., 1886–93; married Mrs. Ella Blanchard
Howard of Rochester Oct. 11, 1884; resumed the
practice of law in Buffalo in 1894.

*PHILIP GERST*

**Philip Gerst** has attained high public station
in Buffalo at an unusually early age, and is among
the youngest of the prominent city officials. The
chronology of events in his comparatively short
career bespeaks an energy, determination, and ability that may be expected to lead to yet higher
positions in the public service in coming years.
He has made an excellent start, and bids fair to
maintain his present rate of progress.

Mr. Gerst is a native of Buffalo, and still lives
in the house in which he was born thirty-odd years
ago. Few men know the beautiful city so intimately
and thoroughly as he; and his accurate acquaintance with both the people and the history of Buffalo
has doubtless stood him in good stead in his political
campaigns. His educational training preparatory

to entering upon a vocation was obtained in the
public schools of Buffalo, and in a business college.
He graduated from Public School No. 20, and after
a period of study at the Central High School entered Bryant & Stratton's Business College, where
he acquired a knowledge of commercial
forms and usages.

After completing his school course he
began the study of law in the office of
James A. Roberts. Practical business
life, however, attracted him strongly, and
he soon laid aside his text-books to enter the railway service. He was in the
employ of the Erie railroad for several
years, rising from the position of messenger to that of cashier. Resigning
from the railroad company in 1886, he
went into the coal business with the firm
of Dakin & Sloan; and afterward embarked in the real-estate business, forming a partnership with Michael Doll.
He is still engaged in this, having lately
purchased the interest of his partner.

While earning the reputation of an
active and enterprising business man,
Mr. Gerst at the same time was coming
to the front as a forceful factor in
the politics of Erie county. He has
been conspicuous in the reform movements that have so much benefited the
city politics of Buffalo. In 1892 he was
nominated for his first office, that of
assessor. Though defeated, he ran ahead
of his ticket several hundred votes in his
own ward; and his friends maintain
that he was deliberately counted out.
His strength having been thus demonstrated, he was elected in the following
year to the state assembly. He represented the 6th
Erie district in the legislature two years, and established a record that entitled him to further consideration at the hands of his party. In 1895,
accordingly, he was nominated for the responsible
position of treasurer of the city of Buffalo, and was
elected by a large majority. On the first of January,
1896, he began his four years' term of office; and
he is already fulfilling the predictions and anticipa-
tions of his friends.

Mr. Gerst is an enthusiastic fraternity man, be-
longing to Occidental Lodge, No. 766, of the
Masonic order, and having membership in the
Valley of Buffalo Ancient Accepted Scottish Rite
Masons, 32d degree. He is also a member of the
North Buffalo Lodge of Odd Fellows, No. 517.

*PERSONAL CHRONOLOGY— Philip Gerst was born at Buffalo September 17, 1864; was educated in the public schools and Bryant & Stratton's Business College; was in the employ of the Erie railroad, 1879–86, and of Dakin & Sloan, coal dealers, 1886–88; was member of assembly, 1884–85; was elected treasurer of the city of Buffalo in 1895, for the term 1896–98; has carried on a real-estate and insurance business since 1888.*

•••    ---

**Edward W. Hatch,** though still in the prime of life, long ago attained a position of dignity and importance in the affairs of men. The judicial calling, probably more than any other, requires a combination of qualities and a thoroughness of mental equipment that can rarely be found outside the ranks of men well advanced in years and experience. That Judge Hatch was found to possess early in life the requisite experience in the law, and the penetration and general maturity of mind appropriate to the bench, stamps him at once as a man of exceptional ability and character.

Heredity doubtless had something to do with all this. Judge Hatch's grandfather was Captain Jeremiah Hatch, who obtained his title through heroic action in the War for Independence. His son Jeremiah inherited, with his father's name, something at least of his father's spirit, for he raised a company at the outbreak of the Civil War, and went to the front as captain of the 130th New York volunteers. He died at Suffolk, Va., in December, 1862.

Judge Hatch was born in Friendship, Allegany county, and attended the academy there in the fall and winter months until he was sixteen years old. Unable to pursue his studies further in a systematic way at that time, he turned his hand to the blacksmith's trade, and also engaged in lumbering in the Pennsylvania forests and in Wyoming county, New York. These occupations — not altogether prophetic of his later career — occupied about four years, between 1868 and 1872. In the latter year he found an opportunity to take the first step towards satisfying an ambition that he had long cherished. Andrew J. Lorish, afterward county judge of Wyoming county, was then postmaster of Attica, and was also practicing law there. He gave Mr. Hatch a clerkship in the post office, with the

understanding that a considerable part of the time might be devoted to the reading of law. This divided allegiance to business and to study was a poor substitute for a law school; but the young student made the most of his opportunities, and had accomplished a great deal when the chance came, in 1874, to go to Buffalo and enter the law office of Corlett & Tabor. Mr. Corlett afterward became a justice of the Supreme Court, and Mr. Tabor the attorney-general of the state; and in their office a broad and thoroughly practical training in the law could be obtained by a diligent student. Mr. Hatch remained with them until the dissolution of the firm in 1875, and continued with Mr. Corlett until admitted to the bar the next year. He then practiced law alone for two years, when he was invited by Mr. Corlett to form a partnership

*EDWARD W. HATCH*

with him. This association, significant of Mr. Hatch's fidelity and success as a law student, continued until Judge Corlett went upon the bench in 1883. After that, in January, 1884, Mr. Hatch, together with Porter Norton and H. W. Box, formed the law firm of Box, Hatch & Norton, with which Mr. Hatch continued to practice until his elevation to the bench January 1, 1887.

A firm believer in the principles of the Republican party, Mr. Hatch early rose to prominence in political circles. In 1880, and again three years later, he was nominated by acclamation for the office of district attorney of Erie county. He was elected by large majorities on both occasions, and discharged with conspicuous ability the important duties of the office. He was next a candidate for public honors in the fall of 1886, when he was elected by a large majority for a term of fourteen years one of the judges of the Superior Court of Buffalo. The new state constitution, prepared by the convention of 1894, abolished that court, and provided that the judges thereof should be transferred to the state Supreme Court on January 1, 1896, for their unexpired terms. This feature of the constitution would have affected Judge Hatch, had he not been nominated in the fall of 1895 as justice of the Supreme Court for the 8th judicial district. He was elected, with many votes to spare, and thus entered upon a new term of fourteen years from January 1, 1896. Under the new constitution the Supreme Court has four appellate divisions, to which justices are assigned by the governor; and Judge Hatch was appointed for five years one of the appellate judges for the 2d department, comprising Kings and adjoining counties. He entered upon his new duties at Brooklyn January 1, 1896.

A justice of the Supreme Court of the state of New York cannot discharge his duties ably and conscientiously and have much time left for outside pursuits. Judge Hatch is subject to this limitation, but he contrives, nevertheless, to maintain close relations with many movements affecting the public welfare. He delivers occasional lectures on literary and social topics as well as on questions of the day. His career thus far has been rich in results, and promises a future of honorable achievement.

*PERSONAL CHRONOLOGY— Edward Wingate Hatch was born at Friendship, N. Y., November 26, 1852; received a common-school education; began the study of law at Attica, N. Y., in 1872, and was admitted to the bar in 1876; married Helen Woodruff of Conneaut, O., in 1878; practiced law in Buffalo, 1876-89; was district attorney of Erie county, 1881-86; was judge of the Superior Court of Buffalo, 1887-95; became judge of the Supreme Court January 1, 1896, and was appointed by Governor Morton appellate judge for the 2d department of that court for a term of five years.*

**Lucian Hawley** has considerably exceeded the scriptural limitation of life, and has never in all these years been false to the trust reposed in him. As counselor, public official, corporation officer, and trustee, the chief business of his life has been to guard and preserve the interests of others. With what vigilance and fidelity he has done this our opening statement shows. The more critically and minutely his career is examined, the more clearly will this aspect of his life appear.

Born not long after James Monroe entered the White House, in Saratoga county, New York, Mr. Hawley spent his boyhood in that part of the state. His education was begun at Glens Falls, and was finished at Buffalo, whither he had moved in April, 1837. In those days the opportunities for academic and collegiate instruction were far less abundant than now, and Mr. Hawley was unable to study for a degree. He had the best possible substitute, however, in a long term of service with the legal firm of Fillmore, Hall & Haven. Millard Fillmore, afterward President of the United States, and his associates, were giants at the Erie-county bar; and Mr. Hawley, as managing clerk of the firm, could hardly have been better placed to acquire valuable experience in the actual practice of the law. He held this position for four years, and was thus enabled to obtain admission to the bar in November, 1844.

His first partnership was with Isaiah T. Williams, a brother of the late Gibson T. Williams. In 1846 the firm was strengthened by the addition of Nelson K. Hopkins, and the style became Williams, Hopkins & Hawley. This association was dissolved in 1847, when Mr. Hawley formed a partnership with his brother, Seth C. Hawley. An appointment in 1849, as deputy collector of customs for the district of Buffalo Creek, caused Mr. Hawley to abandon the law for about four years. At the end of that period he became successively managing clerk in the law office of John Ganson, secretary of the company publishing the *Commercial Advertiser*, traveling collector for the famous house of Pratt & Co., and secretary of the Buffalo Agricultural Machine Works.

This brings us down to 1865, when Mr. Hawley began his long career in the United States internal-revenue service. During the eleven years thus employed he was legislated out of office three times and resigned twice; but on each occasion he was restored to office with a better position. This came about, not from solicitation on his part, but from the desire of the treasury officials to perfect the service, and as a reward of merit. The internal-revenue officers of the government were subjected to subtle temptations in those days, and were not always above suspicion:

so that an officer of Mr. Hawley's fidelity and absolute honesty was correspondingly valuable to the
treasury department. After eight years of service
in subordinate capacities Mr. Hawley was appointed,
in 1873, supervisor of internal revenue by President
Grant, and was assigned to duty in New York city,
with the state of New York as his district.

The most important and interesting
part of Mr. Hawley's work as supervisor
was his agency in the downfall of the
"whiskey ring," the popular name for
the association of revenue officers and
distillers who so largely defrauded the
government of the internal revenue on
distilled spirits. The ring originated in
St. Louis, but extended its nefarious operations throughout the country. President Grant and Secretary Bristoc, however, were equal to the emergency, and
on May 10, 1875, a simultaneous raid
was made on the implicated distilleries
of St. Louis, Milwaukee, and Chicago.
As a result the government was able to
bring into court about $3,500,000 worth
of seized property, and indictments
against 238 persons, including distillers,
rectifiers, wholesale liquor dealers, and
many officers of the internal-revenue
service. Mr. Hawley was placed in
charge of the raid at St. Louis, and carried out his end of the movement with
exceptional vigor and success. In the
fall of the same year he was sent to the
Pacific coast, and confirmed the suspicion that a corrupt ring there was
defrauding the government. The ring
was so powerfully protected by local
allies that Secretary Bristoc and his
faithful supervisor were unable to repeat here their
St. Louis success. In February, 1876, Mr. Hawley
submitted his resignation, but at the request of the
commissioner of internal revenue remained in office
until May. He then returned home, poor in pocket
and broken in health, having given some of the best
years of his life to the service.

Since then he has engaged in the management of
individual estates, and in executive and fiduciary
work of various kinds. His legal training, broad
experience, and spotless integrity make him particularly efficient and valuable in such matters.

*PERSONAL CHRONOLOGY — Lucian
Hawley was born at Moreau, N. Y., November 8,
1818; received a common-school education, and was
admitted to the bar in 1844; practiced law in Buffalo,
1844–49; was appointed deputy collector of customs in
1849; was engaged in the United States revenue
service, 1865–76; married Irene Burt Leech of Buffalo April 19, 1848, and Lida Williams Jennings of
Lockport, N. Y., December 18, 1877; has made his*

*LUCIAN HAWLEY*

*home in Buffalo since 1876, and has been a resident
of the city since 1877.*

* * *

**Charles E. Hayes** is a member of one of
the most prominent lithographic companies in the
United States. For years the work turned out from
the establishment of Koerner & Hayes has elicited
universal praise and admiration, and few houses
have done more to educate popular taste in the art of
illustration. The standard of the general public in
such matters is higher now than ever before, and
bespeaks for the future a race more appreciative of
the nature and function of pictorial representation.

Mr. Hayes was born in Canada of American parents, and he is an American by training. His

parents were residents of Rochester, N. Y., but
moved to Steubenville, Ohio, the year Charles was
born. Mr. Hayes had the benefit of a thorough
public-school education in the Buckeye State, and
graduated from the Steubenville High School when
only seventeen years of age. He supplemented this

CHARLES E. HAYES

scholastic training by a course in the well-known
business college of Bryant & Stratton at Buffalo.
Having thus prepared himself for a commercial
career, he became a clerk in the office of Drullard &
Hayes of Buffalo, and filled a position with that firm
for three years. His next employment was as bookkeeper for Cosack & Co., makers of the famous
"Buffalo Lithographs." Here he showed such business judgment and skill in managing the affairs of
the firm that he was eventually placed in charge of
the office, and of the financial interests of the concern. The natural result followed, and Mr. Hayes
became a member of the firm. The other members
were H. Cosack and H. T. Koerner. On the death
of Mr. Cosack in 1892, the firm was reorganized,

the surviving partners buying out Mr. Cosack's interest, and forming a new partnership under the style
of Koerner & Hayes. The new firm has continued
to uphold the reputation, and enjoy the prosperity, of
the old house. Their factories on Lakeview avenue in Buffalo afford employment to a large number
of people, from skilled artists and engra-
vers down to laborers and truckmen.
The product of their works is found
everywhere, and has carried the name
of Koerner & Hayes, not only over
the United States, but also to foreign
lands.

While devoting himself assiduously to
his private business, Mr. Hayes has been
a potent influence in local political
affairs. He is a Republican in political
belief. His popularity among his fellow-
townsmen is shown by his strong candidacy for the office of councilman in
1892, a losing year for his party, when
he ran ahead of his ticket, and was
defeated by only forty-five votes.

In Masonic circles Mr. Hayes occu-
pies a prominent place. He is a Knight
Templar; Junior Warden of Hugh de
Payens Commandery, No. 30; Senior
Warden of Rose Croix Chapter; and for
two years he was Worshipful Master of
Ancient Landmark Lodge. He is a
member of the Westminster Presbyterian
Church.

*PERSONAL CHRONOLOGY*—
*Charles Eugene Hayes was born at Oak-
ville, Canada, March 24, 1858; was
educated in the public schools of Steubenville, O., and Bryant & Stratton's Business College, Buffalo; became bookkeeper
for the firm of Cosack & Co., Buffalo,
in 1878, and was admitted to the firm in 1881;
married Carrie Fairchild Spencer of Buffalo October
11, 1881; has been a member of the firm of Koerner & Hayes, successors to Cosack & Co., since
1892.*

•••

**Frederick Howard** comes of good old New
England stock. Both his parents were born in Vermont, and were among the early settlers of Erie
county. The Green Mountain State, like the rest of
New England, has furnished many substantial and
reliable citizens to the Empire State. Any community is fortunate whose early history was determined
largely by New Englanders. Their enterprise, thrift,
honest dealing, sense of justice, and devotion to

school and church, have made them everywhere bulwarks of industrious, loyal citizenship.

Mr. Howard was born at East Aurora, Erie county. When he was three years old his parents moved to Elma, and in the district school of this little town he received his elementary education. He had the usual struggle of boys of limited means to obtain a higher education, but he managed to overcome various difficulties, and to take a course at the Aurora Academy. A college education was beyond his financial reach, and he went to Buffalo and read law in the office of Milo A. Whitney. He served a faithful apprenticeship as a law clerk, and after gaining a theoretic and practical knowledge of legal science he was admitted to the bar by the Supreme Court, when twenty-two years of age. For two years after this he practiced alone. Impressed with the ability and capacity of his former clerk, Mr. Whitney then invited Mr. Howard to become his associate. The partnership was formed, and was maintained for several years. Having resumed practice alone and continued the same five years, Mr. Howard associated himself, in January, 1888, with Myron H. Clark of Elma, becoming senior member of the firm of Howard & Clark. This partnership still continues.

In his chosen profession Mr. Howard has sought solidity of learning in particular branches of the law rather than a smattering of the whole field. He has steadily gained clientage, and long ago passed the uncertain stage in the life of every professional man who begins his career without influential backing. With the spirit of a true American, Mr. Howard has not selfishly confined himself to his office, and wrapped himself up in the gains and rewards of his profession. He has given freely of his time and thought to philanthropic and church work, and the advancement of political morality. He is especially devoted to the promotion and improvement of the Children's Aid Society, commonly known as the Newsboys' and Bootblacks' Home, of which he is a trustee and most efficient member. For several years he was secretary of the Buffalo Orphan Asylum, and ungrudgingly gave many hours of valuable time to its affairs.

Coming of a race nurtured in Congregationalism, Mr. Howard naturally possessed a predilection for the church of his fathers; and though originally a member of the Lafayette Street Presbyterian Church, he became identified with the First Congregational Church of Buffalo at its organization. He was one of its charter members, and is now a member of the board of trustees. He is deeply interested in church music, believing that the spirit of worship can be raised by means of it to higher planes.

Mr. Howard's political affiliations have always been with the Republican party, of which he is a consistent, loyal, and active member. He sincerely believes that the welfare of his party means the welfare of his country. He is not, however, blind to the fact that all human organizations contain many imperfections; and he is an enthusiastic member of the Good Government Club, and has identified himself with its many measures for the correction of

*FREDERICK HOWARD*

abuses in municipal government, and for the purification of local politics. As might be inferred from the foregoing, he is an active member of the Buffalo Republican League.

*PERSONAL CHRONOLOGY — Frederick Howard was born at East Aurora, N. Y., September 12, 1855; was educated in the district schools of Elma and at Aurora Academy; moved to Buffalo in 1874, and began the study of law in 1875; was admitted to the bar in 1878; married Harriet Elizabeth Mabie of Buffalo October 25, 1881; has practiced law in Buffalo since 1878.*

GEORGE H. HUGHSON

...

**George H. Hughson** is a genuine American, and has the Yankee trait of adapting himself to circumstances. He has been a worker all his life, and when not occupied at one thing has found something else to keep him busy. He is a native of western New York, and few men have so intimate an acquaintance with that part of the state as he. His early years were spent in Cattaraugus county, whither his parents had moved when he was an infant. His boyhood was passed on a farm, and he hired out his services to a farmer when most boys enjoy the advantages of school life and frequent holidays. From the farm he entered a gun factory. Disliking the trade of a gunsmith, he went to work in a woolen factory at Gowanda, N. Y., and later at Wattsburg, Penn. It was not until he went to Buffalo, in 1850, that he was able to attend the public schools regularly. But he was soon obliged to earn his own living again, and this time he entered the grocery business, in which he continued a number of years. Then he spent one year as a clerk in a clothing store at Rochester. At this period he felt the need of a better education, and attended the Normal School at Fredonia for one term.

After his father's death in 1854, Mr. Hughson returned to Buffalo, and spent another year in a clothing house. His next employment was in the office of Howard & Co., the well-known iron founders. He maintained his relations with this house till 1872, when he entered into partnership with Joseph M. Blake in the packing-box business. He soon sold out his interest, and turned his attention to the manufacture of silk hats. But Mr. Hughson's versatility was not yet exhausted, and he next embarked in the carriage and harness business, and later in the shoe business.

So far in life Mr. Hughson had taken part in almost every occupation dealing with the supply of man's bodily wants in the way of protection. His energies were employed in a new field when he became connected with the celebrated Niagara Bakery, then under the control of Walter S. Ovens. Mr. Hughson next interested himself in the national game of baseball, and was chosen secretary and treasurer of the Buffalo Baseball Club. When he gave up that he entered the real-estate and insurance business, and to-day he is a member of the well-known fire-insurance firm of Edward C. Roth & Co. As will readily be seen, Mr. Hughson is an all-round man; and in every occupation and calling that he has pursued he has made friends, from his genial disposition and fidelity to those who trusted in his worth.

*PERSONAL CHRONOLOGY — George Hiram Hughson was born at Gowanda, Erie county, N. Y., August 1, 1843; was educated in the public schools, and in the Normal School at Fredonia, N. Y.; moved to Buffalo in 1850, and has been actively engaged in various commercial pursuits there; married Helen*

McLeroth of Chicago April 8, 1858, and Mrs. Juliet Ferguson of Buffalo March 30, 1892; has been engaged in the fire-insurance business at Buffalo since 1885.

...

**Edgar B. Jewett**, mayor of Buffalo, was born in Michigan somewhat more than fifty years ago. His parents, John Cotton Jewett and Priscilla Board man Jewett, moved to Buffalo when he was a boy, and his father established there the business house that afterward became known as the John C. Jewett Manufacturing Co. Mr. Jewett received his early education in the public schools of Buffalo; but he had a strong aptitude for business life, and was impatient to enter upon a commercial career. He closed his schoolbooks, therefore, at the age of sixteen, and went into his father's establishment This was in 1860. He made rapid progress in acquainting himself minutely with every branch of the business, and he has now for many years been the chief guiding hand in controlling the destinies of the concern. How efficient his management has been may be seen in the fact that the output of Jewett refrigerators has enormously expanded, until the house has become everywhere known as one of the foremost of the country in its line.

When the Civil War broke out Mr. Jewett was actively engaged in the conduct of his business affairs; but he did not hesitate to sacrifice personal interests in serving the cause of his country. He joined as a private company C, 74th regiment, N. G., S. N. Y. Becoming second sergeant in May, 1863, he served as such during the campaign that followed Lee's invasion of Pennsylvania in the summer of that year. Returning to Buffalo as first sergeant of his company, he was commissioned first lieutenant June 29, 1865; promoted to the captaincy April 3, 1866; appointed major and inspector of rifle practice of the 31st brigade April 11, 1877; made inspector of the 14th brigade October 9, 1879; appointed lieutenant colonel and chief of staff of the 14th brigade October 25, 1880; and elected brigadier general of the 8th brigade March 29, 1884.

To his business record and military life Mr. Jewett has made in recent years a most important addition — a career as a public official. His success

and prominence in commercial and social circles naturally called attention to his eligibility for public office; and his name was often considered by party managers in connection with the nomination for high offices. He did not enter public life, however, in an important capacity until March 1, 1894, when Mayor Bishop appointed him one of the police commissioners of Buffalo. He discharged the duties of this office vigorously, wisely, and with an eye single to the public good. When, therefore, he became the Republican nominee for the office of mayor of Buffalo, in November, 1894, he was elected by a majority of nearly 10,000, the largest ever received by a candidate for that office.

Without attempting to consider in detail Mr. Jewett's work in the mayoralty, one may safely assert that he has fulfilled the expectations of his

*EDGAR B. JEWETT*

supporters, and has justified the faith of his electors. Bringing to the office a mind thoroughly disciplined by years of military and business service, a character impervious to the subtle temptations of power, and an experience finely fitted to prepare him in material ways for the work before him, Mayor Jewett could not fail to achieve substantial success. As might have been expected from his past, he has shown singular executive ability in conducting the business of his office, and has required similar capacity in all

*FREDERICK KENDALL*

the departments of the city government. Without resorting to the petty arts of the demagogue, he has at the same time shown himself in various ways a vigilant guardian of the public rights. He believes in enlarging the sphere of municipal government, or at least the sphere of municipal control, to a certain extent ; but he would do this in a conservative way, and with due regard to vested interests. He has been a staunch advocate of civil-service reform, and early in the year 1896 made a new classification of all the city offices, the marked feature of which was the sweeping extension of the merit system. It is now applied to nearly every municipal position.

In social life Mayor Jewett has been conspicuous for many years, and has been widely popular. He

has taken high degrees in Masonry, and is a member of the Acacia Club, to which only Master Masons are eligible. He belongs, also, to the Buffalo Club, and to other fraternal and social organizations.

*PERSONAL CHRONOLOGY— Edgar Board-man Jewett was born at Ann Arbor, Mich., December 14, 1843 ; was educated in the Buffalo public schools ; married Elizabeth Foster Danforth of Ann Arbor October 4, 1865 ; was appointed commissioner of police of Buffalo March 1, 1894, and elected mayor of the city in November of the same year ; has been president and general manager of the John C. Jewett Mfg. Co. since January 1, 1885, having been connected with the same since 1860.*

• • •

**Frederick Kendall** has for fifty years watched the city of Buffalo grow and expand from little more than a village to its present industrial and territorial limits. During that period he has been a part of its business and political life, and has been at all times a faithful guardian of its interests.

Mr. Kendall comes from a race of Vermonters born and bred for generations among the rocks and hills of that grand old state. He inherited from them a love of country, a belief in honesty and in the brotherhood of man, a spirit of industry, a fairness of judgment, and a proper toleration of the sentiments of others. His father, Jacob W. Kendall, moved into the western part of New York state when the ox cart was almost the only means of transportation. He settled in the town of Darien, Genesee county, and there Frederick was born. The latter's boyhood was spent on his father's farm, amid such incidents as befall the pioneer everywhere. In those primitive days, when Indians and wolves were more numerous than white neighbors, educational institutions in the country were far from what they are now. But Darien was not lagging behind her sister towns : she boasted of a brick schoolhouse, where the font of education flowed for all who came. It was there that Mr. Kendall obtained his early book training.

Farm life in a crude country possessed no attractions for the young man. The fame of Buffalo was heralded abroad. The Erie canal had been built, traffic on the lakes was already of great importance, and Buffalo was feeling the impetus. Here, then, was the place for the young and the ambitious. So Mr. Kendall went to Buffalo. After a short time word came of Chicago, at the far end of the Great Lakes. Mr. Kendall went there. This was in 1846. Swamps and prairie wolves were the chief sights of the place in that year, and after four months Mr. Kendall returned to Buffalo. He engaged in business there until 1849, when he moved to Detroit, opening a large hardware and stove store. But Buffalo's attractions were still potent, and in 1851 he returned thither again. Shortly afterward he opened one of the first exclusively fancy-goods stores on Main street, continuing there for a number of years, until ill health compelled his retirement.

Mr. Kendall has always taken a deep interest in politics, and for years he was active in Republican-party affairs. When the part of Buffalo included in the old 2d ward was of much greater importance than it is now, Mr. Kendall was its representative on the board of supervisors for six years; and later he represented the same district on the board of aldermen for two years. In both these bodies he was known as a worker, and the interests of his constituents were never permitted to suffer.

While Mr. Kendall was a member of the board of aldermen he became connected with the movement for abolishing grade crossings. He was selected as the aldermanic member of a joint committee representing various interests, formed for the purpose of carrying on a warfare against the evil from which Buffalo had so greatly suffered. From that joint committee an executive committee, of which Mr. Kendall was a member, was formed to devise measures to accomplish the desired result. Finally, in 1888, the legislature created the grade-crossing commission, and Mr. Kendall was named as one of the original commissioners. Through various changes he has remained in that body, giving much time and thought to the solution of the many vexed questions that have arisen, persistent in the face of much opposition, determined that the great work should go on, and striving to be absolutely fair to all interests concerned.

Mr. Kendall is a member of Hiram Lodge, No. 105, F. & A. M., having become a Master Mason in 1863. He is also a member of the Universalist Church of the Messiah.

*PERSONAL CHRONOLOGY— Frederick Kendall was born at Darien, N. Y., January 6, 1825; attended district schools; went to Buffalo in 1847; engaged in business in Detroit, 1849-51; returned to Buffalo in 1851, and engaged in various mercantile pursuits; married Elsey L. Saunders at Buffalo March 23, 1854; was supervisor of the old 2d ward of Buffalo, 1871-78 and 1881-84, and alderman of the same ward, 1887-88; has been a member of the Buffalo grade-crossing commission since its creation in 1888.*

...

**Charles Lamy** is a scion of the old German stock that has been so prominent in the history of Erie county. His father came with his parents as a child from Germany in 1829, and settled upon a farm in East Eden. There the family remained,

CHARLES LAMY

and there Charles Lamy was born twenty years later. One of his brothers, who looks back to the same old home, is George H. Lamy, the present sheriff of Erie county.

Charles Lamy's early days were those of the ordinary farmer's son. He worked on the farm, and began going to district school when about six years old. At fifteen he left the school, as his parents were unable to provide further instruction. Then he began work for himself. He entered a grocery in Buffalo, and learned the business. He learned it well, and in 1874 set up for himself as a grocer. He began by paying heavy rent for quarters at Nos. 301-305 Elk street. Eight years later he bought the building, a large four-story brick structure. He is now sole owner of the property, does a large grocery, flour, and feed business employing seven clerks, and is one of the best known merchants of South Buffalo.

Mr. Lamy gave his grocery undivided attention until 1886, when he became a heavy stockholder in the Magnus Beck Brewing Co. He served the company as its president for nearly four years. During his administration a new brewery was erected, at a cost of nearly a quarter of a million dollars, Mr. Lamy acting as chairman of the building committee until the structure was completed. In 1895 he sold his stock, and retired from the business. He is extensively interested in real estate at the present time, not as a speculator, but as a conservative investor who believes in Buffalo's future.

Mr. Lamy's life was merely that of a quiet, prosperous business man until 1893. In that year Buffalo rose in revolt against "boss" rule, and to Mr. Lamy, who had never been a candidate for political preferment, there came a summons to office. He received the Republican nomination for state senator in the 30th district, which comprised various wards in the city of Buffalo. He accepted the nomination with reluctance, and only from a feeling that such was his duty in the existing crisis. The year was remarkable in local politics, and one of its most striking incidents was the result of the election in the 30th district. In a constituency having a normal Democratic majority of 4100, Mr. Lamy, the reform candidate, was elected by a plurality of 940. The following winter he had the satisfaction of pressing through the legislature to final enactment measures that restored to Buffalo her rights of home rule. He was the author of other bills of benefit to Buffalo, and in 1895 he was unanimously renominated to the senate, this time in the new 47th district, and was re-elected by a plurality of 3889. In the legislature of 1896 he was the chairman of the senate committee on canals, and a member of two other important committees. Among the measures connected with his name was that making an appropriation for beginning work on the new 74th-regiment armory in Buffalo.

Mr. Lamy is a member of various societies and orders. He is a Mason, and has reached the 32d degree in the order. He is a member of St. Mark's Methodist Church.

*PERSONAL CHRONOLOGY—Charles Lamy was born at East Eden, Erie county, N. Y., May 1, 1849; was educated in the district schools; went to work in a grocery in Buffalo when a boy, and commenced business for himself May 1, 1874, as a grocer; married Magdalena Urban June 10, 1875, and Clara B. Demever June 10, 1885; was president of the Magnus Beck Brewing Co. for nearly four years, retiring from the company in 1895; was elected to the state senate as a Republican in 1893, and was re-elected in 1895.*

* * *

**George L. Lewis** is one of the younger lawyers of Buffalo, but he has been for some time a prominent member of the Erie-county bar. The influence and prestige of a family name justly honored in legal circles and everywhere respected, account in part for his success; but the chief cause must be sought in his own ability and character as developed and tested in years of earnest professional endeavor.

Born in Buffalo four years before the outbreak of the Civil War, Mr. Lewis spent his boyhood and youth in that city. He prepared for college at the Briggs School, Buffalo, entering Yale in the fall of 1875, and graduating therefrom with the class of '79. The superiority of a law school over office training in the attainment of legal knowledge is now commonly conceded; but Mr. Lewis had the best of reasons for preferring the latter method because he had the best of practical schools in his father's office. Judge Lewis was then at the height of his fame as a successful attorney, and his magnificent practice brought to his office all the material that a student of law could desire. With such a preceptor and such a field of study, Mr. Lewis could not fail to make rapid progress, and he was able to obtain admittance to the bar in 1881 after devoting to the task much less time than is commonly consumed in a law school.

Mr. Lewis began practice January 1, 1882, with his father and Adelbert Moot, under the firm name of Lewis, Moot & Lewis. When the senior member of the partnership became justice of the Supreme Court of the state on January 1, 1883, and thus withdrew from the firm, the remaining partners continued their association under the style Lewis & Moot until January 1, 1890. On that day Loran L. Lewis, Jr., was admitted to the firm, and the old name of Lewis, Moot & Lewis was revived. Since September

1, 1894, George L. Lewis and his brother Loran have
practiced together under the style Lewis & Lewis.

This firm, as might be inferred from its origin
and history, has been altogether successful, and now
enjoys a large and growing practice of a very desirable kind. George L. Lewis rarely appears in court,
devoting his time to the office part of
the work. Actual litigation in open
court usually forms a small proportion of
an attorney's labor, and Mr. Lewis is so
situated that he need not take part in
the contested work of his firm. He has
been forced by the nature and extent of
his practice to acquaint himself with all
branches of the law; but he has paid
special attention to the law of real property, and to banking and general corporation law. This specialization is
consistent with his tastes, and is also
desirable because of the fact that a large
part of Lewis & Lewis's business has to
do with real-estate titles and transfers,
and with corporation affairs.

Viewing the man rather than the lawyer for a moment, we may note the fact
that Mr. Lewis is a great lover of
horses, and knows their points from A
to Z. For several years he was an
active member of the Buffalo Polo Club.
He has long been interested in photog-
raphy, and has attained much skill in an
art that is not so easy as it seems, if
only the best results are accepted. His
mind has a somewhat remarkable mechanical bent, and grasps at once the
essential points of a complicated machine. In political belief Mr. Lewis
has always been a Republican, though
he has not taken a prominent part in
politics. He could hardly be called a clubman, as
his tastes are not such as find satisfaction in the
routine life of the average club; but he belongs to
the University, Buffalo, Ellicott, and Country clubs,
and is *persona grata* at all of them.

*PERSONAL CHRONOLOGY—George Lester
Lewis was born at Buffalo May 11, 1857; graduated
from Yale College in 1879; was admitted to the bar in
1881; married Nellie Augusta Sweet of Buffalo May
11, 1883; has practiced law in Buffalo since 1881.*

***

**Alfred Lyth** was but six years of age when he
moved to Buffalo from England with his parents.
The family was in humble circumstances, and no one
who saw the little lad at that time, in homemade

clothes of cheap material, could have dreamed that
before many years he would make his influence felt
in the whole community. But he possessed a habit
of industry, and other sterling qualities that are sure
to lead to success. Attending school in the winter,
working at whatever he could turn his hand to during

*GEORGE L. LEWIS*

the other months, and studying evenings the whole
year round, he reached the age of thirteen. It was
then that his father began in a small way the manufacture of sewer and drain tile, hollow brick, and
architectural terra cotta. He needed the help of his
sons, and to this new industry they gave all their time.
The firm of John Lyth & Sons was established before
the boys were of age, and they began laying tile to
educate farmers and gardeners to its use. This firm
was the first in the United States to manufacture hol-
low-clay, fireproof, flat arches and partitions, Francis
Lyth of England being the inventor of the hollow flat
arch. The struggle was a hard one at first, for during two years not more than fifty dollars' worth of
tile was sold. The business increased rapidly, how-

ever, when fairly started, and their plant was for a long time one of the most flourishing in Buffalo. Branch works were established at Wellsville, Ohio, and Angola, N. Y., Alfred Lyth remaining in charge of the firm's business in Buffalo. Fireproof construction has been taken up by the concern, and fireproof

ALFRED LYTH

ing contracts of many of Buffalo's largest buildings have been executed by the firm.

When the Civil War broke out Alfred Lyth was under age, and his parents would not consent to his enlistment under Lincoln's first call for volunteers. A few months later, however, he joined the 100th regiment New York volunteers in the field, and went directly to the front. At the battle of Drury's Bluff, May 16, 1864, he was wounded and taken prisoner in the morning. In an hour he made his escape, but was captured in the afternoon, on the Weldon railroad, with two hundred other wounded soldiers. They were surrounded by rebel cavalry, and taken to jail at Petersburg, Va., afterwards to Andersonville, Ga., and then to Florence, S. C., where they were paroled and

released from prison in December, 1864. Mr. Lyth received an honorable discharge at the close of the war. He afterward enlisted and served seven years in various positions in the 74th regiment, N. G., S. N. Y., resigning as major. He is prominent in Grand Army affairs, having been many times a delegate to state and national encampments, and having acted as inspector general of the organization for New York state, and general in command of the 8th division of the New York State Veterans' parade at Washington, D. C., in the National Encampment of 1892.

As a public-spirited citizen Mr. Lyth is well known. His services as alderman were distinguished by an unswerving honesty of purpose, and his exertions in relation to school matters won for him hearty commendation.

*PERSONAL CHRONOLOGY — Alfred Lyth was born at York, England, April 21, 1843; moved to Buffalo in 1850; was educated in the public schools; enlisted in the 100th regiment New York volunteers in 1864, and served until the close of the war; was a member of the 74th regiment, N. G., S. N. Y., 1867–74; married Kate Kappler of Buffalo December 6, 1869; was supervisor of the old 7th ward of Buffalo, 1872–74, alderman for the same ward, 1884–86, and civil-service commissioner, 1889–91; has been a member of the firm of John Lyth & Sons since 1869; was elected president of the Builders' Exchange, Buffalo, in 1896.*

•••

**John A. McCann** was earning his own living at the age of thirteen; he was a bookkeeper and cashier at the age of sixteen; he was in business on his own account at twenty; and he has been a successful journalist since his thirtieth year. The opportunities that come to one of versatile and vigorous activity have been about the only curriculum in which Mr. McCann has been trained; for his schooling, obtained in his native town of Batavia, N. Y., was confined to the "three R's," with the exception of a course subsequently pursued in a business college. Thus equipped, Mr. McCann entered immediately upon the responsible duties of bookkeeper and cashier in the firm with which he had previously spent three years in a subordinate position. His ambition soon led him to seek a larger field, and the following year found him employed by the firm of Sherman & Barnes, dry-goods merchants in Buffalo. From this time he held positions ranging from clerk to manager in various mercantile firms of that city until 1870, when he moved to Savannah, Ga., to embark in business there.

The means acquired by years of devotion to business finally enabled Mr. McCann to enter a new field of activity whose power and prestige had attracted him. With Norman E. Mack he became joint proprietor of the *Chautauqua Lake Gazette;* and the success of this publication enabled him two years later to found the Jamestown *Sunday Leader.* While this journalistic venture met with immediate favor, Mr. McCann nevertheless desired larger scope for his ability, and he therefore returned to Buffalo as editor of the Buffalo *Times.* This position he has filled at intervals since.

In 1885 Mr. McCann established the *National Coopers' Journal,* a trade publication devoted to the interests of cooperage work in all its branches. This venture was strikingly successful, and the *Journal* has become the recognized organ of the coopers' trade. Mr. McCann has been owner and editor of this publication from the beginning.

While actively engaged in public affairs, as every journalist must be, Mr. McCann has not aspired to political leadership, but is content to be one of the powers behind the throne. He is a Democrat on national lines, but he has not allowed questions of general public policy to interfere with his political conduct in local matters. He believes in the absolute divorce of national and state from local government.

In addition to his journalistic work, other enterprises have engaged Mr. McCann's time and attention. In 1885, in connection with Robert McCann, he planned an exposition in Buffalo, which was held in the Becker building, and proved a notable success. The plan included the practical exhibition of silk weaving, paper making, Japanese handiwork, etc. Before the formation of the Niagara Falls Power Co. Mr. McCann secured from the Ontario council a charter for the use of the Canadian side of the Niagara river and falls for the purpose of generating power. This company, however, had not been fully formed when the charter lapsed, and the right was granted to the present company. Other enterprises have been carried to success under

the guidance of Mr. McCann, such as the Jamestown Permanent Loan and Building Association, whose prosperity does credit to his organizing skill. Mr. McCann is a firm believer in Buffalo and its future greatness, and has given substantial evidence of this faith by large and successful real-estate operations and improvements. His interest in the business has not been exclusively commercial, as he has acquired for himself a handsome residence in the beautiful Elmwood district of Buffalo.

*PERSONAL CHRONOLOGY— John Alexander McCann was born at Batavia, N. Y., September 9, 1850; was educated in public schools and a business college; engaged in mercantile pursuits, 1866–79; became part owner and editor of the "Chautauqua Lake Gazette" in 1879, and founded the Jamestown "Sunday Leader" in 1881; married Chloe Anna Doane of*

JOHN A. McCANN

*Buffalo September 9, 1886; has been editor of the Buffalo "Times" at intervals since 1884; founded the "National Coopers' Journal" in 1885, and has been owner and editor of the same since.*

**William Macomber** has lived in Buffalo during the whole of his professional career, and through his connection with industrial enterprise has identified himself with the progress of the city. Born in Genesee county, New York, less than forty years ago, he began his education in the

WILLIAM MACOMBER

district schools, which have started so many American youths on the road to learning. Later he attended the Cary Collegiate Seminary in his native town of Oakfield, and then took a college-preparatory course at Colgate Academy, Hamilton, N. Y. He next entered the University of Rochester, from which he was graduated in 1885.

To a young man of Mr. Macomber's studious temperament and fondness for painstaking investigation, a professional life naturally seemed attractive, and among the professions the law appealed to him most strongly. He began his legal studies in the office of the late William S. Oliver of Rochester. A little later he moved to Buffalo, and completed his course there in the office of Lewis & Moot.

In January, 1887, Mr. Macomber was admitted to the bar, and in the following March he opened a law office alone, and began the somewhat tedious process of building up a clientage. Possessed of natural mechanical ability, and considerably experienced in machine-shop practice, Mr. Macomber had from the beginning a special fondness for the subject of patent law; and he soon decided that it would be both agreeable and profitable to devote his attention to this specialty. In 1889, therefore, he associated with himself as Washington counsel General E. M. Marble and Robert Mason, both of whom were widely experienced in patent law. Since then Mr. Macomber has confined his practice to this branch of his profession, and has already become a recognized authority on the subject. Since 1893 his Washington associate has been John S. Barker.

The law of patents is exceedingly intricate and confusing, but Mr. Macomber's acquaintance with the subject is at once minute and extensive. For the past six years he has been collecting material for a text-book upon patents and the patent law. His plan involves a detailed study of every enactment relating to the subject on the statute books of the land, and of every case involving such questions reported since the organization of the American patent system. Such an exhaustive treatment of the subject requires long and careful preparation, and it will be some time yet before the work is ready for publication.

Mr. Macomber is lecturer on the subjects of patent law and trade-marks in the Buffalo Law School. He is a careful student of economics, and of the complicated problems involved in the production and exchange of commodities in the United States. He has published a number of essays on such subjects in different magazines and political-science publications. While he takes scant interest in party politics, his continued study of history and economics gives him a peculiar interest in the problems of government. He is a persistent advocate of honest money, of home rule, and of civil-service reform.

Mr. Macomber is a member of Alpha Delta Phi college fraternity, of the American Economic Association, and of the American Institute of Civics. Among local organizations he belongs to the Liberal Club, the Good Government Club, and the Pundit

Club; and he is a member of the Delaware Avenue Baptist Church.

*PERSONAL CHRONOLOGY—William Macomber was born at Oakfield, N. Y., November 4, 1857; was educated in various preparatory schools, and at the University of Rochester, from which he graduated in 1885; was admitted to the bar at Buffalo in January, 1887; married Augusta S. Woodruff of Hamilton, N. Y., May 18, 1887; has practiced law in Buffalo since 1887.*

### Louis Franklin Messer,

prominent at the bar of Buffalo, his native city, spent his boyhood on a farm, and obtained his early education in district schools. Subsequently he completed the public-school course in Buffalo, and in 1878 entered Columbia College, New York city. There he took the complete course in the schools of arts and of political science, and graduated in 1882 with the degree of Ph. B. He was an earnest student, and possessed much literary ability, as is shown by the fact that for two successive years he tried for and captured the much coveted Pheilolexian prize for essay writing.

While yet in college Mr. Messer determined to make the legal profession his life-work; and accordingly during his senior year he availed himself of the privileges of the Columbia Law School, where he attended the lectures of the learned Theodore W. Dwight and John F. Dillon. Immediately after his graduation he entered the law office of James A. Roberts of Buffalo as a student, and in 1884 was admitted to the bar at Rochester.

Mr. Messer's professional career has been singularly free from changes in the matter of business connections. His preceptor, Mr. Roberts, foreseeing the success that awaited Mr. Messer as a lawyer, took him into partnership when he was first admitted to the bar, and the connection has lasted ever since. The clientage of the firm has steadily increased, and the large amount of business committed to its charge has made it necessary, from time to time, to take in new partners. The present style is Roberts, Becker, Ashley, Messer & Orcutt, and the firm is known throughout western New York as one of the strongest and most successful in that part of the state.

Much of the business of the firm is connected with real estate, and from the first Mr. Messer has made a specialty of this branch of the law. His experience in the examination of titles to real property led him to appreciate the advantages of a system of abstracting more nearly perfect and complete than any hitherto existent; and in 1891 he organized the Erie County Guaranteed Search Co., one of the first title companies in Buffalo. Of this company he was one of the original incorporators, and has been president from the beginning. He devotes much time to the supervision of its affairs, while still taking an active part in the work of the legal firm with which he is connected.

Seeing the advantage to any city of a thriving suburban population, Mr. Messer for several years has been largely interested in various projects for

*LOUIS FRANKLIN MESSER*

the improvement of the outlying districts of Buffalo. He is a director and secretary of the Bellevue Land & Improvement Co., and holds similar offices in the Buffalo, Bellevue & Lancaster Railway Co.

In his private and social life Mr. Messer is a fine type of the cultured gentleman. Although his many business and professional duties leave him scant leisure for purely literary or artistic pursuits, he has the tastes of a scholar and a connoisseur. His fondness for literature is not confined to the English tongue nor to the present day. The ancient Latin and Greek classics, and the modern writings of French, German, and Italian authors, all claim a share of his attention. His favorite subjects are history and biography, the lives of nations and the lives of individuals; for he agrees with Pope that "the proper study of mankind is man." Mr. Messer is also a warm lover of the fine arts, and is a Fellow of the Buffalo Society of Artists. His club life consists of membership in the Buffalo and University clubs. He is a life member of the Buffalo Republican League.

*PERSONAL CHRONOLOGY—Louis Franklin Messer was born at Buffalo February 1, 1856; graduated from Columbia College in 1882, and was admitted to the bar in 1884; organized the Erie County Guaranteed Search Co. in 1891, and has been president thereof since; has practiced law in Buffalo since 1884.*

* * *

**William J. Morgan** has been active in his country's service ever since he put aside his schoolbooks in the hour of the country's need, and became a volunteer soldier in the War of the Rebellion.

Born in Canada somewhat more than fifty years ago, Mr. Morgan was taken to Buffalo in his tenth year, and has lived there ever since. He was a senior in the Central High School, preparing for college, when the outbreak of the Civil War caused a change in his plans. He enlisted in the 116th New York volunteer infantry as a private, serving until the close of the war, and receiving successive promotions, for attention to duty and meritorious conduct, through the subordinate ranks to that of captain. He participated in all the battles in which his regiment took part, including that of Cedar Creek, where General Sheridan, by his famous ride from Winchester and his wonderful influence over his men, changed a terrible defeat into a glorious victory. In the attack on Port Hudson May 27, 1863, Mr. Morgan led the fascine carriers, who formed the advance of the assaulting column, composed of volunteers for the desperate undertaking, and was wounded four times.

At the close of the war Captain Morgan, with several other retiring officers, engaged in the customs service, with a view to breaking up a desperate gang of smugglers that had overrun the northern frontier and were defying the customs officials. In this work he had several combats quite as dangerous as any experienced during the war; and in one of them he was seriously injured, coming to so close quarters with his adversary that his clothes were set on fire by the discharge of the smuggler's weapon.

In 1869 Mr. Morgan joined the forces of the Buffalo *Commercial Advertiser*, and for twenty years served on its editorial staff. During the railroad riots of 1877, when the police and militia of Buffalo failed to maintain order, the veterans of the late war volunteered their services, and Captain Morgan was elected their commander. The presence of this brave and experienced body of men under arms did much to prevent in Buffalo the destructive scenes enacted elsewhere during the same riotous period.

In 1880 Mr. Morgan was appointed canal appraiser by Governor Cornell, and was elected chairman of the board by his associates. The record of this board during their three and a half years of service was so free from the scandal that had attached to some preceding boards that the governor, in his last message to the legislature, complimented them for the care with which they had kept their important trust, and guarded the interests committed to them. Mr. Morgan was made collector of customs for the district of Buffalo Creek in 1889, and held the position for over four years, making one of the best collectors the port ever had.

In January, 1894, Comptroller James A. Roberts appointed Mr. Morgan to the responsible position of deputy state comptroller, which he still fills. How faithfully he has discharged its duties may be judged from the following extract from the comptroller's report for the year 1895: "In view of my recent protracted illness and long absence from official duty, I desire thus publicly to express my appreciation and recognition of the satisfactory manner in which my able and efficient deputy, Colonel William J. Morgan, performed the very responsible and laborious work of this department."

Mr. Morgan has taken great interest in all measures for enhancing the prosperity of the city of Buffalo, in whose future greatness he has always been a firm believer. He was one of the original promoters of the Buffalo & Jamestown railroad, now the Buffalo & Southwestern. He took an active part for years in the Commercial Union, an organization formed for the purpose of freeing the canals from tolls and securing their improvement, and productive of great good to the canal commerce of Buffalo. He has been secretary of the Buffalo grade-crossing commission from the beginning, and has taken a prominent part in its important work.

Mr. Morgan is a member of Queen City Lodge, F. & A. M., and Keystone Chapter, R. A. M., as well as William Richardson Post, G. A. R., and the Military Order of the Loyal Legion. He belongs to the Buffalo and Ellicott clubs, Buffalo, the Albany Club, Albany, and the Knickerbocker Club of New York city. He is a member of the Richmond Avenue Methodist Church of Buffalo.

*PERSONAL CHRONOLOGY—*
*William James Morgan was born near Peterboro, Canada, October 16, 1840; moved to Buffalo in 1850, and was educated in the public schools there; served in the Union army, 1862-65; married Mary C. Reese of Buffalo September 23, 1869; was on the editorial staff of the Buffalo "Commercial Advertiser," 1869-80; was appointed canal appraiser in 1880, and collector of customs for the district of Buffalo Creek in 1889; has been deputy state comptroller since January, 1894.*

•••

**Edmund Janes Plumley,** during the twenty-odd years that he has practiced law in Buffalo, has devoted the energies of an able and a vigorous mind unremittingly to his profession, and has attained no slight degree of distinction therein.

Mr. Plumley was born in Seneca county, New York, rather more than fifty years ago. After the usual preliminary training in district schools, at the age of fifteen he entered Middlebury Academy, Wyoming, N. Y., where he studied for one year. He then completed his preparatory studies at Genesee Wesleyan Seminary, Lima, N. Y., and afterward spent two years at Genesee College, now Syracuse University. His ambition for a full college course, however, was not to be gratified. More than once he had been obliged to interrupt his studies and spend a short time in teaching, in order to obtain the means for further study; and after completing his sophomore year he was compelled to leave college.

During the next few years Mr. Plumley taught in different public and private schools; and finally, in the spring of 1868, he entered the law office of Hiram C. Day of Buffalo as a student, thus fulfilling a long-cherished purpose. He remained with Mr. Day four years, during which he was duly admitted to the bar. In February, 1872, he received an

unsolicited and wholly unexpected appointment as deputy city clerk, and for three years he faithfully discharged the duties of this position.

In March, 1875, Mr. Plumley retired from the city clerk's office, and associated himself with E. C. Robbins in the law firm of Robbins & Plumley, thus

*WILLIAM J. MORGAN*

beginning the practice of his profession. Since the dissolution of this partnership in 1877, Mr. Plumley has been associated with William M. Hawkins in the firm of Hawkins & Plumley, afterwards enlarged by the admission of Clinton B. Gibbs, and known as Hawkins, Plumley & Gibbs; and with George L. Kingston in the firm of Plumley & Kingston. On May 1, 1894, he formed a partnership with Irving W. Cole, under the name of Plumley & Cole, which still exists. During all these years Mr. Plumley's practice has steadily increased, and he has established a reputation for legal ability and devotion to the interests of his clients that any man might be proud to possess. This success has been fairly won, for he has devoted himself wholly to his profession.

With the exception of his three years' service as deputy city clerk, Mr. Plumley has never held a political office. Yet he maintains an active interest in public affairs, and is willing to give both time and talent to promote the welfare of the community. This fact was abundantly proved by the active part

EDMUND JAMES PLUMLEY

that he took, several years ago, in the investigation of the condition of the school department of Buffalo. This investigation resulted at once in the establishment of the present examining board, to decide on the qualifications of candidates for teachers in the public schools of the city, and in the creation of a strong sentiment favoring a municipal board of education.

Mr. Plumley was one of the charter members of the First Congregational Church of Buffalo. This church was organized in 1880, and he has acted as clerk of its board of trustees for fifteen years. He is also a Mason, holding membership in Queen City Lodge, No. 358, of Buffalo. Mr. Plumley possesses the tastes of a student, and has read widely and

thought deeply. Literature and general history are especially congenial to him, and he has devoted some attention to theological questions. This latter taste he inherits, no doubt, from his father, the Rev. Albert Plumley, who was for nearly forty-five years a well-known Methodist clergyman in western New York. Mr. Plumley has written a number of poems that have been published, and that evince no small amount of literary ability.

PERSONAL CHRONOLOGY— Edmund James Plumley was born at Canoga, Seneca county, N. Y., October 7, 1845; attended Genesee Wesleyan Seminary, Lima, N. Y., and Genesee College (now Syracuse University); taught school at intervals, 1863–48; was admitted to the bar in 1871; married Flora Ella Crandall of Buffalo July 9, 1874; was deputy city clerk of Buffalo, 1872–75; has practiced law in Buffalo since 1875.

William Warren Potter long ago obtained a place in the front rank of the medical profession: and he has since strengthened his position by skill and judgment as a surgeon, by acumen and originality as a student of medical science, by accuracy and depth as a writer on medical subjects. His career was foreshadowed, as to its success and the line of achievement, by his lineage, since his father, his grandfather, and his great-grandfather, not to mention collateral issue, were all distinguished physicians.

Dr. Potter was born in what is now Wyoming county, on the last day of the year 1838. His preparatory studies were carried on in private schools, at Arcade (N. Y.) Seminary, and at Genesee Seminary and College, at Lima, N. Y. His medical education was obtained at Buffalo University Medical College, from which he graduated in February, 1859. In the spring of that year he formed a partnership for the practice of medicine with his uncle, Dr. M. E. Potter, of Cowlesville, N. Y.

The Civil War broke out two years after this, and Dr. Potter made haste to offer his services to the government. He passed the examination of the army board at Albany a few days after Fort Sumter was taken, and in the summer of 1861 was commissioned by Governor Morgan assistant surgeon of the 49th regiment New York volunteers, Colonel D. D. Bidwell, which he had helped to organize in

Buffalo. He accompanied this regiment throughout its early eventful career with the Army of the Potomac, during the peninsular campaign, under McClellan in Maryland, and under Burnside in the Fredericksburg disaster. Left in charge of wounded soldiers while the army was retreating to Harrison's Landing, Dr. Potter fell into the hands of the enemy in June, 1862, and had an interesting interview with the redoubtable "Stonewall" Jackson. He was confined in Libby prison, but was released among the first exchanges, and rejoined his regiment after an absence of only three weeks. In December, 1862, after the battle of Fredericksburg, he was promoted to the rank of surgeon, and served with the 57th regiment New York volunteers during the Chancellorsville and Gettysburg campaigns. Soon after the battle of Gettysburg he was assigned to the charge of the 1st division hospital, 2d army corps, and continued upon that duty until mustered out of service with his regiment at the close of the war. He was brevetted by the President of the United States, for faithful and meritorious service, lieutenant colonel of United States volunteers; and by the governor of New York state, for like reasons, lieutenant colonel of New York volunteers.

Returning to civil life, Dr. Potter followed his profession at Batavia, Genesee county, for a time, but soon returned to Buffalo, where he has since resided. His professional taste, cultivated largely by association with his father, who was also his preceptor, early led him into the field of surgery, and he has performed many of the more important operations in both military and civil practice. Of late years he has given his entire attention to the treatment of the diseases of women, and has performed many difficult operations in the department of gynecic, pelvic, and abdominal surgery.

Dr. Potter belongs to many professional societies, in accordance with this incomplete statement: permanent member of the American Medical Association in 1878, and chairman of its section of obstetrics and diseases of women in 1890; permanent member of the Medical Society of the State of New York, and its president in 1891; member of the Medical Society of Erie County, and its president in 1893; member of the

Buffalo Medical and Surgical Association, and its president in 1886; president of the Buffalo Obstetrical Society, 1884–86; secretary of the American Association of Obstetricians and Gynecologists since 1888; president of the section of gynecology and abdominal surgery of the first Pan-American Medical Congress in 1893. He is examiner in obstetrics for the New York state examining and licensing board; president of the national confederation of state medical examining and licensing boards; consulting gynecologist at the Women's Hospital, Buffalo; and a companion of the Military Order of the Loyal Legion of the United States.

Dr. Potter has been a voluminous contributor to medical literature, and a list of his writings would suggest by its length the Homeric catalogue of ships. Since July, 1888, he has been managing editor of

*WILLIAM WARREN POTTER*

the Buffalo *Medical Journal*. He also edits the annual volume of *Transactions* of the American Association of Obstetricians and Gynecologists, and is the author of the history of the medical profession and its institutions, as related to Erie county, in "Our County and Its People."

*PERSONAL CHRONOLOGY— William Warren Potter was born at Strykersville, N. Y., December 31, 1838 ; was educated at Arcade Seminary, and Genesee Seminary and College, Lima, N. Y.;*

EDWARD C. RANDALL

*graduated from the Buffalo University Medical College in 1859; married Emily A. Bostwick of Lancaster, N. Y., March 23, 1859; engaged in the practice of medicine at Cowlesville, N. Y., 1859–61; served as a surgeon in the Union army, 1861–65; has followed his profession in Buffalo since 1866.*

\*\*\*

**Edward C. Randall** has impressed himself upon the community in which he lives as a man of unusual force and energy. He is a well-known lawyer, and since his admission to the bar thirteen years ago he has figured as counsel in many important legal controversies. He is still so young that the success already achieved may fairly be regarded as the forerunner of continued and higher achievements.

Mr. Randall was born thirty-six years ago in the town of Ripley, N. Y., and had the usual experience of a country boy seeking a liberal education. He received his preliminary training in the district school and academy of his native place, and was prepared for college under private tuition. He pursued his classical studies at Allegheny College, Meadville, Penn. In 1879 he entered the office of Morris & Lambert at Fredonia, N. Y., and commenced a course of legal study. He subsequently moved to Dunkirk, and completed his preparation for the bar in the office of Holt & Holt. After four years spent in mastering the theory and practice of the law, Mr. Randall was admitted to the bar by the Supreme Court April 3, 1883, at Rochester. He at once opened an office in Dunkirk, and met with unusual success from the start. The professional field there was limited, however, and he decided to seek a larger sphere of labor. Turning over his office and business to Eugene Cary, a local attorney, in the fall of 1884 he moved to Buffalo, in whose future growth and development he had great faith, and formed a partnership with Joseph P. Carr, under the firm name of Carr & Randall. Mr. Carr retired from the profession two years later, and Mr. Randall continued to practice alone for the next ten years. He formed a partnership with Jeremiah J. Hurley on January 1, 1896, becoming senior member of the firm of Randall & Hurley.

Mr. Randall first became prominent in Buffalo for his celebrated defense of Frank Curcio, who was tried for murder in 1887. For five years Mr. Randall was counsel for the receivers of the Tonawanda Valley & Cuba railroad ; and he acted in a similar capacity for the supply creditors of the New York, Lake Erie & Western railroad, and participated in the reorganization of that company.

In politics Mr. Randall has been an active Republican. A graceful and an earnest speaker, he has taken the stump in behalf of his party in the various campaigns of the last twelve years. He has never accepted a nomination for political office, preferring to devote his entire attention to the building up of a legal clientage. Believing in the great destiny in store for Buffalo, he has invested largely and successfully in real estate in that city. He is a loyal citizen, interested in many charities, and an earnest promoter of every measure that tends to the permanent welfare of the Queen City. He is a member of the Masonic order, and is widely known in social circles.

*PERSONAL CHRONOLOGY— Edward Caleb Randall was born at Ripley, Chautauqua county, N. Y., July 19, 1860; was educated at Ripley Academy and Allegheny College; studied law at Fredonia and Dunkirk, and was admitted to the bar at Rochester in 1883; has practiced law in Buffalo since 1884.*

* * *

**Adolph Rebadow** was born in Buffalo in the year of Lincoln's first election as President, and has always lived in the Queen City of the Lakes. His education was obtained chiefly in the common schools, and even these he left at an early age. He made up for the lack of academic training, however, by self-instruction. For several years he worked in the Grosvenor Library, Buffalo, and his experience there fitted him to enter upon the study of law.

Mr. Rebadow decided as early as his eighteenth year what his life-work was to be, and he began at that age the great task of learning law. Entering the office of Marshall, Clinton & Wilson as a student, he passed the bar examinations in three years. He began practice at once, opening an office in the American block, Buffalo.

After carrying on his profession alone for about four years, he associated himself, in 1885, with George T. Quinby and Willis H. Meads, under the firm name of Quinby, Meads & Rebadow. This partnership was altogether successful, and the firm conducted a large practice for upwards of eight years, or until the fall of 1893. At that time Mr. Rebadow returned to his old preceptors, Charles D. Marshall and Spencer Clinton, forming with them the present firm of Marshall, Clinton & Rebadow. As Messrs. Marshall and Clinton are veteran members of the Erie-county bar, and two of the strongest and most influential lawyers of western New York, their invitation to the younger man to ally himself with them must be regarded as highly complimentary to Mr. Rebadow's legal capacity. He has fulfilled their expectations, and has done his part in conducting successfully the large and important practice with which the new firm has been favored. The numerous clients of the firm

display the same confidence in Mr. Rebadow that Mr. Marshall and Mr. Clinton continue to exhibit. For so young a man, Mr. Rebadow has appeared in many important trials before juries. Few men of his years, in fact, have conducted so many momentous cases in the Appellate Division, the Court of Appeals, and the Circuit Court of the United States; and the results have been such as to justify the confidence reposed in him by his clients and his partners. Quick, alert, persuasive, ever the advocate when his clients' interests are involved, Mr. Rebadow has attained before juries and judges a degree of success that is easy to understand. Personally he is very likable, and his genial, vivacious temperament endears him to a host of friends.

*PERSONAL CHRONOLOGY— Adolph Rebadow was born at Buffalo June 4, 1860; was*

ADOLPH REBADOW

*educated in the public schools of the city; studied law in the office of Marshall, Clinton & Wilson, and was admitted to the bar in June, 1881; has practiced law in Buffalo since.*

**Joseph P. Schattner** is a genuine Buffalonian. He was born and educated in that city,
and all his business interests are connected with it.
In the thirty-odd years of his career he has seen the
place attain an enviable prominence in the great
sisterhood of American cities, and more than fulfill

*JOSEPH P. SCHATTNER*

the ardent prophecies of its founders. In 1859, the
year of his birth, Buffalo was in the midst of the
hard times following the panic of 1857. This
interruption of the prosperity hitherto characteristic
of the growing city since the crash of 1837, had
been caused by speculation and general financial
recklessness, with inflation and depreciation of the
currency. The acme was reached when specie payments were suspended. The banks succumbed, real
estate sank until it was said "the whole town was not
worth a dollar," and numberless failures followed.
The financial stringency that prevailed was over-
shadowed by the greater anxiety of approaching war.

Mr. Schattner's parents were among the many
sufferers from this depression, and were unable to
give him more than a few years at school before
he was thrown upon his own resources. He attended
St. Mary's Roman Catholic School until the age
of twelve, and then entered the employ of Abram
Bartholomew, a Buffalo lawyer, as office boy. Amid
the law books and the legal atmosphere of the office,
the young lad soon became ambitious to
practice law. This proved to be no mere
air castle. In due time he became a student in the same office where he had
served in the humbler capacity, and at
the age of twenty-one he was admitted
to the bar. He has practiced in Buffalo
ever since, and is counted among the
most successful lawyers of the city, with
a clientage that few men of his age can
boast.

The brewing and malting business is
one of the oldest interests of Buffalo.
Since the time when the third German
settler built a brewery, and gave his
neighbors the first taste of their favorite
beverage made at home, the industry
has grown steadily, and has now reached
enormous proportions. The situation of
the city, in the center of a large barley-
growing district, is favorable to the manufacture. Among the largest establishments is the plant of the Broadway
Brewing & Malting Co. Mr. Schattner
was one of the charter members of this
concern, and is its secretary and attorney. In the eight years of its existence the output has increased from
10,000 to 25,000 barrels a year. The
capital stock is $100,000, while the
assets are $300,000, and the liabilities
$125,000.

Mr. Schattner has also been for several
years secretary of the Erie County Natural Gas &
Fuel Co., Limited. This company was organized
in 1891 with a capital stock of $500,000. It has
a franchise of the entire city, and has piped about
forty miles of streets. The gas is obtained from
wells in Canada, and is conducted across the river
by two pipes.

Mr. Schattner was nominated on the Democratic
ticket as a delegate to the constitutional convention
of 1894, but he shared the fate of his party that
year. He is a member of the Democratic state
committee from the 48th senatorial district, and is
prominent in the councils of his party. He is a
member of St. Mary's Roman Catholic Church, and
belongs to the Catholic Benevolent League.

*PERSONAL CHRONOLOGY—Joseph Peter Schattner was born at Buffalo August 5, 1859; was educated at St. Mary's Roman Catholic School; studied law in the office of Abram Bartholomew, and was admitted to the bar in 1881; has been secretary of the Broadway Brewing & Malting Co. since 1886, and of the Erie County Natural Gas & Fuel Co., Limited, since 1893; has practiced law in Buffalo since 1881.*

***

**Allen D. Scott** has been a factor for many years in the affairs of western New York, and especially of Erie and Cattaraugus counties. He was born not far from the boundary between the two counties, in Andrew Jackson's first administration. His education was threefold, consisting of scholastic training in various institutions, of teaching in the public schools (not the least part of any man's education), and of legal study. First attending the district school in the town of Otto, Cattaraugus county, he continued his studies at the old Springville Academy, and completed them at Lima, N. Y. After teaching the public school at Ellicottville, Cattaraugus county, in 1853, he read law for several years, and was admitted to the bar in 1857.

Mr. Scott commenced practice at once in Ellicottville. His first partnership was formed with Judge Nelson Cobb, under the firm name of Cobb & Scott. After Judge Cobb went to Kansas, Mr. Scott practiced with Patrick H. Jones until the latter went into the army in 1861. Mr. Scott then associated himself with Addison G. Rice, and continued with him until 1868, when Mr. Rice moved to New York city. William G. Laidlaw, afterward district attorney of Cattaraugus county and member of congress, was Mr. Scott's next partner. Scott, Laidlaw & McVey and Scott, Laidlaw & McNair were later associations.

This brief summary of Mr. Scott's partnership connections has taken us past some important events in his public career. In 1857, the year of his admission to the bar, he was appointed surrogate of Cattaraugus county by Governor E. D. Morgan. He was elected to the same office in the fall of that year, and was again elected in the fall of 1861. Legislative as well as juridical honors came

to him, since he was elected to the state senate in 1869 from the 32d district, composed of Cattaraugus and Chautauqua counties. The next important service to which he was called by the public was that involved in his election as county judge of Cattaraugus county in the fall of 1875. He discharged so faithfully the duties of this office that he was re-elected in 1881, and thus served another term of six years.

In May, 1892, Judge Scott brought to a close his long residence in Ellicottville, and moved to Buffalo. His departure was a decided loss to the smaller place. Among the benefits accruing to the town wholly or in part through him may be mentioned its railroad facilities. Judge Scott became very much interested in the construction of the Rochester & State Line railroad, now the

*ALLEN D. SCOTT*

Buffalo, Rochester & Pittsburg, and he was largely instrumental in causing the line to go through Ellicottville. He was the attorney of the road for several years.

Judge Scott has spent the greater part of his life in the country, and has naturally been interested in farming. He has given special attention to the process of preserving green fodder called ensilage, and has built several silos. He is a firm believer in the practicability of raising ensilage for winter fodder.

———

*SIMON SEIBERT*

For about two years after going to Buffalo Judge Scott was connected with the law firm of Sprague, Morey, Sprague & Brownell. In 1893 he became one of the counsel for the executors of the David S. Ingalls estate. This estate amounted to about $700,000, and there was a sharp contest over the will. When the Alleghany & Kinzua Railroad Co. got into financial straits, in 1892, Judge Scott was appointed receiver, and he is still operating the road.

For the last two years Judge Scott has been a lecturer in the Buffalo Law School. He has taken great interest and pleasure in the discharge of this duty, and has the prosperity of the school very much at heart.

*PERSONAL CHRONOLOGY* —*Allen Darius Scott was born at Springville, N. Y., January 15, 1831 ; was educated at Springville Academy and Genesee Wesleyan Seminary, Lima, N. Y.; was admitted to the bar in 1857, and began practice at Ellicottville, N. Y.; married Elizabeth Louisa Noyes of North Collins, N. Y., in September, 1854, and Vina Cox of Otto, N. Y., in May, 1867 ; was elected surrogate of Cattaraugus county in 1855 and again in 1861; was state senator, 1870-71, and county judge, 1876-87; has operated the Alleghany & Kinzua railroad as receiver since 1892; has practiced law in Buffalo since 1892.*

\*\*\*

**Simon Seibert** has attained unusual political popularity, having represented his fellow-citizens in both houses of the state legislature, as well as in the state and other conventions of the Republican party. Indeed, for the last ten years or thereabouts he has been sent as a delegate to almost all the important conventions of his party. He was born in Buffalo, and has always lived there. At the age of five he was sent to the public schools, where his general education was received. Having completed the course of instruction there, he entered Bryant & Stratton's Business College, from which he graduated in 1878. The knowledge thus obtained was first put to practical use in his father's coal business. Later he carried on a men's furnishing store at East Buffalo for several years, and his prudence and sagacity brought their due reward of success.

In 1889 Mr. Seibert retired from business to accept an appointment as United States gauger under President Harrison. When the Democrats came into power in 1893 he found himself free to embark in business once more, and became connected with the Magnus Beck Brewing Co. as traveling salesman, a position that he still holds. He is also president of the Buffalo Clearing Co.

Mr. Seibert has for many years interested himself actively in the welfare of the Republican party. He has been one of its bulwarks in the section of Buffalo known as the East Side, and has been president of the East Side Republican League. No man in that part of the city has been more constantly engaged in the service of the party, or more continuously honored by preferment in its councils. His devotion to public affairs was rewarded, in 1893, by a nomination for member of assembly; and though the normal Democratic majority in his district was 600, and the opposing candidate was one whose popularity had been attested in several former elections, Mr. Seibert was elected by a majority of 1356 votes. After a year's faithful service at the state capital he was renominated in the fall of 1894, and was elected by an increased majority. At the end of his second term he received the higher honor of a nomination to the upper house of the state legislature from the 48th senatorial district. The convention that established his candidacy was composed of representative business men, and he was nominated by acclamation. In 1892 Grover Cleveland had carried this district by a majority of 2000 votes; but Mr. Seibert was elected by a majority of 2206, though he lost nearly 1000 votes under the new ballot law. In 1896 he was elected an alternate delegate to the Republican national convention at St. Louis.

Mr. Seibert's uninterrupted success may well lead one to look for the secret of his political popularity. He himself attributes it chiefly, not to any remarkable genius on his part, but to the simple fact that he has always treated his constituents fairly and honestly, and has not made promises that he was not able to fulfill. In this way he has gained the confidence and respect of all, and those who have known him longest are his best friends — a statement that speaks volumes for the character of any man of whom it can be made.

Mr. Seibert is a member of Mystic Star Lodge, Independent Order of Odd Fellows, and of Millard Fillmore Lodge, Knights of Pythias. He belongs, also, to the Teutonia Maennerchor, one of the chief musical societies of Buffalo; and he has been president of the Sprudel Fishing Club and the Silver King Fishing Club.

*PERSONAL CHRONOLOGY —*
*Simon Seibert was born at Buffalo September 12, 1857; was educated in public schools and Bryant & Stratton's Business College; was in business, 1878–89; was United States gauger, 1889–93; was elected member of assembly in 1893 and 1894, and state senator in 1895; has been connected with the Magnus Beck Brewing Co., Buffalo, since 1893.*

**Albert J. Sigman** was born in Cattaraugus county, New York, somewhat more than forty years ago. His early education was obtained in the public schools of his native town of Cattaraugus, and he also received the benefit of a classical course at Chamberlain Institute, Randolph, N. Y. Beyond that his scholastic training did not go. After leaving Chamberlain Institute, however, Mr. Sigman devoted considerable time to teaching, and he regards this experience as constituting not the least valuable part of his education. He taught ten terms altogether, beginning the occupation when he was only seventeen years of age. At first his field of labor was in the district schools of Cattaraugus county, but his success was such that he was soon placed in charge of more important work, and he finally became principal of a large school at Otto.

ALBERT J. SIGMAN

As Walter Scott deemed journalism an excellent cane but a poor crutch, so Mr. Sigman looked upon country teaching as good enough for a makeshift but not suitable for a permanent calling. All through his career as a teacher he was devoting his days and nights, so far as he could, to the study of law. He was registered at an office, and doubtless derived some benefit from his experience there; but his legal education was acquired almost entirely by himself, without the aid of school or preceptor. Knowledge won in that way is often hard to get; but it sticks when once acquired. Mr. Sigman, at all events, found the self instructing method of reading law highly effective, and he had no difficulty in passing the bar examination in Buffalo in June, 1877.

Opening an office in that city January 1, 1878, Mr. Sigman has since practiced his profession there. He has traveled extensively in Europe and in this country, but his main interests have been in Buffalo, and his professional work has been done in western New York. If repeated victories in contested cases may be made the basis of judgment, he must be regarded as a lawyer of marked ability and success. He has carried on his work from the beginning without associates. He has not specialized his field, but conducts a general practice, and devotes himself alike to court work and to office consultation. His profession brought him into connection a few years ago with certain real-estate operations of some magnitude, and he has since devoted a good deal of profitable time to such interests.

In political matters Mr. Sigman's sympathies were formerly Democratic. He was a charter member of the Cleveland Democracy, and was one of the executive committee that organized the movement. He is a strong protectionist, however, and when Mr. Cleveland came out in favor of a liberalized tariff Mr. Sigman resigned from the Cleveland Democracy, and joined the Buffalo Republican League. He has never been a candidate for public office, though his name has often been mentioned in connection with political nominations. He usually makes speeches, and otherwise takes an active part in campaign work.

Mr. Sigman has been much interested in Free Masonry. He is a Past Master of Hiram Lodge, No. 105, F. & A. M., and a member of the Buffalo Chapter of Royal Arch Masons. He is also Vice Grand of Red Jacket Lodge, No. 238, I. O. O. F.

*PERSONAL CHRONOLOGY—Albert Jay Sigman was born at Cattaraugus, N. Y.; was educated in district schools and Chamberlain Institute, Randolph, N. Y.; taught school, studied law, and was admitted to the bar at Buffalo in June, 1877; has practiced law in Buffalo since January 1, 1878.*

* * *

**Jonathan L. Slater,** prominent at the bar of Buffalo, and widely known in connection with church affairs, was born somewhat less than forty years ago on a farm in Chautauqua county. He started in life with the latent advantage of excellent descent, his ancestors having come to this country from England in colonial times, and having taken an active part in the revolutionary war. Samuel Slater, who built a cotton mill at Pawtucket, R. I., in 1790, and thus established the cotton industry on this side of the Atlantic, was a member of the family; and Hosea Ballou, the eminent Universalist clergyman, belonged to another branch.

Mr. Slater's earliest instruction was obtained from his maternal great-grandmother, who was related to John Quincy Adams and was a schoolmate of his. Further education was acquired at irregular intervals, as the exigencies of farm work permitted, in the public schools of his native town and in Ellington Academy. Upon leaving the farm his ambition to obtain at least a part of the higher education induced him to enter Chamberlain Institute, where he paid his way largely by means of tutoring. He graduated from the institute with high standing in 1880. He then began the study of law in the office of B. F. Congdon, Randolph, and engaged in teaching at the same time. These two occupations have constantly been united by young men ambitious to enter the legal domain, and not infrequently with entire success. So it was in the case of Mr. Slater, since he was able, in October, 1883, to pass the bar examinations at Rochester.

Some eighteen months before this Mr. Slater had left Cattaraugus county to seek the wider opportunities and greater promise of a large city. In the office of Morey & Inglehart of Buffalo he found favorable conditions for continuing the study of law; and he remained there several years after his admission to the bar. January 1, 1887, he opened an office on his own account in Buffalo, and has since carried on a successful practice in that city. Mr. Slater's progress in the law has been made quietly, but steadily. He spends much more time in his office than in the court room, and believes in adjusting legal difficulties, whenever possible, without resort to trial. Reason, common sense, and calm discretion are weapons of legal warfare that seem to him not only less expensive than those commonly used, but also much more efficient and generally satisfactory. Court litigation is sometimes inevitable, of course, but in most cases Mr. Slater finds that he can serve the cause of his client best by consultation, study, and other means of settlement outside the court room. His specialty is domestic corporation work, but his range of practice covers a wide field.

The other side of Mr. Slater's life is to be found in his church work and philanthropic pursuits. For a long time he has concerned himself with such matters — not passively, with a languid interest limited to the contribution box, but actively and vitally, and in a direct, personal way. He is a member of the Delaware Avenue Methodist Episcopal Church, and has long been prominent in the beneficent work of that institution. He served on the official board, and was superintendent of the Sunday school from 1887 to 1890.

This branch of church work has particularly interested Mr. Slater, and he has devoted a good deal of time and thought to the betterment and perfection of Sunday-school service. He was a delegate from New York state to the World's Sunday School Convention held in London, England, in June, 1889. He was president of the Buffalo Sunday School Association from December, 1890, to December, 1892. During his administration the work prospered greatly, and the number of schools represented in the association increased from 67 to 103. A larger organization devoted to similar ends, and known as the Erie County Sunday School Association, has been effective in promoting Sunday-school work not only in Erie county, its special field of activity, but throughout the state as well. Mr. Slater was elected president of this association in May, 1893, and has carried on its work with vigor and wisdom.

Other forms of church and charitable organization have received the benefit of Mr. Slater's judgment and executive ability. He has interested himself for many years in the work of the Young Men's Christian Association, and served as a director of the Buffalo branch from 1886 to 1888. He was largely instrumental in the formation of the Prison Gate Mission, though perhaps the chief credit for this work should be assigned to Mrs. Slater. There are only two other institutions of this kind in the United States, though they are most deserving, and constitute splendid examples of practical philanthropy. The purpose of the mission is to establish quarters near the penitentiary, and to meet prisoners at the critical moment of their discharge; to invite them into the mission, where food and lodging may be obtained, and labor provided to cover the expense thus incurred; and afterward to assist the prisoners to begin life anew under favoring auspices. Mr. Slater is a director of the

Buffalo mission. He gives hearty and intelligent support to every kind of charitable work and Christian endeavor.

*PERSONAL CHRONOLOGY* — *Jonathan Lambert Slater was born at Ellington, Chautauqua county, N. Y., March 26, 1857; attended public*

*JONATHAN L. SLATER*

*schools and Ellington Academy, and graduated from Chamberlain Institute, Randolph, N. Y., in 1880; taught school and studied law, and was admitted to the bar in 1883; married Susan A. Jameson of Dublin, Ireland, September 16, 1885; was president of the Buffalo Sunday School Association, 1890–92, and has been president of the Erie County Sunday School Association since 1894; has practiced law in Buffalo since 1884.*

* * *

**Charles D. Stickney** comes of pure English stock. Two hundred years ago, when the population of New England was made up almost entirely of Dissenters from the eastern counties of England, his ancestors emigrated to Massachusetts from the town of Stickney, near Liverpool. The first great Puritan exodus, which ceased half a century before, had brought to this country a people of unswerving religious standard. As Stoughton, the governor of Massachusetts, said, "God sifted a whole nation that He might send choice grain over into this wilder-

*CHARLES D. STICKNEY*

ness." It was among such that the Stickney family was planted. How this "choice grain" flourished, in spite of harsh climate and niggardly soil, one may see from the early records of New England. Thrifty towns and enduring commonwealths sprang up, public education was provided for, and the principles of popular government were successfully put in practice. In commerce, domestic trade, and manufactures New England soon surpassed all the other colonies. It was gathering wealth, numbers, and fortitude for the second great sifting of the Revolution. Meanwhile the fair pasturage lands that dot the rocky surface of Vermont attracted the descendants of the Stickney emigrants, and there they made their home until the early years of this century.

When the Erie canal was opened many new settlers went to western New York. Among them was our Vermont family, and Erie county became and is still their abiding place. The population of the New England colonies was then homogeneous in the extreme, but that of New York was noted for its heterogeneous character. The Dutch and English element predominated, but there were many French Huguenots, Germans, Swedes, Finns, Welsh, and Jews. The names of many of the towns bear permanent witness to the nationality of the people who christened them. The little village of Holland was doubtless so called by some homesick Netherlander, who hoped to prove that there was more in a name than the popular quotation admits. It was in this village that Charles Stickney was born, early in the second half of the century.

The district school furnished his rudimentary education, and he then completed the course offered at Ten Broeck Academy. Deciding to make the law his profession, he undertook the study in the office of Judge Spring of Franklinville. Going to Buffalo in 1879, he continued his studies with Judge Corlett and Judge Hatch, and was admitted to practice in the New York Supreme Court at Rochester in 1882, and in the United States Court three years later. He opened a law office in Buffalo at once, and has been in active practice there ever since. During almost the entire period he has practiced alone, but recently he formed a partnership with Major E. O. Farrar.

In addition to his office duties Mr. Stickney has given a term of service as clerk of the board of supervisors of Erie county, and is at present attorney for the state of New York in the transfer-tax department. His active participation in politics began with the first Harrison campaign. A member of both state and national Republican leagues, he has spoken in every town and ward in Erie county, as well as in many other places in the state. In the second Harrison campaign, as the official organizer for Erie county, he formed over fifty Republican clubs.

Mr. Stickney attends the Lafayette Avenue Presbyterian Church, and belongs to the Masonic fraternity and other similar organizations.

*PERSONAL CHRONOLOGY — Charles D. Stickney was born at Holland, N. Y., August 9, 1857; was educated at Ten Broeck Academy, Franklinville, N. Y.; was admitted to the bar at Rochester in 1882; married Ida M. West of West Valley, N. Y., April 30, 1882; was clerk of the board of supervisors of Erie county in 1888; has been attorney for New York state in the transfer-tax department since 1894; has practiced law in Buffalo since 1882.*

***

**Jared Hyde Tilden** was born in Franklin, Conn., somewhat less than seventy years ago. He moved to the Empire State in boyhood, traversing Long Island sound in a sloop, and proceeding to Buffalo via the Hudson river and Erie canal. Reaching Buffalo in September, 1837, he attended the public schools of the city, and later a private school, until he was nineteen years old. After working for a short time in the office of his father, Thomas B. Tilden, a prominent builder of Buffalo, Jared decided to study medicine and lead a professional life. With this end in view he went to Cincinnati, and attended the Eclectic Medical Institute until June, 1850, when he received the degree of M. D.

After practicing his profession during the summer of 1850 in Westfield, N. Y., with Dr. Alvin Shattuck, he passed the winter of 1850–51 at the Central Medical College, Rochester, as demonstrator of anatomy. He then spent several months visiting the hospitals in New York city, and attending clinics in Cincinnati. In May, 1851, at Pittsburg, Penn., he was elected vice president of the National Eclectic Medical Association. Taking up his residence again in Buffalo in the fall of 1851, Dr. Tilden renewed his connection with Alvin Shattuck in the practice of medicine. Dr. Shattuck withdrew from the partnership after about a year, and Dr. Tilden practiced alone thereafter. In June, 1854, he was commissioned surgeon's mate of the 74th regiment, N. G., S. N. Y., and for the next ten years he was actively interested in the affairs of the National Guard. He was also a prominent member for thirty years of company D, Buffalo City Guards.

People have long ceased to think of Mr. Tilden as a practicing physician. He followed his profession in Buffalo, however, for several years, or until

the fall of 1859, when he formed a partnership in the building business with his father. The two conducted their operations with marked success until 1869, when Thomas B. Tilden died. Since that time Jared H. Tilden has carried on the business alone. He has long been one of the foremost contractors of western New York, and a transcript from his books would convey a fair idea of Buffalo building operations during the last forty years. Mr. Tilden's pay roll has averaged for many years not far from $50,000 annually. He has built many of the finest structures in Buffalo, including the Palace hotel (destroyed by fire), First Presbyterian Church, Delaware Avenue Baptist Church, Star Theatre building, Union Central Life building, the Red Jacket flats, the north wing of the Sisters of Charity Hospital, and a section of the new Buffalo General Hospi-

*JARED HYDE TILDEN*

tal. He has also built many of the notable dwellings of Buffalo. With the exception of three years, he was secretary of the Builders' Exchange, 1869–89; and he is still an active member of that organization.

Having lived in Buffalo the greater part of the last sixty years, Mr. Tilden knows the city thoroughly, and is identified with many of its social institutions. Like other prominent Buffalonians in earlier times, when the volunteer fire companies took the place of latter-day clubs, Mr. Tilden entered the fire depart-

FREDERICK A. VOGT

ment, "running" with Washington engine, No. 5, from 1846 to 1854. He is a life member of the Buffalo Fine Arts Academy, and of the Buffalo Library. For twenty years or more he has belonged to the Buffalo Historical Society. He was one of the original members of the Oakfield Club, a family association on Grand Island, and has been on the board of directors for many years. He has attended the Central Presbyterian Church for forty years, and has been a trustee of the same for twenty years.

PERSONAL CHRONOLOGY — Jared Hyde Tilden was born at Franklin, Conn., April 30, 1828; moved to Buffalo in 1847, and attended public and private schools there; studied medicine in Cincinnati, and took the degree of M. D. in 1850; married Caro-

line Elizabeth Hedge of Buffalo October 4, 1855; practiced medicine in Buffalo, 1854–59; has conducted a building business in Buffalo since 1859.

⁂

**Frederick A. Vogt** has been a teacher for nearly half his life, and a student from the time he became old enough to study at all. The story of his career has two sides, one recording continuous study and self-development, and the other showing continuous success in his profession as a teacher. Though still a young man, he has won his way in the face of serious obstacles to a position in the foremost rank of Buffalo educators.

Mr. Vogt's life has all been spent in Buffalo. He was born there, of Alsatian parentage, and began his education in the Buffalo public schools at the age of six. At twenty-one he graduated from the high school with honors, receiving the Jesse Ketchum gold medal for high standing in the studies of the graduation year. He had taken a classical course, in the expectation of going to college, but his father died during the senior year, and he had to set about earning his own living.

In the September following his graduation from the high school, Mr. Vogt became principal of Public School No. 9, which was then opened as a new school. Two years later he was promoted to the principalship of school No. 26. There he remained for nine years. Then he became professor of English history and literature in the high school. His stay in this position was short; for a few months later Henry P. Emerson, principal of the high school, was elected superintendent of schools, and as one of his first acts in the new office appointed Mr. Vogt to his earlier position. Thus in less than a dozen years Mr. Vogt advanced from the rank of a graduate of the high school to the principalship of the institution.

Mr. Vogt has proved himself a very successful teacher and an excellent administrator. A feature of his work in the Buffalo High School is the variety of broadening influences that he has found it possible to add to the ordinary school routine. The silent educative influences that come from daily contact with fine specimens of art have received particular attention. Casts from antique sculptures are scattered throughout the building in profusion;

and in the chapel there is an excellent collection of pictures by Buffalo artists, lent to the school at the instance of Mr. Vogt by the artists themselves. The stimulus springing from contact with superior minds is also utilized. Many a distinguished visitor to Buffalo is prevailed upon to address the scholars, and the Wednesday-morning talks in chapel form one of the most interesting and valuable features of school life.

Along with his work in the schools, Mr. Vogt has found time to do outside a great deal of what is practically university extension work. He believes in disseminating the benefits and pleasures of knowledge as widely as possible. In particular, he has delivered many lectures on the natural sciences, a department of study in which he is especially interested ; and certain free courses of lectures by him on geology and botany before the Field Club were exceedingly popular and drew large audiences. He was, indeed, one of the founders of this branch of Field Club work.

All this represents but one side of Mr. Vogt's life. There is another side, as was said at the beginning — his work as a student. All the time that he has been so busy as an instructor, he has been patiently and steadily carrying on his own studies, in Hebrew, the classics, natural science, and the higher mathematics, aiming to secure by self-help the practical results of the university course originally planned.

Mr. Vogt is a member of a number of societies, social, scientific, and literary. Among them are the Liberal Club, the Field Club, the Saturn Club, the Buffalo Orpheus, and the Pundit Club.

*PERSONAL CHRONOLOGY.—*
*Frederick Augustus Vogt was born at Buffalo March 24, 1860; was educated in the Buffalo public schools, graduating from the high school in 1881; was appointed principal of Public School No. 9 in September, 1881, principal of school No. 26 in 1883, and professor of English history and literature in the Buffalo High School in March, 1892; has been principal of the high school since January, 1893.*

* * *

**Ellis Webster** has lived a long and busy life, and his home has been in Buffalo ever since he reached manhood's estate. Nothing more vividly calls to mind the marvelous growth of that city and

of the surrounding country than a consideration of the changes that have taken place within the experience of a man still in active life. When Mr. Webster was born, in the town of Eden, Erie county had been in existence but two years, having been formed from Niagara county in 1821. The new county contained only ten post offices and thirteen towns. It was just emerging from a pioneer settlement into a farming community, and comfortable frame houses had begun to take the place of the log cabins of the first settlers.

Among these early pioneers had been four brothers, sons of Hugh Webster, who moved to what is now the village of Eden Valley, then called Tubbs' Hollow, in 1813, the year after the formation of the town of Eden. One of these brothers was Edward Webster, the father of the subject of

*ELLIS WEBSTER*

our sketch. Ellis Webster attended the primitive district school of those early days, and lived the healthful, hardy life of a country boy. But he was ambitious to achieve greater success than the limited opportunities of a rural community could offer, and a few months before attaining his majority he went to Buffalo.

This was in 1844, the year of the "great flood" in Buffalo, and the financial conditions of the city were most favorable for the young man's success. For several years previous to 1840 the population there had barely held its own; the greatest depression prevailed in business circles, and house after house went down in the general panic. The city recovered slowly from the crash, but by 1845 it had regained a healthy financial condition, and from that time increased rapidly in both population and commercial prosperity.

Mr. Webster had been in the city but three years when he began business on his own account as a member of the firm of D. R. Hamlin & Co., conducting a grocery and produce business on Seneca street. Mr. Hamlin furnished most of the capital, but shared the profits equally with his young associate. For over twenty years Mr. Webster carried on the business, in association with George W. Scott for five years.

In 1868 Mr. Webster embarked in the coal trade, and in 1875 extended his business to include the ice industry, thus connecting his name with the branches of trade in which he has ever since been engaged. In 1875 his son, E. H. Webster, was taken into partnership, and the firm name became E. Webster & Son. In 1886 William Germann was admitted to a share in the business, and the present style of E. Webster, Son & Co. was adopted. Mr. Webster has devoted his energies unremittingly to the business, and it has grown and prospered steadily until it is to-day one of the largest of its kind in Buffalo.

Public affairs have had no great attraction for Mr. Webster; but he has always believed in doing his duty as a loyal citizen, and in 1873-74 he served as alderman of the old 2d ward of Buffalo. He has been a member of the First Baptist Church of Buffalo for more than thirty years. For the first five years he was a trustee and treasurer, and since then he has been a deacon. For about twenty years he has been a life member of the Buffalo Library, and he has belonged to the Buffalo Historical Society nearly as long.

*PERSONAL CHRONOLOGY—Ellis Webster was born at Eden, N. Y., August 3, 1823; was educated in district schools; engaged in the grocery and produce business in Buffalo, 1847-68; married Charlotte W. Whitney of Kenosha, Wis., September 11, 1850; was alderman of the old 2d ward, Buffalo, 1873-74; has carried on a coal and ice business in Buffalo since 1868.*

**Abram Bartholomew,** who has practiced law in Buffalo for more than a quarter of a century, was born in Collins, Erie county, New York, somewhat less than sixty years ago. An affliction of curvature of the spine prevented him from attending school until he was ten years old. He then went to the district schools of Collins for four years, afterward attending the union school at Gowanda one term, and Springville Academy two terms. As his father was not able to provide further education, Mr. Bartholomew resolved to defray his own expenses of tuition and board rather than forego the benefits of learning. At the unusual age of fifteen, accordingly, he began to teach school in the town of Eden. After teaching for several years at select and district schools in various towns of Erie county, he had saved sufficient funds to warrant attendance at the Albany State Normal School; and he had the satisfaction of graduating from that institution with the class of 1857.

The next year Mr. Bartholomew, having decided to make the legal profession his life-work, began to read law in the office of the late C. C. Severance at Springville. He also studied in the office of W. W. Mann, and in that of John L. Talcott, late justice of the Supreme Court. He was not yet firmly established in a pecuniary way, and he paid his living expenses while studying law by further school teaching. All difficulties were happily overcome at last, and in November, 1861, he was admitted to the bar at Buffalo. He was then twenty-four years old, and the struggle for a professional education had been long and arduous; but he has never doubted that the result was worth all that it cost in time and labor and privation.

For about two years after his admission to the bar Mr. Bartholomew remained at home taking care of his father, who was an invalid and needed his assistance. After spending three years in the Oil-creek region, speculating in oil lands in a vain quest for fortune, Mr. Bartholomew wisely settled down to the steady-going practice of law in Hamburg, N. Y. This was in 1866. He remained in Hamburg one year, but the town was well supplied with lawyers — ex-Governor Boies of Iowa, Judge Robert C. Titus of Buffalo, and three others were practicing there at the same time — and he decided to move to Ebenezer in the same county. At the latter place he practiced two years, and established a good country clientage. The outlook, however, was not sufficiently promising to satisfy his ambition, and in 1869 he took up his residence in Buffalo, where he has practiced ever since with gratifying success. He has considerable office work, but is better known as a trial lawyer, as his practice has to do with contested cases largely, and takes him into court much of the time. He has conducted his law business without the aid of associates, though of late years his son Niles, who is also an attorney, has occupied offices with him.

Mr. Bartholomew has never thought it worth while to seek political honors; but he has taken keen interest in public affairs, and has ardently supported the Democratic party. He has taken part in political campaigns for many years, having addressed numerous public meetings in Erie county. He is a member of Orient Lodge, Ancient Order of United Workmen, and attends Westminster Presbyterian Church.

*PERSONAL CHRONOLOGY—Abram Bartholomew was born at Collins, N. Y., February 28, 1837; attended Gowanda Union School and Springville Academy; taught school for a time, and graduated from the State Normal School at Albany in 1857; was admitted to the bar in 1861; married Florence Cutler of Holland, N. Y., December 29, 1864; engaged in oil operations, 1864-65; practiced law at Hamburg and Ebenezer, N. Y., 1866-69; has practiced law in Buffalo since 1869.*

**Charles Berrick**, a builder and contractor of Buffalo for more than forty years, is an Englishman by birth, and possesses many of the best traits of his native people. His very name discloses his origin, since his family in early times adopted for their cognomen a phonetic spelling of Berwick, the famous town between Scotland and England. Charles Berrick, one of thirteen children, was born at Coleshill, near Birmingham, England, nearly seventy years ago. His education was obtained in the common schools of Warwickshire, his native county. After serving his time as an apprentice to the mason's trade, he worked as a bricklayer for various employers, including Geo. Stephenson & Son, the famous locomotive designers, until he was twenty-three years old. That is not the age at which most men attain breadth of view and sagacious foresight; but Mr. Berrick was not like other men, and he resolved to escape from the hard conditions of industrial life in overcrowded England, and try his fortunes amid the ampler opportunities of America.

This determination was not long in maturing to the point of action, and the spring of 1850 found Mr. Berrick on board the bark "Henry," outward bound from London for Sandy Hook and the new world. Winnebago, Wis., was his objective point, as he had English friends in that place; and he started

*ABRAM BARTHOLOMEW*

thither soon after landing in New York, by way of the Hudson river to Albany, and railroad thence to Buffalo. Fortunately for the latter city, and for Mr. Berrick as well, it would seem, Lake Erie was full of ice, steamers could not leave port, railroads west there were none, and Wisconsin was accessible only by tedious stagecoach traveling. Under such conditions, Mr. Berrick decided to stay in Buffalo for a few months, and resume his westward journey in the fall. He obtained employment easily, and became so well satisfied with the outlook by the autumn of 1850 that he postponed indefinitely his trip to Wisconsin, and determined to make Buffalo his permanent residence. Time has shown the wisdom of this decision.

In the middle of the century Buffalo had only 40,000 people, and few buildings that would now be deemed noteworthy in any commendable respect. In the transition from such a city to the present metropolis, with its magnificent public and private structures, Mr. Berrick has had an important part.

CHARLES BERRICK

His training on the other side of the ocean had been long and thorough, and he had worked here only a short time before his employer saw his value and made him foreman. But Mr. Berrick had not left his country, and traveled oversea 3000 miles, to become a foreman merely; and after working for others two years he established himself in business on his own account as a master mason and contractor. His commissions at first were not large, but he did so well such work as was entrusted to him, and showed himself so reliable and honest in all his dealings, that he soon received more important contracts. A list of the buildings erected wholly or in part by him would give one an accurate idea of the architectural emergence of Buffalo from mid-century

conditions to the modern city. Among his early contracts were those made with the Lake Shore and Erie railroads for the erection of roundhouses and machine shops at Buffalo. He laid the foundation work and did the masonry of several of the elevators for which Buffalo is famous. The Tifft House, German Insurance building, Barnes-Hengerer block, St. Louis Church, Coal and Iron Exchange, Bank of Buffalo, Hotel Iroquois, and Marine Bank are well-known Buffalo structures of Mr. Berrick's. He also built many of the elegant dwellings that adorn Delaware avenue, and other beautiful residence districts of the Queen City.

Until 1892 Mr. Berrick conducted his business without partners, but in that year his sons, Alfred and John, were admitted to the firm. They had both grown up in the calling with their father, learning it thoroughly under his superior guidance, and they were thus finely equipped for the work of carrying on the large business built up by Mr. Berrick in forty years of faithful service. The sons now constitute alone the firm of Charles Berrick's Sons, the father having retired in 1894. He continues, however, to take an active interest in the welfare of the concern, and his advice is of great value in the conduct of the business.

Mr. Berrick has devoted most of his time and energy to his work as a builder. His calling, however, has kept him more or less in touch with real-estate operations; and he has himself done something in that line, as the marvelous growth of Buffalo, and consequent expansion of real-estate values, encouraged such ventures. Mr. Berrick has never cared for political office, but has taken the interest of all good citizens in the public well-being. In state and national politics he has always voted the Republican ticket, but in local matters he has voted for the best men without special or exclusive regard to the party ticket on which they ran. He has visited his native land only once since he left it nearly fifty years ago. In 1889 he spent a most enjoyable vacation abroad, traveling on the continent and in Scotland for a while, but naturally devoting more time to his mother country, and the scenes of his youth and early manhood.

*PERSONAL CHRONOLOGY—Charles Berrick was born at Coleshill, Warwickshire, England,*

*December 11, 1826; was educated in the common
schools of England, and learned the mason's trade;
engaged in the same in England until 1850, when he
came to this country; married Margaret Callan of
Buffalo December 24, 1852; carried on the business
of a contractor in Buffalo, 1852-94.*

...

**W. J. Conners** is certainly a remarkable man.
Twenty years ago he was a dock laborer, and fifteen
years ago he was running a saloon on the East Side,
Buffalo; to-day he is a powerful factor in the welfare of thousands of people, and exerts a wide influence in several important lines of commercial
activity — as a brewer, banker, real-estate promoter,
newspaper owner; and his business in the trans-
shipment of freight is larger than that of any other
individual or any concern in the world.    An explanation of this marvelous transformation
may be found in certain qualities of
mind and traits of character — in his
unconquerable energy, native shrewdness of wit, sound judgment on basic
and essential points, fair-mindedness,
large-heartedness.

Mr. Conners was born in Buffalo in
1857.  He attended the public schools
until he was thirteen years old, when
he took to the lakes, running for several
years between Buffalo and Duluth as
a porter on various steamers.  Seeing
clearly that neither fame nor fortune lay
in that direction, Mr. Conners resolved
to make a fresh start on shore.  He had
no money, but he managed to set up a
saloon in Buffalo.  Good results have
sometimes come from poor beginnings,
and so it was with Mr. Conners.  In a
few years he had accumulated sufficient
capital, and had acquired sufficient business experience, to take advantage of an
opportunity that led to fortune.  In the
spring of 1885 he made a contract with
Washington Bullard for handling all the
freight in Buffalo of the Union Steamboat Co.   Mr. Conners fulfilled his
contract with such efficiency, and the
superiority of his system was so obvious,
that other carriers hastened to make
similar contracts with him; and he soon
acquired a virtual monopoly of the business in Buffalo and some other lake ports.  The
work was done before by many more or less irresponsible contractors employing disorderly, un-
trained laborers, with incessant changes of foremen,

troubles with the men, and costly detention of
steamers in consequence.  Mr. Conners made himself the sole responsible head of the entire business,
gained the confidence of his workmen by fair treatment, systematized and organized the work in a
multitude of ways, and ran the business generally
with machine-like smoothness, precision, and efficiency.  He now has contracts for the loading and
unloading at Buffalo, Chicago, Milwaukee, and
Gladstone, Mich., of all vessels belonging to the
following transportation companies:  Union Steamboat, Western Transit, Lackawanna, Lehigh Valley,
Northern Steamship, Union Transit, and "Soo"
line.  In the season of 1895 Mr. Conners handled
3,300,000 tons of bulk freight.  He employs about
3000 men, and is far and away the largest contractor in the world in this business.   It is a

H. J. CONNERS

remarkable and significant fact that he has never
had to face a strike on the part of his laborers.

This vast industry is by no means the only enterprise in which Mr. Conners has engaged.   In

February, 1889, he was made president of the Buffalo Vulcanite Asphalt Paving Co., and conducted the business successfully for several years. In 1890 he acquired a large block of the stock representing the property of the Roos (now the Iroquois) brewery, and carried on the plant for about a year. In the spring of 1895 he made another venture in this business, purchasing a large interest in the Magnus Beck Brewing Co. He has been president of this company since the date mentioned, and has increased the output of the plant fully one third. He owns a quarter interest in the Union Transit Co., operating a line of steamers between Buffalo and Duluth. He is a director in one bank and a stockholder in several others. He is a large owner of real estate, having shown rare judgment in the purchase and development of property in South Buffalo.

December 23, 1895, Mr. Conners bought a controlling interest in the Buffalo *Enquirer*, and since then he has given a large part of his time to the management of the business. He has thoroughly energized the institution, and has increased the circulation of the paper threefold. In September, 1896, he established a modern newspaper plant consisting of independent light and power engines, a battery of linotype machines, equipment for photo-engraving, and a Hoe sextuple press weighing sixty tons, consisting of 30,000 separate pieces, fed from three continuous webs of paper, and able to print, paste, fold, register, and count 72,000 eight-page papers an hour.

In the summer of 1896 Mr. Conners launched the yacht "Enquirer," which has brought him additional fame and pleasure. She is one of the handsomest steam yachts in existence, and her record of over twenty miles an hour at top speed is said to make her the fastest boat on fresh water anywhere in the world.

*PERSONAL CHRONOLOGY—William James Conners was born at Buffalo January 3, 1857 ; attended public schools, but began work as a porter on lake steamers at the age of thirteen ; has carried on a freight-transfer business at Buffalo and other lake ports since 1885 ; married Catherine Mahany of Buffalo in November, 1881, and Mary A. Jordan of West Seneca, N. Y., August 2, 1895 ; has been president of the Enquirer Co., and of the Magnus Beck Brewing Co., Buffalo, since 1895.*

•••

**Daniel J. Kenefick** cannot be said to exemplify the maxim that old men should be chosen for counsel and young men for action — hardly that, as he was born in the midst of the Civil War, and is thus a young man still ; but his success in the trying office of district attorney shows that the common practice need not in all cases be followed. Mr. Kenefick, indeed, has the energy and enthusiasm of youth tempered and governed by the wisdom and discretion of maturity — a particularly happy combination of qualities for the chief prosecuting officer of a populous county.

Born in Buffalo thirty-two years ago, Mr. Kenefick has lived there all his life. He was educated in the public schools of the city, pursued his professional studies in a Buffalo office, sought out his life companion among the charming daughters of Buffalo, and has otherwise been thoroughly loyal to the place of his nativity. Public School No. 4 was his first source of educational inspiration, followed by the high school, from which he graduated with the class of '81. Foregoing the advantages of a systematic training in a law school, Mr. Kenefick carried on his legal studies in the office of Crowley & Movius, and in that of their successors, Crowley, Movius & Wilcox. With some drawbacks, there are in like manner certain advantages in that method of reading law, and Mr. Kenefick must have minimized the obstacles and made the most of the offsetting advantages ; for he was admitted to the bar in October, 1884, having accomplished that end in about the same time that a course in a law school would require.

He began at once the laborious and sometimes discouraging task of building up a clientage. His progress was as rapid as could be expected, and was somewhat facilitated, perhaps, by his early professional enlistment in the public service. After practicing only slightly more than a year, he was appointed to a clerkship in the law department of the city. He retained this position throughout the calendar year 1886, and then resigned to accept an appointment as second assistant district attorney under George T. Quinby, then district attorney. Holding this position five years, and ably discharging its duties, he was appropriately rewarded, on January 1, 1893, by an appointment as first assistant district attorney. On the resignation of Mr. Quinby, in November, 1894, Governor Flower appointed Mr. Kenefick district attorney for the unexpired term.

Mr. Kenefick had now been in the office of the district attorney nearly eight years. Throughout this period he had performed zealously and efficiently the work assigned to him ; and in the latter part of his service, owing to the illness of the district attorney, the chief responsibility of the office rested upon him, and was adequately borne by him. Quite properly and naturally, therefore, the Republican party in 1894 placed Mr. Kenefick in nomination for the office of district attorney. The choice of the convention was emphatically ratified at the polls, as Mr. Kenefick was elected by the surprising vote of almost two to one. That the judgment of the Republican party and of the voters was sound has been amply demonstrated by Mr. Kenefick's efficient service. Always alert and vigorous in protecting the legal interests of Erie county, he is at the same time regardful of the rights of others, and scrupulously careful not to overstep the proper bounds of his authority. His evident fair-mindedness and just disposition of the difficult questions constantly arising in the district attorney's office, have gained for him universal respect and confidence among his professional associates.

Mr. Kenefick's first legal partnership was formed with Joseph V. Seaver. On the latter's election as county judge, Mr. Kenefick associated himself with Messrs. Cuddeback and Onchie. This connection lasted until May, 1893, when Mr. Kenefick and William H. Love combined forces in the existing successful firm of Kenefick & Love.

*PERSONAL CHRONOLOGY —
Daniel Joseph Kenefick was born at Buffalo October 15, 1863; was educated in the public schools of the city, and graduated from the high school in 1881; was admitted to the bar in 1884; married Maysie Germain of Buffalo June 30, 1891; was second assistant district attorney of Erie county, 1887–91, and first assistant district attorney, 1893–94; was appointed district attorney by Governor Flower to fill an unexpired term in November, 1894, and was elected to the office the same year; has practiced law in Buffalo since 1884.*

* * *

**William C. Krauss,** though he has practiced his profession only a few years, has already become recognized as an authority in his specialty of nervous diseases. Present-day life, with its many undeniable advantages, has also some drawbacks; and one of the greatest of these is the excessive demand that it makes on human energy. Men of business, women of fashion, even the very school-children, break down under the strain, and become the victims of nervous ailments of one kind or another, until one doubts whether any healthy minds or

bodies will be found in the years to come. Under such circumstances it is but natural that many of the younger generation of physicians should devote themselves to special investigation of such troubles; and few have done this more exhaustively, or with brighter promise of brilliant success, than Dr. Krauss.

DANIEL J. KENEFICK

Born in Wyoming county in 1863, he obtained his preparatory education in the Attica Union School, from which he graduated in 1880 as the valedictorian of his class. He then entered Cornell University, receiving the degree of Bachelor of Science in 1884, as well as a two-year certificate for extra work done in the medical preparatory course. From the beginning his studies were directed in the line to which he has steadily devoted himself; since this preparatory work at Cornell, under Dr. Burt G. Wilder, concerned the anatomy and histology of the nervous system. Dr. Krauss's medical degree was obtained from the Bellevue Hospital Medical College in 1886, when he stood second in the honor class. After spending the summer of that year in Bellevue

Hospital, he went abroad in the fall, and passed three years in the special study of nervous and mental diseases. He attended the famous universities of Munich, Berlin, and Paris, receiving the degree of M. D., *magna cum laude*, from the University of Berlin in 1888. In the spring of 1889

WILLIAM C. KRAUSS

he visited the London medical schools, returning home in June of that year.

Dr. Krauss had some acquaintance with Buffalo, where his father was well known in commercial circles; and he had already acquired a reputation among the members of his profession there as special correspondent of the Buffalo *Medical Journal* during his years of study abroad. He decided, therefore, to settle in that city. So long and thorough a preparation for any calling could hardly fail to ensure success therein — certainly not when united with such natural ability as Dr. Krauss possesses. His success has been uninterrupted, and he has already built up a large special practice. He has also made a reputation as an expert on insanity, and has been

called upon to testify before the courts in nearly every important case calling for such testimony in central and western New York.

As a medical writer and instructor Dr. Krauss has been prominent ever since he began practice. He has been professor of pathology in the medical department of Niagara University (1890–95), and is now professor of nervous diseases there. In 1890 he delivered a course of lectures at Cornell University. He is associate editor of the Buffalo *Medical Journal*, and of several other medical publications in both Europe and America. He has published sixty-five scientific papers, treating of a variety of subjects, and embodying the results of much original research in his special line. His connection with professional societies is unusually extensive: he is a Fellow of the Royal Microscopical Society of London, and of the American Neurological Association; he is a member of the American Microscopical Society (of which he is secretary), the Buffalo Microscopical Society (of which he was president in 1892–93), the New York State Medical Society, the Medical Association of Central New York (of which he was elected first vice president October 20, 1896), the Lake Erie Medical Society, and the Erie County Medical Society. He was one of the founders of the Buffalo Academy of Medicine in 1892, and was its secretary for several years. In 1890–92 he was secretary of the Buffalo Obstetrical Society. He belongs to the Buffalo Medical Club, as well as to the Liberal and University clubs of Buffalo, and the Buffalo Association of Cornell Alumni. He holds the position of neurologist in a number of the city hospitals, including the Erie County Hospital, the Sisters of Charity Hospital, and the Asylum and Hospital of the Sisters of St. Francis.

*PERSONAL CHRONOLOGY— William Christopher Krauss was born at Attica, N. Y., October 15, 1863; graduated from Cornell University in 1884, and from Bellevue Hospital Medical College, New York city, in 1886; studied in European universities, 1886–89; married Clara Krieger of Salamanca, N. Y., September 4, 1890; has practiced in Buffalo since 1889, confining his work to diseases of the mind and nervous system; has been professor in Niagara University since 1890.*

**Edward C. Shafer** is well and favorably known in commercial circles, and in the political life of Buffalo. Few men have been so thoroughly occupied with business, and at the same time so prominent in local affairs. But Mr. Shafer possesses unusual capacity for grappling with, and quickly solving, the many perplexing problems that arise in the course of a mercantile career. The growing demands of his business have in recent years restricted his activity in matters of public concern, but he is thoroughly informed on all public questions.

Mr. Shafer is a native of the Keystone State, and received there a common-school and an academic education. After taking up his residence in Buffalo he pursued a commercial course at Bryant & Stratton's Business College in that city. He began life's work with the firm of Barnes, Bancroft & Co. of Buffalo, from whose employ he went to serve as bookkeeper for O. S. Garretson. With this training he embarked in the hardware business as a partner in the Buffalo Hardware Co., and was connected with this enterprise for six years. He then became manager of the Buffalo School Furniture Co. The growth of their business rendered incorporation desirable, and upon the organization of the concern as a stock company Mr. Shafer became director, treasurer, and general manager. He has retained these positions to the present time. The improvement in school furnishings in recent years has been marvelous, but Mr. Shafer has kept his company in the van of the industry.

In politics Mr. Shafer is a Republican, but could not be fairly called a partisan. His popularity was shown when he ran for alderman on the Republican ticket in the old 3d ward of Buffalo, time out of mind a Democratic stronghold. Mr. Shafer came within 132 votes of an election. Two years later he was appointed police commissioner by Mayor Becker, and diligently performed the duties of that office. In the year 1889 he was elected to the office of city comptroller. He served one term to the satisfaction of the people, and would have been renominated by his party, had not the pressure of private business compelled him to decline. In the same year there was a movement afoot to elect Mr. Shafer mayor of the city, but the same reasons that obliged him to decline a renomination for comptroller made it necessary to renounce as well all thought of the mayoralty.

The development and expansion of the business of the Buffalo School Furniture Co. is due in large part to Mr. Shafer's tireless energy and foresight. His duties with this company absorb nearly all his time. Recently, however, he has been elected president of the Standard Paving Co. of Buffalo; and for years he has been a director of the Hydraulic Bank. He is a member of many fraternities, in all of which he takes a prominent part, and has filled various high offices. In short, since taking up his residence in Buffalo, Mr. Shafer has proved himself not only a sound business man, but also one who has the best interests of his community at heart. He enjoys accordingly in large measure the respect and good will of his fellow citizens.

*EDWARD C. SHAFER*

*PERSONAL CHRONOLOGY— Edward C. Shafer was born at Honesdale, Penn., April 17, 1850; received a common-school and an academic education in Pennsylvania; moved to Buffalo in 1872.*

*married Elizabeth Anderson of Buffalo June 25, 1874; engaged in the hardware business, 1871–84; was appointed police commissioner of Buffalo May 1, 1881; was city comptroller, 1890–91; has been connected with the Buffalo School Furniture Co. since 1884.*

***

**Ernest Wende**, well known as a successful physician in a difficult specialty, and more widely known for his remarkable efficiency as health commissioner of Buffalo, was born in Erie county about forty years ago. After graduating from the Buffalo High School in 1874, Dr. Wende engaged in teaching two years, and then took up the study of medicine. His medical education consumed the greater part of the next twelve years, and included attendance at Buffalo University, from which he graduated with honors in 1878; at the College of Physicians and Surgeons, Columbia; and at the University of Pennsylvania, whence he graduated with honors of the first class in 1884, and from which he received the degree of Bachelor of Science in 1885. In 1885–86 he crowned with the latest results of medical research an education that was already remarkably thorough, studying in Vienna and Berlin, and specializing his work on skin diseases and microscopy in the private laboratories of Virchow and Koch. In the course of his medical studies Dr. Wende won a West Point competitive examination, and attended the Military Academy one year (1875–76). He practiced medicine at Alden, Erie county, in the intervals of his advanced professional training. In 1879 he was elected school commissioner from the first district of Erie county. Since his return from Berlin in the fall of 1886, he has practiced continuously in Buffalo, and has made himself famous for his successful treatment of diseases of the skin.

We have saved most of our space for an account of Dr. Wende's work as health commissioner of Buffalo. Under this head it is not too much to say that his services to the city have been invaluable, and will benefit Buffalonians for many years to come. Taking office January 1, 1892, by appointment from Mayor Bishop, he entered upon his duties admirably equipped for the work before him. His exhaustive professional studies and rare skill as a physician were only a part of his qualifications. Added to these he possessed unusual executive ability, and was thereby enabled to organize a department of health that has become a model for other cities. Under his administration the death rate in Buffalo has steadily decreased, having fallen from 23.48 per thousand of population in 1891 to 11.67 for the first six months of 1896. The deaths

recorded in 1891 were 6001 in number, while in 1895, notwithstanding an increase of 80,000 inhabitants, the number of recorded deaths had fallen to 4684. These and other statistics are regarded as proof that Buffalo is the healthiest city of its size in the world.

The following are some of the ways in which Dr. Wende has brought about this most beneficent result. Formerly records of contagious diseases were made by mail at the convenience of the attending physician; now all such cases must be reported immediately by telephone. Thereupon the health office, open at all hours day and night, will dispatch a man to inspect the premises, attach placards to the house, and adopt such other sanitary precautions as may be advisable. To guard against the pollution of the city water, daily bacteriological and chemical examinations are made. One of the first results of this system was to close forever an emergency inlet which was formerly used in times of low water, and which sometimes let sewage into the public mains. Over half the wells formerly used for domestic purposes were found on examination to contain water charged with germ life, and were accordingly filled up. The periodical visitation of the public schools and annual vaccination of the pupils, minimizes the danger of epidemics in the schools. All police stations, fire-department quarters, and schoolhouses are minutely inspected at stated intervals, to ensure hygienic conditions.

The inspection and purification of the milk supply of Buffalo involved a difficult piece of organization. The banishment of cow barns from thickly peopled districts, and the compulsory observance by milk producers of regulations designed to reduce the risks of mothers and children, were at last effected; and now a record is kept of every milkman, so that any diseases on his route ascribable to impure milk may lead to investigation and appropriate punishment. Another feature of the Wende administration that abolishes disease by preventing its birth, may be found in the system of inspecting supplies of vegetables, meats, and the like, at markets and produce houses. Frozen oranges, rotten bananas, and other dangerous food, have frequently been condemned. Tenement houses, minor hotels, and lodging places are often visited, lest infectious diseases take root and spread undetected. A vast amount of sickness has doubtless been headed off by municipal supervision of plumbing and drainage. No plumbing can now be done unless plans therefor are first filed, and approved by experts; and no householder need pay for his plumbing until the completed work is passed upon by inspectors and accepted. Without

recounting further the means employed by Dr.
Wende to protect the city from disease, suffice it to
say that he has conducted the department of health
on a scientific basis from first to last.

Dr. Wende is professor of diseases of the skin in
the medical department of the University of Buffalo,
and of botany and microscopy in the
College of Pharmacy. He is greatly
interested in geology, botany, and the
natural sciences generally, and is profoundly erudite in these subjects. He is
also an archæologist, and has brought to
light many interesting relics in his numerous country walks around western
New York and Ontario. The Buffalo
Society of Natural Sciences is indebted
to him for many valuable contributions.

Dr. Wende belongs to the Erie County
Medical Society, the New York State
Medical Association, the American Mi-
croscopical Society, and the Pan-Ameri-
can Medical Association. He was re-
cently elected vice president of the
American Public Health Association.
He is a Fellow of the Electro-Thera-
peutic Association, and of the Royal
Microscopical Society of England.

*PERSONAL CHRONOLOGY —
Ernest Wende was born at Mill Grove,
N. Y., July 23, 1853; graduated from
the Buffalo High School in 1874, from
the medical department of the University
of Buffalo in 1878, and from the University of Pennsylvania in 1881; studied in
the medical department of Columbia College, 1881-82, and in the universities of
Berlin and Vienna, 1883-84; married
Frances Harriet Cutler of Omaha, Neb.,
August 25, 1881; has practiced his profession at Buffalo since November, 1886; has been
health commissioner of Buffalo since January, 1892.*

* * *

**Deman M. Blasdell,** for years past one of
the leading citizens of North Collins, Erie county,
was born in Perrysburg, N. Y., in 1840. His education was varied, beginning with the district school,
and including attendance at Gowanda Academy and
Oberlin College. He also taught school two winters
in the town of Persia, Cattaraugus county, before
going to Oberlin. He left college to continue his
education in one of the finest possible schools of
discipline — the Union army during the Rebellion.
Enlisting in the first year of the war, in company
H, 44th New York volunteers, he remained in the

army until July, 1862, when he was wounded so
seriously in the fight at Malvern Hill, the last of the
"Seven Days' Battles," that he was compelled to
leave the service.

Like thousands of other bright young men, Mr.
Blasdell began his business career as a telegraph

ERNEST WENDE

operator. He was soon promoted to the position of
station agent, and served in that capacity for nine
years at Smith's Mills, Chautauqua county. Wisely
concluding that such work was not likely to result in
financial independence or an assured position in life,
Mr. Blasdell formed a partnership with David Sherman at North Collins, for the conduct of a general
mercantile business. They commenced operations
April 1, 1872, and carried on a successful business
for the next five years.

To many people Mr. Blasdell is known chiefly
through his connection with the suburb of Buffalo
founded by him and bearing his name. In 1883 he
bought a large tract of land in the northern part of
Hamburg, Erie county, and laid out there the town

of Blasdell. He caused a post office to be established at the place, and was the first postmaster; and he conducted a general store there for several years. He still owns much valuable property at Blasdell, and is naturally greatly interested in the prosperity of the town; but in 1887 he returned to

*HEMAN M. BLASDELL.*

North Collins, and has since resided there. In a business way he has concerned himself chiefly with real estate.

As might be expected from his prominence in business affairs, Mr. Blasdell has likewise attained distinction in political life. He was supervisor of the town of North Collins for the three years, 1878–80. In November, 1895, he was elected to the state legislature from the 8th assembly district by the largest majority ever given to a candidate in his district, and in November, 1896, he was re-elected. He was appointed by Governor Morton in 1895 a trustee of the Thomas Asylum, an institution for orphan Indians on the Cattaraugus Indian reservation. He is now treasurer of the institution as well.

His service in the Civil War has given Mr. Blasdell a place in the Grand Army of the Republic, and he is a Past Commander of the S. C. Noyes Post. He has taken an active part in Masonry, having membership in Fortune Lodge, No. 788, F. & A. M., Gowanda Chapter, No. 136, R. A. M., and Salamanca Commandery, No. 62, K. T.

*PERSONAL CHRONOLOGY— Heman M. Blasdell was born at Perrysburg, Cattaraugus county, N. Y., January 28, 1840; took part in the Civil War, 1861–62; married Lusannah Sherman of North Collins, N. Y., June 8, 1863; was telegraph operator and station agent at Smith's Mills, N. Y., 1863–72; conducted a general store at North Collins, 1872–77; was supervisor of North Collins, 1878–80; founded the town of Blasdell, Erie county, N. Y., in 1883, and engaged in business there, 1883–87; was elected member of assembly in November, 1895, from the 8th Erie-county district, and was re-elected in 1896; has lived in North Collins since 1887.*

**William Bookstaver,** mayor of Dunkirk, N. Y., and for many years thoroughly identified with all that is good in the city, is of Dutch descent, and was born in Montgomery, N. Y., in the last days of the year 1833. His ancestors are traceable in this country, through various paths of honor, from the year 1732, when his great-grandfather, Jacob Bookstaber (as the name was then spelled), came from Holland, and settled in Orange county, New York.

Mr. Bookstaver graduated from Montgomery Academy in 1852, and afterward taught in the same institution for one year. His ultimate purpose was to practice law, and in April, 1855, he went to Dunkirk to prepare himself for the legal profession. After studying in the office of Brown & Bookstaver he was admitted to the bar in 1858.

A sound knowledge of law is an invaluable piece of equipment for any business man, and this fact has not infrequently encouraged lawyers to use their talents chiefly in the conduct of business affairs. So it has been in great part with Mr. Bookstaver. He has transacted a good deal of office law business; but he engaged in real estate ventures on a large scale soon after his admission to the bar, and these operations, together with other business pursuits, have absorbed his time and attention to the exclusion of active legal practice. He showed his faith in the future of Dunkirk by making large real-estate investments in different parts of the city; and he has long been one of the heaviest individual tax-payers of the place. He is president of the Dunkirk Savings and Loan Association, which has helped many worthy men to acquire homes and property. He was prominent in the organization of the Dunkirk, Warren & Pittsburg railroad, now the Dunkirk, Allegheny Valley & Pittsburg, and was one of the original directors of the company.

The story of Mr. Bookstaver's political career is long and interesting, and extremely significant of the esteem in which he is held by his fellow-citizens. He has served Dunkirk, as village and city, in every department of municipal administration. While the place remained a village he was successively its clerk, attorney, treasurer, and president. In 1875 he was elected supervisor from the town of Dunkirk, and remained on the board, with the exception of a single twelvemonth, for sixteen years. At the end of that period, in 1890, he declined a unanimous nomination for re-election, as he was about to make an extended foreign tour. In 1885 he was appointed one of the water commissioners, and is still on the board. In 1887 he was appointed mayor of Dunkirk to fill the vacancy caused by the resignation of M. L. Hinman, and the next year he was elected to the same office. He was re-elected in 1889 and again in 1890, and in 1896 he was once more summoned to the mayor's chair.

While mayor, in 1888, Mr. Bookstaver devoted much time to the establishment of a system of municipal electric lighting, believing that in this way the city could secure the best results at a minimum cost. Dunkirk was the pioneer in this movement in the state, and the plan met with fierce opposition. The mayor, supported by the common council, argued the matter before the governor and both branches of the legislature, and carried it through the courts. It was a test case of municipality *versus* monopoly, and Mayor Bookstaver's untiring efforts were finally crowned with success. So high an authority as Professor Richard T. Ely, the well-known economist and advocate of municipal ownership, gives Mr. Bookstaver great credit for

this achievement; and the fact that lights are furnished in Dunkirk at 15 cents a night each as compared with 50 cents in Baltimore and 65 cents in Boston, where the service is obtained from private corporations, is a strong argument in favor of his theory.

For many years Mr. Bookstaver has been well known in state political circles as an earnest Democrat. In 1876 he was a delegate to the Democratic national convention at St. Louis that nominated Samuel J. Tilden for the presidency. In 1887 he was appointed by Governor Hill a member of the committee on prison-labor reform, and served as chairman of the same.

*PERSONAL CHRONOLOGY—William Bookstaver was born at Montgomery, Orange county, N. Y., December 28, 1844; was educated in Montgomery*

*WILLIAM BOOKSTAVER*

*Academy; studied law in Dunkirk, N. Y., and was admitted to the bar in 1858; married Mary A. Leonard of Augusta, Me., July 18, 1861; was supervisor for the town of Dunkirk, 1875-90, with* the exception of one year; was a delegate to the Democratic national convention in 1876; was mayor of Dunkirk, 1887-90, and was again elected in 1896; has practiced law in Dunkirk and engaged in real-estate operations there since 1858.

*JAMES CHALMERS*

**James Chalmers** is one of the sturdy, energetic sons of Scotland who form so respectable an element of the population of western New York. He was born near Edinburgh, a poor boy, and owes his success to his pluck, perseverance, and intelligence. His schooling was brief. It began when he was seven years old, and ended at thirteen when he left Gillespie's Free School, in Edinburgh, with the medal awarded for the highest average in all branches of the curriculum. He then taught school in Edinburgh until he was sixteen, and afterward became an apprentice to an Edinburgh machinist. But his work in the school, and later in the machine shop, was only a part of what the boy did. From the age of eight, in addition to his other duties, he had worked in a gelatine factory. His father had a

contract to produce gelatine at a fixed price, and to reduce the expense of manufacture James had to labor in the factory from early morning until the school bell rang, and again after school until bedtime. Thus he had no chance for study at home, and his award of honors at school is the more noteworthy. When he became a machinist's apprentice, his extra labor continued; and after walking three miles night and morning to and from the machine shop, he had to spend a few hours at the gelatine factory assisting his father. This manner of life lasted until he was twenty-one.

This was a hard apprenticeship, but it is the kind that develops and strengthens character if the soil is fit. When, therefore, James Chalmers came to this country, in 1872, to seek his fortune, he was possessed of qualities that ensured his success. He worked first at the spring-hammer works in Williamsville, Erie county, N. Y., and then in the Erie-rail-road repair shops at Susquehanna, Penn. While he was thus working for others he formed the determination to engage for himself in the manufacture of gelatine. He had no means, but he did have a knowledge of the methods of manufacture acquired by many years' weary labor; and, what was no less valuable, he had confidence and perseverance, willing hands, and a robust constitution. He began business as a manufacturer in 1873 at Williamsville, where there was an abundant supply of the pure spring water essential to the production of gelatine. Without money, progress at first was slow; but the result was what might have been expected — success.

Mr. Chalmers's brother, Peter Chalmers, was a partner in the business until 1882, when he moved to Texas. Since then James Chalmers has conducted the business alone, with steadily increasing success. His product is sold throughout the United States. The original factory has been greatly enlarged, and recent improvements include a drying room one hundred and fifty by fifty feet in area, containing over five thousand feet of pipe, and capable of evaporating eight hundred gallons of water a day.

Mr. Chalmers has always refused to accept nominations for political office, but his townsmen have insisted upon his filling several positions of trust and honor. He is a member of the board of education of the Williamsville High School, president of the board of trustees of the village, and president of the Williamsville board of water commissioners. He has always taken an interest in educational matters, and has shown himself in many ways a man of public spirit. He was instrumental in having Williamsville connected with Buffalo by electric railway, and was at one time vice president and manager of the road. His standing among food-producers was shown by his election as a director of the National Pure Food Manufacturers' Association. Mr. Chalmers is a member of all the Masonic bodies up to the 32d degree, and of the Nobles of the Mystic Shrine.

*PERSONAL CHRONOLOGY— James Chalmers was born at Gorgie Mills, near Edinburgh, Scotland, October 15, 1844; was educated at Gillespie's Free School, Edinburgh; married Helen Wilson of Peebles, Scotland, August 23, 1866; came to America in 1872; established the Chalmers gelatine factory at Williamsville, N. Y., in 1873, and has conducted the same since.*

...

**Joseph M. Congdon,** a prominent lawyer of Cattaraugus county, and otherwise well known in western New York, was born about fifty years ago. His general education was obtained in the district schools of his native county and in Randolph Academy, while his professional studies were carried on in the office of Jenkins & Goodwill at East Randolph. He rounded out his legal knowledge by taking a course at the Albany Law School. Completing his work there in the summer of 1870, he was admitted to the bar in October of the same year. Mr. Congdon had spent most of his life in Randolph and vicinity, and wisely decided to cast in his lot with those who knew him best. He began the practice of law, therefore, at East Randolph on June 1, 1871, in partnership with his brother, Benjamin F. Congdon. The firm of Congdon & Congdon carried on a successful legal business until September 1, 1873, when Mr. Congdon associated himself with his father-in-law, M. T. Jenkins, for the purpose of practicing law in Fredonia, Chautauqua county. This partnership lasted two years, or until Mr. Congdon decided to leave Fredonia, and carry on his profession in the neighboring town of Gowanda.

This was in September, 1875, and since then, with the exception of three years' residence in Buffalo, in 1882-84, Mr. Congdon has made Gowanda his abiding-place. That the choice of location was wise seems clear from his subsequent success, though equal prosperity might have rewarded his efforts elsewhere. He rose to prominence quickly in the political and social life of Gowanda, while his professional practice became gratifyingly large and important. By the year 1880 he was so well established in the regard of his fellow-citizens that they elected him to the state legislature from the 2d assembly district of Cattaraugus county; and in 1881 he was re-elected. While in the assembly he was a member of the judiciary committee, one of the most important in the legislature, becoming chairman of the committee in his second year of service. In

JOSEPH M. CONGDON

November, 1895, he again received substantial evidence of his popularity in his election to the office of district attorney of Cattaraugus county. He is now discharging efficiently the duties of this office, the term of service running for three years from January 1, 1896. His firm is now styled J. M. & G. M. Congdon, his son Glenn having been taken into partnership.

One feature of Mr. Congdon's work in the legislature is worthy of special mention. During his first

TIMOTHY E. ELLSWORTH

term in the assembly he became greatly interested in the codification of law. Year after year penal, criminal, and civil codes had been introduced, but had died in one house or the other; and nothing more than this had been accomplished up to the end of Mr. Congdon's first year in the legislature. In his second year there, as chairman of the committee on judiciary, he was in a position to indulge his interest in codification, and to accomplish something where others had failed. During the first week of the session he introduced all three codes, and pushed them unremittingly through all the necessary stages of legislation until they were before the governor for approval. The penal and criminal codes were approved by Governor Cornell, though the civil

code was returned without approval after the adjournment of the legislature. This work placed Mr. Congdon in close connection with David Dudley Field, and a friendship was formed between the two men that lasted until the death of Mr. Field. Mr. Congdon naturally regards with much satisfaction his part in the work of codifying civil law and criminal procedure.

Mr. Congdon has membership in various fraternal societies. He is a Mason, belonging to Phoenix Lodge and Gowanda Chapter; he is a charter member of Lodge No. 46, Ancient Order of United Workmen; and he belongs to Gowanda Lodge, Knights of the Maccabees.

*PERSONAL CHRONOLOGY— Joseph Miller Congdon was born at Napoli, Cattaraugus county, N. Y., January 12, 1846; attended district schools and Randolph Academy; was admitted to the bar in 1870; married Alice M. Jenkins of East Randolph, N. Y., May 24, 1871; practiced law at East Randolph and at Fredonia, 1871–75; was member of assembly from Cattaraugus county, 1880–81; was elected district attorney of Cattaraugus county in November, 1895; lived in Buffalo, 1882–84, but has otherwise practiced law at Gowanda, N. Y., since September, 1875.*

\*\*\*

**Timothy E. Ellsworth** is a lawyer. He is descended from New England stock. For generations the Ellsworths were a Connecticut family, and there the subject of this sketch was born, in the ancient town of East Windsor. His early training was received in public and private schools, and he took his bachelor's degree from the University of Rochester. He then studied law, and after his admission to the bar settled at Lockport.

When the Civil War broke out, Mr. Ellsworth raised a company of volunteers at Lockport, and became its captain. This company was attached to the 7th regiment, New York volunteer cavalry, and served till disbanded in 1862. Mr. Ellsworth continued in the army, and was on the staff of General Wadsworth in the battles of Chancellorsville and Gettysburg. He was honorably discharged in September, 1865, having attained the rank of major by brevet.

Resuming the practice of his profession at Lockport, Mr. Ellsworth soon became known in legal circles and in public affairs. He was an ardent Republican, and a warm supporter of General Grant. Mr. Ellsworth held the office of collector of customs at Suspension Bridge, N. Y., during Grant's two administrations. In the conduct of political campaigns Mr. Ellsworth has been active; and his availability, as well as ability, has been recognized by his party, which has three times elected him to the state senate. He has taken high rank in that body, and has served on its important committees, such as the committee on judiciary and the committee on rules. He is at present senator from the 45th district, and president *pro tempore* of the senate. As a legislator he is industrious, conservative, and sagacious, and strives to give his constituents the best service in his power.

In Mr. Ellsworth's practice at the bar he has two partners, who with him form the firm of Ellsworth, Potter & Storrs. Aside from his law business he is connected with a number of banking and mercantile houses. He is president of the National Exchange Bank, and vice president of the County National Bank; and a director in the Holly Manufacturing Co., the Niagara Paper Mills, the Traders' Paper Co., and the Hartland Paper Co. To these enterprises, as well as to his profession and his public duties, he devotes himself with conscientious effort. He is a member of the Episcopal church, and of the Grand Army of the Republic.

*PERSONAL CHRONOLOGY—Timothy Edwards Ellsworth was born at East Windsor, Conn., September 21, 1836; was educated at public and private schools, and graduated from the University of Rochester in 1857; was admitted to the bar at Rochester in 1858, and began practice at Lockport, N. Y.; served in the Union army, 1861-65; married, on February 2, 1864, Orissa M. Shoemaker of Lockport, who died October 28, 1865; was collector of customs at Suspension Bridge, N. Y., 1870-78, and state senator, 1882-85; was elected state senator from the 45th district in 1895; has practiced law at Lockport since 1865.*

petence, and established himself firmly among the leading men of his community. All this he has done in less than forty years of life. Tireless energy, keen business judgment, and strict integrity have been the main factors in his success.

Mr. Jackson's grandfather was a pioneer in Erie county, going thither early in the century from Vermont, and opening up a farm in Holland on some high land that still recalls his origin in the name "Vermont hill." There Mr. Jackson was born in March, 1858. His early years were as busy as his whole life has been, since he lost his father at the age of eight. His mother, left with limited means, worked with untiring zeal and energy, thereby helping and encouraging her five children to help themselves and each other. After working on a farm most of the time, and attending

### William B. Jackson is a self-

made man. Starting with nothing whatever, in a small country town, without advantage from family connection, and entirely dependent from the first on himself alone, he has acquired a substantial com-

the district and a select school some of the time, William secured a clerkship when sixteen years old in the general store of Morey & Stickney, Holland. He worked three months for nothing, merely to show what he could do, and several months more at a trifling salary ; but he gave his whole time to the business day and night, working as hard and as faithfully as if the store had been his own. All this was duly appreciated by his employers, and in less than two years Mr. Stickney surprised his youthful clerk by inviting him to become his partner. Mr. Jackson had only $204, which he had saved from his earnings, but his character and reputation enabled him to borrow enough to form the partnership. On March 24, 1876, accordingly, when he had just turned his eighteenth year, the firm of Stickney & Jackson began its successful career. Five years later, on March 3, 1881, they purchased the general store of O. W. Childs at Protection, N. Y., which was carried on in connection with the store at Holland. The partnership continued seven years, during which Mr. Jackson made rapid progress in establishing himself as a prosperous business man and respected citizen. In March, 1883, Mr. Stickney found it convenient to retire from the business ; and Mr. Jackson had so prudently conducted his personal affairs that he was able to buy out his partner, and become sole proprietor of the establishment that he had entered as a boy nine years before. Since the date mentioned Mr. Jackson has carried on the business alone with entire success. His place to-day is one of the most complete country stores in western New York. In addition to this enterprise Mr. Jackson has various outside interests that require some of his business attention. He owns pine lands in Mississippi, farm lands in South Dakota, and suburban property in Buffalo, together with choice bits of real estate in Holland.

The proprietor of a general store in a small town has an excellent chance, if he have also the requisite ability, to make himself a power for good in the public affairs of the community. In the case of Mr. Jackson ability was not lacking, and for many years he has had something to do — usually a good deal to do — with everything of much importance that has gone on in Holland. Beginning with the position of town clerk in 1880, he has been successively overseer of highways for three years, during which he was largely instrumental in bringing the roads of Holland to a high degree of excellence ; postmaster of Holland during Harrison's administration, 1889-93 ; and supervisor for the years 1895-96. He has also been Republican committeeman from his district for a number of years. In semi-public, non-political affairs he has been equally active, and many improvements in Holland are ascribable in large part to his efforts. In 1891 he

helped to organize the Holland Water Works Co., and has been president thereof from the start. In 1893 he interested himself in the establishment of a local bank, subscribing for a large block of the stock, and has been president of the institution from the beginning. He has been local treasurer of the Farmers' Fire Relief Association since 1887, and of the Rochester Savings and Loan Association for several years. He has also been treasurer of the Holland fire department since 1894, besides holding other offices that require much of his time. Mr. Jackson belongs to various fraternal societies, including the Masons, Odd Fellows, Knights of the Maccabees, and Order of the Iroquois.

*PERSONAL CHRONOLOGY—William Byron Jackson was born at Holland, Erie county, N. Y., March 20, 1858 ; attended district and select schools ; was clerk in a country store, 1874-76 ; married M. Zina Vaughan of Holland January 12, 1881 ; was town clerk in 1880, overseer of highways, 1887, 1888, and 1894, and postmaster of Holland, 1889-93 ; has been a member of the Erie-county board of supervisors since 1895 ; has conducted a general store at Holland since 1876 ; has been president of the Bank of Holland since its organization in 1893.*

**Wilber Fisk Persons** is still comfortably distant from the prime of life, but has already achieved business success and attained political distinction in a noteworthy degree. He was born in Delevan, Cattaraugus county, N. Y., and has lived there most of his life. In his youth he spent five years, however, on the western frontier, and graduated from the high school in Omaha, Neb.

Mr. Persons began his business career at the age of nineteen, as a telegraph operator on the Union Pacific railroad. After returning to western New York in 1876, he resumed railroad work, becoming assistant division superintendent of the Buffalo, New York & Philadelphia railroad (now the Western New York & Pennsylvania). Concluding that greater rewards awaited him in an entirely different calling — a conclusion amply justified by the result — Mr. Persons purchased the Delevan *Press* in 1887, and thus embarked in the business of newspaper publishing. The venture prospered from the beginning, insomuch that he was emboldened two years later to establish the *Review* at Holland, Erie county. The next year, 1890, brought into being the *Censor* of Sardinia, Erie county ; and in 1893 Mr. Persons purchased the *Wyoming County Record*. Since the latter date he has conducted with increasing success the four weekly newspapers mentioned. They are published in places conveniently situated with reference to each other and to the general territory served, and Mr. Persons is able to handle with dispatch the numerous details of his business. The country covered by his papers is filled with intelligent, conservative, and prosperous people, who appreciate duly and support faithfully such publications as Mr. Persons issues.

Mr. Persons has naturally become prominent in the social and political life of the communities with which he has connected himself. In 1886 he was elected justice of the peace on the Republican ticket over the fusionist representative of the normal majority. In 1891 he was a delegate to the Republican state convention at Rochester, and in 1896 he was a delegate to the convention at New York city. He is a Past Master of Arcade Masonic Lodge, No. 419. He also belongs to Springville Lodge, R. A. M., and to St. John's Commandery, K. T., Olean, N. Y. He is a Past Grand of Delevan Lodge, No. 616, I. O. O. F. Mr. Persons has always taken great interest in everything relating to the welfare of Delevan. He is president of the Delevan Electric Light & Power Co. He was secretary of the building committee during the construction of the new Delevan Union School. He is superintendent of the Yorkshire Water Co.

In his home life and surroundings Mr. Persons is particularly fortunate, and his commodious and elegant dwelling in Delevan is a social center for many friends.

*WILBER FISK PERSONS*

*PERSONAL CHRONOLOGY—Wilber Fisk Persons was born at Delevan, N. Y., November 24, 1858; lived in the West, 1870-76, graduating from the Omaha High School in June, 1875; married Alice Catharine Strong of Delevan June 2, 1880; was in the service of the Union Pacific railroad, 1875-76, and of the Buffalo, New York & Philadelphia railroad, 1876-84; has conducted various weekly newspapers in western New York since 1887.*

•••

**Adam L. Rinewalt** has long been a factor in the newspaper world of western New York, and in the political and business affairs of Williamsville, where he has spent the greater part of his life. It may probably be safely asserted that in proportion to the number of its readers the journal of a small

community is more influential in molding public opinion than the great newspaper of a metropolis. The columns of the village paper are more thoroughly read, and more completely, because more leisurely, digested. The great dailies illustrate the well-known economic principle of the division of labor, and the work upon them is specialized to a degree that would surprise the uninformed. Each has its political editor, its financial editor, its news editor, its religious editor, and its sporting editor. But the editor of a country newspaper must, to a certain extent, combine in himself all the varied functions of these writers. Therefore a successful editor of such a paper is naturally a man of parts, and a controlling influence in the lives and thoughts of his community.

Mr. Rinewalt was born in Williamsville, where his parents were among the early settlers. He attended the district school and academy of his native town. At the age of sixteen he went to Beloit, Wis., where he learned the printer's trade, thus laying a practical foundation for the profession that was to be his life-work. He returned to New York state in his twenty-first year, and secured a position with the *Commercial Advertiser*, Buffalo, then under the control of Matthews & Warren. He remained with them for nine years, when he established

ADAM L. RINEWALT

the *Amherst Bee* at Williamsville, which he has successfully conducted ever since.

Mr. Rinewalt is prominent in Williamsville not only as a newspaper man, but as a promoter of many commercial enterprises. He was among the first to urge the building of the Buffalo & Williamsville electric railroad, and he is one of the stockholders of the company, holding also the offices of director and secretary. He has been largely engaged in real-estate transactions, and is connected with creamery and other business enterprises. No man in the community is more devoted to its interests. He has concerned himself especially with the public schools of the town, the establishment of waterworks, and other movements tending to the advancement of Williamsville.

Always an active Republican, Mr. Rinewalt has frequently been called upon to fill various positions connected with the organization of his party. He was elected collector of Amherst in 1881, and declined a renomination for that office. For nine years he was a trustee of the village of Williamsville, and during five of those years he was president of the village. In 1886 he was elected a school trustee. He has served continuously in that position since, and is now president of the board of education. During President Harrison's administration Mr. Rinewalt was postmaster of Williamsville. He has served on many occasions as a member of campaign committees. Mr. Rinewalt is a representative man among his fellow-citizens, who have time and again displayed their appreciation of his services to the community, and their confidence in his ability and character. He is a member of the Masonic order, and of several other fraternal organizations.

*PERSONAL CHRONOLOGY— Adam Lorenzo Rinewalt was born at Williamsville, N. Y., May 4, 1849; was educated in district schools and Williamsville Academy; learned the printer's trade at Beloit, Wis., 1865–70; worked at his trade in Buffalo, 1870–79; married Sarah Filena Bloker of Williamsville September 18, 1878; was postmaster at Williamsville, 1889–93; established the "Amherst Bee" at Williamsville in 1879, and has conducted the same since.*

**✱✱✱**

**Frank E. Sessions** has an interesting and honorable lineage. His great-grandfather, John Sessions, was of English descent, and was probably born in Massachusetts; his early history is obscure, but it is known that he lived for a time at the foot of the Green mountains in Vermont, and afterward moved with his son to the Empire State. This son, Schuyler Sessions, after clearing up a farm in Chautauqua county and tilling the same for a few years, joined again the westward tide of emigration, and settled on the prairies of Iowa. One of his sons was Columbus Sessions, the father of our present subject. Mr. Sessions's mother was Cordelia French, the daughter of Samuel French, who was born in Massachusetts, but who became a resident of Chautauqua county, settling in the town of French Creek.

Frank E. Sessions was born at the head of Lake Chautauqua, shortly before the middle of the century. When he was five years old his father moved to Wisconsin; and there, by traveling three miles each way every day, Frank was able to obtain such training as the country schools afforded. He continued to attend the district schools of Fond du Lac county until he was fifteen years of age, when his attainments were such that he was able to obtain a position as teacher. He taught for seven years in the Badger State, reading and studying law himself all the time; and engaged in the same occupation after his return to Chautauqua county. There he taught several terms in Sherman, French Creek, and the union-school district of Clymer Village.

Like a multitude of others, Mr. Sessions abandoned teaching for the law. His uncle, Walter L. Sessions, was a prominent attorney of Panama, Chautauqua county, and in his office Mr. Sessions began the study of law in 1869. His progress was checked by a business engagement in virtue of which he became superintendent of the tanning works at Clymer; but he persevered in his legal studies so far as opportunity permitted, and gained admission to the bar in April, 1874. In the summer of 1876 he opened an office in Jamestown, and has since practiced his profession in that city. He was associated with Henry O. Lakin from 1878 until Mr. Lakin's death in 1884, and with E. E. Woodbury for one year thereafter. He has otherwise practiced alone.

Men value most highly and utilize best, as a rule, the things that come to them with difficulty; and Mr. Sessions has improved to the utmost the general and legal education that he acquired so hardly. His thoroughness and accuracy in drawing up legal papers, and his general vigilance in guarding the interests of those who entrust their litigation to him, were soon observed and duly appreciated; and for many years he has enjoyed an extensive and a lucrative practice. His professional ability was fittingly recognized in 1880, when Governor Cornell appointed him special county judge of Chautauqua county. His work in that capacity was so well done that at the end of his appointive term he was elected to the same office for three years. In 1895 he was elected an alderman from the 1st ward of Jamestown, and

was made chairman of the finance committee. In April, 1896, he was unanimously elected president of the city council, and still holds the position. He has always been a public-spirited citizen, and has given his time freely to various movements promoting the welfare of his city. He has taken an active part in the organization and management of the Jamestown Permanent Loan and Building Association, and has been for several years the attorney and a director of the institution. The association was organized in November, 1884, and by means of it hundreds of families in Jamestown have obtained comfortable dwellings of their own.

Mr. Sessions is a Mason, belonging to Mt. Moriah Lodge, No. 145, F. & A. M. He is a prominent member of the Methodist Episcopal Church of Jamestown, having served the society for many years

*FRANK E. SESSIONS*

as treasurer, superintendent of Sunday school, and otherwise. In political life he has acted with the Republican party. He has always been an enthusiastic "Chautauquan," joining the first Normal class in 1871, and graduating with the first Chautauqua Literary and Scientific Circle class in 1882. Mr. Sessions is a devoted student of history, and his private library is remarkably complete in its collection of standard works on this fascinating subject.

OLIVER S. VREELAND

*PERSONAL CHRONOLOGY—Frank Edgar Sessions was born at Chautauqua, N. Y., May 22, 1847; was educated in the common schools of Wisconsin; taught school, in Wisconsin and in Chautauqua county, N. Y., 1863-69; studied law and engaged in business, 1869-74, and was admitted to the bar in the latter year; married Julia R. Bush of Jamestown, N. Y., June 1, 1876; was appointed special county judge in 1880, and elected to the same office for a term of three years in the same year; has practiced law in Jamestown since 1876; has been an alderman of Jamestown since 1895.*

• • •

**Oliver S. Vreeland,** who is now serving his second term as county judge of Cattaraugus county, is a native of the neighboring county of Allegany,

and has always lived in western New York, with the exception of four years spent in college. Notwithstanding the constant movement of our population from the East to the West and from the country to the city, there are still many men who have spent their lives in a single locality, and have risen to prominence among those who have known them from boyhood. This happy combination of change and permanence prevents alike stagnation and instability, and adds greatly to the strength of a community.

Judge Vreeland was born in the village of Cuba somewhat more than fifty years ago. His education, begun in the district schools, was unusually thorough, including two years' study at Olean Academy, a year at Rushford Academy, and two years at Alfred University. He then took a four years' course at the University of Michigan, graduating from that institution in 1869 with the degree of A. B. In 1876 his *alma mater* conferred upon him the degree of A. M.

Having decided to enter the legal profession, Judge Vreeland read law for three years in the office of the late E. D. Loveridge of Cuba, and in January, 1872, he was admitted to the bar. He was somewhat older at this time than most men beginning legal practice; and he had thus the advantage of greater maturity of mind and a more intimate acquaintance with men and affairs. His knowledge of law, moreover, had been gained under an excellent master, as Mr. Loveridge was an able attorney, and one of the most prominent members of the Allegany-county bar. The opportunities for professional advancement afforded by his native village were meager, and Judge Vreeland determined to begin work as a lawyer in the neighboring town of Salamanca. Accordingly, in the April following his admission to the bar, he opened an office there in partnership with Hudson Ansley. The new firm was successful from the first, and soon built up an extensive clientage in Salamanca and the surrounding country. In 1879 the connection was dissolved, and from that time Judge Vreeland practiced alone.

Public affairs were always interesting to Judge Vreeland, as they are to every good citizen; and in 1879 he became president of the village of Salamanca, holding the position for four years. He was then elected supervisor of the town, and served on the board five years. His legal and executive ability had thus been amply demonstrated, and he was soon to have an opportunity to display his judicial ability. In 1887 he was elected to the office of county judge, and began a term of six years January 1, 1888. So well did he discharge the duties of this position that he was re-elected in 1893. Judge Vreeland has many qualities that peculiarly fit him for judicial duties, and his decisions are generally regarded as both able and impartial.

In 1888 Judge Vreeland acted as special counsel for the committee appointed by the assembly to investigate the Indian problem of the state, and wrote the report of the committee.

*PERSONAL CHRONOLOGY— Oliver S. Vreeland was born at Cuba, N. Y., September 28, 1842; attended various schools and academies, and graduated from the University of Michigan in 1869; married Anna M. Guilford of Cuba September 15, 1869; was admitted to the bar in 1872, and began practice at Salamanca, N. Y.; was president of the village of Salamanca, 1879–82, and supervisor, 1882–86; has been county judge of Cattaraugus county since January 1, 1888.*

***

**Walden M. Ward,** a prominent citizen of North Collins, Erie county, is somewhat younger than his well-established place in the medical profession might indicate, as he was born at Perrysburg, N. Y., not long before the outbreak of the Civil War. His early education was obtained in the district school of his native town, and this training was supplemented by attendance at Angola Academy. He then taught school for several years. Having decided to make the doctor's calling his life-work, he availed himself of an opportunity to read medicine with Dr. A. D. Lake of Perrysburg. His professional education was completed, so far as schools and colleges go, at the University of Buffalo, from which he graduated in February, 1885, with an "honorable mention."

Dr. Ward's preparation for the work of a physician had been long and unusually varied, so that he felt able to begin practice soon after graduation. He decided upon North Collins as his field of action, correctly judging that the pleasant and

prosperous country town, with its accessibility to large places, would prove a desirable location for both residential and professional purposes. He opened an office there, accordingly, in May, 1885, and has ever since followed his profession in North Collins and its vicinity. His practice has grown from the small beginning almost inevitable with young physicians until he now has a large and desirable body of patients. He keeps in touch with his fellow-practitioners, and belongs to the Erie County Medical Society and the Lake Erie Medical Society. He has been president of the latter association.

In social life Dr. Ward has naturally been prominent, as his calling has taken him into the homes of the people, and has made him intimately acquainted with large numbers of his fellow-citizens and neighbors. He is a firm believer in the benefits of

*WALDEN M. WARD*

Masonry, and has taken high rank in the order, belonging to Fortune Lodge, No. 788, F. & A. M., Gowanda Chapter, No. 136, R. A. M., and Salamanca Commandery, No. 62, K. T.

Dr. Ward has had neither the time nor the inclination to run for office, but he is an enthusiastic Republican, and takes an active part in the conduct of local political affairs.

*PERSONAL CHRONOLOGY   Walden Manley Ward was born at Perrysburg, Cattaraugus*

CHARLES H. WICKS

*county, N. Y., January 11, 1859; attended district schools and Angola Academy; married Jennie Waters of Versailles, N. Y., January 1, 1884; graduated from the University of Buffalo in February, 1885; has practiced medicine at North Collins, N. Y., since May, 1885.*

• • •

**Charles D. Wicks,** well known in Jamestown and the surrounding country, is a native of Chautauqua county, and has spent practically his whole life there. At present his name is connected with real-estate operations chiefly, but during the greater part of his life he has devoted his best efforts to the cause of education. Realizing the paramount importance to the country of the public-school

system, he has striven as teacher, school commissioner, and member of the school board, to improve that system and make it effective, bringing its benefits within the reach of all.

Mr. Wicks's native town was Ellery, where he was born in President Taylor's first year in the White House. He received a thorough common-school education, afterwards taking a four years' course at the Jamestown Union School and Collegiate Institute. He graduated thence in 1869, at the age of twenty, and began his work as a teacher in the following year. His first position was in the Clymer Union School, and later he taught at Panama, N. Y., and at Corry, Penn.

After a highly successful career as a teacher, Mr. Wicks was elected, in 1878, a commissioner in the first district of Chautauqua county, and held the office for four consecutive terms, or until January 1, 1891. His sphere of activity was thus enlarged from one school to many, and the schools of his district profited greatly by his able and conscientious oversight. Having been so long a teacher himself, he possessed a practical rather than a mere theoretical knowledge of what was needed for the perfecting of the school system; and the excellent condition of the schools to-day is largely the result of his twelve years of faithful and efficient service.

Since 1891 Mr. Wicks has made his home in Jamestown's beautiful suburb, Lakewood, where he has large real-estate interests. The firm of Wicks Brothers had an important part in the establishment of this village, as well as in the development of real estate in the city of Jamestown itself, and Mr. Wicks has the prosperity of the new community greatly at heart. He has been a member of the board of trustees of the village ever since its organization. His well-known devotion to educational interests, and long experience in the management of schools, led to his election as a member of the school board of Lakewood in 1891; and he has held the office continuously since, having recently been elected for another term of three years. He takes an active interest in all movements for promoting the welfare of the village, and is widely known in both business and social circles. He is a member of Lakewood Lodge, No. 628, Independent Order of Odd Fellows, and of Jamestown Lodge, Benevolent and Protective Order of Elks.

*PERSONAL CHRONOLOGY— Charles Henry Wicks was born at Ellery, N. Y., October 15, 1849; graduated from Jamestown Union School and Collegiate Institute in 1869; married Florence R. Robbins of Spartansburg, Penn., November 6, 1874; taught school, 1870-78; served as school commissioner in the first district of Chautauqua county, 1878-81; has been a member of the school board of Lakewood, N. Y., since 1891, and of the board of trustees of the village since 1893; has lived at Lakewood since 1891, engaged in real-estate business there and in Jamestown.*

\* \* \*

**George Baltz** belongs to that class of energetic, self-reliant, and progressive business men, happily found in every thriving American city, who are best described as good all-round men. He is a type of the popular citizen, who knows everybody, and whom everybody is glad to know.

Mr. Baltz is a native of Buffalo, having been born in the Queen City less than forty years ago. He has lived there all his life, and few men who have grown to manhood since the Civil War are so well acquainted as he with events in the recent history of Buffalo. His earliest remembrance is of the closing days of the war, when Buffalo's brave regiments were returning from their posts of duty and of danger. He is a genuine New Yorker, and has compressed into a comparatively short life all the activity and push characteristic of the closing years of the nineteenth century.

The educational opportunities within reach of Mr. Baltz's boyhood were such as the public schools of Buffalo afforded. He received a good common-school training, but lacked the means to pursue a collegiate course. Fortunately, however, with a fair knowledge of reading, writing, and arithmetic, a young man endowed with a sound mind in a sound body need have no doubt of winning success in this land of promise. After spending a number of years in various mercantile pursuits, in order to find his bent, Mr. Baltz at last entered the commission business at the Elk-street market in Buffalo. Beginning as a clerk in the house of Oatman Brothers, he obtained an accurate and a detailed knowledge of the commission business. For thirteen years he labored early and late, and succeeded in establishing himself firmly among the merchants of Buffalo on the produce exchange.

Meanwhile Mr. Baltz had exerted himself in the political affairs of the community, and had become a local factor in the ranks of the Republican party, with which he has always acted. In 1891, when Edward C. Shafer was elected comptroller of the city of Buffalo, he appointed his friend and supporter, Mr. Baltz, to the responsible position of tax collector. Mr. Baltz filled this office so acceptably that two years later he was nominated by acclamation, by the Republican convention of Erie county, for the important office of county treasurer. The result of the ensuing election evinced the wisdom of the convention's choice, and attested the popularity

GEORGE BALTZ

larity of Mr. Baltz, since he secured a majority of over 11,000 votes. He is still performing the duties of this position, and is proving a safe and conservative guardian of public funds.

Mr. Baltz is a man of genial disposition, and is connected with several social and fraternal bodies in Buffalo. He is a member of the Buffalo Turn Verein, and of three branches of the Independent Order of Odd Fellows.

*HERBERT P. BISSELL*

*PERSONAL CHRONOLOGY— George Baltz was born at Buffalo September 17, 1855; was educated in the public schools; engaged in the produce commission business, 1878-91; married Ida A. Becherer of Buffalo October 1, 1885; was tax collector of the city of Buffalo, 1891-94; was elected county treasurer of Erie county in 1894, for the term 1894-96.*

* * *

**Herbert P. Bissell** is one of the best known of the younger professional men of Buffalo. He has been prominent in both law and politics, and has shown that such prominence is compatible with high standards of citizenship and personal conduct.

Born in a little hamlet of Oneida county, he obtained the beginnings of his education in the district school there, and in the public schools of Lockport, whither his family moved when he was nine years old. Four years later he entered De Veaux College at Suspension Bridge. Then came the unusual experience of two years at the Gymnasium Catharinaeum, a public school at Braunschweig, Germany. From this he returned to enter Harvard College, whence he graduated with the degree of A. B. in the class of 1880.

That summer Mr. Bissell became a resident of Buffalo, and began studying for his chosen profession, the law. In due time he was admitted to the bar. For several months he remained as managing clerk with the firm in whose office he had studied. Finally, on January 1, 1885, he began practice for himself. At first he was alone. Then, on July 1, 1886, he became a member of the firm of Brundage, Weaver & Bissell. Six months later he entered the firm of Bissell, Sicard, Brundage & Bissell as junior partner; and with this firm, under the style of Bissell, Sicard, Bissell & Carey, he remained until its dissolution October 1, 1896. This firm, founded in 1834 by Orsamus H. Marshall, was one of the oldest and most distinguished in Buffalo. Nathan K. Hall, who was President Fillmore's postmaster-general, was one of its early members. President Cleveland was its head when he was elected governor in 1882; and its recent head was President Cleveland's late postmaster-general, Wilson S. Bissell. Thus a President of the United States and two postmasters-general have been members of the firm. Its list of clients was equally noteworthy, including corporations like the Lehigh Valley and the Philadelphia & Reading railroad companies, the Lehigh Valley Coal Co., the Lehigh Valley Transportation Co., and several Buffalo banks.

Among the duties of a good citizen is attention to political affairs. Mr. Bissell is a good citizen, and he has been active in politics ever since Grover Cleveland was a candidate for governor. In 1885 Mr. Bissell was nominated by the Democratic party for state senator for the Erie-county district; and though he was defeated by 1500 plurality, he ran 1500 ahead of his ticket. That campaign is yet remembered in Buffalo because of the series of speeches in German that Mr. Bissell delivered in the East Side. He showed a command of classical German that won the admiration of the Germans themselves. In 1892 he was nominated for district attorney, and this time, out of a total vote of 65,000, he was defeated by 44. Mr. Bissell was one of the founders, and for a time president, of the organization called the Cleveland Democracy. In his political career the governing qualities throughout have been devotion to principle and strict integrity.

Mr. Bissell is a member of the Buffalo, Saturn, and University clubs of Buffalo, and of the Reform Club of New York. He has been a trustee of De Veaux College since 1887 ; and has also served as a trustee of the Cary Collegiate Seminary at Oakfield, N. Y., and as curator of the Buffalo Library.

*PERSONAL CHRONOLOGY— Herbert Porter Bissell was born at New London, N. Y., August 30, 1856 ; was educated at public schools, De Veaux College, and the Gymnasium Catharinareum, Braunschweig, Germany, and graduated from Harvard College in 1880 ; studied law in Buffalo, and was admitted to the bar in 1883 ; married Lucy Agnes Coffey of Brooklyn October 30, 1884 ; received the Democratic nomination for state senator in 1885, and for district attorney in 1892 ; has practiced law in Buffalo since 1885.*

* * *

**Rollin L. Banta,** one of the best known and most successful physicians of Buffalo, is descended from excellent Dutch stock. The family tree, taking deep root in American soil in 1650, is an imposing specimen of genealogical development. One member of the family bore the name of Rip Van Winkle — not the same good-for-naught Rip, perhaps, that Jefferson makes so lovable, but possibly the mundane source of Irving's delightful fancy. Dr. Banta's own father was a famous steamboat builder in his day. The firm of Bidwell & Banta launched from their yards at Buffalo some of the largest and most magnificent steamers that had ever sailed the lakes, or even the oceans, up to that time.

Born in Buffalo in November, 1846, Dr. Banta has spent most of his life in that city. After attending Public School No. 4 he went to St. Joseph's Academy three years, and afterward to Manhattan College, New York city, for a like period. Having thus formed an excellent preparatory groundwork on which to rest a professional structure, he entered the

medical department of the University of Buffalo in 1868, and graduated therefrom three years later with the degree of M. D. In the spring of 1873 he opened an office in Erie, Penn., and continued to practice his profession in that city for the next five years. At the end of that period he returned to Buffalo, concluding that his old home was preferable to any other city for both professional and personal reasons. Since then he has carried on his profession in Buffalo with uniform success, and with an increasingly large practice.

Dr. Banta has made no effort to specialize his work, and as a matter of fact his general practice is still extensive. He has been so successful, however, in the department of obstetrics, that he has come to be regarded as a specialist in this subject. His standing in the medical profession is shown by

*ROLLIN L. BANTA*

his appointment to many positions of trust and importance. For four years, ending in 1895, he was professor of therapeutics in the medical department of Niagara University ; and he is now associate professor of obstetrics in the same institution. He has membership in the Buffalo Medical Society, of which he has been president; in the Buffalo Academy of Medicine: in the Erie County Medical Society, of which he has been president; and in the American Association of Obstetricians and Gynecologists, of which he has been vice president. He is consulting physician in the Buffalo Maternity Hospital and in other institutions. He has written many scientific papers on medical subjects, which have appeared in various professional publications.

*PERSONAL CHRONOLOGY— Rollin L. Banta was born at Buffalo November 14, 1846; was educated in public and private schools in Buffalo, and in Manhattan College, New York city; graduated from the medical department of the University of Buffalo in 1871; married Sarah M. Ayer of Buffalo October 27, 1875; practiced medicine at Erie, Penn., 1874-78; has been a professor in the medical department of Niagara University since 1891; has practiced medicine in Buffalo since 1878.*

•••

**Marcus M. Drake** was born in Cortland county, New York, in 1835. His ancestors, English on one side and German on the other, came to America in colonial times, settling in New Jersey. His father moved to Chautauqua county in 1837, and there Mr. Drake spent his boyhood on a farm. His education was acquired in the common schools of Sheridan, near Fredonia, and in the academy at the latter place. When sixteen years old he gave up schools and farm alike, resolved to lead the life of a sailor; and ever since, with the exception of an honorable interruption during the Civil War, Captain Drake, as he came to be called, has been connected in some way with the transportation interests of the Great Lakes.

Betaking himself to Buffalo in 1851, he shipped before the mast, and sailed the lakes as a common seaman for the next four years. At the age of twenty he became a mate, and served as an officer on various sailing vessels and steamers until 1861. In that year he was appointed captain of one of the Erie-railway steamers. He had thus secured a fine start in his chosen calling, and might reasonably have expected continuous advancement and prosperity. By the summer of 1862, however, everyone saw that the Civil War must be fought out in a life-and-death struggle, and Captain Drake did not hesitate to exchange his $1200 position and excellent prospects for the $13 a month perils and hardships of a private in the regular army. In August, 1862, he enlisted in the 72d New York volunteers,

and went to the front at once with the Army of the Potomac.

Captain Drake's career as a soldier would make an interesting narrative in itself. He took part in many important engagements, but was neither wounded nor captured. He was in the battles of Fredericksburg and Chancellorsville, and at Gettysburg his company was ordered forward on the first day to a most exposed position, not unlike the "bloody angle." The engagement at Wappinger Heights, though less memorable than the foregoing battles, was sufficiently serious to many of Captain Drake's comrades in arms. He took part, also, in the dangerous operations around Petersburg, in the battle of Five Forks, and in the closing scenes of the war at Appomattox. He was promoted at various times for valorous conduct in the field, and at the close of the war had reached the rank of first lieutenant. The document recording his honorable discharge from service contains this fine characterization of Captain Drake as a soldier: "An officer whose strict attention to duty, gentlemanly deportment, and cool courage has won the respect of all his comrades."

Taking up his life on the lakes where he had left it three years before, Captain Drake remained in the service of the Erie railway, in command of various steamers, from the close of the war until the fall of 1869. He was then promoted from the position of master to that of superintendent of repairs of the Union Steamboat Co., controlled by the Erie lines. Two years later the Union Dry Docks Co. was organized as a part of the Erie system, and Captain Drake, in addition to his existing cares, was made superintendent of the company. These multifarious duties occupied his time until the fall of 1889, when he resigned his position, and thus terminated his long service with the Erie. He was soon made superintendent of the Lackawanna Transportation Co., organized in the same year, and has since held that position. After his retirement from marine service, where he had made a reputation as a prudent and successful navigator, Captain Drake built up another and a more important reputation as a business manager of unusual ability. He is noted for his uniform courtesy and fair dealing, for his fidelity to the interests of his company, for his prompt and vigorous dispatch of business.

In political life Captain Drake has always acted with the Republican party. In 1878 he was elected an alderman of Buffalo from the 11th ward, and was re-elected five times, thus serving twelve years altogether. In November, 1882, he was chosen mayor of Buffalo by the common council, to fill the unexpired term of Grover Cleveland, governor-elect of New York state. In December, 1895, he was appointed by Mayor Jewett a commissioner of public works of Buffalo for a term of four years from January 1, 1896. Captain Drake has shown in the discharge of public duties the same integrity and ability that have brought him success in business life; and his fellow-citizens, without regard to party, congratulate themselves that Buffalo is to have the benefit of his counsel in the management of an important department for some time to come.

For more than thirty years Captain Drake has been a member of the Masonic order. He belongs, also, to the Grand Army of the Republic, having been the first commander of William Richardson Post, No. 254. He helped to organize the Niagara Bank of Buffalo, and has been vice president of the institution from the beginning. He was largely instrumental in the erection at the park meadows, Buffalo, of the bowlder monument that marks the burial trench of three hundred unknown soldiers of the war of 1812. Another subject in which Captain Drake has interested himself to excellent purpose in recent years is the deepening of the Erie canal. As chairman for the last three years of the Merchants' Exchange committee on harbor and canal improvements, he has labored in season and out of season in behalf of Buffalo's lake and canal commerce. Largely to his efforts will be due both the extension of the outer breakwater in Buffalo harbor to Stony Point, and the enlargement of the Erie canal to a uniform depth of nine feet. Both these improvements will strengthen the commercial position of Buffalo.

*PERSONAL CHRONOLOGY— Marcus Motier Drake was born at Homer, N. Y., September 7, 1844; attended common schools and Fredonia (N. Y.) Academy; served as sailor, officer, and master on the Great Lakes, 1851-62; served in the Union army from August, 1862, until the close of the war; married Mary A. Ludlow of Buffalo December 17, 1867; was on the staff of the Erie railway as captain and superintendent, 1865-88; has been superintendent of the Lackawanna Transportation Co. since August, 1888; was alderman of Buffalo, 1879-90; is commissioner of public works, Buffalo, having been appointed for the term 1896-99.*

**John Kelderhouse** is descended on one side, as his name suggests, from Dutch ancestors, while his mother's people were from Connecticut. His life and character have been influenced by both lines of descent, and his prosperity is the natural outcome of a happy combination of Dutch indus-

*MARCUS M. DRAKE*

try and prudence with Yankee enterprise and energy.

Born in Albany county, New York, in 1823, Mr. Kelderhouse passed his infancy and early boyhood in that part of the state. When he was nine years old he went West with his father, reaching Buffalo in the fall of 1832. That was before the days of trunk lines, and they made the journey by the Erie canal, which had been opened seven years before. At that time Buffalo contained only nine or ten thousand people, so that Mr. Kelderhouse has seen the place grow from a mere town to a metropolitan community, excelling in several important respects every other city on the continent. After attending the common schools of Buffalo he engaged in various

occupations, as a young man often will in casting
about for his proper niche in life. By the year
1845, however, when he was twenty-two years old,
Mr. Kelderhouse had established himself as a wood
dealer, and he remained such for nearly twenty
years, attaining a high degree of success in the busi-

*JOHN KELDERHOUSE*

ness. As the country around Buffalo became more
thickly settled, and the forests gave way to farms
and habitations, and as coal supplanted wood more
and more for domestic purposes and as a generator
of steam on the Great Lakes, Mr. Kelderhouse
wisely adapted his business to the shifting conditions of the industry. Curtailing his dealings in
wood, he branched out gradually as a builder of
vessels, thus preparing himself to participate in the
extension of lake commerce. This extension, as
everyone knows, has been enormous; and those
who, like Mr. Kelderhouse, were wise enough to
foresee the trend of events, have naturally and
properly profited from their sagacity. Mr. Kelderhouse went into the business of building ships

prudently, but gradually enlarged his plant, establishing yards at Bay City and East Saginaw, Mich.,
as well as in Buffalo. His earlier ventures were
carried on alone, but afterward his operations
assumed such proportions that he deemed it wise
and desirable on various accounts to ally himself
with other capitalists in carrying out his
plans. The "Kelderhouse syndicate,"
accordingly, was formed for the purpose
of building and operating large and modern steamers; and such splendid examples of modern naval architecture as the
"Thomas Maytham," "America," and
"Brazil" came into existence as a consequence of this organization.

It was natural for Mr. Kelderhouse to
become interested in Buffalo real estate,
since the bent of his mind is such that
he foresees clearly the natural order of
things, and makes such plans as will best
harmonize with natural developments.
This long-headed discernment of the
future explains his evolution from a
wood merchant to a steamship owner;
and the same precious quality of intel-
lect accounts for his success in real
estate. He is now one of the largest
owners of real property in Buffalo, and
his holdings are not confined to the city
limits. He has extensive farms along
the lake shore of Erie county, on which
he spends happily a good deal of his time.

Mr. Kelderhouse has been a Mason
for forty years or more, belonging to
Erie Lodge, No. 161, F. & A. M. In
political matters he votes for the best
man without regard to party. He has
attended for many years Trinity Episcopal Church.

*PERSONAL CHRONOLOGY — John Kelder-
house was born at Bethlehem, N. Y., March 18,
1823; moved to Buffalo in 1842, and was educated
in the common schools there; began business as a wood
merchant in Buffalo in 1845; married Jane Elizabeth Coatsworth of Buffalo June 9, 1851; has been
engaged in lake commerce, as ship builder and owner,
since 1864.*

\*\*\*

**Frank C. Laughlin,** railroad lawyer, city
attorney, corporation counsel, and justice of the
Supreme Court, has risen rapidly in a profession
that yields its honors grudgingly, and as a rule only
after years of devoted service. Not yet in the
prime of life, and doubtless possessed of latent

powers greater even than those foreshadowed by his past, he has already attained a position that will splendidly employ his ripening talents.

Mr. Laughlin was born shortly before the outbreak of the Civil War in a country town of Erie county. When he was six years old his parents moved to Wilson, Niagara county, and his youth was spent in that place. He attended the district school in winter, worked on the farm in summer, and otherwise followed the usual life of young men brought up in the country. In 1876 he moved to Lockport, and attended for three years the well-known union school of that place.

Having decided to become a lawyer, Mr. Laughlin entered the office of John E. Pond as a student. He was admitted to the bar in 1882, and shortly afterward went to Buffalo for the purpose of practicing law in the office of Sprague, Morey & Sprague. This was a strong firm, to which railroads and other corporations had entrusted their legal interests, and Mr. Laughlin had an excellent chance to justify his choice of a profession. He was equal to the opportunity. He was placed in charge of important cases, and handled with conspicuous ability a large amount of the legal business devolving upon his firm.

In the fall of 1885 William F. Worthington was elected city attorney of Buffalo, and thus had occasion to appoint an assistant. He did not know Mr. Laughlin personally, but he heard so favorable reports of his ability and character that he decided to offer him the position. At that time Mr. Laughlin had been admitted to the bar only about three years, and this unsolicited appointment was a striking tribute to his ability in the law. He accepted the offer, and began his new duties January 1, 1886. Soon after this Mr. Worthington's title was changed from that of city attorney to corporation counsel, and the former designation was given to Mr. Laughlin. He retained the office until 1891, and discharged its duties most efficiently. In a single case — that of the Ellicott-street extension — the issue involved more than $200,000, and Mr. Laughlin won the decision for the city. His success was so marked, indeed, that he became in 1890 the logical candidate of the Republican party for the office of corporation counsel. He ran more than 2000 votes

ahead of his party, but on this occasion the entire Democratic ticket was successful.

For the next few years Mr. Laughlin practiced law on his own account, at first alone, but subsequently in association with Thomas Penney. His success was as marked as it should have been from his previous career, and he would undoubtedly have become one of the leaders of the Erie-county bar, had he not been destined for a higher branch of jurisprudence. Selected again in 1895 by his party as its nominee for the office of corporation counsel, he was elected over his former opponent by a sweeping majority of nearly 8000. This victory presaged his success two years later as a candidate for the position of Supreme Court justice. He was nominated by acclamation for this high office by a convention composed mainly of attorneys representing a bar of

*FRANK C LAUGHLIN*

more than 1200 lawyers in the eight western counties of the state. Everyone acknowledged his fitness for the position, and he was elected by a magnificent majority.

*PERSONAL CHRONOLOGY— Frank C. Laughlin was born at Newstead, N. Y., July 29, 1859; was educated at the Lockport (N. Y.) Union School; studied law, and was admitted to the bar in 1882; began practice in Buffalo in 1884; was assistant city attorney and city attorney of Buffalo, 1886–91; was elected corporation council of Buffalo in 1894, and justice of the Supreme Court in 1895; married Mrs. Martha Bartlett of New York city, formerly Martha Taylor of Buffalo, June 2, 1896.*

...

## Rowland Blennerhassett Mahany,

though still a young man, may be characterized as follows — student, teacher, *littérateur*, diplomat, and congressman. His life so far recalls to mind the biographies of the founders of the Republic, whose precocity enabled them to enter public life and fill high offices before other young men got fairly launched on their careers.

Born in Buffalo in the last year of the Civil War, Mr. Mahany is a representative of the *post-bellum* generation, into whose hands the destinies of the Republic are soon to pass. He received his early education in the public schools of his native city, graduating with highest honors from the high school in 1881. Dependent upon his own exertions, he spent the summer after his graduation working upon a farm in Chautauqua county. In the fall of the same year he became an instructor in Latin and Greek in the Buffalo Classical School, and continued in that position for one year. In 1882 he entered Hobart College, where he studied two years, standing at the head of his class. Actuated by an ambition to secure the broadest education possible, he entered Harvard University in the fall of 1884. He won a prize the first year there. He became secretary and treasurer, and was three times vice president, of the Harvard Union, the chief debating society of the university. He was vice president and president of St. Paul's Society, the Episcopalian organization of Harvard College. In the field of scholarship he attained equal distinction. He was one of the first eight scholars in his class, and in his junior year was chosen a member of the Phi Beta Kappa society, which is annually augmented by the election of students of the highest standing in all the leading colleges of the country. In the same year he was chosen first marshal of the society, and headed the procession of its members in one of their historic marches to Memorial Hall. For two successive years he was a Boylston-prize man, winning one of the prizes awarded to the best speakers in the junior and senior classes. His crowning honor came in 1888, when he graduated from Harvard with the *summa cum laude* degree.

On returning to his home in Buffalo Mr. Mahany became an editorial writer on the Buffalo *Express*. Newspaper work, however, was less congenial to him than study and literature, and he soon abandoned journalism to become an instructor in history and literature in the Buffalo High School.

When James G. Blaine was running for the presidency in 1884 Mr. Mahany, then a student at Harvard College, was one of his most ardent supporters in that hotbed of "mugwumpery." The fact came to Mr. Blaine's attention, and afterward, when secretary of state, he offered Mr. Mahany the position of secretary of legation to Chile. This offer Mr. Mahany thought it wise to decline. In 1892 Mr. Blaine induced President Harrison to nominate Mr. Mahany envoy extraordinary and minister plenipotentiary to the South American republic of Ecuador. The nomination was unanimously confirmed by the senate, and Mr. Mahany betook himself to Quito. Several ministers had died at that post of duty, and Mr. Mahany soon after his arrival there was attacked by the dread fever of the place. Obliged to return home to regain his health, he was nominated for congress on the Republican ticket. He was defeated on this occasion, but the normal Democratic majority was reduced over 1000 votes.

Mr. Mahany returned to Ecuador in 1893, and concluded in nineteen days the Santos treaty, negotiations for which had been pending for nearly ten years. It was said at the time of Mr. Mahany's appointment that he was the youngest diplomat in the world holding the responsible position of foreign minister, and the youngest man in the United States ever appointed to such an office. Mr. Mahany's ambition to enter public life in this country was gratified in the fall of 1894, when the Republican cyclone struck the country. He was elected in that year to the 54th congress over four competitors. Speaker Reed fittingly recognized Mr. Mahany's ability by placing him upon several important committees. The best and practically most effective work in congress is done in committee, and these assignments enabled the young congressman to exert his full share of influence in shaping legislation. His most important work for Buffalo consisted in having the project for the completion of the breakwater placed under the "continuous contract" system. The finest harbor on the lakes will be a monument to Mr. Mahany's first six months in congress. Through his efforts, also, work was resumed on the new post office, and its speedy construction assured. In the memorable election of November, 1896, he was returned to congress with a plurality of nearly 4000 votes. This result, in a district that has always been regarded as a strong-hold of Democracy, testifies most eloquently to Mr. Mahany's popularity.

Though far from the prime of life, Mr. Mahany has already attained honors sought in vain by many older men. With a start in life so splendid, an experience so wide and helpful, an intellectual equipment so thorough, his star can hardly yet have reached its zenith.

*PERSONAL CHRONOLOGY—Rowland Blennerhassett Mahany was born at Buffalo September 28, 1864; was educated in the public schools of Buffalo; studied in Hobart College two years, and graduated from Harvard University in 1888; engaged in journalism and taught school, 1888–92; was appointed minister to Ecuador in 1892; was elected representative to the 54th congress in 1894, and to the 55th in 1896.*

* * *

**Daniel Hugh McMillan**, in the various spheres of his professional, civic, and political life, may justly be said to merit and to enjoy in an exceptional degree the confidence and esteem of his fellow-men. He was born and reared in the valley of the Genesee, New York. He is of Scotch origin, tracing his lineage from Alexander McMillan, whose monumental cross, erected in 1348, still stands with its inscriptions at the family burial place in Kilmory, Scotland. His grandfather, John McMillan, was "John the Upright," arbiter of the Hollanders of the Mohawk valley during the latter part of the eighteenth century. His father, Daniel McMillan of York, was revered and honored by all who knew him as a man of high integrity, kind and generous, of the utmost purity of character; it has been justly said of him, "His hand gave bread and his voice spake peace to the needy and stricken-hearted." His mother, a daughter of Malcolm McNaughton, was a woman of pre-eminent Christian culture. Her father's family took much interest in public affairs, three of her brothers having occupied seats in the Canadian parliament; while a fourth, active in the organization of Wisconsin as a state, was a member of its legislative body.

Mr. McMillan attended the district and village school, and completed his education at Le Roy Academy and Cornell University. In 1869 he went to Buffalo, and began the study of law with Laning, Cleveland & Folsom, gaining admission to the bar in 1871. He is now the head of the firm of

*ROWLAND BLENNERHASSETT MAHANY*

McMillan, Gluck, Pooley & Depew, and local counsel for the Vanderbilt railway companies centering in Buffalo.

In 1885 Mr. McMillan was elected by the Republican party to represent the Buffalo district in the state senate. His career in that body was most satisfactory to his constituents, and was so thoroughly endorsed by his party and friends that he was renominated in the fall of 1887. This nomination he declined. While in the senate he was chairman of the committee on canals, and a member of the committees on judiciary, cities, claims, and Indian affairs.

In addition to the extensive legislation relating to his own district, Senator McMillan found much time to devote to general legislation. As chairman of the canal committee, he prepared and carried through the legislature, against strong opposition, the bill providing for the lengthening of the locks on the Erie canal, by which the cost of transportation between the Great Lakes and tide water was reduced

DANIEL HUGH McMILLAN

upwards of forty per cent. He prepared the following bills, and secured their enactment: one providing for a uniform policy of fire insurance, to be used by all companies doing business in the state; another providing for a commission to report upon the most humane method of carrying into effect the death penalty in capital cases — the bill resulting in the application of electricity in such cases in New York state; another authorizing the utilization of the power of Niagara Falls; another reforming prison labor and discipline; and another regulating the employment of women in manufacturing establishments.

Even before his election to the senate Mr. McMillan was active in behalf of many reforms relating to the affairs of Buffalo. It was through his efforts that the Municipal Court was established; he was also chairman of the committee that formulated the plan embodied in the revised charter of 1892, which provided for a board of aldermen and a board of councilmen, one originating all legislation, and the other having an absolute power of veto.

In 1893 Mr. McMillan was elected by the people of the state one of the fifteen delegates at large to the convention to revise and amend the constitution. In this body he took an active and leading position. He was chairman of the committee on the governor and other state officers, a member of the committees on judiciary and on rules, and also one of the special committee to prepare an address to the people of the state setting forth the work accomplished by the convention.

Mr. McMillan's success has been largely due to a high sense of personal and professional honor, and to untiring industry, coupled with a sagacity that enables him to direct and utilize other men. As a lawyer he takes high rank, as his frequent appearance in the highest courts of the state and nation fully attests. No member of the legal profession possesses the confidence and esteem of the bench and bar in a greater degree. He has a kind and considerate nature, but it does not blind him to his duty, nor swerve him from it. As a politician he has had few equals, for he has demonstrated that a man may enter politics, and discharge the duties of political life, with untarnished honor. As a scholar he has fine literary discrimination, and the cultured tendencies of his mind are mirrored in a choice and well-selected library at his home. For some years past he has devoted much of his leisure to the study of Scottish history and literature, and his collection of works relating to this subject takes high rank among similar collections in America.

Mr. McMillan has been president of the Buffalo Library, and was one of the managers of that association during the erection of the library building and the Hotel Iroquois. He is a manager of the Buffalo State Hospital, a trustee of the State Normal School, a member of the Buffalo Historical Society, and of the Society of Natural Sciences.

In 1888, 1892, and again in 1896, he was chosen at the Republican state convention one of the alternate delegates at large to represent the state in the Republican national convention. He has been a member of the Republican state committee; belongs to the American and the state bar associations; and for twelve years was one of the examiners of applicants for admission to the bar. He is a member of the Presbyterian church, the Buffalo and Liberal clubs, the Chi Psi fraternity, the Consistory, and the Temple. He has two sons, Morton and Ross.

*PERSONAL CHRONOLOGY— Daniel Hugh McMillan was born at York, N. Y.; was educated at Le Roy Academy and Cornell University; studied law in Buffalo, and was admitted to the bar in 1871; was state senator, 1886-87; was chosen alternate delegate at large to the Republican national conventions of 1888, 1892, and 1896, and delegate at large to the state constitutional convention of 1894; has practiced law in Buffalo since 1871; married Delphia Jackson of Sandusky, N. Y.*

***

**William L. Marcy,** one of the most successful of the younger lawyers at the Erie-county bar, was born in Madison county, New York, in 1858. He was taken to Lockport during infancy, and lived there until he was twelve years old. Moving to Buffalo in 1870, he completed his education in the public schools of that city, graduating from the high school in 1876. He had decided to follow the legal profession, and with that end in view he entered an office soon after his graduation from the high school, and read law for three years. In 1879 he was admitted to the bar.

Mr. Marcy was only twenty-one years old at this time, but he determined to make an early start on his professional career, and opened an office at once in Buffalo for the general practice of law. He had no associate for the first four years, but by 1883 his business had assumed such proportions that he thought it desirable to form a partnership. He did so, accordingly, with Joseph V. Seaver, and the firm of Seaver & Marcy carried on a successful practice until 1886. Mr. Marcy then associated himself with Manly C. Green. The partnership of Green & Marcy continued until the senior partner was elected to the Supreme Court in the fall of 1891, when Mr.

Marcy formed a partnership with Emory P. Close. The firm of Marcy & Close has existed ever since, and has built up, from the substantial foundation afforded by the original clientage of the associating members, an imposing column of court litigation and general office practice. Mr. Marcy was appointed assistant district attorney of Erie county by George T. Quinby, serving two terms or six years altogether, from 1887 to 1893. In that responsible position he confirmed his previous reputation as an able and trustworthy guardian of legal rights.

It is evident from all this that Mr. Marcy is a highly successful attorney; but he is a good deal more than that. From the beginning of his active career he has interested himself in various matters connected with the civic welfare, and has been a power for good in the endless struggle with the foes

*WILLIAM L. MARCY*

of honest government. Believing that the ends sought by all good citizens may be most effectively secured through party co-operation, and convinced that the Republican party is altogether the best organization for the purpose, Mr. Marcy has been one of the leading advisers among the younger men who shape the policy of the Republican party. He is a member of the Buffalo Republican League, and has been vice president of the same. The cause of civil-service reform appealed to him powerfully, and he was appointed by Mayor Becker one of the civil-service commissioners.

Aside from his profession and from political and public affairs, Mr. Marcy has concerned himself with various forms of social life. He is a Mason, attending Ancient Landmark Lodge, No. 441; and an Odd Fellow, attending Niagara Lodge, No. 25. He is a member of the Buffalo, Liberal, and Thursday clubs, and of the Idlewood Association. He belongs, also, to the Buffalo Historical Society, and to the Sons of the American Revolution. He has been a trustee of the Buffalo Library, and is now a trustee of the Buffalo School of Pedagogy.

*PERSONAL CHRONOLOGY—William Lake Marcy was born at Peterboro, N. Y., August 29, 1858; was educated in the public schools of Lockport and Buffalo, graduating from the Buffalo High School in 1876; was admitted to the bar in 1879; was assistant district attorney of Erie county, 1887–93; married Carrie Childs of Medina, N. Y., October 7, 1885; has practiced law in Buffalo since 1879.*

* * *

**Charles D. Marshall,** the son of a distinguished lawyer, has inherited his father's legal talents, and has perpetuated the family fame in the annals of the Buffalo bar. His ancestors were French-Italian on one side and English on the other. Mr. Marshall's father, Orsamus H. Marshall, was not only a lawyer of ability, but also an historical scholar of renown. How important his work in American history was may be seen in the circumstance that Francis Parkman, in the later editions of his historical writings, changed numerous passages in consequence of Mr. Marshall's researches. It is hardly too much to say that Orsamus Marshall, in certain departments of American history, was the foremost scholar of his day.

With such a family prestige to maintain, Charles Marshall needed the best of educations. This he obtained. Thorough training in both public and private schools, added to the general culture unconsciously absorbed in the atmosphere of a cultivated home, enabled him to make the most of his special professional preparation. The public schools of Buffalo, Springside Academy, near Auburn, N. Y., and the famous Hopkins Grammar School at New Haven, Conn., amply qualified him to take up the study of law without the interposition of a college course. He went through the Albany Law School, accordingly, in the years that many young men now spend in college, and was admitted to the bar in 1861.

At that time Orsamus H. Marshall was carrying on an extensive practice at the Erie-county bar, and he was glad of an opportunity to receive able assistance by taking his son into partnership. The firm of O. H. & C. D. Marshall served many clients acceptably for about three years, or until the senior partner was appointed clerk of the United States District Court. After carrying on alone for a year both his own and his father's practice Mr. Marshall wisely sought assistance, and began his long association with Spencer Clinton by forming with him, in 1868, the firm of Marshall & Clinton. This was the style until 1873, when Robert P. Wilson was admitted to the firm, and the name became Marshall, Clinton & Wilson. This association was dissolved in 1892, and for a short time thereafter Messrs. Marshall and Clinton practiced together as before. In 1893 they admitted to the firm Adolph Rebadow, who had studied law with them some years earlier; and the present familiar style of Marshall, Clinton & Rebadow was thus acquired. The three attorneys so associated admirably complement each other, and constitute together one of the strongest firms in western New York. Mr. Marshall concerns himself more or less actively with all the business of his firm, but he has paid special attention for many years to the law of real property, and to the management of trust estates. He has been the attorney of the Buffalo Savings Bank since 1878, as his father was for twenty-eight years before that date.

Mr. Marshall is one of the best known clubmen in Buffalo, resorting habitually to the Buffalo Club (of which he has been a director), the Saturn Club, and others. He has a summer residence on Beaver island in the Niagara river, and his friends deem "Beaver Lodge" more attractive than any club. This property Mr. Marshall acquired on the dissolution of the Beaver Island Club, of which he was director and treasurer when Grover Cleveland was president. Mr. Marshall was one of the founders of the Buffalo Society of Natural Sciences, and has been an officer in the organization from the first. He was a director of the Buffalo Library for several years, and in 1887 was elected a member of the real-estate committee. He did not favor, however, the use of the property of the association for hotel purposes, and resigned from the board in 1888. He is at present a director of the Buffalo Fine Arts Academy, the Buffalo Society of Artists, the Buffalo

City Cemetery, and the Third National Bank. He has also served as trustee, treasurer, and vice president of the Thomas Asylum for orphan Indian children on the Cattaraugus reservation.

Mr. Marshall has been for many years one of the trustees of the First Presbyterian Church of Buffalo, and was prominently identified with the movement that resulted in the removal of the church from its former location, where the Erie County Savings Bank now stands, to its present site on the Circle. This step was bitterly opposed by some of the members of the society, and entailed a long legal contest, which Mr. Marshall's law firm, acting in behalf of the trustees, conducted to a successful issue.

Mr. Marshall takes great interest in early American history, and has one of the richest private libraries in this subject anywhere to be found. His father established the library years ago, and collected from a multitude of sources early and rare pieces of Americana. Since his father's death Mr. Marshall has continued the search for choice editions, and has enriched the library in various respects.

*PERSONAL CHRONOLOGY—* *Charles DeAngelis Marshall was born at Buffalo November 14, 1841; was educated at public and private schools; graduated from the Albany Law School, and was admitted to the bar in 1864; has practiced law in Buffalo since 1864.*

**Price A. Matteson** has lived in Buffalo over forty years, has practiced law there thirty-five years, and has made himself well and favorably known throughout western New York. He was born in Darien, Genesee county, in 1840, and spent his boyhood in that town. He obtained his early education in one of the little red schoolhouses that dot the country landscape, and attended for two years Darien Academy, an institution that was never very robust, and that pined away and died long ago. His scholastic training was not carried further, and was thus inadequate to the needs of a professional man. Fortunately Mr. Matteson has a studious disposition and love of learning for its own sake, so that the scanty stock of knowledge originally acquired in the schools of his youth has been augmented throughout his life by systematic and persistent

reading. Literature has always been one of his delights, and he is well acquainted with the standard works of English and American authors.

At the age of fifteen, in 1855, Mr. Matteson left the country for the attractions of city life. Buffalo was growing rapidly at that time, almost doubling

*CHARLES D. MARSHALL.*

its population in the decade before the Civil War; and foretokens of its later prosperity were already at hand. Deciding that a young man who should study law and grow up with the city might reasonably expect to see his professional practice expand with the population, Mr. Matteson entered the office of Houghton & Clark, Buffalo, and read law diligently for several years. His preparatory studies had been insufficient, as we have seen, and he was unable to avail himself of a law school; but he passed the bar examinations in due season, and began to practice in Buffalo in 1861.

Mr. Matteson was then twenty-one years of age, and thus obtained an early start on his professional career. In 1862–64 he was associated with Judge

George W. Houghton, with whom he had studied law, under the firm name of Houghton & Matteson; but otherwise he has practiced alone. The process of building up a legal clientage is not easy, but Mr. Matteson surmounted one obstacle after another until his position at the bar was well assured. So

PRICE A. MATTESON

prominent, indeed, had he become by the year 1877 that he was mentioned as a suitable candidate for the position of city attorney; and he was elected to the office for a term of two years, 1878-79.

Mr. Matteson has found relaxation from professional cares in various fraternal societies. He belongs to the Order of United Friends and to the Ancient Order of United Workmen. He is also a member of Queen City Lodge, No. 358, F. & A. M., and of Keystone Chapter, No. 162, R. A. M. He has attended for many years the Delaware Avenue Methodist Episcopal Church in Buffalo. His social life is divided between Buffalo, where most of his practice is carried on and where he usually lives in winter, and Darien, his native town in Genesee

county. He is fond of country life, especially as it is found in Darien; and he takes delight in spending the summer months amid the scenes of his boyhood.

*PERSONAL CHRONOLOGY* — *Price A. Matteson was born at Darien, N. Y., January 12, 1840; was educated in district schools and Darien Academy; moved to Buffalo in 1855; studied law, and was admitted to the bar in 1861; married Frances E. Brown of Buffalo May 20, 1865; was a member of the Erie-county board of supervisors in 1863, and city attorney of Buffalo, 1878-79; has practiced law in Buffalo since 1861.*

* * *

**Charles G. Pankow**, a commissioner of public works, and otherwise prominent in the political and commercial life of Buffalo, was born near Feldberg, in the grand duchy of Mecklenburg-Strelitz, Germany, in 1851. When he was thirteen years of age he came to this country, whither two brothers had preceded him. Forced to look for employment at once, he became an apprentice in the bakery and confectionery business, and for a long time followed this calling under various employers. His work prevented school attendance during the day, but he did what he could to remedy this privation by attending an evening school. By the year 1880, when he was twenty-nine years old, Mr. Pankow felt that he had worked for other people long enough, and that it was time to make a beginning for himself if he was ever to get ahead in the world. He set up a grocery and saloon, accordingly, in the part of Buffalo where he was well known, and soon had his business on a secure footing. In 1885 he moved his store to its present location at the corner of William and Pratt streets, where he carries on a large and growing business.

The grocery, however, is only one of several enterprises engaging Mr. Pankow's time. He has been connected with the Harmonia Mutual Fire Insurance Co. since its organization in 1877, and has been president of the company continuously since January, 1886. In 1882 he acquired an interest in the Clinton Co-operative Brewing Co., and has been president of the concern since January, 1883, with the exception of the year 1885. Since 1888 he has been president of the Western

Bottling Co., Limited, which manufactures all kinds of "soft" and carbonated drinks. Since May, 1890, he has been president of the Brewers' Association of Buffalo. He is one of the trustees of the United States Brewers' Association, having been elected to the board at Philadelphia, in 1895, for a term of three years.

A man possessed of such business ability as the foregoing record necessarily ascribes to Mr. Pankow, cannot long keep out of politics; especially if such ability be united to uprightness of character and genial personal qualities. All these conditions coexist in Mr. Pankow, and his political success is only what might have been expected. He first came prominently into public notice in the fall of 1883, when he was elected alderman from the old 5th ward for the term of 1884-85. After that he held no official position for a number of years, though he continued to be an active force in the counsels of Republican leaders in his part of the city. In the fall of 1894 he received the nomination for the important position of commissioner of public works, and was elected for a term of three years beginning January 1, 1895.

Mr. Pankow is highly sociable in his nature and habits, and belongs to various organizations designed to satisfy this healthy instinct of mankind. Among these may be mentioned the Masonic order, the Independent Order of Odd Fellows, and the Ancient Order of United Workmen. He is a member of the Evangelical Lutheran St. John's Church.

*PERSONAL CHRONOLOGY—Charles George Pankow was born near Feldberg, Germany, January 27, 1854; learned the baker's and confectioner's trade, and worked at the same, 1868-80; married Mary Graf of Tonawanda, N.Y., June 30, 1870; has conducted a grocery business in Buffalo since 1880; was alderman from the 5th ward, Buffalo, 1884-85; was elected commissioner of public works, Buffalo, in November, 1894, for the term 1895-97.*

∴

**Lee H. Smith** is well known in Buffalo in both professional and social circles. As a medical practitioner and scientist he has won deserved repute, while in military circles he has attained fame as an expert marksman, having been

for six years inspector of rifle practice in the 74th regiment.

Dr. Smith is an Ohio man by birth, but went to Buffalo when a boy, and has since resided in the Queen City. He attended the public schools, including the high school, and afterwards entered the medical department of the University of Buffalo. He pursued the regular three-year course, and passed his examinations; but was not permitted to take his degree, as he had not then attained the age of twenty-one. The degree of M. D. was duly conferred upon him the year following. Dr. Smith's remarkable maturity of mind, and natural talent for the science of medicine, are shown by the early age at which he graduated, and especially by his high rank on commencement day. He took the first Stoddard prize for the best examination in

CHARLES G. PANKOW

materia medica, and shared the Fillmore prize for the best thesis.

Wisely concluding that at his age he could afford to spend a few more years in perfecting his professional knowledge, Dr. Smith went to New York, and matriculated at the College of Physicians and Surgeons, the medical department of Columbia University. Having graduated thence in 1881, he returned to Buffalo to begin his professional work. He has ever since followed his calling in that city.

*LEE H. SMITH*

Dr. Smith has confined his practice to special lines, chiefly of a surgical nature. Early in his professional career he was appointed surgeon in Dr. Pierce's Palace Hotel. This magnificent hostelry was destroyed by fire in 1881, and in its place was erected the Invalids' Hotel, with which Dr. Smith has been connected from the first. He has also been for seven years vice president of the World's Dispensary Medical Association, an auxiliary of the hospital. His opportunities there for varied practice have been numerous and valuable.

Dr. Smith belongs to the eclectic school of medicine, adopting what is best from all schools. He is president of the board of medical examiners representing the Eclectic Medical Society of the State of New York. He has written much on subjects connected with his profession. He is a prominent member of various scientific clubs, having been president of the Buffalo Microscopical Club one year, and of the state Eclectic medical society two years. He has been first vice president of the Buffalo Society of Natural Sciences for the past two years, and devotes all his leisure hours to this institution.

Dr. Smith is an enthusiastic rifleman, and was a member of the 74th regiment's rifle team that won the trophy of the state for four successive years. His relations with the military entitle him to the rank of captain. He is a member of St. Paul's Episcopal Church, of the Buffalo Club, and of Ancient Landmark Lodge, F. & A. M.

*PERSONAL CHRONOLOGY—*
*Lee Herbert Smith was born at Conneaut, O., August 10, 1856; moved to Buffalo in 1868; graduated from the medical department of the University of Buffalo in 1877, and from the College of Physicians and Surgeons, New York city, in 1881; married Corrie Emma Lacy of Buffalo October 5, 1880; has been vice president of the World's Dispensary Medical Association since 1889.*

\* \* \*

**John Strootman**, who has been identified with the shoe industry of Buffalo as a manufacturer for over twenty years, was born in the Queen City of the Lakes. His people are old Buffalonians, his grandfather having cultivated a farm in a part of the city that is now covered with business blocks. Mr. Strootman himself was born, and lived for over forty years, in the same house that sheltered his mother from her childhood.

After attending Public School No. 7, and later a private school, Mr. Strootman at the age of fourteen closed his books to learn his father's business. The latter was for many years a manufacturer of custom shoes, and had in his service some of the best shoemakers of the old world. In such a school Mr. Strootman could not fail to learn the business perfectly in every detail; and the seven years that he spent in his father's employment gave him the finest possible training for his career as a manufacturer. In addition to this long experience he spent about eighteen months with John Dorschel & Co. of Buffalo, taking charge of their pattern and shoe-cutting department. Soon after attaining his majority he began business for himself, having saved an amount of capital that most people would deem wholly inadequate. He knew the business so thoroughly, however, and exercised so much care and judgment in his ventures, that success attended his efforts from the first. He enlarged his operations gradually, as his trade relations extended and his capital increased, until to-day his goods are in demand not only in western New York, but in the South, the West, and the Northwest as far as the Pacific coast. His fourteen experienced shoe salesmen reside at convenient points in various states, and visit each important town and city at frequent intervals. For this purpose samples of new styles and shapes are made up twice a year, and displayed by the salesmen six months ahead of the season. Mr. Strootman usually sells his specialties to but one store in a town. He manufactures shoes for ladies, misses, and children exclusively. The official records of the factory inspectors show that Mr. Strootman employs more people than any other individual manufacturer in Buffalo. His interest and amusement from boyhood has been shoemaking and shoe machinery, and his factory contains an unusually complete equipment of the finest modern appliances used in progressive shoemaking.

In recent years the subject of gold and silver mining has engaged Mr. Strootman's attention to a considerable extent. He has been much more successful in the shoe business than the average manufacturer; but the conditions of trade in that industry have become more and more keenly competitive, until the margin of profit has sunk to a point not far removed from zero. Mr. Strootman has filled his factory with expensive labor-saving devices and costly machinery of various kinds; but competitors have done the same, and the net result has been that customers have bought their shoes at lower and lower prices, while the manufacturers have reaped little or no benefit from the decreased cost of production. In the case of gold and silver mining the conditions are so far different that improved processes of extracting ores, more productive refining methods, and various economies in getting the metal from the mine to the smelter, are all directly effective in swelling the profits of

the business. Having convinced himself of the soundness of this view, Mr. Strootman next sought an opportunity to apply his reasoning practically. A little research among the mining properties of Colorado discovered such opportunities, and he is now largely interested in some of the most productive mines of the Centennial State. He is a director of the Buffalo & Colorado Development Co., and is president of the Golconda Consolidated Mining, Milling & Tunnel Co. The former corporation has its general offices in Denver, its property lying in Fremont county, Colorado. The Golconda company operates mines and mills in Clear Creek county in the same state.

Mr. Strootman has been much absorbed in his business, and has taken little part in outside matters. He belongs to various clubs in Buffalo and the east-

*JOHN STROOTMAN*

ern cities, but rarely visits them. He is a director of the Union Bank, Buffalo.

*PERSONAL CHRONOLOGY — John Strootman was born at Buffalo April 2, 1851; was educated in public and private schools ; learned the shoemaker's business, and worked for his father in the same, 1865–72 ; has been a director of the Union Bank, Buffalo, since 1892 ; has carried on a shoe manufactory in Buffalo since 1874.*

DE WITT G. WILCOX

**De Witt G. Wilcox**, who has made himself widely known in Ohio and in western New York as a physician and surgeon, was born less than forty years ago in Akron, Ohio. He attended the public schools of that city, graduating from the high school in June, 1876. In the following September he entered Buchtel College, where he pursued elective courses for two years. The Cleveland Homeopathic Hospital College was his next educational resource, and in 1880 he received the degree of Doctor of Medicine from that institution. He began practice in the same year at Akron, in partnership with Dr. William Murdoch.

From the beginning of his medical studies Dr. Wilcox had looked forward to the career of a surgeon rather than that of a general physician ; and

in order to equip himself still more thoroughly for such work, he gave up for a while his practice in Akron, and crossed the water to study under the best surgeons abroad. He spent the year 1882 in the hospitals of London and Paris, thereby acquiring an invaluable experience in the theory and practice of surgery. Dr. Wilcox is one of the few Americans who have received appointments in European hospitals ; for six months in 1882 he held the position of resident house surgeon in the London Temperance Hospital.

Having returned to this country early in 1883, Dr. Wilcox resumed the practice of medicine at Akron, and continued to follow his profession there for the next five years. In 1888–89 he associated himself with Dr. Joseph T. Cook of Buffalo, taking up his residence in that city February 1, 1888. There was then no member of the homeopathic school in Buffalo who was giving special and exclusive attention to surgery, and several prominent physicians of the city requested Dr. Wilcox to supply the deficiency. He did so, as stated, and obtained a large practice almost at once. By May, 1890, his surgical patients were so numerous that he found it convenient to establish for their use the Wilcox Private Hospital. This institution served his purpose so well that Dr. Wilcox, at the request of many fellow-practitioners in Buffalo and Erie county, enlarged the hospital, and made it general instead of private. In 1894 the name was changed to the Lexington Heights Hospital. The staff of the institution includes twenty or more of the best-known physicians of Buffalo and western New York, and the enterprise must be regarded from every point of view as highly successful.

Dr. Wilcox was one of the original staff members of the Erie County Hospital, and he is still an attending surgeon in the institution. He is likewise one of the staff of the Buffalo Homeopathic Hospital. He has membership in the New York State Homeopathic Medical Society, in the American Institute of Homeopathy, and in the Buffalo Society of Natural Sciences ; and he has been president of the Homeopathic Medical Society of Western New York. He has frequently written on professional subjects in various medical journals. In 1891 he delivered before the Society of Natural Sciences a lecture on

"Heredity of Crime," which was published in the Buffalo *Express*.

*PERSONAL CHRONOLOGY— De Witt Gilbert Wilcox was born at Akron, O., January 15, 1858; was educated in the Akron public schools and Buchtel (O.) College; graduated from the Cleveland Homeopathic Hospital Medical College in 1880; married Jennie Irene Green of Alfred Centre, N. Y., September 5, 1884; practiced medicine in Akron, 1880–88, with the exception of a year spent in surgical study abroad; has practiced in Buffalo since 1888, devoting himself especially to surgical and hospital work.*

\*\*\*

**James A. Campbell,** one of the most popular insurance men of Buffalo, is a native of Canada, having been born in Niagara Falls, Ont., forty-odd years ago. His parents moved to Buffalo, however, when James was seven years old, and the boy's education was received at Public School No. 1 in that city, and at Bryant & Stratton's Business College.

Mr. Campbell made an early beginning in the business of his life thus far, entering at the age of sixteen the office of the old Buffalo City Insurance Co., of which William G. Fargo, then mayor of the city, was president. Mr. Campbell found the business congenial from the first, and devoted himself assiduously to his duties. He received rapid promotions, and had attained a position of considerable importance when the great Chicago fire of 1871 forced his company into bankruptcy, together with many others throughout the country. So able an assistant as Mr. Campbell had proved himself had no difficulty in finding a new opening, and he soon entered the general insurance office of Worthington & Sill as policy clerk. The following year he was promoted to take charge of the fire business of the firm, holding that position for several years. Having made himself thoroughly familiar with the working details of the establishment, Mr. Campbell determined to start in business for himself. Accordingly, in October, 1876, he obtained the local agency for several prominent companies, and opened an office in Buffalo. For seventeen years he carried on alone a prosperous business. Writing all kinds of insurance — life, fire, accident, plate-glass, and steam-

boiler — he has established a reputation for courteous and business-like dealing, and prompt and satisfactory adjustment of losses, that easily accounts for his success. By October, 1893, his business had grown to such proportions that it became desirable to obtain the help of an associate, and he consolidated his agency with that of John S. Kellner. At the same time they moved their offices to prominent and spacious quarters on Niagara street, where the firm of Campbell & Kellner has continued to the present time, doing a large and steadily increasing business.

When the Buffalo Association of Fire Underwriters was organized in August, 1879, Mr. Campbell was one of the incorporators of the institution, and he has always taken an active part in its work. He was president of the association in 1889.

*JAMES A. CAMPBELL*

Aside from his lifelong connection with the business of insurance, Mr. Campbell is known throughout the state for his interest in co-operative savings and loan associations. As early as 1871, when such societies were a good deal of a novelty, he helped to organize the Prospect Hill Savings and Loan Association, and was made its president. This company was conducted on the old "limited" plan, and in 1877 the stock matured, and the company liquidated its obligations and passed out of existence. In January, 1884, the Erie Savings and Loan Association was organized in Buffalo, and Mr. Campbell was made one of the directors. This position he soon resigned to accept the office of president of the Irish-American Savings and Loan Association, organized in the following April. He remained at the head of the management of this institution for a number of years, finally resigning in January, 1894. During this time he was active in promoting a union of similar associations throughout the state, and when the New York State League of Co-Operative Savings and Building Loan Associations was organized at Rochester in June, 1888, Mr. Campbell was chosen second vice-president. The following year he was unanimously elected president of the state association, and ably discharged the duties of the office.

Twelve years' service in the National Guard must also be recorded in any account of Mr. Campbell's life that aims at completeness. He enlisted as a private in company B, 74th regiment, in May, 1868, received promotions in due course, and on the organization of company F was made first lieutenant of that company. In September, 1876, he became commander of the company, and retained this position until his resignation from the Guard in May, 1880.

*PERSONAL CHRONOLOGY—James Arthur Campbell was born at Niagara Falls, Ont., July 24, 1852; was educated in Buffalo public schools and Bryant & Stratton's Business College; was a clerk in insurance offices, 1868-76; married Emeline A. Short of Buffalo September 17, 1888; was president of the Irish-American Savings and Loan Association, 1884-94; has conducted a general insurance agency in Buffalo since 1876.*

\*\*\*

**Moses W. Dake** has been identified, ever since he went to Buffalo fourteen years ago, with the bakery business. His earlier career as a hardware merchant in a country town seems quite distinct from this, but the experience thus acquired doubtless made possible the success that has attended the later undertaking.

Mr. Dake was born in Livingston county, New York, fifty-six years ago. His father was a farmer in the beautiful Genesee valley; and the boy's education consisted of a little book learning, obtained

at the district school of his native town of Portage, and a large amount of practical experience gained on the farm. Not altogether content with the results of this curriculum, he spent a short time at Nunda Academy in his twentieth year; but an extended course there seemed impracticable, and he soon returned home, and devoted himself for several years to farming.

In December, 1864, he began mercantile life as a clerk in a hardware store in Albion, N. Y., remaining there somewhat more than three years, and learning the business thoroughly in all its details. Commercial life was more attractive to him than farming had been, and he determined to engage in business on his own account. He returned to Nunda, therefore, and established with his father the firm of J. M. Dake & Son, hardware merchants. The father furnished most of the capital, but the son had the entire management of affairs, and was practically the head of the concern. Mr. Dake carried on this business for ten years or more, and built up a good country trade in that part of Livingston county. In March, 1879, he sold his interest to a younger brother, and the business is still conducted under the old firm name of J. M. Dake & Son.

For the next few years Mr. Dake was variously occupied in settling up his affairs at Nunda, and in operations in the oil country; but in January, 1883, he moved to Buffalo, and bought an interest in the Niagara Baking Co. there. In this new line of activity he was successful from the first, and the rapid growth of the business furnishes abundant evidence of his fitness for the management of large interests. When he became connected with the establishment it employed about twenty-five men, and was comparatively a local concern; the plant now employs 125 hands, and its product is sold in New York, Pennsylvania, and Ohio.

In 1890 the United States Baking Co. was organized for the purpose of absorbing into a single corporation numerous baking plants in the central and eastern part of the country, thus unifying their methods of doing business, perfecting their policies, and preventing disastrous competition. The company has been highly successful, and has grown to be one of the largest concerns of its kind in the world. Mr. Dake was a prime mover in this consolidation of interests; and in October, 1890, he merged his business into the United States Baking Co. under the special name of the Niagara Bakery Branch. He has been one of the directors of the corporation since this time, and was assistant general manager of the company in 1891. In that year he spent several months in Boston, building a large bakery for the United States Baking Co., and getting the plant into smooth running order. Returning to Buffalo, he resumed the active oversight of the Niagara Bakery, and has since been so employed. In 1893 he erected for his branch of the business a large four-story building on Michigan street, complete in all its appointments, and admirably adapted to the needs of the extensive business.

Mr. Dake has always been a stanch Republican, and for many years during his residence in Livingston county took an active part in public affairs, serving on the county committee, and otherwise advancing the interests of his party. He attends the Delaware Avenue Baptist Church, Buffalo.

*PERSONAL CHRONOLOGY* — *Moses William Dake was born at Portage, N. Y., March 23, 1841; was educated at district schools and Nunda Academy; was clerk in a hardware store at Albion, N. Y., 1863–68; married Harriet T. Hallenbake of Albion December 24, 1867; engaged in the hardware business at Nunda, 1868–79; has carried on the Niagara Baking Co., now known as the Niagara Bakery Branch U. S. Baking Co., Buffalo, since 1883.*

• • •

**William C. Dambach,** unlike many men of the present day, has confined himself wholly to one line of activity, and has won success in the same calling in which he first found employment as a boy. The story of such a life contrasts markedly with that of the man who has tried his hand at various occupations in the way of trade or manufacture. Though the latter may gain something as regards general experience, he unquestionably loses much valuable time in the battle of life.

Mr. Dambach was born in Buffalo just two months from the day Fort Sumter fell into the hands of the Confederates. He was educated in the public schools of his native city, but left school at the age of fourteen, and began to earn his own living. Having obtained a situation with C. M. Lyman, a Buffalo druggist, he was set to work washing bottles, running the soda fountain, and making himself generally useful about the store. After spending a year in this position he entered the drug store of Thurstone & Co., Buffalo, remaining in their service until he attained his majority. He

was then taken into the firm, which assumed the style of George T. Thurstone & Co.

At the expiration of two years Mr. Dambach sold his interest in the drug business, and entered the medical department of Niagara University as a student. He spent one year there, and gained a

*MOSES H. DAKE*

practical knowledge of medicine that has since been of great value to him in his business. Having decided that a commercial career was likely to be more congenial than a profession, he abandoned his medical studies, and opened a drug store on Seneca street, Buffalo. This was in 1885, and he continued to do business there for ten years. In the meantime, on January 1, 1892, he established an uptown store on Main street; and since May 1, 1895, he has confined his business to the latter location.

In addition to his ordinary drug business Mr. Dambach devotes considerable attention to the manufacture of various pharmaceutical preparations. He has recently completed a laboratory admirably equipped for this purpose, where he will be able to conduct the manufacturing branch of his business on a larger scale than has hitherto been practicable. Mr. Dambach concentrates his whole energy upon his business, and it is already apparent that this singleness of aim will be rewarded by unusual success.

WILLIAM C. DAMBACH

*PERSONAL CHRONOLOGY— William C. Dambach was born at Buffalo June 14, 1861; was educated in the public schools; served as clerk in a drug store, 1875-84; was a member of the drug firm of George I. Thurstone & Co., 1882-84; studied medicine for one year; has conducted a drug business in Buffalo since 1885.*

***

**Conrad Diehl,** though still in the prime of life, is classed in the popular mind with the older physicians of Buffalo. This comes about from the fact that he has always lived in the city, began the practice of his profession there early in life, and attained public office, and consequent prominence, while yet a young man.

After attending public and private schools in Buffalo, and obtaining thereby an excellent preparatory education, Dr. Diehl entered upon his professional studies in the medical department of the University of Buffalo. During the last two years of his course he held the position of resident physician at the county almshouse. After graduating from the University of Buffalo with the class of '66 he determined to round out his professional equipment with a course of study in the old world, and with this end in view he went abroad in the summer of that year. Having studied under the best instructors on the continent for a year, he returned to this country, and opened an office in Buffalo May 1, 1867, for the general practice of medicine. He has followed his profession in that city continuously since the date mentioned.

Dr. Diehl was well and favorably known in the city of his birth even at this early period of life, and the fact was strikingly evidenced in his nomination for the position of coroner in the fall of 1867. He was elected by an extremely large majority, and filled the office efficiently for a term of three years. He declined a renomination, deeming it best to devote his whole time to private practice and hospital work. In February, 1874, he was appointed attending physician at the General Hospital, holding that position until the death of Dr. Rochester, when he was appointed consulting physician; he is still serving in the latter capacity. For the last twenty-three years Dr. Diehl has been secretary to the medical staff of the General Hospital. He served as surgeon to the 65th regiment from 1870 to 1878; and for six years, beginning in 1871, he was attending surgeon at the Erie-county almshouse. He has been a member of the Buffalo board of school examiners since its organization, and was chairman of the board until February, 1896, when he declined a re-election. He is president of the medical board of the German Deaconess Society. He is a strong supporter of the movement for civil-service reform, and was a member of the first civil-service commission of Buffalo. He belongs to various professional and other societies.

*PERSONAL CHRONOLOGY— Conrad Diehl was born at Buffalo July 17, 1843; was educated in public and private schools; graduated from the medical department of the University of Buffalo in 1896; was coroner of Erie county, 1868-70; married Caroline Trautman of Weissembourg, Alsace, May 5, 1869, and Lois M. Masten of Somerset, Mass., May 28, 1892; has been a member of the Buffalo board of school examiners since its organization in 1892; has practiced medicine in Buffalo since 1867.*

***

**Wesley C. Dudley** is so well known in western New York, and has been in the public eye so long, that most people will be surprised to learn that the Civil War antedated his birth by several years. After attending district schools and the Aurora Academy in his native county, Mr. Dudley began his active career at the age of seventeen as a teacher. In this way he procured means to complete his course at Aurora Academy, graduating therefrom in 1888. He then resumed teaching, becoming principal of the Sardinia Union School, and afterward of the Alden Union School. His success as an educator was such that in 1890 he was nominated by the Republican party for the office of school commissioner of the eight Erie-county "south towns." The county itself on this occasion went Democratic by a plurality of 2000, but Mr. Dudley's reputation and personal popularity carried him to victory in the face of general defeat. He seems to have made a specialty of holding important positions and doing remarkable things at an age younger than that of other people similarly circumstanced; and in this case, for example, when he became school commissioner at the age of twenty-three, he was the youngest man in the state holding that office.

But Mr. Dudley had other ends in view than the attainment of a high position among educators. Seeing clearly that his talents would find abundant room for exercise in the legal profession, he declined a renomination to the position of school commissioner, and entered the office of Rogers, Locke & Milburn as a student. The lawyers thus associated constitute one of the strongest legal firms of Buffalo, or even of the state, and in their office Mr. Dudley made rapid progress in the mastery of the law. He was admitted to the bar at Rochester in October, 1894, and began the practice

*CONRAD DIEHL*

of his profession at once in Buffalo. For about two years he practiced alone, but on September 1, 1896, he formed a partnership with Milford W. Childs, son of Justice Henry A. Childs, under the firm name of Dudley & Childs. The new firm begins business with all antecedent conditions highly favorable, and substantial success may safely be predicted.

In some quarters Mr. Dudley is better known as a public man than in his professional capacity. We have already noted his early political prominence in the southern part of Erie county. He has retained this personal following in that locality, and has at the same time extended his influence in other parts of western New York. In October, 1894, he was elected clerk of the Erie-county board of supervisors, and twice since then he has been re-elected. In the spring of 1896 he exerted himself actively in support of McKinley's nomination for the presidency, and was elected a delegate to the Republican national convention at St. Louis. He was the youngest delegate in the convention.

Mr. Dudley is a member of Livingstone Lodge, No. 255, F. & A. M., of Colden, Erie county, and of Aurora Chapter, No. 282, R. A. M. He belongs also to the Independent Order of Odd Fellows, and to the Royal Arcanum.

*WESLEY C. DUDLEY*

*PERSONAL CHRONOLOGY—Wesley Coleman Dudley was born at Colden, Erie county, N. Y., May 31, 1867; attended district schools and East Aurora (N. Y.) Academy; taught school, 1884-90; was elected school commissioner of the southern part of Erie county in 1890; studied law in Buffalo, and was admitted to the bar in 1894; married Flox Belle Stickney of Buffalo April 18, 1895; has been clerk of the Erie-county board of supervisors since October, 1894; has practiced law in Buffalo since 1894.*

...

**Arthur W. Hickman,** prominent at the bar of Erie county for the last twenty years, and well known otherwise as a public-spirited citizen, was born in Calhoun county, Michigan, in the mid-century year. His parents, Isaac Hickman and Eliza Bale

Hickman, were from Devonshire, England, and came to this country in 1847. Mr. Hickman was taken to Buffalo during his infancy, and has lived there ever since. He attended the public schools of the city, and went through the high school, graduating therefrom with the class of '68. Having determined to make the legal profession his life-work, Mr. Hickman entered the office of Austin & Austin, Buffalo, soon after his graduation from the high school, for the purpose of learning law by studying text-books, and by observing the actual routine practice of the profession in a busy office. There were few law schools in those days, and these were not looked upon with favor by the bench or bar, being regarded as places for the easy manufacture of lawyers. Their students were not required to pass qualifying examinations, and so were often admitted with little knowledge of the law. Mr. Hickman found the office method of learning law entirely practicable and successful. He was admitted to the bar at Rochester in September, 1871, and was thus able to begin the practice of his profession when he had been out of the high school but three years.

As he was then only twenty-one years old, he thought it unnecessary to open an office of his own at once, and he continued with Austin & Austin for about a year as their managing clerk. In the fall of 1872 Benjamin H. Austin, Sr., retired from the firm, and Mr. Hickman formed a partnership with the younger Mr. Austin. The firm of Austin & Hickman carried on a successful practice until 1879, when Mr. Austin moved to the Hawaiian Islands to accept a judgeship. For the next few years, during which his time was largely taken up with political matters, Mr. Hickman practiced alone. In 1884 he formed a partnership with Nathaniel S. Rosenau, under the style Hickman & Rosenau. This association continued less than two years, as Mr. Rosenau withdrew in 1885 to take charge of the charity-organization work in Buffalo. For eight years after this Mr. Hickman carried on an important practice without partnership assistance; but in 1893 he formed with William Palmer the firm of Hickman & Palmer. This association still continues, and the firm serves acceptably a large number of individual and corporate clients. Mr.

Hickman began practice so young that his experience rivals that of many older men ; and his judgment in legal affairs is such as might be expected to result from twenty-five years of conscientious service at an exceptionally able bar. He is a lecturer on pharmaceutical jurisprudence in the Buffalo College of Pharmacy.

Mr. Hickman has enjoyed a large practice during almost all his professional life ; but he has not permitted his private interests to absorb his energies, and he has taken a good deal of time for public duties, and for certain matters promoting the general welfare. Municipal reform, the enlargement and betterment of the Buffalo system of docks, the improvement of the public schools, and good government in general, are subjects that have engaged his attention with resultant benefit to his fellow-citizens. His service in the state legislature in the years 1881–82 affords abundant evidence of his public spirit. He shaped his conduct in the assembly with reference to the welfare of his constituents, unmindful of his own political preferment, and without regard to the wishes of machine politicians. His honest independence and refusal to become the tool of a political "boss," cost him the party nomination for re-election. On this occasion, however, the politicians were reckoning without their host, and the people chose to exercise their right of self-government. A petition signed by 1500 of the most prominent men in the district urged Mr. Hickman to become a candidate for re-election on an independent ticket. He did so, and was elected by a majority of 1849 votes, the Democrats making no nomination.

In social life Mr. Hickman has enjoyed the prominence to which his professional standing and his engaging personal qualities entitle him. He belongs to many social organizations, including the Oakfield, Yacht, Island, and Ellicott clubs. For fifteen years he has been a trustee of the First Baptist Church. He takes an active interest in practical philanthropy, and belongs to most of the charitable organizations of Buffalo. He is one of the directors of the German Young Men's Association, and was secretary of the building committee during the construction of Music Hall. He belongs to the Buffalo Orpheus and Liedertafel, and is a life member of the Buffalo Library.

*PERSONAL CHRONOLOGY—Arthur Washington Hickman was born at Marshall, Calhoun county, Mich., June 18, 1850 ; was educated in the Buffalo public schools ; was admitted to the bar at Rochester in 1874 ; was member of assembly from the 3d Erie-county district, 1881–82 ; has practiced law in Buffalo since 1874.*

* * *

**Devoe P. Hodson,** well known in western New York as a member of the Erie-county bar, was born at Ithaca, Tompkins county, in 1856. His general education was acquired in the public schools of Ithaca, in the academy at the same place, and in Cornell University. His legal education was obtained in the office of Samuel D. Halliday and in that of Judge Marcus Lyon. Both of his preceptors were prominent attorneys of Ithaca,

ARTHUR W. HICKMAN

and his clerkship in their offices proved an excellent substitute for a law school. He was admitted to the bar at Saratoga Springs in September, 1877.

Beginning practice at once in Ithaca, Mr. Hodson followed his calling in that city for the next ten years. He was successful as regards both his professional practice and the outside affairs with which most lawyers become more or less concerned; but in 1887 he made a radical change in his vocation

*DEVOE P. HODSON*

and his residence. In the year mentioned he purchased a half interest in the newspaper and printing plant of the Ithaca *Republican*, a paper then published by Walter G. Smith. Messrs. Smith and Hodson determined to move their plant bodily to southern California, and accordingly they established in San Diego a large printing office, publishing in connection therewith the *Morning Telegram*. This business proved unsuited to Mr. Hodson, and after a few months he sold his interest to his partner, returned to Ithaca, and resumed the practice of law.

Concluding that Buffalo offered greater attractions as a place of residence than the smaller city, and greater promise of material rewards as a field of professional practice, Mr. Hodson left Ithaca in

February, 1889, and opened an office in the metropolis of western New York. He practiced alone there for four years, and then associated himself with George B. Webster in the firm of Hodson & Webster. They have continued to practice together since 1893. Mr. Hodson concentrates his efforts on the contested work of his firm, and is regarded as a successful and effective advocate before judge or jury.

During his student days Mr. Hodson espoused the cause of Democracy, and has ever since been prominent in the councils of that party. In 1882–83 he was clerk of the board of supervisors of Tompkins county. In 1885–86 he was corporation counsel of Ithaca. Shortly after moving to Buffalo he received the unusual distinction of an election by the municipal authorities of Niagara Falls as non resident corporation counsel; this office he held two terms. In 1892 he was appointed by the state comptroller a commissioner to report upon the accounts of surrogates throughout New York state relative to the collateral-inheritance law. In 1893 he was nominated for the office of delegate to the constitutional convention, but shared the general defeat of the Democratic party in that year. Mr. Hodson is a prominent platform speaker, and has taken a leading part in every important political campaign since he has lived in Buffalo. He is an active member of the Masonic fraternity, belonging to Ancient Landmark Lodge, No. 441, F. & A. M.; he is also a member of other fraternal societies.

*PERSONAL CHRONOLOGY—Devoe Pell Hodson was born at Ithaca, N. Y., March 24, 1856; was educated in the public schools of Ithaca and in Cornell University; studied law in Ithaca law offices, and was admitted to the bar in 1877; married Mariette Wood of Painted Post, N. Y., December 24, 1880; was clerk of the Tompkins-county board of supervisors, 1882–84, and corporation counsel of Ithaca, 1885–86; practiced law in Ithaca, 1877–89, with the exception of a few months spent in southern California, and has practiced in Buffalo since 1889; was non-resident corporation counsel of Niagara Falls, N. Y., 1890–92.*

* * *

**John W. Reff**, now auditor of Erie county, and heretofore well known in western New York as a public official, was born in Buffalo in 1862. He was educated in the public schools of that city, attending them from the time he was eight years old until the age of sixteen. At the latter stage of life he became a messenger boy for the Western Union Telegraph Co., and followed that interesting calling for the next two years. Deciding then to connect himself with some business in a permanent capacity, he obtained a suitable position with the freight-carrying company known as the Red Line, and began his long service in the transportation industry. He learned the business rapidly, and soon became an expert in the computation and auditing of mileage records. He remained with the Red Line for eight years, or until he was twenty-six years old. By that time he had decided to stop working for others, and to embark in business on his own account. In 1886, accordingly, he opened an office in Buffalo for the writing of insurance, and has since carried on that business with marked success. He makes a specialty of steam-boiler, plate-glass, and accident insurance.

At the relatively early age of twenty-nine Mr. Neff entered upon the political career by which he is best known to the public at large. He had taken a keen and intelligent interest in public affairs from his early manhood, affiliating with the Republican party; but he held no office until 1891, when he was elected one of the supervisors of Erie county from the 7th ward, Buffalo. His work in this office was so satisfactory to his constituents that he was re-elected in 1893. He served upon the purchasing and auditing committee of the board of supervisors, one of the most important assignments. When that committee was abolished in 1895, and the office of county auditor was created to take its place, Mr. Neff was unanimously nominated for the position by the Republican county convention, and was elected to the office by a majority of 15,000 votes. He is now discharging efficiently the duties of this responsible position, his term of office running until December 31, 1899.

Mr. Neff is fond of social life, and belongs to various fraternal societies. He is a member of Ancient Landmark Lodge, No. 441, F. & A. M., and of Buffalo Lodge, No. 36, I. O. O. F. He belongs, also, to the Royal Arcanum, and is a charter member of the Odd

Fellows' Club. He attends Calvary Presbyterian Church.

*PERSONAL CHRONOLOGY*— *John William Neff was born at Buffalo March 23, 1862; attended public schools; worked for the Red Line fast-freight company, 1880–88; married Eva J. Sloan of Buffalo May 10, 1881, and Elizabeth A. Menzies of Buffalo January 27, 1896; was elected a county supervisor from the 7th ward of Buffalo in 1891, and was re-elected in 1893; was elected auditor of Erie county in November, 1895, for the term 1896–99; has conducted an insurance business in Buffalo since 1888.*

***

**George R. Stearns** has practiced his profession in Buffalo, his native city, for nearly a score of years. Indeed, with the exception of the time spent in college, his whole life has been passed in

*JOHN H. NEFF*

the Queen City. The story of his career, made up of successful work in high school, university, and medical college, from each of which he graduated with honors, followed by more successful work in his chosen profession, is not an eventful one : but it is none the less interesting.

Born in Buffalo somewhat more than forty years ago, Dr. Stearns obtained his preliminary education in the city schools, beginning with Public School No. 11, and ending with the Buffalo High School.

GEORGE R. STEARNS

from which he graduated in 1871. He then entered the University of Rochester, graduating with the class of '75 and receiving the degree of A. B. In 1878 the same institution gave him the degree of A. M. in course. Dr. Stearns went to New York city to obtain his medical education, becoming a student in the New York Homeopathic Medical College and Hospital and receiving his M. D. degree in 1878. He then spent a year at Ward's Island Homeopathic Hospital, to which he had received, in competitive examination, an appointment as senior member of staff. The practical experience there gained was of the utmost value to the young physician, and finely fitted him to begin the practice of his profession.

In 1879, therefore, Dr. Stearns returned to Buffalo, and opened an office on Linwood avenue, where he has since remained. He has resisted the modern tendency to limit his field to certain specialties, and has conducted a general practice with gratifying success. In addition to his private practice he holds the position of obstetrician in the Buffalo Homeopathic Hospital, is president of the Training School for Nurses connected with that institution, and is medical director of the Ingleside Home of Buffalo. He has served the public as district physician and physician at the county jail.

Dr. Stearns is a member of the Erie County Homeopathic Medical Society, the Homeopathic Medical Society of Western New York, and the New York State Homeopathic Medical Society : he was elected president of the Western New York society in 1896. He has written articles for these and other scientific and professional associations, which have been published in their journals and transactions. While in college Dr. Stearns joined the Alpha Delta Phi fraternity, and after graduation he was elected a member of the Phi Beta Kappa society. He is a charter member of both the Liberal and University clubs of Buffalo, and expects to become a member of the Sons of the Revolution, in virtue of the active part taken by his ancestors in the early struggle for independence.

From his childhood Dr. Stearns has been connected with the Lafayette Street (now the Lafayette Avenue) Presbyterian Church, and since 1886 he has been a member of the Session of the society.

PERSONAL CHRONOLOGY—George Raynolds Stearns was born at Buffalo March 30, 1854; attended Buffalo public schools, and graduated from the University of Rochester in 1875 ; graduated from the New York Homeopathic Medical College and Hospital in 1878, and spent the following year in Ward's Island Homeopathic Hospital, New York city; married Jennie S. Olver of Buffalo May 25, 1880; has practiced medicine in Buffalo since 1879.

* * *

**John Trefts** has been a foremost figure in the iron industry of Buffalo for half a century. He lived in Pittsburg when a young man, and learned there the trade of an iron molder. His long residence in Buffalo began in the year 1845, when he took charge of the foundry department of the Buffalo Steam Engine Works. He remained with this concern and its successors nearly twenty years, acquiring stock in the company, and taking an important part in the business. The panic of 1857 brought disaster to the Buffalo Steam Engine Works, as to thousands of other concerns; and the business was reorganized under the style of George W. Tifft, Sons & Co. Mr. Trefts remained with the new firm seven years, and contributed very materially to the success of the business in that period. Chiefly through his skill as an iron worker and knowledge of iron ores, the Tifft firm was able to carry through profitably in 1860 a contract for the manufacture of the rails used in laying the first street railway in Buffalo.

A greater degree of historical interest attaches to Mr. Trefts's connection with the petroleum industry. Soon after Colonel E. L. Drake "struck oil" in August, 1859, near Titusville, Penn., and thereby set in motion one of the greatest industrial forces of the century, Mr. Trefts interested himself actively in the oil business both as an operator and as a manufacturer of mechanical appliances used in the production of oil. He made the castings for the engine used to pump the Drake well. In 1860 he associated himself with P. S. Willard, and leased a part of the Shaffer farm, not far from Colonel Drake's original discovery. In operating their well here they used the first engine that ever drilled with a rope, as well as the first set of jars ever employed in oil production. These jars were invented by Mr. Willard, and were ill adapted to their purpose, so that the well was not a success, resulting in a "plugged hole." Relic hunters interested in the subject may pleasantly employ themselves in excavating these jars, as they are still in their untimely grave, buried under $1800 worth of experience.

Mr. Trefts's next venture was on the Ham McClintock farm, near Oil City. In attempting to drill this well his workmen became discouraged, and were disposed to abandon operations, so that Mr. Trefts took charge of the work personally. After dislodging three sets of tools left in the well by former drillers, he vindicated his faith by discovering a well that yielded 200 barrels of oil a day. A few weeks after this he succeeded in completing the well-known Van Slyke well on the Widow McClintock farm. He had no interest in this well, which was owned by John Van Slyke and C. M. Farrar. Work had been abandoned on the well, but Mr. Trefts felt so confident that oil could be found there that he undertook further explorations at his own expense. His judgment proved excellent, as the well produced 2500 barrels of oil a day.

These ventures in the oil country had not interfered with Mr. Trefts's regular occupation at the Tifft works in Buffalo. On the contrary, his experience as an actual producer of oil helped him materially in later life as a manufacturer of the various machines used by oil operators. In other parts of the business as well Mr. Trefts was particularly successful. For many years the propeller wheels made by him

*JOHN TREFTS*

were deemed more durable than any wheels elsewhere obtainable. This superiority was the result of his knowledge of iron, and ability in mixing various kinds of ore so as to produce the maximum strength in the finished product. By the year 1864 he had acquired such a mastery of his business, and had attained such a reputation among buyers of foundry products, that he felt able to give up his position at the Tifft concern, and embark in business on his own account. He formed a partnership,

*EDWARD K. EMERY*

accordingly, with Chillion M. Farrar and Theodore C. Knight, under the style of Farrar, Trefts & Knight, for the purpose of establishing a foundry, machine shop, and general iron works. In 1869 Mr. Knight retired from the firm; but the other partners, under the well-known style of Farrar & Trefts, have carried on the business ever since. Their resources at first were slight; but their experience, energy, and character ensured ultimate success. The business expanded year by year until now the firm is known throughout the iron trade as one of the most successful concerns in its line in the country. Boilers of all kinds, propeller wheels, steam engines, iron and brass castings, and a multitude of special mechanical appliances used in various industries, are some of the famous " F. & T." products. The works of the concern occupy three acres of valuable land in Buffalo.

*PERSONAL CHRONOLOGY—John Trefts passed his youth in Pittsburg; was in the employ of the Buffalo Steam Engine Works and their successors, 1845–64; engaged in oil production, 1859–64; has conducted a foundry and general iron works at Buffalo since 1864.*

***

**Edward K. Emery,** elected to the bench of the Erie County Court in 1895, has worked hard all his life, and has reaped a reward consistent with his efforts and deserts. Though not far beyond the period of life allotted to "young men," he has already solved the problem of prosperity, and has made his future secure. His success is the more noteworthy from the fact that he selected a field of labor in which rewards are long delayed, and never come by chance, or as the result of anything but work and worth.

Born in East Aurora, Erie county, in 1851, Judge Emery spent his youth and early manhood after the manner of many young men in the country dependent on themselves for a professional education. By teaching school in winter and farming in summer he acquired sufficient means to pursue the study of law. Proceeding to Buffalo for that purpose, he gave his days and nights to legal research with characteristic earnestness, and was admitted to the bar in 1877. He began the practice of law in Buffalo at once, and soon became known as a trustworthy adviser in all legal matters. This favorable reputation was confirmed in his further practice, and he was regarded during his later years at the bar as one of the ablest of the younger attorneys in Erie county.

Like so many other lawyers, Judge Emery began early in his career to take a keen interest in political affairs. His convictions on public questions have harmonized with the principles of the Republican party, and for many years he has enjoyed the confidence of Republican leaders and shared their counsels. He first came prominently before the public as a candidate for office in the fall of 1886, when he received the Republican nomination for the assembly in the old 5th Erie-county district. He was elected that year and again the next, and served on important committees in the assembly in the sessions of 1887–88. For the next few years his law practice was so large that he thought it inexpedient to re-enter political life, though he continued to follow public affairs closely. In the fall of 1895, however, when the Republican party offered him professional and political honors at once in the nomination for the office of county judge, he wisely decided to accept the candidacy. He was elected by a majority of more than 8000 votes over his Democratic opponent, and on January 1, 1896, began his term of six years.

Judge Emery has many traits of mind and character that make him prominent in social life, and he has a wide circle of friends. He belongs to various fraternal organizations, including the Masonic order, the Odd Fellows, and the Royal Arcanum.

*PERSONAL CHRONOLOGY—*
*Edward Kellogg Emery was born at East Aurora, N. Y., July 29, 1851; attended the district schools and academy of his native town; taught school and studied law, and was admitted to the bar in 1877; married Clara B. Darbee of East Aurora October 7, 1884; was member of assembly, 1887–88; practiced law in Buffalo, 1877–95; was elected judge of the Erie County Court in 1895 for the term 1896–1901.*

**Byron D. Gibson,** long a leading merchant of East Aurora, N. Y., and latterly a prominent man in the public affairs of the town, was born there in September, 1859. He was educated in the district schools of his native town, and in the academy at the same place. His father, Chisman Gibson, carried on a clothing and boot and shoe business at East Aurora for nearly forty years, and Byron entered the store at the age of nineteen for the purpose of acquainting himself thoroughly with mercantile affairs. He remained with his father until the latter's death in 1890, when he purchased the business from the estate. He has since conducted the enterprise with the success that might have been predicted from his long experience and excellent school of commercial training. The store is still located in the same place where the elder Mr. Gibson began business in the middle of the century; the establishment has been for many years one of the landmarks of the village.

East Aurora has come to be a good deal of a town, and its population extends over a correspondingly wide area. The original Gibson establishment was located in the western part of East Aurora, in the village called Willink. Deeming it desirable to reach the important trade at the other end of the town, Mr. Gibson formed a partnership, in March, 1891, with A. E. Hammond, for the purpose of carrying on a business in clothing and general furnishings in the territory not covered by the Willink store. This project was successfully carried out, and Mr. Gibson now has a flourishing trade in both his individual establishment and his partnership concern.

Having lived in East Aurora all his life, and taken a leading part in the business and social affairs of the community, Mr. Gibson gradually attained

*BYRON D. GIBSON*

political prominence as well. In March, 1892, he was elected trustee of the village for two years. At the expiration of this term he received the honor of an election as president of the village of East

Aurora, and in the following year he was re-elected to this office. In March, 1895, he was also elected supervisor from the town of Aurora for two years. On this occasion the Democrats paid him the indirect but conspicuous compliment of nominating no one against him. On November 20, 1889, Mr. Gibson

*East Aurora September 4, 1882; was postmaster at Willink, 1890-93; was trustee of the village of East Aurora, 1892-94, and its president, 1894-96; was elected supervisor of the town of Aurora in March, 1895, for two years; has conducted a clothing store at East Aurora since 1890.*

\*\*\*

**Warren B. Hooker,** a son of John and Philena Hooker, was born in Perrysburg, Cattaraugus county, New York, in 1856. His father was a native of Vermont, and his mother, Philena Waterman, of Massachusetts. They settled on a farm in Cattaraugus county, and lived honorable and useful lives prolonged in each case beyond the psalmist's allotment of three score years and ten.

Warren was reared upon his father's farm, and became accustomed early in life to such toil and discipline as gave him strength for future achievement. Aside from the district school he was educated at Forestville Academy, from which he graduated with honor in 1875. Soon after this he began the study of law with the late John G. Record of Forestville. He was admitted to the bar of the Supreme Court in 1879, and practiced law in Chautauqua county until he moved to the West in 1882.

In 1884 he returned to western New York, and entered upon the active practice of his profession in Fredonia. He has remained there ever since, and has attained abundant success in both professional and political life. In 1878 he was elected special surrogate of Chautauqua county for a term of three years.

*WARREN B. HOOKER*

was appointed postmaster of Willink, and held the office four years, 1890-93.

Mr. Gibson is a firm believer in fraternal societies, and supports several by membership and regular attendance. He belongs to Blazing Star Lodge, No. 694, F. & A. M.; to East Aurora Chapter, No. 282, R. A. M.; and to the Masonic Life Association of Western New York. He is also an Odd Fellow, attached to Aurora Borealis Lodge, No. 642, and a member of the Royal Arcanum.

*PERSONAL CHRONOLOGY— Byron D. Gibson was born at East Aurora, N. Y., September 14, 1859; was educated in district schools and Aurora Academy; was a clerk in his father's store at East Aurora, 1878-90; married Hattie A. Holmes of*

He was elected supervisor of the town of Pomfret in 1889 and again in 1890, receiving at the latter election the unusual compliment of the support of both political parties.

In the fall of 1890, at the age of thirty-three, Mr. Hooker received the nomination of the Republican party for congress in the 34th congressional district, comprising the counties of Chautauqua, Cattaraugus, and Allegany, and was elected by a majority of 5726. He was re-elected in 1892, and again in 1894, when he received 15,300 plurality. In 1896 he was nominated once more, and was elected to the 55th congress by a plurality of 27,426 votes. These repeated political triumphs have been achieved in a district distinguished for intelligence, and for the zeal and ability with which political honors are contested.

In the 54th congress Mr. Hooker held the important and coveted position of chairman of the committee on rivers and harbors. The bill that he then presented to the house in that capacity was not only passed in both branches of congress by large majorities, but was afterward carried over a presidential veto. The measure provided for an appropriation larger than that of any previous bill on the subject; but the expenditures authorized were so judicious and so equitably distributed that the bill was not attacked by the press, nor by the opposition speakers in the campaign of 1896.

Mr. Hooker's success as a politician is not accidental, but is due to his able discharge of duty, and to the benefits that he has conferred upon his constituents. Industrious, ambitious, self reliant, pleasing in manner, commanding in presence, Mr. Hooker may confidently look forward to a continuance of public favor and of political honors.

In September, 1884, Mr. Hooker was united in marriage with Etta E. Abbey, a daughter of Chauncey Abbey, lately president of the Fredonia National Bank, and long a prominent citizen of Chautauqua county. They have two children, Sherman Abbey and Florence Elizabeth.

*PERSONAL CHRONOLOGY — Warren Brewster Hooker was born at Perrysburg, N. Y., November 24, 1856; was educated at Forestville (N. Y.) Academy; studied law, and was admitted to the bar of the Supreme Court in 1879; was elected special surrogate of Chautauqua county in 1878; married Etta E. Abbey of Fredonia, N. Y., September 11, 1884; was supervisor of the town of Pomfret, 1890-91; has been member of congress since 1891; has practiced law in Fredonia since 1884.*

* * *

**John McEwen**, well known among the successful business men of Allegany county, was born in New York city in 1849. His father, Duncan McEwen, came from the Highlands of Scotland, and learned the machinist's and millwright's trades in Glasgow. He was a man of high character and exceptional ability, and ultimately obtained the position of superintendent of one of the large government shipyards at Liverpool. He was ambitious, however, to have a busi-

ness of his own, and wisely decided that America promised the quickest realization of his hopes. In April, 1849, accordingly, he embarked with his family from Liverpool in one of the first steamships constructed for ocean traffic. They made the passage in eighteen days, then regarded as marvelously quick. John was born the day they landed in New York city.

After sojourning in various places, Duncan McEwen finally established himself in Wellsville, Allegany county, in May, 1854. Beginning operations modestly — a lathe and a drilling machine, indeed, comprised his entire plant at first — he enlarged his business prudently as opportunity offered, and laid the foundations in his little foundry and machine shop for the magnificent business afterward developed therefrom by his sons. At the time of his death,

*JOHN McEWEN*

however, in February, 1864, the works were hardly self-sustaining, and John McEwen, his eldest son, was still a boy. The shop was rented for a few years, therefore, while John and William, the next son, prepared themselves to take up the business. By 1868 they felt ready to carry on the work, and formed the firm of McEwen Brothers.

This was nearly thirty years ago, when both the brothers were under age and comparatively inexperienced. They had traits of mind and character, however, that more than countervailed these deficiencies, and they achieved a rare degree of success. Suffering a temporary setback in October, 1876, when their plant was burned, they at once erected a substantial brick building, and equipped the same with the finest and latest machinery. The firm now employs about sixty workmen, and manufactures annually engines, boilers, mill and general machinery valued at $125,000 or more. They make a specialty of fitting up tanneries, and for twenty-five years past they have furnished the machinery for all the tanneries within 150 miles of Wellsville, including the enormous plant at Costello, Penn., the largest in the world. John McEwen has been the head and front of the concern from the beginning, and its success may be ascribed in a superior measure to his energy and business sagacity.

Aside from his career as a manufacturer Mr. McEwen deserves mention as a public-spirited citizen. In political matters he has long been an important factor in the Republican party of Allegany county, though he has felt unable to neglect his business interests in the way that public office might require. He was a delegate, however, to the Republican national convention held at Minneapolis in 1892. He is a Knight Templar Mason of St. John's Commandery, Olean. His connection with the Wellsville, Coudersport & Pine Creek railroad illustrates both his public spirit and his ability as a financier. The road was originally planned many years ago, but work was abandoned after eight miles had been graded. In 1890 it was rumored that Hornellsville capitalists intended to build a competing line that would seriously retard the growth and prosperity of Wellsville. Under the circumstances Wellsville deemed it highly important to put its road through at once. Mr. McEwen personally circulated the paper for subscriptions; and he was elected president and general manager of the new company, and gave close attention to the construction, equipment, and operation of the road. The enterprise was highly successful, and when the road was sold, in 1895, the stockholders realized a handsome profit on their investment.

*PERSONAL CHRONOLOGY—John McEwen was born at New York city April 21, 1849; moved to Wellsville, Allegany county, N. Y., in 1854; married Emma Alger October 30, 1879; began business as a manufacturer of machinery at Wellsville in 1868, and has continued the same since.*

**Sheridan McArthur Norton,** though he has barely reached the prime of life, has already attained success in various lines of activity — as a teacher, lawyer, promoter, farmer, banker, and judge. His lineage will bear close scrutiny, and will lead the examiner back to Puritan stock. He was born in a country town in Allegany county, New York, shortly before the middle of the century, and spent his boyhood and youth under the harsh but wholesome discipline of farm life. His early education was obtained in the common schools, in Friendship Academy, and in the Belmont graded school. At the age of seventeen he began to teach, and continued in that occupation during a great part of the time for the next seven years. Before he had reached his majority he was made president of the Allegany County Teachers' Association.

He was fond of teaching, and would doubtless have been very successful in the profession, had he decided to make that his life-work. The law was attractive to him, however, and in 1871, simultaneously with his teaching, he began to fit himself for the bar. He studied first at Angelica with Judge James S. Green and D. P. Richardson, afterward reading law at Belmont with Judge Hamilton Ward and General Rufus Scott. He was admitted to the bar January 8, 1874, and began practice three weeks later at Friendship.

He built up rapidly a valuable clientage, and obtained a wide reputation for adjusting disputes without litigation, and for winning his suit in contested cases. He acquired distinction, also, as a referee, and ever since his admission to the bar he has had an extensive business in hearing references.

Judge Norton has shown great aptitude for business, and has been strikingly successful as a promoter of business enterprises. He has been president of the Citizens' National Bank of Friendship since its organization in 1882. He was interested in the first oil well at Richburg, Allegany county, and devoted considerable attention to the development of the oil industry. He showed rare good judgment in withdrawing from his operations at an opportune time. He had an active part in the construction of the railroad from Friendship to Bolivar, holding a directorate in the company. As a practical farmer conducting operations on a large scale, Judge Norton has likewise demonstrated his business ability. He owns a farm in Friendship of over 200 acres, which he personally superintends, and to which he turns for relief from the exhausting labors of his profession.

Judge Norton has always taken great interest in the affairs of his town and county. For three years, beginning in 1879, he was supervisor of Friendship, and was chairman of the board during the last two years of his service. For a number of years he was a member of the board of education. He is an effective and entertaining speaker, and is in great demand on Fourth of July and other patriotic occasions.

In 1889, and again in 1895, he was elected county judge, and has faithfully discharged the duties of that office, and of the Surrogate's Court of the county. His decisions are characterized by strict integrity and judicial fairness. His thorough knowledge of the law was tested in the notable Miner will case. This was carried to the Court of Appeals, which sustained Judge Norton's decision. In the fall of 1895 he presided at Geneseo for Judge Nash during the fiercely contested Father Flaherty case, and won much approval for his conduct of the trial.

Judge Norton takes a deep interest in Masonry, in which he has attained the 32d degree.

*PERSONAL CHRONOLOGY—Sheridan McArthur Norton was born at Belmont, N. Y., May 1, 1848; was educated in Friendship Academy and the Belmont graded school; taught school at intervals, 1865-72; was admitted to the bar January 8, 1874, and began practice at Friendship, N. Y.; married Mary Laban Robinson of Friendship September 1, 1880; was supervisor of Friendship, 1879-81; has been president of the Citizens' National Bank of Friendship since 1882; has been county judge and surrogate of Allegany county since 1890.*

\*\*\*

**Lewis S. Payne** has been one of the foremost citizens of Niagara county, New York, for more than half a century. Born in the town of Riga, Monroe county, in 1819, he obtained such instruction as the imperfect common schools of the time afforded, his parents feeling unable to provide education at better schools away from home. Resolving, at the age of sixteen, to start out for himself in the world, Lewis proceeded to Tonawanda, where an uncle lived, and there found

employment as a general-utility boy in one of the variety stores so common in the country. His aptitude for business was marked even at this early day, and by the time he had reached his majority he was able to buy out his employers and conduct the establishment on his own account.

*SHERIDAN McARTHUR NORTON*

General stores in the country, managed prudently by men of character and weight in their community, have often become the basis of substantial fortunes; and Colonel Payne's career illustrates the general truth. Branching out into one enterprise and another as his means increased and experience broadened, he became long before the period of middle life one of the most successful business men in the county. Tonawanda had not then become the second greatest lumber market in the world, but its subsequent prominence in that industry was already foreshadowed; and Colonel Payne, with many others, found it profitable to engage in the business. In 1847 he built the first steam sawmill in Tonawanda. He also engaged for several years in the forwarding, shipping, and commission business. In 1858 he turned his attention to farming, and has ever since maintained a large and beautiful estate in the town of Wheatfield.

When the Civil War broke out Colonel Payne was in the prime of vigorous manhood, and he threw

*LEWIS S. PAYNE.*

himself into the contest with the same persistence and energy that had brought him success in business life. Raising a company of volunteers at his own expense in the fall of 1861, he ultimately reached McClellan's army, and took part in the famous Peninsular campaign. Enlisting as a private, he was promoted through the various grades until he reached the rank of lieutenant colonel. He participated in some of the hottest battles of the war, and in less than four months lost more than a third of his regiment. Williamsburg, Seven Pines, White Oak Swamp, and Malvern Hill were the scenes of some of his earlier battles. In the spring of 1863 he made many daring expeditions with his company, particularly distinguishing himself by able and suc-

cessful operations in Charleston harbor. In August, 1863, while attempting to intercept the communications of the enemy between Charleston and Fort Sumter, he was attacked by a superior force, and after a desperate engagement was wounded and taken prisoner. Confined for a while in the hospital at Charleston, he was afterward taken to Columbia, S. C., where he was kept in close confinement until February, 1865.

With such a record in war and in the mercantile world, Colonel Payne has naturally been prominent in public life. Originally a Whig, he became, after the dissolution of that party, a Douglas Democrat. As early as 1844 he was elected one of the supervisors of Wheatfield, and served on the board for eleven terms. He was the first collector of canal tolls appointed at Tonawanda, holding the office in 1850–51. Elected clerk of Niagara county in the fall of 1851, he discharged the duties of the office efficiently and faithfully during the years 1852–54. Eleven years later he was again made county clerk, and held the office for the term 1866–68. In the fall of 1869 he was elected to the state assembly. He was made chairman of the committee on claims in that body, and was also a member of the committee on canals, and of that on military affairs. In November, 1877, he received the Democratic nomination for the office of senator from the 29th district. This district ordinarily went Republican by about 2000 votes, but on this occasion Colonel Payne was elected by a narrow margin. He was the first Democrat ever elected in the 29th senatorial district. In 1882 he was nominated for congress, but even his great popularity was unequal to the task of overcoming the usual Republican majority.

In recent years Colonel Payne has withdrawn from active pursuits, confining his attention to the oversight of his farm and the maintenance of his property. His memory has become somewhat uncertain with advancing age, but in most respects his seventy-eight years rest lightly upon him. His knowledge of pioneer conditions in western New York, his stirring experiences in the Civil War, and other eventful periods of his career, give unusual charm and interest to his reminiscent talks. He is widely respected in Niagara county, and holds a warm place in the regard of those who know him best. Everyone wishes him a twilight of life as long and as lovely as the fading of day in midsummer on the peaks of Ben Nevis.

*PERSONAL CHRONOLOGY—Lewis Stephen Payne was born at Riga, N. Y., January 21, 1819; was educated in common schools; was clerk in a country store, 1845–49; married Mary Tabor of Ithaca, N. Y., November 22, 1850; served in the Union army throughout the war; was elected a member of the Niagara-county board of supervisors in 1844, and served eleven terms; was clerk of Niagara county, 1852–54 and 1866–68; was member of assembly in 1870, state senator, 1878–79, and candidate for congress in 1884; has been engaged in various mercantile enterprises at North Tonawanda, N. Y., since 1841.*

\*\*\*

**William H. Proudfit** has been identified with the city of Jamestown for more than half a century, and may almost be regarded as a native of the place. He was born, however, in Milwaukee, Wis., and was two years old when he was brought to western New York. He received his education in the Jamestown common schools and academy, but left school at the age of fifteen to begin business life. His first employment was that of clerk in a dry-goods store, and he subsequently served as cashier and finally as bookkeeper in dry-goods and clothing stores in Jamestown. By the year 1862 he had made a good start on a successful mercantile career; but he interrupted it, like so many other men in those fateful years, at the call of his country. Enlisting in company F, 112th New York volunteers, in August, 1862, he served until the close of the war, and was honorably discharged June 13, 1865.

Returning to Jamestown, he established the clothing house of Proudfit & Osmer in December, 1866, buying out the firm of Andrews & Preston. He has conducted this business at the original location ever since, and has become one of the foremost merchants of Jamestown. Mr. Osmer died in 1880, and from that date Mr. Proudfit has been sole owner of the business, devoting his best energies to the enterprise, and achieving most gratifying and well-deserved success.

All public movements for the general good have received Mr. Proudfit's active support. He is a

Republican in politics, and takes a proper interest in party affairs; but he has no aspirations for public office, and has never accepted a political nomination. He is deeply interested in the growth and prosperity of the city that has been his home for so many years, and in its benevolent and charitable work. He is an elder in the First Presbyterian Church there; and took a prominent part in the organization of the local Young Men's Christian Association, serving on its first board of directors. When the James Prendergast Free Library was established in Jamestown, as a memorial of the man to whom the city owes its name, Mr. Proudfit was appointed one of the first trustees of the institution. He is also a trustee of the Cemetery Association, a member and trustee of the Grand Army of the

WILLIAM H. PROUDFIT

Republic, and a director of the Chautauqua County Trust Co.

*PERSONAL CHRONOLOGY—William Henry Proudfit was born at Milwaukee, Wis., December 15, 1841; was educated in the common schools*

and academy of Jamestown, N. Y.; was employed
as clerk and bookkeeper in Jamestown, 1856–62;
served in the Union army, 1862–65; married Ellen
E. Hall of Jamestown October 2, 1866; has conducted a clothing house in Jamestown since 1866.

*HARVEY S. SPENCER*

**Harvey S. Spencer,** one of the best-known
and most respected citizens of the village of Hamburg, was born in Lewis county, New York, fifty-
seven years ago. His father, Stephen Spencer, was
a farmer, and Harvey passed his early years after the
usual manner of farmers' sons. As a boy he attended the district school in Turin, his native town.
He continued his education at the academy at Lowville, the county seat, and at the Fairfield Academy
in the neighboring county of Herkimer, finally completing his scholastic training at Whitestown Seminary, Oneida county. Like so many country boys,
he was compelled to make persistent efforts and many
sacrifices in order to obtain an academic education,
and he availed himself with corresponding eagerness
of all the opportunities that came within his reach.

Having qualified himself for teaching, Mr. Spencer
gave several years to that work in various places in
Lewis and Oneida counties. He had no mind to
make this his life work, however, and in 1865 he
moved to western New York, and took up his residence in Hamburg, Erie county, where
he established an insurance agency. This
business he carried on continuously for
over twenty years, writing both fire and
life insurance, and representing many of
the leading companies of the country.
In 1883 he helped to organize the Bank
of Hamburg, and was made cashier of
the new institution. He has filled this
position ever since, and has proved himself an able and efficient official, serving
the patrons of the bank with uniform
courtesy, and guarding their interests
most faithfully.

Mr. Spencer has identified himself
thoroughly with the pretty village where
he has lived so long, and every worthy
enterprise designed to promote its growth
and add to its business facilities has
received his hearty co-operation and
support. He has taken an active part in
the organization of several local corporations of this kind, notably the Hamburg
Canning Co., the Hamburg Water &
Electric Light Co., and the Hamburg
Investment & Improvement Co., and is
a stockholder in each. He is also secretary and treasurer of the two last-named
corporations. His fellow-citizens appreciate his public spirit, and gave unmistakable evidence of the fact by electing
him to the office of supervisor when he
was nominated by the Republican party
in 1884. The peculiar significance of this election
lies in the circumstance that Mr. Spencer is the
only Republican who has won the office upon party
issues in the history of the town.

Mr. Spencer takes the prominent part in the social
life of Hamburg to which his high standing in business circles naturally entitles him. For many years
he has been a member of Fraternal Lodge, No. 625,
F. & A. M., and served several terms as Worshipful
Master. He belongs, also, to the Royal Arcanum
Council, the local lodge of Odd Fellows, and to the
Ancient Order of United Workmen. He is at
present a director of the Masonic Life Association
of Western New York.

*PERSONAL CHRONOLOGY — Harvey S.
Spencer was born at Turin, N. Y., July 15, 1840;*

*was educated at Lowville and Fairfield academies and Whitestown Seminary; taught school, 1864-65; established an insurance agency at Hamburg, N. Y., in 1865; married Julia A. Bunting of Eden, N. Y., October 11, 1870; was a member of the Erie-county board of supervisors, 1881-82; has been cashier of the Bank of Hamburg since its organization in 1884.*

...

**Edward B. Vreeland** occupies a prominent position in the town and county of his residence — a position that he has attained by force of native ability and elements of personal popularity. He was born in Cuba, Allegany county, N. Y., in December, 1857. He received his education in the public schools of his native town, and in Friendship Academy, from which he graduated in 1876. He then became a resident of Salamanca, N. Y., and for a period of five years was principal of the Salamanca public schools. He was a successful educator, and made an enviable record as a disciplinarian and instructor.

While teaching, Mr. Vreeland was also studying law, and he was ultimately admitted to practice in the courts of the state; but his tastes ran more to business than to the routine of legal practice, and he never engaged actively in his profession. In 1882 he opened an insurance office in Salamanca, and his skillful management and upright dealings converted the enterprise into a large and successful business. He is still connected with the agency. In 1891 he was elected president of the Salamanca National Bank, and yet holds the position.

Ever since early manhood Mr. Vreeland has taken an active interest in political affairs. He is a vigorous and entertaining speaker, and his oratorical services are sought not only for campaign work, but also on social occasions. Believing heartily in the principles of the Republican party, he has done much, on the stump and otherwise, to explain and popularize those principles. He is thoroughly informed on questions of the day. He was elected supervisor of Salamanca in 1893, and still represents his town on the county board. He is regarded as one of the most efficient members of that body. He has been president of the Salamanca Board of Trade for five years, and in that capacity has promoted the mate-

rial interests of the community in various ways. He was postmaster of Salamanca during President Harrison's administration.

Mr. Vreeland has devoted himself principally to business, and has been eminently successful in that regard. He has excellent judgment, is conservative in his methods of thought and action, and has enjoyed in a marked degree the confidence and respect of his fellow-citizens. He is now in the prime of vigorous manhood, and it is the confident belief of his many friends that the future has in store for him a degree of success even higher than that already attained.

Mr. Vreeland has been interested in Masonry for many years, and has reached a high rank in that order. He was the first Eminent Commander of Salamanca Commandery, No. 62, K. T.

*EDWARD B. VREELAND*

*PERSONAL CHRONOLOGY—Edward Butterfield Vreeland was born at Cuba, N. Y., December 7, 1857; was educated in common schools and Friendship Academy; was principal of the Salamanca ( N. Y.)*

*public schools, 1877–82; studied law, and was ad-
mitted to the bar in 1881; married Myra S. Price
of Friendship, N. Y., July 27, 1881; established an
insurance agency in Salamanca in 1882; was postmaster of Salamanca, 1889–93; has been supervisor of*

*DAVID J. WILCOX*

*the town of Salamanca since 1894; has been president
of the Salamanca National Bank since 1894.*

•••

**David J. Wilcox,** like so many other successful
sons of the Empire State, is of New England parentage, his ancestors having been among the early settlers of Vermont. His father, Elihu Wilcox, left the
Green Mountain State more than half a century ago,
and became one of the pioneers of Cattaraugus county,
New York. Born at Leon in that county, shortly
before the middle of the century, Mr. Wilcox spent
his boyhood on his father's farm, attending common
schools in winter and working hard the rest of
the year. He was ambitious to go to college, but
had to practice great self-denial to gain his end.
By teaching school, however, and making sacrifices

of various kinds, he managed to work his way along,
taking preparatory courses at Chamberlain Institute
and Fredonia Normal School, and attending Cornell
University three years in the class of '77.

Having decided to make the practice of law his
life-work, Mr. Wilcox began his reading in the office of King & Montgomery
at Ithaca, N. Y., continued his study
with Henderson & Wentworth at Randolph, N. Y., and finished his legal education at the Albany Law School. He
graduated from this institution in 1878,
and was admitted to the bar at Buffalo
the same year. The lawyers with whom
he studied were exceptionally able attorneys, and in their offices he enjoyed an
unusually good opportunity to acquire a
thorough knowledge of legal forms and
procedure. When this practical experience had been supplemented by a course of
systematic study in a law school, he was
excellently equipped for the attainment
of honors in a keenly competitive calling.

Moving to Springville, Erie county,
in November, 1878, Mr. Wilcox has followed his profession there continuously
since. The practice of a country lawyer
is likely to be varied, and to give one a
wide knowledge of law, and of business
and life in general. Mr. Wilcox has
now received the benefit of such a calling
for nearly twenty years, and he is naturally a lawyer of learning and ability.
He has taken part in many important
cases, besides transacting a large amount
of routine legal business. In the famous
controversy over the estate of David S.
Ingalls, Mr. Wilcox was one of the counsel for the contestants, and had an important part
in securing the compromise that ended the struggle.

In political affairs Mr. Wilcox has always espoused
the principles represented by the Democratic party.
His first public position was that of clerk of the board
of supervisors of Cattaraugus county, which he held
in 1873. A few years after taking up his residence
in Springville he was elected to the state assembly,
representing the southern district of Erie county in
that body in 1883–84. In 1888 he was appointed
by President Cleveland receiver of the United
States land office at Walla Walla, Wash., and spent
the next two years in the Evergreen State. He then
returned to New York, and filled the position of
financial clerk of the state assembly in the years
1890–91.

Mr. Wilcox has long been interested in the Masonic order, belonging to Springville Lodge, No. 351, F. & A. M. He is also an Odd Fellow.

*PERSONAL CHRONOLOGY— David James Wilcox was born at Leon, N. Y., October 27, 1847; was educated at preparatory schools and Cornell University; graduated from the Albany Law School, and was admitted to the bar in 1878; married Happie H. Stowell of East Ashford, N. Y., August 22, 1878; was clerk of the Cattaraugus-county board of supervisors in 1873, member of assembly, 1883-84, and financial clerk of the assembly, 1890-91; has practiced law in Springville, N. Y., since 1878, with the exception of two years spent in Walla Walla, Wash., as receiver of the United States land office.*

...

**Egburt E. Woodbury,** for the past two years surrogate of Chautauqua county, has had a remarkably successful career for so young a man. Though only thirty-six years old, he has had a seat in the state legislature for three years, and has also won distinction in his chosen profession.

Born in the village of Cherry Creek in 1861, Mr. Woodbury spent the first eleven years of his life there, attending district schools when he became old enough. At the end of that time, his parents having died, he moved to Randolph, Cattaraugus county, and there continued his education. He finished his scholastic training with a three years' course at Chamberlain Institute, one of the best and most popular schools in western New York. Having thus acquired as much education as his circumstances permitted, Mr. Woodbury taught school for two winters, and worked as a farm hand for several years; but he had no mind to devote his life to either of these occupations, and in 1880 he began reading law with Rodney R. Crowley of Randolph. His legal studies were completed in the office of Lakin & Sessions at Jamestown, and in the spring of 1884 he was admitted to the bar.

It is always a compliment to the ability and zeal of a young lawyer when those with whom he has studied are glad to retain his services, and to admit him into partnership when he begins practice. Mr. Woodbury received this mark of confidence, and on July 1, 1884, the firm of Lakin, Sessions & Woodbury was organ-

ized. This association was destined to be of short duration, as Judge Lakin, the senior partner, died before the expiration of the month. Messrs. Sessions and Woodbury continued to practice together until July 1, 1885, when Mr. Woodbury formed, with George R. Butts, the firm of Woodbury & Butts. This connection lasted until the election of the senior member as assemblyman in the fall of 1890. For several years thereafter Mr. Woodbury practiced alone; but in December, 1894, he associated himself with Eleazer Green, at that time mayor of Jamestown, and since elected district attorney of Chautauqua county. The firm of Green & Woodbury still exists, and naturally receives much of the legal business of Jamestown and vicinity.

Mr. Woodbury's political career extends over the last ten years. On the organization of Jamestown

*EGBURT E. WOODBURY*

as a city, in 1886, he was elected one of its first justices of the peace, and served for nearly four years, declining re-election at the end of that time. For three years, beginning in 1889, he was a member of the Republican county committee, acting as its chairman in 1889, and as manager of the campaign in 1891. In the fall of 1890, when less than thirty years old, he was elected member of assembly from the 2d Chautauqua-county district by a plurality of 1721, and his re-election in 1891 was effected

HENRY ALTMAN

by a plurality of 2669. In 1892, after the consolidation of the two Chautauqua districts, he was elected to represent the entire county. He was prominently mentioned as a candidate for a fourth term; but refused to allow his name to be used, feeling that he could no longer make the sacrifice of business interests that the office required.

Mr. Woodbury's latest public service, of which he is justly proud, is the part he took in securing the nomination of Major McKinley for President. One of the first champions of this cause in western New York, he became a candidate for the office of delegate to the national convention at the earnest solicitation of the McKinley men of Chautauqua county. Though he was defeated by a few votes in the

district convention, the strong fight made by him and other friends of the great protectionist resulted in the choice of a delegate from the 34th congressional district who went to St. Louis under positive instructions to support the candidacy of William McKinley.

*PERSONAL CHRONOLOGY.*— *Egbert E. Woodbury was born at Cherry Creek, Chautauqua county, N. Y., March 29, 1861; attended district schools and Chamberlain Institute, Randolph, N. Y.; married Florence E. Holbrook of Randolph December 25, 1880; studied law, and was admitted to the bar in 1884; was justice of the peace, 1884–89, member of the Chautauqua-county Republican committee, 1889–91, and member of assembly, 1891–93; has been surrogate of Chautauqua county since January 1, 1895; has practiced law in Jamestown since 1884.*

**Henry Altman** is an excellent example of the American business man, who, in conducting large private affairs, finds inclination and leisure to interest himself also in politics and all worthy enterprises. Although he has not often held public office, nor been officially connected with party management, he has always been regarded in Buffalo as one of the staunchest and most influential Republicans in the city. When any public enterprise has to be carried through, he is one of the first men called upon to help in the movement. He has the ability of interesting other men in whatever interests himself.

Mr. Altman has been a Buffalonian virtually all his life, although he was born in Rochester, and spent his first two years there. He is the youngest son of Jacob Altman, who settled in Buffalo in 1854, establishing the clothing house of Altman & Co., still existent. Henry Altman was educated in the Buffalo public schools and the Buffalo Academy, and graduated from Cornell University in the class of 1873, with the degree of Bachelor of Science. Upon his return home from college he entered business life as a member of the firm of Altman & Co., and quickly developed into an able and successful man of affairs.

Mr. Altman is a good citizen, as well as a good business man, and has always taken a deep, unselfish interest in public affairs. He has been a leader in various movements designed to promote the welfare of Buffalo. When an effort was made there to obtain one or both of the great national political conventions of 1896, Mr. Altman was one of the committee of Republicans appointed by the mayor to work in the interest of the city ; and the Republicans and Democrats together chose him as chairman of the committee of one hundred representative citizens that had in charge the official prosecution of the matter. Such offices as this come naturally to Mr. Altman because it is felt that they could not be in safer or more able hands.

When, under the new charter, a board of school examiners was created in Buffalo, one of the five members of the first board, appointed in February, 1892, was Mr. Altman. The position was an important one. He proved himself a conscientious and highly capable officer, and was reappointed ; and at the reorganization of the board in 1896 he was chosen its chairman.

Mr. Altman has been prominent for years in the counsels of the Republican party in Buffalo, and has served as president of the Buffalo Republican League. He has been connected with many of the public and social institutions of the city. He has served for twenty-one terms as trustee of the Buffalo Library. He is president of the local Alumni Association of Cornell University, and ever since his graduation has been president of the Cornell class of 1873. He is a 32d degree Mason, and has held positions of honor in various lodges, associations, and clubs.

*PERSONAL CHRONOLOGY—
Henry Altman was born at Rochester August 12, 1854; moved to Buffalo in 1856, and attended the public schools there; graduated from Cornell University in 1873; married Mrs. Sadie Strauss Rayner of Baltimore, Md., at London, Eng., July 4, 1887; has been engaged in the clothing business in Buffalo since 1874.*

***

**Irving W. Cole,** who has practiced law in Buffalo since 1893, was well known in both legal and political circles in Schuyler county before he took up his residence in the Queen City of the Lakes. He was born in Seneca county in 1859, and received his early education in the district schools of his native town of Covert. When he had exhausted their limited resources he became a student at the Farmer Village Union School near

by, and finally completed his general education at Cook's Academy, Havana, N. Y., shortly before attaining his majority.

Mr. Cole had determined to become a lawyer, and for that purpose betook himself to Watkins, the county seat of Schuyler county, where his brother was already established in that profession. This was early in the spring of 1880. For somewhat more than two years he read law at Watkins, and then finished his professional studies by a year at the Albany Law School, graduating in May, 1883, with the degree of LL. B. He had been admitted to the bar earlier in the year. Returning to Watkins in September, 1883, he formed a partnership with his brother, Fremont Cole, under the name of Cole Brothers. This style lasted until January, 1889, when E. O. Bolyen was admitted to the firm, which

*IRVING W. COLE*

then became known as Cole, Cole & Bolyen. In the fall of 1890 Fremont Cole withdrew from the firm, but Irving W. Cole and Mr. Bolyen continued to practice together until January 1, 1892. At that time Mr. Cole formed a partnership with a younger brother, Elbert Cole, that lasted about two years.

Circumstances combined to give Mr. Cole an unusual amount of professional experience during his ten years' practice in Watkins. During the greater part of their professional association his brother,

WALTER D GREENE

Fremont Cole, was in the legislature, and thus much of the work of the firm fell upon the younger brother. Later, his partner Mr. Bolyen was elected district attorney, and for the next few years Mr. Cole took an important part in the prosecution of the principal criminal trials in Schuyler county. Thus well equipped with experience, he determined to seek a wider field for the exercise of his talents, and in the fall of 1893 he moved to Buffalo. For a short time he practiced alone, but on May 1, 1894, formed his present partnership with E. J. Plumley, under the firm name of Plumley & Cole.

Since taking up his residence in Buffalo Mr. Cole has confined his attention exclusively to his profession, feeling that at such a time the most important thing was to win the place at the Erie-county bar to which his attainments elsewhere entitled him. He took an active part for many years, however, in political affairs in Schuyler county, and it would not be surprising if he should soon find opportunity to employ his talents in this direction in his new home.

During his law-student days in Watkins he held the position of clerk of the Surrogate's Court, and for the last two years of his residence there he was the chairman of the Republican county committee. He also did good service for his party as the writer of the political editorials for one of the local papers during two years. Mr. Cole's interest in party affairs was stimulated, no doubt, by his brother's noteworthy public career: Fremont Cole represented his district in the assembly for five consecutive years, and was the speaker of that body for two years.

*PERSONAL CHRONOLOGY —
Irving W. Cole was born at Covert,
N. Y., September 21, 1859; attended
public schools and Cook's Academy, Havana, N. Y.; was admitted to the bar in
1884; practiced law in Watkins, N. Y.,
1884–94; was chairman of the Schuyler-county Republican committee, 1892–94;
married Mrs. Nelle E. Ingham of Elmira,
N. Y., June 27, 1894; has practiced law
in Buffalo since 1894.*

•••

**Walter D. Greene,** prominent in Buffalo alike in professional, public, and private life, is a native of the Green Mountain State. His ancestors came from England in early colonial times, and settled in Boston. Later they journeyed into the wilderness of Vermont; and there, in the town of Starksboro, Walter was born forty-odd years ago. His early education was received in the district schools of his native town, and he then took a course of study in the academy at Union Springs, N. Y., from which he graduated in 1871.

Betaking himself to Buffalo at the close of his preparatory studies, Dr. Greene matriculated in the medical department of the University of Buffalo, and received his professional degree from that institution in 1876. He spent the next two years in the Rochester City Hospital, serving first as junior assistant physician, and afterwards in the more responsible post of house physician. In the latter position he had an excellent practical school for the application of the knowledge previously acquired; and he was thus unusually well qualified, when he left the hospital, to begin private practice. This he did, in 1878, at Mendon, Monroe county, New York.

The opportunities for usefulness and for professional success in a country town are necessarily limited, and in 1880 Dr. Greene sought a more extended field. Accordingly, he moved to Buffalo, where he has since conducted a general medical and surgical practice; and in this he has been markedly successful, attaining the high rank to which his talents and professional skill entitle him.

Buffalo has benefited largely by Dr. Greene's sound learning and practical common sense, in his long connection with the health department of the city. In 1882, soon after his arrival there, he was appointed district physician in this department, and served most acceptably for seven years. At the end of that time he was appointed health physician of the city, and for two years filled this responsible position with credit to himself and with profit to his fellow-citizens. In December, 1896, Dr. Wende, on his reappointment as health commissioner of Buffalo for the five years 1897–1901, at once made Dr. Greene his deputy. In this highly desired and most responsible post Dr. Greene will doubtless add to his prestige as a physician and executive officer.

Dr. Greene is a member of all the local and state medical societies, and since 1892 he has held the professorship of hygiene in the medical department of Niagara University. He is prominent in Masonic circles, having taken the 32d degree in the Ancient Accepted Scottish Rite. He also has membership in the Acacia Club, and is a director in the Masonic Library Association of Western New York. He is well known and much liked in social life. He is a member of the Buffalo Club.

*PERSONAL CHRONOLOGY—Walter David Greene was born at Starksboro, Vt., April 29, 1854; was educated in district schools and Union Springs (N. Y.) Academy, and graduated from the medical department of the University of Buffalo in 1876; served on the staff of the Rochester City Hospital, 1876–78; married Mary E. Pursel of Buffalo November 28, 1878; practiced medicine in Mendon, N. Y., 1878–80; was district physician in the health department of Buffalo, 1882–*

*89, and health physician of the city, 1889–91; has practiced medicine in Buffalo since 1880; has been deputy health commissioner of Buffalo since January 1, 1897.*

* * *

**Samuel McGerald,** widely known in western New York for many years in the ministry and in journalism, was born in County Antrim, Ireland, in 1833. He came to this country early in life, and at the age of sixteen began a systematic course of instruction at Genesee Wesleyan Seminary, Lima, N. Y. He devoted the next seven years to a thorough preparation for the ministry, completing his scholastic education in his twenty-fourth year at the Rochester Collegiate Institute.

In August, 1856, Dr. McGerald entered the ministry of the Methodist Episcopal church, and

SAMUEL McGERALD

was stationed at Conesus, Livingston county, N. Y. After serving the usual term in that place he had pastorates successively at Bath, Warsaw, Medina, Albion, Tonawanda, and Buffalo. It was apparent soon after Dr. McGerald entered the ministry that he had chosen a vocation admirably suited to his talents and temperament; and his work in all the places mentioned was exceptionally fruitful of good. While he was pastor of the Riverside Church in Buffalo the society's debt of $16,000 was liquidated.

He has been twice elected a delegate to the General Conference of the Methodist Episcopal church, attending the conference held in New York in 1888 and that in Omaha in 1892. In 1893 his ability and services were fittingly recognized by Nebraska University, which conferred upon him the degree of Doctor of Divinity.

For the last decade or more Dr. McGerald has given most of his time to certain publications intimately connected with the religious world. By no means lacking in the qualities always desired and frequently found in ministers of the gospel, he has in addition to these a practical bent of mind that helped him materially as a pastor, and has been indispensable in his later career as an editor and publisher. Appointed by the Genesee Conference in 1885 to edit the Buffalo *Christian Advocate*, Dr. McGerald found the work so much to his liking that he purchased the paper, and has since conducted the same on his own account. His son Arthur is business manager of the enterprise. The paper is now called the *Christian Uplook*. Dr. McGerald also edits and publishes the monthly organ of the Royal Templars of Temperance. He is profoundly interested in the work of this society, and has conducted its journal with much success.

Dr. McGerald was one of the original "Chautauquans" in 1874, believing heartily in the movement, and has ever since actively supported the cause. He taught normal classes in the summer school at Chautauqua under Dr. John H. Vincent, and for twelve seasons delivered a course of lectures there on Palestine and Jerusalem.

*PERSONAL CHRONOLOGY—Samuel McGerald was born in County Antrim, Ireland, June 29, 1844; was educated at Genesee Wesleyan Seminary, Lima, N. Y., and Rochester Collegiate Institute; married Eunice Ada Durand of Canandaigua, N. Y., August 19, 1858; entered the ministry in 1856, and held various pastorates in New York state until 1885; was a delegate to the General Conference of the Methodist Episcopal church in 1888 and 1892; has been editor and owner of the Buffalo "Christian Advocate," now the "Christian Uplook," since 1885.*

***

**Alexander McMaster** has lived long enough in Buffalo to be reckoned among the "old residents," but the first twenty years of his life were spent in Canada. Born in the village of Fort Erie, Ont., in the early '40's, as a child he could look across the broad Niagara to the city that was later to be his home—a thriving place of nearly 30,000 souls then, though very different from the modern metropolis. Afterward, while still a lad, he moved to Brantford, Ont., and completed his education in the public schools of that place.

The natural bent of his mind led him to a practical calling, and at the age of sixteen he became an apprentice to the machinist's trade in the Waterous Engine Works at Brantford. After a long and thorough preparation there Mr. McMaster moved to Buffalo in 1862, and quickly obtained employment with the King Iron Works of that city. He remained with this concern ten years, receiving promotions from time to time, and finally reaching a position of considerable importance. In 1872, however, he received an appointment as chief engineer of the Commercial line of steamers, and gladly availed himself of the increased opportunities that the greater responsibilities of the position brought to him. During the next decade he became widely known in his profession, and established a reputation as a practical engineer of great ability.

In 1883 Mr. McMaster severed his connection with the Commercial Line, and accepted an appointment as United States local inspector of boilers for the district of Buffalo. He discharged the duties of this office ably and efficiently, and in 1889 President Harrison appointed him United States supervising inspector of steam vessels for the 9th district. This position he held throughout Harrison's administration, and until 1894.

During the thirty-odd years of his residence in Buffalo Mr. McMaster has taken considerable interest in public affairs. In 1879 he was elected alderman from what is now the 20th ward, and served in that capacity for eight consecutive years. He has also been active in various financial enterprises, and since 1893 has been vice president of the Union Bank of Buffalo. He is a Mason and a member of the Acacia Club, and attends the Presbyterian church.

*PERSONAL CHRONOLOGY.— Alexander McMaster was born at Fort Erie, Ont., October 10, 1842; was educated in public schools; learned the machinist's trade at Brantford, Ont., 1858–62; married Malinda Cripps of Buffalo May 3, 1862; was in the employ of the King Iron Works, Buffalo, 1862–72, and of the Commercial line of steamers, 1872–84; was appointed United States local inspector of boilers in 1883, and United States supervising inspector of steam vessels in 1889; has been vice president of the Union Bank, Buffalo, since 1893.*

\*\*\*

**Lewis Stockton,** well known at the bar of Buffalo and in the social world of the Queen City, is descended from the old New Jersey Stockton family, famous in our history from colonial and revolutionary times. His father was the late Rev. W. R. Stockton, D. D. Born in

Montgomery county, Pennsylvania, while the Civil War was still raging, Mr. Stockton obtained his early education in the public schools, and higher instruction at Ursinus College, Collegeville, Penn. This institution was ambitiously named, but Mr. Stockton regarded his work there as preparatory only. Entering Lehigh University, South Bethlehem, Penn., in the fall of 1877, he received there, in 1881, the degree of A. B., graduating at the age of nineteen as valedictorian of his class. Mr. Stockton's rank as a scholar is sufficiently evident in the foregoing statement. His general standing with the college authorities is further attested by his appointment as instructor in South Bethlehem.

While teaching in the charming college town for the next two years Mr. Stockton was looking forward to permanent professional work at the bar, and

*LEWIS STOCKTON*

was preparing himself therefor by reading law under the guidance of General W. E. Doster, a prominent attorney of the Keystone State. At the close of the college year in 1883 he took up his residence in

Buffalo, and entered the office of Bissell, Sicard & Goodyear for further legal training. Devoting all his time now to the mastery of law, he made rapid progress, and was admitted to the bar in June, 1885. After rounding out his legal knowledge with fifteen months' additional observation of and participation in actual practice with the firm of Bissell, Sicard & Goodyear, he set up an office of his own in September, 1886. In the decade since elapsed he has made a reputation as a painstaking and trustworthy adviser in legal affairs. He has had some important contested cases, but he is a discourager of litigancy, and his practice has resolved itself largely into office consultation and research. He has never felt it necessary or advisable to form a partnership for the practice of law.

Without holding public office or receiving political nominations, Mr. Stockton has still concerned himself actively with public affairs. A firm believer in the wisdom of a liberalized tariff, and profoundly impressed with the need of sound money, he has exerted himself zealously in the presidential campaigns concerned with those subjects. He has delivered numerous speeches, contributed articles to the press, and otherwise made himself a factor in the campaigns of recent years. In local affairs, likewise, he has taken critical interest in the principles and practice of municipal government, allying himself with the Good Government clubs, Civil Service Reform Association, and Municipal Ownership League. He was formerly vice president of the Cleveland Democracy. If all good citizens followed public affairs as Mr. Stockton does, the professional politician would lose his occupation, and many of the faults deemed inherent in popular government would be no more.

Having been one of the prime movers in the organization of the University Club of Buffalo, Mr. Stockton has taken great interest in the welfare of the institution ever since its formation in the spring of 1895. He is chairman of its committee on literature and art, and in that capacity devotes much time and thought to the extension and enrichment of the club library. The result is apparent to all members who frequent the delightful literary corner of the clubhouse. Mr. Stockton is also a member of the University Club of New York city.

Mr. Stockton has taken a prominent part for several years in the councils of the Episcopal church in the diocese of Western New York; and he represented the diocese at the Minneapolis General Convention of 1895. He helped to organize the Laymen's League, and became one of the officers of the institution. This body of active laymen

works directly under the bishop, and is the channel through which a good deal of practical philanthropy becomes beneficently effective.

*PERSONAL CHRONOLOGY— Lewis Stockton was born at Evansburg, Penn., March 12, 1862; graduated from Lehigh University in 1881, and taught at South Bethlehem, Penn., 1881–83; was admitted to the Buffalo bar in 1885; married Eloise Gilbert of Glencoe, Md., April 5, 1885; has practiced law in Buffalo since 1886.*

\*\*\*

**George Howard Thornton**, known throughout the Empire State as an expert stenographer, was born in Watertown, N. Y., in 1851. He received an excellent education early in life, attending the common schools, Jefferson County Institute, and the Watertown High School. Having thus obtained a thorough preparation for college, he entered Rochester University in 1868, and graduated therefrom four years later. In 1882 he received the higher degree of Master of Arts from his *alma mater.* He first became interested in stenography when a schoolboy, and learned the Gurney system of shorthand at that time. Most experts in the subject agree that the Benn Pitman system of phonography is one of the very best, and Mr. Thornton thought it worth while to forget his earlier method and start in anew with the Pitman *Manual.* He did so, accordingly, while in college, and acquired such proficiency in the new system that he was able to earn $2000 by court reporting in his senior year. He kept up his college studies all the time, moreover, passing creditably the periodical examinations. If college men of limited means only knew it, there is no better pecuniary resource for them than shorthand; and there is the further advantage that the fascinating art would help them greatly in their college work, and would be of perpetual assistance in after life.

In August, 1872, Mr. Thornton moved to Buffalo, and has ever since resided there. In the same year he became assistant stenographer of the Supreme Court in Buffalo, and continued in that position until 1882, when he was made official stenographer of the Supreme Court; the latter office he still holds. He was elected official stenographer of the New York state assembly in 1889; of the state senate in 1890; of the state constitutional commission in 1892; and one of the stenographers of the state constitutional convention in 1894. He has reported the proceedings of many important legislative committees, including the Fassett committee of 1890, whose report filled 4600 printed pages. For several years he reported the Chautauqua Assembly, under a contract to furnish at least twenty-six newspaper columns daily. His stenographic notes are written so perfectly that they can be turned over to others familiar with his system to be transcribed. He has reported many conventions concerned with professional and scientific subjects, and thus requiring not only highly expert shorthand writing, but also some knowledge of the topics discussed. His collegiate education gives him an advantage in this respect over most professional stenographers, and he has further equipped himself for efficient and intelligent work by a wide course of general reading. In addition to this he studied law, for its value in court reporting, and was admitted to the bar in 1882. He is familiar with French and German, and has interpreted both languages in court. His private library contains over two thousand volumes, including many works of reference and a large number of books in French.

It is clear from the foregoing that Mr. Thornton stands in the very front rank of stenographers. This fact has received official recognition, so to speak, at various times. In 1882 he was elected president of the New York State Stenographers' Association, and was again elected to that office in 1896. He was made president of the International Stenographers' Association in 1884. In 1882 he published a text-book on phonography entitled "The Modern Stenographer."

Mr. Thornton has now lived in Buffalo nearly a quarter of a century, and has become well and favorably known in that city. He is a member of the leading clubs there, including the Buffalo, University, Acacia, Yacht, Whist, and Chess clubs.

*PERSONAL CHRONOLOGY—George Howard Thornton was born at Watertown, Jefferson county, N. Y., April 28, 1851; attended Jefferson County Institute, the Watertown High School, and Rochester University, whence he graduated in 1872; married Della L. Cragin of Troy, N. Y., May 30, 1874; was assistant stenographer of the Supreme Court, Buffalo, 1874–82; was admitted to the bar in 1882; was elected president of the New York State Stenographers' Association in 1882, and again in 1896, and of the International Stenographers' Association in 1884; has been official stenographer of the Supreme Court, Buffalo, since 1882.*

**Nelson O. Tiffany,** widely known in Masonic and insurance circles in western New York, was born in Erie county in 1842. He is of excellent New England stock, his ancestors having come to this country over two centuries ago. His mother dying when he was five years old, Nelson was

*GEORGE HOWARD THORNTON*

brought up by his uncle, William A. Whitney, a farmer and manufacturer of furniture at Scotland, Ontario. His early life was filled with hardship and disappointment. Leaving his uncle's at the age of seventeen he knew no home thereafter until he had made one for himself many years later. After starting out in the world he obtained a place on a farm, where he worked hard from dawn till dark for seven dollars a month. A few months of this sufficed to show that prosperity lay not that way, and the young man sought to improve his position by taking work as a general laborer in a lumber camp. His duties there were comprehensive, ranging from the driving of oxen in the woods to accounting, timekeeping, and the measurement of timber.

In this unsatisfactory way Mr Tiffany passed his youth. Concluding that a lumber camp was not the best place for a young man ambitious to establish himself in the world, he went to Buffalo, and entered a business for which his training had particularly adapted him. Becoming general foreman in the

NELSON O. TIFFANY

furniture manufactory of W. Chase & Son, he remained with them about three years, and became, in 1868, general superintendent for the furniture house of A. H. Andrews & Co., Chicago. Not liking the western metropolis as well as Buffalo, he returned to the latter city after about two years, to become superintendent in the factory of Chase & Co. While with them he was much more than a superintendent, as he invented and patented three improvements in school seats and desks, and made illustrative models with his own hands. In 1871 he deemed it best to leave the furniture business, and become a traveler for the Howe Sewing Machine Co.; and for the next ten years he was a manager and superintendent of agencies for that house.

Having resigned the position of manager for the Howe company, Mr. Tiffany became the general agent for their goods in Buffalo, where he conducted a successful business for over five years. During this time he figured in a somewhat famous tax suit. The owner of the block in which his store was located having failed to pay the taxes on the premises, the city attorney directed the tax collector to make a levy on the personal property of Mr. Tiffany in his store. Naturally indignant, Mr. Tiffany protested against what seemed to him an inexcusable outrage. The case finally reached the Court of Appeals, where Mr. Tiffany won. The suit was a great annoyance to him at first, but proved to be a blessing in disguise, as it advertised his business most effectively.

In 1882 Mr. Tiffany took the management of the New York office of the Household Sewing Machine Co., controlling the trade of the company in New York, Brooklyn, and Jersey City. After conducting the office a year he resigned his position for the purpose of engaging in the business with which he is now identified — that of insuring the lives of Free Masons.

Mr. Tiffany has changed his calling several times, but he has always learned thoroughly any business that he has followed. In the case of insurance he began his preparation by attending a course of lectures in the medical department of the University of Buffalo in 1883-84. As soon as he had completed this course he was elected secretary and general agent of the Masonic Life Association of Western New York. For twelve consecutive years he has been re-elected to this position by the unanimous vote of the board of directors. It need hardly be added that Mr. Tiffany has conducted the affairs of the association with equal skill and success, and that he is regarded among insurance people as an exceptionally able executive officer. During the years 1893-95 he was secretary of the national convention of mutual-insurance underwriters.

On the personal side Mr. Tiffany's biography presents several interesting features. Passionately fond of flowers ever since childhood, he has cultivated a garden with his own hands for many years, partly from love of the pastime, partly for the sake of the exercise. He is likewise fond of sports, such as hunting, fishing, and yachting ; and he is a director of the Buffalo Yacht Club. Devoted to science and art and general literature, he has accumulated a library of over a thousand standard and choice volumes. In religious opinion Mr. Tiffany was always a Unitarian by instinct, as he says, long before he heard of such a church or creed : and for twenty-five years he has been a regular attendant of the Church of Our Father, the first Unitarian society of Buffalo. As might be surmised from his occupation, he has been active in Masonry, having taken all the degrees in all the branches of the order except the 33d degree in the Scottish Rite.

*PERSONAL CHRONOLOGY — Nelson Otis Tiffany was born at Lancaster, N. Y., February 1, 1842; worked on a farm and in a lumber camp, 1859–61; engaged in the furniture business as manager and designer, 1864–67; married Julia Charlotte Chase of Buffalo January 28, 1868; traveled for the Howe Sewing Machine Co. as manager and superintendent of agencies, 1867–77; conducted the sewing-machine business in Buffalo on his own account, 1877–82; was manager of the New York office of the Household Sewing Machine Co. in 1884; has been secretary and general agent in Buffalo of the Masonic Life Association of Western New York since 1884.*

∴

**Frank Brundage,** essentially a young man, has had a career full of achievement. No lawyer at the western end of the state is more widely or more highly appreciated for professional or personal merit. He commenced the practice of his profession in the little town of Angelica, in Allegany county. He was born and reared in that county, was married there, and still keeps alive his connection with his old friends, neighbors, and relatives in that section. They insist that Frank Brundage is an Allegany boy, though it is twenty-five years since his professional career carried him into broader fields.

His first move was to Lockport. Ten successful and fortunate years were spent there in the practice of the law, mostly in connection with Hiram Gardner and the firm of Ellsworth, Potter & Brundage. Niagara county was a pleasant and appreciative second home. All that it had to give to a lawyer it gave to him. When he had been in the county only three years

he was nominated by acclamation, and elected district attorney ; and after he had declined a unanimous renomination to that office he was elected county judge. Niagara county, too, made him its candidate for judge of the Supreme Court in the 8th judicial district, and he came within two votes of being nominated. Few men ever had political experiences pleasanter or more promising than those that surrounded the last seven years of Judge Brundage's life in Lockport.

But for a man with the natural gifts of a trial lawyer, nothing that politics or office has to offer compares in attraction with the active practice of his profession in a great city. Buffalo knew of Judge Brundage's powers as an advocate, and Judge Brundage knew of the opportunities to exercise his abilities which Buffalo could give ; and the inevitable

*FRANK BRUNDAGE*

happened. When he was barely thirty-five he had received about all that there was to get through politics in his profession. The prospect was bright for promotion in the same lines, but another kind of success was infinitely more attractive to him. He decided that, having tried both, he preferred the private to the public station; and he enrolled himself in the exceedingly small class of office-holders who have resigned. Subsequent events show that he has not repented his decision, for

*FREDERICK HALLER*

though temptations have been offered to him he has steadfastly declined to be a candidate for anything.

Frank Brundage, lawyer, of Buffalo, has had about what he desired when he left Lockport. He has practiced law under the most favorable auspices, and with a goodly measure of success. Before he moved to Buffalo he was engaged as counsel in the Lyon case, growing out of the Bork treasury matters; and succeeded in reversing the conviction in the Court of Appeals after having been defeated in all the other courts. There were not many big cases in Buffalo during the eight years of his connection with the firm of Bissell, Sicard, Brundage & Bissell in which he did not make an appearance at some stage of the proceedings. He has had

leisure to travel, and to enjoy the society of his friends; he has been able to exercise his ardent Republicanism by making campaign speeches without recompense; and, in short, he has found life as a whole well worth living. The only serious cause for complaint that he has had against fortune was a prolonged and severe attack of ill health, the result of an accident. In 1894 this necessitated his withdrawal from the practice of his profession. However, he has recovered his health completely, and since 1895 has been in active practice as the senior member of the firm of Brundage & Dudley.

*PERSONAL CHRONOLOGY— Frank Brundage was born at Allen, Allegany county, N. Y., January 4, 1847; completed his education at Friendship (N. Y.) Academy; was admitted to the bar at Albany in December, 1868; practiced law at Angelica, N. Y., 1869-72; married Ella S. Brown of Angelica February 15, 1871; moved to Lockport, N. Y., in October, 1872, and resided there until 1883; was district attorney of Niagara county, 1875-77, and county judge, 1879-83; moved to Buffalo in February, 1883, and has practiced law there since.*

\*\*\*

**Frederick Haller** was born in Augusta, Ga., two years before the outbreak of the Civil War. Becoming an orphan during infancy, he was brought up by relatives. He began to go to school at the age of six, and continued to obtain instruction in fundamental subjects until he was twelve years old. By that time his people felt unable to provide further education, and he was indentured for a term of three years as an apprentice to a cigar manufacturer at Savannah, Ga. This was not the most ideal method of attaining distinction in the law, but Mr. Haller's career shows that such an end may sometimes follow this beginning.

Serving out the prescribed time, and devoting himself diligently to all parts of his work, Mr. Haller learned the cigar maker's trade from A to Z. Passing mention may be made of his fortunate escape from yellow fever during the epidemic of 1876 at Savannah. In 1880 he left the Empire State of the South, determined to seek the larger opportunities of metropolitan life. Taking up his residence in New York city, accordingly, about the time he became of age, he worked at his trade there for the next eight years. The cigar makers of New York have frequently been at odds with their employers, and Mr. Haller, who soon became a leader among his fellow-workmen, was a strong force on the side of the employees. In all controversies he was conservative and wise in his counsels and leadership.

In 1888 Mr. Haller left New York and betook himself to Buffalo. He carried with him the tools of his trade, and soon found work. He had been in Buffalo only a few months, however, when he made a radical departure from his previous vocation. At the suggestion of Tracy C. Becker, a prominent attorney of Buffalo, who had become interested in Mr. Haller, the latter resolved to study law. This decision was not so strange as it might appear, since Mr. Haller had been for years a persistent reader and student on a small scale. While living in New York he visited the Cooper Institute frequently, and attended the lectures at that institution. Entering the Buffalo Law School in the fall of 1888, he pursued his studies with great energy. His rapid progress, indeed, was remarkable, when the adverse conditions under which he labored are taken into account. Not only was he somewhat handicapped at the beginning by reason of inadequate preparation, but he was also obliged, in order to support himself and family, to work at his trade while attending the law school. All these difficulties were happily overcome at last, and he obtained the degree of Bachelor of Laws in 1890.

Admitted to the bar at Buffalo in June, 1891, Mr. Haller began practice at once. His first partnership was formed in that year with James C. Fullerton, with whom he continued to be associated until January 1, 1894. After practicing alone for sixteen months, Mr. Haller formed a partnership with L. P. Hancock, under the firm name of Haller & Hancock. This association still exists. Mr. Haller has already established a substantial practice, and attained an excellent position at the bar of Buffalo. His capacity in the law was recognized in January, 1896, when he was appointed one of the assistant district attorneys of Erie county.

*PERSONAL CHRONOLOGY—Frederick Haller was born at Augusta, Ga., April 8, 1859; was educated in common schools; learned the cigar maker's trade and worked at the same, in Savannah, Ga., and in New York city, 1874–88; married Anna Zeip of New York city May 7, 1884; studied law, and was admitted to the bar in 1891; has been assistant district attorney of Erie county since January 1, 1896; has practiced law in Buffalo since 1891.*

● ● ●

**Mark Sibley Hubbell** is one of the best-known men in Buffalo and in western New York, although he is barely forty years old. Newspaper men and public officials are necessarily much in the public eye, and he has already won distinction in both lines of activity.

Mr. Hubbell was born in Buffalo, where his father, John Hubbell, was city attorney in 1854–55, and was otherwise prominent as lawyer and citizen for many years. Mark Hubbell's education, begun in

*MARK SIBLEY HUBBELL*

Buffalo schools, was completed at military academies in Montrose and Newark, N. J.; and he then entered the office of Bangs, Sedgwick & North of New York city as a law student, with a view to following his father's profession. After due prepa ration he was admitted to the bar in 1878, and prac ticed for about a year in his father's office in Buffalo; but at the end of that time he determined to yield to his strong predilection for journalism and a literary career.

Mr. Hubbell's first work in the newspaper world was for the Buffalo Express, and it soon became evident that he had acted wisely in changing his profession. Before long an opportunity offered to go to New York, and he spent four years there in the service of the Times and the World. These great dailies proved an excellent training school for the young journalist, and he profited much by the experience gained there. After making a trip around the world, via Australia and the Orient, he returned to Buffalo in 1883, and took a position with the Buffalo Courier. Later he acted as managing editor of the Buffalo Times for two years, and then served on the staff of the News for six years. Buffalo readers do not need to be told of his work during this time. His natural ability, cultivated and enriched by extensive travel and accurate observation, gave him a foremost place among local editorial writers. His descriptive style was easy, yet vivid; his political articles were keen and discriminating; but the work for which he is best known is his poetry. Here his talent for satire had full play, though he could be also pathetic at times; and these verses, treating in his own inimitable style the topics of the day, whether of local or more extended interest, did much to influence popular opinion on many important questions.

The change from journalism to the work of a city official is a radical one in some respects, but Mr. Hubbell has acquitted himself with equal credit in the latter calling. Elected city clerk for the year 1894, he has been re-elected each succeeding year, and is now serving his fourth term in that capacity. These continued re-elections sufficiently attest the fact that he has discharged the duties of the office to the complete satisfaction of the common council and of the public generally. He has done much to systematize the working of his department, and has compiled an excellent "Manual" of the city government. He has also prepared and published a unique and most serviceable annotated edition of the "Charter and Ordinances."

Mr. Hubbell's connections with the social life of Buffalo are many and varied. He is a Mason, belonging to Ancient Landmark Lodge, No. 441, F. & A. M.; and a member of the Orpheus Society, the Buffalo Historical Society, the Buffalo Republican League, the Press Club, and the Ellicott Club. His gifts as a writer and public officer, and his ardent devotion to the prosperity of Buffalo, have given him a large circle of friends and acquaintances.

*PERSONAL CHRONOLOGY— Mark Sibley Hubbell was born at Buffalo February 5, 1857; was educated in Buffalo schools, and in New Jersey military academies; was admitted to the bar in 1878, and practiced law a short time; married Elizabeth J. Oliver of Buffalo January 3, 1884; was connected with various newspapers in New York and Buffalo, 1882-94; has been city clerk of Buffalo since January 1, 1894.*

\*\*\*

**George E. Matthews,** editor of the Buffalo *Express* and president of the Matthews-Northrup Co., is following closely the course mapped out for him by nature. He is the son of a distinguished editor and printer, and his career has been the natural result of inheritance and surroundings.

Mr. Matthews was born in Westfield, Chautauqua county, at his mother's old home; but his parents lived in Buffalo at the time, and he may fairly be regarded as a Buffalonian from first to last. His education was obtained there, in private schools, until he was sixteen years old. He was ready to enter college then, but his parents thought him too young to get the full benefit of a college course. For two years, therefore, he gave up school life, and devoted himself partly to travel and partly to learning the rudiments of the printer's trade as typesetter, copyholder, and proof reader. His father, J. N. Matthews, was at that time editor of the Buffalo *Commercial Advertiser*, and part owner of the large printing plant connected therewith; and in that establishment Mr. Matthews, while waiting for time to catch up with him before entering college, laid the foundations of his knowledge of the printing and publishing business. By the fall of 1873 he was rather more than eighteen years old, and was ready to go on with his education. Entering Yale, accordingly, with the class of '77, he received in due course the Bachelor of Arts degree.

In January, 1878, J. N. Matthews became editor and proprietor of the Buffalo *Express*, and his son entered the service of the paper in the business department. At first only a clerk behind the counter of the public office, he soon rose to more responsible stations, and ultimately held the position of business manager for several years. He also filled various places on the staff of writers, as occasional vacancies made opportunity for such experience. He was telegraph editor for a time, city editor for several periods, and literary editor for three years, thus obtaining adequate training for his present work of editor in chief. In the printing business, likewise, Mr. Matthews served a long and wholesome apprenticeship. He was correspondence clerk in the old house of Matthews Bros. & Bryant, had charge of various departments in the establishment of Matthews, Northrup & Co., and finally became treasurer of the latter concern. He has always been interested in the various arts of typography, and has a comprehensive general knowledge of the subject.

The death of J. N. Matthews in December, 1888, charged his son with the responsibility of managing both the Buffalo *Express* and the printing business; and since then Mr. Matthews has been editor of the paper and president of the Matthews-Northrup Co. As an editor he has obtained generous commendation for independence, sympathy with all movements promoting good government, and consistent and unyielding opposition to "machine" politics. Whatever else has been said of the Buffalo *Express*, no one has ever seriously thought that it could be frightened off or bought off. Its editor's birth synchronized with the birth of the Republican party, and Mr. Matthews has always been a strong supporter of Republican doctrines. He has never been a candidate for public office, but his duties as an editor have made him conversant with some of the discomforts, as well as some of the pleasures, connected with a public position.

The life of Mr. Matthews has been devoted so exclusively to the business of printing and newspaper making, that it has been fortunate for him that his relations with those having similar interests have always had a strong infusion of friendship. He has been for several years president of the Buffalo Typothetæ, and of the Buffalo Newspaper Publishers' Association. He is a member, though not a very active one, of almost all the leading clubs and many of the associations of Buffalo.

*PERSONAL CHRONOLOGY— George Edward Matthews was born at Westfield, N. Y., March 17, 1855; prepared for college in private schools at Buffalo, and graduated from Yale College with the class of 1877; held various positions in the business and editorial departments of the Buffalo "Express," and with the printing establishment of*

*Matthews, Northrup & Co., 1878-88; married Mary Elizabeth Burrows of Buffalo July 12, 1887; has been editor of the Buffalo "Express," and president of the Matthews-Northrup Co., since January 1, 1889.*

GEORGE E. MATTHEWS

**Ottomar Reineeke,** editor of the Buffalo *Freie Presse*, was born somewhat more than fifty years ago in the German principality of Schwarzburg-Sondershausen, near the romantic Harz mountains. His early education was received in the schools of his native land; but in his twelfth year his parents came to the new world and settled in Buffalo, and the lad's studies were completed in the public schools of that city. His father was a printer by trade, ingenious and possessed of the sturdy determination that compels success. Two years after arriving in Buffalo he started a printing office, with a capital of $80 and no credit, and with a press built by himself of wood and iron. This machine bore more resemblance to the early inventions of Gutenberg than to the sextuple press of a modern newspaper office; but it served the purposes of its maker so well that when he died a dozen years later he left his son a substantial business, which included the publication of a weekly German newspaper, the Buffalo *Freie Presse*.

From the time the printing office was started, Ottomar Reinecke had helped his father in the

OTTOMAR REINECKE

afternoons while attending school in the morning ; and he soon left school altogether, and devoted his whole time to the office. He was thus well qualified to take charge of the business at his father's death in 1866. The following year he formed a partnership with Frank H. Zesch that has continued ever since. Five years later George Baltz was admitted to the firm, and the *Freie Presse* became a daily journal. This was in 1872, and for the past twenty-five years the paper has held its place as the recognized organ of the German Republicans of Buffalo, and under Mr. Reinecke's able leadership has won deserved success. Mr. Baltz retired from the business after two years, and since then the firm of Reinecke & Zesch have been the owners and pub-

lishers of the paper, and have carried on an extensive job-printing business.

Mr. Reinecke is connected with various business enterprises outside of his newspaper interests. He has been for a number of years a director and stockholder in the Erie Fire Insurance Co., and holds a similar position in the Citizens' Gas Co. He is a member of the Buffalo Typothetae, an association of employing printers for business and social purposes. He is a life member of the German Young Men's Association and of the Buffalo Turn Verein, and belongs to the Saengerbund, the second oldest singing society in the city. In January, 1896, Mayor Jewett appointed him one of the park commissioners of Buffalo.

Mr. Reinecke is an enthusiastic naturalist, and has devoted his leisure time for years to study and research in this line. Beetles, butterflies, birds, and birds' nests and eggs have interested him particularly, and his collection of such specimens is probably one of the largest belonging to a private individual in the United States. He has published a complete list of local Coleoptera that is exceedingly valuable. He has taken great interest in the Buffalo Society of Natural Sciences ever since its organization in 1861, and has done much to enrich its collections in the special subjects that have received his attention.

*PERSONAL CHRONOLOGY—Ottomar Reinecke was born at Sondershausen, Germany, November 20, 1840 ; came to the United States in 1852 ; was educated in German schools and in Buffalo public schools ; worked for his father at the printer's trade, 1854-66 ; married Eva Engel of Buffalo September 25, 1866 ; has been a member of the firm of Reinecke & Zesch, job printers and proprietors of the Buffalo "Freie Presse," since 1867 ; has been one of the park commissioners of Buffalo since 1896.*

\* \* \*

**Perry Champlin Reyburn** numbers among his ancestors so many names famous in the early history of our country that passing mention must be made of them in any sketch of his own life. Benedict Arnold, governor of Rhode Island in 1663, Thomas Hazard, one of the founders of Newport in the same state, Christopher Champlin, first Grand Master of Masons there, and many revolutionary heroes and heroines are included in the list; while in the present century we find the Perry brothers, Oliver Hazard and Matthew Calbraith, one of whom won a signal victory over the English at Put-in Bay in the war of 1812, while the other commanded the expedition to Japan in 1853 that opened to American commerce the harbors of that inhospitable island empire. Oliver Hazard Perry, it may be remembered, announced his victory to General Harrison in the words so often quoted, " We have met the enemy, and they are ours."

The subject of our present sketch has spent his life thus far — less than forty years in all — in Buffalo. He was educated in the public schools of the city, leaving the high school at the age of seventeen to begin the study of law. The next four years were passed in Buffalo law offices, at first with Joseph V. Seaver and Brainard T. Ball, and later with David F. Day and Frank R. Perkins. At the end of that time he was admitted to the bar at Rochester, and began the practice of his profession in Buffalo. After practicing alone for some time he became a member of the firm of Ballymore, Reyburn & Griffin in March, 1890. When this association was dissolved by an act of the legislature that prohibited Mr. Griffin, as clerk of the Surrogate's Court, from practicing law, Mr. Reyburn continued his connection with Mr. Ballymore until the spring of 1896. Since then he has practiced alone. Mr. Reyburn has made a specialty of the settlement of estates, real-estate titles, and mortgages; and has had charge of a number of important cases and suits.

In religious, social, and fraternal circles Mr. Reyburn has long been prominent and active. Left an orphan at the age of eight years, he was brought up by his grandfather, Gordon Bailey, a deacon in the Unitarian church; and he has attended that church from childhood, working in the Sunday school for many years as librarian and teacher. He was for a long time a member of the Unity Club of Buffalo, holding the office of secretary and treasurer, and taking a foremost part in the amateur theatrical work of the club. He was a charter member of the Buffalo City Guard Cadet Corps, organized in 1873. Following in the steps of his early ancestor, he has taken great interest in Masonry, in which he reached

the 32d degree when but twenty-three years of age. In 1882 he joined Washington Lodge, No. 240, F. & A. M., of which his grandfather had been Master in 1854, and after ten years in the various chairs was made Worshipful Master January 1, 1896. He is also a member of Buffalo Chapter, No. 71, R. A. M.; Hugh de Payens Commandery, No. 30, K. T.; Buffalo Consistory, A. A. S. R.; and Ismailia Temple, Nobles of the Mystic Shrine. He served five years on the Masonic board of relief. He has been for many years a member of the Buffalo Republican League, and belonged to the famous " 306 " organization in 1880. He has membership, also, in the Buffalo Whist Club and in the Acacia Club.

*PERSONAL CHRONOLOGY— Perry Champlin Reyburn was born at Buffalo September 10, 1859; was educated in public schools there; studied*

*PERRY CHAMPLIN REYBURN*

*law, and was admitted to the bar at Rochester October 8, 1880; married Ida A. Schneider of Buffalo January 30, 1895; has practiced law in Buffalo since 1880.*

**George B. Webster**, well under forty, is still classed among the young lawyers of Buffalo, but he has already won success such as many men are content to struggle a lifetime to secure. A law student under President Cleveland when the President was still a Buffalo lawyer, Mr. Webster has

GEORGE B. WEBSTER

retained a warm personal interest in the fortunes of his old employer, and this has naturally impelled him to take a prominent part in politics on the Democratic side. His success as a lawyer, however, is in no way dependent on his activity as a politician. He stands high socially, as the kind of man that other bright men like to know.

Mr. Webster's education was all obtained in Buffalo, first in the Rev. J. F. Ernst's private school, then in Public School No. 16, and afterward in the Normal School and the Heathcote School. When fourteen years old he closed his books, and set about earning his own living. Having obtained a situation in the treasurer's office of the Buffalo, New York & Philadelphia railroad, he remained there till

he was sixteen years old, and was industrious and faithful in the performance of all duties assigned to him. Moreover, unlike many boys who go to work at an early age, he did not regard the pleasure of spending a salary from week to week as the only object in earning it. He looked to the future, husbanding his resources, and thus was able, at an earlier age than is possible in the case of most self-dependent young men, to prepare for the profession that he had determined to make his life-work. After spending somewhat more than a year in the law office of Bowen, Rogers & Locke, he entered the office of Bass, Cleveland & Bissell, a firm that was destined to give the city a mayor, the state a governor, and the nation a president and a postmaster-general. Mr. Webster was admitted to the bar about a year and a half after entering the service of the firm, but he remained with it for three years longer.

After Mr. Cleveland assumed the office of governor, Mr. Webster was called to Albany to take a position in the capitol commissioner's office. He remained there for more than three years, and then, returning to Buffalo, resumed the practice of law, first by himself, and later in partnership with Devoe P. Hodson.

When the election for delegates to the constitutional convention was held, Mr. Webster was named as one of the Democratic candidates. The nomination was made in the expectation that he would be elected, and would have a part in the work of revising the constitution, as the Democratic party was then in apparently impregnable control of the state. But 1893 proved to be a Republican year, and Mr. Webster was defeated with most of the other candidates of his party in his part of the state.

Mr. Webster belongs to the Buffalo Club, the Ancient Landmark Lodge, F. & A. M., the Royal Arcanum, and the Sons of the American Revolution. He has served terms of enlistment in both the 65th and the 74th regiments. He is a member of the Church of the Ascension (Episcopal).

*PERSONAL CHRONOLOGY—George Buell Webster was born at Buffalo March 8, 1859; was educated in public and private schools in Buffalo; was admitted to the bar in 1880; married Agnes Jeanette Ovens of Buffalo June 27, 1883; has practiced law in Buffalo since 1886.*

**Wadsworth J. Zittel,** one of the proprietors of the Buffalo Candy Co., was born in Detroit, Mich., a little more than forty years ago. His parents were natives of the province of Alsace-Lorraine who came to this country in the early '30's and settled in Buffalo. Later they moved further westward to Michigan, where Wadsworth was born. He graduated from the public schools of Detroit, and afterward took a course at Bryant & Stratton's Business College there; and at the age of fifteen, with a sound fundamental education and plenty of native pluck and energy, he started in business life. He went first to Akron, Ohio, where he spent three years in a wholesale drug and grocery house, and gained considerable insight into practical business methods. He then betook himself to Buffalo, his parents' former home, and entered the employ of Philip Becker & Co., one of the largest wholesale grocery firms in the city. He began with them at the bottom of the ladder, but soon worked his way up to more important positions, and eventually became a traveling salesman, with territory in western New York and Pennsylvania. In fact the greater part of the fifteen years that he remained with this house was spent "on the road." But falo's wonderful development along all the lines of business and commercial activity began during this time, and Mr. Zittel's employers were not slow to take advantage of the favorable conditions. Progressive, and at the same time conservative, their house furnished an excellent practical school in which to learn sound business principles and successful business methods. Mr. Zittel was an apt pupil, and his connection with the firm was profitable alike to them and to himself.

But when a favorable opportunity offered to embark in business on his own account, Mr. Zittel, like most other men, was willing to leave even a good position as an employee for the sake of the greater independence to be found in an establishment of his own. In company, therefore, with Michael Hausauer, who had been one of his employers in the firm of Becker & Co., and his son George M. Hausauer, Mr. Zittel in 1891 established the Buffalo Candy Co., manufacturers and wholesale dealers in confectionery. He has conducted this business ever since, and has met with a gratifying

measure of success. A spacious building on Ellicott street is now occupied by this company.

Mr. Zittel is a consistent Republican, and has long taken an interest in party politics. He has never held public office, but his name has been mentioned in connection with various political nominations. He is a Mason, and belongs to all the bodies of the order up to and including the 32d degree. He is also an Odd Fellow, and a member of Holy Trinity Lutheran Church. He belongs to various social organizations, among them the Old German Society and the Ellicott Club.

*PERSONAL CHRONOLOGY* — *Wadsworth J. Zittel was born at Detroit, Mich., November 24, 1855; was educated in public schools and Bryant & Stratton's Business College; was clerk in a wholesale drug and grocery house at Akron, O., 1870-74; was*

WADSWORTH J. ZITTEL

*in the employ of Philip Becker & Co., Buffalo, 1874-88; married Sarah Goetz of Buffalo May 14, 1889; has been a proprietor of the Buffalo Candy Co. since 1891.*

**Carl Otto Hultgren**, the only Swedish pastor in the United States who has served a single congregation so long as thirty-two consecutive years, is widely known in western New York and Pennsylvania, and as widely beloved. Born in one of the southern provinces of Sweden on Christmas day,

*CARL OTTO HULTGREN*

1832, he has lived a long life consistently with the happy omen of his birthday. He came to America with his parents in September, 1853, and took up his residence in the old Swedish settlement at Andover, Ill. He had then reached his majority, and had already made some progress in obtaining an education. At Andover this progress was much accelerated by the tuition of the gifted pastor of the local church, the Rev. Jonas Swensson, who was Mr. Hultgren's predecessor in the pastorate at Jamestown. Continuing his studies in Chicago, Springfield, and Paxton, Ill., Mr. Hultgren was ordained Lutheran pastor by the Augustana synod June 19, 1864.

Before this date he had received a call from the First Swedish Lutheran congregation at Jamestown.

Accepting this opportunity gladly, he threw himself into his work with the ardor of youth, the energy of his race, the devotion of his noble character. Success could not long withstand such forces, and the little church with which he started flourished exceedingly. In 1864, when he took charge of the Jamestown church, the communicant membership was eighty. This figure had risen to 1233 when he resigned in 1895, while the total membership amounted to 2252. The first church was built by him in 1866, and was afterwards enlarged; and the congregation now worship in a superb Medina-stone structure valued at $100,000. In 1895 failing health made it prudent for Mr. Hultgren to give up active service, and his appreciative and affectionate congregation voted him a liberal annual pension.

But Mr. Hultgren has been more than a pastor — or rather, he has been a perfect pastor, in the full etymological meaning of the word: he has cared for his flock most tenderly and most faithfully. Unnumbered poor immigrants from his native land bless him for his kindness to them in their hour of need. He furnished transportation, clothing, meals, and overflowing cheer. His little home was often crowded, but room was always made for the helpless. His services were not confined to his immediate congregation. For years he was the only Swedish Lutheran clergyman in western New York, and his countrymen both there and in Pennsylvania came to rely upon him implicitly for services in matters spiritual.

Mr. Hultgren has taken a broad view of his work, and has served the cause of Christian advancement in many ways not directly connected with his pastoral duties. He organized and nurtured into abounding vitality a great number of the Swedish churches that now exert their beneficent influence over the western counties of the Empire State and adjacent parts of Pennsylvania. He was one of the organizers, in 1870, and the first president, of the New York Conference of the Augustana synod, a body that now has 35,000 members, and owns property valued at over $1,000,000. In 1883 he became the chief founder and one of the incorporators of the Gustavus Adolphus Orphans' Home, located at Jamestown. Ever since then he has given the institution untiring care.

Mr. Hultgren is a singularly modest man, and his countless benefactions would never have been known from any act or word of his. This biography, indeed, would never appear if he could have his way ; but thousands of readers will welcome even an inadequate sketch of his inspiring life and exalted character.

*PERSONAL CHRONOLOGY — Carl Otto Hultgren was born at Urena, Sweden, December 25, 1842 ; came to the United States in 1853 ; was educated at Illinois State University, Springfield, Ill., and at Augustana College and Seminary, Paxton, Ill., from which he graduated in 1864 ; married Annie Truedson at Galesburg, Ill., June 6, 1866 ; was pastor of the First Swedish Lutheran Church, Jamestown, N. Y., 1864-95 ; has been president of the board of directors of the Gustavus Adolphus Orphans' Home, Jamestown, since its organization in 1883.*

...

**Frank S. Oakes,** long prominent in his native county of Cattaraugus, and of late actively connected with many enterprises in Buffalo, was born of New England parentage fifty-odd years ago in what is now the village of Arcade. His career as inventor, manufacturer, public official, and private citizen, presents an unusual variety of interesting details, and displays throughout a conscientiousness and a desire to benefit his fellows that are not so common as optimists would have us believe.

In his boyhood Mr. Oakes attended the district schools of Cattaraugus county ; and later spent several terms at a "select" school at Yorkshire Center, which he organized by securing pupils and teacher himself. Just before his majority he entered a hardware and tin store at Otto, N. Y., of which his brother was one of the proprietors. He remained there several years, acquiring a practical knowledge of tinsmithing in addition to a general knowledge of the retail business of the store. His boyhood having been spent on a dairy farm, he was familiar with the handling of milk and all dairy products ; and in 1873 he made practical application of this early knowledge by inventing and patenting the "common-sense milk pans" for cream raising. The peculiarity of these pans consisted in the setting of the milk at the unusual depth of ten to twenty inches, and

their introduction was hindered by the prejudice of even the most intelligent dairymen against such an innovation ; but in 1878 the invention was awarded the first prize at the New York State Fair, and to-day Mr. Oakes's theory has become generally accepted. Since 1874 he has been successfully engaged in the manufacture of his invention in Cattaraugus, and of late years has greatly extended his operations. A large tinning and stamping plant has been established, and a general line of dairy and cheese-factory apparatus is manufactured. The present style of the firm is Oakes & Barger, and their goods are sold throughout the dairy sections of the United States.

Since 1891 Mr. Oakes has been a member of the firm of Rich & Oakes, dealers in real estate in Buffalo and vicinity. An enthusiastic believer in

*FRANK S. OAKES*

the future of the Queen City, and in the tremendous impetus which the advent of electric energy from the Falls may be expected to impart to the manufacturing interests of the Niagara frontier, he has identified himself with many movements for promoting the prosperity of "greater Buffalo." He took a prominent part in the building of the Buffalo, Kenmore & Tonawanda electric railway, and was vice president and a director of the company until it was sold to the Buffalo Traction Co. He is a member of the Buffalo Real Estate Exchange, and was a director of the association for one year. He represented the Exchange in the World's Real Estate Congress in Chicago during the exposition of 1893. He served as chairman of the improvement committee of the Exchange ; and he is now chairman of the forestry committee, a body that aims to secure the establishment of a municipal bureau that shall plant and care for the shade trees of the city. He was a member of the Exchange committee that obtained from the municipal authorities the right of entrance for Niagara Falls electric power.

Mr. Oakes has taken a keen interest in public affairs for a long time. Twenty years ago he was elected excise commissioner of the town of New Albion, in which the village of Cattaraugus is situated, and used his office to rid the town, through the courts, of the traffic in intoxicating liquors ; and he accomplished the work so thoroughly that there has been no return of the evil since. He has served as president of the village of Cattaraugus for three successive terms, during which the present system of waterworks, deemed one of the best in the country, was constructed. His latest re-election, in 1896, without opposition, was a strong endorsement of his able and vigorous administration. On questions of general public policy his sympathies are with the Republicans, though his interest in the cause of temperance, both from a moral and economic standpoint, compelled him to vote with the Prohibition party for a number of years. He was a delegate to the Prohibition national convention in 1884 and again in 1888. In the crucial campaign of 1896, however, he gave his active support to the Republican ticket, making a number of speeches in favor of McKinley and sound money.

Consistently with his principles, Mr. Oakes abstains from the use of tobacco and strong drinks. He is a member of the Congregational church, but is liberal in his religious views, believing in practical rather than theoretical Christianity. He is much interested in Sunday-school work, and is a supporter of home and foreign missionary enterprises. He is a member of the Ellicott Club of Buffalo, of the Ancient Order of United Workmen, and of the Royal Templars of Temperance.

PERSONAL CHRONOLOGY— Franklin Stacey Oakes was born at China (now Arcade),

N. Y., December 26, 1844 ; was educated in district and "select" schools ; was employed in a hardware store at Otto, N. Y., 1865-429 ; married Jennie Calver of Marblehead, Mass., September 11, 1874 ; has been president of the village of Cattaraugus, N. Y., since 1894 ; has engaged in the manufacture of dairy and cheese-factory apparatus at Cattaraugus since 1874, and in real-estate and other enterprises in Buffalo since 1891.

***

**Lauren W. Pettebone** has taken a prominent part in the recent development of Niagara Falls from a town of small commercial importance to a thriving and growing manufacturing city. The story of the "harnessing of Niagara" is a familiar one, and each successive step in the great achievement has been watched with eager interest. A wonderful impetus has been given to all kinds of business activity in that locality, and men like Mr. Pettebone have not been slow to avail themselves of the opportunities thus presented.

Born in Lockport less than fifty years ago, Mr. Pettebone was taken to Buffalo in early childhood, and was educated there in private schools. In the meantime his family moved to Niagara Falls, and when he left school in 1865 he entered the office of the Niagara Falls Paper Mfg. Co. He remained with this concern eighteen years, becoming thoroughly conversant with the business in all its branches, and developing from an inexperienced kid into a shrewd and sagacious business man. Finally, in 1883, he organized the Pettebone Paper Co., and was made its secretary and treasurer. Five years later he became president of the corporation, and held the office until 1892. At that time the Pettebone-Cataract Paper Co. was organized, with Mr. Pettebone as vice president and director ; and these positions he still holds.

Mr. Pettebone has thus been connected with the manufacture of paper for over thirty years, or during the whole of his business life ; and his best energies have been devoted to this, his chief enterprise. His business interests, however, are varied and extensive, and several corporations have received the benefit of his counsel in their boards of directors, among them the Niagara County Savings Bank, the Niagara Falls Power Co., and the Niagara Falls Water Works Co. He was at one time, also, vice president of the Cataract Bank.

Military affairs have interested Mr. Pettebone greatly for a long time, and for six years, beginning in 1885, he was first lieutenant of the 42d Separate Company at Niagara Falls. In 1891 he was made major and inspector of rifle practice of the 4th brigade, N. G., N. Y., and since 1894 he has been inspector of the brigade. In political matters he is a Republican, and he was his party's candidate for supervisor several years ago; but he has never had the time or the inclination to interest himself greatly in politics. He took an active part for many years in the work of Rescue Hook & Ladder Co., of which he was foreman from 1871 to 1881, and president for several succeeding years. Since 1888 he has been junior warden of St. Peter's Episcopal Church at Niagara Falls. Of late he has found it convenient as well as agreeable to spend his winters in Buffalo; but he still maintains a summer home at Niagara Falls, and is bound to the smaller city by many social as well as business ties.

*PERSONAL CHRONOLOGY— Lauren W. Pettebone was born at Lockport, N. Y., June 29, 1848; was educated in private schools in Buffalo; was in the employ of the Niagara Falls Paper Mfg. Co., 1865–84; married Lavinia Porter Townsend of Niagara Falls, N. Y., September 14, 1881; was secretary and treasurer of the Pettebone Paper Co., 1884–88, and president, 1888–92; has been vice president and director of the Pettebone-Cataract Paper Co. since its organization in 1892.*

\*\*\*

**Peter A. Porter,** one of the most eminent men of Niagara Falls, and elsewhere widely known and respected in western New York, is descended from a line of ancestors renowned in history. His father, Colonel Peter A. Porter, was killed at the battle of Cold Harbor while gallantly leading his regiment over the breastworks in a magnificent charge. Two nights later five brave men of his command rescued the body under the very breath of the enemy's guns. General Peter Buel Porter, the grandfather of our present subject, was even more distinguished, attaining high honors in both civil and military life. He was elected to congress three times, and was the right arm of the American forces in the battles of Fort Erie, Chippewa, and Lundy's Lane. He was, indeed, the chief figure in the great historic drama enacted in western New York in the early decades of the century.

With such inspiration in the past, Mr. Porter has found it easy to maintain the splendor of the family

name. Born in Niagara Falls shortly after the middle of the century, he attended St. Paul's School, Concord, N. H., one of the best preparatory schools in the country. The course of study there was appropriately followed by higher educational training at Yale College, and by extended foreign travel

*LAUREN W. PETTEBONE*

thereafter. Since then he has made his residence continuously in Niagara Falls, and has had much to do with almost everything of importance that has gone on there in the last twenty years. A good deal of his time has necessarily been given to the care and development of the family estate, which originally included much of the land now contained in the beautiful state reservation at Niagara.

Mr. Porter has been a prime mover in many projects designed to promote the welfare of Niagara Falls, and his fellow-citizens have frequently sought his counsel and leadership in municipal matters. In 1885 he was elected a member of the state legislature, and was re-elected the next year. While in the assembly he introduced and effected the passage of the "Niagara Tunnel" bill providing for the cyclopean undertakings of the Cataract Construction Co., and making possible the development of electrical energy in enormous volume from the Falls. Mr Porter was deeply interested in this wonderful conquest of nature. He wrote the historical chapter

*PETER A. PORTER*

in the special number of Cassier's magazine describing the tunnel scheme in all its aspects.

As might be inferred from the last statement, Mr. Porter is a brilliant scholar, and is particularly well versed in local history. He has made minute and painstaking researches among original documents relating to the past of the Niagara region, and is regarded as a high authority on questions relating thereto, his special library on this subject being the most extensive in the country. His interest in such matters has doubtless been stimulated by the fact that his forefathers had so large a part in the making of history along the Niagara frontier.

*PERSONAL CHRONOLOGY — Peter Augustus Porter was born at Niagara Falls, N. Y.,* October 10, 1853; graduated from Yale College in 1874; married Alice Adele Taylor in 1877; was member of the New York state assembly, 1886-87.

...

**Arthur Schoellkopf,** mayor of the city of Niagara Falls in 1896, belongs to a family that has been prominent in business circles in western New York for many years. His father, Jacob F. Schoellkopf, came to America more than half a century ago and settled in Buffalo, where Arthur was born in 1856. After some elementary education in private schools at home, the boy was sent to Germany at the age of nine, and for four years attended the academy at Kirchheim, his father's native place, in the province of Württemberg. Returning to Buffalo in 1869, he received further education at St. Joseph's College, and then took a course at Bryant & Stratton's Business College as a final preparation for active business life.

In 1873 Mr. Schoellkopf left school, and devoted the next four years to acquiring a thorough practical knowledge of the milling trade in the North Buffalo and Frontier mills, operated at first by Thornton & Chester and later by Schoellkopf & Mathews. In 1877 his father, with A. M. Chesbrough, bought the property of the Hydraulic canal at Niagara Falls, and Mr. Schoellkopf was sent thither to take charge of it, and to assist in the erection thereon of the Niagara Flouring Mills, of which he became local manager. These mills are among the largest in western New York, having a capacity of 2000 barrels daily. In 1878 the Niagara Falls Hydraulic Power & Mfg. Co. was organized to develop the Hydraulic canal, and to furnish water power for other mills in the vicinity. Jacob F. Schoellkopf was president of the company, and Arthur Schoellkopf became its secretary and treasurer and general manager, and has held these positions ever since.

In addition to the business interests outlined above, Mr. Schoellkopf is actively connected with other enterprises so many and varied that it is possible in a brief sketch merely to give a list of them. He is president of the Park Theater Co.; vice president of the Cliff Paper Co.; secretary and treasurer of the International Hotel Co. and of the Niagara Falls Brewing Co.; a director of the New York Mutual Savings and Loan Association, and president of the local branch; president of the Power City Bank; a director of the Bank of Niagara; and a trustee of the Niagara County Savings Bank. He built the first street railway in Niagara Falls, managed it for seven years, and established it on a paying basis. The man who has made such a record at forty years of age must possess unusual ability and a character that inspires the confidence of others. Mr. Schoellkopf's success may be ascribed to a happy combination of the progressive spirit of the native American with the habits of industry and application inherited from his German ancestors.

In political belief Mr. Schoellkopf is a Republican; but the positions of responsibility to which he has been called have come to him, not as a politician, but as a public-spirited citizen in whose sound judgment and unquestioned integrity his fellow-citizens could rely. He was one of the first sewer commissioners of the village of Niagara Falls, and has been a commissioner of public works ever since the organization of the community as a city. His election to the mayor's chair took place in March, 1896, and his administration of the office was most business-like and thorough.

A man of Mr. Schoellkopf's importance in business and public life naturally becomes interested in all the complex developments of modern existence. Mr. Schoellkopf belongs to Niagara Frontier Lodge, No. 132, F. & A. M., is a Knight Templar and a Noble of the Mystic Shrine, and Exalted Ruler of lodge No. 346, B. P. O. E. He is a member and trustee of the First Presbyterian Church of Niagara Falls, and vice president of the city's Chamber of Commerce. He has membership in the Ellicott Club, Buffalo.

*PERSONAL CHRONOLOGY —*
*Arthur Schoellkopf was born at Buffalo June 14, 1856; was educated in Buffalo and in Germany; learned the miller's trade in Buffalo, 1874-77; married Jessie Gluck of Niagara Falls, N. Y., October 14, 1890; has been local manager of the Niagara Flouring Mills since 1877, and secretary and treasurer and manager of the Niagara Falls Hydraulic Power & Mfg. Co. since 1878, and is also an officer in many other commercial and financial organizations in Niagara Falls; was elected mayor of Niagara Falls in 1896.*

**Willis H. Tennant** is descended from Scottish ancestry, and may have acquired thence his sturdy determination and strength of character. His grandfather, a full-blooded Scotchman, entered the revolutionary army at the age of eighteen, and was present at West Point at the time of Benedict Arnold's treason. Notwithstanding decided drawbacks in his early surroundings, Mr. Tennant, by untiring energy and perseverance, has placed himself in the ranks of the prominent lawyers and business men of western New York.

His early life was spent on a Chautauqua-county farm, and his education began at the age of fourteen at the district school. This continued for four years, about twelve weeks each year, and at the end of that time his father deemed his tuition complete. But the son had a far different ambition — that of

*ARTHUR SCHOELLKOPF*

obtaining a fair education — and, with the same determination that has characterized his subsequent career, he proceeded to achieve his purpose. After much coaxing he obtained his father's consent to enter the Mayville Union School, five miles away, on condition that he should do "chores" at home night and morning, and walk to and from school. He remained at school in Mayville somewhat more than a year, and during nearly all of that time these difficult conditions were faithfully fulfilled, until he

*WILLIS H. TENNANT*

had traveled on foot over 1700 miles between the farm and the Mayville schoolhouse.

Having received a certificate to teach in the district schools, Mr. Tennant was so occupied for one winter. He then took a course in a business college at Painesville, Ohio, and the following December began the study of law. From the time he entered school at Mayville he was entirely dependent upon his own resources; but these proved quite sufficient. He read law three years with a prominent attorney of Mayville, and paid for the privilege by taking care of the office, and making himself generally useful there; while he earned his board during the entire time by working as porter and barn boy in a hotel.

Mr. Tennant was admitted to the bar in January, 1880. He began practice in Mayville the following summer, and has followed his calling there continuously since. In November, 1880, he was admitted to practice in the United States District Court, and in March, 1882, the same privilege was obtained in the United States Circuit Court. Among the important cases that he has successfully conducted was that of the town of Ellery against the board of supervisors of Chautauqua county. Its purpose was to review and correct the equalized valuations of the several towns and cities of the county made by that board; and the result was a reduction of $3,000,000 in the equalized valuations of the country towns, and a corresponding increase in the valuations of the cities of Jamestown and Dunkirk. Mr. Tennant has made a specialty of corporation, real-estate, and investment law, and has an extensive and profitable practice. For several years he has been the general counsel for the Equitable Aid Union, a fraternal benefit society that receives and disburses nearly $1,000,000 annually; he has charge of all its legal affairs in the United States. In 1892 he assisted in organizing the State Bank of Brocton, and became its attorney.

In 1889 Mr. Tennant became interested in Buffalo real estate, and his investments, made with prudence and sound business judgment, have been uniformly successful. Since 1891 he has been a member of the Buffalo Real Estate Exchange. He took an active part in building the first electric railway between Buffalo and Tonawanda, in 1891.

Mr. Tennant is a member of the Independent Order of Odd Fellows, and of other fraternal societies. In politics he is an ardent Republican, and has worked early and late to promote the political fortunes of his friends and party. He has always taken an active part in public affairs, has served for several years as a member of the Mayville board of education, and has been president of the village. Mayville owns and operates its own water and lighting systems, having assumed the control thereof largely through Mr. Tennant's advocacy and leadership.

Mr. Tennant has barely reached the prime of life, and the prophecy may safely be made that additional honors await him, and a position even higher than that already attained, in social, business, and professional life.

*PERSONAL CHRONOLOGY - Willis Hale Tennant was born at Chautauqua, N. Y., April 20, 1854; was educated in district schools and the Mayville (N. Y.) Union School; was admitted to the bar in 1880; married DeEmma Van Valkenburgh of Mayville December 24, 1884; has practiced law in Mayville since 1880; was elected president of the village of Mayville in March, 1896, and supervisor in February, 1897.*

···

**George Douglas Emerson** was born at Abbott's Corners, Erie county, New York, in December, 1847. This little settlement is near Buffalo, and Mr. Emerson may fairly be deemed a Buffalonian from the first, since he moved to the city in infancy, and has lived there ever since. His family history is interesting. His uncle, General Mason Brayman, was a distinguished officer in the Civil War, and was afterward governor of Idaho for several years. Nathaniel Emerson, the paternal grandfather of our present subject, settled in East Aurora, Erie county, in 1804; and other members of the family also helped to open up western New York to civilization. Lower down, the family tree is more interesting still, taking the investigator, by way of Bunker Hill and other famous scenes in colonial history, back to the original immigrant in Connecticut two and a half centuries ago.

Mr. Emerson began his education by entering public school No. 4 in 1853, and passed through the various grades until he graduated from the Buffalo High School in July, 1865. After some minor clerkships he entered the service of the Central-Hudson railroad at Buffalo in May, 1874. He found the railroad calling congenial, and remained with the company in their freight department at Buffalo and East Buffalo until October, 1887. From April, 1888, until December, 1889, he was connected with the inspection bureau of the Central Traffic Association, with headquarters in Buffalo. He had a part in the preparation of the eleventh United States census, serving as special agent of the census bureau for eleven months in 1890-91. He supervised the gathering of statistics

of the manufacturing industries in Buffalo and Tonawanda.

For the last few years Mr. Emerson has devoted most of his time to political affairs and his duties as a public official. He has frequently represented Republican voters at city, assembly, and congressional conventions, and has twice been a delegate to state conventions. He was assistant secretary of the Republican general committee of Erie county during the four years 1891-94, and was secretary of the same committee in 1895-97. Since January 1, 1894, he has been deputy clerk of the state senate at Albany.

In social and society matters Mr. Emerson has been active. He has served the High School Alumni Association as vice president, president, and class historian. He belongs to the Buffalo Society

GEORGE DOUGLAS EMERSON

of Natural Sciences, and to the American Academy of Political and Social Science, Philadelphia. He is first vice president of the Independent Club of Buffalo, a popular dining association. His interest in the cause of temperance is evident in the fact that he has served seven terms as presiding officer of a council of the Royal Templars of Temperance, and was also on the executive committee of the Grand Council of the order for seven years. He is fond of historical research, and is chairman of the

WILLIAM S. GRATTAN

Indian memorials committee of the Buffalo Historical Society. He is one of the guarantee subscribers for the *American Historical Review* published in Boston. He is a member of the Delaware Avenue Methodist Episcopal Church, Buffalo, and of Washington Lodge, No. 240, F. & A. M.

*PERSONAL CHRONOLOGY— George Douglas Emerson was born at Abbott's Corners, N. Y., December 4, 1847; was educated in Buffalo public schools, and graduated from the high school in 1864; married Susan K. Corwin of Buffalo December 11, 1872; was connected with the freight department of the Central-Hudson railroad at Buffalo, 1874-87, and with the inspection bureau of the Central Traffic Association, 1888-89; was special agent*

*of the United States census bureau, 1890-91; has been deputy clerk of the New York state senate since 1894.*

\*\*\*

**William S. Grattan** was born in Monroe county, Pennsylvania, about fifty years ago. He attended the district schools of his native town, and Blairstown (N. J.) Seminary; but closed his books at the age of sixteen, and became an apprentice in the works of the Lackawanna Iron & Coal Co. at Scranton, Penn. In December, 1864, he entered the service of the Delaware, Lackawanna & Western Railroad Co. as a clerk in their coal office. He remained with the Lackawanna company until March, 1870, when he engaged with David C. Henderson and went to Westfield, Mass., to build the Holyoke & Westfield railroad. In 1871-72 he built a part of the Greenwood Lake railroad in New Jersey, and a dam and bridge for the Lackawanna railroad at Montclair, N. J. In February, 1873, he began work on the "Fourth avenue improvement" in New York city. In January, 1875, he opened a quarry at Randolph, N. Y., and quarried the stone needed for a bridge across the Hackensack river. In September, 1877, he made a contract to build the stone foundation for the steel works at Pompton, N. J. In 1878, the year the New York elevated railroads were first operated, he worked for the company as a foreman mason. The next year he acted as assistant to the superintendent of the Brighton Beach railroad; and in January, 1879, he returned to the elevated railroad company as dispatcher.

The business of a contractor, however, was more to Mr. Grattan's liking than railroad operating; and in July, 1880, he made an engagement with the contracting firm of Smith & Ripley, taking charge for them of eighteen miles of work on the New Haven & Northampton railroad. A year later he was sent to Genesee county, New York, to supervise the construction of six miles of road for the Lackawanna company. In December, 1881, he went to Buffalo to do some masonry for the firm of Smith, Ripley & Andrews; and after that he continued his acquaintance with western New York by overseeing the construction of the West Shore road through a part of Erie county.

Since then the story of Mr. Grattan's career is little more than a record of repeated successes as a general contractor. In April, 1883, he made an important contract with the Delaware, Lackawanna & Western railroad providing for the construction at Buffalo and East Buffalo of shops, coaling stations, a trestle at Erie street, and freight houses at the foot of Main street. In February, 1887, Mr. Grattan built the Lackawanna trestle at Cheektowaga, near Buffalo, the largest coal trestle in existence at that time. The success of these independent ventures and the magnitude of his operations induced Mr. Grattan to seek partnership assistance; and in January, 1888, accordingly, he formed with Alva M. Jennings the firm of Grattan & Jennings. The partnership has been maintained ever since, and the firm has taken a high stand among the general contractors of the country. A complete account of their business during the last nine years would give one a fair idea of the building conditions of western New York in that period. The work of the firm covers a wide range, and includes pile driving, dock building, excavating and concreting for structural foundations, large buildings requiring fine finish, and general masonry. In addition to these styles of contracting, they do a good deal of special work for railroads, making culverts, bridge approaches and foundations, concrete engine beds, and the like. Grattan & Jennings have executed several large construction contracts in a remarkably short time. In 1896, for example, on a contract with the Erie railroad, they took down an old coal trestle on the Blackwell canal, and erected in its place in sixty days, with lumber brought from Georgia, a new trestle containing about 2,500,000 feet board measure of lumber and 2800 oak piles.

Mr. Grattan has always been a consistent Republican voter, but has never cared to hold public office. In December, 1896, however, Mayor Jewett appointed him one of the three fire commissioners of Buffalo, and he is now discharging capably the duties of that office. The term runs six years from December 1, 1896.

*PERSONAL CHRONOLOGY— William S. Grattan was born at Shoemaker's, Penn., June 8, 1846; was educated in district schools and Blairstown (N. J.) Seminary; was in the employ of the Lacka-* wanna Iron & Coal Co., and the Delaware, Lackawanna & Western Railroad Co., at Scranton, Penn., *1862-70; married Amelia C. Mickens of Hewitt, N. J., August 30, 1877; had charge of various railroad and other contracts in Massachusetts, New Jersey, and western New York, 1870-83; has done a general contracting business in Buffalo since 1883.*

**M. J. Healy,** recently appointed by Mayor Jewett of Buffalo one of the commissioners of public works of that city, was born in Buffalo in November, 1859. He attended public schools until he was fifteen years old, but closed his books then in order to satisfy his desire for a business career. Entering the service, accordingly, of Leonard Hinkley, who conducted a general store at the corner of Niagara street and Forest avenue, Buffalo, young

M. J. HEALY

Healy learned the rudiments of business in the thorough way possible in such an establishment. He had not been in business more than a year, however, before he saw that even a commercial career demanded considerably more education than he had yet obtained. He changed his plans abruptly, therefore, entering St. Joseph's College and studying there three years — 1873-75.

Making a fresh start in 1876 with an intellectual equipment much broader than before, Mr. Healy went to work for Pratt & Co., Buffalo. He remained with this famous concern until 1878, when a favorable chance came to go into business with his brothers, in the firm of P. & M. Healy. They conducted a flourishing trade in groceries, meats, hardware, glass, etc., until February, 1895, when the business was divided, and a new firm, styled B. J. & M. J. Healy, was formed. This concern has also prospered markedly, and the Healy brothers may be said to control a large part of the trade in their line in the section of Buffalo known as Black Rock. Besides conducting a large retail business, they are the wholesale representatives of the Niagara Flouring Mills, the Akron Flouring Mills, and the New York Rubber Paint Co. The success of the business is due largely to the energy, long experience, and general ability of M. J. Healy.

For several years Mr. Healy has taken an active interest in political affairs, and has had much influence with the local leaders of the Democratic party. He held no public office, however, until January, 1897, when he was appointed commissioner of public works for the four years 1897-1900. Mayor Jewett's selection was regarded with general satisfaction, and it was felt that Mr. Healy would bring to the duties of his office excellent judgment and unusual executive ability.

Mr. Healy's capacity in business affairs has been recognized by various associations that have sought his guidance. He is a director, for example, of the Irish-American Savings & Loan Association of Buffalo, a stockholder in the Niagara Bank of Buffalo, and first vice president of the Black Rock Business Men's Association. He is president of St. Joseph's College Alumni Association, a director of the Knights of Columbus, and an active member of various other fraternal and social organizations.

*PERSONAL CHRONOLOGY— Michael John Healy was born at Buffalo November 4, 1859 ; was educated in public schools and St. Joseph's College, Buffalo ; was in the employ of Pratt & Co., 1876-78 ; married Elizabeth Warner of Buffalo February 9, 1897 ; was appointed commissioner of public works of Buffalo for the term 1897-1900 ; has carried on a grocery and meat business at Black Rock since 1878.*

* * *

**Robert Rodman Hefford**, widely known in the business and political circles of western New York, was born in Buffalo in 1845. He obtained his education in his native city, attending private and public schools and Bryant & Stratton's Business College. Reasonably well equipped in that way for a commercial career, he became a clerk at the age of seventeen in a wholesale salt and cement house. After remaining with this concern a short time, and serving as a clerk about a year in the canal-collector's office, he formed a partnership in 1865 with E. E. Hazard to conduct a coal business. Mr. Hefford was then only twenty years old, and he has been connected with the coal industry ever since. The firm of E. E. Hazard & Co. carried on a flourishing trade until 1871, when Mr. Hefford succeeded to the business, and conducted operations on his own account. In recent years his business has resolved itself largely into the shipping and forwarding of coal ; and he has had an important part in making Buffalo one of the greatest coal markets in the world.

Though Mr. Hefford has been strikingly successful as a business man, he has attained even more distinction in public life. He began to interest himself in political matters in early manhood, serving as alderman from the 2d ward of Buffalo nearly twenty years ago. He took high rank at once in the municipal legislature, and was elected thereto for three consecutive terms. He acted as president of the common council during the last two years, and as president of the board of health during a part of his service. He was conscientious and aggressive, and especially distinguished himself in opposing the notorious street-cleaning contract which was vetoed by Mayor Cleveland, and which indirectly started Cleveland on his way to Albany and Washington. In January, 1883, Mr. Hefford was sufficiently prominent in the Republican party to receive the nomination for the Buffalo mayoralty when the vacancy caused by Cleveland's election as governor had to be filled ; but John B. Manning, the Democratic candidate, was elected.

Mr. Hefford has always been a strong supporter of the Erie canal, and has done a good deal to maintain and improve that highway of commerce. He is chairman of the executive canal committee of the state, which is composed of representatives from the important commercial organizations of New York, and which carried through the constitutional convention of 1894 and the legislature of 1895 the $9,000,000 canal-improvement appropriation. The canal committee also did efficient work among the people at large, and was the chief agency in effecting the approval of the measure by the voters at the elections of 1894 and 1895.

In December, 1895, Mayor Jewett of Buffalo appointed Mr. Hefford a commissioner of public works, and the press of the city, without regard to party, warmly commended the appointment. There was general regret when the fact transpired that Mr. Hefford's private business was sometimes concerned with municipal contracts, and that he did not think it proper under the circumstances to accept the appointment.

Mr. Hefford has lately been made a member of the New York state commission to the Tennessee Centennial Exposition.

The list of offices in party organizations held by Mr. Hefford is almost as long as his list of public positions. He has been one of the recognized leaders of the Republican party in western New York for many years. He has been a member of the Republican general committee several times, and was chairman of the county committee in 1885–86. In 1887 he was made the first president of the Republican League of the State of New York, and was re-elected in 1888. He was a member of the executive committee of the state league for several years, and was vice president of the National Republican League during the years 1889–93. He is now a member of the Buffalo Republican League and of the State Republican League.

Mr. Hefford has naturally been prominent in the social life of Buffalo. He is chairman of the board of trustees of the First Baptist Church, a life member of the Buffalo Library, and first vice president of the Buffalo Club. He was president of the Buffalo Merchants' Exchange and of the Board of Trade for the three terms included in the years 1894–96; he was unanimously elected for the last two terms.

*PERSONAL CHRONOLOGY— Robert Rodman Hefford was born at Buffalo February 25, 1845; was educated in Buffalo schools; was clerk in a wholesale house in Buffalo, 1862–64, and in the canal-collector's office in 1864; married Harriet Rosalia Whittaker of Catskill, N. Y., January 4, 1870; was alderman from the 2d ward, Buffalo, 1879–82, and president of the common council, 1884–84; was president of the Republican League of the State of New York, 1887–88, and vice president of the National Republican League, 1889–93; was president of the Buffalo Merchants' Exchange and of the Board of*

*ROBERT RODMAN HEFFORD*

*Trade, 1894–96; has been engaged in the coal trade in Buffalo since 1865.*

---

**John C. Jewett**, the founder of the great manufacturing company in Buffalo that bears his name, was born in Cayuga county, New York, February 2, 1820. Central New York was not then dotted with schools of every grade, and Mr. Jewett was unable to obtain much education. Spending his summers on the farm with his father, he attended district schools during the winter, alternating work and study in this way until he was seventeen years old. He then made a start in the outer world by changing his residence to Ann Arbor, Mich., where his brother Samuel was engaged in business. Mr. Jewett went to work in his brother's store, and showed such aptitude for business that he was soon taken into the firm. By far the most important thing that happened to him in Ann Arbor was his meeting with Miss Priscilla Boardman in December, 1840. This acquaintance ripened into courtship,

and the courtship culminated in marriage on Mr.
Jewett's birthday in 1843. Miss Boardman was
then in her seventeenth year only, but her strong
and lovely character was already well developed.
She was a remarkable woman in many ways, and
Mr. Jewett's great success in life was doubtless due

JOHN C. JEWETT

in a large degree to the splendid intellectual and
moral qualities of his faithful wife.

Soon after his marriage Mr. Jewett left Ann
Arbor, and embarked in business on his own account
in Albion, Mich. He remained there for several
years, reaping as much success as could reasonably
be expected in so small a place. The inevitable
limitations of the town in a business way ultimately
caused Mr. Jewett to seek the larger opportunities of
a growing city ; and in October, 1849, accordingly,
he took up his residence in Buffalo. Setting up at
once a small manufacturing plant, he turned all his
energy and wonderful power of application upon the
enterprise. For nearly forty years he gave himself
up to the business, until he had made it one of the

great industries of the country. Refrigerators,
water filters, and a multitude of other household
utensils, have been distributed in enormous quantities over every part of the United States and of
some foreign lands, from the mammoth works of the
John C. Jewett Mfg. Co. Mr. Jewett, of course,
did not build this magnificent commercial structure without substantial assistance — no man could have done that ;
but his was the dominating mind and
guiding hand for many years. His
sons, Edgar B. Jewett, the present president of the company, and Frederick A.,
the present treasurer, and his son-in-law,
Risley Tucker, the secretary of the company, have all grown up with the house,
and have had an important part in the
marvelous growth of the business.

In January, 1886, after having worked
hard for many years — too hard for his
own physical good — Mr. Jewett retired
from the active cares of business life.
In May of the next year he received a
severe shock in the sudden death of his
beloved consort. This blow sapped his
declining strength, and for the last few
years ill health has forced him to live in
Los Angeles, southern California. Under the sunny skies of that favored clime
he is quietly passing the closing years of
a useful and honorable life.

*PERSONAL  CHRONOLOGY —
John Cotton Jewett was born at Moravia,
N. Y., February 2, 1820 ; attended district schools ; married Priscilla Boardman
of Ann Arbor, Mich., February 2, 1843 ;
engaged in business in Michigan, 1847-
49 ; established in Buffalo in 1849 the
business afterwards styled the John C.
Jewett Mfg. Co., and actively carried on the same
until 1885 ; has lived a retired life in southern California since 1888.*

•••

**Fayette Kelly,** one of the foremost citizens
of Hamburg, N. Y., and an able member of the
bar, was born in the town of Boston, Erie county,
in 1849. He received a better education than most
young men brought up in the country are able to
acquire. Attending first the common schools of
Hamburg, he there prepared himself for a course at
Aurora Academy, from which he graduated in 1872.
This paved the way for additional training at Hamilton College, from which he received the degree of
A. B. in 1876, and that of A. M. in 1879. This

thorough education along general lines was followed by professional study; and he was admitted to the bar in 1881.

Long before this date Mr. Kelly had attained marked success in a calling often made the gateway to a legal career. After leaving college in 1876 he obtained an appointment as instructor in Greek and Latin at the Tarrytown Institute, and taught for the next five years in the famous town by the Hudson. He decided, however, not to make teaching his life-work, but to practice law; and with that end in view he devoted much of his time during his residence in Tarrytown to legal study. After gaining admission to the bar he thought it worth while to teach a little longer, and thus acquire sufficient capital to tide over the briefless period in almost every lawyer's early experience. He became principal of the Hamburg Academy, accordingly, holding the position during the school year 1882–83. The next year he began the practice of law at Hamburg.

Mr. Kelly doubtless acted wisely in changing his vocation, though he thereby handicapped himself, so to speak, by several years' delay in the race for legal honors. He was thirty-five years old when he began to practice law, whereas the average attorney probably gets to work nearly a decade earlier. Mr. Kelly, however, was admirably equipped for rapid progress when he finally opened an office among people who had known him all his life. Possessed of their good will in advance, he soon built up a substantial clientage in Hamburg and the surrounding country; and he has long enjoyed rather more than his share of the legal business in his part of the county. By the year 1890 he had his country interests so well in hand that he resolved to open an office in Buffalo, and carry on a city practice in addition to his outside clientage. This plan worked successfully, and since then Mr. Kelly has transacted a large volume of legal business through his offices in Buffalo and Hamburg. He continues to live in the latter town, but his professional work is becoming more important in the larger place.

Mr. Kelly is a Democrat in his way of looking at political questions, and has long been prominent in local public affairs. He has represented the town of Hamburg on the Erie-county board of super-

visors for seven consecutive years; and for three years, 1890–92, he was chairman of the board. Taking special interest in the cause of education, as might be expected from his early career as a teacher, he has done what he could to improve the school service of his community. He belongs to the Masonic order, and to similar fraternal associations. He is a member of the Presbyterian church, and of the Delta Kappa Epsilon college society.

*PERSONAL CHRONOLOGY— Fayette Kelly was born at Boston, N. Y., June 5, 1849; graduated from Aurora Academy in 1872, and from Hamilton College, Clinton, N. Y., in 1876; taught school, 1876–84; was admitted to the bar in 1881; married Katherine B. Keyes of Hamburg, N. Y., August 4, 1886; has practiced law at Hamburg since 1884, and at Buffalo since 1890.*

*FAYETTE KELLY*

**John Lund**, conductor of the Buffalo Symphony Orchestra, and otherwise widely known in western New York as a musician, was born in Hamburg, Germany, in October, 1859. He is commonly regarded as an out-and-out German, but is not really so. Though he is a native of a German state, speaks German fluently, and has in great measure the ideas and instincts of the German people, yet genealogical analysis reduces the pure German element of his blood to one quarter only.

*JOHN LUND*

His father was a Norwegian, while his mother was of combined Russian and German descent.

Mr. Lund's father, who was a merchant, wished his son to enter the legal profession ; but the boy's instinct, inclining him strongly in the direction of music, had its way. His mother was a thorough musician, and encouraged her son to indulge his love of music. She became his first teacher, indeed, when he began the study of the piano at the age of six or seven. A few years later he became a pupil of Dinckler, remaining with him for seven years. Entering Leipsic Conservatory at the age of seventeen, he there enjoyed the tuition of such men as Reinecke, Wenzel, Oscar Paul, Jadassohn, and E. F. Richter, the famous composer of text-books on

harmony. Mr. Lund graduated from Leipsic in 1880, having studied there the piano, violin, oboe, and organ, as well as harmony, counterpoint, and composition. Upon leaving the conservatory Mr. Lund was appointed chorus master at the Opera House in Bremen ; and two years later he was advanced to the post of assistant conductor. In 1883 he went to Stettin as conductor at the Opera House in that city.

Mr. Lund came to this country in 1884. Dr. Leopold Damrosch, conductor at the Metropolitan Opera House in New York, went to Berlin in quest of an assistant. He wanted a young man thoroughly acquainted with the musical dramas of Wagner. John Lund was recommended to him as exactly the man he sought. A little investigation showed that this was so, and Dr. Damrosch engaged Mr. Lund as assistant conductor of the German opera in New York. After the death of Dr. Damrosch John Lund became the leader of Mr. Amberg's forces in that manager's ill-starred attempt to produce German opera in opposition to the Metropolitan Opera House. After a year with Amberg and a short time in Germany, Mr. Lund accepted an offer to become director of the Rochester Liedertafel. He did not stay long, however, in the Flower City. The Buffalo Orpheus was looking for a director, and through William Steinway heard of Mr. Lund. A committee from the Orpheus society attended one of the Rochester concerts, and after the performance made a contract with Mr. Lund.

That was in the spring of 1887. During the following fall and winter the Buffalo Symphony Orchestra was organized, and Mr. Lund was invited to become its conductor. The organization at that time consisted of thirty-three men, of whom several were amateurs. It was not until the fourth year of the orchestra's existence that an entire symphony was presented. By hard and conscientious work Mr. Lund has made the organization favorably comparable with any of similar size in the United States. His work with the Buffalo Orpheus has likewise borne excellent fruit. In 1888 he took the Maennerchor to Baltimore, where the best singing societies in the country competed ; and the Buffalo society won first prize in the second class. In New York, in 1895, the Buffalo organization won third prize in the first class.

Although Mr. Land was educated in the strict classicism of the Leipsic school, Mendelssohn representing the extreme limit in modern music, he is naturally liberal in his musical tastes. His favorite composers are Wagner, Beethoven, Tschaikowsky, and Svendsen; but a glance at the Symphony programmes will show that he makes free use of the works of many other composers. Though Mr. Land is a young man, his compositions are already considerable in number. Some of the more important are the "Wanderer's Song," for male chorus and orchestra; "The Flowers' Revenge," a cantata for mixed chorus, solos, and orchestra; "The German War Song," for male chorus, solos, and orchestra; "Scene Amoureuse," for full orchestra; "In the Garden," for string orchestra and harp.

*PERSONAL CHRONOLOGY — John Land was born at Hamburg, Germany, October 20, 1859; studied music under Dinckler, 1869–76, and in the Leipsic Conservatory, 1876–80; was connected with the production of grand opera in Germany and New York, 1880–86; married Ida Louise Zeller of Buffalo in 1888; has been director of the Buffalo Orpheus, and of the Buffalo Symphony Orchestra, since 1887.*

\*\*\*

**Norman E. Mack,** editor and proprietor of the Buffalo *Times,* and widely known in western New York from his prominence in political life, was born in West Williams, Ont., in 1856. His family left Canada when he was still a child, and took up their residence in Pontiac, Mich., in 1868. There Mr. Mack became a clerk in a business house. Both the mercantile knowledge and the disciplinary training thus obtained were of great value in his important business undertakings later in life. After remaining in Pontiac four years, he availed himself of the greater opportunities of a large city by embarking in the advertising business in Detroit and Chicago. This was his first experience in newspaper work, and gave him an insight into a most important part of the publishing business.

In 1874 Mr. Mack established himself in Buffalo. He had then been engaged in the advertising business two years, and was well acquainted with many branches of the difficult subject. He continued, therefore, for several years to conduct various advertising enterprises in Buffalo.

Many of these ventures had to do with the press, and gave him considerable experience in actual newspaper making, and by the year 1878 he felt able to enter the journalistic world as a publisher. Establishing the *Chautauqua Lake Gazette,* accordingly, at Jamestown, N. Y., he conducted the enterprise with fair success for some months; but in 1879 he received a favorable offer for the paper, and disposed of the property.

In September of the same year Mr. Mack began his long career in Buffalo journalism by founding the *Sunday Times.* For a while the printing was done outside the office, and not until 1881 was the first press purchased for the new paper; while the first number of the *Daily Times* was issued December 13, 1883. Since the latter date the paper has made marked progress in both circulation and advertising

*NORMAN E. MACK*

patronage. In 1886 additional space became necessary for dispatching the enlarged volume of business; and the Times building, at Nos. 193–195 Main street, was secured and occupied. In June, 1887, a Hoe perfecting press was placed in operation; in 1892 another Hoe press, a counterpart of the first, was installed; and in 1895 a Goss "three-decker" was added to the plant. In 1893 ten Mergenthaler linotype machines were set up in the composing room, superseding the old system of setting type by hand.

D. NATHANIEL McNAUGHTAN

Until 1884 the *Times* was independent in politics, but in the presidential campaign of that year it came out strongly for Cleveland, and has ever since supported the regular Democratic nominees. Mr. Mack has been very active in political affairs personally as well as journalistically, and has had an important part in the counsels of the Democratic leaders. He has been a delegate to various local and state conventions. He was one of the alternates to the Democratic national convention of 1892, and was the New York member of the notification committee in that year. He represented his congressional district on the Democratic state committee for two terms, declining a third term. He was a delegate to the Democratic national convention of

1896, and was a member of the state committee in the presidential campaign of that year. He supported Mr. Bryan vigorously, and enjoyed his confidence in a high degree. Mr. Mack, indeed, was probably the most prominent advocate of the "regular" Democracy in western New York, and thereby acquired great favor with those who believed in that cause.

Mr. Mack is a member of the Buffalo, the Ellicott, and the Press clubs, of the Orpheus and Liedertafel singing societies, and of other social organizations.

*PERSONAL CHRONOLOGY—Norman E. Mack was born at West Williams, Ont., July 24, 1856; was clerk in a store at Pontiac, Mich., 1868–72; engaged in the advertising business in Detroit and Chicago, 1872–74, and in Buffalo, 1874–78; married Harriette B. Taggart of Buffalo December 22, 1891; established the "Chautauqua Lake Gazette" at Jamestown, N. Y., in 1878, and the Buffalo "Sunday Times" in 1879; was alternate delegate to the Democratic national convention in 1892 and delegate in 1896; has been editor and proprietor of the Buffalo "Times" since its establishment in 1883.*

•••

## D. Nathaniel McNaughtan

was born in Worcester, Mass., less than thirty years ago. Before he was six years old his parents moved to Auburn, N. Y., and the greater part of his life thus far has been spent in that pleasant little city. He attended the public schools there, but completed his education at the academy in the neighboring town of Weedsport, whither his parents moved in 1882. After leaving school he spent about a year working at the shoemaker's trade, and was then employed as an accountant for two years, first with Tompkins & Horton and later with F. B. Tompkins. By this time he had become ambitious to study law, and in January, 1888, he entered the office of F. E. Cady, judge of the City Court of Auburn, as a student. He remained there three years, working as a bookkeeper evenings and at odd intervals as the exigencies of his financial condition required.

Admitted to the bar in March, 1891, Mr. McNaughtan at once commenced the practice of his profession in the office of his former preceptor, Judge Cady; and in the following December he opened an office in connection with John D. Teller, ex-surrogate of Cayuga county, with whom he became closely associated. After a few years, however, he decided to seek a more extended field of professional labor than Auburn could offer, and in June, 1894, he moved to Buffalo. He spent the first year and a half there as managing clerk for F. M. Inglehart; but in February, 1896, he opened an office on his own account. His success in the practice of law at Buffalo has been singularly rapid and substantial. He was fortunate in having a chance to show his capacity while with Mr. Inglehart, who entrusted most of his important work, and all of his court and litigated work, to Mr. McNaughtan. Having established his reputation in this way, and shown his ability to handle complicated pieces of litigation, Mr. McNaughtan has obtained a class of business that does not commonly fall to the lot of young lawyers. From the outset of his career as an independent attorney he has been able to occupy himself with interesting and important cases; and his contested work has taken him almost exclusively into the higher and appellate courts. He has conducted these cases with so much ability, and has obtained a class of clients so substantial in character, that a high position at the bar of Buffalo seems assured for him.

Before taking up his residence in Buffalo Mr. McNaughtan interested himself considerably in the local politics of Auburn, where he did good work in the organization of party forces and the harmonizing of opposing factions. He has never sought nor desired public office, and has declined such openings for political preferment as have been tendered to him. In December, 1891, Adelbert P. Rich, district attorney of Cayuga county, offered him the position of assistant district attorney; and in February, 1894, he was nominated for justice of the peace in Auburn, but did not accept the nomination. As yet he has taken no active part in public affairs in Buffalo.

*PERSONAL CHRONOLOGY —*
*D. Nathaniel McNaughtan was born at Worcester, Mass., August 24, 1869; was educated in Auburn (N. Y.) public schools and Weedsport (N. Y.) Academy; worked at the shoemaker's trade and as a bookkeeper in Auburn, 1885-87; studied law, and was admitted to the bar in*

*1891; practiced law at Auburn, 1891-94; married Elizabeth Manro at Auburn November 5, 1894; was managing clerk in a law office in Buffalo, 1894-96; has practiced law in Buffalo since February, 1896.*

∗∗∗

**Charles W. Miller** enjoys in large measure the esteem and good will of the people of Buffalo, where his name has been a household word for more than a quarter of a century. He has been both a cause and a result of the city's progress, and his fame in the special line in which he has won distinction has penetrated far beyond the state. In the livery and baggage business Mr. Miller has kept pace with improvements in the railway and steamboat service. He has facilitated the movement of baggage and passengers, and rendered travel free from many of its besetting annoyances. He has

*CHARLES W. MILLER*

established an industry employing hundreds of men and operating a large equipment.

Mr. Miller may be said to have been to the manner born. His father, Jacob S. Miller, established in 1828 one of the first livery stables in Buffalo, situated near the present Coal and Iron Exchange. Mr. Miller, senior, added to this business, in 1848, a line of omnibuses running from the foot of Main street to Cold Spring. Young Miller assisted his father in this business, and tells to-day how he used to sell omnibus tickets for sixpence apiece, or twenty for a dollar. Mr. Miller's reminiscences of those early days would make an interesting volume. He laughs as he tells of his father's prediction of ruin because the town council had passed an ordinance forbidding the blowing of the stage horn below Genesee street. On the death of his father, Charles W. succeeded to the business, though he was then only eighteen years of age. Five years later the Buffalo Street Railway Co. came into existence, and a new order of things arose.

While possessed of more than average determination, Mr. Miller had too much sense to sit down, Indian-like, on the track of modern progress. He accepted the inevitable, and sold out his omnibus line to the railway company, which gladly made him superintendent. He remained with the company four years, when his independent spirit asserted itself, and he resumed the coach and livery business. Eight years later he purchased the stables of Cheeseman & Dodge on Pearl street, and removed to that location. Buffalonians will recall the well-known structure, built in twenty-one days, in order to escape the operation of an impending law extending the fire limit against wooden buildings in the business part of Buffalo. Predictions were numerous that the structure would some day go up in smoke, and its many narrow escapes caused it to be known for years as "the only fireproof building in Buffalo."

It was the year after this purchase that Mr. Miller began the coach and baggage-express business. He obtained from Commodore Vanderbilt the privilege of placing agents on the New York Central trains entering Buffalo ; and in time secured the same rights on all roads entering the city. Later he opened a union ticket office, where a traveler can purchase a ticket to any part of the United States, and have his baggage checked through to destination. Few cities can boast a similar convenience. As Buffalo continued to grow, Mr. Miller opened an uptown stable on Delaware avenue, equipping it with the finest horses and carriages for public use seen in the city up to that time. This stable Mr. Miller subsequently disposed of. As a citizen with proper pride in one of the noted residence avenues of the country, he appreciated the fact that the street should not be invaded for business purposes. Moreover, his many

enterprises made it advisable to concentrate all departments under one roof. For this purpose he built the magnificent stables on Huron street. This establishment he justly maintains to be one of the best appointed of its kind in the United States. Here all the repairing incident to his business is done by skillful employees ; and Mr. Miller has facilities for turning out finished carriages if he saw fit to do so.

Mr. Miller's operations are not confined to Buffalo. He is the senior partner in the Miller-Brundage Coach Co., which revolutionized the carriage service at Niagara Falls. Despite fierce opposition, this field was won from extortionate and irresponsible carriers. Mr. Miller furnishes also the transportation equipment for the famous Ponce de Leon hotel at St. Augustine, Fla., and for the Bon Air hotel, Augusta, Ga. An adequate idea of the vast extent and proportions of his business may be obtained by a summary of his force and expenses. All told, he employs more than two hundred vehicles — coaches, victorias, coupés, omnibuses, and moving vans — over five hundred horses, and nearly four hundred men. His pay roll amounts to not far from $4000 a month. It is said that Mr. Miller's entire plant could not be duplicated for less than half a million dollars.

*PERSONAL CHRONOLOGY— Charles W. Miller was born at Buffalo January 19, 1847 ; was superintendent of the Buffalo Street Railway Co., 1869-43 ; married Louise L. Noxon in 1861 ; has carried on a general coach and livery business in Buffalo since 1864, and has recently extended his operations to Niagara Falls, Georgia, and Florida.*

*   *   *

**Francis S. Root** was born in Cayuga county, New York, in 1869. He worked on his father's farm until he was twenty-one years old, attending district schools, however, in winter, and finally graduating from the literary department of the Port Byron Academy in 1889. The next year he went to Cornell. After taking a scientific and literary course for a year, he entered the law school, and graduated therefrom with the degree of LL. B. in 1893. From the time he left home to go to college Mr. Root was dependent entirely on himself for the means of support. He was fortunate enough to obtain a state scholarship, which gave him free tuition ; and he worked in various ways during vacation time to defray the rest of his expenses. It is a remarkable fact, worthy of permanent record, that Mr. Root was able to spend three years at Cornell at a total cost, including board, clothing, books, and everything else but tuition, of $546. In connection with this fact it is interesting to note that he attained distinction in college in both the ways open to students — in scholarship and in athletics. His graduating thesis, entitled "A History of the Evolution of the Modern Law of Real Property," won the first prize in competition with a class of sixty-three members, and was afterward published in the New York *Law Review*. Mr. Root was a member of the freshman crew that defeated Columbia at New London in 1891, and the next year he was on the Cornell "varsity" crew.

Having obtained at Ithaca an excellent training in the theory of law, Mr. Root rounded this out with practical work in the actual dispatch of legal business. Entering first the office of John D. Teller at Auburn, N. Y., he afterward continued his study in Buffalo with Wilcox & Miner and with Harvey L. Brown. Thus amply prepared, he passed the bar examinations easily at New York in January, 1895. He then opened an office at Buffalo, and has since followed his profession in that city. He practiced alone until April 1, 1896, then associated himself for several months with James Harmon in the firm of Harmon & Root, and since September 1, 1896, has carried on his work without partnership assistance.

Mr. Root has been greatly interested in politics and in various economic and sociological questions. He is an ardent advocate of civil-service reform, an income tax, state ownership of railroads and natural monopolies, direct legislation, the single tax, and absolute free trade. In 1895 he was the nominee of the People's party for justice of the Supreme Court, and his nomination was endorsed by the Prohibition party. He was an enthusiastic supporter of Bryan and Sewall and the Chicago platform in the presidential campaign of 1896, and made a few speeches in behalf of the Democratic candidates. He is liberal in religious belief, and is a member of the Unitarian church.

*PERSONAL CHRONOLOGY— Francis Stanton Root was born at Port Byron, N. Y., November 4, 1869; graduated from the literary department of the Port Byron Academy in 1889, and from the law department of Cornell University in 1894; was admitted to the bar in March, 1895, and has practiced law since then in Buffalo.*

**Oscar F. Price** is a true son of Jamestown, having been born there fifty-odd years ago, and having spent all his life there thus far. He may also be regarded, not less truly, as the father of the modern city of Jamestown, since to him more than to any other one man must be ascribed the

*FRANCIS S. ROOT*

evolution of the place from the thriving village of a dozen years ago.

Mr. Price attended the Jamestown schools and academies, and when his general education was completed he took up a course of law study. This legal knowledge has been of great service to him, both in his extensive real-estate dealings, and in his public duties as the chief executive officer of a new city. After completing his law studies Mr. Price embarked in the real-estate business, and in this field did good service to the community. Jamestown well deserves the epithet of "City of Homes," and this is due in no small degree to Mr. Price's efforts. He has built hundreds of houses, and placed them on the market on terms so easy that those who wished to secure homes have been enabled to do so; while in many other cases he has sold the land, and advanced money for those who wished to build for themselves.

In addition to this very practical work for the building up of the city, Mr. Price has always taken

OSCAR F. PRICE

an active part in public affairs, for which his character, at once progressive and conservative, renders him peculiarly well fitted. For a number of years he served as a member of the village board of trustees, and in 1882 and 1883 he was the president of the board. His townspeople were not slow in recognizing his ability for public affairs and his devotion to their interests, and in 1883 and 1884 they sent him to Albany as their representative in the state legislature.

About this time Mr. Price became impressed with the fact that Jamestown had outgrown the conditions of a village, and was prepared to take its place among the cities of the state. He set himself to educate public opinion in this regard, and to over-

come the prejudices of those ultra conservatives who are never ready for a change. Finally, in February, 1885, a petition was presented to the village trustees urging them to call a meeting of citizens to consider the proposal for a city charter. The meeting was called, and a committee of ten was appointed to draft the new charter. Mr. Price was a member of this committee, and had a large part in preparing the charter and in securing its passage by the legislature a year later. When the first election of city officers was held, April 13, 1886, Mr. Price was elected mayor; and he held that trying and responsible position for four consecutive terms. During that time many problems had to be solved by the new city. The questions of paving, electric lighting, street railroads, water, and sewers all demanded attention; and in every case Mayor Price took his stand on the side of the people, and secured for them an economical and satisfactory adjustment of the matter under consideration. During all the years of his administration no whisper of scandal was ever breathed against the city government, no accusation of political trickery was ever dreamed of; and when, at the close of his fourth term of office, he refused to allow his name to be used as a candidate for re-election, he left a record for unselfish devotion to the public welfare that has seldom been equaled in the annals of city government. So great was his popularity that, after an interval of two years, he was again called to preside over the affairs of the city, and in April, 1896, he began his fifth term as mayor of Jamestown.

In private as in public life Mr. Price possesses a manner unassuming and courteous, yet dignified withal. His fellow citizens know him as a man whose sound and accurate judgment can be relied upon, and whose rare kindliness of heart makes him the friend of all who need his aid.

*PERSONAL CHRONOLOGY—Oscar F. Price was born at Jamestown, N. Y., September 11, 1840; was educated in Jamestown schools and academies; was a member of the board of trustees of Jamestown for several years, and served as president of the board, 1882-84; was member of the state assembly, 1883-84; was the first mayor of Jamestown, holding the office, 1886-94, and was elected again in 1896.*

**Edward A. Skinner**, for twenty years past president of the First National Bank of Westfield, N. Y., and its successor, the National Bank of Westfield, was born in the town of Aurora, Erie county, in 1841. His father, who was a Presbyterian clergyman at that time, had moved to western New York from Oneida county five years earlier, and the family another generation back was to be found in Berkshire county, Massachusetts. When Mr. Skinner was thirteen years old his father moved to Westfield, to fill the position of a bank cashier. Between that date, 1854, and the outbreak of the Civil War, Mr. Skinner spent most of his time acquiring an education in the Westfield Academy.

In October, 1861, the 9th regiment, New York volunteer cavalry, was organized in Chautauqua and Cattaraugus counties, and was rendezvoused at Westfield; and in November, 1861, while still under age, Mr. Skinner entered the service. In the same month his regiment joined McClellan's army near Washington, and served there and on the Peninsula, unmounted, until May, 1862. Having returned to Washington at that time to be mounted and equipped, the regiment was assigned to Siegel's corps under Pope's general command in July, 1862, and participated in the unsatisfactory campaign of that summer. After Pope's retreat to Washington Mr. Skinner's regiment became a part of the cavalry corps of the Army of the Potomac, and served therewith throughout the campaign of '63 in Virginia, Maryland, and Pennsylvania. Early in his army life Mr. Skinner was detailed to act as regimental quartermaster, and was soon commissioned such; and during much of the time he discharged the duties of brigade quartermaster. He left the service, owing to ill health, in March, 1864.

In the fall of 1864 the First National Bank of Westfield was organized, and Mr. Skinner, becoming assistant cashier of the institution, began his long career as a banker. The fact that he had made no mistake in choosing his vocation was soon apparent, and he was promoted in a few years to the position of cashier.

In 1870, however, consistently with the unrest of youth, he decided to try his fortunes beyond the Mississippi. Kansas was then one of the most promising states of the West, and in the city of Ottawa

Mr. Skinner assisted in organizing the First National Bank. He remained in Kansas several years, and then, after spending some months in Europe, once more took up his residence in Westfield, in the summer of 1874, becoming vice president of the First National Bank, and taking an active part in its management. Two years later his father died, and he succeeded him in the presidency of the bank. Since then Mr. Skinner has remained at the head of the institution, and has attained a high reputation as a progressive and conservative banker.

Aside from his banking interests Mr. Skinner's chief business connection has been with the fraternal organization known as the Royal Arcanum. Joining this society in 1878, he participated in the organization of the Grand Council of the State of New York in 1879, and was sent as its first representative to

EDWARD A. SKINNER

the Supreme Council of the order. In 1880 he was elected Supreme Treasurer, and has held the position continuously since. The importance of the office may be understood from the statement that the Royal Arcanum now has 190,000 members, disburses annually five million dollars, and has paid in death claims since its organization nearly forty million dollars.

In the social life of Westfield Mr. Skinner has naturally been prominent. He has long been a member of the Presbyterian Church there. He belongs to the Grand Army of the Republic, and to the Loyal Legion. He is a firm believer in the principles of the Republican party, but has held no political office except that of supervisor of the town of Westfield for three years.

*PERSONAL CHRONOLOGY— Edward Alburn Skinner was born at Griffin's Mills, Erie county, N. Y., May 10, 1841; was educated at Westfield (N. Y.) Academy; served in the Union army, 1861–64; was assistant cashier and cashier of the First National Bank of Westfield, 1864–70; engaged in banking at Ottawa, Kans., 1870–74; married Frances M. Barger of Westfield October 29, 1864, who died June 16, 1872; married Augusta Wheeler of Portville, N. Y., August 19, 1874; became vice president of the First National Bank of Westfield in 1874, and has been president of that bank and its successor, the National Bank of Westfield, since 1876; has been Supreme Treasurer of the Royal Arcanum since 1880.*

\*\*\*

**Arthur C. Wade** has won success in both law and commercial life. He possesses the capacity, the activity, and the resolution so characteristic of the modern man of affairs. His experience as a lawyer and business man has been diversified, and of an intensely practical kind. He has been a promoter of new enterprises, an encourager and a supporter of mechanical skill and ingenuity. At the same time he has not allowed private affairs to absorb all his attention, but has been actively engaged in political and public matters that demand the participation of all patriotic citizens.

Mr. Wade is a native of Chautauqua county, and attended its excellent district schools, receiving higher education at Ellington Academy and Chamberlain Institute. He early became desirous of making the law his profession, and pursued a course of study at the famous Albany Law School, from which he graduated twenty years ago. He was admitted to the bar of the Supreme Court in 1877, and opened an office at Ellington, N. Y., the same year, becoming a partner of Theodore A. Case of that town, for many years a prominent lawyer and citizen of western New York. This connection lasted for six years, and was valuable to Mr. Wade in bringing him into contact with a greater volume

of business than ordinarily falls to the lot of a beginner in the law. In 1883 the partnership was dissolved, and he associated himself with Orsell Cook and Jerome B. Fisher of Jamestown, N. Y., with whom he continued to practice until the death of Judge Cook twelve years later. Since then his partners have been Mr. Fisher and M. R. Stevenson. Mr. Wade's legal career has been marked by careful study of his cases, elaborate preparation for trial, and faithfulness to the interests of his clients. Since the days of Madison Burnell the Chautauqua-county bar has not known an abler cross-examiner or a more successful advocate than he. In these qualities he stands conspicuous among the foremost lawyers of western New York. His well-known talent for investigation and his practical knowledge of street-railway management, commended him to the legislative committee that investigated the surface and elevated railways of the state in the summer and fall of 1895; and his skillful and thorough conduct of the investigations elicited the cordial commendation of the ablest lawyers throughout the state.

Mr. Wade's business enterprises have been mainly in the line of manufacturing and transportation. He is president of the Fenton Metallic Mfg. Co., the Jamestown Felt Mills, the Ulster Oil Co., and the United States Voting Machine Co. He is secretary of the Waverly, Sayre & Athens Traction Co., and secretary and treasurer of the Chautauqua Steamboat Co. The mere recital of the names of these organizations indicates the practical bent of Mr. Wade's energies. He is also extensively engaged in real-estate transactions, and has figured in many land-improvement enterprises.

A man so prominent at the bar and in business naturally acquires such influence and prestige in a community as will commend him for political preferment. Mr. Wade is a strong Republican in his political faith, but he has too many interests to find much time for the diversions of politics. For several years, however, his services have been in great demand during campaigns; and he has made numerous tours of the state, and is one of the favorite campaign orators. He is an aggressive, logical, vote-getting speaker, and eloquent enough to control even a hostile audience. His party associates have at various times sought to induce him to become a candidate for public office, and in 1891 he was nominated for state comptroller. He had excellent qualifications for this office, and would doubtless have discharged its duties most acceptably, had he been elected. It happened, however, not to be a Republican year, and he suffered defeat with the rest of the ticket.

As may be easily inferred from the foregoing, Mr. Wade is a progressive force in his community, and has had a large part in the recent development of Jamestown and Chautauqua county. His career is an inspiration to the younger members of the bar, and is a striking example of what brains, energy, and patience can accomplish in this country. Having experienced some of the difficulties with which young men have to contend, he is ever ready to lend them a helping hand. Many young lawyers owe their first impetus to success to his kindly interest and substantial aid.

*PERSONAL CHRONOLOGY —*
*Arthur C. Wade was born at Charlotte, N. Y., December 12, 1852; was educated at Ellington (N. Y.) Academy, and Chamberlain Institute, Randolph, N. Y.; graduated from the Albany Law School in 1877, and was at once admitted to the bar; married M. Frank Briggs of Ellington August 22, 1877; practiced law at Ellington, 1877–82; was Republican candidate for comptroller of the state of New York in 1894; has practiced law in Jamestown, N. Y., since 1883.*

***

**Jerome B. Fisher** is known to the bar and people of western New York as one of the safest counselors and ablest trial lawyers in that section of the state. He was born in the village of Russell, Warren county, Penn., about forty-six years ago, removing to Jamestown in 1864, where he has since resided. His early education was obtained in the common schools of Pennsylvania, and was continued at the Jamestown Union School and Collegiate Institute, from which he graduated in 1872. He also attended Cornell University two years, taking an optional course. After leaving Cornell, he began the study of law in the office of Bootey & Fowler at Jamestown, and was admitted to the bar in 1878.

He began practice alone, but soon formed a partnership with Marvin Smith, under the firm name of Smith & Fisher. This partnership continued till August, 1884, when he became the junior member of the firm of Cook, Lockwood & Fisher. In 1882 Mr. Lockwood retired from the firm, and in 1883 Arthur C. Wade was admitted to membership, the style being Cook, Fisher & Wade until the dissolution of the firm upon the death of Judge Cook in July, 1895. Fisher & Wade continued the business,

and in September, 1895, they associated with them M. R. Stevenson.

In political matters Judge Fisher has been a partisan of the strictest sort, but has enjoyed the confidence and esteem of men of all parties. He has virtually been in public life since his admission

ARTHUR C. WADE

to the bar. Even while studying law he was twice elected clerk of the village of Jamestown, and afterwards represented the city on the board of supervisors. In 1884 he was chosen alternate delegate to the Republican national convention, where he favored the nomination of Blaine; and he was an ardent supporter of Harrison in the national convention of 1888, to which he was a delegate. After the election of President Harrison Judge Fisher was a prominent candidate for the office of United States district attorney, and received the united support of the organization and leaders of the party in the state. Owing to an unfortunate factional fight, he was defeated in 1890 for the position of county judge of Chautauqua county. In 1896 he received the unanimous nomination of the Republican county convention for the same office, and was elected by more than 7000 majority. He has been on the bench only a short time now, but already long enough to demonstrate his impartiality, fairness, and fidelity.

Judge Fisher has had few equals in western New

*JEROME B. FISHER*

York in recent years as a trial lawyer. Two notable recent cases in which he was conspicuously successful were the Broadhead-Lister suit, involving several hundred thousand dollars, and the case of the People against James Rainey, whom he succeeded in acquitting of the charge of murder.

Not only has Judge Fisher been conspicuous in the courts and active in politics, but for many years he has been prominent in lodge and social circles, and identified with many business enterprises. He is president of the Jamestown Shale Paving Brick Co., and of the Lakewood Ice Co., and is a stockholder in other business enterprises. He is a member of Mt. Moriah Lodge, F. & A. M., and of

Western Sun Chapter, R. A. M.; and he was the first Eminent Commander of Jamestown Commandery, No. 61, K. T. He is a Past Exalted Ruler of Jamestown Lodge, No. 263, B. P. O. E., and is chairman of the board of Grand Trustees of the order in the United States. He is a prominent member of the Jamestown Club.

Judge Fisher's services are in almost constant demand for public addresses. As an aggressive campaigner he has acquired a well-deserved fame, while as an occasional orator and after-dinner speaker he ranks with the foremost of the Empire State. From an early period in his career Judge Fisher enjoyed the friendship of the late Governor Fenton, and was named by him as one of his executors, and was made a legatee under his will.

*PERSONAL CHRONOLOGY—Jerome B. Fisher was born at Russell, Warren county, Penn., February 14, 1854; moved to Jamestown, N. Y., May 8, 1863; was educated at Jamestown Union School and Collegiate Institute, and Cornell University; was admitted to the bar in 1878; married Julia E. Hatch of Jamestown December 19, 1878; was alternate delegate to the Republican national convention in 1884, and a delegate in 1888; was elected county judge of Chautauqua county in November, 1891; has practiced law in Jamestown since 1878.*

\* \* \*

**Arthur C. Hastings,** recently elected mayor of Niagara Falls, and previously prominent in political and in business life, is still a young man, having been born in Brooklyn a few months before the beginning of the Civil War. His early education was received in the public schools of Brooklyn; and he afterward attended Smith College at Hatfield, Mass. He commenced his active business career in 1877 at Rochester, with the Rochester Paper Co., becoming secretary of the company after a short term of service. Resigning this position in 1889, he associated himself with John F. Quigley in building and operating pulp and paper mills at Niagara Falls, N. Y. After that he became treasurer and manager of the Cliff Paper Co. at Niagara Falls, and is still so engaged. Mr. Hastings has concentrated his business activity on a single industry, and has in that way acquired a wide knowledge of the field. He knows thoroughly both the manufacturing end of the business, and the difficult market in which the product must be sold. The paper industry has expanded enormously in recent years because of great improvements in machinery and processes ; and men who have grown up with the new order of things are correspondingly valuable in the conduct of paper-making plants.

Mr. Hastings has given his best attention to business, and has not until lately taken an active part in outside pursuits. He has always been interested, however, in public matters, and only the pressure of private business has kept him from participation in political affairs. In 1896 he became president of the police board of Niagara Falls, and made so good a record in the office that his name began to be mentioned in connection with the mayoralty of the city. As the time for deciding upon the nominees approached, his candidacy increased in favor, and he ultimately received the Republican nomination. He was elected in March, 1897, overcoming the usual Democratic majority. Although Mayor Hastings has served but a part of his term as chief magistrate of Niagara Falls, the prophecy may safely be made that his administration will be efficient, business-like, and clean.

In the social life of Niagara Falls Mayor Hastings has naturally been prominent. He is a Knight Templar Mason, and a member of the Order of Nobles of the Mystic Shrine.

*PERSONAL CHRONOLOGY—Arthur Chapin Hastings was born at Brooklyn, N. Y., July 14, 1860 ; was educated in Brooklyn public schools and at Smith College, Hatfield, Mass. ; married Alice W. Brown of Rochester January 14, 1887 ; was connected with the Rochester Paper Co., 1877–89 ; has been treasurer and manager of the Cliff Paper Co., Niagara Falls, N. Y., since 1892.*

**Lee R. Sanborn** has stamped himself indelibly upon the map of Niagara county, and in the hearts of its people. His father was a teacher at Bath, N. H., and afterward an itinerant preacher in the Methodist Episcopal church ; and his mother was likewise a teacher at Worcester, Mass., and a person of culture and character. Under the wholesome influence of their precept and example Mr. Sanborn acquired a thorough moral and a

fair intellectual education. He was born near Brockport, Monroe county, but moved a few miles west, to the place that now bears his name. There he engaged in the lumber business and in manufacturing, and soon became widely and favorably known. In fact his position in the community ultimately became such that the people of the place named the village after him.

The prominence implied in this event was also evident in numerous public trusts to which Mr. Sanborn was called early in his career. At one time or another he has held almost all the town offices. In 1870 and again the next year, he was a member of the state assembly, and took a prominent part in the proceedings of that body. He has often been sent as a delegate to state conventions, and in 1884 was a delegate to the national convention that nom-

*ARTHUR C. HASTINGS*

inated James G. Blaine. For many years he has been regarded as one of the leaders of the Republican party in Niagara county ; and his great influence at home and elsewhere has contributed materially to the strength of the Republican cause in his part of the state. In 1886 he was appointed by the governor of New York a member of the board of management of the state school for the blind at Batavia. He was elected president of the board of trustees in the same year, and still holds that position. He is

*LEE R. SANBORN*

noted for his interest in all philanthropic enterprises, and for many deeds of private benevolence.

Mr. Sanborn has been engaged in various commercial undertakings, and has shown unusual business ability in the conduct of the same. He has been largely interested in the manufacture of lumber in western New York and Michigan, where he has had large timber interests for many years. He has also taken much personal interest in his farm, which is one of the most fertile in the county.

Mr. Sanborn has been since early manhood a firm believer in Masonry, and has risen to high rank in the order. He is a member of Genesee Commandery, No. 10, Knights Templars, Lockport, a Scottish Rite Mason, and a member of Ismailia Temple,

Buffalo. He is also greatly interested in the Royal Templars of Temperance, and other fraternal orders. In 1887 he was elected representative to the Supreme Council of Royal Templars, and by that body was made a life member of the board of directors. In 1892 he was elected Supreme Councilor, and now holds that position.

*PERSONAL CHRONOLOGY—Lee Randall Sanborn was born at Sweden, Monroe county, N. Y., August 8, 1841; was educated in public schools; married Julia C. Crawford of Lewiston, N. Y., September 9, 1859; was a member of the New York state assembly, 1870-71; has lived at Sanborn, N. Y., engaged in lumber dealing, farming, and various commercial enterprises, since 1848.*

* * *

**John G. Wallenmeier, Jr.,** is of German descent, but his life thus far has been spent in western New York. Born in the section of Buffalo known as Black Rock during the early part of the Civil War, he was taken to Tonawanda in childhood, and has made his home there ever since. He received his education in the public schools of the town, and gained his first knowledge of commercial life there.

Shortly before he attained his majority Judge Wallenmeier began business on his own account, opening a grocery store in Tonawanda in May, 1883. He conducted the undertaking with prudence and energy, and met with a good degree of success from the start. After a few years he added a meat market to his establishment; and the combined business was continued until the spring of 1894, when he sold his store in order to devote himself to other duties.

Judge Wallenmeier has always been an active Republican, and has taken a prominent part in public affairs in Tonawanda. His devotion to his party and the cause of good government in general was appreciated by his fellow-citizens; and was appropriately recognized by his appointment by the council of Tonawanda as the first police justice under the act of 1894 establishing a police force in the town. In the spring of 1895 he was elected by the people to the same office for a term of four years. The growing and changing population of the thriving manufacturing town is not always of the most peaceful character, and Judge Wallenmeier has had abundant opportunity to exercise the functions of his office. He has fulfilled its duties with commendable zeal and vigor, and with strict impartiality as well ; meting out due punishment to all offenders without regard for position, and with a sturdy determination to render justice that has gained for him the approval of all right minded persons.

Judge Wallenmeier has taken much interest in the work of the savings and loan associations that have become so popular in recent years. Their facilities for utilizing the small weekly savings of the working man appealed to his German thrift and common sense. In 1890, accordingly, he helped to organize the Niagara Savings and Loan Association, and was its president for several years, retiring in 1896 when he found the cares of the position too arduous to be continued longer in connection with his public duties.

In the general and social life of the community Judge Wallenmeier is naturally prominent, and he has a host of friends. He is the Worshipful Master of Tonawanda Lodge, No. 247, F. & A. M., and belongs to the German Evangelical church. Having served from 1878 to 1886 as a volunteer fireman at Tonawanda, he received his exemption papers from the village council in April, 1886. In April, 1897, he was elected by the active volunteer firemen a member of the Tonawanda Firemen's Benevolent Association then organizing, and was chosen by a unanimous vote its first secretary.

*PERSONAL CHRONOLOGY— John George Wallenmeier, Jr., was born at Buffalo October 10, 1862 ; was educated in the public schools of Tonawanda, N. Y.; married Hattie May Koch of Tonawanda November 14, 1884 ; conducted a grocery and meat market at Tonawanda, 1884-94 ; was president of the Niagara Savings and Loan Association, 1895-96 ; has been police justice of Tonawanda since 1894.*

\* \* \*

**John G. Wicks,** one of the leading attorneys of the Chautauqua county bar, has been prominently identified with the municipal history of the city of Jamestown since its organization. When that community outgrew its village conditions, and assumed the dignity of a city, Mr. Wicks was chosen a member of the first common council from the 1st ward of the city. He had been instrumental, with

others, in drafting the original charter by which the new city was to be governed. On the organization of the common council he took an active part in inaugurating and maintaining the policy of the municipal government.

Mr. Wicks was particularly prominent among those who demanded a municipal control of certain natural monopolies, such as public waterworks, electric lighting plants, and the like. It was largely through his efforts that a municipal electric lighting plant was established at Jamestown. As an abler man of the city he worked for this end in season and out of season ; and the plant has since been enlarged and developed to such an extent as to justify and reward his early activity and energy in its behalf.

After a service of four years in the common council Mr. Wicks retired from public office ; but his

work was too important to the commonwealth to permit of long inactivity, and at the end of a year he was chosen attorney for the city of Jamestown. Acting in this capacity for four years, he drafted many amendments to the city charter; virtually, indeed, he redrafted the entire instrument. During his term of office many public improvements were undertaken; and all the bonds created thereby were issued under his direction, and the contracts for more than half a million dollars' worth of public

*JOHN G. WICKS*

works were drawn by him. To his credit as an attorney it can be said that no flaw has been discovered in any of this work.

Mr. Wicks was born in the town of Carroll, now Kiantone, Chautauqua county. After graduating from the Jamestown High School, and later from the Albany Law School, he was admitted to the bar in 1876, and soon took rank with the leaders of his profession in his native county. Among the attorneys who have graduated from his office are A. C. Pickard, J. Delevan Curtiss, and D. D. Dorn. For several years he was associated with Mr. Curtiss; since the dissolution of this partnership he has preferred to practice alone.

Aside from his connection with the legal pro-

fession, Mr. Wicks has been prominently identified with the Independent Order of Odd Fellows, holding the office of District Deputy Grand Master of Chautauqua county for three years in the '80's. He has always been active in the Republican party.

*PERSONAL CHRONOLOGY — John Gilbert Wicks was born in the town of Carroll, Chautauqua county, N. Y., January 10, 1855; was educated in country schools and the Jamestown High School; graduated from the Albany Law School, and was admitted to the bar in 1876; married Emma L. Russell in December, 1876; was an alderman of the city of Jamestown, 1889–90, and city attorney, 1891–95; has practiced law in Jamestown since 1876.*

★★★

**Fred D. Corey** was born in Jefferson county, New York, during the Civil War. He was educated in the public schools of Watertown, the county seat, and graduated from the high school there in 1884. He at once turned his attention to teaching, and followed this occupation very successfully for the next six years. For the first half of that time he remained in his native county, and held the position of principal successively in the schools at Evans' Mills, Brownville, and Sackett's Harbor. In 1887, however, he accepted the principalship of a grammar school at Norwalk, Conn., and for the next three years labored there. By this time he was in his twenty-eighth year; and it became evident to him that the teacher's calling, though attractive in many ways, did not afford the opportunity for advancement that he desired. Accordingly, he gave up his position in Connecticut, and began, somewhat late in life, to prepare himself for admission to the bar.

Returning to the city of Watertown, Mr. Corey entered the office of Hannibal Smith as a student, and remained with him a little more than a year. In the fall of 1891 he became a member of the Buffalo Law School, and graduated therefrom in the following May. Realizing that the Queen City offered a field of professional activity unsurpassed, perhaps, by any city in the land, he decided to try his fortunes there. For two years he worked in the office of Robert F. Schelling as a clerk, and then, July 1, 1894, formed a partnership with Edward D. Strebel, under the firm name of Strebel & Corey, that still exists. In the years since passed he has made good progress in building up a substantial clientage, and making a place for himself at the bar of Erie county. The fact that he was several years older than the average lawyer when he began practice, has been in his favor in some respects, since he has been able to bring to bear upon legal problems a more mature mind and more ripened judgment.

Mr. Corey devotes himself wholly to his chosen profession. Thus far he has resisted the allurements of political life, which as a rule appeal so strongly to a lawyer, and he is not a member of any social or fraternal organizations. He belongs to the North Presbyterian Church.

*PERSONAL CHRONOLOGY— Fred Daniel Corey was born at Black River, Jefferson county, N. Y., May 27, 1864; graduated from the Watertown (N. Y.) High School in 1884; taught school, 1884-89; married Ella L. Phelps of Sackett's Harbor, N. Y., August 17, 1887; was admitted to the bar in 1892; has practiced law in Buffalo since 1892.*

* * *

**Roland Crangle** is a notable example of the oft-cited fact that in America hard work, when combined with native ability, is sure to be amply rewarded. Even in America, though many men amass large fortunes in a comparatively short time, it is not so common for a man to rise from the position of a day laborer to the ranks of one of the learned professions in a dozen years. Such, however, is the story of Mr. Crangle's career thus far.

Born in the north of Ireland little more than thirty years ago, Mr. Crangle spent his boyhood on the farm in County Down where his parents still reside. At an early age he became a pupil in one of the National Schools of the country, and continued his studies there until his sixteenth year, obtaining thus a good general education. He was ambitious for a far higher career than any that seemed open to him in his native land, and he accordingly determined to emigrate to America. Arriving in New York, he betook himself at once to Buffalo, which has proved a most hospitable home. Without friends or money, he was obliged to begin at the foot of the ladder, and his first employment was that

*FRED D. COREY*

of a laborer on the docks. He afterward worked as a freight hand in the Erie-railroad freight house, and subsequently secured a position as clerk in the freight office of the Lake Shore road.

During the years thus occupied Mr. Crangle devoted his spare time to the study of elocution, for which he had a great liking, and much natural aptitude; and in due time he graduated from the Buffalo School of Elocution. In the presidential campaign of 1888 he used his talents in the service of the Democratic party, making many speeches in favor of its candidates. His political work brought him to the favorable notice of many men prominent in Buffalo; and, as he had now accumulated some capital from his eight years of hard work, he was able to gratify his ambition, and prepare himself for a position where his abilities would have full scope.

In January, 1889, accordingly, he entered the law office of Rogers, Locke & Milburn, Buffalo, where he remained five years, during which he was duly admitted to the bar. This firm stands second to none in western New York, and Mr. Crangle's long connection with the office as student and clerk could not fail to give him a thorough knowledge of the principles and practice of the law. Since January, 1894, he has practiced on his own account, and has attained a most satisfactory measure of

ROLAND CRANGLE

success. He is recognized by his fellow members of the Buffalo bar as a painstaking and careful lawyer of decided ability, and his steady advancement in his chosen profession may be confidently predicted.

Mr. Crangle cares little for club or society life, preferring to devote himself to his profession.

*PERSONAL CHRONOLOGY— Roland Crangle was born at Ballyquintin, County Down, Ireland, August 17, 1864; was educated in the National Schools of Ireland; came to the United States in 1880, and worked as a laborer and clerk at Buffalo, 1880–88; studied law, and was admitted to the bar in June, 1892; has practiced law in Buffalo since January, 1894.*

**F. D. Duckwitz** was born less than forty years ago in the town of Wheatfield, Niagara county, New York. His parents, Augustus and Louise Donath Duckwitz, were natives of Stettin, Germany, who came to the United States in 1853. They spent five years in New York, and then moved to Niagara county, where Augustus Duckwitz bought a farm and carried on a large nursery, selling nearly all the fruit trees in that section of the state. During the war he served as provost marshal, and after his return North bought a large general store in St. Johnsburgh, Niagara county. This he conducted for several years, acting at the same time as auctioneer, insurance agent, and justice of the peace. Ferdinand Duckwitz helped his father on the farm and in the store, attending district schools as he had opportunity, until his fourteenth year. At that time his father sold the store, and the new proprietor was glad to secure the young man's services at a salary. Mr. Duckwitz remained with him two years, and accumulated a sufficient sum to enable him to gratify his desire for a better education than he had thus far obtained. At the age of sixteen, accordingly, he left home and betook himself to Buffalo, where he studied for a year at Bryant & Stratton's Business College. He then went West, and spent a year working on farms and in stores in various places. By this time he had determined to become a lawyer, and had also decided the question of locality in favor of the East. Returning, therefore, to his native county, he entered the office of George C. Greene of Lockport as a student. His preparatory training had not been so thorough as would have been desirable, but he made up for any lack in this respect by close application and natural ability. During his three years in Mr. Greene's office he published the *Lockport Deutsche Zeitung,* a weekly German paper, and also acted as insurance agent and organizer of lodges, managing in this way not only to support himself, but to save enough money to take him to college. He entered the law department of Union University in 1879, graduated May 21, 1880, and in the same month was admitted to practice in all the courts of New York state.

Immediately after his admission to the bar Mr. Duckwitz opened an office in Buffalo, where he has practiced ever since with most gratifying success. In the early part of his legal career he was much helped by his thorough knowledge of the German language, which the large German population of the city rendered particularly useful. In 1884 he formed a partnership with John G. Perkins, which lasted until Mr. Perkins's death in 1883. He then associated himself with Charles K. Robinson, and later with William Armstrong. January 1, 1890, Mr. Duckwitz established the present firm of Duckwitz, Thayer & Jackson, in partnership with Wallace Thayer and Frederick S. Jackson. This association was a most fortunate one, and has become one of the most popular of the younger law firms of Buffalo. Mr. Duckwitz is an excellent counselor and business lawyer, Mr. Thayer possesses decided talent as a trial lawyer, and Mr. Jackson is an able co-worker in the general business of the firm.

Mr. Duckwitz is actively concerned in a variety of matters outside his profession. For a number of years he was the treasurer and a trustee of the Mechanics' Institute, and took the greatest interest in the association. He belongs to many social and fraternal organizations, including the Royal Arcanum, the Improved Order of Heptasophs, and the United Friends. He is a member of the Supreme Council of the Empire Knights of Relief, and of the Supreme Ruling of the Fraternal Mystic Circle of the State of Pennsylvania. He was one of the incorporators of the Order of the Iroquois of Buffalo, and is the Supreme Councilor of the order, chairman of the committee on laws, and a member of the board of trustees. In politics he is a staunch Republican, who never hesitates or wavers in his party allegiance, and has been for many years a member of the Buffalo Republican League. He is one of the wardens of St. Luke's Episcopal Church, and was for a time its treasurer.

*PERSONAL CHRONOLOGY—Ferdinand Herman Duckwitz was born in the town of Wheatfield, N. Y., August 11, 1858; attended district schools and Bryant & Stratton's Business College; studied law in a Lockport office, and graduated from the law department of Union University in 1880; married Henrietta Waldron Springsteed of Albany December 22, 1880; has practiced law in Buffalo since 1880.*

**Joseph L. Fairchild,** who has been prominent in public life for many years, was born in Seneca county, New York, during Andrew Jackson's first administration. After attending the private schools of his native town, and graduating at Waterloo Academy, he continued his studies under a private tutor, and fitted himself for the sophomore class at Hobart College. He changed his mind, however, when about to begin his collegiate course, deciding to study law. His uncle, Harlow S. Love, was then one of the leading attorneys of Buffalo; and in his office, that of Talcott & Love, Mr. Fairchild read law. He was admitted to the bar in 1855, and began his career as a lawyer at once in Buffalo.

For the next fifteen years Mr. Fairchild gave himself unreservedly to his profession, building up a practice that was at once lucrative and gratifyingly

*F. H. DUCKWITZ*

significant of his legal ability. He served acceptably several of the successors of the Holland Land Co., and other individual and corporate clients whose legal interests were important. In the fall of

1867 an important position came to him entirely without solicitation on his part, and Mr. Fairchild abandoned his profession for the office of register in bankruptcy. In the year mentioned congress passed the momentous piece of legislation known as the national bankruptcy act, which called into being an

*JOSEPH L. FAIRCHILD*

important set of officials concerned in the adjustment of bankrupt estates. Their functions were both judicial and administrative, and only men of high character and tried ability were selected for the office. Mr. Fairchild received his appointment from Salmon P. Chase, chief justice of the United States, and was sworn into office January 3, 1868. For the next decade he devoted all his time and strength to his important work, sparing himself in no respect, and discharging most efficiently the trying duties of his office. In 1878 congress repealed the act under which Mr. Fairchild was appointed, except as to cases existing at that time. Mr. Fairchild still retains the office, but its work has been increasingly light since the repeal of the law.

Having lived in Buffalo since the middle of the century, Mr. Fairchild has become one of the best-known men of the city, and has taken a leading part in many public movements. He was prominent in the Young Men's Association for many years; and was a prime mover in effecting the important change of location made in 1864, when the society left its quarters in the old American block and purchased the St. James hotel property on the site of the present Hotel Iroquois. For two years he was on the board of supervisors of Erie county, representing the old 10th ward, Buffalo. He was a park commissioner for eight years, and was a member of the building committee that supervised the construction of the Parade House. He had much to do, also, with the planning of Delaware park, taking great interest in the creation of its charming lake and other beautiful features.

Mr. Fairchild has been a member of the Masonic order since early manhood, and is a life member of Ancient Landmark Lodge, No. 441, F. & A. M. He is also a charter member of Adytum Chapter, R. A. M.

An interesting episode in Mr. Fairchild's life was his visit at the White House just after Lincoln's inauguration. He was related to Lincoln by marriage, and knew him intimately years before the presidency was mentioned in connection with the "Rail-Splitter." During this visit Mr. Fairchild met many of the notable men of the country, and he looks back upon the experience with great interest. It is worthy of note that he has been intimate with another President, as he and Grover Cleveland are old-time chums. Mr. Fairchild does not agree with Mr. Cleveland on political questions; but he has the warmest regard for him personally, and believes thoroughly in his honesty of character and purpose.

*PERSONAL CHRONOLOGY — Joseph Lewis Fairchild was born at Waterloo, N. Y., April 8, 1831; was educated in private schools and Waterloo Academy; studied law in a Buffalo office, and was admitted to the bar in 1854; practiced law in Buffalo, 1854–67; married Anna E. Dennison of Buffalo November 14, 1862; was a member of the Erie-county board of supervisors, 1866–67, and a park commissioner of Buffalo for eight years, beginning in 1874; has held the office of register in bankruptcy at Buffalo since 1868.*

**Charles Cyrus Farnham** was born in Bradford, Orange county, Vermont, in 1861. He is the oldest living son of Roswell Farnham, who was governor of Vermont in 1880–82. The Farnhams were among the earliest settlers in the Massachusetts colony. The first ancestor on this side of the ocean was Ralph Farnham, who sailed from Southampton, England, April 6, 1635, in the brig "James," and landed in Boston after a voyage of fifty-eight days. Settling first in Andover, Mass., not far from Boston, the Farnhams afterward moved to Concord, N. H. They were among the earliest inhabitants of that frontier town, the name of Ephraim Farnham appearing under the date February 5, 1725, in the Proprietors' Records of Pennycook (now Concord). This Ephraim had a son Benjamin, whose son John, born in Concord January 2, 1766, was the grandfather of Governor Roswell Farnham. Governor Farnham's grandfather on the maternal side was Captain David Bixby of Piermont, N. H., who served in the armies of the Revolution from Lexington to Saratoga. Enlisting then on board the privateer "Franklin," he was taken prisoner by a British frigate, carried to England, and confined for seventeen months in Mill (presumably Dartmoor) prison. The mother of Charles Cyrus Farnham was Mary Elizabeth Johnson of Bradford, Vt., who married Roswell Farnham on Christmas day, 1849.

Our present subject prepared for college at the academy in his native town, and entered the University of Vermont at Burlington in the fall of 1882. Graduating thence in due course in June, 1886, he commenced at once the study of law in his father's office. After remaining there a year he went into the law department of Columbia College, New York city, whence he graduated with the degree of LL.B. in 1889. During the vacations of his law course Mr. Farnham employed his time in tutoring the grandchildren of Salmon P. Chase and a son of General Wager Swayne.

Some time before his graduation from Columbia Mr. Farnham had decided to settle in Buffalo, feeling sure that the charm of the city as a place of residence was no greater than its promise as a field of professional practice. Proceeding thither, accordingly, on the day before he received his degree as a Bachelor of Law, he took an examination for admission to the bar, and passed successfully. He was taken at once into the office of McMillan, Gluck & Pooley, where he had at one time read law, and remained with them until November, 1890, when he opened an office of his own. After practicing alone a few months, he formed a partnership in July, 1891, with August Becker, who had also studied law in the office of McMillan, Gluck & Pooley. The firm of Becker & Farnham has prospered from the beginning, and is now regarded as one of the strongest associations among the younger lawyers of the city. Mr. Farnham has proved himself an energetic and prudent business man and lawyer, and has conducted many complicated cases to a satisfactory issue. He enjoys the esteem and confidence of many clients and friends.

*CHARLES CYRUS FARNHAM*

Mr. Farnham has thought it wise to abstain from active participation in political affairs. He belongs to the University Club and various other social organizations; and both he and Mrs. Farnham are consistent members of the First Congregational Church, Buffalo. Mrs. Farnham is the daughter of Edward Hall, who for many years conducted a successful private school at Ellington, Conn.

*PERSONAL CHRONOLOGY — Charles Cyrus Farnham was born at Bradford, Vt., May 9,*

*GEORGE H. FROST*

*1854, graduated from the University of Vermont in 1886, and from Columbia College Law School in 1889; was admitted to the bar at Buffalo in 1889; married Grace Hall of Ellington, Conn., October 30, 1889; has practiced law in Buffalo since 1889.*

•••

**George H. Frost,** who has become well known of late years in both professional and business circles in Buffalo, is a native of Chautauqua county, and had attained prominence there as a lawyer and a citizen before he moved to the Queen City in 1889.

Born in the town of Cherry Creek in the year in which President Fillmore entered the White House, Mr. Frost received his early education in the com-

mon schools of the place, and later attended the Jamestown Union School and the Ellington Union School. His work as an instructor during the next ten years furnished an excellent substitute for regular scholastic training. Before he was twenty he began teaching in the common schools ; and for several years he carried on this occupation during the winter months, and worked on his father's farm in summer. Later he gave all his time to teaching, and had charge of schools at Versailles, Cherry Creek, Kennedy, and other places.

But school teaching as a life-work did not satisfy Mr. Frost's ambition; and he determined to prepare himself for the legal profession. He read law, accordingly, in the office of the late John G. Record of Forestville, N. Y., and was admitted to the bar at Rochester in October, 1883. Feeling that success would be most quickly attained among those who knew him best, he at once opened an office in his native town. He was considerably older at this time than the majority of men beginning legal practice ; but this circumstance in a lawyer's career has some advantages along with some undeniable drawbacks, and a man of ability soon makes up for the years that have been seemingly lost. Mr. Frost was successful from the start. After several years, actuated by the same ambition that had led him to abandon teaching for the law, he gave up his country practice and moved to Buffalo, judging rightly that the increased opportunities in a larger field of action more than compensated for the keener competition of a busy city.

For the first four years of his residence in Buffalo Mr. Frost practiced alone, but on January 1, 1894, he formed, with Fred W. Plato, the firm of Frost & Plato, which still continues. Soon after his arrival in Buffalo Mr. Frost became actively interested in the project for building an electric railway on Delaware avenue from Buffalo to Tonawanda. He was one of the organizers of the Buffalo, Kenmore & Tonawanda Electric Railway Co., and acted as attorney for the corporation during the construction of the road, and until it was sold to the Buffalo Traction Co.

Mr. Frost has always been an earnest Republican. During his residence in Cherry Creek he interested himself actively in public affairs, and in all movements for advancing the prosperity of his town and

county. In the fall of 1886 his services were
fittingly rewarded by a nomination for member of
assembly from the second district of Chautauqua
county. He was duly elected, and was re-elected
in 1887, serving his constituents with zeal and
ability. During both terms in the legislature Mr.
Frost was a member of the committee on general
laws. In March, 1888, the assembly passed a resolution calling for the appointment of a committee to
ascertain the social, moral, and industrial condition
of the several tribes of Indians in the state ; to investigate the tribal organizations and the title to the
lands in the different reservations ; and to afford such
aid as would enable the state to deal wisely and intelligently with the 5000 Indians dwelling within
her borders. Mr. Frost was a member of this committee, and took an active part in its laborious work.
An exhaustive study of the subject, occupying several months, resulted in a report
to the assembly dated January 31, 1889.
This document covers seventy-nine pages,
and with its various appendixes makes
up a volume of more than 400 pages.
The committee recommended the repeal
of most of the existing Indian laws, the
enactment of a compulsory-attendance
school law, and the allotment of the
land of the state reservations in severalty
to the different members of the tribes,
believing that only as the Indian becomes
an American citizen, and not a "ward"
of the government, will the Indian problem be solved. Mr. Frost's work on
this committee amply demonstrated his
fitness for public service ; but since his
removal to Buffalo he has taken a less
active part in public affairs than formerly, wisely preferring to devote his
entire energy for a time to establishing
himself firmly in the ranks of the successful lawyers of the city. He belongs
to no fraternity, church or other associations.

*PERSONAL CHRONOLOGY*
*George H. Frost was born at Cherry
Creek, N. Y., December 15, 1850; attended district schools, and union schools
at Jamestown and Ellington ; taught school
in various towns, 1870–82; married Helen
M. Perrin of Dayton, N. Y., December
18, 1879; studied law, and was admitted to the
bar in 1883; practiced law in Cherry Creek, 1883–
89; was member of assembly, 1887–88; has practiced law in Buffalo since November, 1889.*

**Ethan H. Howard** is one of the oldest residents of Buffalo, since he moved thither in 1827,
and has made his home there continuously for
seventy years. His parents were New Englanders,
his mother a native of Connecticut and his father of
Vermont, where his grandfather fought under General Stark in the battle of Bennington. They
settled on a small farm in the village of Boston,
Erie county, in 1807, and there our subject was
born five years later. He was still an infant when
the burning of Buffalo and Black Rock threw the
neighboring settlers into a panic of fear; and his
mother prepared for flight to the forest with her
children at the approach of the savage foe. Mr.
Howard's childhood, begun amid such stirring
scenes, was continued amid the privations and hardships of pioneer life. But civilization advanced

*ETHAN H. HOWARD*

rapidly in western New York after the news was
received that peace had been declared. Immigration received a fresh impetus, and a greater degree
of prosperity soon became apparent.

By the time the lad had reached the age of fifteen the village of Buffalo had become a thriving town, and already gave unmistakable evidence of its future leadership in the affairs of that part of the state. Thither he went, accordingly, and obtained employment in the post office, where the entire force of

HENRY C. HOWARD

assistants consisted of himself and another boy. Three years later he entered the dry-goods store of S. N. Callender as a clerk, remaining there for the next five years — four years with Mr. Callender and one year with J. P. Darling. Mercantile life proved attractive to Mr. Howard, and he displayed marked ability for it ; and in 1836 he started in business for himself as a member of the dry-goods firm of Dole & Howard. The style was subsequently changed to Fitch & Howard, then to Howard & Cogswell, Howard & Whitcomb, and Howard, Whitcomb & Co. ; and in 1865 the business was sold to the present firm of Flint & Kent. Mr. Howard's excellent judgment, honorable and upright methods, and careful business management brought him un-

usual success ; and during the thirty years of his connection with the firm it attained a foremost position among the retail houses of the city.

After severing his connection with the dry-goods business Mr. Howard associated himself with Joseph Warren, J. M. Johnson, and others in the organization of the Courier Company. He was the treasurer of the concern during the years 1868-69, selling out his interest at the end of that time to Dr. Kenney, son-in-law of Dean Richmond. Since 1870 Mr. Howard has not been actively engaged in business life, though he holds important positions of trust in various organizations. He was a trustee and the second vice president of the Erie County Savings Bank, and a director of the Buffalo Gas Light Co. In 1882 he assisted in founding the Bank of Niagara at Niagara Falls, and became a director of the institution ; and in 1892 he took part in the organization of the Columbia Bank, Buffalo, in which he is likewise a director.

Mr. Howard's peaceful and prosperous old age is a fitting close to an honorable and useful life. Though by nature singularly quiet and unobtrusive, his high character as a business man and a private citizen has won for him the respect of all who know him, and the warm affection of many friends. He has been for years a deacon in the Unitarian church, of which he is one of the oldest members.

*PERSONAL CHRONOLOGY—*
*Ethan How Howard was born at Boston, Erie county, N. Y., February 14, 1812 ; was a clerk in the Buffalo post office, 1827-28, and in a dry-goods store, 1829-36 ; married Mary E. Rumsey of Stafford, N. Y., October 24, 1842, and Caroline H. Cogswell of Peterborough, N. H., September 1, 1846 ; engaged in the dry-goods business at Buffalo, 1836-65 ; was treasurer of the Courier Company, Buffalo, 1868-69 ; has occupied positions of trust in various corporations in Buffalo and vicinity since 1870.*

***

**Henry C. Howard** is thoroughly identified with the Queen City of the Lakes. His family settled in Buffalo in the early days of the city ; his father had an important part in the commercial development of the place ; and he himself was born there, educated there, married there, and has always lived there. He believes in Buffalo heartily, and has no wish ever to shift his allegiance. Mr. Howard left school at the age of eighteen or nineteen, and gave himself up to business. He has never engaged in active commercial life of the routine countingroom order except for a few months early in his career. Ever since then his connection with business affairs has been of that more interesting and independent nature concerned with proprietary supervision. He has been president of the Bank of Niagara at Niagara Falls ever since it was organized in 1882, and vice president of the Bank of Suspension Bridge since its organization. He was for some years vice president of the Columbia National Bank, Buffalo, and is a director in the Bank of Buffalo.

In political matters Mr. Howard supports the Republican party. He does not care for participation in public affairs, however, and has never taken an active part in politics. His time is pleasantly occupied, aside from business hours, with his family and home. He is a member of the Buffalo Club, and of the Ellicott Club. Early in the summer he takes his family to a beautiful country seat on the banks of the Niagara river between Lewiston and Youngstown. Mr. Howard attends Trinity Church, Buffalo, of which he is a vestryman.

*PERSONAL CHRONOLOGY — Henry Cogswell Howard was born at Buffalo September 20, 1847; was educated in public and private schools; married Jennie Matilda Jewett of Buffalo January 4, 1869; has devoted himself to various business enterprises and to the care of the family estate since 1865; has been president of the Bank of Niagara, Niagara Falls, N. Y., since 1882.*

\*\*\*

**W. E. Kisselburgh, Jr.,** well known in both the eastern and the western ends of the Empire State, was born at Troy, N. Y., in 1859. He spent the first thirty years of his life in that city, and received his education there and in Albany. At the time of his graduation from the Troy High School in 1875 he had not fixed upon the practice of law as his vocation, and he began his active work in the world in the capacity of reporter for the Troy *Times*. In 1880 he obtained a position in the office of the secretary of state under J. B. Carr, and devoted his leisure hours to the study of law. Con-

tinuing this work more thoroughly in the celebrated law school at Albany, he received the degree of LL. B. from that institution in 1882. He was admitted to the bar the next year, and commenced to practice in Troy October 1, 1885.

Mr. Kisselburgh was associated with L. E. Griffith from October, 1885, until August, 1889, when he changed his residence from Troy to Buffalo. In the latter city he practiced alone until January 1, 1893, forming at that time a partnership with H. S. Lary. This connection lasted until January, 1895, when he associated himself with C. H. Bennett in the firm of Kisselburgh & Bennett. Mr. Kisselburgh has spent most of his time in Albany since May, 1894, and has therefore been unable to give minute attention to the affairs of his Buffalo clients. He has kept in touch, however, with the business

*W. E. KISSELBURGH, JR.*

connected with his firms, and has given close attention to the more important cases.

Living so near the state capital, Mr. Kisselburgh began to be interested in public affairs at an early age. He has frequently been a delegate to state conventions, and has otherwise been active in political life. In 1892 he was associated with Judge Laughlin and Mr. Moot as special counsel for the Citizens' Committee of Buffalo organized to prevent election frauds. Mr. Kisselburgh was especially

GEORGE E. LATTIMER

well qualified for this work from his experience in Troy four years before, when he had assisted in the legal proceedings that caused the removal from the registration books of about 2000 names wrongfully enrolled. Since May 1, 1894, Mr. Kisselburgh has been one of the deputy attorney generals of the state of New York, having been appointed to the office by Attorney General Theodore E. Hancock.

*PERSONAL CHRONOLOGY— William Edward Kisselburgh, Jr., was born at Troy, N. Y., January 28, 1859; graduated from the Troy High School in 1875, and from the Albany Law School in 1882; married Helen Laura Kittale of Troy May 12, 1889; was admitted to the bar in 1883; practiced law in Troy, 1883–89; was appointed deputy*

attorney-general of New York state in 1894; has practiced law in Buffalo since 1889.

## George E. Lattimer,

well known among the younger business men of Buffalo, was born in that city thirty-three years ago. After attending the public schools of Buffalo until he was sixteen years old, he made an early start on his commercial career by engaging on his own account in the business of carting coal, ice, and sand. He supplied the sand for some of the largest buildings in Buffalo, and built up a flourishing business. Having shown so much ability while still in his teens, Mr. Lattimer developed even more rapidly with increased experience. He attracted favorable notice among the business men of the city; and one of them, William S. Grattan, was glad to form a partnership with the young man. In the spring of 1886, accordingly, the firm of Grattan & Lattimer was organized for the purpose of carrying on a business in general freight contracting.

This venture proved successful from the beginning. Little else could have been expected in view of Mr. Grattan's broad business experience, Mr. Lattimer's special training in the carrying industry, and the excellent judgment of both partners. They were the first firm in Buffalo to contract with the railroads to handle their package freight, and they made such contracts with the Lackawanna, New York Central, and Lehigh Valley railroads. The firm employs at all times a large number of men, and in the busy season as many as a thousand are on its pay roll. At the time of the sound money parade in Buffalo in the presidential campaign of 1896, Mr. Lattimer marched at the head of 500 or more employees of his firm. Mr. Grattan has very important business interests outside of this concern, and necessarily leaves the management of Grattan & Lattimer affairs to the junior partner.

As for personal qualities unconnected with business, reference may be made to Mr. Lattimer's great interest in horses. He has owned at different times some of the fastest trotters ever seen on the magnificent parkways of Buffalo. Early in 1897 he was one of the prime movers in the proposed speedway running along Scajaquada creek in the rear of the Buffalo State Hospital.

Mr. Lattimer is a devoted Mason, and is a member of all the bodies of that order up to and including the 32d degree. He belongs to DeMolay Lodge, No. 498, F. & A. M. ; Buffalo Chapter, No. 71, R. A. M. ; Lake Erie Commandery, No. 20, K. T. ; Buffalo Council ; and Ismailia Temple, Nobles of the Mystic Shrine. He belongs likewise to the Masonic social organization called the Acacia Club.

*PERSONAL CHRONOLOGY — George Edward Lattimer was born at Buffalo June 19, 1847; was educated in the Buffalo public schools; engaged in a general carting business in Buffalo, 1880–86; married Annie Jones of Buffalo December 10, 1890; has been a member of the firm of Grattan & Lattimer, general freight contractors, since 1886.*

***

**Joseph Mischka** fought his way to an enviable position in the musical world of Buffalo by dint of energy and perseverance, coupled with natural gifts of a high order. His success is the more interesting and noteworthy from the fact that his training as a musician has been obtained altogether in Buffalo. He was not born in that city, but was brought thither at the age of six by his parents. The latter were in humble circumstances, and were unable to give their son much education. After attending a kindergarten in his native Bohemia, and one of the Buffalo public schools, he entered the parochial school connected with St. Louis Church, Buffalo. It was evident early in life that he possessed unusual musical talent, and his parents determined to foster this gift as much as possible. At the age of seven, accordingly, they obtained a chance for him to study the violin ; and he became a member of the orchestra that then took the place of an organ in St. Louis Church. A little later he developed a fine voice, and was made the principal alto in the choir. His gifts attracted the attention of the Rev. William Deiters, who was an ardent lover of music and who became the good genius of the boy. Father Deiters was possessed of an ample fortune, and he gave the young musician many advantages that would not otherwise have been his.

At the age of thirteen Joseph Mischka left school to become an errand boy for Blodgett & Bradford,

music dealers. The connection became something more than a business one, since Mr. Blodgett recognized the talent of his employee, and helped him in various ways to acquire a musical education. Young Mischka made the most of these opportunities, and at the age of fifteen was sufficiently advanced in his studies to become the organist of the North Presbyterian Church Sunday school. Soon after this he obtained the position of organist at Calvary Presbyterian Church. From there he went to Westminster, and thence successively to the old Unitarian Church, to the Universalist, and to St. Paul's. Each of these changes constituted a step in advance as regards both dignity of position and compensation. It may be said, indeed, that in all the numerous changes made by Mr. Mischka, he never gave up a place except by voluntary resignation to accept

*JOSEPH MISCHKA*

another position in the line of promotion. His house is filled with valuable gifts received at various times from the societies and churches with which he has been connected.

While organist of the Westminster Church, Mr. Mischka began his career as conductor of singing societies by taking charge of the newly organized Arion Society. This was a chorus of mixed voices, and its concerts, conducted by Mr. Mischka, were very popular. In 1878 he became chorus master of

DANIEL O'GRADY

the Caroline Richings Opera Co., with which he remained one year. Returning to Buffalo at the end of that period, he found the Liedertafel directorship vacant, and was asked to conduct rehearsals until the position should be permanently filled from abroad. He was so well liked, however, that the idea of sending to Europe for a leader was abandoned ; and Mr. Mischka remained in the position twenty-four years, with an interruption of two years between 1877 and 1879. On his retirement in the fall of 1894 the office of honorary director was created in order to bestow it upon him.

Mr. Mischka was the local musical director of the Saengerfest of the North American Saengerbund held in Buffalo in 1883, comprising 3000 singers

and 100 musicians, and of the great musical festivals held in that city in 1884, 1885, and 1887. He was director of the Vocal Society from 1887 to 1894, and brought that organization to a high pitch of excellence. For the last twenty-seven years, with the exception of two years between 1880 and 1882, Mr. Mischka has been organist of Temple Beth Zion ; and since 1887 he has been organist at the Delaware Avenue Methodist Episcopal Church. Since 1873 he has been professor of music in the Buffalo State Normal School. Having been appointed in the fall of 1894 supervisor of music in the Buffalo public schools, he found the responsibility of this position so great that he severed his connection with the Liedertafel and with the Vocal Society. He now has 60,000 children in his charge. It is his ambition and aim, not only to teach music to the children for their own sake, but also to furnish capable singers to the chorus masters of the next generation.

As a promoter of music in Buffalo no man has a record superior to that of Mr. Mischka. He has always been active in support of musical enterprises, and has never been sparing of his time or strength in furthering their success. His generosity toward his colleagues is well known, and many a young musician dates his career from the time when Mr. Mischka brought him to public notice.

*PERSONAL CHRONOLOGY—Joseph Mischka was born at Hermanmestec, Austria, May 8, 1846 ; came to the United States in 1852, and settled in Buffalo ; was chorus master of an opera troupe, 1848-49 ; engaged in business as music dealer and publisher, 1849-72 ; married Catherine Dietz of Buffalo September 5, 1871 ; was director of the Buffalo Liedertafel, 1870-77 and 1879-94 ; has held various prominent positions as teacher of music and as church organist in Buffalo since 1870.*

* * *

**Daniel O'Grady,** one of the deputy excise commissioners appointed under the famous Raines law of 1896, was born in Rochester, N. Y., a short time before the outbreak of the Civil War. His father carried on a prosperous business in Rochester for many years, and there the young man acquired his education and early business experience. After attending the public schools of the Flower City he took a course at Bryant & Stratton's Business College, graduating from the institution in due time.

Mr. O'Grady's real start in the world was made in 1885, when he shifted his residence from Rochester to Buffalo, and established himself in business in the latter city. He selected for his field of operations a part of Buffalo that was then very sparsely settled — the extreme eastern section of the city. Much of this neighborhood is now given up to prosperous manufactories, railroad yards, slaughterhouses, and cattle pens; but when Mr. O'Grady established a grocery at the corner of Broadway and Bailey avenue most of the land near him was used for farming purposes. It was evident, however, that the industrial growth of Buffalo was likely to move in that direction; and Mr. O'Grady soon had plenty of neighbors. A large Polish population ultimately occupied the territory tributary to his business, and he came to know the people well, and to have considerable influence with them. Several railroad and other strikes, of long duration and corresponding severity to employees and their tradesmen, have occurred at East Buffalo since Mr. O'Grady went there; but he has weathered every such industrial gale, though some other commercial craft have foundered.

Under the circumstances indicated in the foregoing statement of Mr. O'Grady's career in East Buffalo, it was natural for him to take an interest in public affairs, and to acquire considerable importance in local politics. There seems, indeed, to be a tendency of that kind in the family, since Mr. O'Grady's brother, James M. E. O'Grady of Rochester, has long been prominent in the politics of Monroe county, and is now speaker of the state assembly. Daniel O'Grady has been identified with the Republican organization in Buffalo for the last ten years as district and general committeeman, and has an important personal following in his part of the city. He has not cared to hold political office, however; and never did so until April, 1896, when H. H. Lyman, state commissioner of excise, appointed him one of his deputies, with headquarters at Buffalo.

Mr. O'Grady has given his chief attention to business and politics. He belongs to various fraternal associations, however, such as the order of Elks, the Red Men, and the Knights of Pythias. He is naturally a member of the Buffalo Republican League, and has served on the executive committee of the organization.

*PERSONAL CHRONOLOGY— Daniel O'Grady was born at Rochester February 1?, 1861; was educated in common schools and Bryant & Stratton's Business College; married Elizabeth Maloney of Spencerport, N. Y., January 30, 1884; was appointed deputy excise commissioner for Buffalo in April, 1896; has been in business at East Buffalo since 1885.*

•••

**John Townsend Pitkin** was born in Wayne county, New York, somewhat less than forty years ago. The Pitkin family has had an important part in the history of America ever since William Pitkin, the third governor of Connecticut, was chosen in

*JOHN TOWNSEND PITKIN*

1754 to prepare a plan of union for the colonies. There were five other members of this committee including the chairman, Benjamin Franklin. Among the descendants of this Pitkin may be found three judges of supreme courts, one United States senator, two state governors, members of congress and state legislatures, and many men prominent in professional and commercial life.

Our present subject went to the union school in his native town of Palmyra, and after moving to Buffalo in early youth attended the well-known Heathcote School, a private institution of excellent standing. At the age of sixteen he closed his books, not expecting then ever to resume systematic academic training. He had always taken great interest in electrical subjects, and his first venture in the outer world was made as an electrician, line repairer, and operator for the Atlantic & Pacific Telegraph Co. This was in 1874. The next year he made a commercial hit by running "electric light" excursions from Buffalo to Niagara Falls. The arc light was then just coming into general use; and the viewing of the Falls in the new light, variously and brilliantly colored, became a popular pastime. In 1876 he entered the service of the Central Hudson road at Buffalo as train dispatcher, telegraph operator, and ticket agent. The next year he was employed by the Buffalo police department as chief telegraph operator; and in 1879 he became an operator for the Western Union company at Buffalo.

Deciding to follow a professional rather than a business career, and having a strong inclination toward the study of medicine, Mr. Pitkin entered the College of Physicians and Surgeons at New York in 1881, and afterward attended the medical department of the University of Buffalo. He received from the latter institution in 1884 the degree of M. D., obtaining at graduation the distinction of an "honorable mention." For several years after this he tutored medical students at the University of Buffalo with much success. Opening an office in Buffalo soon after he obtained his degree, Dr. Pitkin carried on an increasingly large general practice for over a decade. His early interest in electrical matters was maintained all the time, naturally taking a direction harmonious with his professional work.

The application of electrical science to surgery and general therapeutics has become of great importance in recent years, and Dr. Pitkin has devoted a good deal of time to the study of the subject. This investigation convinced him of the wide usefulness of electricity in the art of healing, and he decided to specialize his work to a considerable extent in this line. He founded, accordingly, in November, 1896, the Buffalo Electrical Sanitarium, with executive offices in Ellicott Square and branches at 206 Connecticut street and 619 Prospect avenue. This experiment has already proved successful, and Dr. Pitkin has at times more patients than he can easily care for. He has taken great interest in the "X-ray" discovery as related to surgical operations, and has done a good deal to popularize exact and useful knowledge of the subject. He has contributed articles to the Buffalo *Medical Journal* on stomach and peritoneal washing and on hemorrhages from the nostrils.

On the personal side, mention may be made of Dr. Pitkin's interest in military affairs. In 1879 he organized company F of the 74th regiment, N. G., S. N. Y., serving as captain of the company for some time; and he is now a member of the Buffalo City Guard Cadet Association. In politics he is a Republican, and received the nomination of his party for alderman in 1887. He has observed closely the territorial expansion of Buffalo, and has made some successful ventures in real-estate operations. He is a member of the First Presbyterian Church of Buffalo.

*PERSONAL CHRONOLOGY—John Townsend Pitkin was born at Palmyra, N. Y., May 8, 1858; attended Palmyra Union School and Heathcote School, Buffalo; held various positions as electrician and telegraph operator, 1874-81; studied medicine, and graduated from the medical department of the University of Buffalo in 1884; married Lizzie Simons Youngs of Buffalo March 4, 1886; has practiced medicine in Buffalo since 1884.*

\*\*\*

## Andrew J. Robertson

Andrew J. Robertson was born in Delaware county, New York, in 1851. After attending district schools and the academy in his native town, teaching at intervals and boarding around among the farmers in the old-fashioned way, he sought higher instruction in Delaware Academy at Delhi, N. Y. At the age of twenty he entered Cornell University with the class of '75, hoping to take the full course. He was obliged to meet his own expenses, and after working his way along through the freshman year he decided that it would not pay to follow such a life for three years more. He did not, however, give up the idea of studying law; and after teaching German for a year at Delaware Academy he began to prepare himself in an office at Delhi for the bar examinations. He studied thus three years, supporting himself by his labor, and was admitted to the bar in the fall of 1876.

Beginning practice at once in Delhi, Mr. Robertson concluded after a few months that he need not hesitate to pit himself against the legal lights of a larger place; and in March, 1877, accordingly, he opened an office in Elmira. After practicing alone until January, 1880, he formed a partnership with Gabriel L. Smith, ex-county judge. The firm of Smith & Robertson carried on a successful practice until January 1, 1889. At that time Mr. Robertson associated himself with John Ball, Jr., and the next year Dix W. Smith was admitted to the partnership. The firm of Robertson, Smith & Ball continued until the senior partner moved to Buffalo in April, 1893.

Mr. Robertson had then practiced in Elmira sixteen years, and had, of course, formed valuable business connections; but he felt sure that Buffalo was destined to become a large city, and he knew that the abler members of the legal profession must share in such prosperity. He has been in Buffalo only four years now, but has already attained a position of prominence at the local bar; and the prediction may safely be made that he will repeat in Erie county his earlier success in the Southern Tier.

Like many other lawyers, Mr. Robertson has been much concerned with politics; but unlike many people so occupied, he has not at any time sought public office. His interest in the subject has been that of a public-spirited citizen, believing heartily in the principles of the Republican party, and trying to promote the greatest good of the greatest number in all proper ways. During his later years in Elmira Mr. Robertson frequently acted as counsel for Republican organizations in election contests; and he devoted a good deal of time to the work of instructing election officers as to their legal rights and duties on voting days. He is thoroughly informed in these matters, and the campaign managers of Buffalo have availed themselves of his services in every election since he went to that city. He has also been prominently connected with the Good Government Clubs of Buffalo, having associated himself with the movement from the beginning. He has acted as legal adviser for the organization, and rendered special service in conducting the investigation into the management of the Erie-county almshouse in 1896-97.

Aside from professional and political work, Mr. Robertson has concerned himself with several interesting subjects. He was one of the early devotees of cycling, and was a charter member and the first president of the Kanaweola Bicycle Club of Elmira.

He is an elocutionist of decided talent, and has frequently read in public in a semi-professional way. He is particularly interested in the study of Shakespeare, and is president of one of the Shakespeare clubs of Buffalo. He has written somewhat for publication at various times, and was the poet of his

ANDREW J. ROBERTSON

class at Cornell. He has been for many years a member of the Zeta Phi fraternity of Delhi, and was the poet at its annual dinner in 1874. He is a charter member of the Independent Club of Buffalo, and was the president thereof for the first two years of its existence.

*PERSONAL CHRONOLOGY — Andrew James Robertson was born at Andes, Delaware county, N. Y., March 29, 1851; attended district schools and academies and Cornell University; was admitted to the bar in 1876, and practiced in Delhi, N. Y., 1876-77; married Martha Hoyt Thompson of Elmira, N. Y., December 19, 1878; practiced law in Elmira, 1877-93; has practiced law in Buffalo since April, 1893.*

**Jacob F. Schoellkopf**, a veritable "captain of industry," and widely respected in western New York for his character and personal qualities, was born in Kirchheim-unter-Teck, a small town of Württemberg, Germany, in 1819. After attending the schools of his native town until he was fourteen

*JACOB F. SCHOELLKOPF*

years old, he began his business life by becoming an apprentice in his father's tannery. The tanner's trade might almost be regarded as a part of Mr. Schoellkopf's inheritance, since both his father and his grandfather had been conspicuously successful in the business. Having served as an apprentice the full term of five years, Jacob Schoellkopf broadened his industrial training by following a clerkship in a mercantile house for about two years. European emigration to the United States had already begun on a considerable scale, and Mr. Schoellkopf was sufficiently ambitious and foresightful to wish a part in the movement. Continued reflection only confirmed his purpose; and in December, 1841, when twenty-two years old, he landed in New York city.

Utterly ignorant of the English language, Mr. Schoellkopf was forced at first to accept the readiest employment at hand, and he naturally reverted to his old trade. After following this for two years in New York city, he moved to Buffalo in 1844, and established a small leather store on Mohawk street. His capital was limited to $800, which his father had loaned him. Seeing at once that he had made no mistake in committing himself to business, Mr. Schoellkopf soon embarked in a more ambitious venture by purchasing a small tannery at White's Corners (Hamburg), near Buffalo. His early training was invaluable to him in this enterprise, and ensured his success. In two years, or in 1846, he enlarged his operations by starting a sheepskin tannery in Buffalo; in 1848 he established a tannery in Milwaukee; and in 1850 still another tannery at Chicago resulted from his incessant activity. Both the Milwaukee and the Chicago tanneries are still in successful operation, though Mr. Schoellkopf withdrew his interest from them a few years after their establishment. In 1853 he started another tannery at Fort Wayne, Ind., and in 1854 yet another, at North Evans, N. Y., conducting the latter plant with unusual success for twenty years. In 1864 he bought a site for a tannery at Sheffield, Penn., then a part of the wilderness, and built up there a remarkably successful industry. He is now the senior proprietor of one of the largest sheepskin tanneries in the United States, located in Buffalo.

In 1857 Mr. Schoellkopf engaged in the milling industry by erecting the North Buffalo Flouring Mills. His wonderful business ability brought him success in the new departure, and he ultimately became one of the largest millers in the Empire State. In 1870 he bought the Frontier Mills in Buffalo, and subsequently erected extensive flouring mills at Niagara Falls. He is the senior partner in the famous milling firm of Schoellkopf & Mathews.

Mr. Schoellkopf's brilliant success in the management of his own vast enterprises has induced the directors of various corporations to seek his aid; and in some cases he has been willing to accept such directorates, or to share otherwise in the management of important corporations. He was vice-president of the Buffalo, New York & Philadelphia railroad before its sale to the present Western New York & Pennsylvania company. For a long time he was vice president of the Third National Bank, Buffalo ; and he is still a director in several banks in Buffalo and Niagara Falls. He is also a director and the president of the Citizens' Gas Co., Buffalo. He has been a trustee of the Buffalo General Hospital since it was founded. His varied industrial enterprises at Niagara Falls gave him special interest in the water power there, and in 1877 he bought the Hydraulic canal at the Falls. Seeing clearly the economic possibilities of the undeveloped Niagara power, he began at once to improve the property ; and many large mills, manufacturing paper, flour, aluminium, and other important products, are now using the canal. About 20,000 horse power is now produced, but this quantity will be greatly increased when proposed enlargements and improvements of the canal and power station are completed. For the purpose of developing the property Mr. Schoellkopf, soon after he bought the canal, organized the Niagara Falls Hydraulic Power & Manufacturing Co., of which he is still president.

Mr. Schoellkopf went back to Europe for the first time in 1853, and since then he has revisited his native land on many occasions. Though he is now in his seventy-eighth year, he still enjoys excellent health, and enters actively into business and social life.

*PERSONAL CHRONOLOGY —*
*Jacob Frederick Schoellkopf was born at Kirchheim-unter-Teck, Germany, November 15, 1819 ; was educated in German schools, and learned the tanner's trade in his native land ; came to the United States in 1841, and settled in Buffalo in January, 1844; married Christiana Sophie Duerr of Kirchheim-unter-Teck March 12, 1848 ; has been engaged in the tanning business since 1844, in milling since 1857, and in the management of various corporations for many years.*

•••

**Louis Schoellkopf** was born in Buffalo somewhat more than forty years ago, of German parents. He was favored with unusually careful tuition. Attending private schools until the age of ten, he then studied for four years in Germany, his father having a high opinion of the thorough training to be

obtained there. This excellent educational groundwork facilitated further training in Buffalo by private teachers, at St. Joseph's College, and at Bryant & Stratton's Business College.

The mention of the last-named institution shows the character of the career on which Mr. Schoellkopf had decided. It was natural and easy for him to choose a mercantile life, since his father, Jacob F. Schoellkopf, had vast business interests, and wished to have his son versed in commercial affairs. At the age of eighteen, therefore, Mr. Schoellkopf went to work in his father's tannery, learning the tanner's trade there thoroughly in the course of the next four years. If heredity counts for anything in such matters, the young man had every reason to take kindly to this occupation ; since his grandfather and his great-grandfather had been tanners in Ger-

*LOUIS SCHOELLKOPF*

many, and his father, after learning the trade in his native land, had established himself in the same business in Buffalo thirty years before. Having acquired a firm grasp of the business, Louis

Schoellkopf thought it advisable to set up a plant of his own ; and in 1877, accordingly, he formed a partnership with his brother Henry, under the style of J. F. Schoellkopf's Sons. This firm conducted a successful tanning business until Henry Schoellkopf died in 1880, when a new firm was organized, consisting of Louis and Alfred P. Schoellkopf and John Ross. This organization was well planned, and the concern has transacted a large volume of business. The original firm name is still used.

Mr. Schoellkopf has been concerned with various business undertakings, both in Buffalo and elsewhere, aside from that just described. In connection with his father and brother, he has devoted much time of late years to a number of enterprises in Niagara Falls, including the Power City Bank, International hotel, Cliff Paper Co., and Niagara Falls Hydraulic Power & Manufacturing Co.

In the social life of Buffalo Mr. Schoellkopf is highly regarded ; and as a lifelong resident of the Queen City, and a trusted and trustworthy citizen, he has an extensive circle of friends. In political matters his sympathies are with the Republican party, and he is a member of the Buffalo Republican League ; but he has taken no active part in politics, and has never sought nor held public office. He attends the Westminster Presbyterian Church, and is a member of the Westminster Club. He belongs, also, to the Ellicott Club, the Merchants' Exchange, the Orpheus Singing Society, and the Charity Organization.

*PERSONAL CHRONOLOGY — Louis Schoellkopf was born at Buffalo March 25, 1855 ; studied in Buffalo schools and colleges and in Germany ; learned the tanner's trade in Buffalo, 1873-77 ; married Myra Lee Horton of Sheffield, Penn., May 18, 1881 ; has been engaged in the tannery business in Buffalo since 1877 as a member of the firm of J. F. Schoellkopf's Sons.*

***

**Rodney Macauley Taylor** is a type of many distinguished Americans, who have by their own efforts risen from poverty to affluence. Colonel Taylor himself is fond of saying that "the good Lord is sure to help them that try to help themselves in this glorious country of ours—the very best that the world has ever known."

In the spring of 1847 Mr. Taylor was a clerk in a commission and shipping house on Broad street, New York city. When returning from the bank one day he met face to face an officer in uniform, who proved to be his brother, Captain Taylor, just arrived from Mexico. After the capture of Vera Cruz, General Scott had ordered Captain Taylor to go to Cincinnati

on some army business, and his brother Rodney decided to accompany him thither. The two went West together, accordingly, by way of Buffalo. Colonel Taylor remembers clearly how he and his brother registered at the Mansion House June 7, 1847 — the twenty-second anniversary, as they were told, of the hanging of the three Thayer brothers in Niagara square. Captain Taylor took a steamer from Buffalo to Cleveland *en route* to Cincinnati ; but the younger brother, having received an offer of a clerkship in a dry-goods store on Main street, resolved to accept the opportunity, and make Buffalo his permanent abiding-place.

Mr. Taylor had not been in Buffalo long before the dry-goods business became dull, and at his own request he was released from service. He had deposited in a bank on his arrival in Buffalo a few hundred dollars, which he now drew out, and devoted to the purchase of a carload of cheese. He sold this in central New York in six days, returning to Buffalo with a clear profit of $107. This successful transaction led to further ventures in the same direction, and in the spring of 1848 Mr. Taylor felt competent to manage a grocery and provision business of his own. He established such a store, accordingly, on Main street near where the Tifft House now stands. The sequel showed that he had not overrated his powers, and in 1849 he opened another store near the northeast corner of Main and Swan streets. He enjoyed a prosperous trade until December, 1854, when he closed out his business in order to go to Florida for the health of his wife.

After returning from the West Indies, whither he had gone from Florida, Mr. Taylor devoted himself for a few years to his real-estate interests in Buffalo and Erie county. In the spring of 1858 he cleared away the trees and stumps on some of his land in the southern part of the city, and erected the house in which he has since dwelt. Soon after this he began to take a prominent part in public affairs. In the fall of 1860 he was nominated for the office of supervisor, and in the following year he was elected alderman from the 13th ward, Buffalo.

In the War of the Rebellion Colonel Taylor had an active and highly patriotic part. In 1862 he became one of the government enrolling officers, and in November of that year he was made one of a committee of three from the 13th ward to raise funds, and otherwise recruit the northern armies. As soon as the draft of his ward was completed, he went to New York, purchased there a uniform for himself and clothing and other equipments for soldiers, and obtained authority from the governor of the state at Albany to raise recruits for the 12th New York volunteer cavalry. Returning to Buffalo then, he unfurled the United States flag from his office on Main street, over handbills headed "Recruits Wanted." After only two weeks of hard work and considerable expense -- there was no bounty paid for recruits at that time -- Colonel Taylor was able to send out of Buffalo on December 8, 1862, 102 men. Having received a captain's commission December 13, he recruited four more companies of a hundred men each. On January 5, 1864, he was commissioned major. After having been honorably mustered out July 19, 1865, he was made a first lieutenant in the regular army July 28, 1866. This appointment was the more gratifying as it came entirely without solicitation on Colonel Taylor's part, at a time when many officers who had served in the Civil War were making strenuous efforts to obtain commissions in the regular army. Colonel Taylor was personally recommended for the honor by President Grant and Secretary Stanton ; and as he felt unwilling, for family reasons, to serve in the cavalry, to which he was first appointed, he was transferred to the 12th infantry, and later to the 20th infantry. He was made captain October 22, 1876. He was also brevetted, for faithful and meritorious service, lieutenant colonel and colonel. After serving at many posts in the regular army for nearly twenty years, he was honorably retired by act of congress, for age, September 19, 1884.

Since then Colonel Taylor has devoted himself for the most part to the development of his property in South Buffalo. He has effected many improvements in that part of the city, and has radically changed the general aspect of the locality as a place of residence. He has paid over $40,000 in local taxes within a decade ; and his annual tax to city, county, and state has increased from $200 to more than ten times that amount.

*PERSONAL CHRONOLOGY--Rodney Macauley Taylor was born at Dryden, Tompkins county, N. Y., September 19, 1820 ; was educated in common schools ; was a clerk in stores in New York city and Buffalo, 1847-48 ; carried on a grocery business in Buffalo, 1848-54 ; married Elizabeth Beers of Jerusalem, N. Y., September 4, 1844, her sister Mary Beers June 21, 1851, and Sarah J. Dash of Angola, N. Y., February 5, 1857 ; was a commissioned officer in*
the volunteer army of the United States, 1862-65, and in the regular army, 1866-84 ; has been engaged since 1884 in the care and development of his extensive property.*

### ***

**William David Walker,** recently elected bishop of the Protestant Episcopal diocese of Western New York, is a native of the Empire State, and had a long career there as a parish priest ; though in recent years he has been so thoroughly identified with the missionary work of the Northwest that many people think of him as a westerner only.

Bishop Walker was born in New York city in 1839, and made his home in the metropolis for more than forty years. Attending first the public schools, he afterward prepared for college at Trinity School, a classical institution of high standing in his

*RODNEY MACAULEY TAYLOR*

native city. At the age of sixteen he entered Columbia College, from which he graduated in 1859, receiving the McVickar prize. He had already determined to devote himself to the church, and accordingly became a student at the General Theological Seminary in the same year. He completed the course there in 1862, and received deacon's orders at the hands of Bishop Horatio Potter in the Church of the Transfiguration on his twenty-third birthday.

He was at once elected vicar of Calvary Chapel, New York, and entered upon his work in the following October, serving also as special assistant in Calvary Church. On his next birthday, June 29, 1863, he was ordained priest in Calvary Church. By the year 1870 the building previously occupied by the chapel had become too small for the congregation, and the large church known as Calvary Free Chapel was built at an expense of $130,000. Here Bishop Walker labored until 1883, when he was chosen by the house of bishops first bishop of the missionary district of North Dakota. His consecration took place in Calvary Church December 20, 1883. Bishop Clark of Rhode Island acting as consecrator, and bishops Potter and Clarkson as presenters. Many other bishops assisted at the ceremony, including the two bishops Paddock, bishops Littlejohn, Scarborough, and Starkey. The preacher on this occasion was Bishop Coxe, who had presented the new bishop for ordination to the priesthood in the same church twenty years before.

No greater contrast could well be imagined than that between the conditions of work in a large and prosperous city parish and those in a district comprising 180,000 souls scattered over 70,000 square miles of territory. But Bishop Walker possessed the faith and devotion, the zeal and energy needed for his new work; and the history of his years of labor in the Northwest is a history of continual achievement in the cause of Christianity and of general civilization. Many of those committed to his pastoral care were Indians, and much of his time and effort was given in behalf of this unfortunate race. In 1887 he was appointed by President Cleveland one of the board of United States Indian commissioners, a body of ten men having general oversight of the interests of the Indians throughout the country; and he was ever the friend of the red man, and accomplished much for his elevation.

Bishop Walker's strong common sense and practical methods of work were peculiarly well fitted for the administration of a missionary diocese. His "cathedral car" was one of the most effective expedients for ministering to a scattered population that could possibly have been devised. The name is self-explanatory: a railway car was fitted up as a church, with altar, font, lectern, and organ, and seats for about seventy-five people; and by its means

thousands who could not otherwise have been reached were brought into touch with the ministrations of the church. Its adaptability to modern conditions was so strikingly evident that the idea has since been utilized in all parts of the world. The Greek church of Russia now employs five such itinerant churches on the great new railroad in Siberia; and similar work is carried on at Tiflis in the Caucasus, at old Carthage in the north of Africa, in the diocese of Grahamstown in south Africa, and in other places. Five such churches are now in use by the Baptist church in this country, and two others by the Episcopal church.

At the beginning of his ministry Bishop Walker was associated with Bishop Coxe at Calvary Church, New York; and the friendship then begun strengthened with years, and lasted until the death of the elder man. During the later years of his life Bishop Coxe frequently made use of his friend's help, sending him on episcopal duty to many parishes in the diocese of Western New York. After the death of Bishop Coxe a strong sentiment developed in favor of Bishop Walker for his successor. Many in the diocese knew him personally, and it was believed that the choice would be in accord with the wishes of their late beloved bishop. The special council met in Trinity Church, Buffalo, October 6, 1896, and the next day Bishop Walker was elected third bishop of the diocese. He entered upon his new duties December 20, 1896, after an impressive service of enthronization in St. Paul's Cathedral. While Bishop Walker's work in his eastern diocese is but just begun, it is safe to prophesy that he will not be less successful there than in the West. He has received a hearty welcome from the general public, as well as from the priests and people of his church, and all are ready to bid him Godspeed in his new field of labor.

In addition to many pastoral letters, convocation addresses, and sermons, Bishop Walker has published several writings that possess peculiar interest from the importance either of the subjects treated or of the occasion of their delivery. Among these may be mentioned his report to the President and congress on the Sioux and Chippewa tribes of Indians in North Dakota (1886); a sermon on the "Relations of Wealth to Labor," preached in Westminster Abbey in 1888, and one on "God's Providence in Life," delivered at St. Paul's Cathedral, London, on the death of the Emperor of Germany; an essay on "Domestic Missions," read at St. James Hall, London, at the annual meeting of the venerable Society for the Propagation of the Gospel in Foreign Parts (1888); and an address on "Missions in the United

States," delivered in the same place in 1894. The bishop has received honorary degrees from many colleges and universities both at home and abroad. In 1884 Racine University made him a Doctor of Divinity, and ten years later Oxford University, England, conferred a similar honor upon him. In 1884, also, he received from his *alma mater* the degree of S. T. D. Griswold College gave him the LL. D. degree in 1888, and Trinity College, Dublin, in 1894. He is also a Doctor of Canon Laws of the University of King's College, Windsor, Nova Scotia.

*PERSONAL CHRONOLOGY*
*William David Walker was born at New York city June 29, 1839; graduated from Columbia College in 1859, and from the General Theological Seminary in 1862; was vicar of Calvary Chapel, New York city, 1862-84; was bishop of the missionary district of North Dakota, 1883-96; was elected bishop of the diocese of Western New York October 3, 1896.*

\*\*\*

**George F. Brownell** has had a remarkably successful career and has attained, at the age of thirty-six, a position of trust and responsibility that would test the powers of a much older man. Though he was born in Des Moines, Ia., his parents were originally from eastern New York; and after the war they moved back to the Empire State, and settled in Medina. There Mr. Brownell received his early education, graduating from the Medina High School, and afterward attending the Lockport Union School. Going West again after this, he entered the academic department of the University of Michigan, from which he was transferred later to the law department. His professional training was unusually thorough, since he received his degree as a Bachelor of Laws from the Albany Law School in 1882, and from the University of Michigan Law School the next year.

On his admission to the bar Mr. Brownell spent a few months in the office of Thomas M. Cooley, judge of the Michigan Supreme Court and dean of the University of Michigan Law School, and subsequently chairman of the interstate-commerce commission. He then moved to Buffalo, and entered the office of Sprague, Morey & Sprague as assistant to the late E. Carleton Sprague. The unique prestige of this firm throughout western

New York offered the young man a brilliant field of professional achievement. In 1888 he was admitted to partnership, the style becoming Sprague, Morey, Sprague & Brownell; subsequently this was changed to Sprague, Moot, Sprague & Brownell; and since June 1, 1897,

*WILLIAM DAVID WALKER*

the firm has been known as Moot, Sprague, Brownell & Marcy.

Mr. Brownell's professional work has been concerned chiefly with the railroad and other corporation interests of the firm, which are many and important; and since the death of E. Carleton Sprague early in 1895, he has had charge of these interests. This work has not taken him so much into the courts, nor brought him so conspicuously before the public eye as some of his fellows; but the responsibilities intrusted to him have been very great, and have been ably administered. The Erie railroad, the Grand Trunk railway, and the Buffalo Creek railroad have been among the corporate clients of the firm; and the legal interests of the former corporation in western New York and of the Grand Trunk throughout the state have been committed to Mr. Brownell. One of the important labors of his firm in this connection has been the adjustment of the relations between the Erie road, the other roads entering Buffalo, and the city itself, in the matter of

*GEORGE F. BROWNELL*

abolishing grade crossings; and Mr. Brownell has handled this delicate and complicated question with rare skill. Of late years his service to the Erie railroad has included growing duties as counsel in other parts of the state, and his successful discharge of these duties led to his appointment in May, 1897, as general solicitor for the company. This appointment may be regarded as a signal proof of Mr. Brownell's professional standing, since he owes it, not to moneyed influence or backing, but purely to merit and ability. He will retain his membership in the Buffalo firm with which he has been so prominently identified, but will make his home in New York city.

Outside of his profession Mr. Brownell has been actively identified with many phases of social life,

taking special interest in present-day problems such as are represented by the work of the Liberal and Thursday clubs of Buffalo. He belongs, also, to the Buffalo, Saturn, Country, and Ellicott clubs of Buffalo, the Genesee Valley Club of Rochester, and the Chi Psi college fraternity. He has been actively connected with the Masonic order; and is a Past Master of Ancient Landmark Lodge, No. 441, F. & A. M., a member of Hugh de Payens Commandery, and of the Buffalo Consistory. He belongs to the Buffalo Society of Artists, the Buffalo Historical Society, and the Buffalo Library Association, and is a member of the Episcopal church. His political sympathies are with the Republican party, and he was the first secretary of the Buffalo Republican League.

*PERSONAL CHRONOLOGY— George Francis Brownell was born at Des Moines, Io., June 5, 1861; was educated in New York state public schools, and in the University of Michigan, Ann Arbor; graduated from the Albany Law School in 1882, and from the University of Michigan Law School in 1884; was appointed general solicitor of the Erie railroad in May, 1897; married Anne Kniseley Abbott of Buffalo June 7, 1897; has been connected with the firm of Sprague, Morey & Sprague of Buffalo and their successors since 1884.*

\* \* \*

**George Clinton** belongs to a family that has done much to further the best interests of Buffalo and of New York state, and his own share in that work has been considerable. Ever since Charles Clinton, the first ancestor of the family on this side of the water, settled in Ulster county in 1731, the Clintons have been prominent in the Empire State, both in war and in peace. Born in Buffalo about fifty years ago, George Clinton received his early education in private schools, afterward attending the public schools, and graduating from the old Central High School in 1865, shortly after its organization.

Mr. Clinton's father, George W. Clinton, was a prominent lawyer, and the son determined to follow the same profession. He went to New York, therefore, in 1866, and entered the law department of Columbia College, from which he graduated two years later with the degree of LL.B. For about a year he practiced in New York city, and then decided to try his fortunes in the West. He established himself, accordingly, at Hudson, Wis., where he remained for the next five years. Returning to Buffalo in 1874, he associated himself with Martin Clark in 1882, becoming senior partner in the firm of Clinton & Clark. This firm still exists, and maintains a high standing at the Erie-county bar.

In public affairs Mr. Clinton has long been an active force. Elected to the state assembly on the Republican ticket in 1883, he served with distinction in the ensuing session, working for the best interests of his constituents and of the state at large in an independent spirit that refused to be bound by party dictation. He was made chairman of the canal committee in the assembly — a most fitting appointment, since he shares the interest of his illustrious grandfather, De Witt Clinton, in the canals of the state, and believes them to be a most important factor in its commercial prosperity. His work in this connection has not been confined to that performed in the legislature, for he has taken a leading part in the Union for the Improvement of the Canals, an organization that has had much to do with bringing about the extensive improvements in the Erie canal now in progress. Mr. Clinton served as the second president of this association.

Many other movements affecting the welfare of Buffalo have received Mr. Clinton's support: indeed it may be said that he has taken a more or less active interest in all public questions for many years. He has served as one of the park commissioners of the city, and was also a member of the trunk-sewer commission during the building of the Genesee street and Bird-avenue branches. He worked faithfully to secure the adoption of the present city charter, which he had likewise helped to prepare. He has always been the friend of the public schools, and has taken part in the movement for raising their standard, and removing them as far as possible from political influences. He was instrumental in establishing the Buffalo Law School, and was its professor of admiralty law for several years, until compelled to resign on account of the demands of his private practice. He has long been an active member of the Buffalo Merchants' Exchange, and was its president in 1893. Mr. Clinton is a member of the Buffalo Society of Natural Sciences, the Buffalo Club, and many similar organizations.

He belongs to the Masonic order, and to the Episcopal church.

*PERSONAL CHRONOLOGY— George Clinton was born at Buffalo September 7, 1846; graduated from the Buffalo Central High School in 1865, and from Columbia College Law School in 1868; practiced law in New York city, 1868–69, and in Hudson, Wis., 1869–74; married Alice Thornton of Buffalo January 11, 1872; was a member of the New York state legislature in 1884; has practiced law in Buffalo since 1874.*

***

**Elias S. Hawley** was born on the banks of the Hudson river in Saratoga county, New York, on a farm purchased in 1794 by his grandfather, Amos Hawley. After attending school up to the age of eleven in Moreau, Glens Falls, and Fort

*GEORGE CLINTON*

Edward, he went West with his family to Black Rock, near Buffalo, where his uncles, Nathaniel Sill and Joseph Sill, lived. This was in the summer of 1823, and the journey, made by wagon,

consumed exactly one week. They left what is
now Main street, Buffalo, near Granger's Mills, and
after crossing Scajaquada creek, took the road
through the woods that is now called Lafayette
avenue. This was the only road then open between
Main street and the Niagara river, except the
thoroughfare now called North street.

ELIAS S. HAWLEY

Mr. Hawley's early recollections of Black Rock
and Buffalo are most interesting. A short time
after he reached the village, the third and fourth
steamboats on Lake Erie, named the "Pioneer"
and the "Henry Clay" respectively, were built in
the shipyard at Black Rock. The principal business of the village was done by what was called
the Harbor Company, consisting of Captain Sheldon
Thompson and associates. Some of the principal
families of the place were those of James L. Barton,
Colonel Bird, Captain Bidwell, and General Peter
B. Porter, who built the house, then deemed a fine
residence, occupied in recent years by Lewis F.
Allen. Near them lived Mr. Best, father of the late

Robert Hamilton Best, who kept a public house which
is still standing on Niagara street, and which has
been occupied of late years by the Rev. Mr. Robie.
The old Indian Conjaquada, after whom Scajaquada
creek was named, lived in those days at the mouth
of the creek. Black Rock was then larger than
Buffalo, and was the port of entry, Mr. Hawley's
uncle, Joseph Sill, being the custom-
house officer. Mr. Hawley can recall
only two dwellings between Black Rock
and Niagara square, and only one cleared
field on the west side of Niagara street
south of the present Porter avenue.
What is now Prospect park was dense
woods. In the spring and fall Niagara
street was impassable, and vehicles went
on the beach from Black Rock to Buffalo. Mr. Hawley and his brother Seth,
when driving cows to pasture, used at
times to see wild deer in what is now
the heart of Buffalo.

Having been offered by his uncle an
option between an education and the
gift of a thousand dollars at the age
of twenty one, Mr. Hawley accepted the
former—"unfortunately," as he says.
Attending Cambridge Academy in Washington county for two years, he was
there prepared for Middlebury College,
where he stayed until the end of his
sophomore year. He then taught a
year at Mount Pleasant, Westchester
county, and after that entered the senior
class of Union College, Schenectady,
from which he graduated in July, 1833.
Returning to Buffalo, he taught a private
school in the part of the town at that time
called "Hydraulics." Public School
No. 8 was completed in 1838, and Mr.
Hawley served as its principal for a year.
He afterwards studied law in Barker & Hawley's law
office, receiving a diploma in due course. About
1840 the firm of Hawley & Co., consisting of Seth
C. and Elias S. Hawley, established a money and
package express between Buffalo and Detroit. In
1844 Mr. Hawley was appointed by the common
council superintendent of schools, at a salary of
$300 a year. He was appointed again in 1846
and in 1847. He was connected with the volunteer
fire department about this time, belonging first to
engine No. 8, and afterward to "Eagle 2," located
near the present site of the Buffalo Library.

About the middle of the century Mr. Hawley
began his long service with Pratt & Co. He re-

mained with the house twenty-three years altogether, as collecting attorney at first, and then as superintendent of the Buffalo Iron & Nail Works. He left the concern only when it went out of the iron business. Since then he has devoted himself partly to the management of his own private business, and partly to the care of the Austin estate. He was appointed attorney for this property many years ago, and has guarded it vigilantly at all times.

Mr. Hawley has always been prominent in the affairs of Buffalo, and he has sometimes taken an active part in the political life of the city. In 1868 he was elected alderman from the old 11th ward, and in 1883 he served as member of assembly from the 3d Erie-county district. In the same year he was appointed secretary and treasurer of the Buffalo Insane Asylum, now the Buffalo Hospital, and has ever since discharged the duties of the office. He was largely instrumental in the formation of the Buffalo Historical Society, and has been connected therewith as member or officer from the beginning. He was on the board of trustees for a number of years, serving part of the time as its president. He was connected with the First Presbyterian Church from about 1838 until the formation of the North Presbyterian Church, of which he was one of the trustees. Mr. Hawley has been very much interested in the genealogy of his family, and has accumulated at great expense and infinite trouble a large mass of information regarding the various branches of the family in this country. He has published what is probably as complete a work of this kind as has ever been printed.

*PERSONAL CHRONOLOGY —
Elias Sill Hawley was born at Morean, N. Y., October 28, 1812; moved to Buffalo in 1843; graduated from Union College in 1844; taught school, 1836-39; was superintendent of schools in Buffalo in 1844, 1846, and 1847; married Lavinia Hurd Selden of Buffalo May 30, 1845; was in the employ of Pratt & Co. for twenty-three years; was alderman from the 11th ward, Buffalo, in 1869, and member of assembly in 1883; has been engaged of late years in the management of his own property and of trust estates in Buffalo, and as secretary and treasurer of the Buffalo Hospital.*

**Edward C. W. O'Brien,** of 439 Delaware avenue, Buffalo, is one of the best known physicians of that city. Born in the city of Quebec, Canada, fifty-four years ago, he obtained his early education from the teaching of the Christian Brothers, and at private schools. Thrown upon his own resources at an early age, he acquired by his contact with the world away from home, a large fund of practical experience that must have aided in developing the strength of character and self-resourcefulness for which he has long been noted. Dr. O'Brien's residence in Buffalo began almost forty years ago. Having decided, a few years after he settled there, to become a physician, he took the full course at the University of Buffalo, and graduated from the medical department of that institution in February, 1867. He has

*EDWARD C. W. O'BRIEN*

followed his calling in Buffalo ever since, and has attained high rank in the medical fraternity of Erie county. During his thirty years of active practice he has had numerous cases of exceptional difficulty, but probably none more noteworthy than two instances in which he successfully reduced dislocation of the neck. Both cases were those of adults, requiring exact anatomical knowledge, nice calculation, and rare self-possession.

Dr. O'Brien's prominence in Buffalo came about in part as a result of his notable record as health physician of the city for several years. He obtained this office early in his professional career, by appointment of the board of health, and was reappointed five times. His term began in the winter of 1872-73, and lasted until 1877, when the Democratic party gained possession of the city government, and appointed a Democrat to the office. Dr. O'Brien's administration will be long remembered on account of the great smallpox epidemic then raging. This scourge infested the entire world at that time, and many large cities were frightfully ravaged by the disease. Buffalo alone had about 1900 cases, though Buffalo was rid of the pestilence several months before any other large American city. Dr. O'Brien was physician to the smallpox hospital maintained in Buffalo during the epidemic ; and in addition to his regular duties as health physician, he was obliged twice a day to visit this hospital, located on the outskirts of the city. He often made his second visit as late as midnight. He naturally came into close relations with the physicians of Buffalo at that time, and it is worthy of note that they cordially commended his administration of the health department during that ordeal. The press of the city, also, without regard to party, recognized his efficiency as health physician. Mention should be made of the interesting fact that Dr. O'Brien introduced the use of bovine vaccine virus in Buffalo. There were then only a few vaccine farms in America, and the introduction of the virus met with opposition from a considerable part of the general public, and even from some physicians who did not fully understand the subject, though these soon used it freely.

Dr. O'Brien's record in the health office of Buffalo attracted favorable notice, not only in the city itself, but also in some degree throughout the state. This fact was evidenced in his nomination as a compromise candidate to the position of health officer of the port of New York — a position then comparable in point of compensation to the presidency of the United States, though the enormous fees of the office have since been commuted into a fixed salary. Governor Cleveland nominated for the position the distinguished physician, Austin Flint ; but the nomination had not been confirmed when Mr. Cleveland left Albany to enter the White House. Governor Hill then nominated Dr. Phelps of New

York, whose name was likewise rejected by the state senate. Finally Governor Hill sent in the name of Dr. O'Brien, whose political principles were harmonious with those of the dominant party in the senate. Owing to a factional quarrel among the Republicans of that body, Dr. O'Brien failed by a few votes of confirmation. The general and hearty endorsement of his nomination, however, was very gratifying to his friends. One of the Buffalo papers devoted a page to a report of interviews with leading physicians, other professional men, and prominent citizens generally, who commended Dr. O'Brien's nomination on the ground both of professional fitness and of personal character. A large and representative delegation of Buffalonians, including members of both the medical colleges, went to Albany to urge confirmation upon the senate committee to which the nomination was referred. The Buffalo *Commercial*, in an editorial article, spoke as follows :

" To the senators upon whom the responsibility of the confirmation of Dr. E. C. W. O'Brien rests, the *Commercial* can say this much : that the nominee is a man of irreproachable habits temperate, industrious, and a worthy citizen of any community. As a Republican he has ever been staunch, loyal, and unswerving. As a physician he has been thoroughly tested, and that in the very line of duty in which, as health officer of New York, he would be called upon to serve. Dr. O'Brien was health physician of Buffalo during one of the most trying and perilous visitations that this city has ever experienced. It was during the smallpox epidemic of 1873-74, the most alarming epidemic that ever afflicted Buffalo. By applying to the emergency the most stringent precautions, the best agencies that science and experience could suggest, by insisting upon immediate, positive, and ample measures on the part of the municipality, Dr. O'Brien stamped out smallpox in Buffalo. He met the disease with promptness, intelligence, and courage, and drove it beyond the lines of the city — a service that the people of Buffalo can never forget. Put into the responsible position for which the governor has nominated him, he will bring to the office skill, experience, and a devotion to duty that is sure to find results in a system of quarantine service as intelligent, honest, and rigid as the great port of New York needs and demands. We hope that the Republican senators will confirm this excellent nomination."

Notwithstanding his activity in professional life, Dr. O'Brien has always taken great interest in public affairs, and has been glad to lend himself to any movement likely to promote the welfare of Buffalo. Many positions of trust connected with his profession have been held by him : and all of them, as he is glad to remember, came to him without solicitation. For nearly ten years he was surgeon of the 74th regiment, Buffalo. For several years he was chief medical examiner of the Catholic Mutual Benefit Association of the State of New York. He held the post, for a long time, of physician to St. Vincent's Orphan Asylum at Buffalo. He has been for many years consulting physician to the Providence Asylum for the Insane. He is now surgeon to the Buffalo fire department, and consulting surgeon to the Riverside Hospital, Buffalo. He is a member of the American Medical Association; of the Erie County Medical Society, of which he has been president; and of the Buffalo Academy of Medicine. He has been president of the University Alumni Association of the University of Buffalo, and is one of the curators of that institution. He has had wide experience in examinations of the insane, and for many years has frequently been appointed by the courts of Buffalo as an expert on the question of insanity, and has been called to other cities in that capacity.

*PERSONAL CHRONOLOGY—*
*Edward Charles White O'Brien was born at Quebec, Canada, February 4, 1844; moved to Buffalo in 1859; graduated from the medical department of the University of Buffalo in 1867; was health physician of Buffalo, 1872–77; married Monterey Allis of New York city October 8, 1879; has practiced medicine in Buffalo since 1867.*

**Dilworth M. Silver** was born in Peruville, Tompkins county, New York, somewhat more than forty years ago. His boyhood and youth were passed in this little village, where he received such training as the district schools afforded, as well as the wider and more comprehensive education that comes from contact with other boys and with the world in general. At the age of eighteen he moved to the western end of the state, and spent the next four years in Jamestown. Here he obtained the benefit of a short attendance at the Jamestown Academy, but was obliged to devote himself largely to the task of earning a livelihood. He was ambitious, however, to become a lawyer, and set about attaining that end, acquiring by private reading and study the general culture that his incomplete scholastic preparation had failed to furnish.

Mr. Silver judged wisely that the larger the place the greater the opportunity for advancement, professional and other. Proceeding to Buffalo, accordingly, in 1875, he spent several months in business, and then entered the law office of William C. Fitch as a student. In due time he acquired the necessary legal knowledge, and in January, 1880, was admitted to the bar at Syracuse. The following month

he opened an office in Buffalo, where he has practiced continuously ever since. He was considerably older when he began his professional career than the average lawyer so circumstanced; and this fact undoubtedly gave him greater maturity of mind and a firmer grasp of legal principles than the young

*DILWORTH M. SILVER*

practitioner is likely to possess. He was fortunate, also, in establishing himself in Buffalo when he did. The growth of the metropolis of western New York in the decade then beginning was remarkable; and the many new industrial and commercial enterprises, and consequent development of real-estate operations, necessitated a vast amount of legal business of one kind or another. Mr. Silver profited, as might have been expected, from all these favoring circumstances. It may also be noted that he has devoted himself wholly to his profession, and the measure of success that he has attained may be regarded as the reward of hard and conscientious work in his chosen field. With the exception of about eighteen months, he has always practiced alone, deeming it more advantageous, on the whole, to carry on his work without partnership assistance.

Mr. Silver is an earnest Republican, and has made political speeches throughout Erie county in every important campaign for several years past. Of late he has given considerable time to the study of his

*WILLIAM F. STRASMER*

family genealogy — a subject that seldom fails to prove deeply interesting to one who turns his attention in that direction. On his mother's side he has found little difficulty in tracing the family back to the original settler, who came to this country in 1690 and established himself in New Jersey; and Mr. Silver may be pardoned for feeling some natural pride in the fact that Vice President Hobart is also a descendant of this common ancestor. Mr. Silver is an Odd Fellow, belonging to Idlewood Lodge, No. 652. He attends the Delaware Avenue Methodist Episcopal Church.

*PERSONAL CHRONOLOGY— Dilworth M. Silver was born at Peruville, N. Y., March 10, 1854; was educated in common schools and acade-*

*mies; studied law, and was admitted to the bar in 1880; married Elizabeth Englehart of Batavia, N.Y., in January, 1888; has practiced law in Buffalo since February, 1880.*

...

**William F. Strasmer** is prominent among those members of the Erie-county bar who have combined success in the legal profession with active participation in the various investment enterprises that have characterized the growth of Buffalo in the last decade. He is a native of Buffalo, where he has always lived. To the energy and perseverance that marked his early efforts to gain an education, his later success is partly attributable. When a boy at Public School No. 32, he won the Jesse Ketchum gold medal in a competitive examination open only to graduates of the highest standing in all the grammar schools of the city. He subsequently attended the high school, was graduated in 1876, and in the fall of the same year became a student in the University of Rochester, from which he received the degree of A. B. in 1881. While pursuing his studies at college, he tutored and in his senior year did some literary work for the Rochester papers. Although thus devoting considerable time to matters not pertaining to his course of study, he maintained a high standing; and some years later, when a chapter of the Phi Beta Kappa was formed at the university, the faculty elected him a member because of his scholarly attainments.

On leaving college, Mr. Strasmer accepted an appointment as principal of the academy at Whitney's Point, N. Y., and taught there for two years, reading law at the same time in the office of an attorney in that village. He returned to Buffalo in 1883, and entered the law office of Benjamin H. Williams, then a member of the firm of Williams & Potter. In 1885 he was admitted to the bar. He remained with Williams & Potter for some time after this, in order to familiarize himself with practice in the United States courts, and particularly in admiralty law, of which that firm made a specialty. In June, 1887, he formed a partnership with Wilber E. Houpt, which lasted until October, 1889. Since then he has carried on his practice alone, deeming such a course more desirable in many respects.

Mr. Strasmer began his professional life in Buffalo at a time when the rapid growth of the city favored the promotion of many enterprises in the line of real-estate investment and improvement. Litigation connected with shipping interests, which had especially interested him in the early part of his legal career, had been almost wholly driven from Buffalo by altered conditions of lake traffic; and he drifted, more from pressure of business than from choice, into real-estate and corporation law. A number of organizations for investment in realty were formed under his advice and counsel. These corporations, notwithstanding the depression that began in 1893, are among the most substantial of their kind in Buffalo, and demonstrate Mr. Strasmer's ability and conservative judgment. He has served as an officer and director in some of these organizations; and the duties thus assumed have been inconsistent with active court litigation, and have made him chiefly an office lawyer and counselor. This has been true likewise of some other prominent members of the Buffalo bar having similar interests.

Mr. Strasmer devotes much of his time to the study of public questions. In national politics he is an independent Republican. He supports movements that tend to furnish the best public service, and to secure the application of common-sense and businesslike methods. He has been for some years a member of the Civil Service Reform Association; and in April, 1896, he was appointed by Mayor Jewett a civil-service commissioner of the city of Buffalo. The appointment met with general approval. This is the only public office he has filled.

Mr. Strasmer is a member of Erie Lodge, No. 161, F. & A. M.; and of Niagara Lodge, No. 25, I. O. O. F., of which he is a past grand officer. He belongs, also, to several other social organizations, including the Acacia, Saturn, and University clubs.

*PERSONAL CHRONOLOGY—William F. Strasmer was born at Buffalo; attended the public schools of Buffalo and Rochester University, whence he graduated in 1881; taught at Whitney's Point (N. Y.) Academy, 1881-83; was admitted to the bar in 1885; has practiced law in Buffalo and engaged in various business enterprises since 1887; has been a civil-service commissioner of Buffalo since April, 1896.*

**William F. Wendt**, president of the Buffalo Forge Co., was born in Buffalo less than forty years ago. He received his education in Public School No. 32 and in the old Central High School. His early business training was obtained as a bookkeeper in the office of R. W. Bell & Co. of Buffalo.

Before he was twenty years old Mr. Wendt began his connection with the Buffalo Forge Co. The business had been established only a few months, and had met with little success; and Mr. Wendt was able to purchase a half interest in the concern for a small sum. His keen business foresight was soon evident in the increasing prosperity of the enterprise. At first he took charge of the financial part of the business, but he soon became convinced of the necessity of a knowledge of the practical work of manufacture. Accordingly, while laying the foundation

*WILLIAM F. WENDT*

of his present extensive business, he acquainted himself thoroughly with all the processes and detail of manufacture, and with the general management of the concern; so that, when he purchased the interest of his partner, Charles Hammelmann, in 1883, he was well fitted to assume the control of all departments of the business.

In 1886 Mr. Wendt admitted to partnership a younger brother, Henry W. Wendt; and the two have worked together ever since. The growth of

CRÉTIEN WEYAND

the business has been continuous and rapid, and to-day few concerns are more widely known in its special line than the Buffalo Forge Co. At first but two sizes of forges were made; but new sizes, styles, and improvements have been constantly added to the product of the works, and their business in portable forges is now estimated to be the largest in the United States. The manufacture of heating and ventilating apparatus was begun in 1884, and to-day the firm has few rivals in that line. In 1893 they took up the manufacture of high-speed automatic engines, which now constitute a large part of the output of the factory. The extensive works of the firm are located on Broadway, and among them stands the original frame factory, an eloquent reminder of the

small beginnings from which the business has grown. Selling agencies for the products of the house are maintained in the principal cities of the United States, and in London, Paris, and St. Petersburg. The building up of such a business in less than twenty years is sufficient proof of the ability, enterprise, and energy of the man who has guided the fortunes of the house during all that time.

Although one of the most modest and unassuming of men, and chiefly occupied with the management of his business affairs, Mr. Wendt takes deep interest in political matters and in the questions of the day. He has long been active in local public affairs, and is an old member of the Buffalo Republican League. He was one of the ten men who built the first electric railroad to Tonawanda in 1888; and he is a director of the Citizens' Bank, and a member of the real-estate commission of the German Young Men's Association. He belongs to the Lutheran church.

*PERSONAL CHRONOLOGY —*
*William Franz Wendt was born at Buffalo July 2, 1858; was educated in the public schools; married Mary Gies of Buffalo November 8, 1882; bought an interest in the Buffalo Forge Co. in 1878, and has been at the head of the business since 1883.*

\*\*\*

**Crétien Weyand,** as he was really named in his fatherland, or Christian Weyand, as he is commonly known in this country, was born in Lorraine, France, about seventy years ago. He attended the common schools of his native province, but was not able to carry his education very far. In his twenty-first year he left Lorraine for the wider opportunities of the new world, landing in New York in the spring of 1847. Without delaying long in the metropolis, he betook himself to Buffalo, and there obtained employment as a cobbler. He worked at this trade for several years as an employee, much of the time with Forlush & Brown, and ultimately established a shop of his own.

All this happened so long ago that most people do not recall the facts at all, and always think of Mr. Weyand as a prosperous and wealthy brewer. He has been that for many years; but such a position in life is not attained at a single bound, and in Mr. Weyand's case the evolution from a

hard-working shoemaker to a retired brewer was a long
process. He first engaged in the brewing business in
1866. He had a partner until 1873, but their combined capital was little enough, and their plant was
necessarily small and ill equipped. The purest and
best of barley malt was used from the beginning,
and improved machinery was introduced as fast as
the necessary capital could be saved or secured.
Few people realize the complexity and nicety of
modern brewing methods, or the scientific care and
skill requisite at every stage of the operation. From
the moment when the barley is placed in the malt vat
until the matured liquid is taken from the ice cellar
nine months later, ceaseless supervision must prevail.

Taking the business alone in 1873, Mr. Weyand
devoted himself with renewed energy to the task
of building up a magnificent plant. His efforts
were completely successful, and in a
few years his establishment was one
of the first in its line in Buffalo. As
advancing age made it desirable to give
up active commercial life, he converted
his business into a corporation in 1890,
keeping the office of president for himself, and making his son, John A. Wey-
and, vice president and manager, and
his son, Charles M. Weyand, secretary
and treasurer. Both John Weyand and
his brother Charles had grown up in the
business and knew it thoroughly, so that
the affairs of the new corporation were
safe in their charge. Since this change
was made the business of the Weyand
brewery has increased markedly, and in
1896-97 it became necessary to make
extensive additions to the plant. The
establishment is now one of the best-
equipped breweries in the country, and
its product finds increasing favor in a
wide market.

*PERSONAL CHRONOLOGY—
Cretien Weyand was born in Lorraine,
France, May 11, 1826; came to the
United States in 1847, and settled in
Buffalo; worked at the shoemaker's trade,
1847-66; married Magdalena Maver of
Buffalo May 9, 1852; has carried on a
brewery in Buffalo since 1866.*

\*\*\*

## Eugene M. Bartlett

has long
been prominent in the affairs of Wyoming county,
and like distinction may safely be predicted for him
in Erie county, to which he has recently transferred
a part of his professional practice. He is a son of

Myron E. and Cordelia E. Bartlett, and belongs to a
family that has been honored for generations in both
England and America. He is a lineal descendant of
a brother of Josiah Bartlett, an early governor of New
Hampshire, who conferred lasting distinction on the
name by signing the Declaration of Independence
next after John Hancock. Mr. Bartlett's grandfather moved to Wyoming county from Vermont in
1824, and his father was born there seven years
later.

Mr. Bartlett was born in Warsaw about forty years
ago, and was educated at the academy in his native
town, at Geneseo Academy, and at Cornell University. Before entering Cornell he was employed
for a time as a printer in the office of the *Western
New Yorker*, under William H. Merrill, now
managing editor of the New York *World*. Mr.

*EUGENE M. BARTLETT*

Bartlett has always had a fondness for journalism,
and has frequently contributed articles to newspapers
and magazines; but the legal profession in the end
proved most attractive to him. He took up the

study of law, therefore, in the office of Bartlett &
Bartlett at Warsaw.

In January, 1880, he was admitted to the bar, and
at once assumed all the responsibility that his preceptors and the clients of the office would intrust to
him. His father had long been one of the most
conspicuous members of the Wyoming-county bar,
and the young lawyer soon formed a partnership with
him, under the style of M. E. & E. M. Bartlett.
From the beginning Mr. Bartlett took special interest
in the court work of the firm ; and probably few men
of his age in western New York have argued a
greater number of cases, embracing a more wide and
varied range of subjects, than he. The discovery of
salt in Wyoming county opened new fields for the
exercise of legal ability ; and Mr. Bartlett has been
active in the organization of corporations to utilize
this discovery, and in the protection of their interests. During the fifteen years that he has practiced in Wyoming county his firm has enjoyed an
extensive and lucrative practice, taking part on one
side or the other in nearly every important case in
the county, and becoming widely known in professional circles. January 1, 1896, Hayden H. Tozier
was admitted to partnership, and the firm of Bartlett,
Bartlett & Tozier has succeeded to the prosperity of
the former association.

The county seat of Wyoming county is a delightful town to live in, with a social life and a degree of
general culture not always attained in places of much
larger growth ; but the professional opportunities of
so small a community are necessarily limited, and
Mr. Bartlett decided in the spring of 1896 to extend
his field of practice. He formed a partnership,
accordingly, with Greenleaf S. Van Gorder of Pike,
Wyoming county, and Carleton H. White and Elijah
W. Holt of Buffalo, for the general practice of law in
the Queen City of the Lakes. The firm of Bartlett,
Van Gorder, White & Holt was organized June 1,
1896, and has commodious offices in the Mooney-
Brisbane building, Buffalo.

Although Mr. Bartlett's ambition for distinction
in his chosen calling has left him little time or inclination for the life of a professional politician, he
has always been an uncompromising Republican ;
and in 1886 his party elected him district attorney
of Wyoming county. He protected zealously the
legal interests of the district throughout his term,
but declined to become a candidate for a second
term, as his private practice required his whole time.
In 1892 Wyoming county instructed its delegates
to the judiciary convention to vote for Mr. Bartlett
as the nominee for the office of justice of the
Supreme Court.

In social affairs Mr. Bartlett has taken a position
consistent with his prominence in law and in other
relations of life. He believes in fraternal societies,
and belongs to Crystal Salt Lodge, I. O. O. F.;
Warsaw Lodge, F. & A. M.; Wyoming Chapter,
R. A. M.; and Batavia Commandery, K. T. He is
a member, also, of the Cataract Hose Company,
Warsaw, of the Genesee Valley Club, Rochester, and
of the Buffalo Club. He holds directorates in the
Warsaw Gas and Electric Co., and in the Warsaw
Water Works Co. He is also a member of the New
York State Bar Association. In 1889 he built the
finest business block in Warsaw.

*PERSONAL CHRONOLOGY— Eugene M.
Bartlett was born at Warsaw, N. Y., March 19,
1855 ; attended Warsaw and Geneseo academies
and Cornell University : was admitted to the bar in
January, 1880 ; was district attorney of Wyoming
county, 1887–89 ; married Grace M. Sheldon of
Hornellsville, N. Y., January 24, 1885 ; has practiced law in Warsaw since 1880, and in Buffalo since
June 1, 1896.*

***

**Ossian Bedell**, whose name instantly suggests
Grand Island to a multitude of minds, was born in
Franklin county, Vermont, in 1832. He did not
stay long in the Green Mountain State, as his parents
moved to Tonawanda, N. Y., when he was six years
old. There the lad attended the common schools
of the town, and at the age of eleven commenced
driving a team for his father on the Erie canal.
He followed the canal most of the time for the next
twenty years ; though he obtained some further education meantime at the Genesee Wesleyan Seminary.

Mr. Bedell lived in Tonawanda until 1846, when
he moved to Grand Island. This has been his home
during the half century since then ; and few men are
more thoroughly identified with any locality than is
Mr. Bedell with the interesting island above the
Niagara rapids. By the time he was twenty-one
years old he had a farm of his own on the island, to
which he resorted between the canal seasons, and
which he made the nucleus of large land holdings.
The progress of the little colony on Grand Island was
slow until 1874, when Mr. Bedell and others organized a stock company to equip and operate a ferry
from the head of the island to Buffalo. This service
has been maintained ever since, and has been of
great assistance in developing the island. Many
people think of Grand Island as a summer and excursion resort merely ; but this conception is altogether
incomplete. There are now about 1300 people there,
three churches, eleven schools, and other institutions appropriate to an independent community.

In 1876 Mr. Bedell built the hotel that has since been known as the Bedell House. This structure is three stories high, with a five-story tower, and broad verandas on all sides. Numerous attractions make the resort one of the most popular in western New York.

Mr. Bedell has been active in political affairs for many years. During Lincoln's administration he was appointed inspector of customs for the district of Buffalo Creek. In 1862-63 he was the supervisor of Erie county from Grand Island. He was appointed on March 14, 1881, assistant superintendent of public works for the western division of the Erie canal, holding office until April 1, 1884. During President Harrison's term in the White House Mr. Bedell was appointed United States consul at Fort Erie, Ont., taking office July 24, 1890, and holding the place until the change of administration in the spring of 1893. In July, 1897, he was again appointed to the office by President McKinley. Mr. Bedell has long been regarded by the leaders of his party in Erie county as a stanch supporter of the Republican cause. He has often been an active factor in political conventions, and has otherwise exerted a strong influence in behalf of the Republican party in the western end of the state.

*PERSONAL CHRONOLOGY—
Ossian Bedell was born at Georgia, Vt., June 6, 1842; was educated in common schools and Genesee Wesleyan Seminary, Lima, N. Y.; married Permelia Zimmerman of Tonawanda, N. Y., March 28, 1854; worked on the Erie canal, 1854-63; was inspector of customs at Grand Island, N. Y., under President Lincoln, and county supervisor from the town of Grand Island, 1862-63; was assistant superintendent of public works for the western division of the Erie canal, 1881-84; was United States consul to Fort Erie, Ont., 1890-93, and was reappointed in July, 1897.*

OSSIAN BEDELL

Toward the close of the first half of the century Mr. Brunn's parents came to this country from Germany, and settled in Buffalo. There Charles was born in 1858, and there he has spent his life, barring an interval of three years. He attended the public schools, and evinced there the same ability that has brought him success in later years, since at the age of twelve he had prepared himself to enter the high school. Circumstances prevented further school attendance; but the active business life in which he has since been engaged has supplied abundant opportunities for acquiring the most practical kind of knowledge, and he has made good use of these.

As stated above, Mr. Brunn's first employment was that of a telegraph operator for the Western Union company at Buffalo. After spending two years with them he became operator for the Buffalo & Jamestown railroad, serving in this capacity and as train dispatcher until 1877. In that year he was made assistant superintendent of the road, known by

...

**Charles A. Brunn** has been prominent in railroad circles in Buffalo and its vicinity so long that it will be a surprise to many readers to learn that he is not yet forty years old. The explanation lies in the fact that he began his business career as a telegraph operator when only twelve years old, and has risen steadily ever since.

that time as the Buffalo & Southwestern, and held the position until the line was leased to the New York, Lake Erie & Western road in 1880 under the designation of the Buffalo & Southwestern division. This position he has held ever since, though his duties have been largely extended from time to time

CHARLES A. BRUNN

in various directions. July 1, 1886, he was sent to Meadville, Penn., as superintendent of the eastern division of the New York, Pennsylvania & Ohio railroad, of which the New York, Lake Erie & Western was the lessee. He operated this division, extending from Salamanca, N. Y., to Kent, Ohio, and from Meadville to Oil City in Pennsylvania, for three years, when his headquarters were again moved to Buffalo.

Since his return to Buffalo in 1889 Mr. Brunn has occupied a position of great importance in the management of the Erie road. In addition to the superintendency of the Buffalo & Southwestern division, running to Jamestown, he is superintendent of the Buffalo division, extending to Hornellsville on the main line, and including the Lockport, Niagara Falls, and International Bridge branches. Notwithstanding his comparative youth, Mr. Brunn is the ranking superintendent as to years of service on the Erie system between New York and Chicago. Some idea of his varied duties may be gained from the statement that he has charge of the locomotive and repair shops of the Erie in Buffalo, its elevators and lake warehouses, and the enormous coal trestles and coal-shipping plant at East Buffalo. These last two works have been erected at an expense of more than a quarter of a million dollars since the reorganization of the Erie, and their construction and management have added greatly to Mr. Brunn's already heavy cares.

Mr. Brunn has been interested in Masonry ever since he reached his majority. He belongs to DeMolay Lodge, No. 498, F. & A. M.; Buffalo Chapter, No. 71, R. A. M.; Lake Erie Commandery, No. 20, K. T.; and Ismailia Temple, Nobles of the Mystic Shrine. He is a member of the Acacia Club, and of St. James Episcopal Church.

*PERSONAL CHRONOLOGY— Charles Augustus Brunn was born at Buffalo January 28, 1858; was educated in public schools; was telegraph operator for the Western Union company at Buffalo, 1870-72, and for the Buffalo & Jamestown railroad, 1872-77; was assistant superintendent of the Buffalo & Southwestern railroad, 1877-80; has been in the employ of the Erie railroad as division superintendent since 1880, with headquarters at Buffalo during most of that time.*

\*\*\*

**John L. Crosthwaite** was born in Buffalo, and during the greater part of his business life he has been actively connected with the transportation trade on the Great Lakes. His education was received in public and private schools in his native city, and at the age of seventeen he left school and began business life. Going to Bay City, Mich., he engaged with his father in the building and running of boats. He continued in this occupation for the next five years; but in November, 1876, he lost his vessel in a gale on Lake Erie. After this disaster he temporarily abandoned his connection with lake commerce.

Becoming interested in politics, he devoted some time to that fascinating pursuit; and in the spring of 1878 accepted a position under John Tyler as deputy collector in the customhouse, remaining in the government service for three years. During this time he took up the occupation of newspaper writing. He was correspondent for the Western Associated Press, the Chicago *Inter-Ocean*, and the New York *Truth*; and he did the first marine reporting for the Buffalo *Express* after its reorganization in 1878. He acted as financial secretary of the Buffalo Press Club in 1879 during the presidency of the late Thomas Keene.

In 1884, after a lapse of five years, Mr. Crosthwaite returned to his earlier calling, and established a vessel-broker's office on the old Central wharf. This business he has conducted ever since, owning and operating several vessels on the lakes, and dealing in marine insurance as well. Of late years he has branched out into other activities. He was one of the original subscribers for the stock of the Niagara Falls Paper Co., and still retains his interest in the corporation, having full charge of their water transportation. In June, 1893, with George R. Howard, he organized the Niagara Radiator Co. of Buffalo. He is now associated with D. O. Mills of New York city, and Lewis A. Hall, president of the Export Lumber Co. of New York, in the construction of a steel ship for lake navigation that will be one of the largest ever used on inland waters.

Mr. Crosthwaite's business cares have of late years monopolized his attention almost to the exclusion of other interests. He has, however, reached the 32d degree in Masonry, belonging to Buffalo Consistory, and to Queen City Lodge, No. 358, F. & A. M. He is a member of the Country Club and the Ellicott Club.

*PERSONAL CHRONOLOGY—John L. Crosthwaite was born at Buffalo in 1854; was educated in Buffalo schools; engaged in lake traffic, 1871-76; married Elizabeth Sherman Morgan of Buffalo April 12, 1876; was deputy collector of customs, 1878-84; has owned and operated lake vessels since 1881.*

engaged elsewhere at times, he has regarded the Queen City of the Lakes as his home for more than a score of years.

Mr. Douglass was born in a log house in the town of Busti, Chautauqua county. His parents were pioneers of western New York, having emigrated thither from Jewett City, Conn., early in the '30's. His education was begun in the district schoolhouse about a mile and a half from the farm where he was born. Later he spent one term in the Westfield (N. Y.) Academy, and then took a three years' course in the Union School and Collegiate Institute at Jamestown, N. Y. By this time he had centered his ambition on the study of law, and to fit himself for that profession he attended for two years the law department of Columbian College at Washington, D. C. From this institution he graduated in

JOHN L. CROSTHWAITE

**Silas J. Douglass** is one of the many lawyers and real estate men who have found in Buffalo a profitable as well as a pleasant field for the exercise of their talents. While he has been actively

1872. The next year he formed a law partnership with William H. Cutler in Buffalo, where he has practiced much of the time since, though devoting some time to government work and to business.

Mr. Douglass is known as an expert collector of census statistics, and his ability in this direction has received official recognition on several occasions. In fact, he has been connected, in one way or another, with the last three censuses of the national government — those of 1870, 1880, and

SILAS J. DOUGLASS

1890. It was while studying law at Columbian College, Washington, that Mr. Douglass received his first insight into the difficulties attending these great statistical undertakings. At that time he served, during 1871 and 1872, as a clerk in the Washington census office. When the time came for taking the tenth census, Mr. Douglass was appointed by President Hayes a supervisor of census, having in charge the 11th census district of the state of New York. This district included the counties of Chautauqua, Cattaraugus, Niagara, and Erie. On the completion of his duties in connection with this position he was offered a clerkship in the office of the superintendent of census at Washington, where he remained two years. Before his return to Buffalo

he spent a year as assistant examiner of patents in the patent office. During his connection with the census office Mr. Douglass had displayed so much zeal, energy, and ability in the discharge of his duties, that President Harrison appointed him supervisor of census in 1890, and he was again assigned to the 11th census district. He displayed such fitness for the work, and so much energy in pushing it to a speedy completion, that the census officials at Washington commended him highly.

PERSONAL CHRONOLOGY — Silas Judson Douglass was born at Busti, N. Y., December 9, 1847; was educated in Westfield (N. Y.) Academy and Jamestown (N. Y.) Union School and Collegiate Institute; graduated from the law department of Columbian College, Washington, D. C., in 1872, and began practice in Buffalo in October, 1873; married Leonora Godwin of Buffalo May 8, 1879; was supervisor of census for the 11th census district of New York state in 1880 and in 1890.

***

Richard Hammond has done his full share in building up the manufacturing industries of Buffalo, and in giving employment to many men. The present is often called the age of iron and steel, and the workers in this line perform the heavy labor that lies at the foundation of material prosperity. In the din and dust of shops that the dainty seldom visit, are wrought out the mighty machines and ponderous engines that make modern life possible. Brawn and muscle and brain are all required in the pursuit of these laborious occupations. Just as there is no royal road to learning, so there is none to the trades. Personal contact with the work and long experience are necessary to master the details.

Mr. Hammond's career illustrates anew the power of one man with a strong will bent on the establishment of a business of his own. He had no advantages of birth or early training beyond what came from healthy, honest parents, and an elementary education. Born in a foreign land, he was twelve years old before he came to this country, and had the opportunity given to every American citizen to achieve whatever his ambition and talents can secure. None realize better than those born abroad how different are the conditions and the social customs of this country from those of the old world. Here the race, while not necessarily to the strongest, is to the man who will run and keep at it. A successful start does not necessarily imply a successful finish, and all that our institutions furnish is a start, the rest depending on the man himself.

The basis of every trade or profession is an apprenticeship, and the more thorough this is the better the workman. Thirty years ago one could not jump into a trade at a bound; and to-day as a result we have better journeymen, better master mechanics, and better employers. Mr. Hammond served his apprenticeship as a machinist and boiler-maker in Troy, N. Y., where he lived from the time he came to America until 1871. He then went to Whitehall, N. Y., and engaged in business for himself, afterward moving to Frank-lin, Penn., where he remained until 1882.

In the latter year the advantages of a larger field, and the gradual but sure development of Buffalo into one of the great manufacturing centers of the country, led Mr. Hammond to move thither. With John Coon as partner he started the Lake Erie Boiler Works; and to this enterprise he added in 1890 the Lake Erie Engineering Works, the two concerns employing five hundred men and requiring eight large buildings for their operations. Together they constitute one of the big shops of the city, and by providing work and wages for so many they become real factors in the industrial life of Buffalo. The Lake Erie Engineering Works is a joint-stock corporation, of which Mr. Hammond is president.

The active management of two such plants has kept Mr. Hammond closely confined to the office and shop; and, though an ardent Republican, he has uniformly declined to accept office, refusing at one time a nomination for councilman. But he has none the less been a force with his influence and means in the counsels of his party associates.

While living in Troy Mr. Hammond was a member of the 24th regiment, N. G., S. N. Y., and he has always regretted that he was not old enough to go to the front in the Civil War. He is a member of the Catholic Mutual Benefit

Association and the Catholic Knights of America, and is a parishioner of St. Joseph's Cathedral. In his relations to society and the community he is noted for his cordiality, generosity, and strict integrity—a plain man, without ostentation, enjoying the respect and good will of his neighbors and townsmen, and of all with whom he is connected in business relations.

*PERSONAL CHRONOLOGY—Richard Hammond was born in Ireland January 27, 1849; came to the United States in boyhood, and learned the machinist's trade at Troy, N. Y.; married Johanna Mahar of Troy April 25, 1870; engaged in business in New York and Pennsylvania, 1871-82; has conducted the Lake Erie Boiler Works at Buffalo since 1882, and the Lake Erie Engineering Works since 1890.*

*RICHARD HAMMOND*

**Herman Hennig,** well known at the bar of Buffalo and Erie county, was born in Saxony about forty-five years ago. He was brought to America during infancy by his parents, who had relatives in

Buffalo, and who went thither at once on reaching the country. There Mr. Hennig's father, also named Herman, lived until his death in 1871; and his mother is still a resident of that city. After attending the public schools, Mr. Hennig received further instruction from private tutors. His special

*HERMAN HENNIG*

training in the law was obtained in the office of Corlett & Tabor, famous attorneys of Buffalo, with whom he remained several years.

Having secured in this way a comprehensive knowledge of law as regards both theoretical text-book discussion and actual office experience, Mr. Hennig had no trouble in passing the bar examinations at Rochester in October, 1876. He began to practice at once in Buffalo, and has ever since followed his profession in that city and adjacent territory. He has never thought it desirable to specialize his work, preferring to utilize his broad training in the law by carrying on a general practice. This plan has been consistently followed, and he now conducts a large amount of legal business covering a wide range of

subjects. He does his work without partnership assistance.

Like so many other members of his profession, Mr. Hennig has devoted a good deal of attention to public affairs. Always until the fall of 1896 he was a staunch Democrat, prominent in the counsels of the party, and active in the dissemination and advocacy of Democratic principles. In 1883 he was elected to the office of city attorney of Buffalo, or, as it is now called, corporation counsel; and filled the position with conspicuous ability during the years 1884–85. At the expiration of his term of office his administration was heartily commended, not only by the press and politicians of his party, but also by the Republican papers and some prominent Republican attorneys. In 1894 he was nominated by the Democrats for the important position of district attorney of Erie county. In every campaign since 1872 Mr. Hennig has taken the stump. Most of his political speeches have naturally been made in Buffalo and Erie county; but he has also at times made campaign tours in other counties, and occasionally outside the Empire State. Up to the year of the McKinley-Bryan campaign he spoke in behalf of Democratic candidates; at that time, however, he espoused the cause of the Republicans on account of the money issue, and rendered potent aid to the cause of sound finance.

Mr. Hennig has a social nature, and belongs to various organizations designed to satisfy this healthy tendency of humankind. For some time he was chairman of the committee on laws of the Grand Lodge of the Ancient Order of United Workmen; and for three terms, beginning June 1, 1891, he was Grand Commander of the Select Knights. He belongs, also, to the Improved Order of Red Men, to the Knights of the Maccabees, and to the Odd Fellows.

*PERSONAL CHRONOLOGY — Herman Hennig was born in Saxony October 16, 1852; was educated in Buffalo at public schools and by private tutors; studied law, and was admitted to the bar in 1876; was city attorney of Buffalo, 1884–85; has been twice married, the second time to Sadie G. Rowman of Buffalo May 24, 1893; has practiced law in Buffalo since 1876.*

**William B. Hoyt,** one of the best-known and most successful practitioners at the Erie-county bar, has hardly yet emerged from the ranks of young men, as he is less than forty years old. He was born at East Aurora, Erie county, and has lived in that county all his life with the exception of the time spent in college. He obtained his early education in the academy at East Aurora, and completed his preparatory studies at the Buffalo High School.

Choosing Cornell as his *alma mater*, Mr. Hoyt began his studies at that institution in the fall of 1877, graduating with the class of 1881. In college Mr. Hoyt followed a general course of instruction, but gave especial attention to history and political science. He applied to his college work the same zeal and earnestness that have characterized his entire career, and acquired during his four years at Ithaca an exceedingly valuable foundation for his later professional studies. While in college he interested himself a good deal in the Cornell journalism of his day. He was managing editor of the monthly magazine, one of the editors of the college weekly, and the founder of the Cornell *Daily Sun* — a prosperous organ of campus public opinion that has continued to shine for all ever since. Mr. Hoyt has always been a loyal son of Cornell, and has taken great interest in the welfare of the institution. The fact received proper and gratifying recognition in June, 1895, when the alumni elected him one of the trustees of the university for a term of five years.

Mr. Hoyt was one of the fortunate mortals who have a decided bent for a particular calling, and are thus spared the trouble of weighing the comparative advantages of various possible pursuits. He decided in his college days to make the law his life-work, and with that end in view he became a student with Humphrey & Lockwood, and was admitted to the bar from their office in March, 1883. The firm mentioned was one of the oldest and busiest in Buffalo, and afforded a student all that could be desired in the way of practical experience in the dispatch of legal business. Partly on that account, but more especially because of his previous mental discipline, close application to his work, and rare ability in grasping quickly the essential points of a

subject, Mr. Hoyt made rapid progress in his profession.

After his admission to the bar, Mr. Hoyt was asked to become a member of the firm, which then assumed the familiar style of Humphrey, Lockwood & Hoyt. Additions have been made to the firm, but the original associates have continued to practice together up to the present time, and have established a wide reputation for responsibility and success. Mr. Hoyt does a large share of the court work of the firm, besides transacting a due amount of the office business.

In 1886 Mr. Hoyt was appointed assistant United States district attorney for the northern district of New York, holding the position until 1889. In 1894 he was appointed by Attorney-General Olney counsel to the United States interstate commerce

commission for the states of New York and Ohio, with the official title of assistant attorney-general. Aside from the two places mentioned Mr. Hoyt has not held public office. He is an earnest advocate of the principles of the Democratic party, and has for many years enjoyed the confidence of party leaders in Buffalo and western New York.

*PERSONAL CHRONOLOGY— William Ballard Hoyt was born at East Aurora, N. Y., April 29, 1858; prepared for college at East Aurora*

*JOHN D. LARKIN*

*Academy and the Buffalo High School, and graduated from Cornell University in 1881; studied law, and was admitted to the bar in 1883; married Esther Lapham Hill of Buffalo December 29, 1887; was assistant United States district attorney, 1886–89, and was appointed assistant attorney-general in 1894; has practiced law in Buffalo since 1884.*

* * *

**John D. Larkin,** one of Buffalo's successful business men and respected citizens, was born in that city little more than fifty years ago. His parents were English people; and his father, Levi H. Larkin, was the founder of the Clinton Iron Works, now carried on by Bingham & Taylor. One of Mr. Larkin's first recollections is of the burning of the old

Eagle tavern November 14, 1849, when he was but four years old. This hostelry stood on Main street, on the ground afterward occupied by the American hotel, where occurred the disastrous fire of 1865. At the time of the earlier fire the work of fighting the destroying element was intrusted to the volunteer fire department, of which Mr. Larkin's father was a member; and the apparatus at their disposal was extremely limited. When it was discovered, therefore, that brands from the burning tavern had lodged in the belfry of the old court house on Washington street, the building seemed doomed to destruction, as no water could reach the spot. But Mr. Larkin's father succeeded in climbing the slippery shingles and smothering the fire with his coat, thus saving the building, which was then deemed a most important one.

After attending the public schools of Buffalo in childhood, Mr. Larkin began business life at the age of twelve by entering the employ of William H. Woodward, a dealer in wholesale and retail millinery. He remained with him four years; and then, in 1862, began work in the soap manufactory of Justus Weller. For the next eight years he worked for Mr. Weller in Buffalo, learning thoroughly the business in which he has ever since engaged, and becoming increasingly valuable to his employer. When Mr. Weller moved to Chicago in 1870 Mr. Larkin went with him, and the next year was admitted to partnership in the firm of J. Weller & Co. This connection lasted until April, 1875, when Mr. Larkin sold out his interest in the business to Mr. Weller, and returned to Buffalo.

Mr. Larkin was now intimately acquainted with the details of soap manufacture, and had no desire to lose the results of twelve years' experience by taking up a different occupation. Accordingly he established a small factory on his own account, and set to work to build up a substantial business. In 1878 Elbert G. Hubbard was admitted to a share in the enterprise, and the firm of J. D. Larkin & Co. was organized. This style continued until February, 1892, when the business was incorporated as a stock company, called the Larkin Soap Manufacturing Co., with Mr. Larkin as president and treasurer. Mr. Hubbard withdrew from the concern in 1893.

Mr. Larkin has given his best energies to the undertaking during all these years, and has succeeded by persistent and well directed effort in building up one of the large and successful manufactories of the Queen City.

Mr. Larkin is a man of quiet tastes, and has never taken an active part in public affairs. While interested in politics, he has no desire to hold office, nor has he any of the qualities that make the practical politician. He belongs to no lodges or clubs, but is a member of the Prospect Avenue Baptist Church, Buffalo. He is particularly interested in young men, and is fond of helping them when they show a willingness to help themselves, preferring thus to make his charity private and personal, rather than to work through institutions, whose aid is not always discriminating.

*PERSONAL CHRONOLOGY — John Durrant Larkin was born at Buffalo September 29, 1845; was educated in Buffalo public schools and Bryant & Stratton's Business College; was employed in a wholesale millinery store in Buffalo, 1857-61; was engaged in soap manufacture, as employee and partner, in Buffalo and Chicago, 1862-75; married Frances H. Hubbard of Hudson, Ill., May 10, 1874; has been the head of the business now known as the Larkin Soap Manufacturing Co., Buffalo, since its establishment in 1875.*

* * *

**Eugene M. Ashley** is known throughout Niagara county, and indeed throughout western New York, as one of the brainiest, shrewdest, boldest, and soundest lawyers within that territory. He is more than that. He is a business man of large experience and much foresight, accustomed to the successful handling of immense interests. Further, he is directly and positively interested in all public questions, a hearty partisan in politics, and an active force in many social and other organizations in the city of Lockport.

Mr. Ashley had a variety of experiences before he adopted the profession in which he has won such signal success. He is a Genesee-county boy by birth, and attended the common schools of his neighborhood; afterward taking a course at the Tenbroeck Academy at Franklinville, N. Y., and completing his education under private tutors. Then he taught school for seven years in Genesee county. But his nature was too restless and ambitious to be satisfied with the confines of the schoolroom. He was already taking an active part in politics; and in 1873 he was appointed United States revenue agent, and on September 1 was assigned to duty in Lockport. He held this position for about a year. For the next

three years he studied law, and had the advantage of pursuing his studies in the offices of such men as L. F. & G. W. Bowen and Judge David Millar.

In January, 1880, Mr. Ashley was declared fully qualified to act as an attorney and counselor at law. He immediately launched out alone, but in 1882 he formed a partnership with D. E. Brong. Later Frank M. Ashley became a member of the firm. In 1886 Mr. Brong retired, and the firm of E. M. & F. M. Ashley continued until 1894, when the firm of Roberts, Becker, Ashley, Messer & Orcutt, with offices at Buffalo and Lockport, came into existence.

With all Mr. Ashley's interest in politics, he has not often held public office. He was the very able district attorney of Niagara county for six years, being first elected to the office in 1880 and again in 1883. He was also the unsuccessful Republican nominee for member of assembly in 1892 in a Democratic district. This has been about the extent of his political life, though he is a campaign speaker of much eloquence. He has preferred to devote his energies to the building up of a lucrative law practice, and the development of the many commercial enterprises in which he is engaged. No litigation of great importance has occurred in Niagara county in the past ten years in which he has not appeared on one side or the other. This may seem a broad statement, but it is fully warranted by the facts. Mr. Ashley has been counsel for the board of supervisors of Niagara county, and for the board of education of Lockport; and he successfully carried through the erection of new school buildings after two years of strenuous opposition.

A few instances of Mr. Ashley's connection with large business enterprises may be cited here as an indication of his natural shrewdness and willingness to do all that lies in his power for the material advancement of his city. With the late John Hodge of Lockport, he organized and owned the Lockport street railroad in 1886 and 1887. This road was for a time operated under great difficulties and many embarrassments, but the energy and ability of its owners finally removed all these. In 1892 the motive power was changed to electricity, and the road was started and operated as an electric line in August, 1895, just twenty days after the death of Mr. Hodge, whose interest in the enterprise had been most untiring. In company with James A. Roberts of Buffalo, Timothy E. Ellsworth of Lockport, and William M. Ivins of New York, Mr. Ashley organized the Traders' Paper Co. of Lockport, one of the largest mills in the state. The organization was completed in 1895, and the plant was put in operation in 1896. Mr. Ashley was also the projector of an electric railroad from Lockport to Olcott on Lake Ontario. He was a charter member of the Lockport Electric and Water Supply Co., which has a franchise to build a power canal from Niagara river to Lake Ontario.

*GEORGE W. BRIGGS*

Mr. Ashley is prominent in the club and social life of Lockport, where his many charming qualities make him highly esteemed.

*PERSONAL CHRONOLOGY— Eugene M. Ashley was born at Bethany, Genesee county, N. Y., June 1, 1850; received his education in common schools and Tenbroeck Academy, and from private tutors; moved to Lockport, N. Y., September 1, 1875, as United States revenue agent; was admitted to the bar in January, 1880; married Eliza W. Adriance of Lockport December 29, 1880; was elected district attorney of Niagara county in 1880, and again in 1884; has practiced law in Lockport since 1880.*

* * *

**George W. Briggs** was born in the town of Collins, Erie county, New York, less than fifty years

ago. He attended the common schools of the neighborhood in boyhood, and afterward spent some time at a select school, acquiring a good general education, and fitting himself for the work of a teacher. He followed this profession, indeed, for twelve years, though he had no intention of making it his life-work.

In the spring of 1881 Mr. Briggs moved to Orchard Park, Erie county, where he has since resided. Two years later he began his present business as a dealer in farmers' supplies of all kinds. At first he sold goods on commission only, in a small way; but he soon became firmly established on a more satisfactory basis, and for a number of years now he has done a thriving business in his part of the county. During the greater part of this time he has conducted the undertaking alone; but for several months in 1893 he was in partnership with C. N. Smith, in the firm of Briggs & Smith.

Mr. Briggs has long been interested in public affairs, and has served his fellow-citizens in one capacity or another for many years. He held the office of justice of the peace for two terms, or six years; and has represented the town of East Hamburg on the Erie-county board of supervisors ever since 1889. He has taken a prominent and active part in the work of the board from the first. In 1893 he was a member of the purchasing and auditing committee, and in 1896–97 he was the chairman of the board.

Mr. Briggs is a Mason, and belongs to several other fraternal societies, including the Knights of the Maccabees, Select Knights, and Independent Order of Odd Fellows. He has membership in the following Masonic bodies: Zion Lodge, No. 514, F. & A. M., Orchard Park; Buffalo Chapter, No. 71, R. A. M.; Lake Erie Commandery, No. 20, K. T., Buffalo; Ismailia Temple, Nobles of the Mystic Shrine, Buffalo; and the Acacia Club, Buffalo. He attends the Presbyterian church.

*PERSONAL CHRONOLOGY— George W. Briggs was born at Collins, N. Y., October 10, 1850; was educated in common and select schools; married Orcelia A. Pike of West Concord, N. Y., December 29, 1875; taught school, 1868–80; was justice of the peace, 1884–89; has been a member of the Erie-county board of supervisors since 1889; has conducted a general store at Orchard Park, N. Y., since 1884.*

**Eugene Cary**, prominent in the legal and political circles of Niagara Falls, was born in Dunkirk, N. Y., somewhat less than forty years ago. After attending the public schools of his native place, he obtained higher instruction at Cornell University, graduating thence in 1878 with the degree of B. S. He then devoted a year to business in his father's hardware store at Dunkirk, and the winter of 1879–80 he passed as principal of a school at Sinclairville, Chautauqua county.

By this time Mr. Cary had decided to make the practice of law his life-work. Entering the office of Judge Thomas P. Grosvenor, therefore, at Dunkirk, he applied himself with characteristic zeal to the task of mastering legal science. He continued his reading until August, 1881, when the position of superintendent of schools at Bedford, Ia., was offered to him. He accepted this opportunity, and managed the public schools of Bedford with marked efficiency for the next three years. He found a little time for his law studies during these years in the West, and had no difficulty in passing the bar examinations at Buffalo in June, 1884.

From November, 1884, until October of the next year, Mr. Cary practiced law at Forestville, near Dunkirk, in partnership with Daniel Sherman. Niagara Falls was already beginning to give promise of its later industrial supremacy, and Mr. Cary resolved to settle there. Associating himself, accordingly, with Henry C. Tucker, he practiced at the Falls in the firm of Tucker & Cary from October, 1885, until May, 1887. For the next six years he carried on a large practice without partnership assistance. Since May 1, 1893, he has been associated with William C. Wallace in the well-known firm of Cary & Wallace. He has become a familiar figure in the courts of Niagara county, and is widely known as an able and trustworthy attorney.

Outside of professional work Mr. Cary has been especially interested in politics. He was a member of the executive committee of the Chautauqua-county Republican committee in 1884. In the fall of that year he edited the political columns of a Dunkirk newspaper. Since going to Niagara Falls he has been on the Republican city committee several times, and in the important campaign of 1896 he

was chairman of that committee. He was one of the alternate delegates to the Republican national convention at St. Louis in the same year. He has been a delegate to every Republican judiciary convention in his district for the last ten years, and was chairman of the convention in 1895. Notwithstanding his activity and importance in the counsels of the Republican party, he has never cared to hold public office. He has, however, been a member of the Niagara Falls board of education since March, 1896.

Mr. Cary has been somewhat active in the business life of Niagara Falls as well as in law and politics. He holds directorates in the Power City Bank and in the Bank of Niagara ; and acts as attorney for these institutions, and for the Bank of Suspension Bridge. He is a trustee of the Niagara County

EUGENE CARY

Savings Bank, and president of the Niagara Falls Memorial Hospital.

*PERSONAL CHRONOLOGY* — *Eugene Cary was born at Dunkirk, N. Y., November 21, 1857,*

*graduated from Cornell University in 1878; was
engaged in teaching and as superintendent of schools,
and in reading law, 1879-84; was admitted to the
bar in June, 1884; married Mary M. Wand of Buffalo July 5, 1882; practiced law at Forestville, N. Y.,
1884-85; was an alternate delegate to the Republican*

FREDERICK A. FULLER, JR.

*national convention of 1896; has practiced law at
Niagara Falls since 1887.*

•••

**Frederick A. Fuller, Jr.,** one of Jamestown's most public-spirited citizens, was born in
Rutland, Vt., fifty-odd years ago. He was only two
years old, however, when his parents moved to
western New York and settled in Jamestown, where
his father established a jewelry business. At the
age of eighteen he graduated from the Jamestown
Academy, and at once became an employee in his
father's store. There he remained for the next nine
years; and then went to New York city, where he
engaged for several years in importing fine watches
and precious stones. In 1875, however, he returned

to Jamestown to assist his father once more, and
three years later succeeded him in the charge of the
business. This was nearly twenty years ago, and he
has conducted the establishment ever since.

In the case of many men, a business life monopo-
lizes the largest share, if not the whole, of their
attention; and some such statement as
that briefly given above comprises about
all there is of interest in their careers.
But it is not so with Mr. Fuller. While
devoting himself actively to his private
affairs, he has given much of his best
thought and most earnest work for many
years to public matters, both political
and educational. His fellow-citizens
have special cause to be grateful to him
for his interest in the schools of the
city. He was first chosen a member
of the board of education in 1884, and
has served continuously since, having
been annually elected president of the
board for the past seven years. Much
of the credit for the present admirable
public-school system of the city of
Jamestown belongs to him, since he has
done more, perhaps, than any other man
to create and maintain it.

Mr. Fuller has long been active, also,
in Democratic politics in western New
York, and has been a prominent member
of the Democratic state committee. In
the first Cleveland campaign he was a
presidential elector; and though the
youngest of the New York members of
the electoral college, he was chosen with
Erastus Corning of Albany, to deliver
the sealed electoral vote of the state of
New York for President and Vice-President.

Mr. Fuller is well known in social and business
life in Jamestown and beyond. He has been for
many years a director of the City National Bank of
Jamestown, and is a member of the Jamestown Club.
He takes an active part in the work of the First
Presbyterian Church, and is one of its deacons. He
belongs to the Reform and Democratic clubs of New
York city, and to the Sons of the American Revolution. He has given considerable attention to the
subject of his family genealogy, and takes a pardon-
able pride in the fact that he is a lineal descendant
in the eighth generation of Dr. Samuel Fuller, who
came over in the "Mayflower." By virtue of this
descent Mr. Fuller has membership in the Pilgrim
Society of Plymouth, Mass.

*PERSONAL CHRONOLOGY— Frederick A.
Fuller, Jr., was born at Rutland, Vt., April 10,
1839; was educated in the Jamestown (N. Y.)
Academy; was a clerk in his father's store in Jamestown, 1857-61; married Cornelia Ludlow Benedict
of Brooklyn, N. Y., May 24, 1866; engaged in the
jewelry business as an importer in New York city,
1861-75; was a presidential elector in 1884; has
been a member of the Jamestown board of education
since 1884, and its president since 1890; has conducted a jewelry business in Jamestown since 1878.*

...

**John S. Lambert,** though he has been known
as Judge Lambert for a long time, attained that title
so early in life that he has hardly yet reached the
prime of his powers. He was born in the eastern
part of the Empire State, in Rensselaer county,
shortly after the middle of the century;
and received his education in the common schools, and in Greenwich Academy, Washington county. He then
moved to the western end of the state, becoming a law student in the office of Morris & Russell of Fredonia, from which he
was admitted to the bar in 1877.

Beginning practice at first in Mayville
on his own account, Judge Lambert, in
1878, accepted an invitation from his
former preceptors, who showed their
appreciation of his ability by taking him
into partnership. He continued a member of the firm of Morris, Russell &
Lambert for four years, when Mr. Russell withdrew, and the firm of Morris &
Lambert was formed, which lasted until
Judge Lambert's elevation to the bench
of the Supreme Court. He proved himself during this time to possess unusual
talent as a legal practitioner, and he
would undoubtedly have taken rank with
the leaders of his profession in western
New York had he remained at the bar.

Judge Lambert began to take an interest in public affairs early in his professional career, and served on the board
of supervisors of Chautauqua county in
1880 and 1881 as the member from the
town of Pomfret. In the fall of 1884
he was elected by the Republican party
as county judge of Chautauqua county;
and his work in this position was so well regarded that
his first term was followed by a second, beginning in
January, 1888. He was not permitted to serve out
this term, as he was elected a justice of the Supreme

Court of New York state in the fall of 1889. The
judicial convention met in Buffalo October 3, 1889;
and it was not until ten days had elapsed, and 151
ballots had been taken, that a nomination was made.
The election, however, brought out the strength of
the candidate, and showed the wisdom of the choice;
since Judge Lambert received a large majority
throughout his district. His field of work is the
8th judicial district, which includes the counties of
Erie, Chautauqua, Cattaraugus, Orleans, Niagara,
Genesee, Allegany, and Wyoming.

Judge Lambert's career on the higher bench has
justified his advancement to such a station of trust
and responsibility. He was less than forty years old
when his term as Supreme Court justice began; but
he had a natural aptitude for the judicial calling,
and his training and experience in life were likewise

*JOHN S. LAMBERT*

factors in his success on the bench. He enjoys a
high reputation with the legal profession of western
New York. In social life he is noted for his affabil-
ity and extreme courtesy.

*PERSONAL CHRONOLOGY— John S. Lambert was born at Johnsonville, N. Y., February 4, 1851; was educated at Greenwich (N. Y.) Academy; studied law, and was admitted to the bar in 1877; practiced law at Mayville, N. Y., 1877-78, and at Fredonia, N. Y., 1878-89; married Winni*

*J. C. MORGAN*

*fred Philips of Cassadaga, N. Y., August 19, 1891; was a member of the Chautauqua-county board of supervisors, 1880-81, and county judge of Chautauqua county, 1882-89; has been a justice of the Supreme Court of New York state since January 1, 1890.*

∗∗∗

**J. C. Morgan**, though little more than forty years old, has been connected for nearly twenty years with the business of paper manufacture. Born in Erie county, Pennsylvania, he passed the years preceding his majority in the manner usual to country boys; attending the district school regularly until the age of eleven, and after that working the greater part of the time, and going to school for two or three months each winter when there was no work

to be done. When he was sixteen years old he left school, and went to work permanently. Several years later he took a short course at a commercial college; but his successful business career, and present important position in the industrial world, must be ascribed to natural ability and close application rather than to any very thorough preparatory training.

In the spring of 1878 Mr. Morgan began business on his own account, forming a partnership with H. F. Watson of Erie, Penn., for the manufacture of roofing and building paper. At first they had a small mill at Fairview, Mr. Morgan's native place; but in 1880 they built a mill in the city of Erie. Two years later Mr. Morgan sold out his interest there, and moved to Battle Creek, Mich., where he built another mill, and continued the manufacture of building paper. For several years he carried this on successfully; but in 1890 he disposed of the business to the American Strawboard Co., becoming assistant general manager of the concern, and having charge of their twenty-six mills in the manufacturing department, with headquarters at Anderson, Ind.

Having obtained a thorough knowledge of the paper-making business, Mr. Morgan had been anxious for some time to engage in the industry on a larger scale than had at first been practicable. While carrying on his mill at Battle Creek he had formed a company in Chicago, under the style of the Soo Paper Co., to build an extensive mill at Sault Ste. Marie, Mich.; but this project had been subsequently abandoned on account of difficulties in obtaining a proper title, and in securing the necessary water power. Finally, in 1891, he resigned his position with the American Strawboard Co., and organized the Niagara Falls Paper Co., one of the largest concerns of its kind in the country, of which he has been from the first secretary and general manager. The erection of the plant at Niagara Falls was begun in the following year, and the company has carried on an enormous business ever since. The mill has a capacity of 120 tons of finished paper per day; and the product turned out includes manilla, newspaper, and book-finished paper.

*PERSONAL CHRONOLOGY— John Crook Morgan was born at Fairview, Erie county, Penn.,*

*August 8, 1855; attended district schools and a commercial college; married Hattie E. Dewey of Shelby, Mich., December 22, 1880; engaged in the manufacture of paper at Erie, Penn., and Battle Creek, Mich., 1878-90; was assistant general manager of the American Strawboard Co., 1890-91; organized the Niagara Falls Paper Co. in 1891, and has been secretary and general manager of the same since.*

•••

**Frederick R. Peterson,** well known in the legal and political circles of Chautauqua county, was born in the town of Ellicott, New York. His boyhood and youth were spent in the familiar way that has so often in American life led to eminence — attending district schools, teaching school at times, and working on the home farm more than anything else. This was his life up to his twenty-first year. In 1877 he entered upon a systematic course of instruction in Jamestown Union School and Collegiate Institute, taking a classical course, and graduating from the institution in 1880. Having decided to follow the legal profession, he entered the office of Sheldon, Green, Stevens & Benedict, a prominent law firm of Jamestown, N. Y. After studying there zealously for several years, and acquiring valuable experience in the actual dispatch of legal business, he was admitted to the bar at Rochester in October, 1884.

Opening an office at once in Jamestown, Mr. Peterson has ever since followed his profession there. He practiced alone for the first few years, but in 1888 formed a partnership with Clark R. Lockwood under the style of Lockwood & Peterson. This association continued until 1892, when the firm was dissolved. In the same year Mr. Peterson formed a partnership with Frank W. Stevens under the firm name of Stevens & Peterson. This connection has been maintained ever since, and has been distinctly successful. Mr. Peterson has shown himself a prudent and sagacious adviser on legal questions, and a trustworthy agent in the conduct of litigation. He stands high in the esteem of the bar of Chautauqua county.

Mr. Peterson has taken an active part in political affairs, and his public life antedates by a year his professional career. Becoming clerk of Jamestown in 1883, he continued to discharge efficiently the

duties of the office until 1888. He was one of the supervisors of Chautauqua county from Jamestown in 1892 and again in 1893. In the fall of 1896 he received the Republican nomination for the office of assemblyman from the 1st Chautauqua-county district, and was elected by the extraordinary plurality of 5800. In the legislature he served on the committees on judiciary, revision, and the Soldiers' Home.

Mr. Peterson is fond of social life, and is a member of various social and fraternal organizations. He is especially interested in Free Masonry, and has attained high rank in the order. He belongs to Mt. Moriah Lodge, No. 145, F. & A. M.; Western Sun Chapter, No. 67, R. A. M.; and Jamestown Commandery, No. 61, K. T. He is a member of the Knights of Pythias, the order of Elks, and the Knights of the Maccabees, as well as

FREDERICK R. PETERSON

the Jamestown Club, Albany Club, and the First Methodist Church of Jamestown.

*PERSONAL CHRONOLOGY— Frederick R. Peterson was born in the town of Ellicott, Chautauqua*

*county, N. Y., January 21, 1857; graduated from
the Jamestown (N. Y.) Union School and Collegiate
Institute in 1880; was admitted to the bar in October,
1884; married Edith S. Osgood of Jamestown April 8,
1885; was clerk of Jamestown, 1884-88, and a
member of the board of supervisors, 1892-93; was*

CHARLES J. SHULTS

*elected to the state assembly in 1896; has practiced
law in Jamestown since 1884.*

***

**Charles J. Shults,** one of the youngest
newspaper publishers in western New York, was born
in Cattaraugus county thirty years ago. He was
educated in the union school at Ellicottville, his
native town, and learned the printer's trade with R.
H. Shankland in the office of the *Cattaraugus Union,*
published at Ellicottville. Mr. Shankland was a
friend of Horace Greeley, and a co-worker with the
founder of the *Tribune,* and under him Mr. Shults
obtained an excellent knowledge of the printer's
craft. At that time, however, he had not decided
definitely to engage in the printing and publishing

business; and he therefore spent several months as a
student in a law office, and also studied medicine for
a short time.

Deciding at last that a business career offered
greater advantages on the whole than professional
work, Mr. Shults gave up both the law and medicine, and embarked in the business with
which he has since been identified —
that of newspaper publishing. His first
venture was the purchase of the *Pine
Valley News* of South Dayton, N. Y.,
which he conducted successfully for three
years. In 1885 he bought the Cherry
Creek *Monitor,* and consolidated the two
papers, issuing a new sheet called the
Cherry Creek *News.* He is still publishing this paper, and is making it more
and more valuable to its readers. In
1890 he bought the Gowanda *Herald,*
and has conducted that publication with
vigor and success ever since. In addition to these undertakings he acted for
a time as state editor of the Buffalo
*Enquirer.*

Mr. Shults is well known to the newspaper fraternity of the state, having
served for two terms as a member of the
executive committee of the New York
State Press Association. At the annual
meeting of that organization in 1896 he
read a paper entitled "A Year's Experience as an Advertising Agent," that
attracted considerable attention for its
able and intelligent treatment of the
question of advertising, so important to
all newspaper publishers. His state-
ments carried additional weight as being
the result of practical experience rather
than of theoretical speculation. This
experience had been gained not only in his work
as a publisher, but largely in connection with the
Consolidated Country Press; which he organized
in Buffalo in 1892, and which he still conducts, in
company with Edward Rutherford, under the name
of Chas. J. Shults & Co. This association controls
the advertising of about a hundred papers published
in the territory tributary to Buffalo, and carries on
a general advertising agency as well. Mr. Shults
is now the secretary and treasurer of the Chautauqua County Press Association. He is a firm Republican in political belief, and conducts his papers in
the interest of that party. He has never thought
it worth while to seek public office, but served as
town clerk of Cherry Creek in 1887 and 1888.

Mr. Shults has been greatly interested in Masonry ever since he joined the order soon after attaining his majority. He was Master of the lodge in Cherry Creek for two years; and in September, 1894, he was appointed by John Hodge, Grand Master of Masons of New York State, as District Deputy Grand Master of the 26th Masonic district. This appointment was unsought by Mr. Shults, and was highly acceptable to the fraternity throughout the district, where he was widely known and respected. In June, 1896, he was again appointed to the position by Grand Master John Stewart, and served a second term with credit and distinction. He is the youngest Mason ever holding a position of this character.

*PERSONAL CHRONOLOGY—Charles Julius Shults was born at Ellicottville, N. Y., February 23, 1867; was educated in common schools; married Eva M. Morian of Cherry Creek, N. Y., May 4, 1887; learned the printer's trade at Ellicottville; was appointed District Deputy Grand Master of Masons in 1894, and again in 1896; has been a newspaper owner and publisher in western New York since 1882.*

...

**Albert R. Smith** was born in the village of North Tonawanda little more than twenty-five years ago. He spent his childhood on a farm on the banks of the Niagara river; and attended the public schools up to the age of eleven, when he became a clerk in a grocery store. His active career, begun at this early age, has thus been considerably longer than that of most men of his years; and has also been unusually varied, embracing as it does both business and professional life.

When he was fifteen years old Mr. Smith became connected with the lumber trade, the great industry that has made the present city of North Tonawanda one of the most important commercial centers in western New York. For a time he acted as tally boy and shipper. He then spent a winter at Bryant & Stratton's Business College, Buffalo, where he took a general business course, learning stenography and typewriting as well. In the spring of 1889 he entered the office of Smith, Fassett & Co., lumber dealers in North Tonawanda, as stenographer and confidential clerk, and remained with them for the next four years.

By this time Mr. Smith was twenty-two years old, and had made a good start in business life. He was anxious, however, for a different kind of success from any to be obtained as a lumber dealer; and as he had now accumulated some money he was able to gratify this ambition, and prepare himself for the legal profession. Entering the office of Lewis T. Payne in the spring of 1893, he applied himself for the next three years to the task of acquiring the necessary knowledge; reading Kent and Blackstone, and familiarizing himself with the practical work of a lawyer's office at the same time. He took the bar examinations at Rochester June 17, 1896, and was admitted to practice July 29. For several months thereafter he remained in Mr. Payne's office, but on January 4, 1897, he opened an office on his own account.

*ALBERT R. SMITH*

It does not happen to many men to assume judicial duties within a year of their admission to the bar, but this was Mr. Smith's experience. The act of the legislature passed April 24, 1897, created the city of North Tonawanda ; and on April 27 Mayor McKeen appointed Mr. Smith the first city judge of the new municipality. This appointment was the more noteworthy inasmuch as the mayor is a Republican and there were three Republican applicants for

*August 18, 1874 ; was educated in public schools and a business college ; was clerk for a lumber firm in North Tonawanda, 1889—93 ; studied law, and was admitted to the bar in 1896 ; has been city judge of North Tonawanda since May 1, 1897.*

\* \* \*

**R. B. Bickford** has been prominently connected with the leather industry in Buffalo ever since he first went thither thirty years ago. He was born in the southeastern part of New Hampshire in 1830, and at an early age began attending the district schools. After he became old enough he spent his summers at work on a farm ; but he continued his attendance at school during the winter until he attained his majority, and in this way secured an excellent general education. When he was eighteen years old he gave up farming, and spent a short time as a brick maker, and then went to work at his present trade of belt and hose making.

In 1849 Mr. Bickford left home, and went to Lowell, Mass., where he worked at the latter trade for eighteen years for Josiah Gates. For the first four years he was employed as a journeyman ; but after that he became superintendent of the factory, and continued in that position while he remained in the establishment. By this time he had acquired a thorough knowledge of the business, and was desirous of starting out on his own account. Accordingly, in January, 1867, he went to Buffalo ; and established himself as a manufacturer of leather belting and fire hose, forming

R. B. BICKFORD

the position, while Mr. Smith has always been identified with the Democratic party.

Military and fraternal organizations have always been attractive to Mr. Smith, and have received his active support. He is first sergeant of the 25th Separate company, N. G., S. N. Y., of Tonawanda ; and a member of the Young Men's Christian Association and of Alert Hose Company of the same place. He belongs to Niagara Council, No. 718, Royal Arcanum ; is Junior Warden of Tonawanda Lodge, No. 247, F. & A. M. ; and a charter member of Electric City Lodge, No. 663, I. O. O. F., and of Court Warwick, Independent Order of Foresters.

*PERSONAL CHRONOLOGY— Albert Rockwell Smith was born at North Tonawanda, N. Y.,*

with Fred B. Curtiss the firm of Bickford & Curtiss. Two years later Fred Deming was admitted to partnership, and the style became Bickford, Curtiss & Deming. In 1875 Mr. Deming retired, and the original firm name was resumed until 1883, when William C. Francis bought out Mr. Curtiss's interest, and the firm became Bickford & Francis. Mr. Francis died in April, 1889 ; and the business was reorganized as the Bickford & Francis Belting Co., Walter T. Wilson purchasing the interest of Mr. Francis in the working capital, and Mr. Bickford's son, R. K. Bickford, being admitted to a share in the concern.

Mr. Bickford established his business in the beginning at 53 and 55 Exchange street, and he has remained there ever since. But though the location has been unchanged, the business has entirely outgrown the limited proportions of thirty years ago. More space has been required from time to time for the conduct of the business, and the staff of employees has been greatly increased; and to-day the concern carries on the manufacture of leather belting and fire hose on an extensive scale, and enjoys a high reputation in the commercial world.

Mr. Bickford is an earnest Republican, and a firm believer in the distinctive Republican doctrine of protection for American industries; but he has never taken an active interest in party affairs, nor cared to hold public office. He is a 32d degree Mason, and Past Master of DeMolay Lodge, No. 498, and attends the Baptist church. His greatest interest outside of his business has been the subject of music. For over forty years, beginning as a young man in Lowell, he sang in different churches, acting much of the time as choir conductor; and he has also composed considerable church music.

*PERSONAL CHRONOLOGY—Richmond H. Bickford was born at Rochester, N. H., February 8, 1830; was educated in common schools; married Emma J. Tracy of Mercer, Maine, July 18, 1854; learned the trade of a belt and hose maker, and worked at the same in Lowell, 1849-67; has carried on the manufacture of leather belting and fire hose in Buffalo since 1867.*

∴∴∴

**George Bingham** was born in Lancaster, N. Y., and has always made his home there, though his work as a business man and as a public official has been done in Buffalo. He is a son of Henry L. Bingham, a native of Windham, Conn., who settled in western New York when a young man.

After a general education in public and private schools, Mr. Bingham took up the profession of a civil engineer, and at the age of eighteen became a rodman in the employ of the old Buffalo & Washington railroad under William Wallace, chief of the engineering department. He soon rose to more important positions, and finally had charge of a division of the road as assistant engineer. He took part, also, in the planning and construction of other railroads in the western states and Canada, and worked for a year in the city engineer's department

of Buffalo, running the levels for the topographical map of the city. In 1875, however, Mr. Bingham abandoned the calling of an engineer, and embarked in the hide and leather business, forming a partnership with S. W. Nash, Jr., on May 1, 1876. This connection was dissolved six months later, and Mr. Bingham then conducted the business alone until May 1, 1886. In 1888 he became superintendent of the Thomson-Houston Electric Light & Power Co. in Buffalo, and held the position for the next three years.

In 1880 Mr. Bingham was elected to the state assembly from the 4th Erie-county district, and in the memorable contest in the legislature of 1881 over the United States senatorship, he distinguished himself by his vigorous support of the candidacy of Roscoe Conkling. In 1891 President Harrison

*GEORGE BINGHAM*

appointed Mr. Bingham United States appraiser for the port of Buffalo; and since that time he has been occupied with public service, and has filled important positions in Erie county. He held the post of appraiser for three years, or until he was elected county clerk in 1894. His discharge of the duties of this office has been marked by painstaking care and attention to details, and he has made an enviable record as an honest and capable public official. In 1895–96 he was the chairman of the

CLARENCE W. HAMMOND

Erie-county Republican committee, and in 1895 he was elected president of the village of Lancaster. He is also one of the justices of the peace for the same town.

*PERSONAL CHRONOLOGY— George Bingham was born at Lancaster, N. Y., December 21, 1848; was educated in public and private schools; worked as a civil engineer, 1860–75; married Carrie Lee of Lancaster September 4, 1874; engaged in the hide and leather business, 1876–88, and in electrical business, 1888–94; was member of assembly in 1881, United States appraiser, 1891–94, president of the village of Lancaster in 1895, and chairman of the Erie-county Republican committee, 1895–96; has been county clerk of Erie county since January 1, 1895.*

**Clarence W. Hammond** is widely known and highly regarded in business circles in Buffalo, where he has lived for nearly twenty years. Though he is now so closely identified with the interests of the Queen City, he had a business career of considerable length and importance before coming to New York state.

Mr. Hammond was born in the little village of East Jaffrey, N. H., less than fifty years ago. He was taken West in childhood, however, and received his education and early business training in Michigan. After attending the public schools of Saginaw for a time, he finished his studies at Ypsilanti. At the age of sixteen he became a banker's clerk, gaining thus his first insight into the world of finance, which was afterward to be his successful field of labor.

After a short experience there Mr. Hammond engaged in a general mercantile business, becoming manager of a concern manufacturing lumber, salt, etc. He conducted this enterprise for a number of years, and met with much success. In 1879, in company with Wellington R. Burt of Saginaw, Mich., he established in Buffalo a wholesale lumber business and planing mill. The importance of Buffalo as a distributing center, where the product of the western forests could be advantageously prepared for the market, and shipped by rail or canal to all points in the East, was coming to be realized more and more; and the venture of the two Michigan men proved a fortunate one. Mr. Hammond took an active part in the work of the Buffalo Lumber Exchange, an organization formed to secure uniform freight rates, and in other ways to protect the interests of the lumber dealers; and largely instrumental in effecting the passage of the bill to abolish grade crossings within the city limits. His popularity with this association was shown in the fact that when he retired from the lumber business he was elected an honorary member of the exchange, a distinction never before conferred upon a member.

In 1889 Mr. Hammond disposed of his lumber interests and made an entirely new departure, organizing the People's Bank of Buffalo. His long experience in the practical conduct of business affairs had been an excellent preparation for this venture in one respect at least — he knew what the patrons of a bank expect from such an institution. The result has proved that he also possessed the other qualities necessary to ensure success; for he has been the moving and guiding spirit in the organization from the beginning, and the high stand it has taken among the banks of Buffalo is due chiefly to his able and efficient management. He has been cashier of the bank ever since its organization, and has given his undivided attention to it. In January, 1897, he was elected to the office of second vice president as well.

Though political nominations have several times been offered to him, Mr. Hammond has uniformly declined them, deeming any active participation in public affairs incompatible with a proper attention to his other duties. He is much interested in Masonry, in which he has taken all the degrees except the 33d; and he belongs, also, to many other similar organizations. He attends the Unitarian church. He takes an active interest in all things connected with his adopted city, and has done much by his business foresight and acumen to maintain and increase its prosperity.

*PERSONAL CHRONOLOGY—Clarence W. Hammond was born at East Jaffrey, N. H., June 5, 1848; was educated in Michigan schools; began business life in 1864 as a bank clerk, and afterward engaged in lumber manufacture in Michigan; conducted a wholesale lumber business in Buffalo, 1879-89; married Adele E. Sireet of Buffalo June 2, 1881; has been cashier of the People's Bank, Buffalo, since its organization in 1889, and second vice president since January 1, 1897.*

* * *

**John M. Hull**, who for the last dozen years has practiced law at the Erie-county bar, was born in Buffalo thirty-eight years ago. After attending Public School No. 5 and the Buffalo Central High School, he prepared for college at Cook Academy, a well-known institution under the control of the Baptist church located at Havana, or what is now the village of Montour Falls. He then took a full classical course at the University of Rochester, from which he graduated in 1882 with the degree of A. B.

Leaving college then, with the world before him in which to choose his line of work, Mr. Hull determined to fit himself for the legal profession. His studies were completed in due course, and in

October, 1884, he was admitted to the bar. In December of the same year he opened an office in Buffalo, and has practiced there continuously since. He has been content to stand or fall in his professional career entirely on his own merits, forming no partnership associations; and his present assured position and growing clientage prove the wisdom of his course.

Mr. Hull has never taken a very conspicuous part in political affairs, though he has long been known as an earnest Republican who could be counted on to work for his party. His only public office thus far has been directly in the line of his professional duties. In October, 1894, he was chosen by the Erie-county board of supervisors as their attorney; and has held the position ever since, having been reappointed in October, 1895, and again January 1, 1897.

*JOHN M. HULL*

In private as in public life, Mr. Hull is quiet and unassuming; but he has many friends in his native city who know and admire his genial nature and many agreeable qualities. He is a Mason,

belonging to Washington Lodge, No. 240, F. &
A. M.; Keystone Chapter, No. 162, R. A. M.;
Hugh de Payens Commandery, No. 30, K. T.;
and Ismailia Temple, Nobles of the Mystic Shrine.
He attends the Delaware Avenue Baptist Church.

*PERSONAL CHRONOLOGY — John M. Hull
was born at Buffalo December 15, 1858; attended
Buffalo public schools and Cook Academy, Havana,
N. Y., and graduated from the University of Rochester in 1882; was admitted to the bar in 1884; has
been attorney for the Erie-county board of supervisors
since October, 1894; has practiced law in Buffalo
since 1884.*

— ∙ — ∙∙∙

**Jewett M. Richmond** is known to all Buffalonians as a business man of unusual sagacity and
spotless integrity, and a citizen whose time and
means for many years have been freely bestowed in
behalf of every deserving public movement. The
Richmond family came to America in early colonial
days, and settled in Massachusetts. Mr. Richmond's
grandfather, Josiah Richmond of Taunton, was a
soldier in the Revolution; and afterward removed
to Barnard, Vt., with his son Anson. Anson Richmond took part in the war of 1812; and at its close
emigrated to central New York, and settled in the
village of Salina, afterward part of the city of Syracuse, where he engaged in the manufacture of salt
until his death in 1834.

Jewett Richmond was born at Syracuse in 1830,
and received a common-school education there. At
the age of seventeen he became a clerk in a country
store in the neighboring village of Liverpool, where
he remained four years. He then went back to Syracuse as clerk in the grocery store of William Gere.
In 1853 Mr. Richmond and two older brothers, with
William Gere and William Barnes, began the manufacture of salt and flour on an extensive scale.
Branch stores were opened in several large cities, in
each of which Mr. Richmond had an interest; and
in the spring of 1854 he went to Buffalo as manager
of the branch in that city.

In 1860 Mr. Richmond disposed of his interest in
this concern, and established a grain commission
business in partnership with Henry A. Richmond.
The venture was successful from the first, and in
1863–64 the Richmond elevator was built by the
firm, which was known as J. M. Richmond & Co.
Mr. Richmond had now been actively engaged in
business for nearly twenty years. He had worked
with tireless energy, and had met with unusual success; and he felt entitled to a long vacation. He
gave up his business, accordingly, in 1864, and went
abroad, where he spent the greater part of a year in

travel. Returning to Buffalo in 1865, he formed a
partnership with his two brothers, Alonzo and Moses
M., and resumed the commission business, which he
conducted for the next fifteen years with much success. In 1884 he retired from active business, and
has since devoted himself to the care of his extensive real estate and other interests.

Early in his business career Mr. Richmond established a reputation for conducting to a successful
issue any enterprise that he undertook; and his fellow-citizens have frequently been glad to avail themselves of this ability. The case of the Buffalo &
Jamestown railroad, well known to the older generation of Buffalonians, is perhaps the most conspicuous
instance of his public-spirited zeal. On the organization of the road in 1872, Mr. Richmond was
elected the first president. He accepted the position with reluctance; but having once accepted it,
he threw himself heartily into the work of raising
funds, and building and equipping the road. The
financial depression of 1873 proved a serious obstacle to the progress of the undertaking, and only the
most prompt and energetic measures saved it from
failure. Mr. Richmond gave himself unreservedly
to the care of the enterprise; and, though his private interests suffered materially, he succeeded in
completing the road, and putting it in successful
operation in 1875. He then resigned the presidency, and turned his attention once more to private
affairs.

Mr. Richmond has been president of the Buffalo
Mutual Gaslight Co. for twenty-five years, resigning
in the spring of 1897. In 1867 he was elected
president of the Marine Bank of Buffalo, and held
the office two years, when he resigned on account of
pressure of other business. He afterward served as
vice president of the institution, and from 1892 to
1894 was again its president; and he is now a member of its board of directors. He is vice president
of the Buffalo Savings Bank, and has been president
of the Board of Trade.

When the new charter of the city of Buffalo went
into operation January 1, 1892, an upper house was
provided in the city legislature, known as the board
of councilmen, and consisting of nine members
elected on a general ticket for a term of three years.
Mr. Richmond, who had often before declined to
let his name be used for political office, yielded to
the wishes of his friends, and accepted the Democratic nomination for this new office. He was
elected for the years 1892–94, and during the last
two years he was president of the board of councilmen. Throughout his term he was acknowledged
by both parties to be a most valuable public servant;

and it was a matter of general regret that he could not be induced to accept a second term.

Though he has been so active in business life, and so successful in the management of business enterprises, Mr. Richmond has never been wholly absorbed in such matters; but has maintained a hearty interest in all that concerns the intellectual development of the community. He is a life member of the Buffalo Fine Arts Academy, the Society of Natural Sciences, and the Buffalo Library; and was president of the latter association for three years, and a member of the building committee at the time of the erection of the society's handsome building, on Lafayette square. He belongs to the Buffalo and Falconwood clubs.

*PERSONAL CHRONOLOGY.— Jewett Melvin Richmond was born at Syracuse December 9, 1830; attended common schools; was a clerk in country stores, 1847–54; engaged in the manufacture and sale of salt, 1854–60; married Geraldine H. Rulderow of New York city November 10, 1830; conducted a grain commission business in Buffalo, 1860–81; was president of the Buffalo & Jamestown railroad, 1872–75; since 1881 has been occupied with the care of his estate, and with his duties as an officer in various corporations.*

...

**Robert R. Smither** is well known in Buffalo not only as an enterprising and successful business man, but also for his intelligent and active interest in public affairs. Any city is fortunate that can command the services of practical, clear-headed men in carrying on its government; and few men have been more efficient in this regard than Mr. Smither.

Mr. Smither was born in England, in the historic city of Winchester, in 1851, and is therefore well under fifty years of age. He was brought to America by his parents in childhood, and has made his home in Buffalo since 1868, when he secured a situation as a clerk in the drug store of W. H. Peabody. From that time on — almost thirty years now — Mr. Smither has been connected with the drug business in Buffalo; and he long ago became one of its leading pharmacists. After occupying a responsible position with Mr. Peabody, and becoming widely and favorably known in his profession, he acted for a time as manager of a similar establishment for W.

R. Crumb; and in 1875 began business for himself at the corner of Niagara and Jersey streets. He still carries on this store, which has become, with the lapse of years, one of the most extensive in the city. About ten years ago he opened a second store at the corner of Elmwood avenue and Bryant street,

*JEWETT M. RICHMOND*

in the midst of a new and rapidly growing section of the city; and since that time he has conducted the two stores with continued success.

Mr. Smither is devoted to his profession, and has done much to raise the standard of its membership in Erie county and throughout the state. He was active in support of the bill to restrict the practice of pharmacy to persons properly qualified and licensed therefor, and had an important part in securing its passage in the legislature. He has been president of the Erie County Board of Pharmacy since its organization in 1884; and is ex-president of the Erie County Pharmaceutical Association, and chairman of the Board of Curators of the Buffalo College of Pharmacy. In 1896 he was unanimously elected president of the New York State Pharmaceutical Association, and was re-elected in 1897.

Mention has been made above of Mr. Smither's public service. This began in 1879, when he was elected a member of the board of supervisors from the old 9th ward, Buffalo, on the Republican ticket.

*ROBERT K SMITHER*

He was re-elected three times, thus representing the ward on the county board for eight years, or until his removal to another part of the city. Although but twenty-eight years old when first elected, his natural aptitude for public affairs soon asserted itself; and he became known as one of the most efficient members of the board, and served as its chairman for three terms. In the first election under the new city charter, in 1891, he was the Republican candidate for alderman in the 24th ward, and was elected by a substantial majority. Two years later he was re-elected by a largely increased majority; and in 1895 he was nominated by acclamation for a third term, and elected by the largest majority ever given for a ward officer under the

revised charter. In 1894 he was the president of the common council, and in 1895 he was unanimously elected president of the board of aldermen. Mr. Smither's work in behalf of a clean, business-like administration of city affairs, and his successful efforts in securing various necessary reforms, are known to all Buffalonians; and it may be confidently expected that they will make further use of his administrative talents in the future.

*PERSONAL CHRONOLOGY—Robert Knight Smither was born at Winchester, Eng., October 10, 1851; came to America in 1858; became a clerk in a Buffalo drug store in 1868; married Lucretia C. Newkirk of Buffalo August 25, 1874; was a member of the Erie-county board of supervisors, 1880–87; has been alderman from the 24th ward, Buffalo, since 1891, acting as president of the common council in 1894 and president of the board of aldermen in 1895; has conducted a drug business in Buffalo since 1875.*

**A. P. Thompson** has been intimately connected for half a century with the manufacturing and other interests of Buffalo. His father, Sheldon Thompson, had an important part in the early development of western New York, and his more remote ancestors were prominent in the Connecticut colony in ante-revolutionary days. Anthony, the first of the family to emigrate, came to America in 1637, and was one of the founders of New Haven. Major Jabez Thompson, the great-grandfather of A. P. Thompson, served in the Colonial wars; had command of the first troops sent from Derby, Conn., immediately after the fighting at Lexington; and as colonel of his regiment was killed in the retreat from New York, September 15, 1776. His son, also named Jabez, born in 1759, spent his life as a sailor, and was lost with his vessel when only thirty-five years old. His son Sheldon, a boy of ten at the time, was thus obliged to care for himself, and shipped as a cabin boy on a vessel of which his brother William was the master. He followed the sea for the next fifteen years, and eventually obtained command of a fine ship in the West India trade. At this time, however, the hostilities between the great European nations rendered commerce on the ocean exceedingly dangerous and difficult; and in

1810 Sheldon Thompson was induced to join some other adventurous spirits and emigrate to the wilderness of western New York with a view to building up a trade on the lakes. The firm of Townsend, Bronson & Co. was organized, accordingly; and during the first year one schooner of a hundred tons was built and launched on Lake Ontario, and another on Lake Erie. About the year 1816 Mr. Thompson moved from Lewiston to Black Rock, and at once became one of the most influential citizens of Erie county. In addition to his part in extending and firmly establishing the commerce on the lakes and on the Erie canal, he has the distinction of being the first mayor of Buffalo elected by the people, and one of the founders and first vestrymen of St. Paul's Church, the first Episcopal church in Buffalo.

Augustus Porter Thompson was born at Black Rock in 1825, when that settlement was still a rival of its neighbor, Buffalo. The question of the future supremacy of the two places had been practically settled, however, several years before in favor of Buffalo, when that village was chosen as the terminus of the Erie canal; and in 1830 Mr. Thompson's father took up his residence there. Porter Thompson received an excellent education for those early days, attending academies at Lewiston and Canandaigua, and private schools in Buffalo. After that he spent several years in his father's establishment as a clerk, acquiring a general knowledge of business principles and methods.

On attaining his majority Mr. Thompson received an interest in the firm of Thompson & Co., manufacturers of white lead; and he has always been connected with this industry with the exception of a short interval in the '60's. In 1860, having disposed of his interest in the lead works, he associated himself with Edward S. Warren and De Garmo Jones, and built a large anthracite blast furnace — the second of the kind in Buffalo. Later these two furnaces were united under the name of the Buffalo Union Iron Works, and a third furnace was built, and one of the largest rolling mills ever erected up to that time. In 1866 Mr. Thompson severed his connection with the iron works, and bought an interest in the lead factory of S. G. Cornell & Son, afterward the Cornell Lead Company. He

became vice president of this concern, and afterward president; and held the latter office until the business was transferred to the National Lead Company in 1887. Since that time he has been a director of that company and the manager of its Buffalo branch.

Mr. Thompson has naturally been interested in various enterprises outside of his work as a manufacturer. He was for some years cashier of the Buffalo City Bank, and a member of its board of directors. He was also a member of the first board of directors of the old railway company that built the road on Niagara street in 1860. He has taken an active and public-spirited part in many movements for promoting the intellectual well-being of Buffalo. He is a member of the Buffalo Historical

*A. P. THOMPSON*

Society, and a life member of the Buffalo Library and the Buffalo Fine Arts Academy. He is one of the wardens of St. Paul's Church, and a trustee of St. Margaret's School, Buffalo, and occupies other positions of trust and responsibility.

*PERSONAL CHRONOLOGY—Augustus Porter Thompson was born at Black Rock, N. Y., February 14, 1825; was educated in private schools and academies; married Matilda Cass Jones of Detroit, Mich., June 9, 1853; was a member of the firm of Thompson & Co., Buffalo, manufacturers of*

*HENRY W. WENDT*

*white lead, 1845-49; engaged in iron manufacture in Buffalo, 1849-67; was a member of the Cornell Lead Co. from 1867 until it became the Buffalo branch of the National Lead Co., and has been its manager since.*

...

**Henry W. Wendt,** though still less than thirty-five years of age, has filled an important place in the manufacturing world for more than fifteen years. Born in Buffalo in the early '60s, he has always made his home there. Even during his schoolboy days, he evinced a natural bent for mechanics, which he lost no opportunity to gratify. After receiving a good practical education in the public schools of his native city, he entered the employ of the Buffalo Forge Co., beginning at the bottom, and working at the bench and lathe, and thus gaining a practical knowledge of the machinist's trade. In the same manner he mounted step by step through all the different departments until in January, 1886, he was admitted to partnership in the concern; his brother, William F. Wendt, having a few years previously acquired entire ownership and control of the business.

The association was a most fortunate one, as has been proved by the continued prosperity and the steady enlargement of the concern. The important place that it occupies to-day in the manufacturing world is due in no small part to Mr. Wendt's thorough practical knowledge of the mechanical and engineering parts of the business, and to the faculty for going to the bottom of things, which was so marked a characteristic when he was a mere lad. His wide experience in designing, and in the practical installation of some of the largest heating and ventilating plants in the country, supplemented by his natural mechanical ability, has gained for him a standing in the foremost rank of heating and ventilating engineers; and there is, perhaps, no one to-day whose advice on weighty matters in this line is more frequently in requisition, or whose standing as an authority is more widely recognized.

Of a sanguine temperament and a naturally genial disposition, Mr. Wendt has the power, so common to self-made men, of inspiring in his subordinates some portion of his own enthusiasm, and comprehensive grasp of mechanical problems: the result is, that he is surrounded by a corps of engineers whose loyalty to, and unquestioned faith in, their employers has contributed very materially to the success of the firm. Their uninterrupted prosperity, which has suffered no check in good or bad times, and their reputation for being always fully abreast with the latest developments in engineering science and improved processes of manufacturing, are due in no small degree to his personal influence.

As consulting engineer in the larger and more important work engaged in by his firm, Mr. Wendt travels considerably and enjoys an enviable acquaintance among scientists and engineers at home and abroad. In the field of invention he has made a considerable mark, several patents having been granted him for improvements in various lines of engineering.

Although enjoying a wide acquaintance among public men, with whom he comes in contact almost daily in his own city and elsewhere, he has never allowed his name to be used in connection with a public office. He is a member of the board of trustees of the Buffalo Builders' Exchange, and prominent in Masonic circles.

*PERSONAL CHRONOLOGY — Henry W. Wendt was born at Buffalo June 19, 1864; was educated in Buffalo public schools; learned the machinist's trade with the Buffalo Forge Co., and has been a member of the corporation since 1886.*

* * *

**C. Lee Abell**, well known among the younger business men of Buffalo, was born in that city about forty years ago. For several generations his family has been prominent in western New York, his grandfather, Thomas G. Abell, having moved from Vermont to Fredonia in 1814. He was one of the foremost men of the place, as was his brother Mosely; and had an important part in the development of Chautauqua county. In company with two others, Thomas Abell established in 1829 a line of stagecoaches between Buffalo and Erie; and he is said to have made the first stagecoach in the country. He was one of the founders of Fredonia Academy. He moved to Buffalo in 1852, and died there five years later. His son, William H. Abell, the father of our present subject, was also a prominent man. Born in Vermont in 1814, he was taken West during infancy; graduated from Fredonia Academy; lived in Austin, Texas, during the years 1839–42, holding several important public offices there; and spent the rest of his life in Buffalo in various successful commercial pursuits. He died there in 1887.

Mr. Abell's maternal grandfather, Oliver Lee, was a native of Connecticut, but moved to western New York in early life. He took a prominent part in the operations on the Niagara frontier during the war of 1812, and afterward engaged extensively in lake commerce and in other mercantile pursuits. He was a man of strict integrity and unusual business ability; and throughout his career enjoyed the confidence and esteem of a large circle of friends. At the time of his death in 1846 he was president of the Attica & Buffalo railroad, and of Oliver Lee & Co.'s Bank, Buffalo. This latter institution was founded by him, and conducted successfully for a number of years.

C. Lee Abell began his active business career at the age of sixteen in the office of a wholesale coal dealer in Buffalo, with whom he remained for about four years. The next few years were devoted to various clerkships in Buffalo, and two years' service in Bradford, Penn., with the United Pipe Lines. After the burning of the Marine elevator in 1879, he formed a partnership with his father and Daniel O'Day for the purpose of building and operating the new Marine elevator. This purpose was effected in 1881, and the business was successfully conducted

*C. LEE ABELL*

as a partnership until 1894. At that time the elevator was enlarged, and the business was transferred to a stock company of which Mr. Abell was made president and manager. The Marine elevator

handles easily 20,000 bushels of grain an hour, and
stores at one time 700,000 bushels. This business
is Mr. Abell's chief commercial interest; but the
care of his father's estate devolves largely upon
him, and requires a part of his time and attention.

*PERSONAL CHRONOLOGY*— *Charles Lee
Abell was born at Buffalo October 4, 1856; held
various clerkships in Buffalo and Bradford, Penn.,
1872–80; married Emma L. Farthing of Buffalo
March 5, 1880; was a member of the National
Guard in Buffalo, 1881–94; has been
manager and part owner of the Marine
elevator, Buffalo, since 1884.*

***

**Robert F. Atkins** was born in
London, England, sixty years ago, but
has made his home in Buffalo ever since
his fifteenth year. He was educated at
Knox's College, Toronto, and afterward
attended Bryant & Stratton's Business
College in Buffalo. He then obtained a
situation in an undertaker's establishment
in Buffalo, and this vocation he followed
until 1861.

When the war broke out it found General Atkins with a wife and two small
children, and a newly established business that needed his attention. He gave
up all his personal interests, however,
and at once prepared to go to the defense of his country. He probably
shared the general belief at that time
that the struggle would be a short one;
but having once set out, he never faltered, but remained in active service
until the last rebel company had laid
down their arms. In April, 1861, he
helped to organize a company from the
ranks of the volunteer fire department of
Buffalo, and was elected its first lieutenant. They presented themselves for duty
in New York two months later, and were
temporarily stationed at Castle Garden.

*ROBERT F. ATKINS*

As for personal matters, mention should be made
of Mr. Abell's long and distinguished career in the
National Guard. Beginning as a private and a
charter member of the Buffalo City Guard Cadets,
he served successfully as sergeant, second lieutenant,
and first lieutenant. He was elected captain of
company C, 74th regiment, October 3, 1884; and
became major in July, 1891, and lieutenant colonel
the next year. He resigned from the National
Guard in April, 1894. He is a 32d degree Mason,
belonging to Buffalo Consistory, A. A. S. R., and
to Hugh de Payens Commandery, No. 30, K. T.
He has membership, also, in various other fraternal
organizations. He has been an active force in the
Democratic party for many years, attaining special distinction in connection with the Cleveland Democracy.

When Colonel Cochran's regiment, the 1st United
States chasseurs, was organized, General Atkins
received an appointment as third sergeant of company B. The regiment was assigned to General
Graham's brigade, Couch's division, 4th corps;
and was in active service at Ball's Bluff, Williamsburgh, Yorktown, Fair Oaks, and Seven Pines.
In the latter engagement Sergeant Atkins was
wounded, and sent home on furlough; and while
there he was promoted to the rank of first lieutenant, and assigned to company C, the color company of the 116th New York volunteers, of which
Colonel Chapin was the heroic commander. The
regiment served with General Banks in Louisiana, and
Lieutenant Atkins acted as brigade quartermaster and
commissary on the staff of Brigadier General Chapin

throughout the campaign, and in the engagements of Baton Rouge, Plains Store, Coxe's Plantation, and the siege of Port Hudson. During this campaign he was advanced to the captaincy of his company; and in August, 1863, he was made lieutenant colonel in the 18th United States infantry, and appointed to the board of examiners of officers for United States troops, with headquarters at Port Hudson. In the examination for this position Colonel Atkins stood first among a large number of officers, and was assigned as commanding officer of the 4th United States engineers at Fort Brashear. He was mustered out at New Orleans in September, 1865, and in 1868 received a brevet commission as colonel, for meritorious service.

Returning to Buffalo in 1865 after an absence of nearly four and a half years, General Atkins became local editor of the *Evening Post*, and in 1870 paymaster of the Anchor line of steamboats. In 1877 he took up again his former business, and he has long been known as one of the leading undertakers of Buffalo. He was president of the New York State Undertakers' Association in 1881 and 1882; and took an active part in the formation at Rochester, fourteen years ago, of the National Undertakers' Association, and was elected a delegate to the first convention of the association.

General Atkins has been actively interested in the Grand Army of the Republic from the time of its organization, and has five times been elected commander of Chapin Post, No. 2, of Buffalo. He is also a member of the Union Veteran Legion, as well as a number of other societies — military, patriotic, and fraternal. He takes special interest in the Independent Order of Odd Fellows, and has been an active worker in that organization for many years. He was the first department commander of the Patriarchs Militant of the Empire State, and derived his title of brigadier general from that position. He increased the number of Cantons in the state from seventeen to twenty-six, and Canton Persch, No. 26, of Buffalo, was mustered in by him. He belongs to Canton Buffalo, No. 5, and was its first captain. He was for two years president of the Odd Fellows' Club of Buffalo. He is a member of the English Lutheran Trinity Church, and is the

only American member of the order of the Harugari in this country.

*PERSONAL CHRONOLOGY— Robert Forsyth Atkins was born at London, Eng., February 24, 1847; was educated at Knox's College, Toronto, and Bryant & Stratton's Business College, Buffalo; married Susan E. Wheeler of Buffalo June 24, 1857; served in the Union army, 1861-65; was local editor of the "Evening Post," 1866-69, and paymaster of the Anchor line of steamers, 1870-76; was Commander of the Patriarchs Militant of the Empire State in 1886; has conducted an undertaking establishment in Buffalo since 1877.*

**⁂**

**William H. Bradish** was born in Wayne county, New York, about forty years ago; but his parents moved to Batavia when he was only two

*WILLIAM H. BRADISH*

years old, and there he obtained his education and his early business experience. Having graduated from the Batavia High School, he served for a time as recorder in the office of the county clerk of

Genesee county, and was afterward employed by his father, who owned a large wood and iron working establishment in Batavia. In 1877 he went into the newspaper business, establishing with Malcolm D. Mix the Batavia *Daily News*. When this enterprise was well under way he sold out his interest therein,

*BRONSON C. RUMSEY*

and sought a wider field of activity in the neighboring city of Buffalo.

Notwithstanding his varied experience, Mr. Bradish was but twenty-three years old when he began his residence in the Queen City. His first employment was that of stenographer for Sprague, Milburn & Sprague, one of the leading law firms of the city, with whom he remained for four years. He then acted as superintendent of the Gilbert starch works at Black Rock for a time. Subsequently he was connected with the firm of Bell, Lewis & Yates, coal dealers, and with Richard Humphrey, a flour and feed merchant at Black Rock. For several years past Mr. Bradish has carried on an insurance office and a brokerage business in real estate and mining stocks, and in this he has been wholly successful.

Mr. Bradish is an earnest Republican in political belief, and has interested himself actively in public affairs for many years. In 1892 he was his party's candidate for alderman in the 25th ward, and his popularity was so great that he was elected although the district is usually strongly Democratic. Two years later he was re-elected by a largely increased majority, and in 1896 he occupied the important position of president of the board of aldermen.

For eleven years Mr. Bradish was prominently connected with the National Guard, serving most of the time in the 74th regiment. He was for a time first lieutenant of company B, Spaulding Guards; and afterward first lieutenant and captain of company A. He was also elected president of company D, Buffalo City Guard, comprising the old company D, the Gordon Highlanders, and the mounted Buffalo City Troopers. When he retired from the National Guard he held the rank of major on the staff of General William F. Rogers.

Ever since his early newspaper experience in Batavia Mr. Bradish has been more or less interested in the publishing business, and in general newspaper work. He acted for a time as manager of the Black Rock Publishing Co., and he has done occasional work for different papers as a correspondent. He attends the Presbyterian church, and belongs to a number of clubs and other organizations. He is a member of Occidental Lodge, No. 766, F. & A. M.; North Buffalo Lodge, No. 517, I. O. O. F.; and Black Rock Court, I. O. F. His clubs are the Acacia (Masonic), the Fraternity (Odd Fellows), and the Audubon, an association devoted to hunting, fishing, and shooting, and maintaining a well equipped shooting park. He is a prominent member of the Black Rock Business Men's Association.

*PERSONAL CHRONOLOGY— William Hamilton Bradish was born at Lyons, N. Y., April 7, 1856; was educated in Batavia public schools; engaged in various business enterprises in Batavia, 1870-79; married Louise H. Reichert of Buffalo April 25, 1881; was an alderman from the 25th ward, Buffalo, 1893-97, and president of the board of aldermen in 1896; has lived in Buffalo since 1879, and has conducted a brokerage and insurance business since 1892.*

**Edward Bennett**, president of the Buffalo Savings Bank, was born in the Queen City seventy years ago, and has spent almost all his life there. He was just twenty-one when the California gold fever of 1848 broke out ; and, with the enthusiasm of youth, he at once set out for the new El Dorado.

Returning to Buffalo after a year's absence, Mr. Bennett soon established a reputation as one of that city's most trustworthy men of affairs. In 1877 he was elected a trustee of the Buffalo Savings Bank. In August, 1890, he was elected its first vice president ; and in October, 1893, on the death of Warren Bryant, the president, Mr. Bennett succeeded to that office. The Buffalo Savings Bank was established in 1846, and is therefore the oldest institution of its kind in Buffalo.

When the revised charter of the city was adopted in 1853, enlarging its boundaries to include the village of Black Rock, and increasing the number of wards to thirteen, Mr. Bennett was elected one of two aldermen from the 5th ward, and retained his seat in the common council by re-election for four years. In 1872 Mayor Brush appointed him a member of the board of park commissioners, and he held the office for sixteen years by successive reappointments from different mayors. In 1877 he was nominated by the Workingmen's party for mayor of Buffalo, and the nomination was endorsed by the Tax Payers' Association.

Mr. Bennett is a member of the Buffalo Club and of the Orpheus Singing Society. He has been a trustee of the Charity Organization Society of Buffalo ever since its early days, and has taken an active interest in its work of supervising and regulating the charities of the city.

*PERSONAL CHRONOLOGY—*
*Edward Bennett was born at Buffalo February 21, 1827 ; received an academic education ; was a clerk in a dry-goods store, 1841–48 ; engaged in mining and other enterprises in California, 1848–49, and in the real-estate business in Buffalo, 1850–97 ; married Mary Josephine Osier-Auchinleck October 19, 1885 ; was an alderman from the 5th ward, Buffalo, 1854–57, and a park commissioner, 1872–88 ; has been president of the Buffalo Savings Bank since October, 1893.*

**Harlan W. Brush**, editor of the North Tonawanda *Daily News*, is a native of Ohio, and made his home there until his removal to western New York in 1894. Born in Nelson, Portage county, in 1865, he began his education in the public schools at an early age ; and entered Mt. Union College when only thirteen years old. He took a classical course there that lasted two years ; but left college in his sophomore year, and began to make his own way in the world.

Mr. Brush has been connected from the first with the printing and publishing business, and though little more than thirty years of age, his experience therein extends over a period of fifteen years or more. He learned the printer's trade in the office of John G. Garrison, publisher of the Alliance (Ohio) *Weekly Standard* ; and at the age of eighteen purchased a

*EDWARD BENNETT*

job-printing office in Alliance, and began to work for himself. In 1887 he formed a partnership with his former employer, Mr. Garrison of the *Standard* ; and the next year he organized a stock company with a capital of $16,000, for the purpose of purchasing the two Republican papers of the place, the *Review* and the *Standard*. He became manager of the company, and conducted it for about six years with much success. The same year the company was organized he began the publication of a daily

*HARLAN H. BRUSH*

paper called the *Daily Review*, which became, under his vigorous management, a prosperous and well conducted publication.

In December, 1894, Mr. Brush sold out his interests in Ohio, and moved to North Tonawanda, where he purchased the *Daily News*, which he has edited and published ever since. During this time the place has developed from a village into a city which is growing rapidly, and which presents unusual evidences of material prosperity. So thriving a community offers an excellent field for a newspaper man of energy and ability such as Mr. Brush has proved himself to be, and he may be counted on to make the Tonawanda *News* a power in the Lumber City.

Politically Mr. Brush's sympathies have always been with the Republicans, and he has long been an active and efficient party worker. During his residence in Alliance he served for a time as secretary of the Republican committee there. Since moving to Tonawanda he has taken a prominent part in public affairs; and in the fall of 1897 he received an appointment as United States consul at Clifton, Ont., a position that he will doubtless fill with entire credit.

Aside from his newspaper business Mr. Brush has been actively interested in several manufacturing enterprises, and has become thoroughly identified with the general life of the community. He attends the Methodist Episcopal church, and is a member of the Alpha Tau Omega college fraternity.

*PERSONAL CHRONOLOGY—Harlan W. Brush was born at Nelson, O., May 27, 1865; was educated at common schools and Mt. Union (O.) College; learned the printer's trade at Alliance, O., 1880–85; married Annetta Hamilton of Emlenton, Penn., May 16, 1888; conducted a job-printing office in Alliance, 1885–87, and published a newspaper there, 1887–94; was appointed United States consul at Clifton, Ont., in 1897; has been proprietor and editor of the North Tonawanda "Daily News" since December, 1894.*

* * *

**Carl Thurston Chester** has practiced at the Buffalo bar for fifteen years, and is well known in the professional and general life of the Queen City. Born in Connecticut forty-odd years ago, he spent his childhood and youth there, moving to Buffalo at the age of sixteen. He had already received an excellent fundamental education in the public schools of his native state, ending with several years' attendance at the Norwich Free Academy; and he finished his preparation for college in the Buffalo Classical School under Professor Horace Briggs. He returned to Connecticut to complete his education, entering Yale College in 1871, and graduating therefrom four years later with the degree of A. B. He took a high stand in scholarship from the first, and won distinction throughout his course. He received the Junior Exhibition prize and the De Forest medal, the two highest prizes in literature and oratory in the gift of the university; and he was chairman of the board of editors of the Yale Literary Magazine.

Mr. Chester determined to follow the law as a profession, and he spent two years in New York at the Columbia Law School immediately after leaving college, graduating in 1877 with the degree of LL. B. He then became managing clerk in the office of Bowen, Rogers & Locke, one of the most prominent law firms in Buffalo. He remained there for several years, receiving thus an excellent training in the practical work of a busy office, and gaining experience that has been invaluable to him since. After an interval of about a year spent in European travel, Mr. Chester in 1882 opened an office in Buffalo on his own account. His success was marked from the beginning, and proves the value of thorough preparation for such a career. Large and important as is the clientage he has built up, it is the result of his individual effort; for he has steadily refused all offers of partnership associations, preferring to control the entire business of his office with the aid of an able staff of assistants. Though he has devoted himself to general practice, not making a specialty of any particular branch of the law, he has become widely known as the counsel for large estates, corporations, and business houses.

Mr. Chester's sound and accurate learning in the law was recognized in the early years of his professional life by his appointment as a member of the faculty of the Buffalo Law School soon after its organization in 1887. He has retained his connection with this institution ever since; and is at present professor of the law of insurance, wills, special actions, etc. Since 1882 he has been the secretary and attorney of the Buffalo Orphan Asylum; and for upwards of ten years he has acted as secretary and treasurer of the board of trustees of the City and County Hall.

In the social life of Buffalo Mr. Chester is well known, and he is especially popular in club circles. He belongs to the Buffalo, Saturn, and University clubs, and to the Yale Alumni and D. K. E. associations of western New York. He served for two terms as president of the Saturn Club, and is a member of the council of the University Club.

*PERSONAL CHRONOLOGY — Carl Thurston Chester was born at Norwich, Conn., August 1,* *1854; graduated from Yale College in 1875, and from Columbia College Law School in 1877; was managing clerk in the office of Bowen, Rogers & Locke of Buffalo, 1877–81; has practiced law in Buffalo since 1882.*

***

**Gibson L. Douglass,** vice president and general manager of the Western Transit Co., is a lineal descendant on his father's side of William Douglass, who settled in Gloucester, Mass., in 1640, and Major Brian Pendleton, who came to America in 1630 and settled in Watertown, Conn. On his mother's side he comes of a race of sturdy, honorable ship carpenters and seafaring men, who emigrated from Germany in 1630, and settled in New York. His grandfather in this line was Captain John Winans, whose career deserves more than a passing mention.

*CARL THURSTON CHESTER*

John Winans was born in Poughkeepsie, N. Y., June 15, 1766. He learned the trade of a ship carpenter under his father, James Winans, whose shipyard was at that time a noted place for the building of ocean vessels as well as river craft; and he ultimately succeeded his father in the ownership of the business. When Robert Fulton started the first steamboat ever built — the "Clermont" — from New York for Albany September 2, 1807, John Winans was on board. He had been brought in

GIBSON T. DOUGLASS

contact with the great inventor through Robert R. Livingstone, Fulton's friend and partner and the legal counselor of Captain Winans. Chancellor Livingstone appreciated the ability of the latter, and brought the two men together for the purpose of aiding Fulton to perfect his invention. Captain Winans had watched the construction of the "Clermont" with the deepest interest, and had given Fulton many valuable suggestions. When the success of the new invention was secured he immediately contracted with Fulton and Livingstone for the right to build and navigate steamboats on Lake George and the waters of Lake Champlain lying within the borders of New York state. He at once set about the construction of a vessel for this

purpose; and in the spring of 1808 he launched from the foot of King street, Burlington, Vermont, the steamboat "Vermont." This steamer was 120 feet long, twenty feet wide, and eight feet deep; and had a speed of four miles an hour. She was the second steamboat ever constructed in America; and Captain Winans, as her builder, owner, and navigator, may justly claim a high place among the industrial pioneers of the land. The "Vermont" commenced regular trips between Whitehall, N. Y., and St. Johns, Canada, in the spring of 1809; and from that time until she sunk at Isle Au Noix in October, 1815, had an eventful career. During the war of 1812 she was used by Commodore McDonough and General Macomb for the transportation of troops and supplies on Lake Champlain; and she took an active part in the battle of Plattsburgh September 11, 1814. During these years Captain Winans organized the Champlain Transportation Co. and the Lake George Steamboat Co., both of which are still in existence as part of the Delaware & Hudson Canal Co. system. The state of Vermont granted to Captain Winans and his associates, November 10, 1815, the sole right to navigate with steam vessels the waters of Lake Champlain within the boundaries of that state; and this grant, together with his contract with Fulton and Livingstone for New York waters, gave him control of the steamboating on lakes Champlain and George. In 1815 he superintended the building of the steamer "Phoenix" at Vergennes, Vt., for the Champlain company, and the next year he built for himself the steamer "Champlain." Both of these vessels were burned within a few years. The steamer "Caldwell," which was built about this time, and of which Captain Winans was half owner, was the first steamboat ever used on Lake George. This vessel furnished the connecting link in the water transportation between New York city and Montreal, since the great thoroughfare between the north and the south at that time was by way of these two northern lakes. Having successfully established steam navigation on these waters, Captain Winans sold his interest in the two transportation companies and returned to his native city of Poughkeepsie, where he died June 5, 1827. He was married September 2, 1793, to Catherine Stewart of

Poughkeepsie. Many original documents of unusual interest connected with the early history of steamboating on the waters of Lake Champlain and Lake George were left by Captain Winans, and are now in the possession of his grandson, Mr. Douglass.

Whether it be owing to a special interest in the subject of transportation inherited from his grandfather, or to some other cause, the fact remains that Mr. Douglass's entire business life has been devoted to this kind of work; and that few men in the country have had a greater amount of practical experience in that line than he. The altered conditions of the present day have produced many changes in the transportation industry; but Mr. Douglass has exercised the same foresight, energy, and sagacity that were conspicuous in Captain Winans's career, and has met with equal success.

Entering the employ of the Western Transportation Co. as a clerk in their office at Troy, N. Y., at the age of nineteen, Mr. Douglass has ever since been connected with that company and its successor, the Western Transit Co. In 1865 he succeeded to the management of the Troy agency of the company, and held that position for upwards of fifteen years. In 1881 he was appointed general freight agent of the company, with headquarters in New York city; and when the New York Central railroad purchased the organization in 1884, and it became known as the Western Transit Co., he continued to occupy the same position.

During these years Mr. Douglass has been connected with various other freight organizations; and his experience in all branches of inland transportation — canal, rail, and lake — has been remarkably extensive and thorough. During a part of his years in Troy he represented the New York Central road as agent for the Blue Line and subsequently for the Merchants' Despatch Transportation Co., both all-rail fast freight lines. From 1872 to 1877, also, he was the Troy agent for the Northern Transportation Line, a canal and lake line doing business between New York city, northern New York, and Canada via the Champlain canal and Lake Champlain. He was a director in this company, and at one time its general superintendent. In New York city his duties were still more varied and important. In 1890 he was appointed manager of the floating property

of the New York Central railroad used in the harbor of New York, and operated under the name of the New York Central Lighterage Co. At the same time he managed the grain elevators of the New York Central and West Shore railroads, and the East-river piers of these companies. In January, 1897, he was elected vice-president and general manager of the Western Transit Co., and has since made his home in Buffalo.

Mr. Douglass is a Democrat in political belief, but has never had time to interest himself actively in public affairs. He is a Mason; and belongs to the Ellicott Club of Buffalo, and the Transportation Club of New York city. He attends in Buffalo the Delaware Avenue Methodist Episcopal Church.

*PERSONAL CHRONOLOGY— Gibson L. Douglass was born at Chazy, Clinton county, N. Y.,*

*JOHN WINANS*

*January 22, 1839; married Anna M. Ojers of Chicago March 30, 1864; became a clerk in the office of the Western Transportation Co. in Troy, N. Y., in 1858, and has been actively engaged in the handling and transportation of freight ever since ; has been vice president and general manager of the Western Transit Co., with headquarters at Buffalo, since January 20, 1897.*

\* \* \*

**James B. Huff** is one of the most popular citizens of Tonawanda, both politically and socially ;

*JAMES B. HUFF*

and this fact is perhaps best accounted for by his character, which is modest and unpretentious, and generous to a fault. He was born in Tonawanda barely forty years ago, and has always lived there. He received a thorough education in the public schools of the town, which he attended from early childhood until he was twenty years old.

Public affairs have interested Mr. Huff intensely ever since he was old enough to vote, and he began to hold office soon after he attained his majority. Nominated by the Democratic party in 1879 for the position of village clerk, he was elected by a majority of 200. The next year he defeated a different candidate by about the same majority. His popularity was so generally recognized that in the three

succeeding years no one could be found to accept the Republican nomination against him, and he was re-elected each time without opposition. But Mr. Huff does not believe in monopolies, even though they be political ones ; and at the end of five years he refused to allow his name to be used as a candidate, thus leaving the field free to other competitors. His next public office was that of village treasurer, to which he received a unanimous election. He has also served as trustee of the village, and has attended county and other conventions of his party.

Mr. Huff's allegiance to the Democratic party was put to the test in 1896, when the free-silver declaration was inserted in the Chicago platform ; and it was a question whether he should stand by his party or his principles. The latter triumphed, however, and he cast his vote for a candidate who would maintain the currency of the country on a gold basis. In the spring of 1897 Mr. Huff was chosen to bear the standard of the disaffected faction of the Republican party in Tonawanda as their candidate for president of the village. That faction had suffered defeat the previous year, and it was felt that he was the only man who had a chance of succeeding against the regular Republican nominee. The result of the election was most flattering, since he received a large majority of the votes cast. Indeed, Mr. Huff has never been defeated in a contest for any public office, and it is easy to predict for him further political triumphs in the future.

Of late years Mr. Huff has been prominently identified with the great lumber industry at Tonawanda, having established himself as a wholesale lumber dealer in 1892. He is well known in Masonic circles, belonging to Tonawanda Lodge, F. & A. M., and Tonawanda Chapter, R. A. M., as well as to Zuleika Grotto, No. 10.

*PERSONAL CHRONOLOGY — James B. Huff was born at Tonawanda, N. Y., August 14, 1857 ; was educated in the public schools ; married Etta L. Long of Tonawanda December 21, 1881 ; has served as clerk of the village of Tonawanda, village treasurer, and village trustee ; was elected president of the village in March, 1897 ; has carried on a wholesale lumber business at Tonawanda since 1892.*

**Edward C. Roth,** one of the best known insurance men of Buffalo, was born in that city shortly before the beginning of the Civil War. His scholastic education was not carried far and his present fund of general information was acquired by judicious reading and observation after he had left school, and entered the larger world of business. He prepared himself to take the course of study at the high school in Buffalo, but finally decided not to do so. Instead of that he began business life in his early teens by entering the old hardware establishment of De Witt C. Weed & Co. Purposing to learn the business thoroughly, he remained with the house in various grades of service about five years, and thereby acquired not only a minute knowledge of the hardware business in particular, but also an excellent all-round training in general business principles and usages.

The death of the senior Mr. Weed in 1878 produced some unsettlement in the Weed concern, and indirectly resulted in Mr. Roth's retirement from the service of the house. He then engaged in the business with which he has ever since been identified — insurance. Entering the office of William D. Lewis, he remained with him about four years, and learned thoroughly every branch of the insurance business. By that time he had become so well known among insurance people that James Ferguson, a prominent underwriter of New York city, sought his alliance in a partnership in the fire and marine insurance business. Mr. Roth accepted the offer, and the firm of Ferguson & Roth wrote a large volume of insurance up to the time of Mr. Ferguson's death in 1885. Mr. Roth then continued the business under the present well-known style of Edward C. Roth & Co. In 1888 George H. Hughson was admitted to the firm, and in 1891 Frank W. Fiske, Jr., became one of the partners; these two, with Mr. Roth, constitute the existing firm.

Since Mr. Roth has concerned himself with insurance the business has changed in many respects, and has enormously expanded as regards both volume and kinds of risk assumed. Fire and marine risks constituted at first the greater part of his business, and still make up a large proportion of his transactions; but he has added from time to time various branches of insurance — boiler, plate-glass,

burglary, employers' liability, etc. — as new conditions produced new hazards and the need of corresponding safeguards. He is now the Buffalo representative of some of the strongest companies in the world, providing insurance against a multitude of casualties.

*PERSONAL CHRONOLOGY— Edward C. Roth was born at Buffalo October 22, 1859; was educated in the public schools of the city; was employed in a hardware store, 1873-78; was clerk in an insurance office, 1878-81; married Hattie Weller of Buffalo September 29, 1891; has conducted a general insurance business in Buffalo since 1881.*

***

**John L. Schwartz,** vice president of the Buffalo Brewers' Association, is a native of the Queen City, and is well known in its business, social, and

*EDWARD C. ROTH*

political life. Born in 1859 in the old 4th ward, at the corner of Washington and Chippewa streets, he received his early education in St. Michael's parochial school; and when St. Canisius College was opened in 1870 he became one of its first students. After a course of four years there he left school at the age of fifteen, and began business life.

At this time Mr. Schwartz's father and brother carried on a planing mill in Buffalo, and the young man went into business with them for several years.

*JOHN L. SCHWARTZ*

Four years later the father died, and the business was dissolved ; and Mr. Schwartz became a clerk in the office of Joseph Berlin, who conducted a general insurance and coal business. After about a year in this capacity he established a coal and wood business on his own account. He was just twenty-one years old at this time ; but he had had considerable business experience, and was well qualified by natural ability and training to carry on such an undertaking. He conducted the enterprise with entire success for twelve years, when he sold out to his brothers, Edward J. and Joseph A. Schwartz.

Having disposed of his coal business, Colonel Schwartz took up an entirely different line of work. In company with John S. Kellner, Edward A.

Diebold, and Joseph Phillips, he bought the plant of the Queen City Brewing Co., at the corner of Spring and Cherry streets, and established the Star Brewery for the conduct of a general brewing and bottling business. He has devoted himself to the management of this enterprise ever since, and has become widely known in one of Buffalo's most important industries.

Though he has never held public office, Colonel Schwartz has long been prominent in the counsels of the Democratic party. He is actively interested in several fraternal societies, and has membership in many such. He was for many years one of the board of trustees of the Buffalo Catholic Institute, and is still a member of the organization. Since 1892 he has been Grand Treasurer of the Catholic Mutual Benefit Association, having been elected for the third time at Syracuse in 1897. He owes his military title to his connection with the Uniformed Catholic Knights, having been colonel of the 2d regiment of that organization in the state of New York for the past eight years. He belongs, also, to the Buffalo Orpheus, the Catholic Benevolent Legion, and the Royal Arcanum ; and is a trustee of St. Michael's Church. He has been a member of the board of directors of the Buffalo Volksfreund Printing Co. since 1887, and president of the Alumni of St. Canisius College since 1894.

*PERSONAL CHRONOLOGY—John Leo Schwartz was born at Buffalo April 14, 1859 ; was educated at St. Canisius College, Buffalo ; worked in his father's planing mill, 1874-78, and in a coal office, 1878-79 ; carried on a coal and wood business in Buffalo, 1880-92 ; married Elizabeth J. Zegewitz of Rochester October 12, 1887 ; has been manager and part owner of the Star Brewery, Buffalo, since 1892.*

•••

**Thomas Eugene Warner,** well known for many years in the journalism of Niagara county, was born in Orleans, Ontario county, fifty-odd years ago. He received his education in the schools of his native town, and at the age of sixteen began to earn his own living. He was fortunate in choosing at first a trade that proved congenial, and that led naturally to the position of newspaper publisher which he has filled now for upwards of fifteen years.

Becoming a printer's apprentice in an office at Phelps, N. Y., in 1860, he worked at his trade for the next seventeen years. His apprenticeship was completed in the office of the Geneva *Gazette*, under Stephen H. Parker, one of the best-known representatives of the Democratic press in the state; and his practical experience of the printer's craft was gained in a number of newspaper offices in some of the largest cities in the United States, where he became thoroughly conversant with the different departments of the business. In 1877 he took up an entirely new line of activity, accepting an appointment as warden of the Jersey City Charity Hospital, where he remained for the next two or three years.

In September, 1880, Mr. Warner moved to Tonawanda, and became associated with Thomas M. Chapman in the publication of the Tonawanda *Herald*. He had already had considerable experience in newspaper work, serving at first as a reporter on the Detroit *Free Press*, and later as state editor of that well-known journal, at the same time furnishing reportorial correspondence from the several cities of Michigan. He was therefore well qualified by training as well as by natural ability for the new work which he undertook in Tonawanda, and which he carried on for seventeen years with much success. In the fall of 1897 he sold his interest in the *Herald* to Mr. Chapman, the senior partner; and established the daily, semiweekly, and weekly *Argus* in the "Twin Cities" of the Tonawandas. For the conduct of this enterprise he formed a partnership with Frank P. Hulette, for many years the successful editor of the *Wyoming County Leader* of Arcade, N. Y., and widely known as the secretary of the New York State Democratic Editorial Association. The new paper is the only one in its territory devoted to the interests of the Democratic party; and as Messrs. Warner and Hulette are both ardent supporters of that party, and newspaper men of trained ability, the success of the venture need not be regarded as doubtful.

During his residence in Tonawanda Mr. Warner has become well and favorably known in both public and private life. In 1886 he was appointed clerk of the village of North Tonawanda, and held the office continuously until the adoption of the city charter in April, 1897,

when he was unanimously chosen the first city clerk. He is a Mason, and holds the office of Past Master in Tonawanda Lodge, No. 247, F. & A. M., and that of High Priest in Tonawanda Chapter, No. 278, R. A. M. He is a member of St. Mark's Episcopal Church.

*PERSONAL CHRONOLOGY—Thomas Eugene Warner was born at Orleans, N. Y., March 23, 1844; was educated in common schools; learned the printer's trade and worked at the same in various cities, 1860-77; married Florence Elizabeth Hansford of Jersey City, N. J., September 18, 1876; was warden of the Jersey City Charity Hospital, 1877-80; was one of the publishers of the Tonawanda (N. Y.) "Herald," 1880-97; has been clerk of the village and city of North Tonawanda since 1886; established the Tonawanda "Argus" in October, 1897.*

*THOMAS EUGENE WARNER*

**Irving Emmet Waters,** cashier of the Citizens' Bank of Buffalo, has had an important part of late years in the commercial activities of the Queen City; and, though comparatively a newcomer there, has done much to further its prosperity. His public-spirited zeal has been unflagging, and he is widely known in business circles as a man of unusual energy and sagacity.

Mr. Waters is a native of Herkimer county, New York, and a large part of his life thus far has been

*IRVING EMMET WATERS*

spent there. Born in Little Falls about fifty years ago, he received his education in the common schools and academy of that place, and at the age of seventeen began to earn his own living. His first position was with the American Express Co., where he remained four years. He then secured a situation as clerk in the Herkimer County National Bank, where he gained his first insight into the management of a financial institution. After several years in this position he went to Buffalo in July, 1873, as teller in the Bank of Commerce, which had just been organized.

Banking was to be Mr. Waters's life-work, and Buffalo the scene of his success as a banker; but he did not stay long in the city at that time, returning to Little Falls in May, 1876, and engaging in business there for the next four years. This was quite long enough to convince him that his talents were better suited to a financial than a mercantile career; and accordingly, in 1880, he again entered the employ of the Herkimer County National Bank, this time as general bookkeeper. He remained in this position for ten years, becoming thoroughly familiar as time went on with the science of banking, and gaining experience that has been invaluable to him since.

In 1890 the Citizens' Bank of Buffalo was organized; and Mr. Waters's friends in that city, who had recognized his ability during his short connection with the Bank of Commerce fifteen years before, suggested to the board of directors that the post of cashier of the new institution be tendered to him. The offer was made and accepted, and from the time the bank first opened its doors Mr. Waters has filled that responsible position. Under his energetic and efficient management the new institution prospered from the beginning, and soon became recognized as one of the solid financial concerns of the city. In the conduct of its affairs Mr. Waters for the first time had an opportunity to exercise his talents as a financier, and the high standing that it has attained shows how well he has availed himself of that opportunity. The Citizens' Bank has been in existence only seven years, and during much of that time the financial condition of the country has been far from prosperous; furthermore, it is one of the smaller institutions of the city, having a capital of only $100,000. In spite of these facts it occupies a foremost position in the financial world, and is deemed one of the strongest institutions of its size in the country.

Mr. Waters has had the best interests of Buffalo closely at heart ever since he took up his residence there, and has had a part in many enterprises that have been productive of good to the city. He has been very successful in attracting outside capital thither, and thus promoting business activity. He was one of the organizers of the Lenox Corporation, that completed in 1897 the Lenox apartment house, a large and elegant structure on North street near Delaware avenue, that compares favorably with the finest buildings of its class in any city in the United States.

All his best energies Mr. Waters devotes to business, spending little time in politics or society matters. He is a member, however, of the Buffalo Orpheus.

*PERSONAL CHRONOLOGY — Irving Emmet Waters was born at Little Falls, N. Y., August 13, 1846; was educated at Little Falls Academy; was employed in various capacities in Little Falls, 1863–74; married Eliza I. Waterman of Little Falls February 4, 1875; was teller of the Bank of Commerce, Buffalo, 1874–76; engaged in business in Little Falls, 1876–80; was bookkeeper of the Herkimer County National Bank of Little Falls, 1880–90; has been cashier of the Citizens' Bank, Buffalo, since 1890.*

* * *

**Albert J. Wright** is well known in both business and social circles in Buffalo, where he has lived since childhood. He is descended from good old English stock that settled in the American colonies in early days, the most illustrious member of the family being Silas Wright of Canton, N. Y.— governor, congressman, United States senator, and an able statesman in the days of Clinton, Clay, and Webster.

Mr. Wright was born in Oswego, N. Y., where his father, Alfred P. Wright, also a native of the place, carried on a large business in canal transportation. When he was eight years old his father moved to Buffalo, and the boy began his education there. After spending about two years in Public School No. 14 he prepared for college in the Buffalo Classical School under Professor Horace Briggs, and then took a scientific course at Wesleyan University, Middletown, Conn.

Returning to Buffalo in 1878 in his twentieth year, Mr. Wright was fortunate enough to find an excellent opening ready for him. The firm of Preston & Wright, established by his father a dozen years before for the handling and transfer of grain, had met with marked and continuous success; and the young man at once entered their office, and set himself to master the intricacies of the business. Two years later Mr. Preston was compelled by ill health to give up active business, and the firm of A. P. Wright & Son was organized, with Albert J. Wright as the junior partner.

The new firm soon became one of the most widely known in the country; and the long experience of

the father and the enterprising and energetic spirit of the son were alike factors in its remarkable success. In the first year the enormous amount of 33,000,000 bushels of grain was handled by them during the season of navigation. After ten years of uninterrupted success the firm was dissolved in 1890, and since that time Mr. Wright has carried on alone a business as banker and broker in grain and stocks. His earlier experience as a grain merchant has been of value to him in this new enterprise, and he has met with the success to which his unquestioned ability entitles him.

In 1884, when only twenty-six years old, Mr. Wright was elected president of the Buffalo Merchants' Exchange. He was the youngest man ever chosen for that responsible position, and the fact is evidence of the high opinion of his powers

*ALBERT J. WRIGHT*

entertained by the business men of Buffalo. After his retirement from the presidency of the association he served for several years as a trustee. He also served in 1884 as president of the Buffalo Board of Trade.

He was for a time trustee of the Buffalo Library, and was a member of the board at the time the money was raised for the erection of the present library building.

Mr. Wright is a prominent member of several exclusive clubs in Buffalo and elsewhere. He was one of the incorporators of the Country Club of Buffalo in 1889, and is still a governor of the institution. He is also a governor of the Buffalo Club, and belongs to the Ellicott and Yacht clubs of Buffalo and the Chicago Club of Chicago.

*PERSONAL CHRONOLOGY - Albert J. Wright was born at Oswego, N. Y., August 24, 1858; was educated in Buffalo schools and Wesleyan University, Middletown, Conn.; married Gertrude Bent of Middletown September 25, 1878; engaged in the grain commission business in Buffalo, 1878–90; was president of the Merchants' Exchange and the Board of Trade of Buffalo in 1884; has carried on a banking and brokerage business in Buffalo since 1890.*